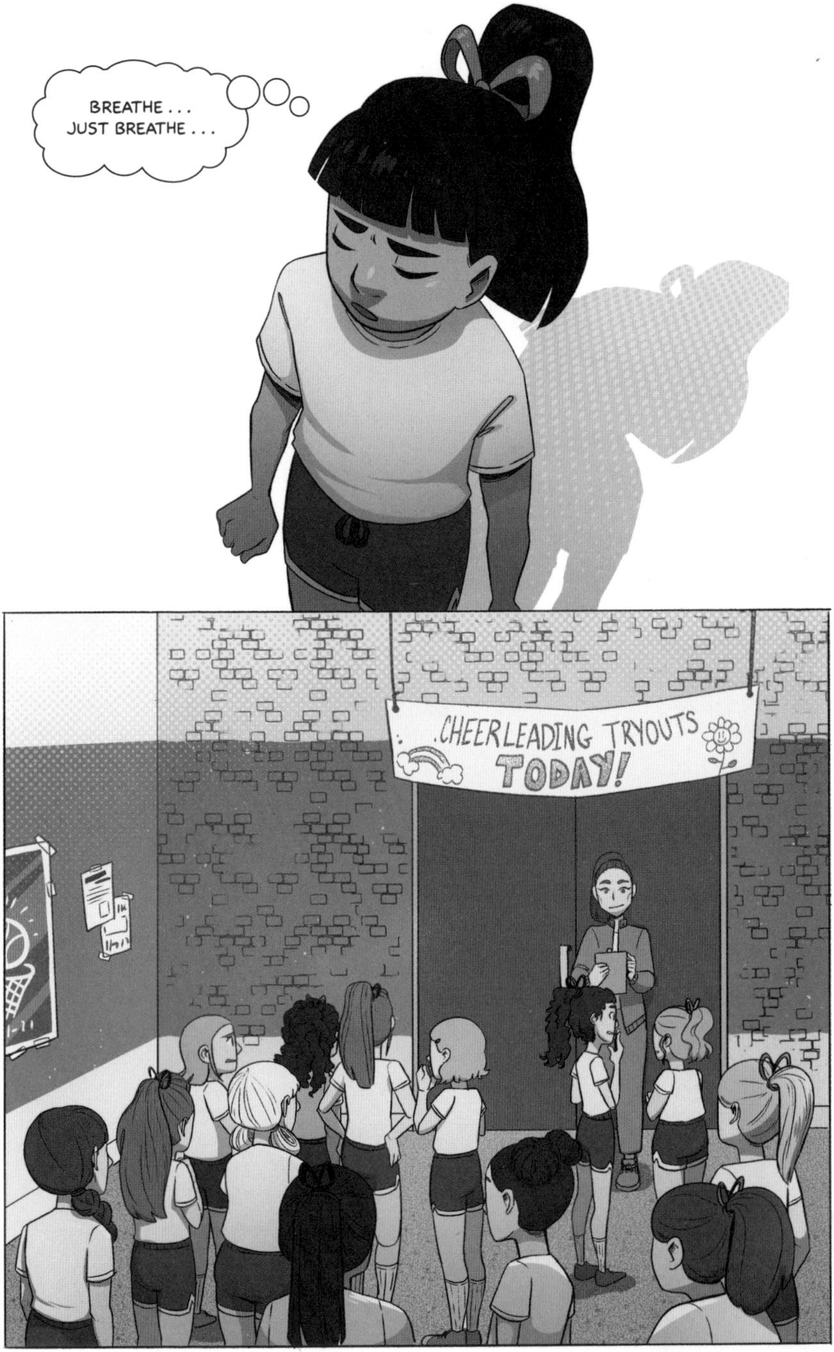
BREATHE . . .
JUST BREATHE . . .
CHEERLEADING TRYOUTS
TODAY!

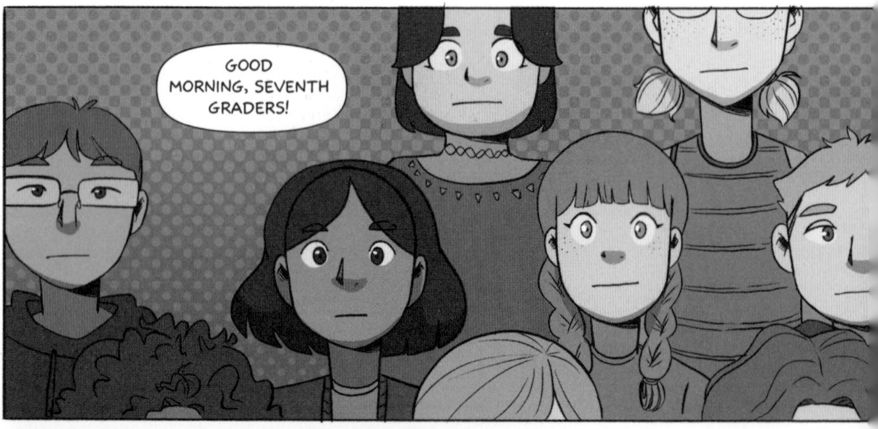
GOOD MORNING, SEVENTH GRADERS!

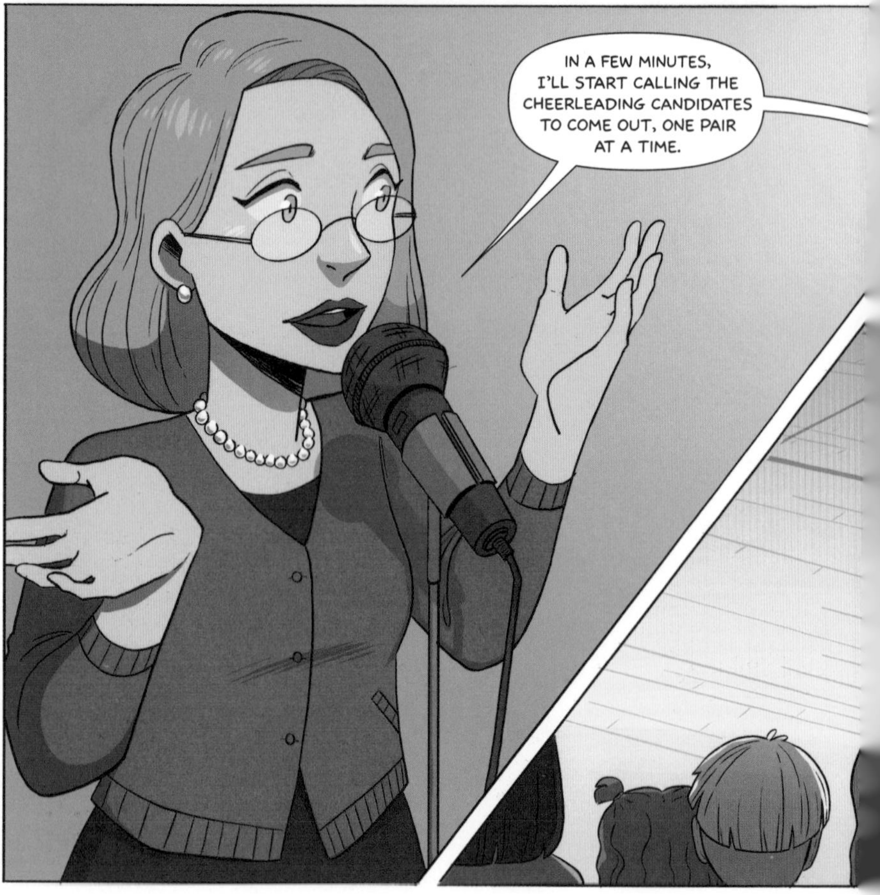
IN A FEW MINUTES, I'LL START CALLING THE CHEERLEADING CANDIDATES TO COME OUT, ONE PAIR AT A TIME.

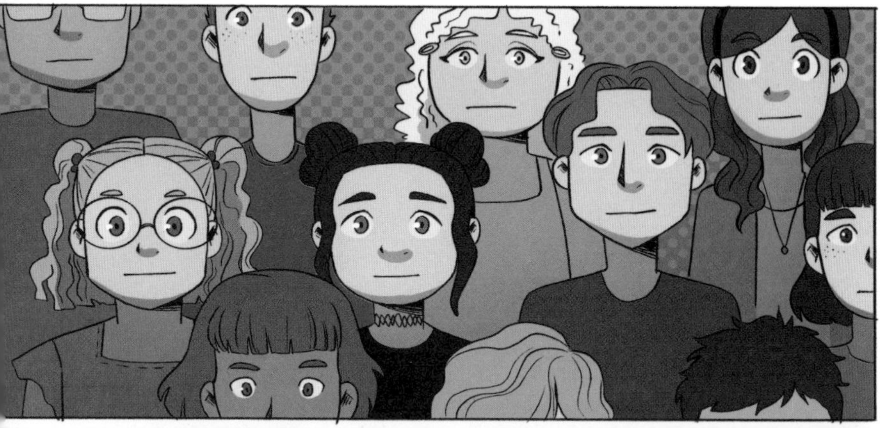

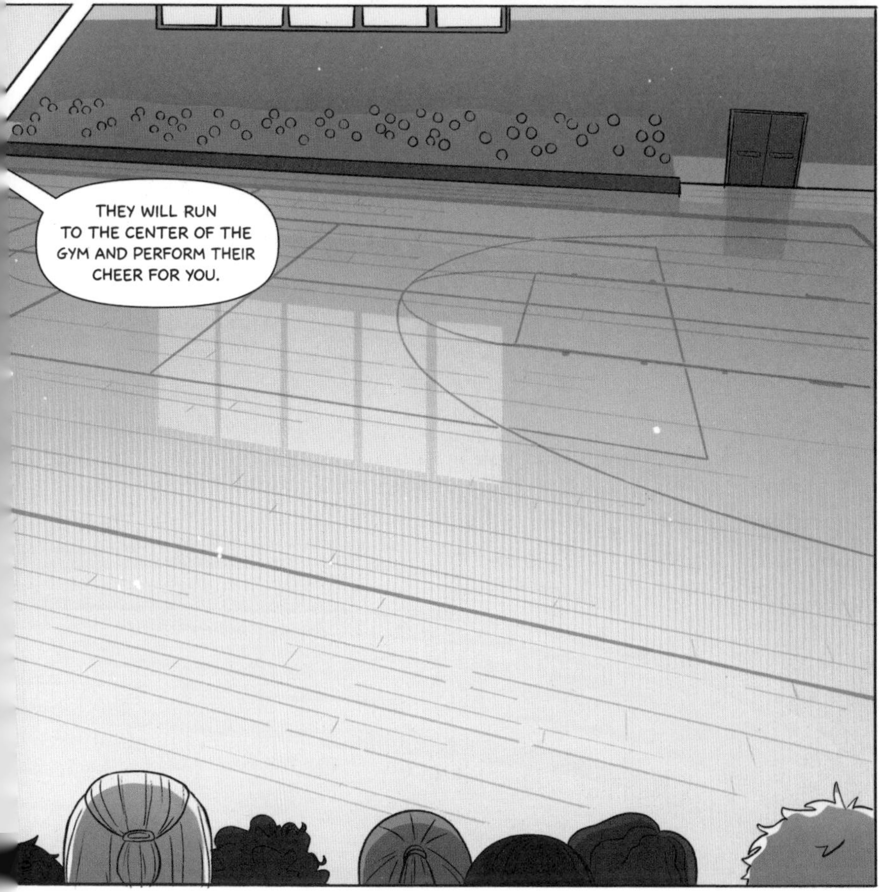
THEY WILL RUN TO THE CENTER OF THE GYM AND PERFORM THEIR CHEER FOR YOU.

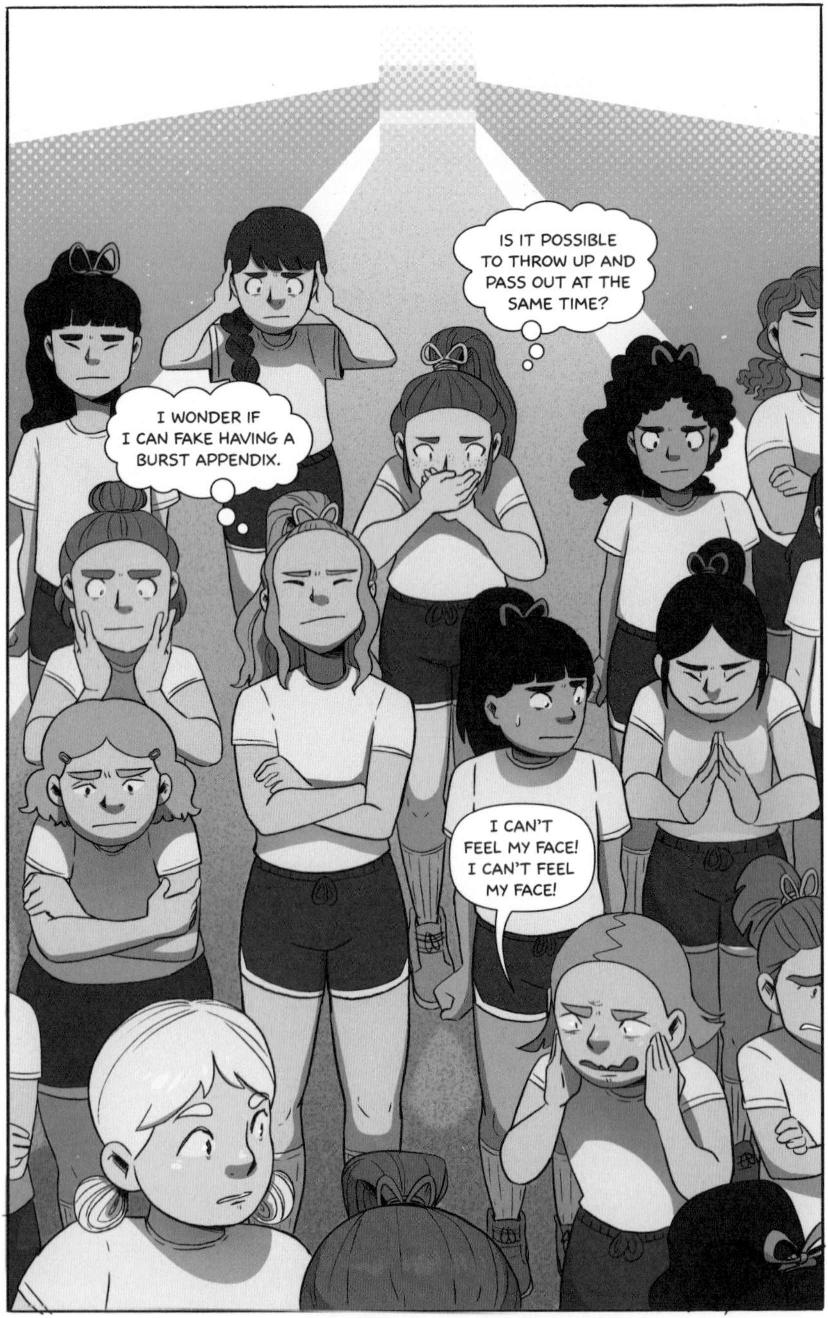
IS IT POSSIBLE TO THROW UP AND PASS OUT AT THE SAME TIME?
I WONDER IF I CAN FAKE HAVING A BURST APPENDIX.
I CAN'T FEEL MY FACE! I CAN'T FEEL MY FACE!

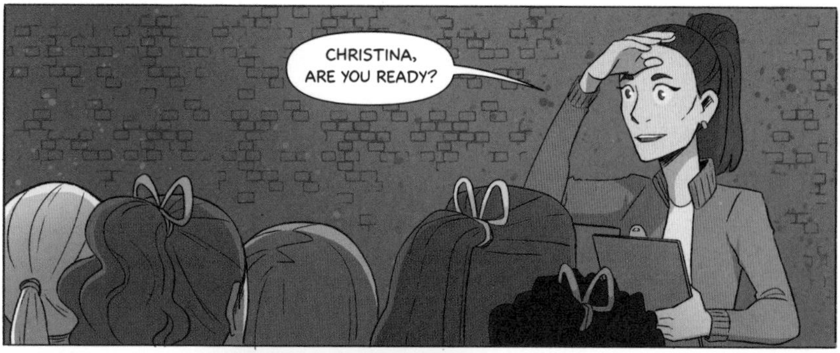
CHRISTINA,
ARE YOU READY?

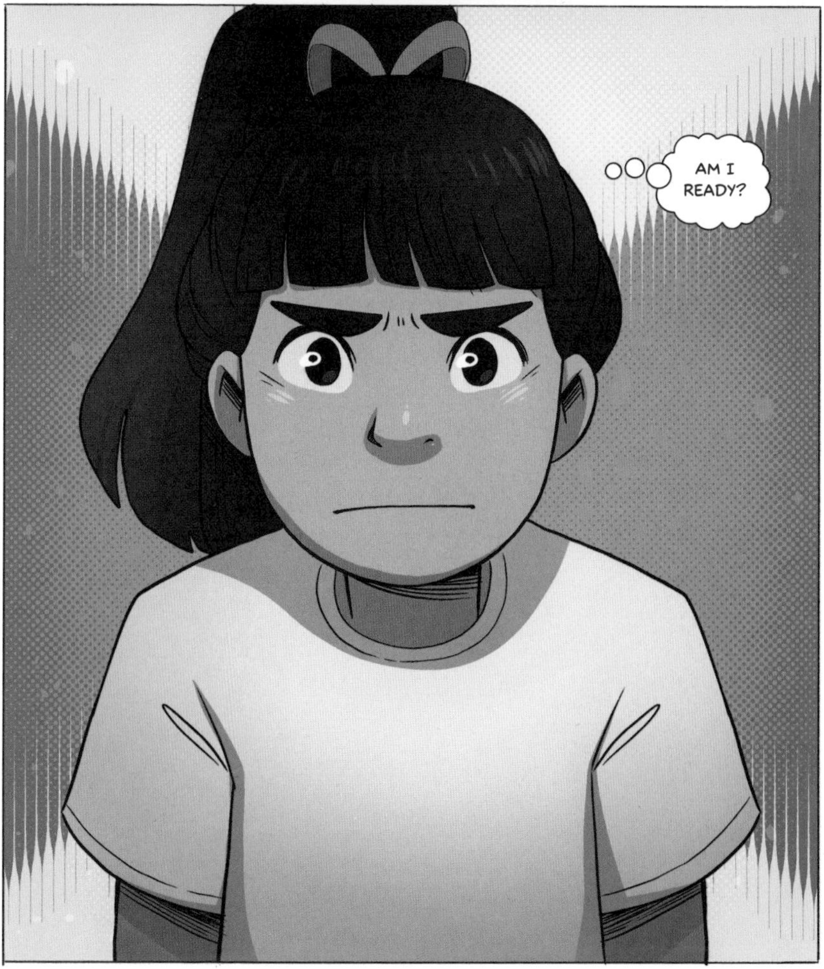
AM I
READY?

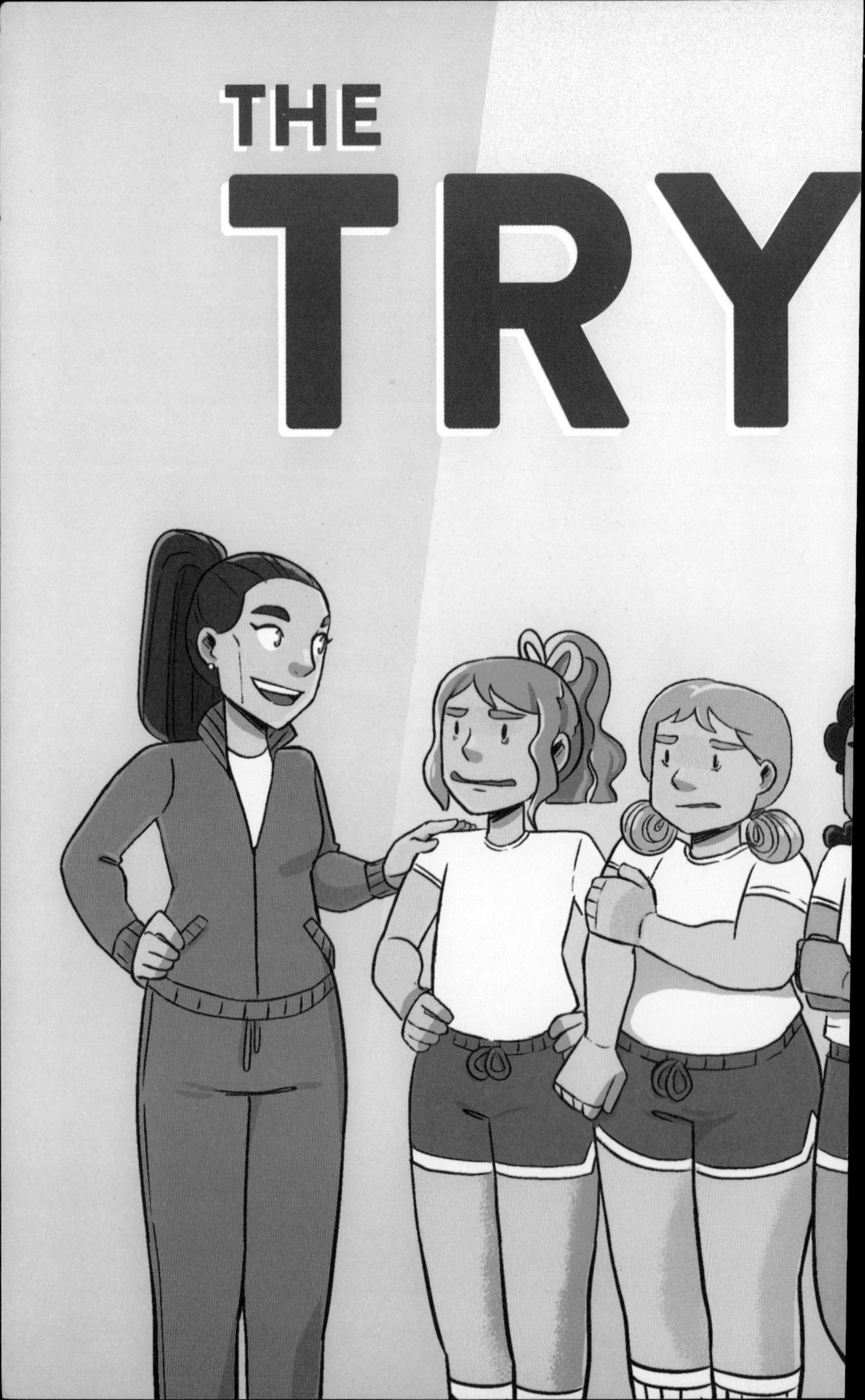
THE
TRY

OUT

WRITTEN BY **CHRISTINA SOONTORNVAT**

ILLUSTRATED BY **JOANNA CACAO**

COLORS BY AMANDA LAFRENAIS

graphix

An Imprint of

SCHOLASTIC

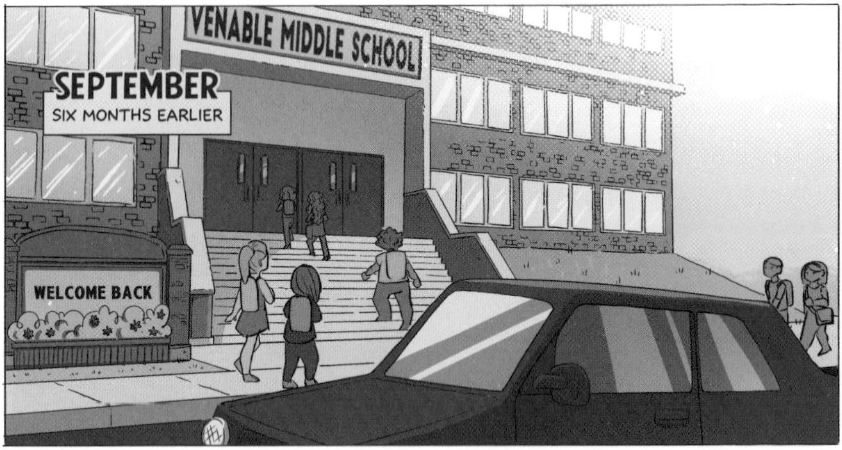
VENABLE MIDDLE SCHOOL
SEPTEMBER
SIX MONTHS EARLIER
WELCOME BACK

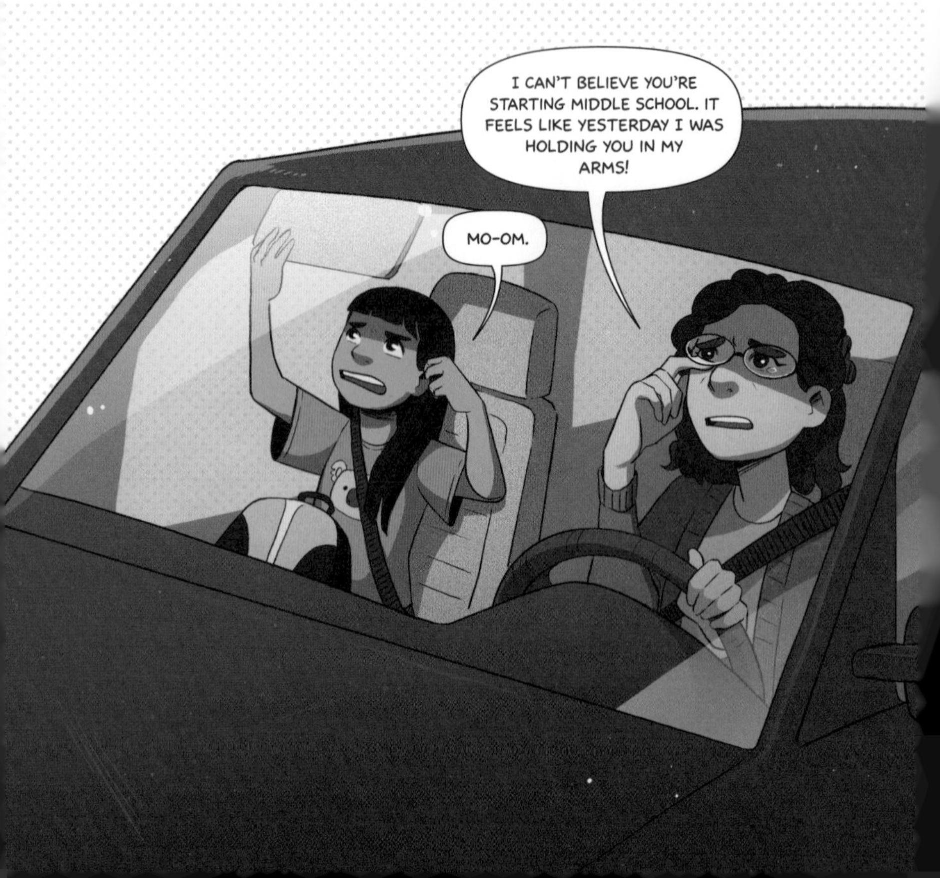
I CAN'T BELIEVE YOU'RE STARTING MIDDLE SCHOOL. IT FEELS LIKE YESTERDAY I WAS HOLDING YOU IN MY ARMS!
MO-OM.

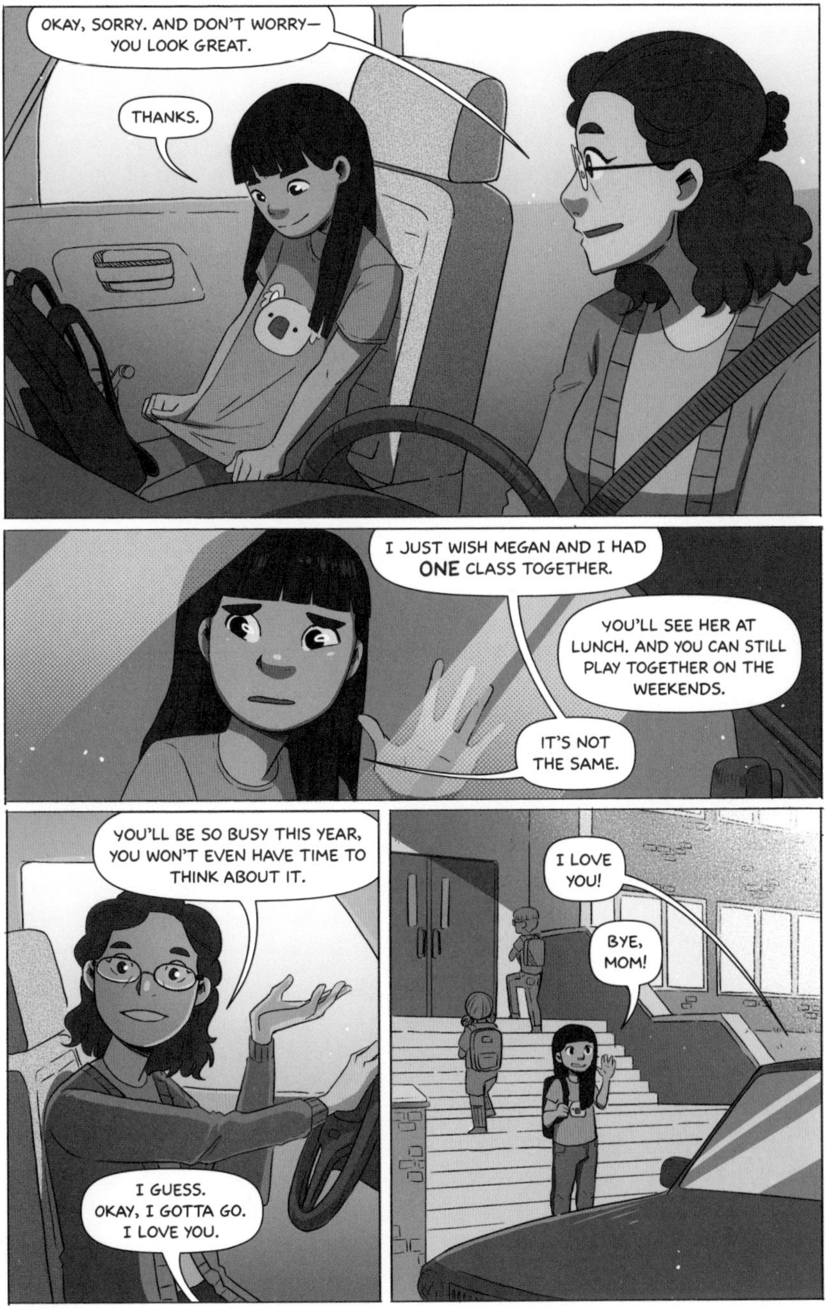
OKAY, SORRY. AND DON'T WORRY— YOU LOOK GREAT.
THANKS.
I JUST WISH MEGAN AND I HAD **ONE** CLASS TOGETHER.
YOU'LL SEE HER AT LUNCH. AND YOU CAN STILL PLAY TOGETHER ON THE WEEKENDS.
IT'S NOT THE SAME.
YOU'LL BE SO BUSY THIS YEAR, YOU WON'T EVEN HAVE TIME TO THINK ABOUT IT.
I GUESS. OKAY, I GOTTA GO. I LOVE YOU.
I LOVE YOU!
BYE, MOM!

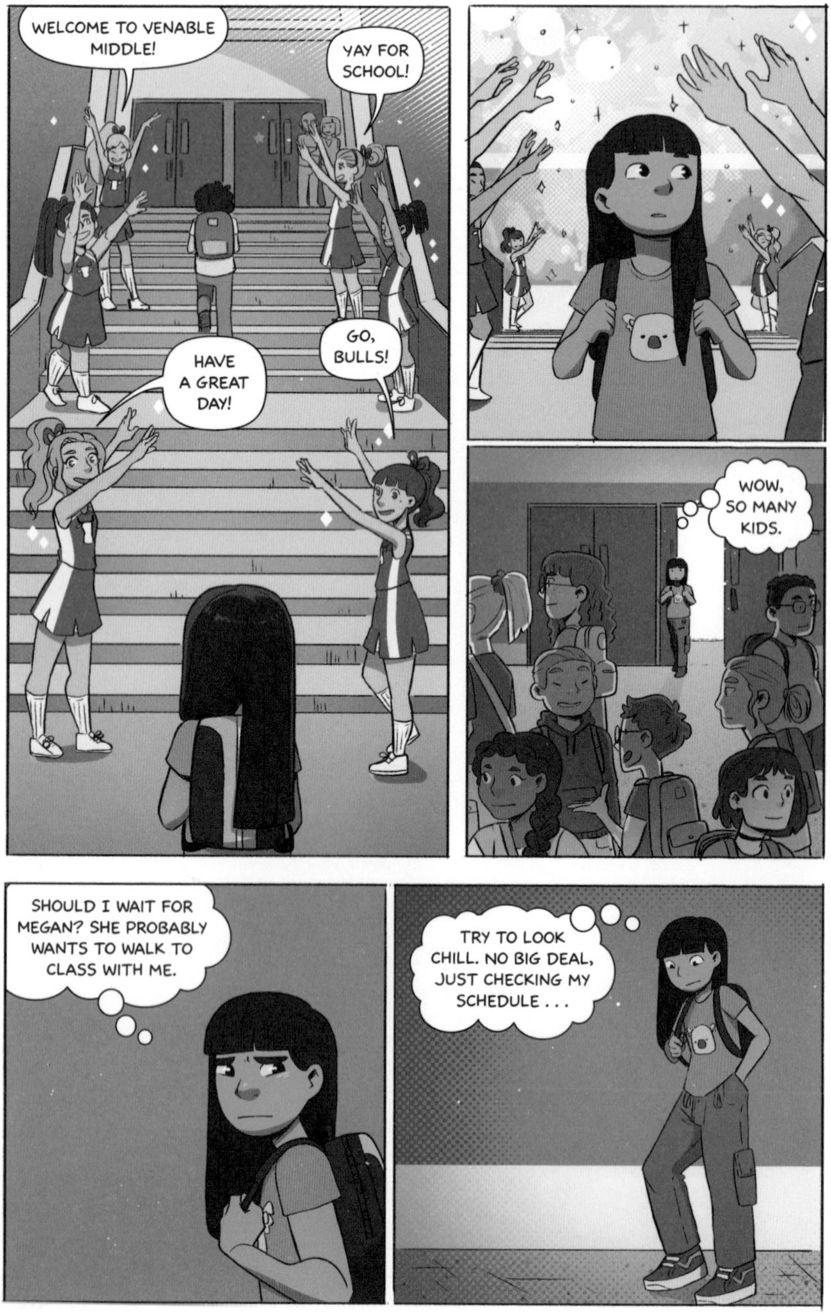
WELCOME TO VENABLE MIDDLE!
YAY FOR SCHOOL!
HAVE A GREAT DAY!
GO, BULLS!
WOW, SO MANY KIDS.
SHOULD I WAIT FOR MEGAN? SHE PROBABLY WANTS TO WALK TO CLASS WITH ME.
TRY TO LOOK CHILL. NO BIG DEAL, JUST CHECKING MY SCHEDULE . . .

SCHEDULE
1-Homeroom-Language Arts
2-Social Studies
3-Math
4-Home Economics
Lunch!
5-Science
6-Art
7-PE
I GUESS I CAN'T WAIT ANY LONGER OR I'LL BE LATE.
CLASS, CLASS, WHERE IS MY ROOM?
RM 112
NO BULLY ZONE
WHOA, THOSE MUST BE THE EIGHTH GRADERS. LOOK AT THEIR COOL SHOES.

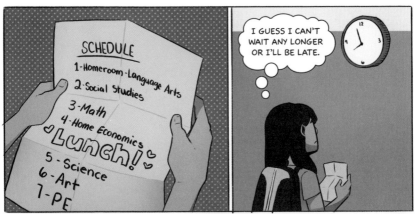

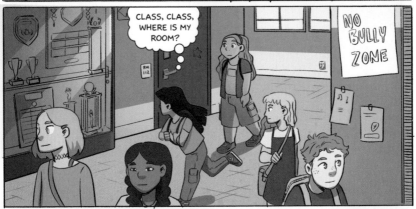

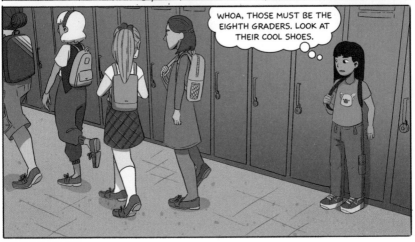

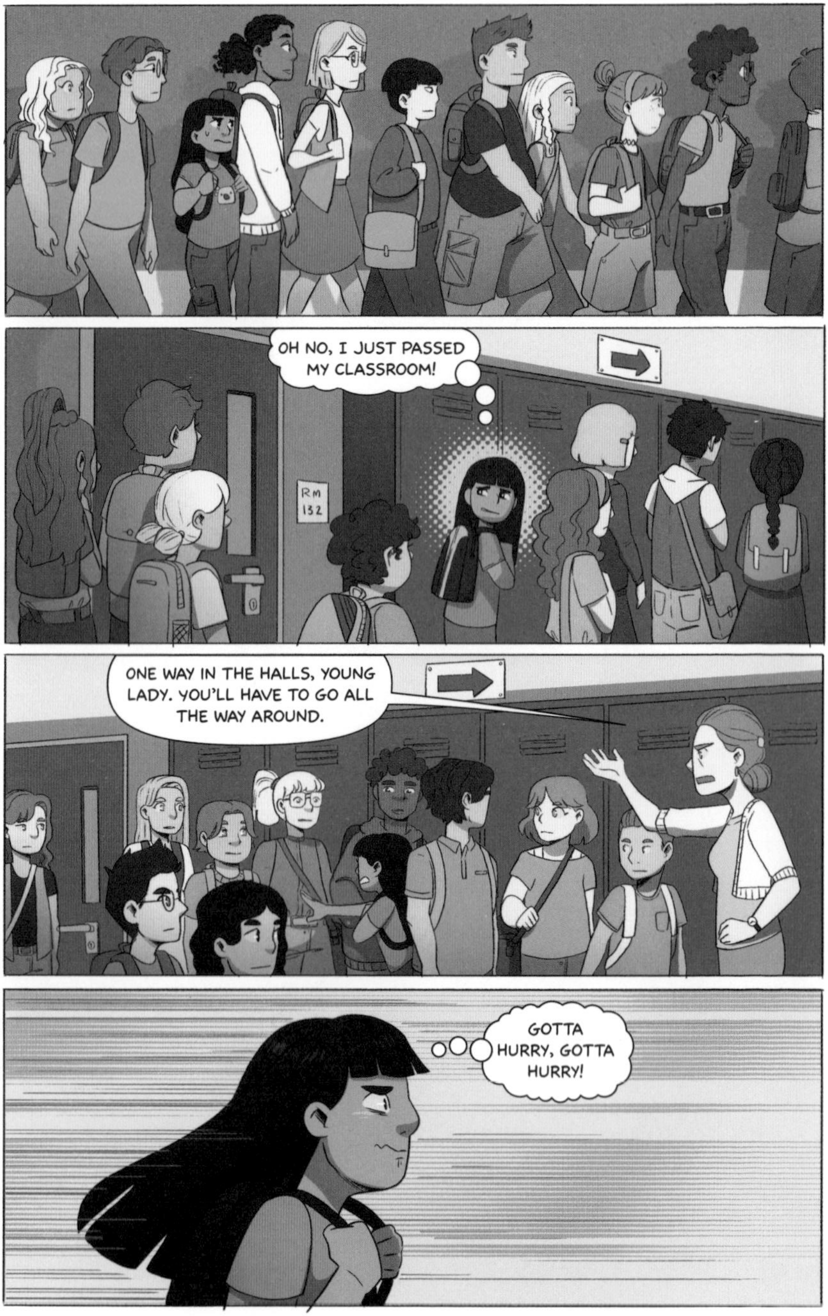
OH NO, I JUST PASSED MY CLASSROOM!
RM 132
ONE WAY IN THE HALLS, YOUNG LADY. YOU'LL HAVE TO GO ALL THE WAY AROUND.
GOTTA HURRY, GOTTA HURRY!

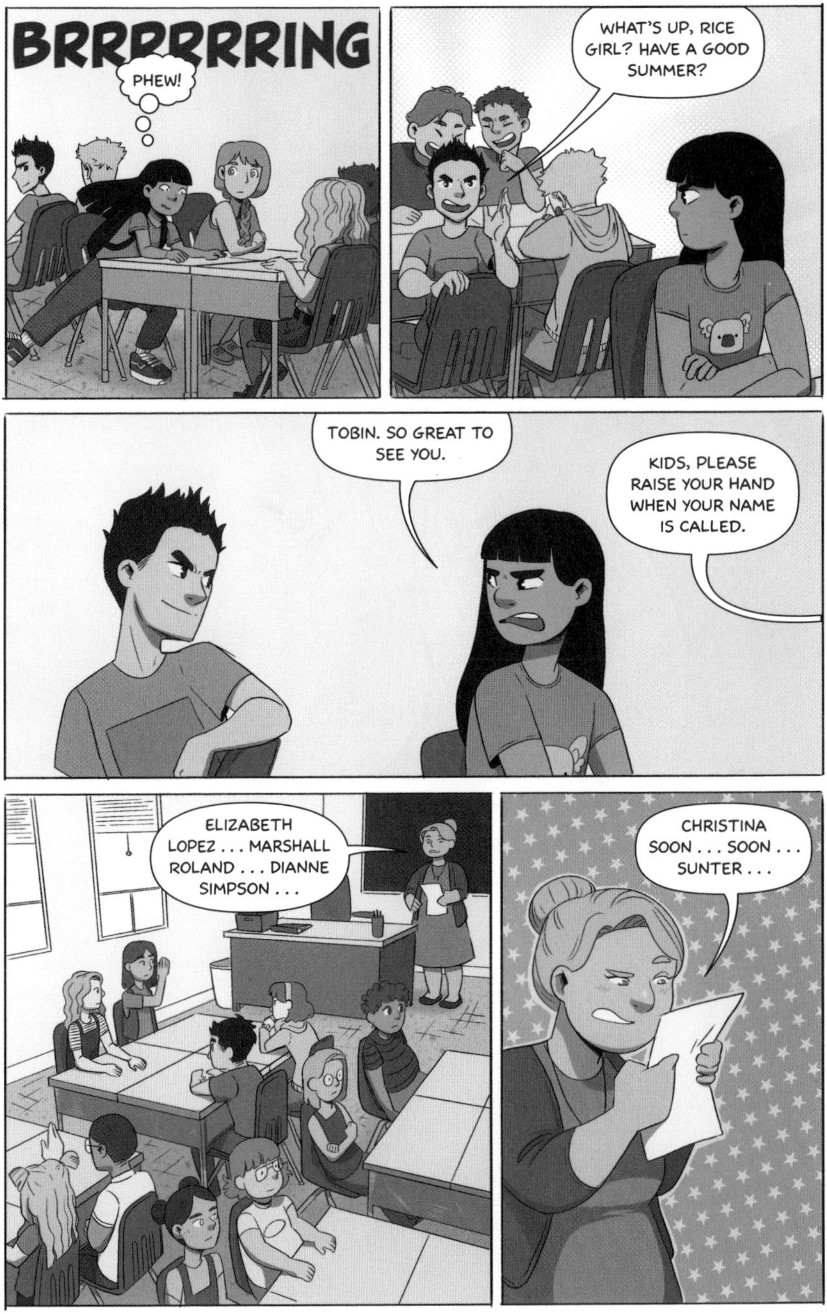
BRRRRRRING
PHEW!
WHAT'S UP, RICE GIRL? HAVE A GOOD SUMMER?
TOBIN. SO GREAT TO SEE YOU.
KIDS, PLEASE RAISE YOUR HAND WHEN YOUR NAME IS CALLED.
ELIZABETH LOPEZ . . . MARSHALL ROLAND . . . DIANNE SIMPSON . . .
CHRISTINA SOON . . . SOON . . . SUNTER . . .

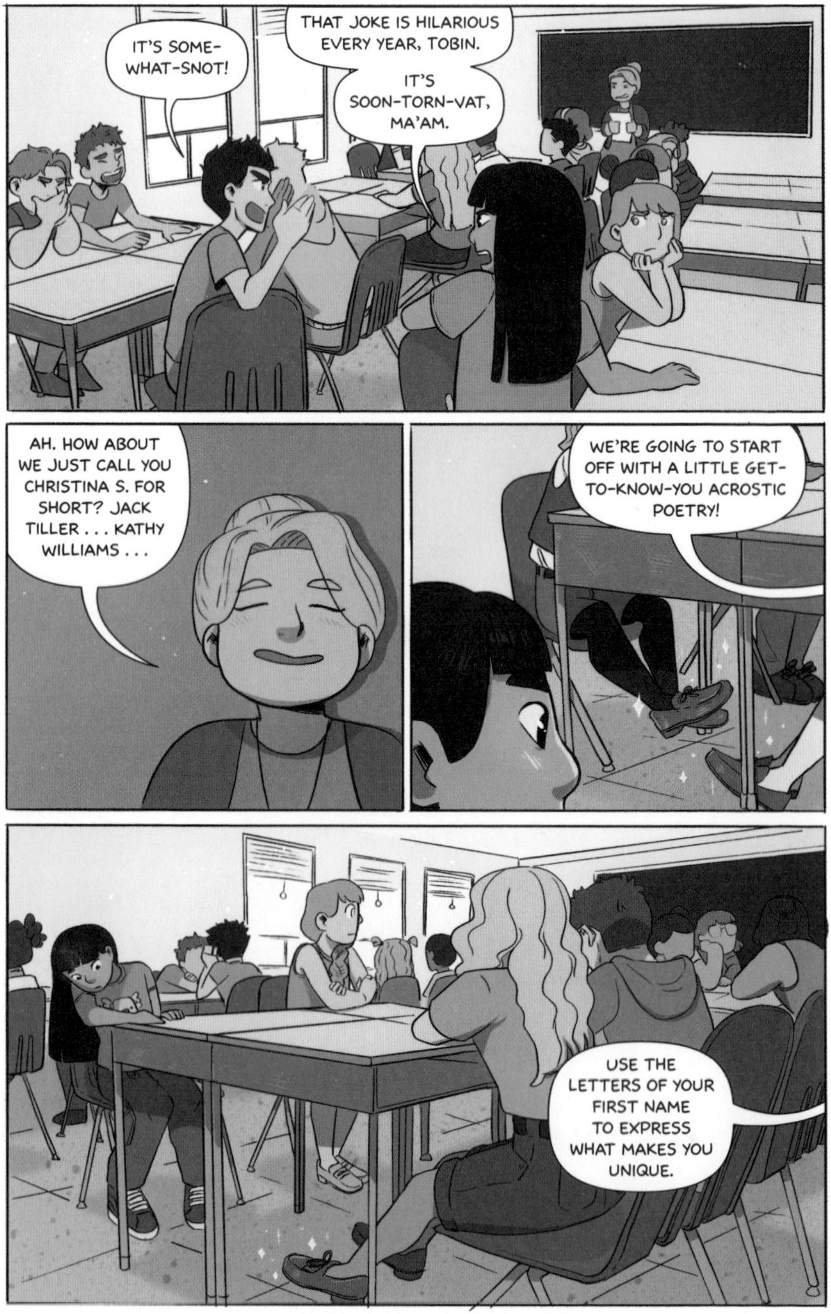
IT'S SOME-WHAT-SNOT!
THAT JOKE IS HILARIOUS EVERY YEAR, TOBIN.
IT'S SOON-TORN-VAT, MA'AM.
AH. HOW ABOUT WE JUST CALL YOU CHRISTINA S. FOR SHORT? JACK TILLER . . . KATHY WILLIAMS . . .
WE'RE GOING TO START OFF WITH A LITTLE GET-TO-KNOW-YOU ACROSTIC POETRY!
USE THE LETTERS OF YOUR FIRST NAME TO EXPRESS WHAT MAKES YOU UNIQUE.

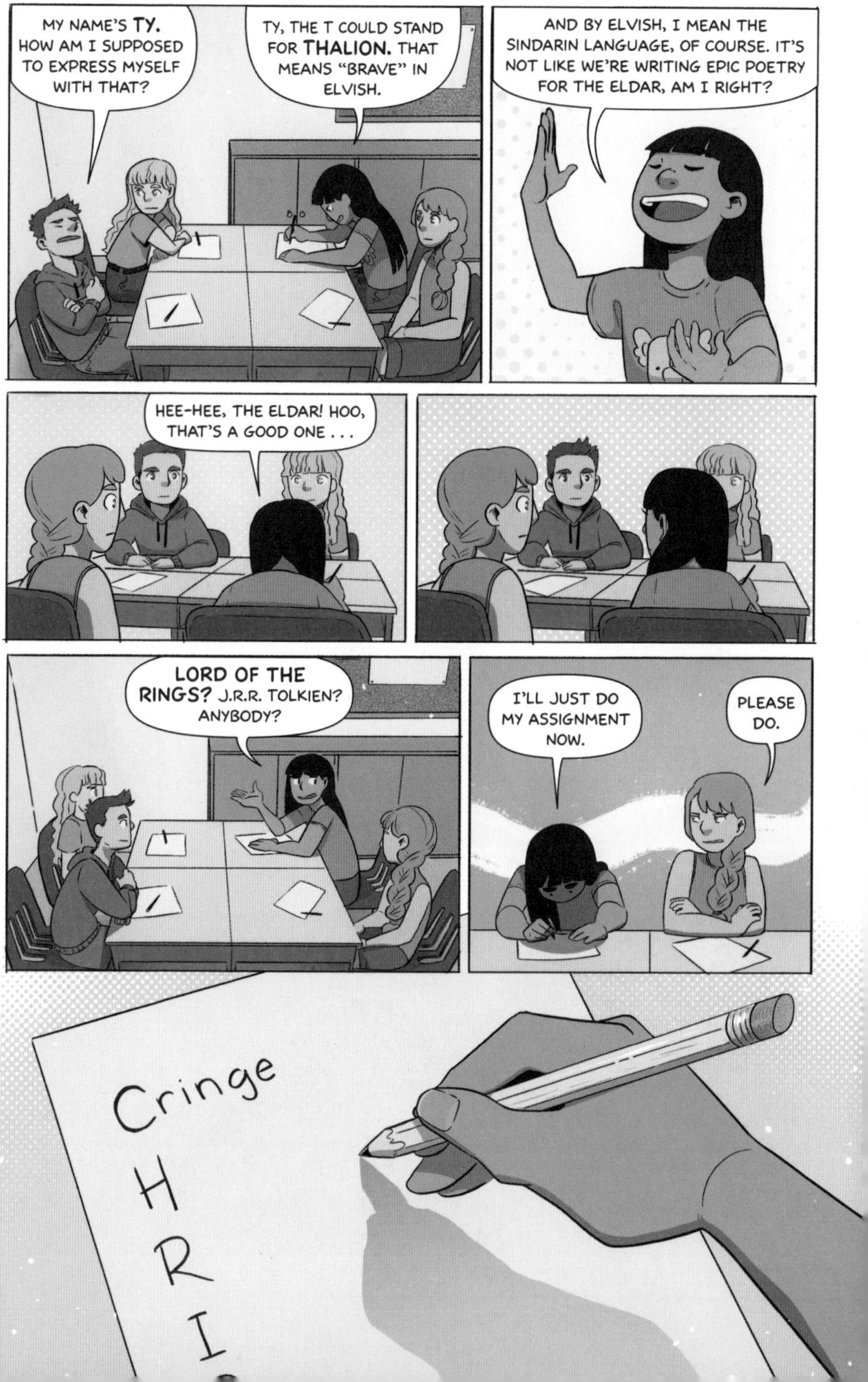
MY NAME'S TY. HOW AM I SUPPOSED TO EXPRESS MYSELF WITH THAT?
TY, THE T COULD STAND FOR THALION. THAT MEANS "BRAVE" IN ELVISH.
AND BY ELVISH, I MEAN THE SINDARIN LANGUAGE, OF COURSE. IT'S NOT LIKE WE'RE WRITING EPIC POETRY FOR THE ELDAR, AM I RIGHT?
HEE-HEE, THE ELDAR! HOO, THAT'S A GOOD ONE . . .
LORD OF THE RINGS? J.R.R. TOLKIEN? ANYBODY?
I'LL JUST DO MY ASSIGNMENT NOW.
PLEASE DO.
Cringe
H
R
I

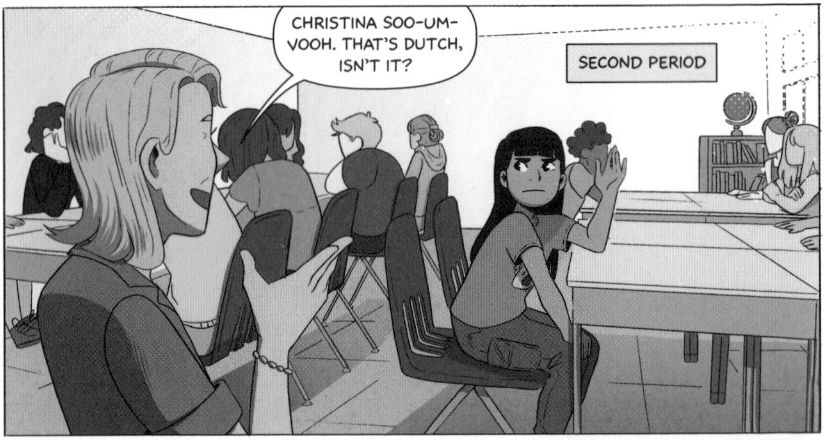
CHRISTINA SOO-UM-VOOH. THAT'S DUTCH, ISN'T IT?
SECOND PERIOD

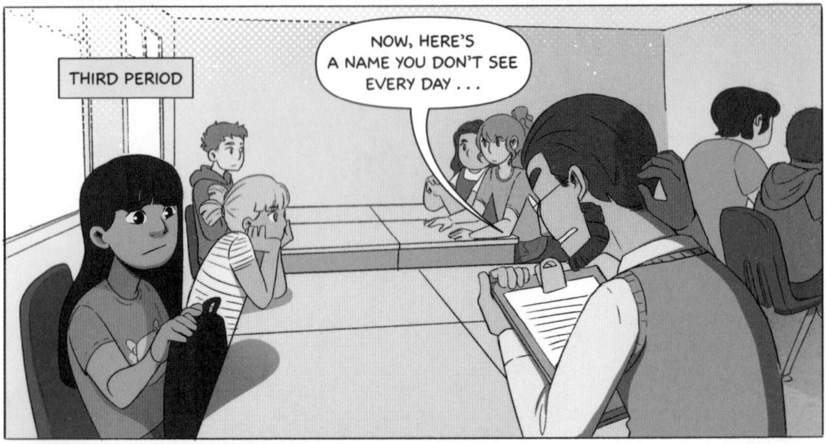
THIRD PERIOD
NOW, HERE'S A NAME YOU DON'T SEE EVERY DAY . . .

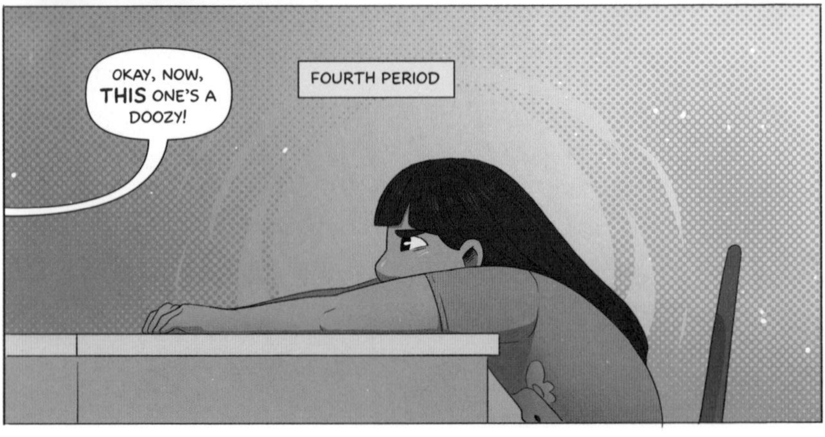
OKAY, NOW, **THIS** ONE'S A DOOZY!
FOURTH PERIOD

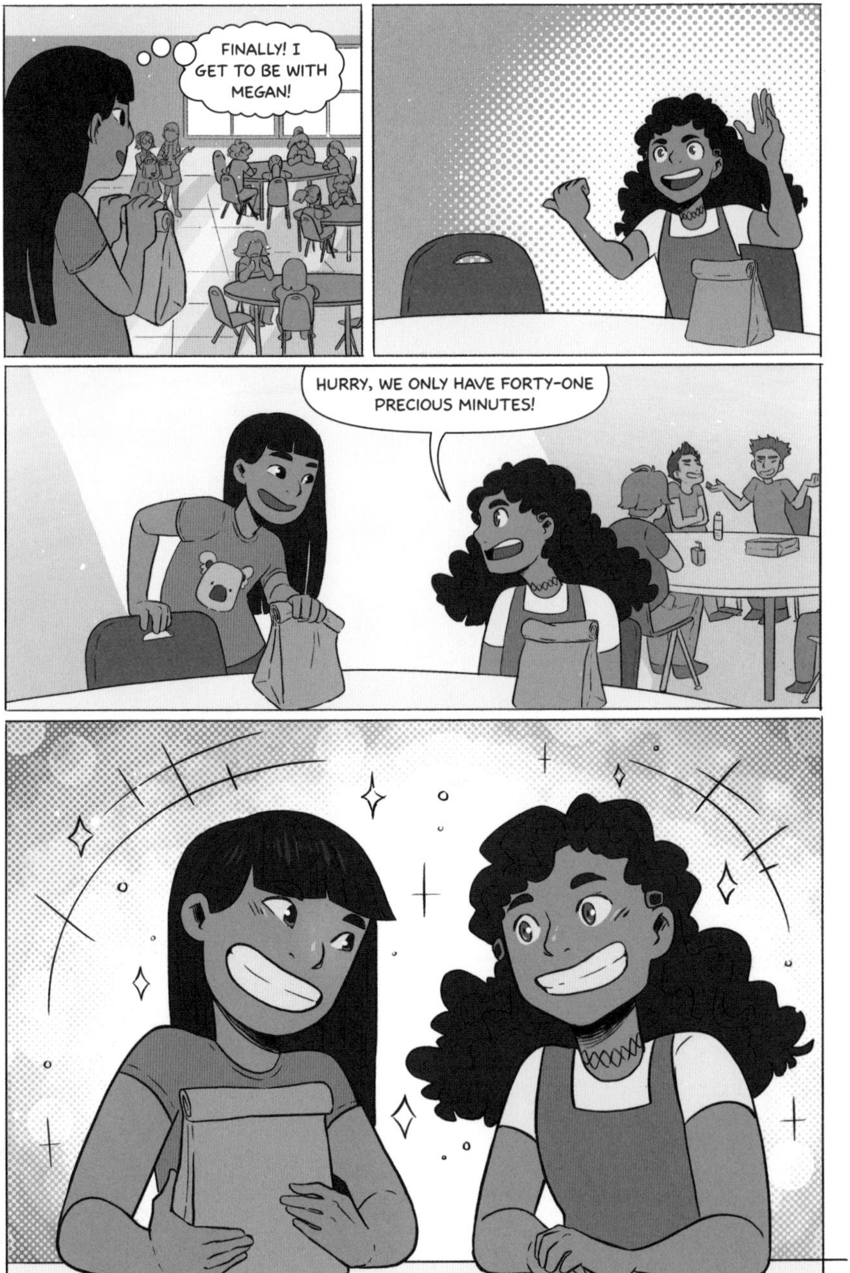
FINALLY! I GET TO BE WITH MEGAN!
HURRY, WE ONLY HAVE FORTY-ONE PRECIOUS MINUTES!

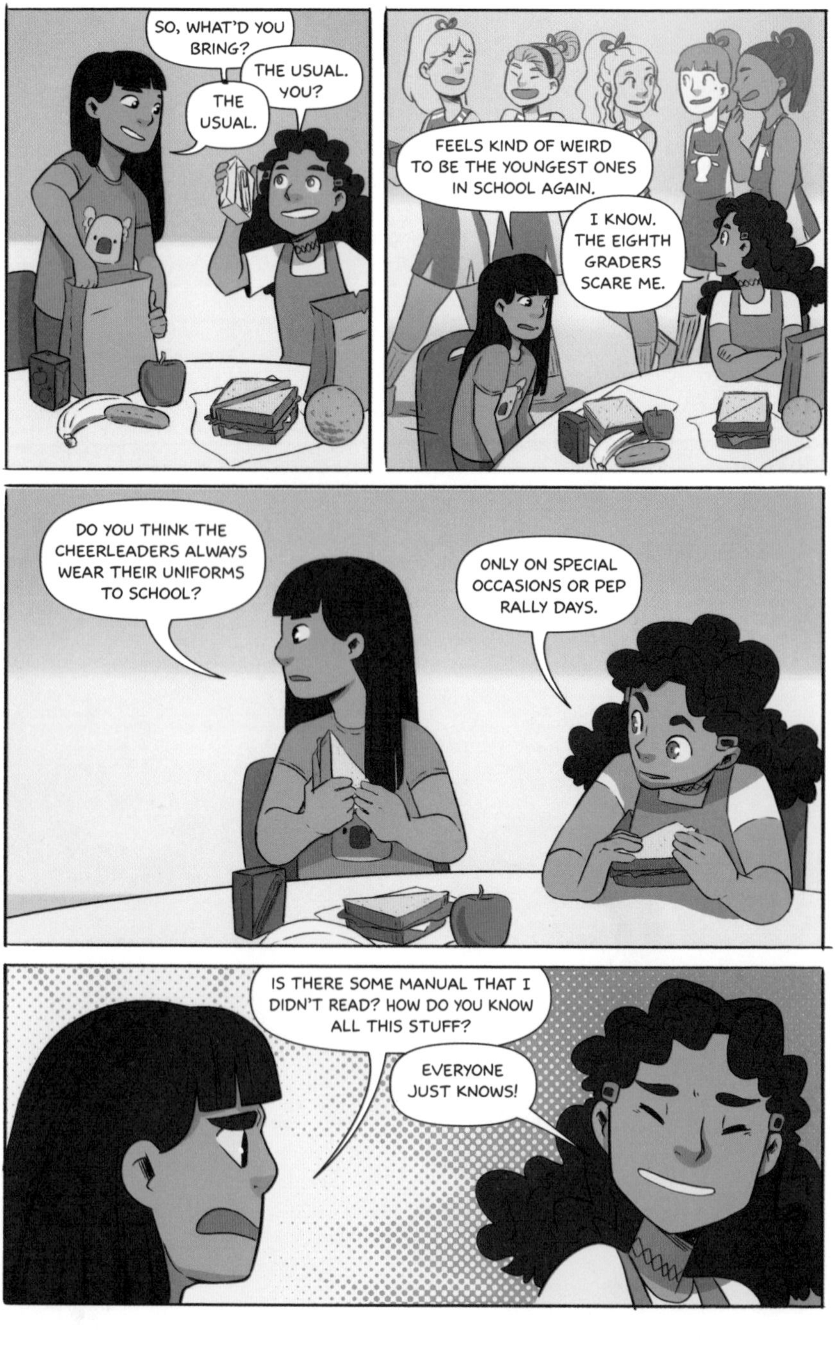
SO, WHAT'D YOU BRING?
THE USUAL. YOU?
THE USUAL.
FEELS KIND OF WEIRD TO BE THE YOUNGEST ONES IN SCHOOL AGAIN.
I KNOW. THE EIGHTH GRADERS SCARE ME.
DO YOU THINK THE CHEERLEADERS ALWAYS WEAR THEIR UNIFORMS TO SCHOOL?
ONLY ON SPECIAL OCCASIONS OR PEP RALLY DAYS.
IS THERE SOME MANUAL THAT I DIDN'T READ? HOW DO YOU KNOW ALL THIS STUFF?
EVERYONE JUST KNOWS!

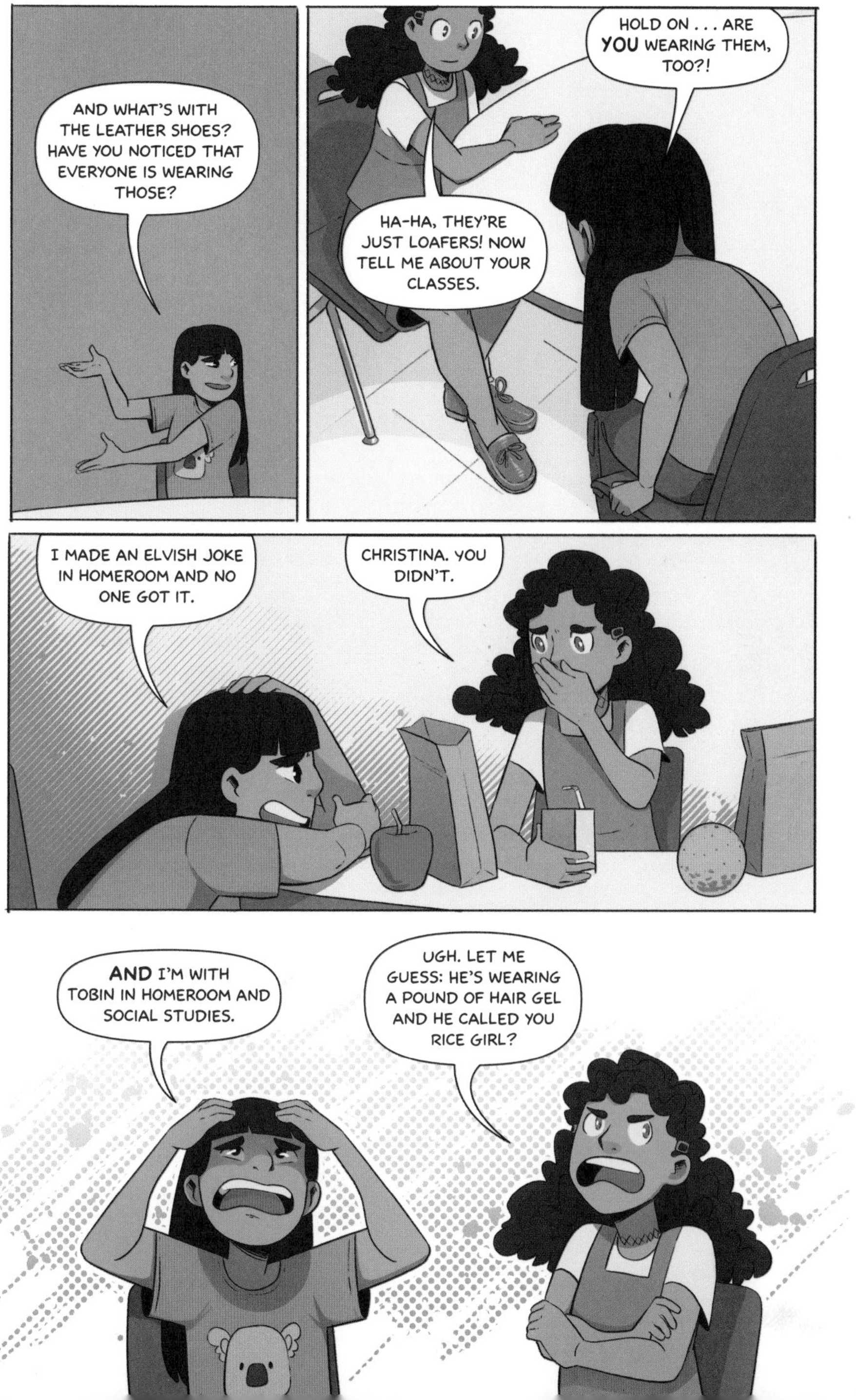
AND WHAT'S WITH THE LEATHER SHOES? HAVE YOU NOTICED THAT EVERYONE IS WEARING THOSE?
HOLD ON . . . ARE YOU WEARING THEM, TOO?!
HA-HA, THEY'RE JUST LOAFERS! NOW TELL ME ABOUT YOUR CLASSES.
I MADE AN ELVISH JOKE IN HOMEROOM AND NO ONE GOT IT.
CHRISTINA. YOU DIDN'T.
AND I'M WITH TOBIN IN HOMEROOM AND SOCIAL STUDIES.
UGH. LET ME GUESS: HE'S WEARING A POUND OF HAIR GEL AND HE CALLED YOU RICE GIRL?

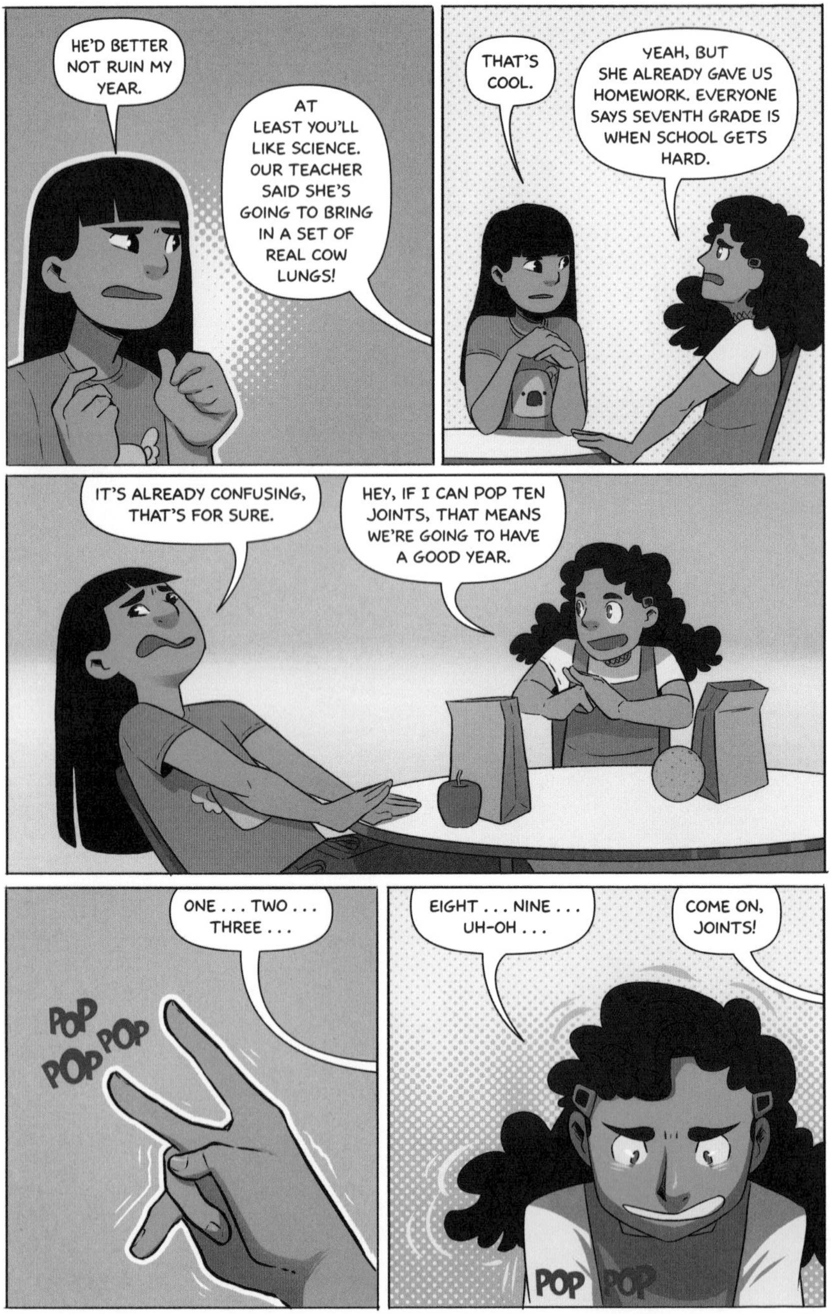
HE'D BETTER NOT RUIN MY YEAR.
AT LEAST YOU'LL LIKE SCIENCE. OUR TEACHER SAID SHE'S GOING TO BRING IN A SET OF REAL COW LUNGS!
THAT'S COOL.
YEAH, BUT SHE ALREADY GAVE US HOMEWORK. EVERYONE SAYS SEVENTH GRADE IS WHEN SCHOOL GETS HARD.
IT'S ALREADY CONFUSING, THAT'S FOR SURE.
HEY, IF I CAN POP TEN JOINTS, THAT MEANS WE'RE GOING TO HAVE A GOOD YEAR.
ONE . . . TWO . . . THREE . . .
POP
POP
POP
EIGHT . . . NINE . . . UH-OH . . .
COME ON, JOINTS!
POP
POP

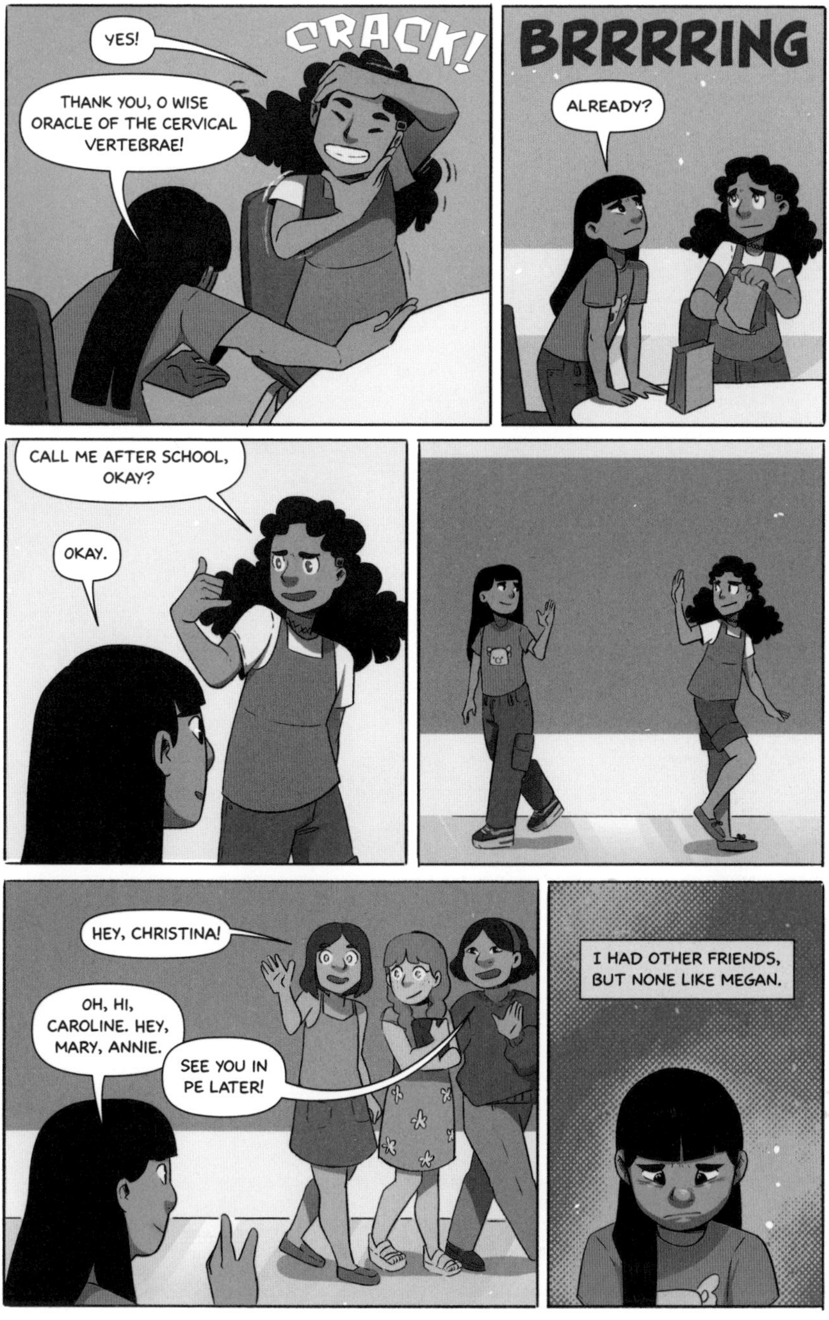
YES!
CRACK!
THANK YOU, O WISE ORACLE OF THE CERVICAL VERTEBRAE!
BRRRRING
ALREADY?
CALL ME AFTER SCHOOL, OKAY?
OKAY.
HEY, CHRISTINA!
OH, HI, CAROLINE. HEY, MARY, ANNIE.
SEE YOU IN PE LATER!
I HAD OTHER FRIENDS, BUT NONE LIKE MEGAN.

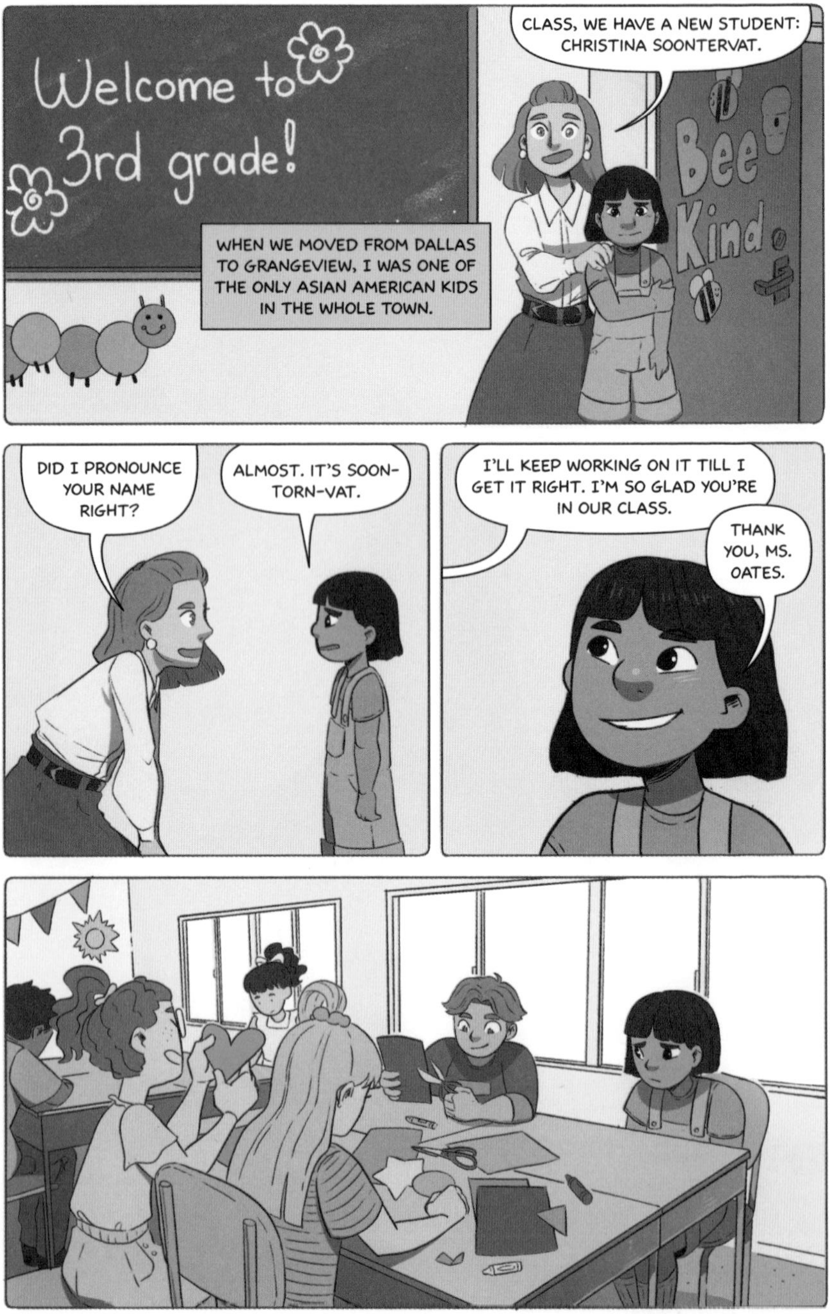
Welcome to 3rd grade!
CLASS, WE HAVE A NEW STUDENT: CHRISTINA SOONTERVAT.
WHEN WE MOVED FROM DALLAS TO GRANGEVIEW, I WAS ONE OF THE ONLY ASIAN AMERICAN KIDS IN THE WHOLE TOWN.
Bee Kind
DID I PRONOUNCE YOUR NAME RIGHT?
ALMOST. IT'S SOON-TORN-VAT.
I'LL KEEP WORKING ON IT TILL I GET IT RIGHT. I'M SO GLAD YOU'RE IN OUR CLASS.
THANK YOU, MS. OATES.

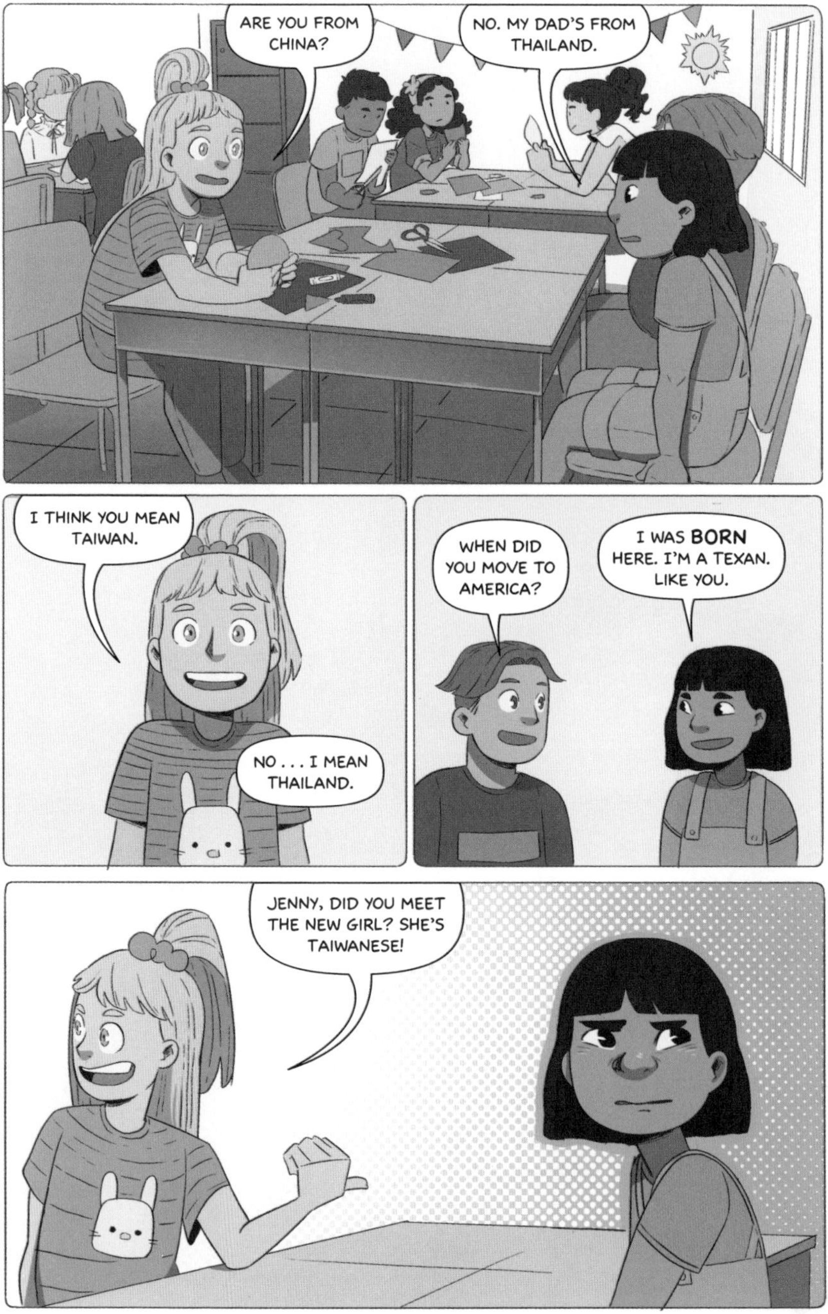
ARE YOU FROM CHINA?
NO. MY DAD'S FROM THAILAND.
I THINK YOU MEAN TAIWAN.
NO . . . I MEAN THAILAND.
WHEN DID YOU MOVE TO AMERICA?
I WAS **BORN** HERE. I'M A TEXAN. LIKE YOU.
JENNY, DID YOU MEET THE NEW GIRL? SHE'S TAIWANESE!

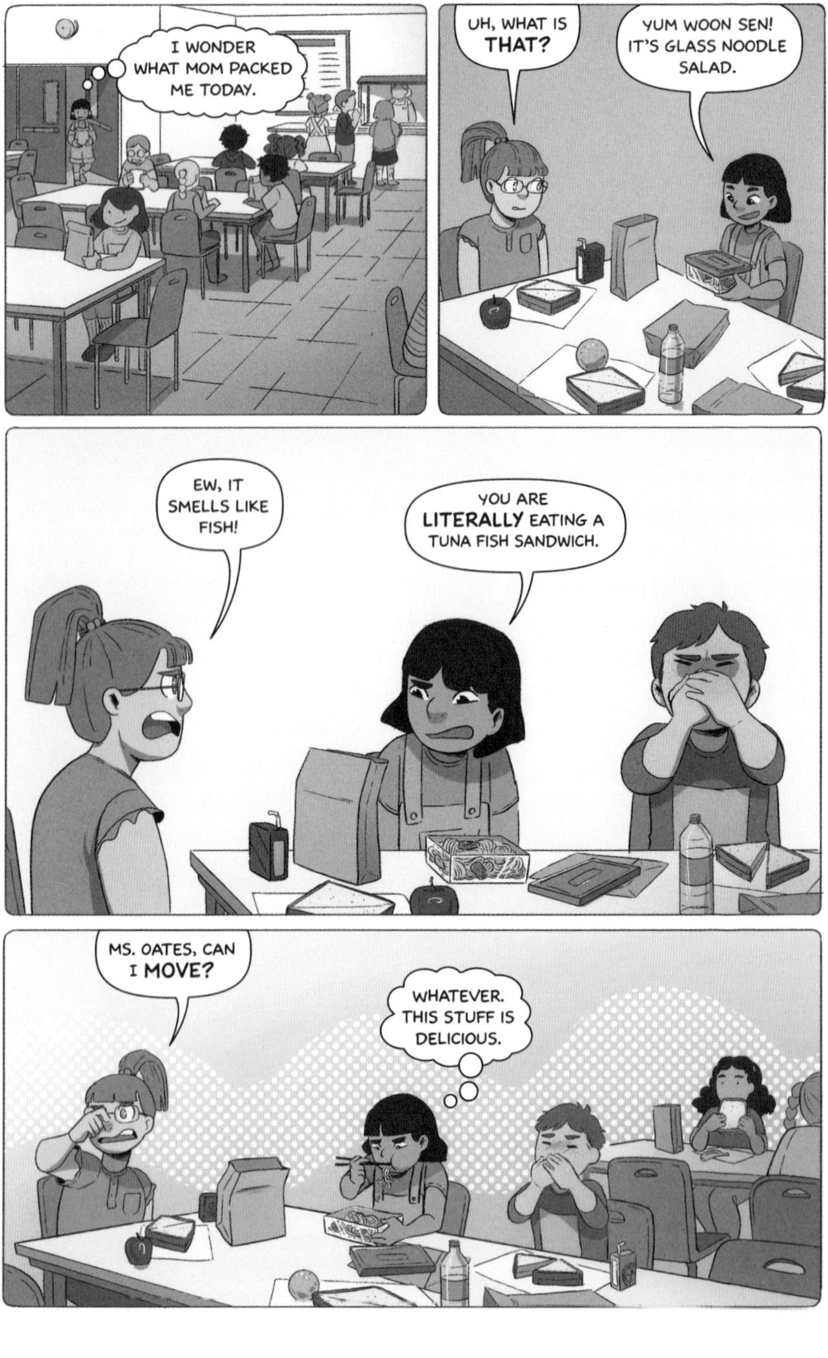
I WONDER WHAT MOM PACKED ME TODAY.
UH, WHAT IS **THAT?**
YUM WOON SEN! IT'S GLASS NOODLE SALAD.
EW, IT SMELLS LIKE FISH!
YOU ARE **LITERALLY** EATING A TUNA FISH SANDWICH.
MS. OATES, CAN I **MOVE?**
WHATEVER. THIS STUFF IS DELICIOUS.

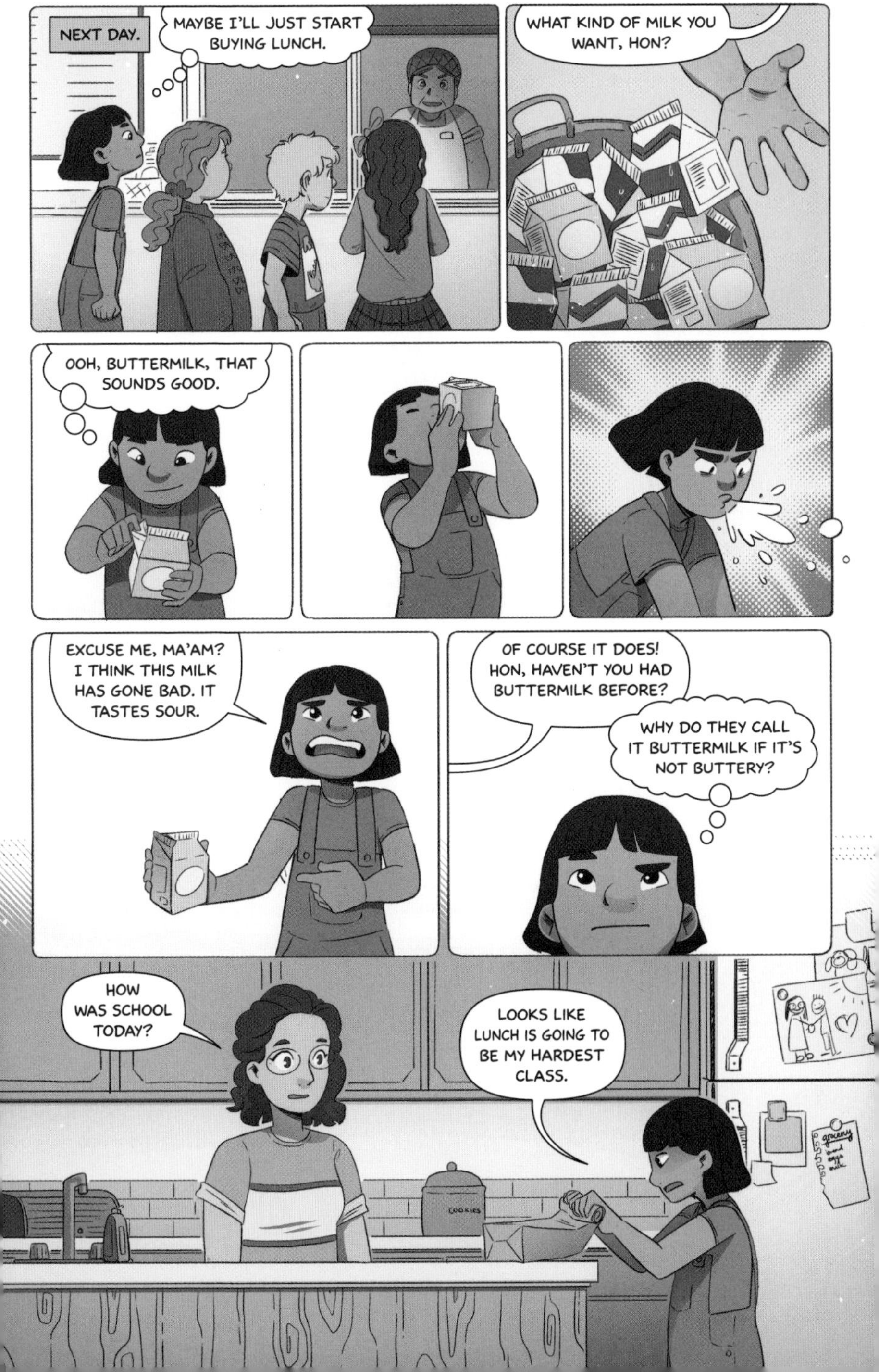
NEXT DAY.
MAYBE I'LL JUST START BUYING LUNCH.
WHAT KIND OF MILK YOU WANT, HON?
OOH, BUTTERMILK, THAT SOUNDS GOOD.
EXCUSE ME, MA'AM? I THINK THIS MILK HAS GONE BAD. IT TASTES SOUR.
OF COURSE IT DOES! HON, HAVEN'T YOU HAD BUTTERMILK BEFORE?
WHY DO THEY CALL IT BUTTERMILK IF IT'S NOT BUTTERY?
HOW WAS SCHOOL TODAY?
LOOKS LIKE LUNCH IS GOING TO BE MY HARDEST CLASS.
COOKIES

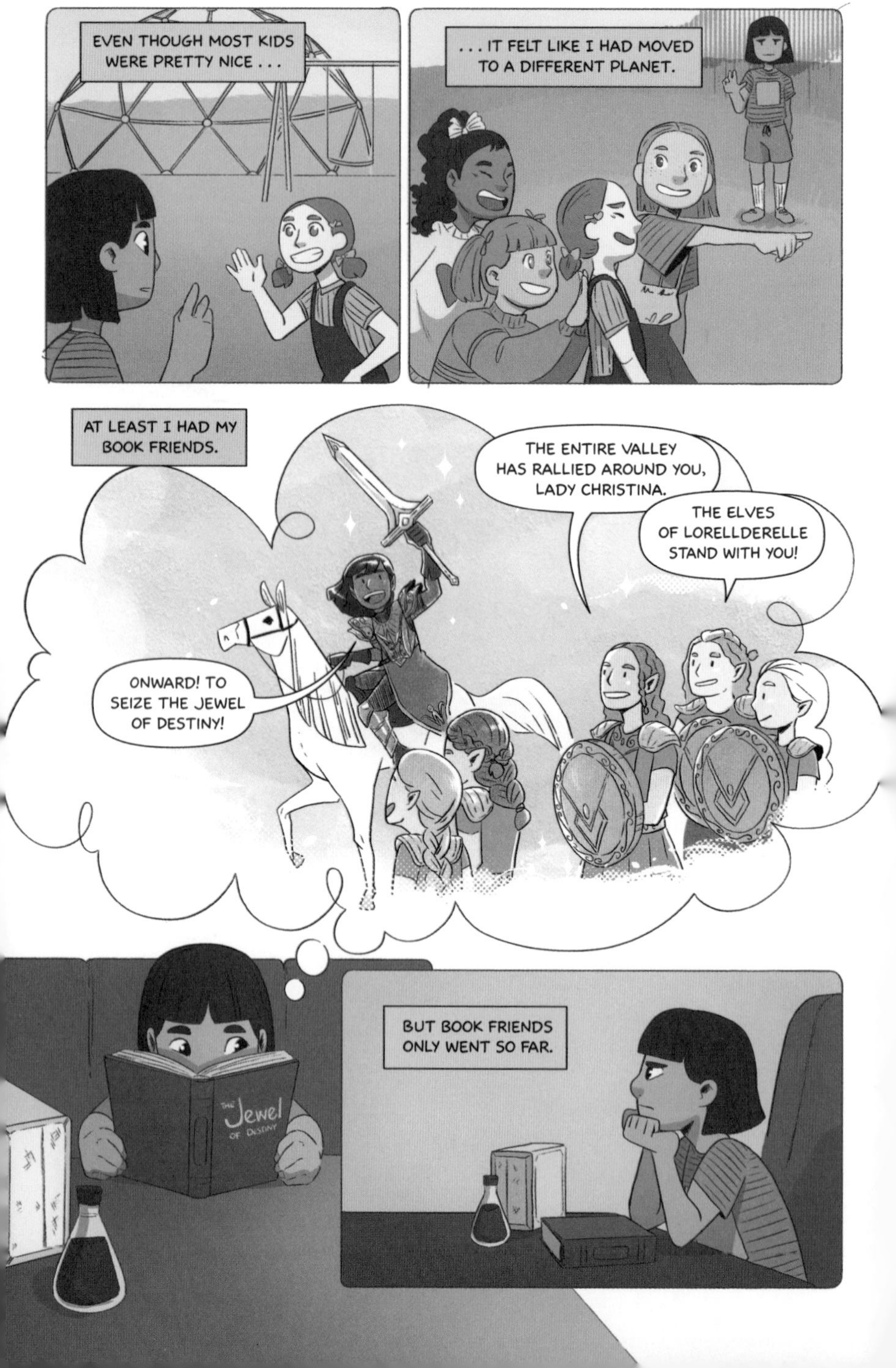
EVEN THOUGH MOST KIDS WERE PRETTY NICE . . .
. . . IT FELT LIKE I HAD MOVED TO A DIFFERENT PLANET.
AT LEAST I HAD MY BOOK FRIENDS.
THE ENTIRE VALLEY HAS RALLIED AROUND YOU, LADY CHRISTINA.
THE ELVES OF LORELLDERELLE STAND WITH YOU!
ONWARD! TO SEIZE THE JEWEL OF DESTINY!
THE JEWEL OF DESTINY
BUT BOOK FRIENDS ONLY WENT SO FAR.

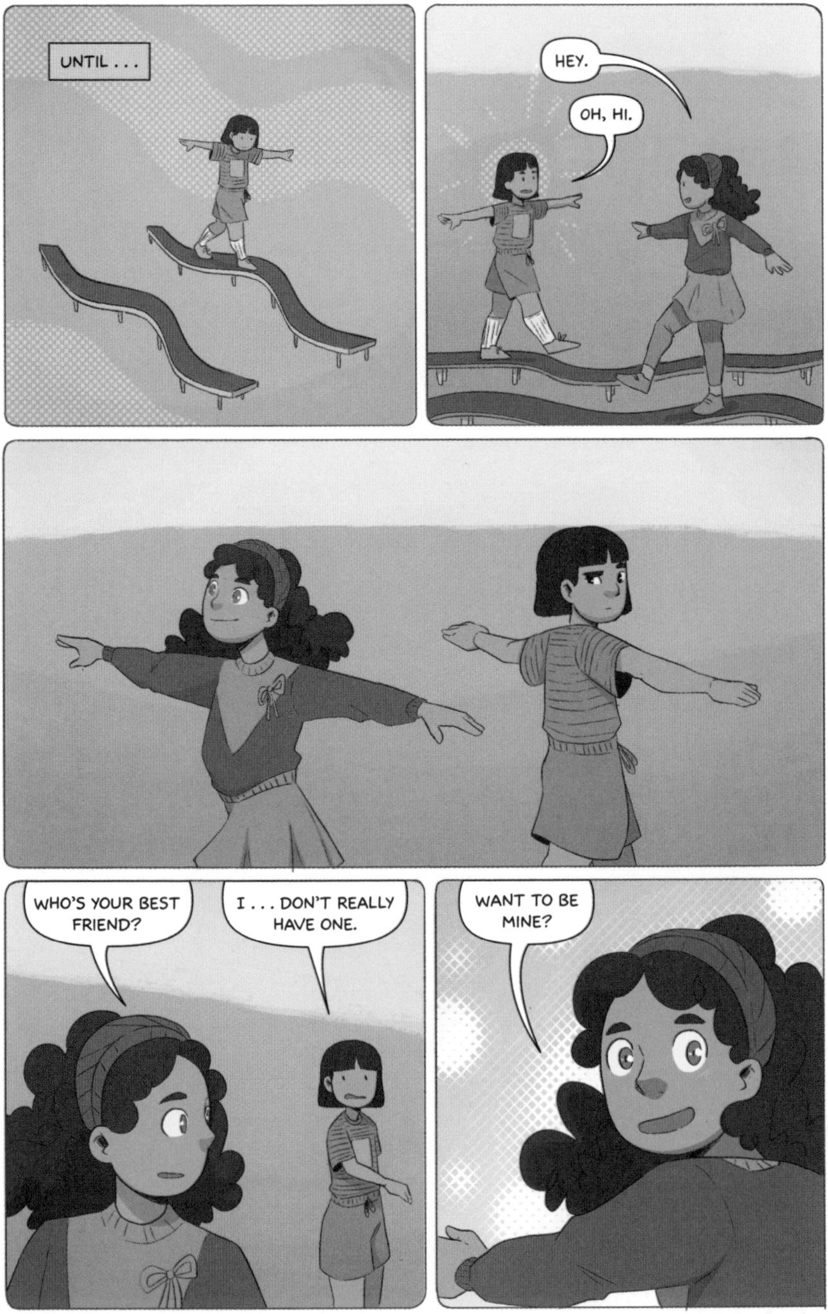
UNTIL . . .
HEY.
OH, HI.
WHO'S YOUR BEST FRIEND?
I . . . DON'T REALLY HAVE ONE.
WANT TO BE MINE?

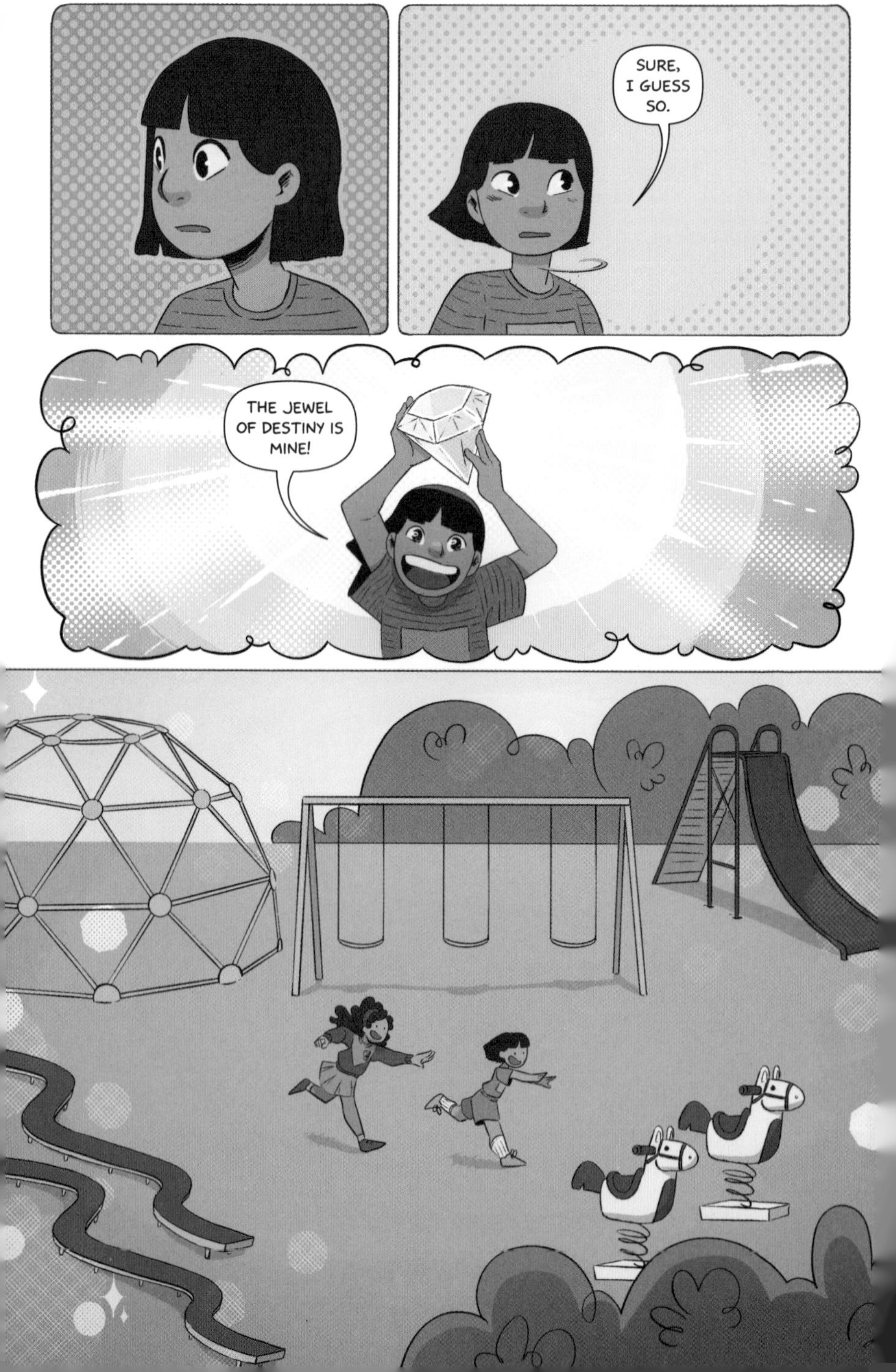
SURE, I GUESS SO.
THE JEWEL OF DESTINY IS MINE!

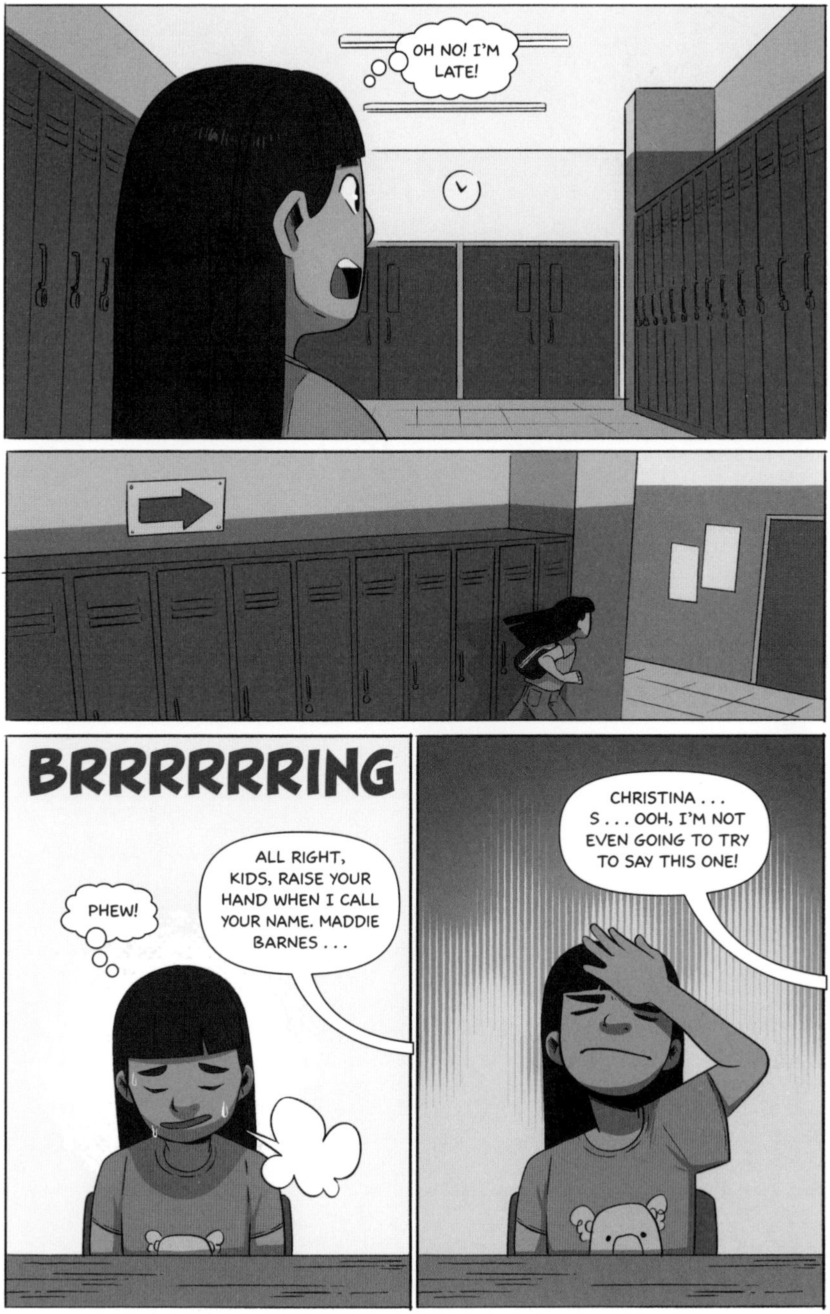
OH NO! I'M LATE!
BRRRRRRING
PHEW!
ALL RIGHT, KIDS, RAISE YOUR HAND WHEN I CALL YOUR NAME. MADDIE BARNES . . .
CHRISTINA . . . S . . . OOH, I'M NOT EVEN GOING TO TRY TO SAY THIS ONE!

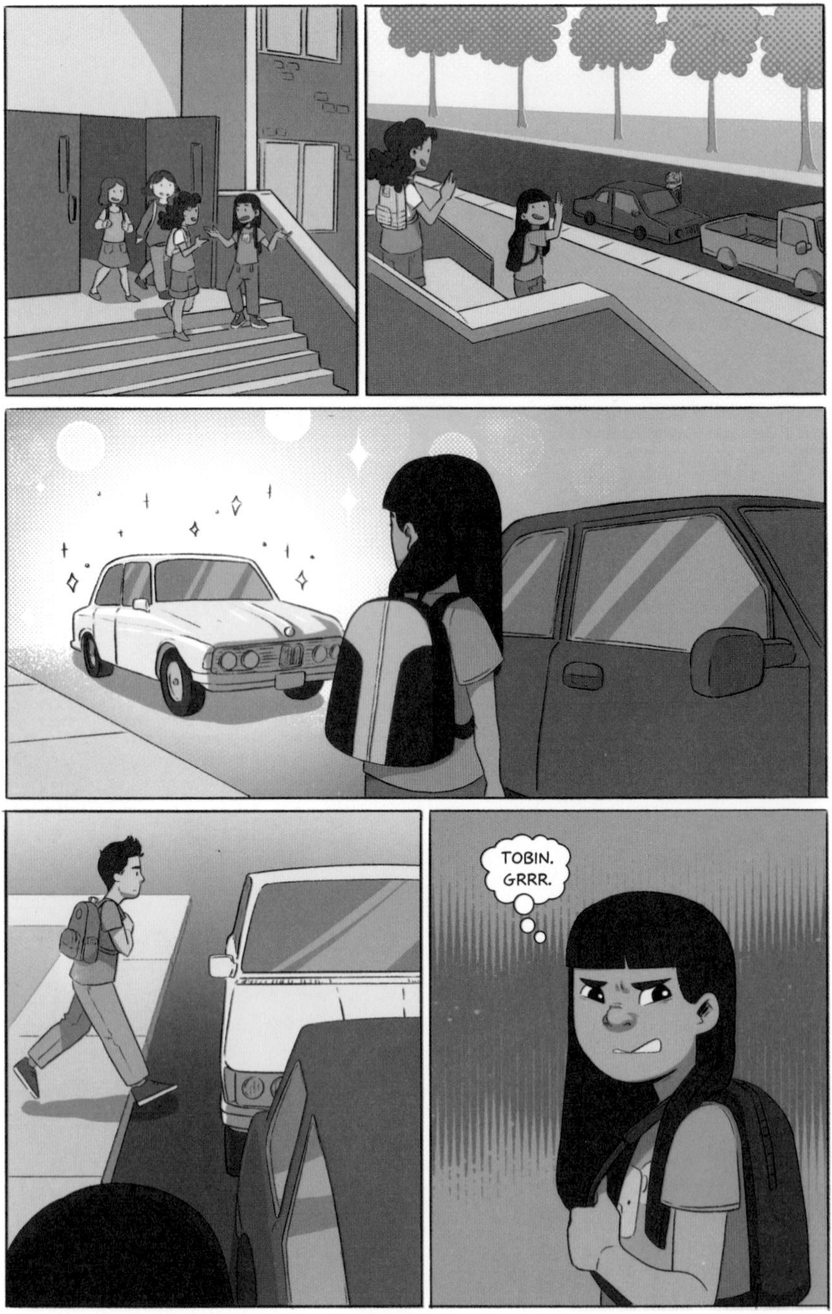
TOBIN.
GRRR.

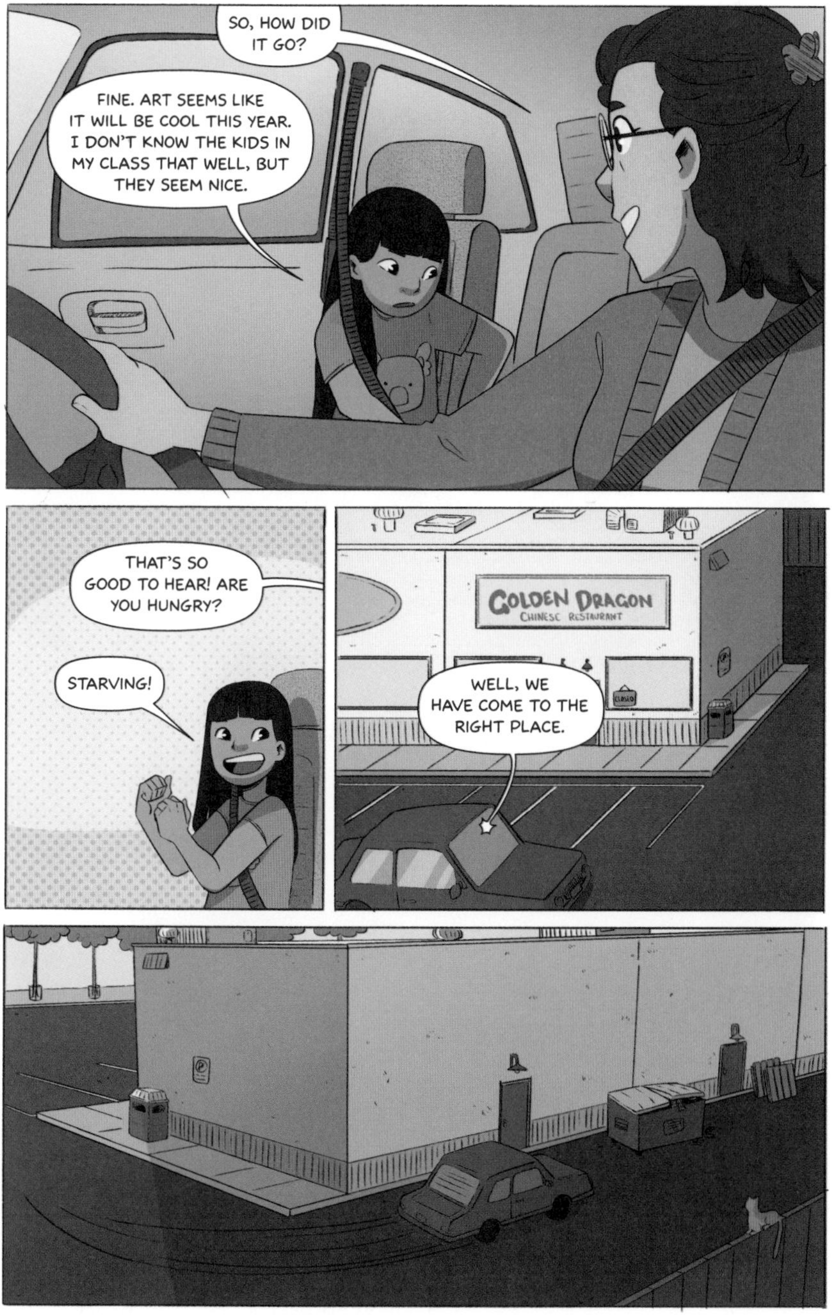
SO, HOW DID IT GO?
FINE. ART SEEMS LIKE IT WILL BE COOL THIS YEAR. I DON'T KNOW THE KIDS IN MY CLASS THAT WELL, BUT THEY SEEM NICE.
THAT'S SO GOOD TO HEAR! ARE YOU HUNGRY?
STARVING!
GOLDEN DRAGON
CHINESE RESTAURANT
WELL, WE HAVE COME TO THE RIGHT PLACE.

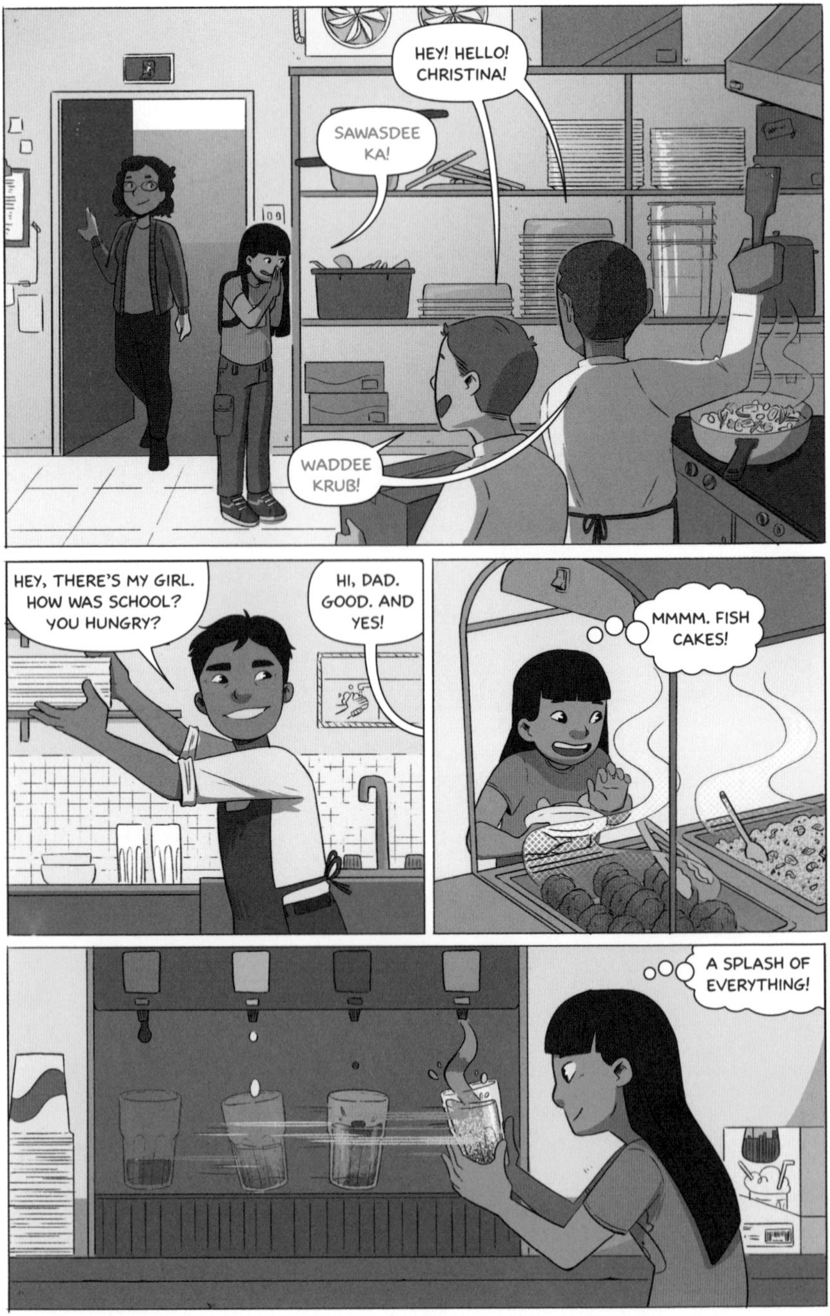
SAWASDEE KA!
HEY! HELLO! CHRISTINA!
WADDEE KRUB!
HEY, THERE'S MY GIRL. HOW WAS SCHOOL? YOU HUNGRY?
HI, DAD. GOOD. AND YES!
MMMM. FISH CAKES!
A SPLASH OF EVERYTHING!

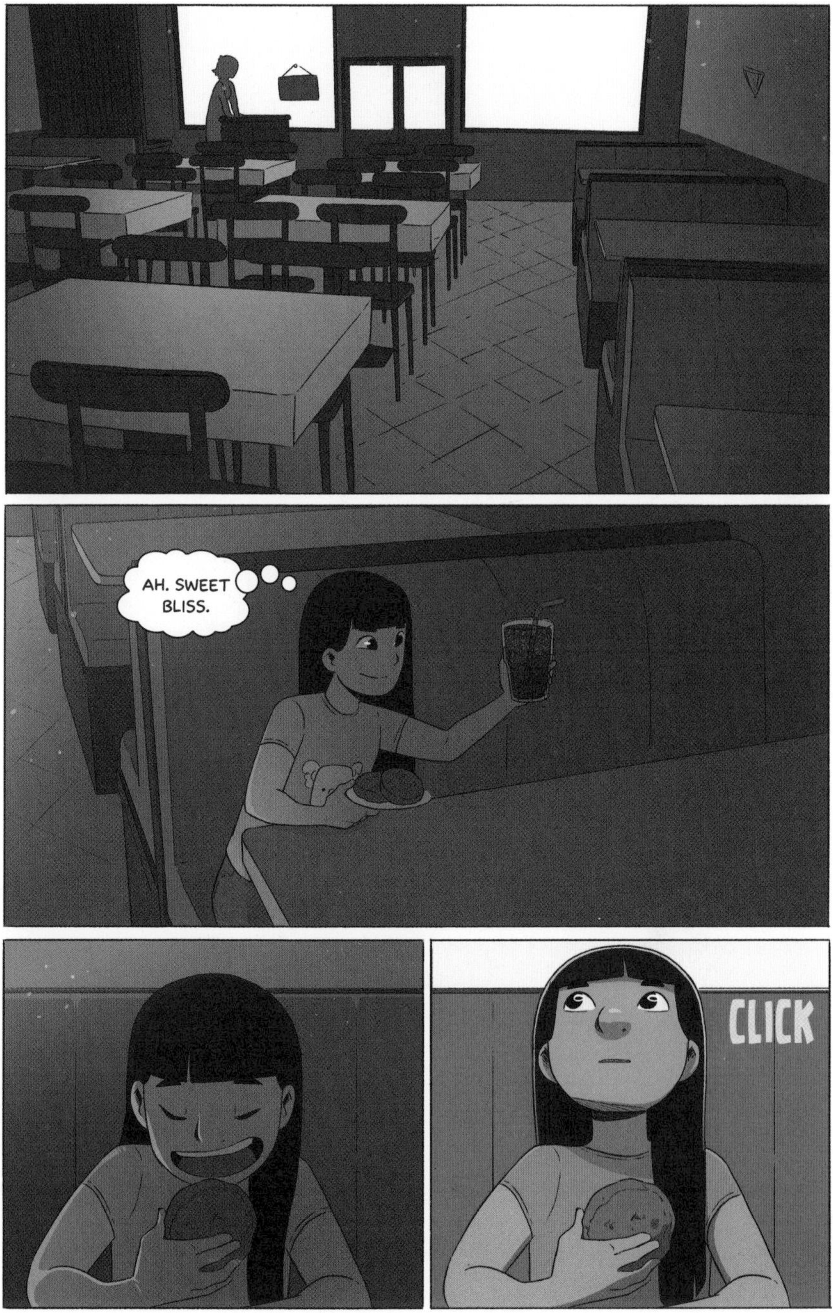
AH. SWEET BLISS.
CLICK

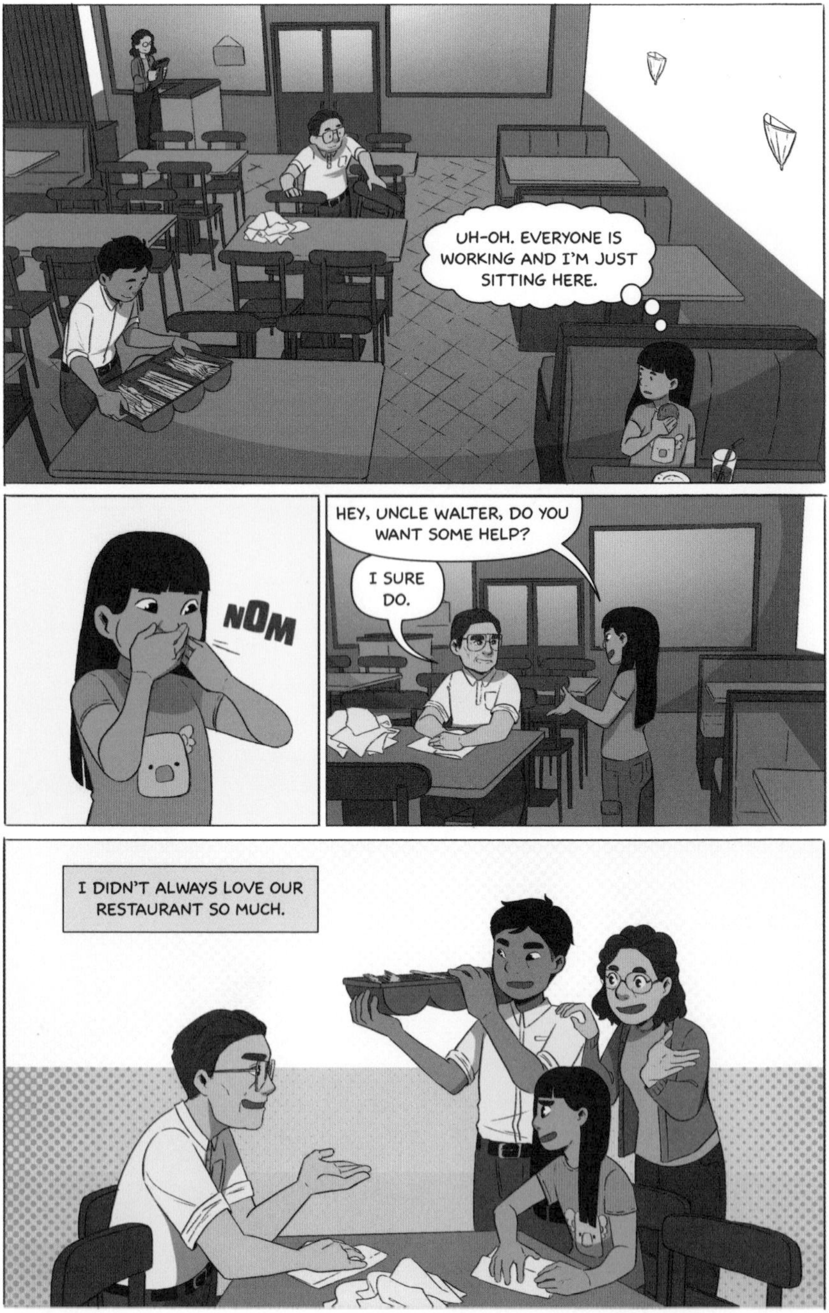
UH-OH. EVERYONE IS WORKING AND I'M JUST SITTING HERE.
NOM
HEY, UNCLE WALTER, DO YOU WANT SOME HELP?
I SURE DO.
I DIDN'T ALWAYS LOVE OUR RESTAURANT SO MUCH.

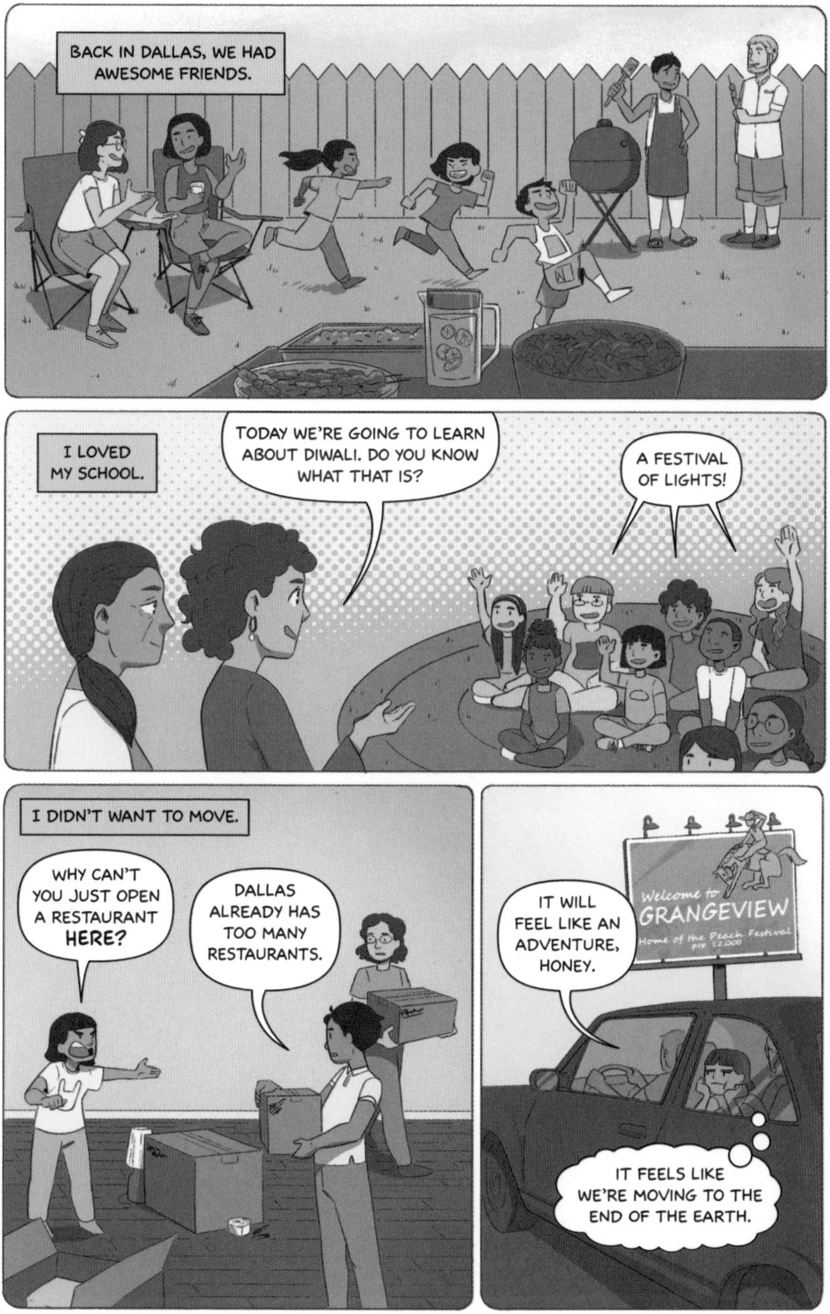
BACK IN DALLAS, WE HAD AWESOME FRIENDS.
I LOVED MY SCHOOL.
TODAY WE'RE GOING TO LEARN ABOUT DIWALI. DO YOU KNOW WHAT THAT IS?
A FESTIVAL OF LIGHTS!
I DIDN'T WANT TO MOVE.
WHY CAN'T YOU JUST OPEN A RESTAURANT **HERE?**
DALLAS ALREADY HAS TOO MANY RESTAURANTS.
Welcome to
GRANGEVIEW
Home of the Peach Festival
IT WILL FEEL LIKE AN ADVENTURE, HONEY.
IT FEELS LIKE WE'RE MOVING TO THE END OF THE EARTH.

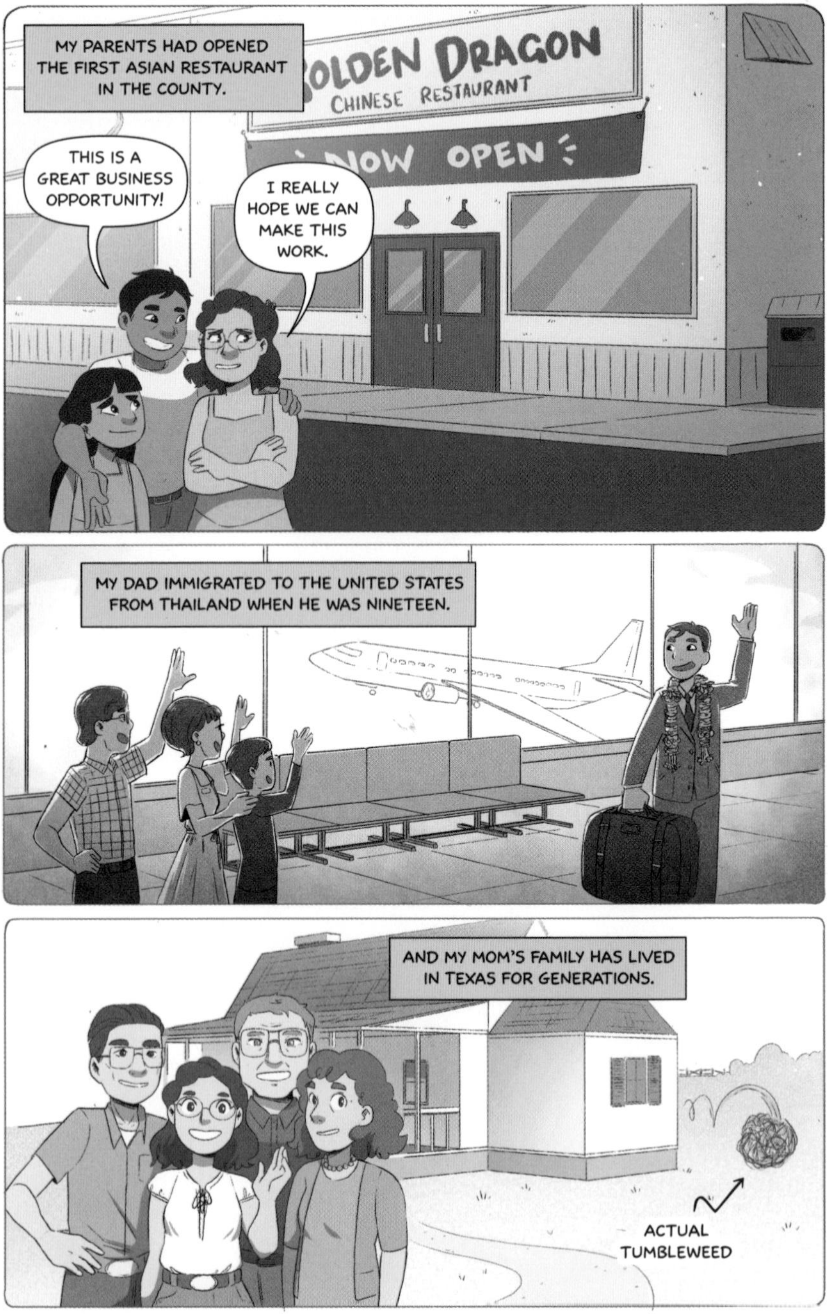
MY PARENTS HAD OPENED THE FIRST ASIAN RESTAURANT IN THE COUNTY.
GOLDEN DRAGON CHINESE RESTAURANT
NOW OPEN
THIS IS A GREAT BUSINESS OPPORTUNITY!
I REALLY HOPE WE CAN MAKE THIS WORK.
MY DAD IMMIGRATED TO THE UNITED STATES FROM THAILAND WHEN HE WAS NINETEEN.
AND MY MOM'S FAMILY HAS LIVED IN TEXAS FOR GENERATIONS.
ACTUAL TUMBLEWEED

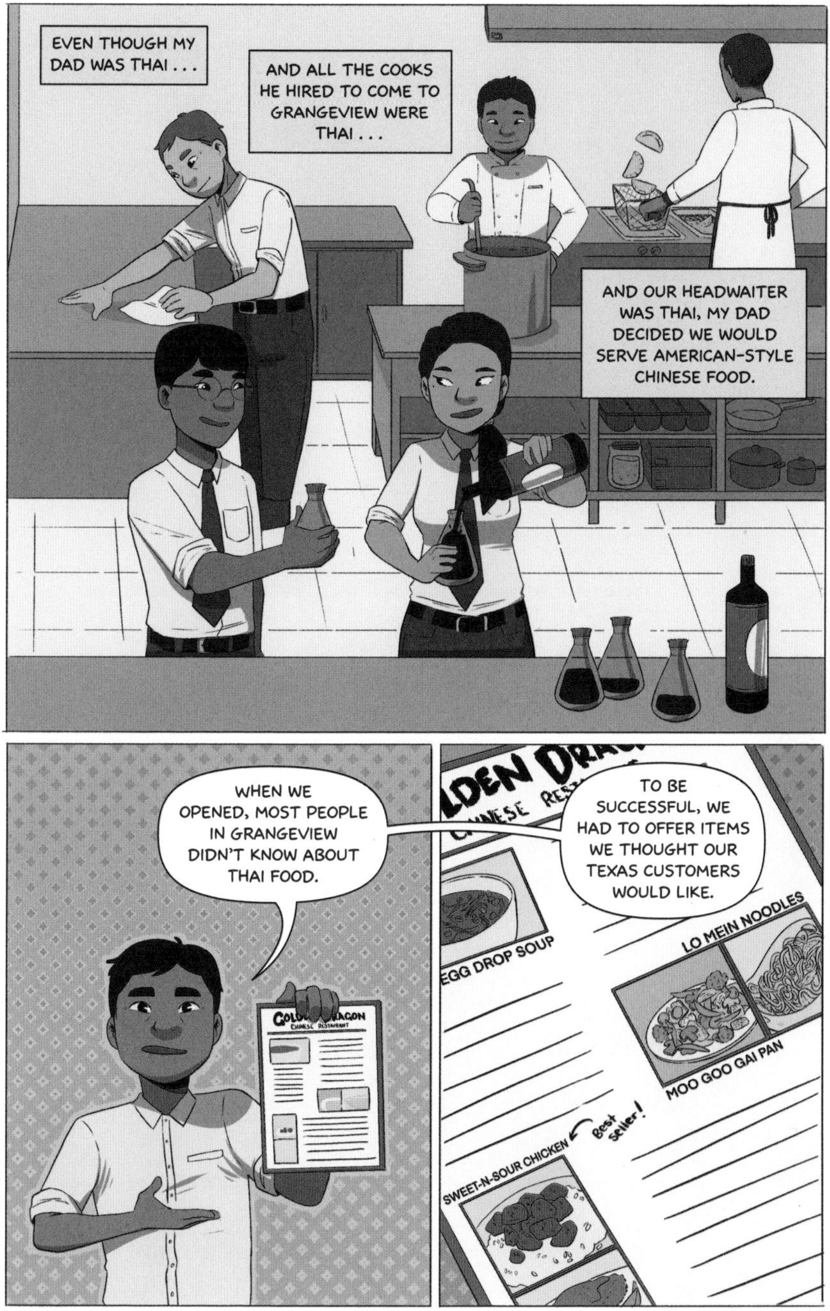
EVEN THOUGH MY DAD WAS THAI . . .
AND ALL THE COOKS HE HIRED TO COME TO GRANGEVIEW WERE THAI . . .
AND OUR HEADWAITER WAS THAI, MY DAD DECIDED WE WOULD SERVE AMERICAN-STYLE CHINESE FOOD.
WHEN WE OPENED, MOST PEOPLE IN GRANGEVIEW DIDN'T KNOW ABOUT THAI FOOD.
TO BE SUCCESSFUL, WE HAD TO OFFER ITEMS WE THOUGHT OUR TEXAS CUSTOMERS WOULD LIKE.
EGG DROP SOUP
LO MEIN NOODLES
MOO GOO GAI PAN
SWEET-N-SOUR CHICKEN
Best seller!

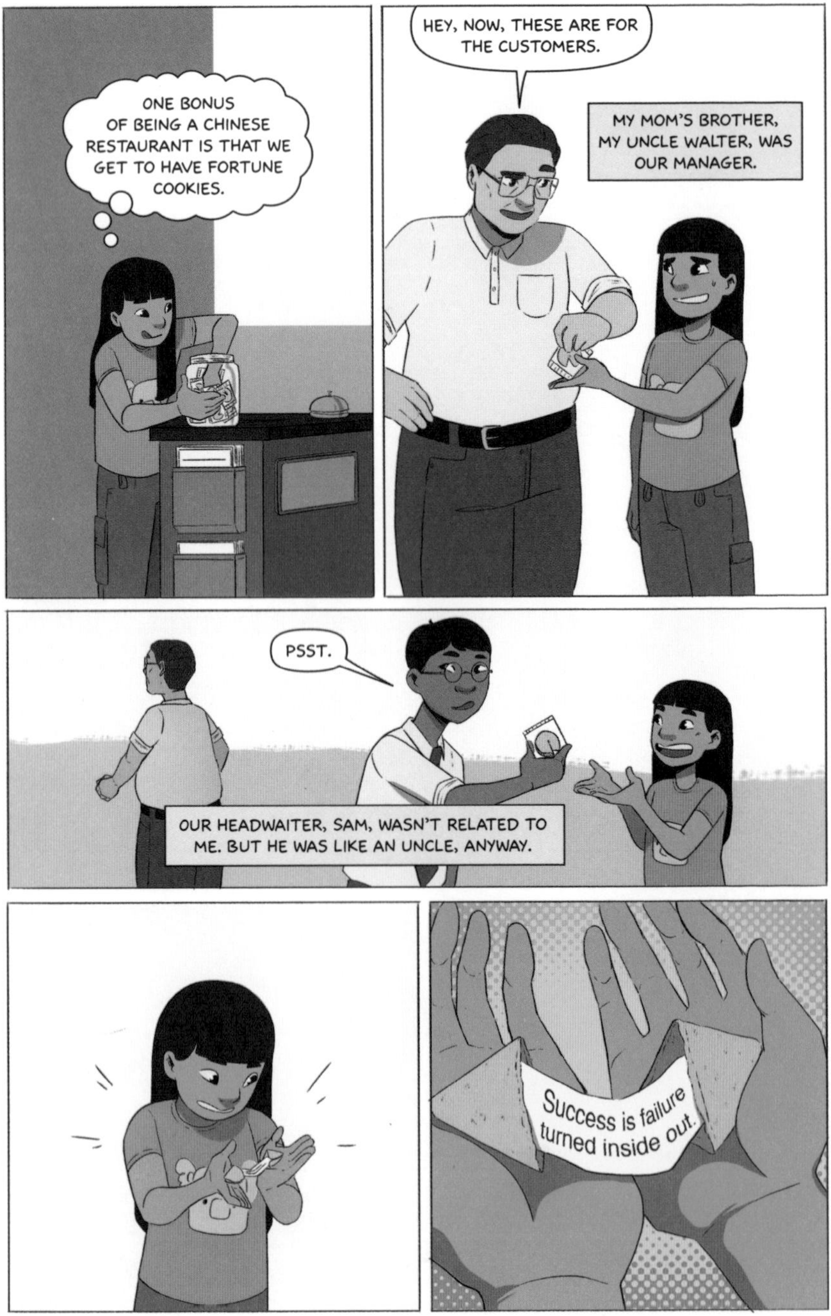
ONE BONUS OF BEING A CHINESE RESTAURANT IS THAT WE GET TO HAVE FORTUNE COOKIES.
HEY, NOW, THESE ARE FOR THE CUSTOMERS.
MY MOM'S BROTHER, MY UNCLE WALTER, WAS OUR MANAGER.
PSST.
OUR HEADWAITER, SAM, WASN'T RELATED TO ME. BUT HE WAS LIKE AN UNCLE, ANYWAY.
Success is failure turned inside out.

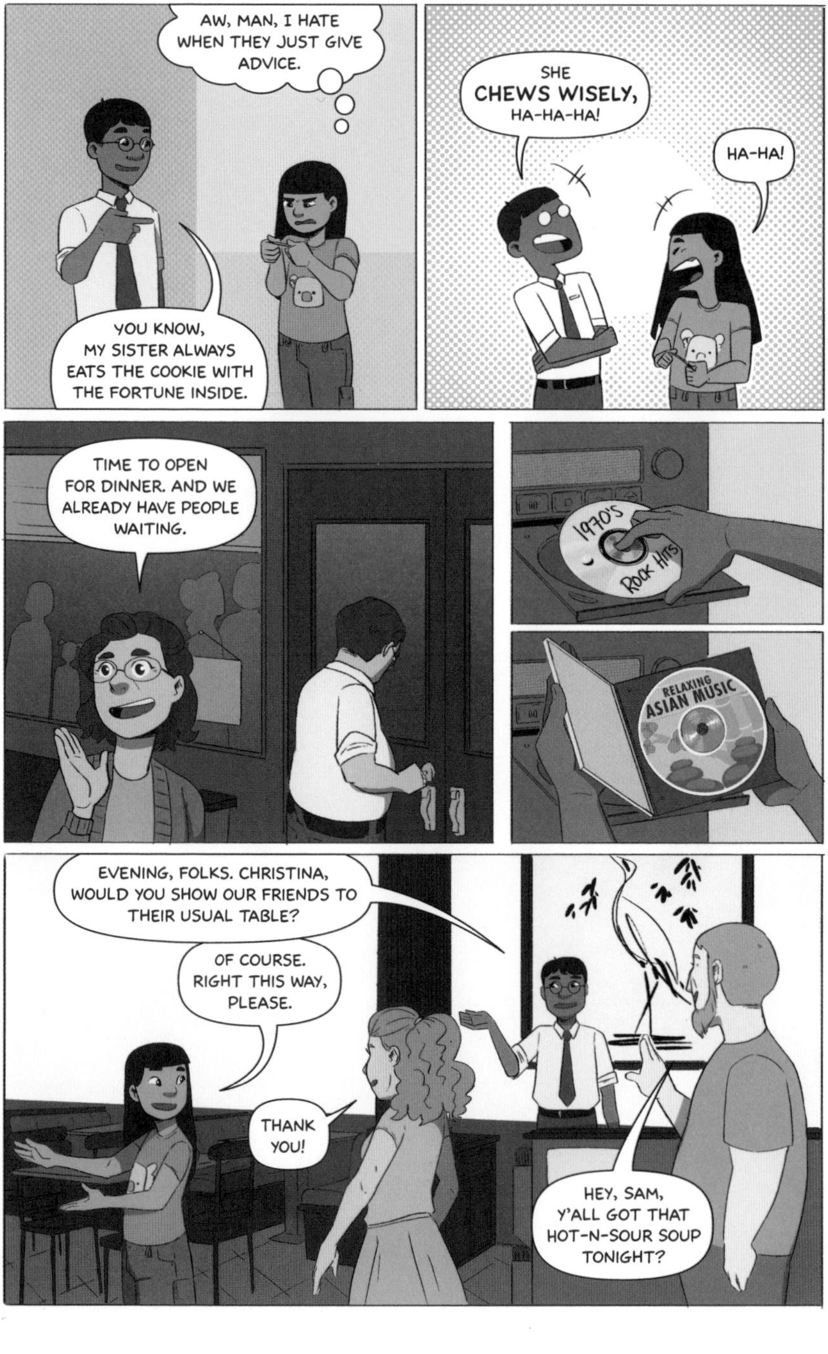
AW, MAN, I HATE WHEN THEY JUST GIVE ADVICE.
YOU KNOW, MY SISTER ALWAYS EATS THE COOKIE WITH THE FORTUNE INSIDE.
SHE CHEWS WISELY, HA-HA-HA!
HA-HA!
TIME TO OPEN FOR DINNER. AND WE ALREADY HAVE PEOPLE WAITING.
1970'S ROCK HITS
RELAXING ASIAN MUSIC
EVENING, FOLKS. CHRISTINA, WOULD YOU SHOW OUR FRIENDS TO THEIR USUAL TABLE?
OF COURSE. RIGHT THIS WAY, PLEASE.
THANK YOU!
HEY, SAM, Y'ALL GOT THAT HOT-N-SOUR SOUP TONIGHT?

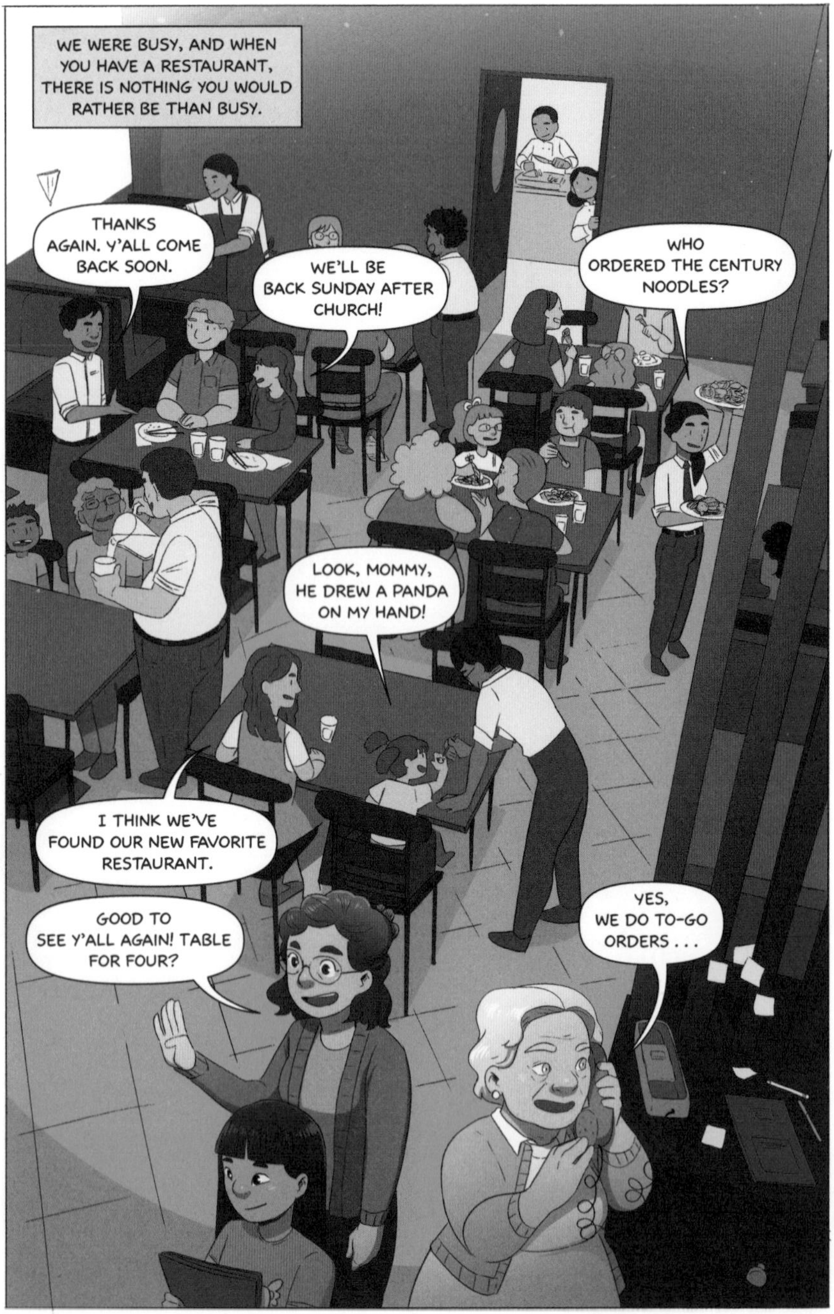
WE WERE BUSY, AND WHEN YOU HAVE A RESTAURANT, THERE IS NOTHING YOU WOULD RATHER BE THAN BUSY.
THANKS AGAIN. Y'ALL COME BACK SOON.
WE'LL BE BACK SUNDAY AFTER CHURCH!
WHO ORDERED THE CENTURY NOODLES?
LOOK, MOMMY, HE DREW A PANDA ON MY HAND!
I THINK WE'VE FOUND OUR NEW FAVORITE RESTAURANT.
GOOD TO SEE Y'ALL AGAIN! TABLE FOR FOUR?
YES, WE DO TO-GO ORDERS . . .

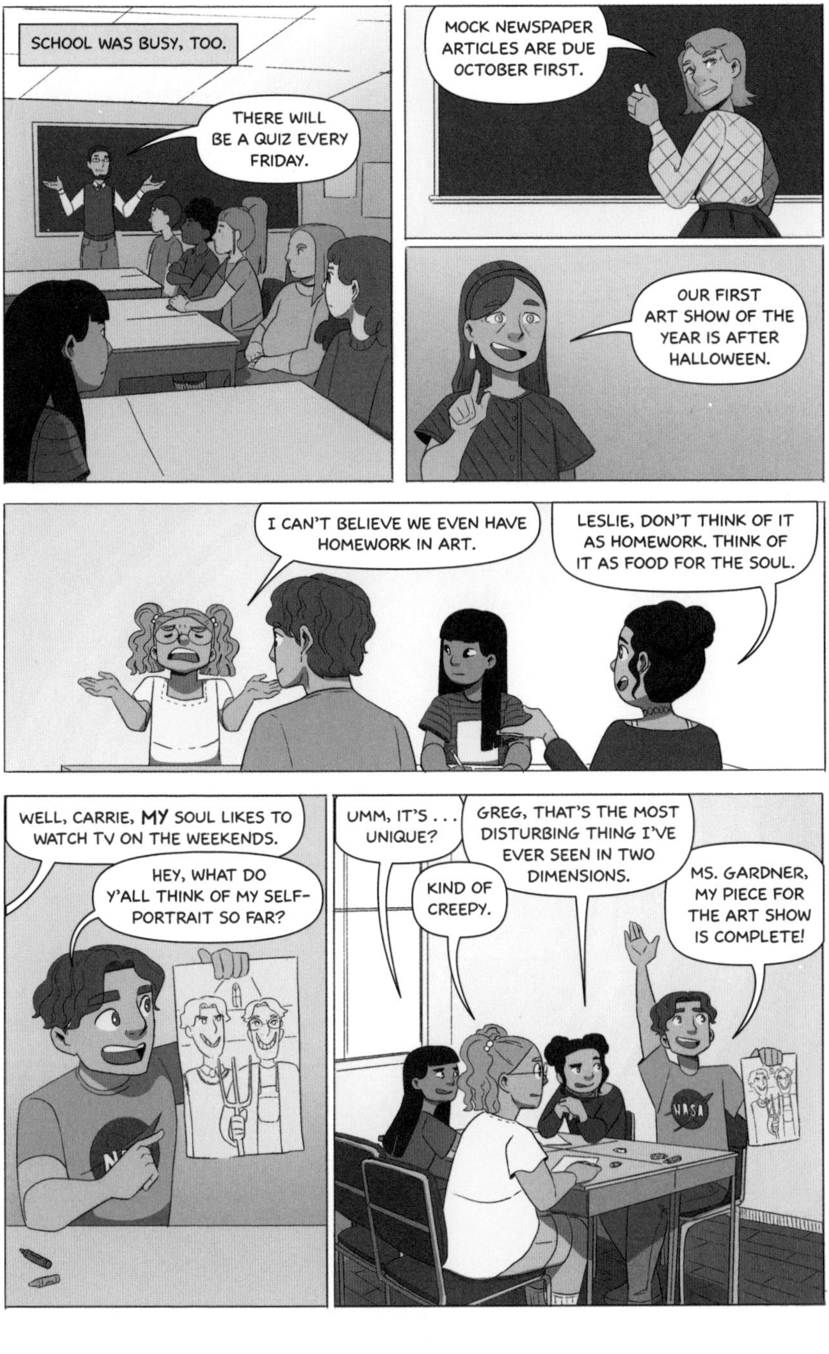
SCHOOL WAS BUSY, TOO.
THERE WILL BE A QUIZ EVERY FRIDAY.
MOCK NEWSPAPER ARTICLES ARE DUE OCTOBER FIRST.
OUR FIRST ART SHOW OF THE YEAR IS AFTER HALLOWEEN.
I CAN'T BELIEVE WE EVEN HAVE HOMEWORK IN ART.
LESLIE, DON'T THINK OF IT AS HOMEWORK. THINK OF IT AS FOOD FOR THE SOUL.
WELL, CARRIE, MY SOUL LIKES TO WATCH TV ON THE WEEKENDS.
HEY, WHAT DO Y'ALL THINK OF MY SELF-PORTRAIT SO FAR?
UMM, IT'S . . . UNIQUE?
KIND OF CREEPY.
GREG, THAT'S THE MOST DISTURBING THING I'VE EVER SEEN IN TWO DIMENSIONS.
MS. GARDNER, MY PIECE FOR THE ART SHOW IS COMPLETE!

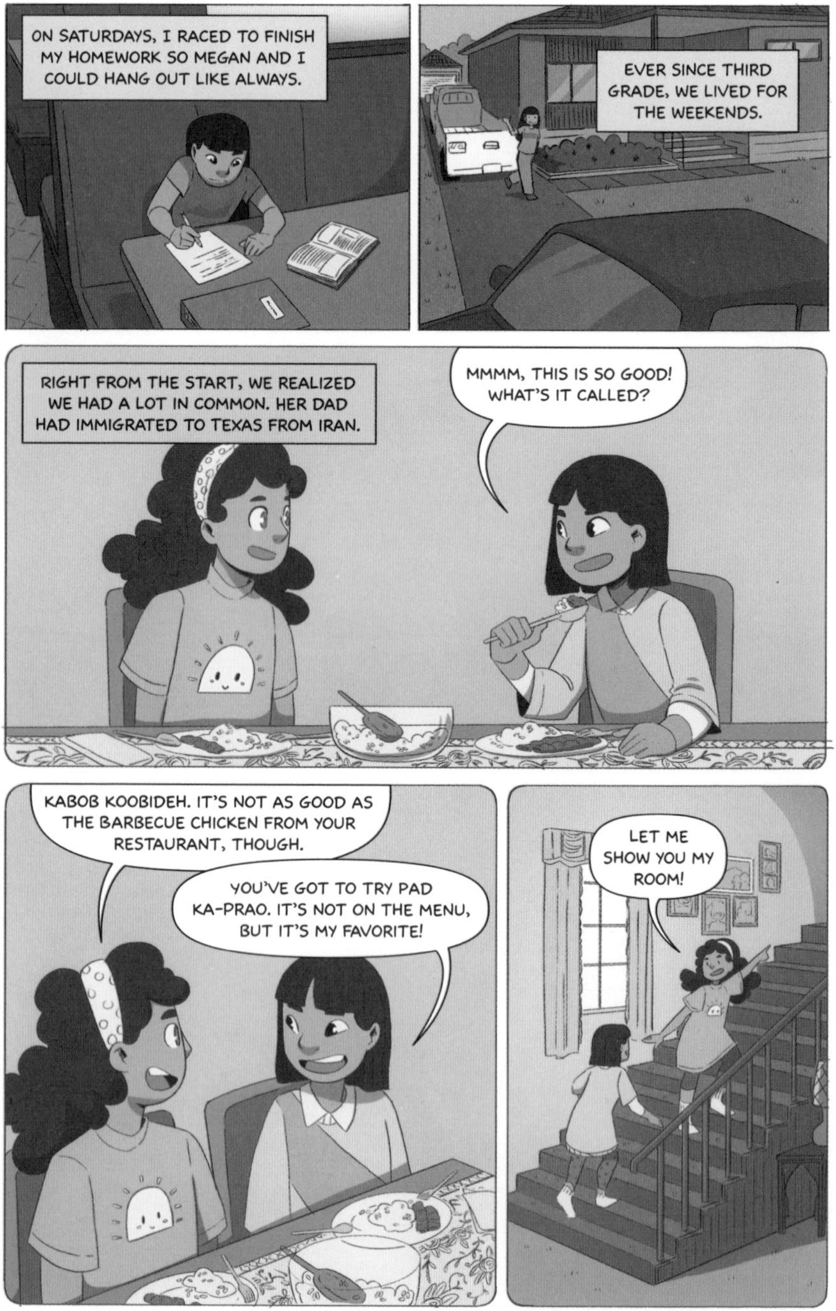
ON SATURDAYS, I RACED TO FINISH MY HOMEWORK SO MEGAN AND I COULD HANG OUT LIKE ALWAYS.
EVER SINCE THIRD GRADE, WE LIVED FOR THE WEEKENDS.
RIGHT FROM THE START, WE REALIZED WE HAD A LOT IN COMMON. HER DAD HAD IMMIGRATED TO TEXAS FROM IRAN.
MMMM, THIS IS SO GOOD! WHAT'S IT CALLED?
KABOB KOOBIDEH. IT'S NOT AS GOOD AS THE BARBECUE CHICKEN FROM YOUR RESTAURANT, THOUGH.
YOU'VE GOT TO TRY PAD KA-PRAO. IT'S NOT ON THE MENU, BUT IT'S MY FAVORITE!
LET ME SHOW YOU MY ROOM!

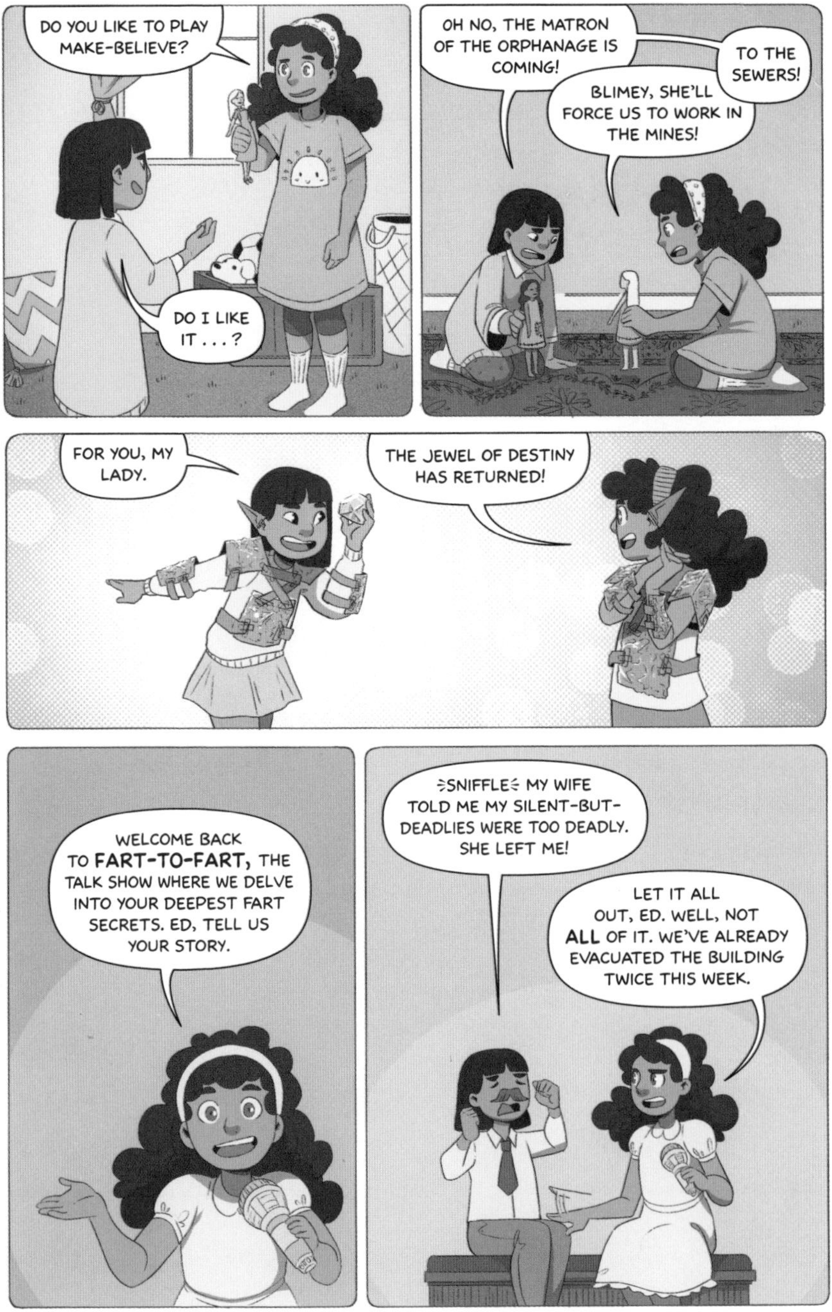
DO YOU LIKE TO PLAY MAKE-BELIEVE?
DO I LIKE IT . . . ?
OH NO, THE MATRON OF THE ORPHANAGE IS COMING!
TO THE SEWERS!
BLIMEY, SHE'LL FORCE US TO WORK IN THE MINES!
FOR YOU, MY LADY.
THE JEWEL OF DESTINY HAS RETURNED!
WELCOME BACK TO FART-TO-FART, THE TALK SHOW WHERE WE DELVE INTO YOUR DEEPEST FART SECRETS. ED, TELL US YOUR STORY.
≥SNIFFLE≤ MY WIFE TOLD ME MY SILENT-BUT-DEADLIES WERE TOO DEADLY. SHE LEFT ME!
LET IT ALL OUT, ED. WELL, NOT ALL OF IT. WE'VE ALREADY EVACUATED THE BUILDING TWICE THIS WEEK.

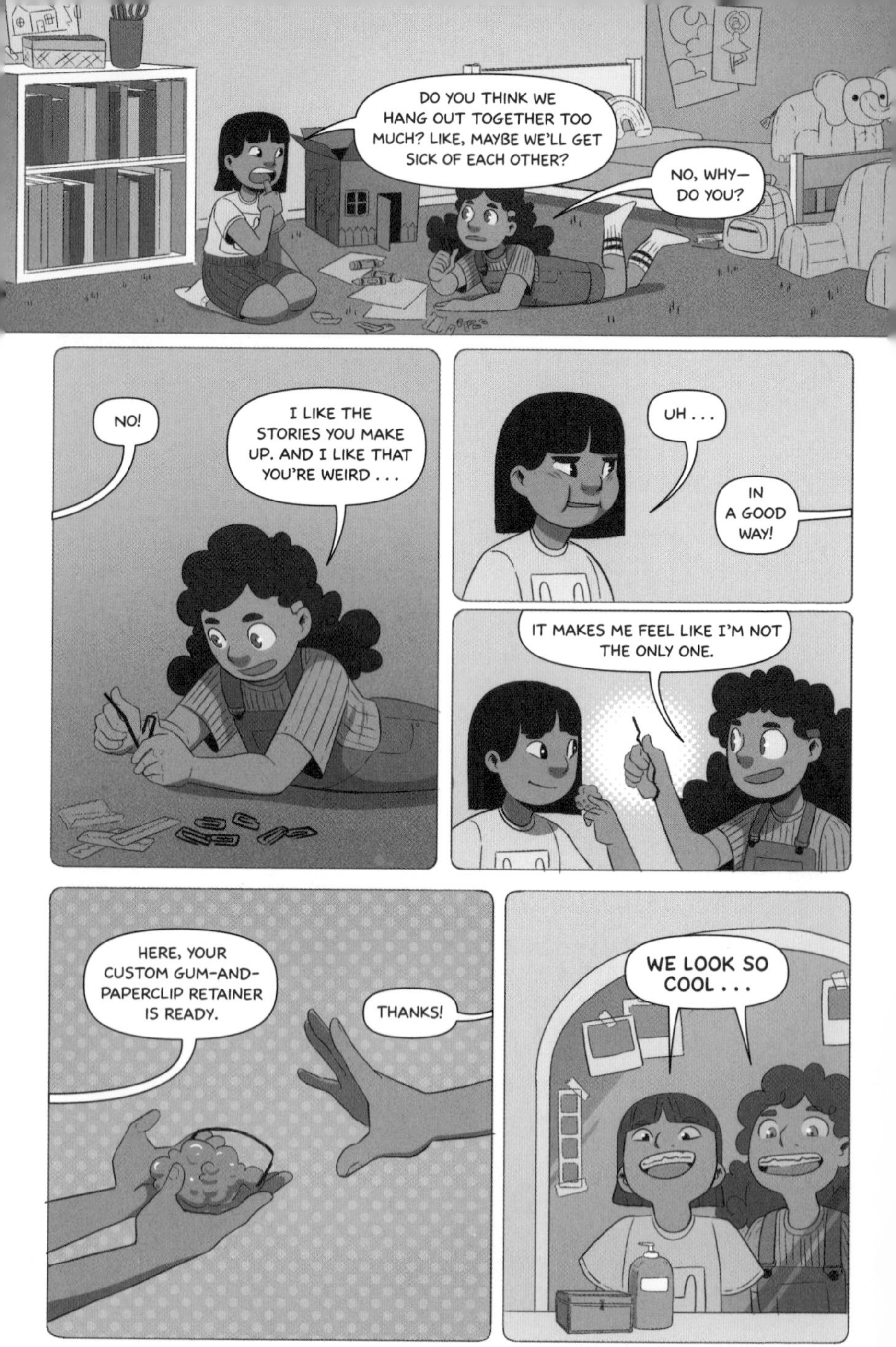
DO YOU THINK WE HANG OUT TOGETHER TOO MUCH? LIKE, MAYBE WE'LL GET SICK OF EACH OTHER?
NO, WHY— DO YOU?
NO!
I LIKE THE STORIES YOU MAKE UP. AND I LIKE THAT YOU'RE WEIRD . . .
UH . . .
IN A GOOD WAY!
IT MAKES ME FEEL LIKE I'M NOT THE ONLY ONE.
HERE, YOUR CUSTOM GUM-AND-PAPERCLIP RETAINER IS READY.
THANKS!
WE LOOK SO COOL . . .

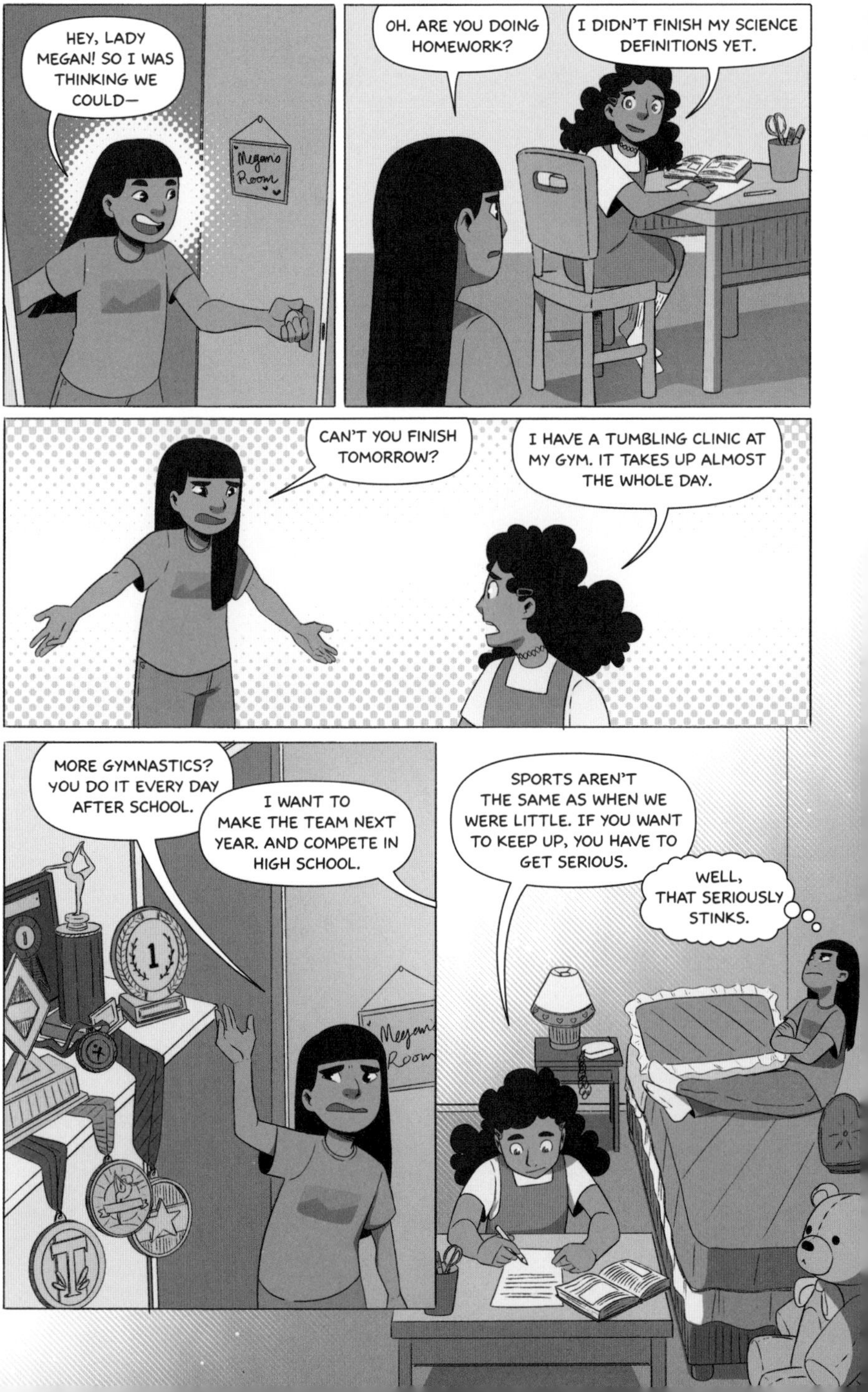
HEY, LADY MEGAN! SO I WAS THINKING WE COULD—
Megan's Room
OH. ARE YOU DOING HOMEWORK?
I DIDN'T FINISH MY SCIENCE DEFINITIONS YET.
CAN'T YOU FINISH TOMORROW?
I HAVE A TUMBLING CLINIC AT MY GYM. IT TAKES UP ALMOST THE WHOLE DAY.
MORE GYMNASTICS? YOU DO IT EVERY DAY AFTER SCHOOL.
I WANT TO MAKE THE TEAM NEXT YEAR. AND COMPETE IN HIGH SCHOOL.
SPORTS AREN'T THE SAME AS WHEN WE WERE LITTLE. IF YOU WANT TO KEEP UP, YOU HAVE TO GET SERIOUS.
WELL, THAT SERIOUSLY STINKS.

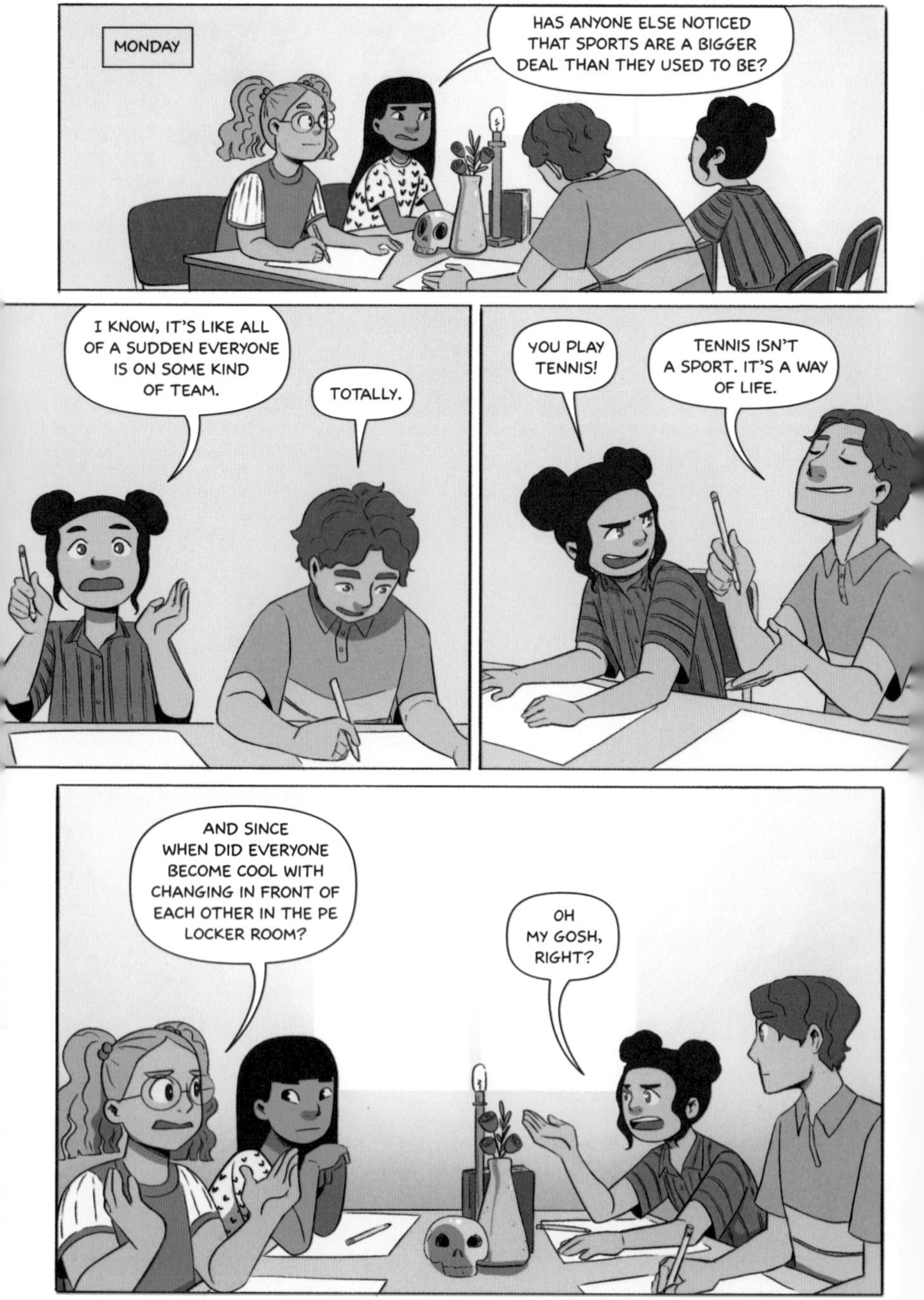
MONDAY
HAS ANYONE ELSE NOTICED THAT SPORTS ARE A BIGGER DEAL THAN THEY USED TO BE?
I KNOW, IT'S LIKE ALL OF A SUDDEN EVERYONE IS ON SOME KIND OF TEAM.
TOTALLY.
YOU PLAY TENNIS!
TENNIS ISN'T A SPORT. IT'S A WAY OF LIFE.
AND SINCE WHEN DID EVERYONE BECOME COOL WITH CHANGING IN FRONT OF EACH OTHER IN THE PE LOCKER ROOM?
OH MY GOSH, RIGHT?

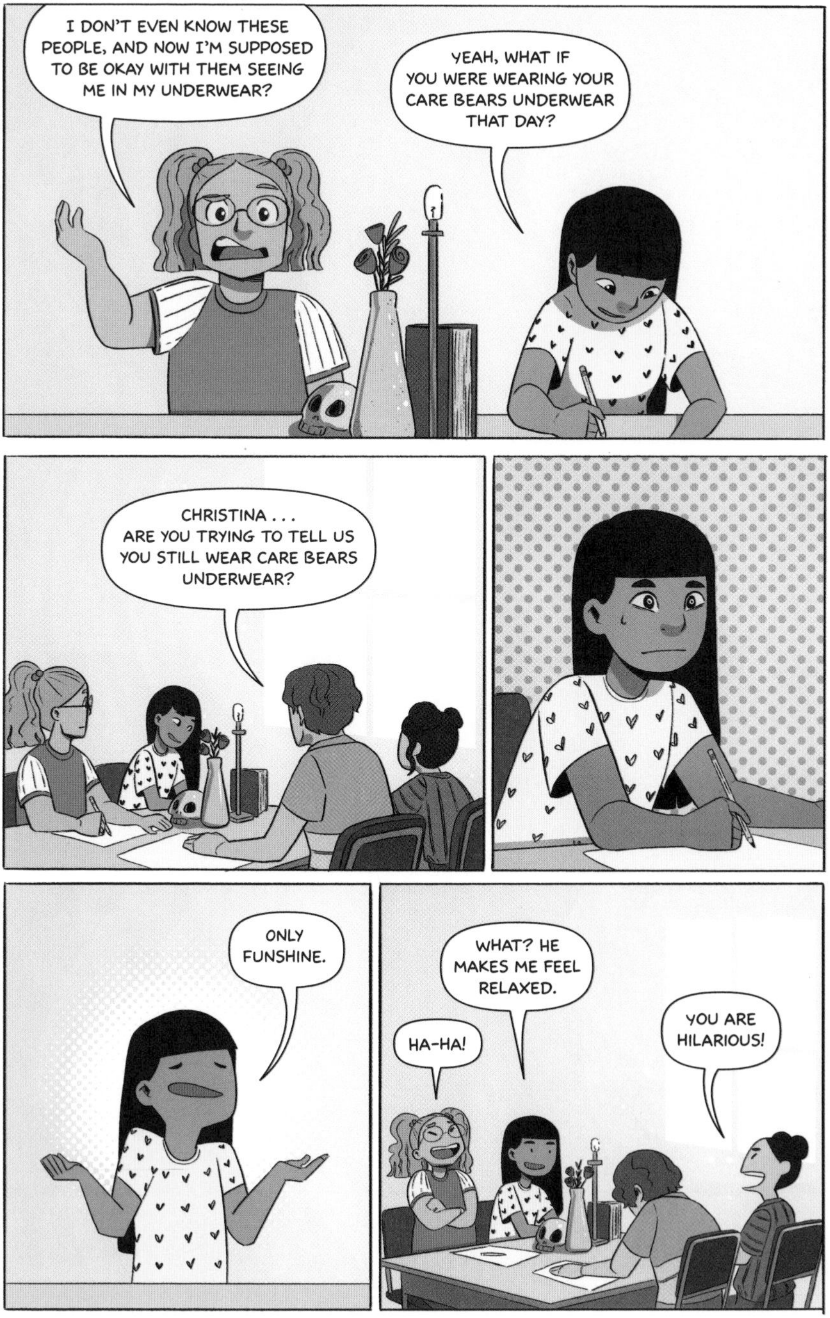
I DON'T EVEN KNOW THESE PEOPLE, AND NOW I'M SUPPOSED TO BE OKAY WITH THEM SEEING ME IN MY UNDERWEAR?
YEAH, WHAT IF YOU WERE WEARING YOUR CARE BEARS UNDERWEAR THAT DAY?
CHRISTINA . . . ARE YOU TRYING TO TELL US YOU STILL WEAR CARE BEARS UNDERWEAR?
ONLY FUNSHINE.
WHAT? HE MAKES ME FEEL RELAXED.
HA-HA!
YOU ARE HILARIOUS!

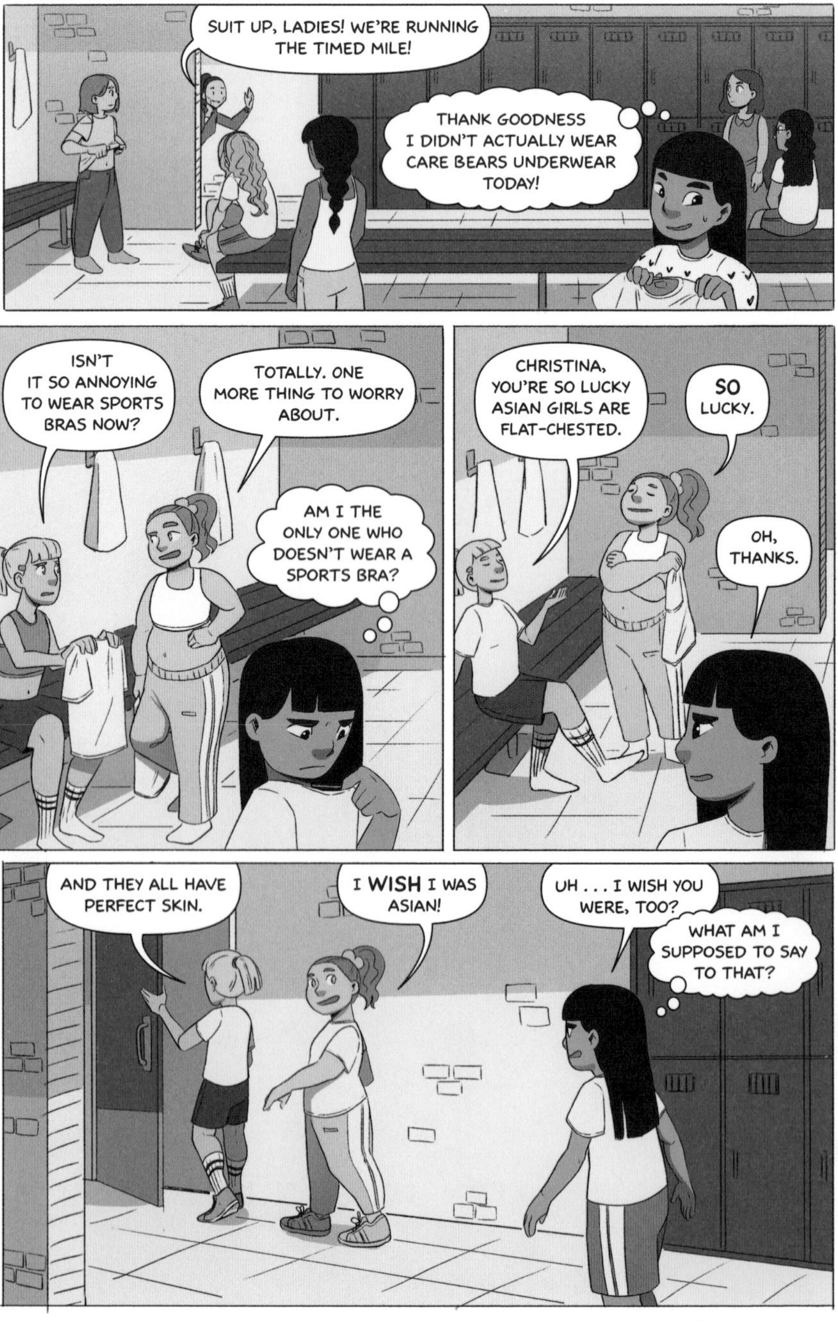

SUIT UP, LADIES! WE'RE RUNNING THE TIMED MILE!
THANK GOODNESS I DIDN'T ACTUALLY WEAR CARE BEARS UNDERWEAR TODAY!
ISN'T IT SO ANNOYING TO WEAR SPORTS BRAS NOW?
TOTALLY. ONE MORE THING TO WORRY ABOUT.
AM I THE ONLY ONE WHO DOESN'T WEAR A SPORTS BRA?
CHRISTINA, YOU'RE SO LUCKY ASIAN GIRLS ARE FLAT-CHESTED.
SO LUCKY.
OH, THANKS.
AND THEY ALL HAVE PERFECT SKIN.
I WISH I WAS ASIAN!
UH . . . I WISH YOU WERE, TOO?
WHAT AM I SUPPOSED TO SAY TO THAT?

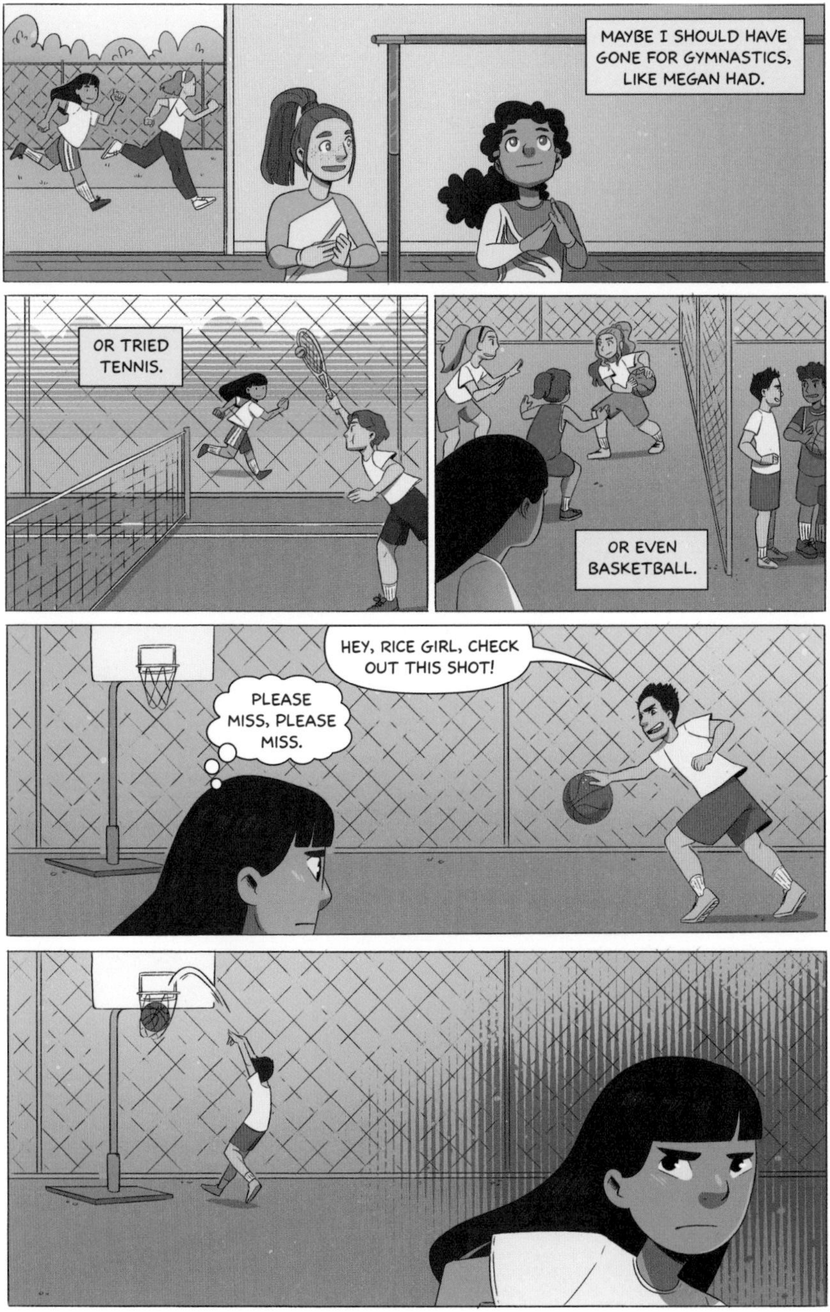
MAYBE I SHOULD HAVE GONE FOR GYMNASTICS, LIKE MEGAN HAD.
OR TRIED TENNIS.
OR EVEN BASKETBALL.
HEY, RICE GIRL, CHECK OUT THIS SHOT!
PLEASE MISS, PLEASE MISS.

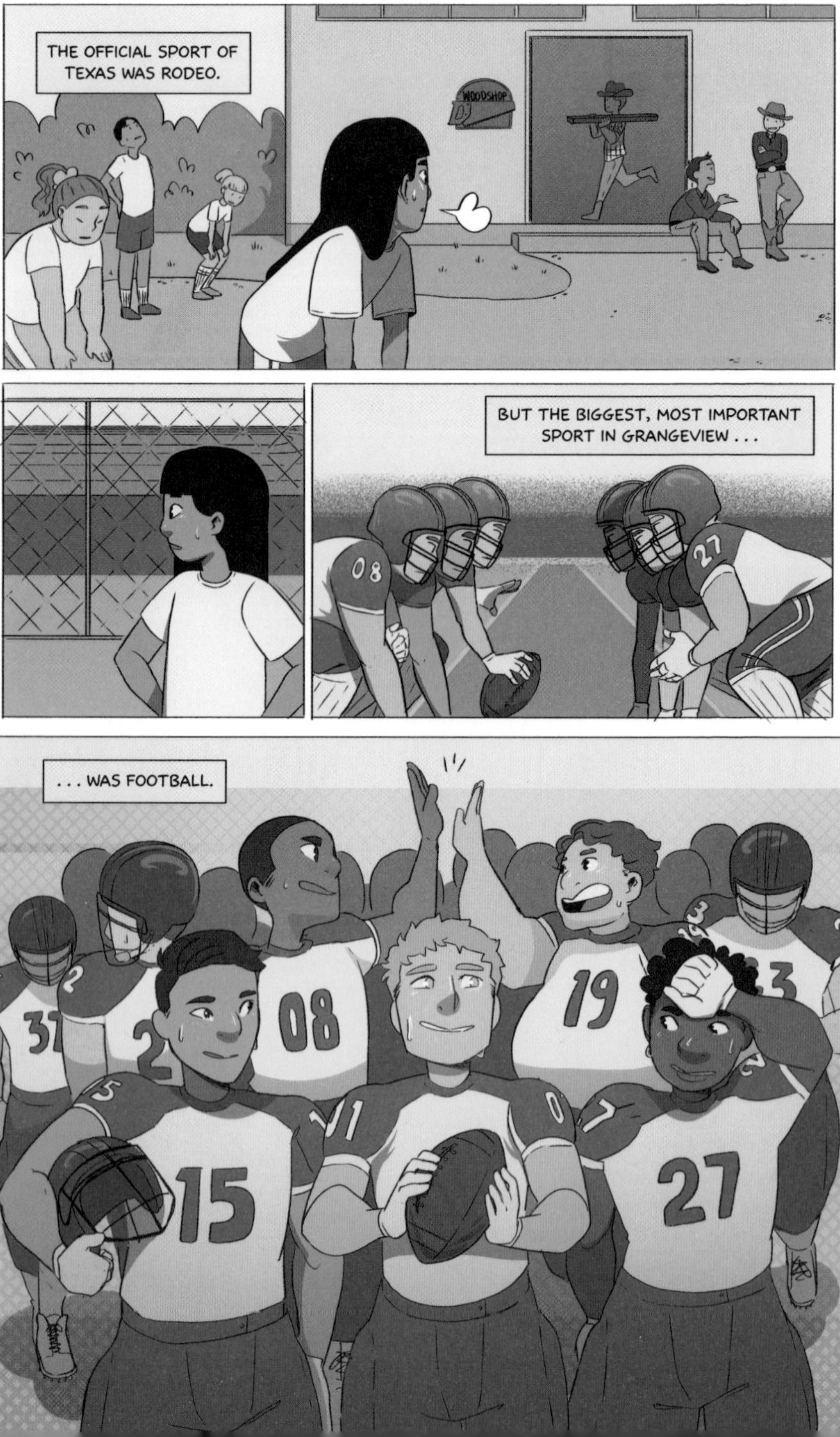
THE OFFICIAL SPORT OF TEXAS WAS RODEO.
WOODSHOP
BUT THE BIGGEST, MOST IMPORTANT SPORT IN GRANGEVIEW . . .
. . . WAS FOOTBALL.

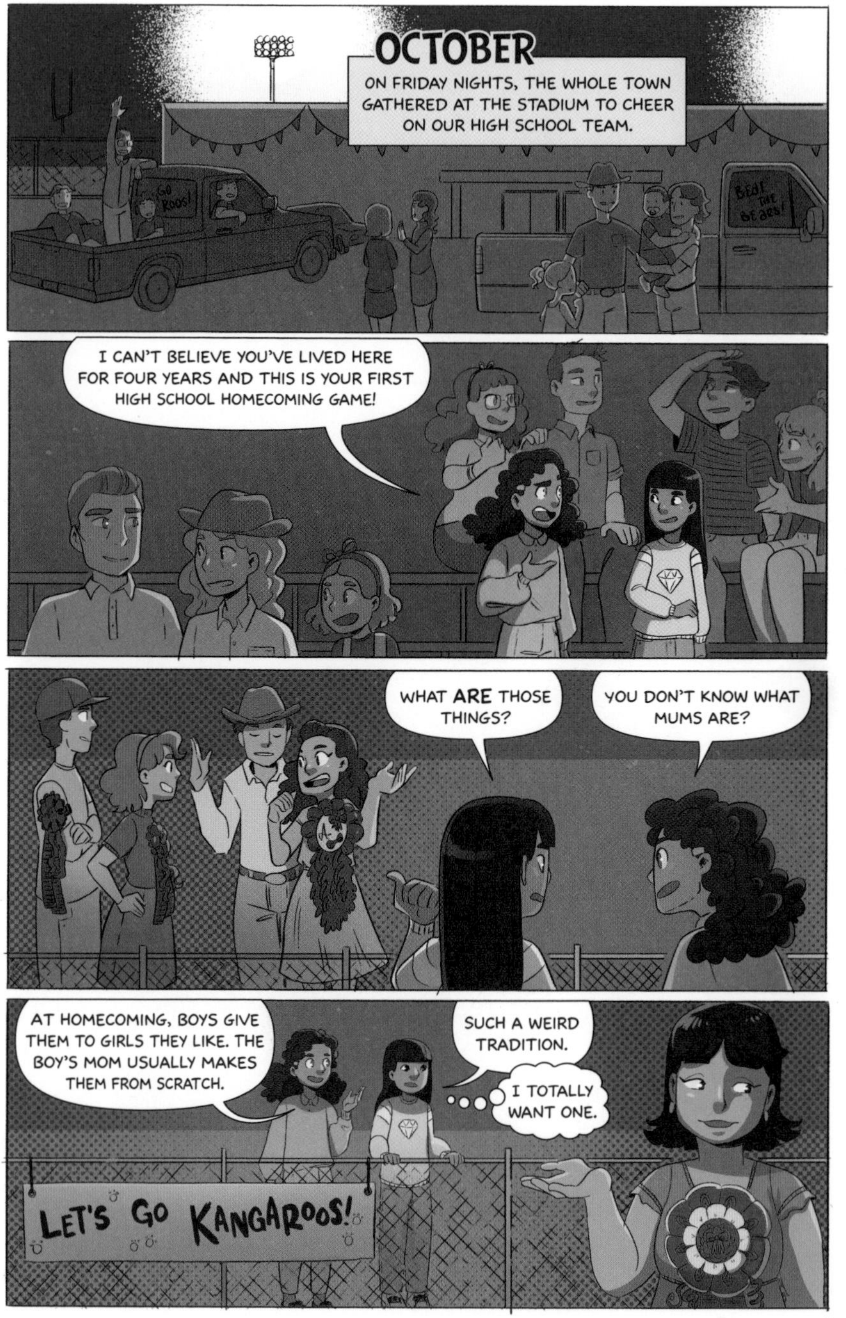
OCTOBER
ON FRIDAY NIGHTS, THE WHOLE TOWN GATHERED AT THE STADIUM TO CHEER ON OUR HIGH SCHOOL TEAM.
GO ROOS!
BEAT THE BEARS!
I CAN'T BELIEVE YOU'VE LIVED HERE FOR FOUR YEARS AND THIS IS YOUR FIRST HIGH SCHOOL HOMECOMING GAME!
WHAT **ARE** THOSE THINGS?
YOU DON'T KNOW WHAT MUMS ARE?
AT HOMECOMING, BOYS GIVE THEM TO GIRLS THEY LIKE. THE BOY'S MOM USUALLY MAKES THEM FROM SCRATCH.
SUCH A WEIRD TRADITION.
I TOTALLY WANT ONE.
LET'S GO KANGAROOS!

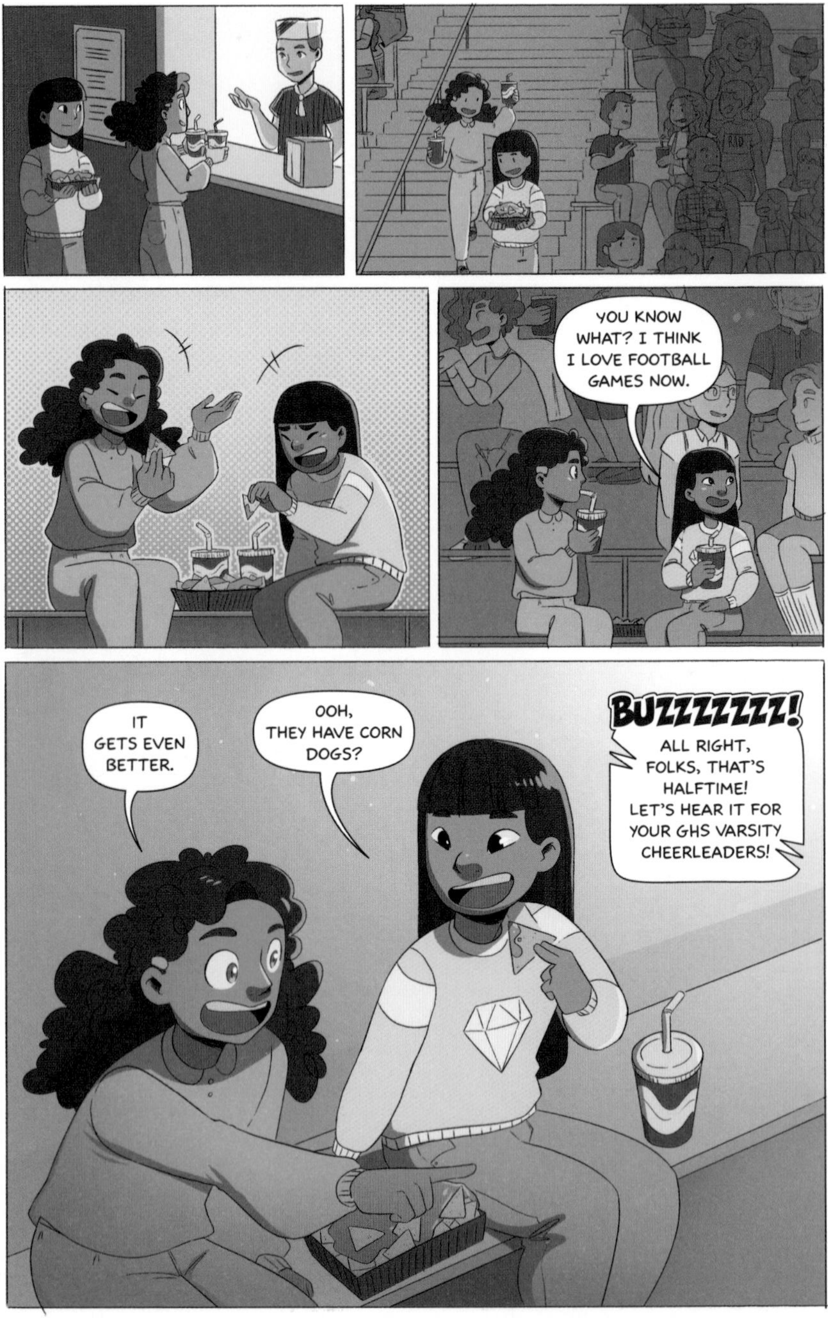
YOU KNOW WHAT? I THINK I LOVE FOOTBALL GAMES NOW.
IT GETS EVEN BETTER.
OOH, THEY HAVE CORN DOGS?
BUZZZZZZZ!
ALL RIGHT, FOLKS, THAT'S HALFTIME! LET'S HEAR IT FOR YOUR GHS VARSITY CHEERLEADERS!

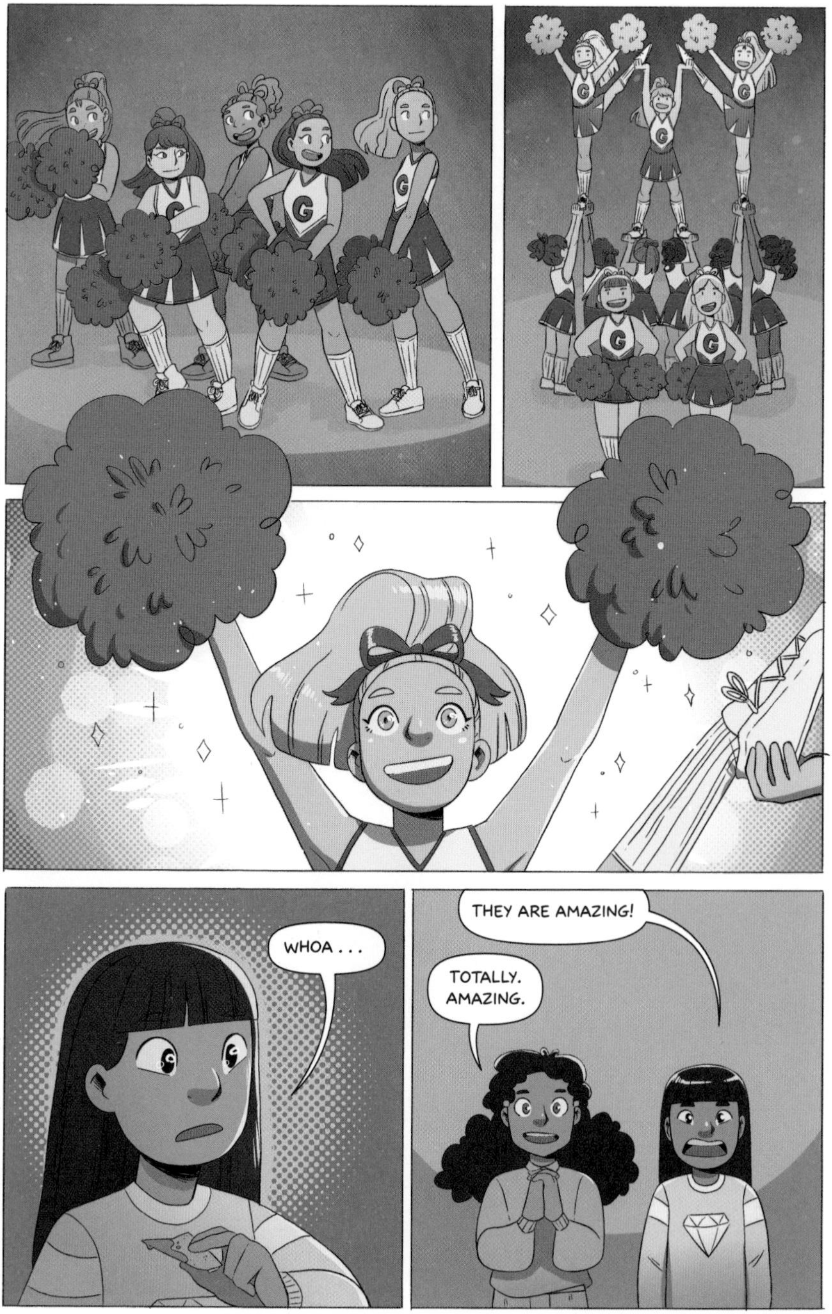
WHOA . . .
THEY ARE AMAZING!
TOTALLY. AMAZING.

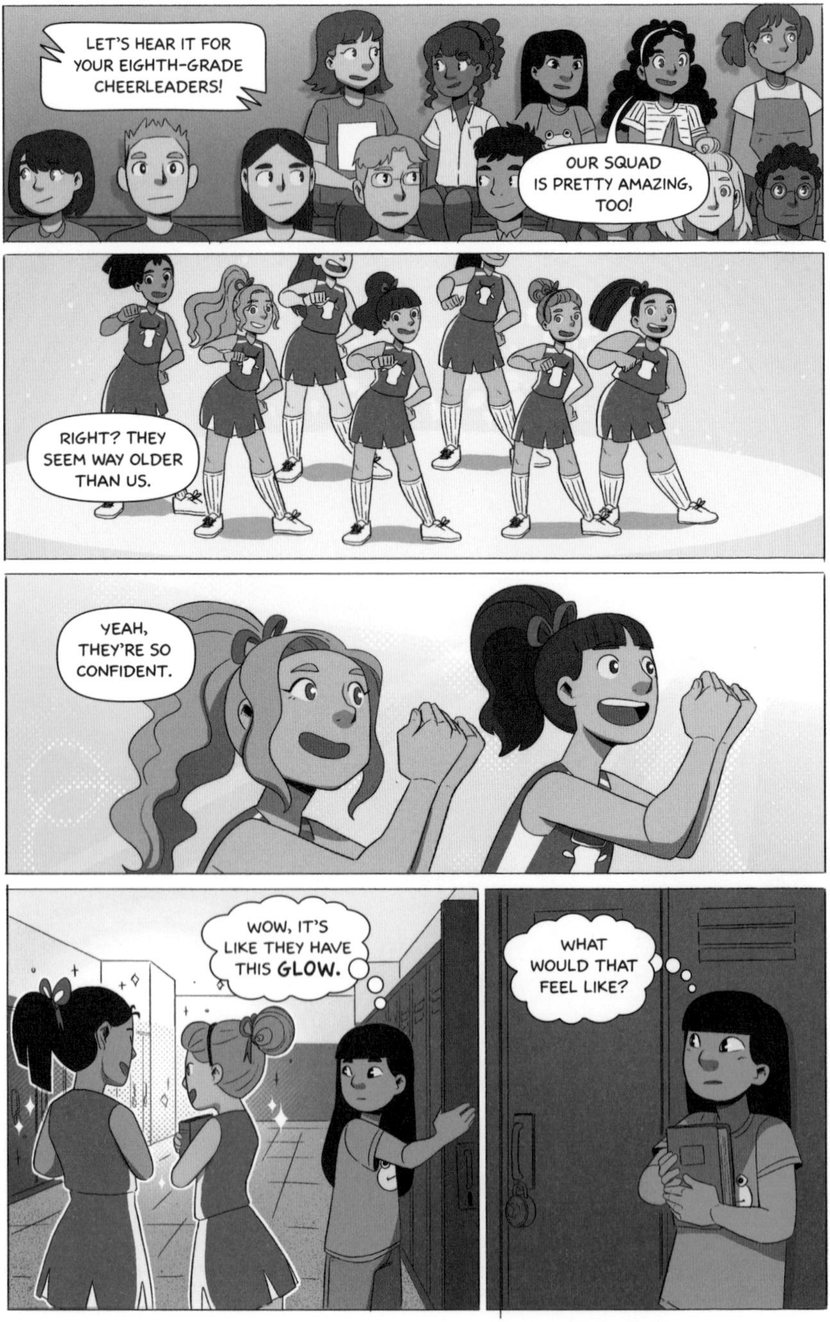
LET'S HEAR IT FOR YOUR EIGHTH-GRADE CHEERLEADERS!
OUR SQUAD IS PRETTY AMAZING, TOO!
RIGHT? THEY SEEM WAY OLDER THAN US.
YEAH, THEY'RE SO CONFIDENT.
WOW, IT'S LIKE THEY HAVE THIS **GLOW.**
WHAT WOULD THAT FEEL LIKE?

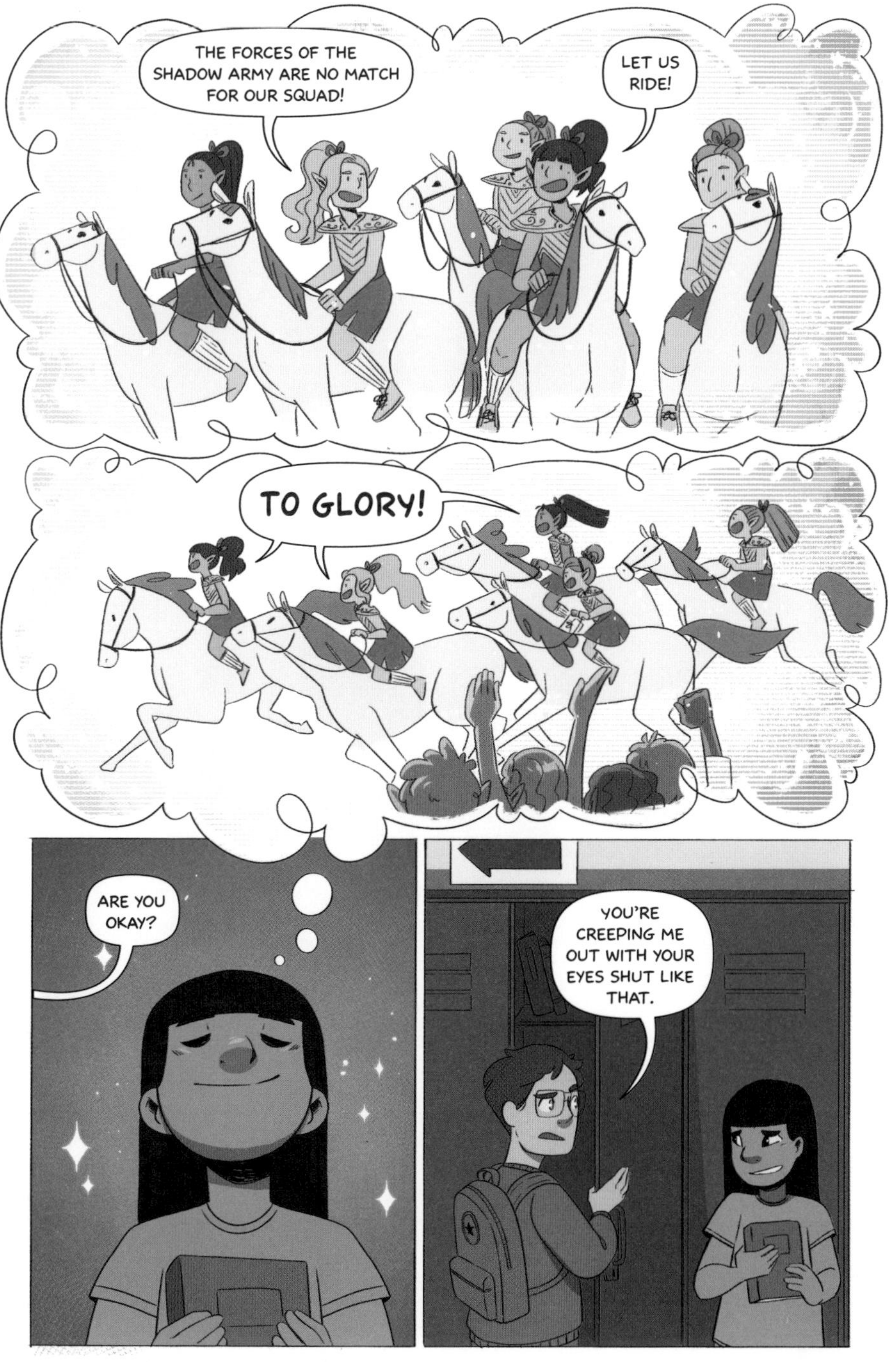
THE FORCES OF THE SHADOW ARMY ARE NO MATCH FOR OUR SQUAD!
LET US RIDE!
TO GLORY!
ARE YOU OKAY?
YOU'RE CREEPING ME OUT WITH YOUR EYES SHUT LIKE THAT.

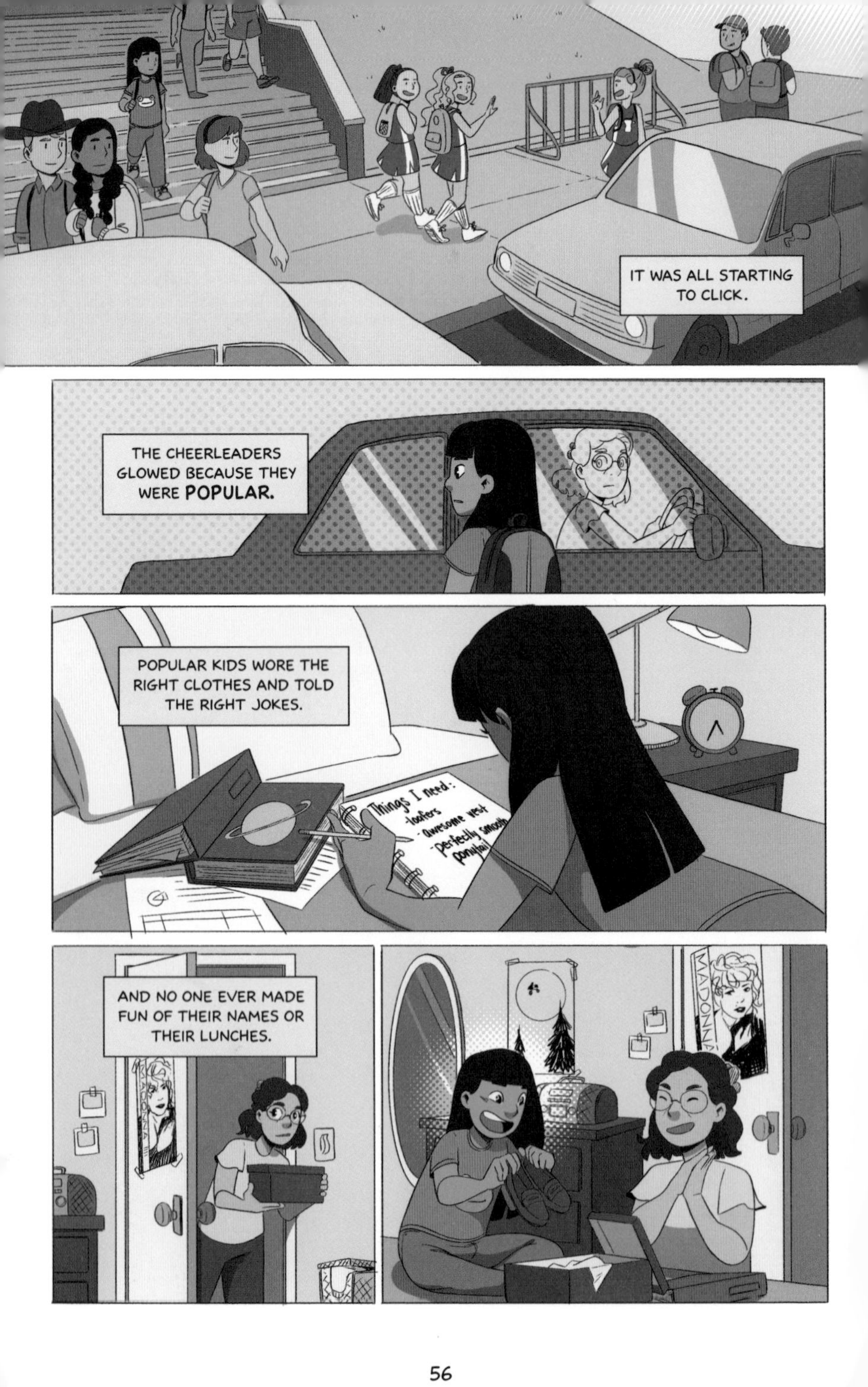
IT WAS ALL STARTING TO CLICK.
THE CHEERLEADERS GLOWED BECAUSE THEY WERE POPULAR.
POPULAR KIDS WORE THE RIGHT CLOTHES AND TOLD THE RIGHT JOKES.
Things I need:
-loafers
-awesome vest
-perfectly smooth ponytail
AND NO ONE EVER MADE FUN OF THEIR NAMES OR THEIR LUNCHES.
MADONNA
MADONNA

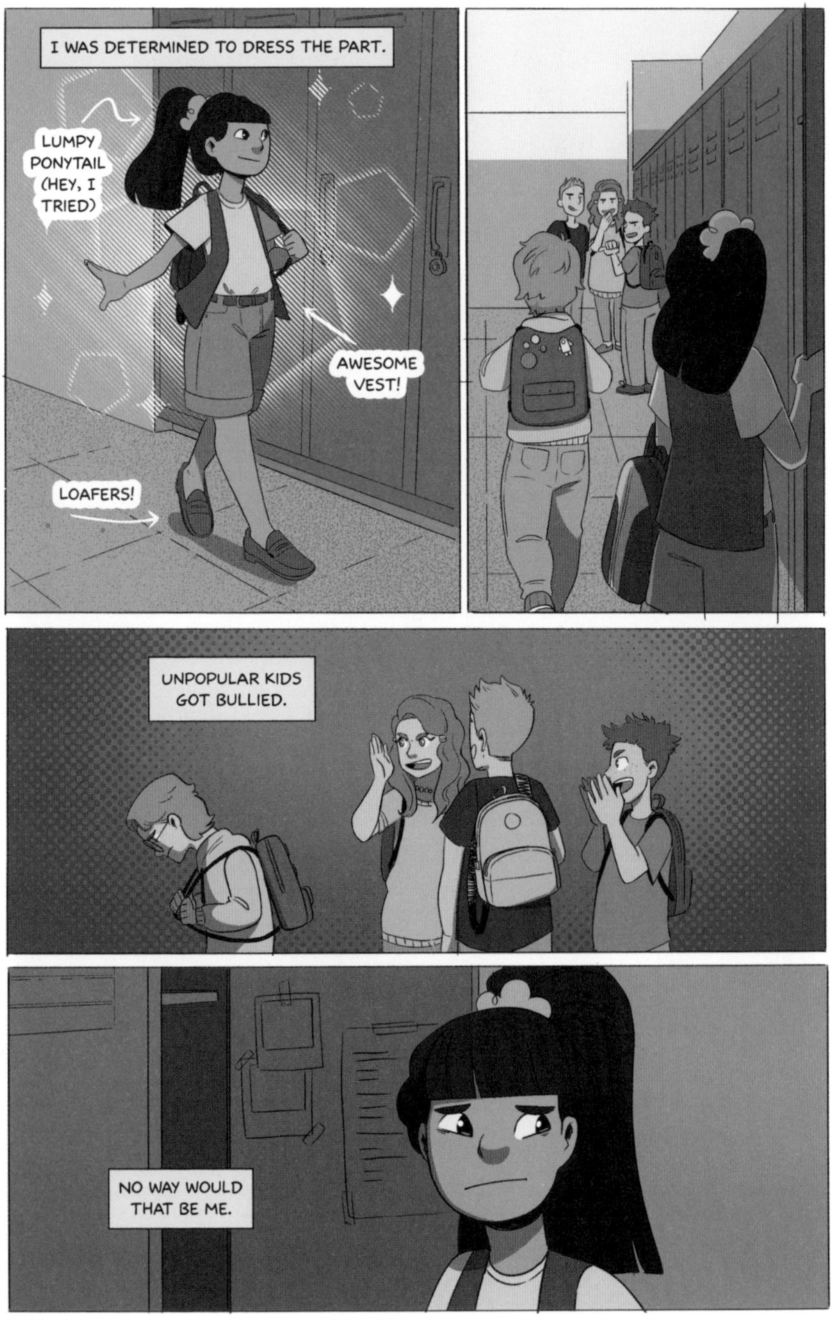
I WAS DETERMINED TO DRESS THE PART.
LUMPY PONYTAIL (HEY, I TRIED)
AWESOME VEST!
LOAFERS!
UNPOPULAR KIDS GOT BULLIED.
NO WAY WOULD THAT BE ME.

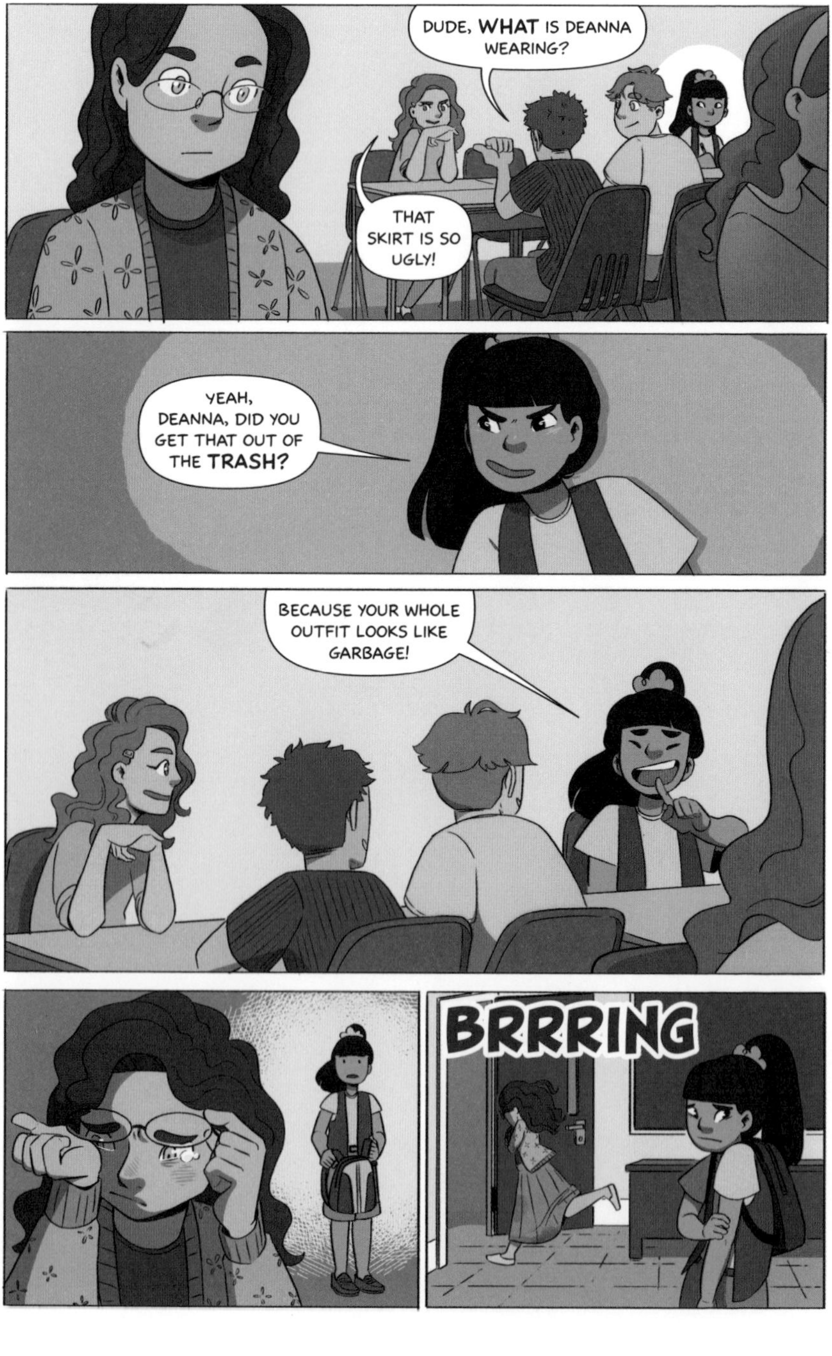
DUDE, WHAT IS DEANNA WEARING?
THAT SKIRT IS SO UGLY!
YEAH, DEANNA, DID YOU GET THAT OUT OF THE TRASH?
BECAUSE YOUR WHOLE OUTFIT LOOKS LIKE GARBAGE!
BRRRING

LATER THAT AFTERNOON

YOUNG LADY, THOSE ARE FOR CUSTOMERS.

HEY, CHRISTINA, YOU WANT TO HELP ME MAKE THE BABY CHOPSTICKS?

OKAY, SURE.

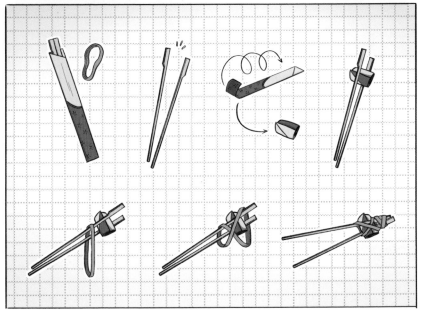

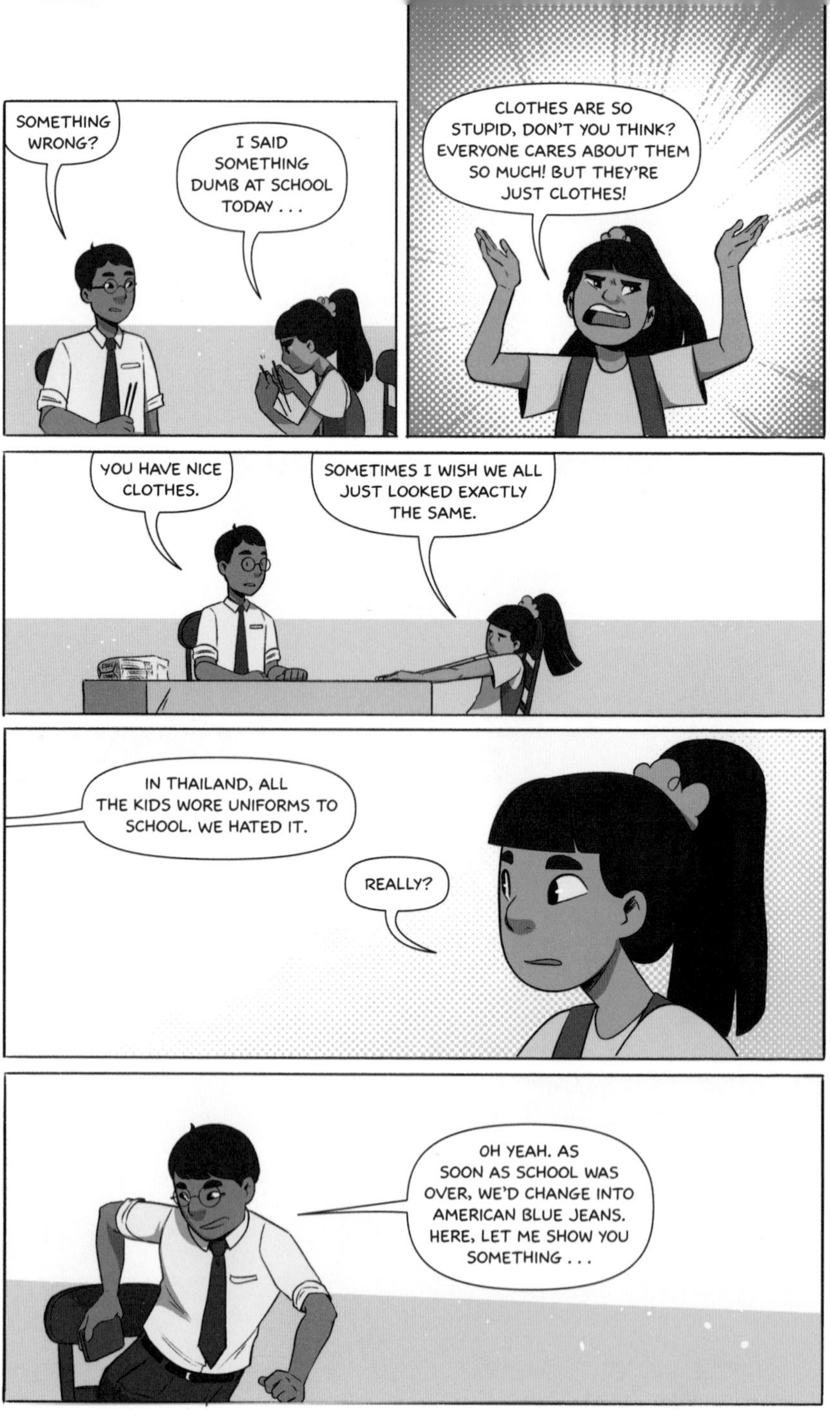
SOMETHING WRONG?
I SAID SOMETHING DUMB AT SCHOOL TODAY . . .
CLOTHES ARE SO STUPID, DON'T YOU THINK? EVERYONE CARES ABOUT THEM SO MUCH! BUT THEY'RE JUST CLOTHES!
YOU HAVE NICE CLOTHES.
SOMETIMES I WISH WE ALL JUST LOOKED EXACTLY THE SAME.
IN THAILAND, ALL THE KIDS WORE UNIFORMS TO SCHOOL. WE HATED IT.
REALLY?
OH YEAH. AS SOON AS SCHOOL WAS OVER, WE'D CHANGE INTO AMERICAN BLUE JEANS. HERE, LET ME SHOW YOU SOMETHING . . .

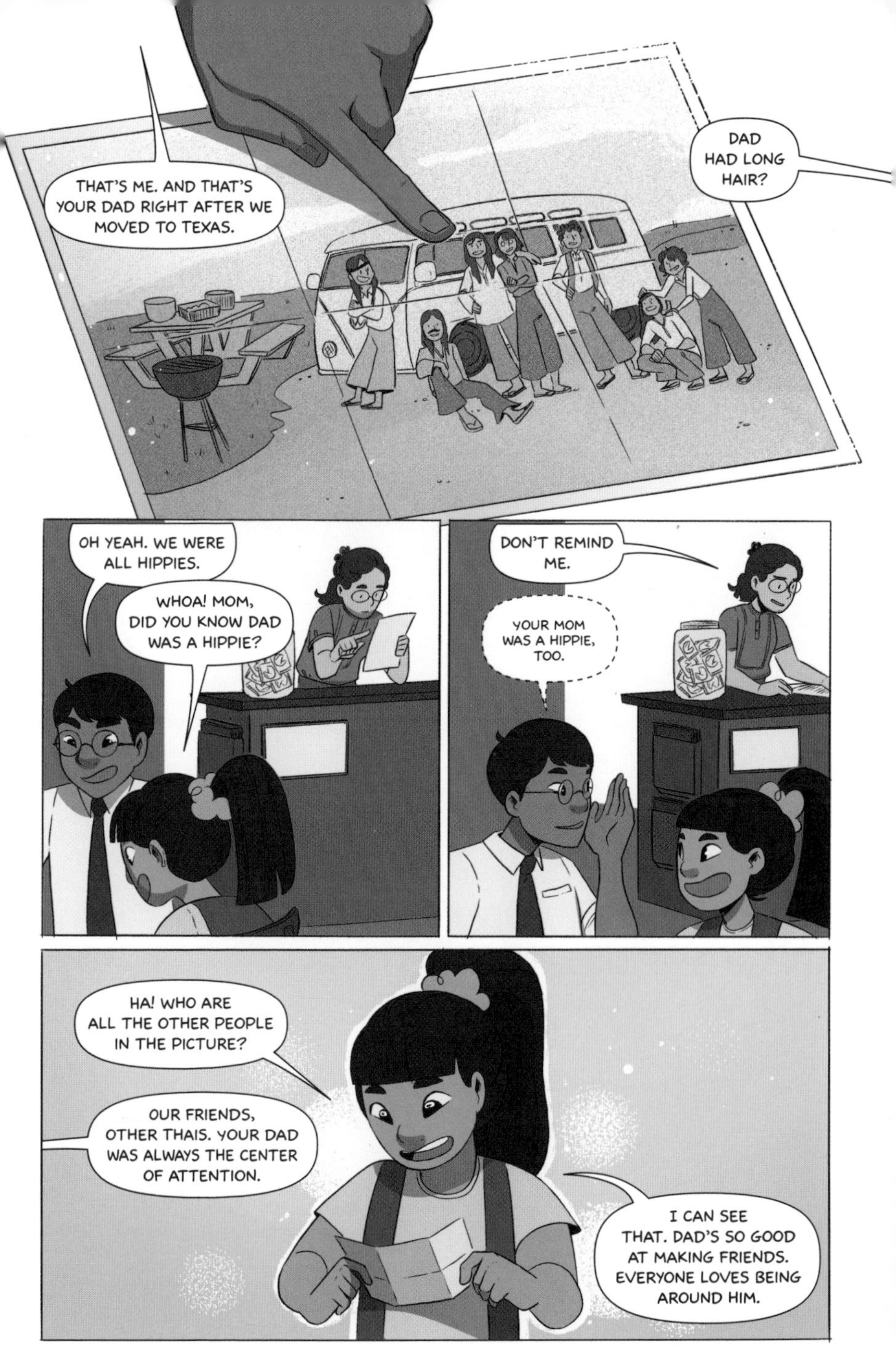
THAT'S ME. AND THAT'S YOUR DAD RIGHT AFTER WE MOVED TO TEXAS.
DAD HAD LONG HAIR?
OH YEAH. WE WERE ALL HIPPIES.
WHOA! MOM, DID YOU KNOW DAD WAS A HIPPIE?
DON'T REMIND ME.
YOUR MOM WAS A HIPPIE, TOO.
HA! WHO ARE ALL THE OTHER PEOPLE IN THE PICTURE?
OUR FRIENDS, OTHER THAIS. YOUR DAD WAS ALWAYS THE CENTER OF ATTENTION.
I CAN SEE THAT. DAD'S SO GOOD AT MAKING FRIENDS. EVERYONE LOVES BEING AROUND HIM.

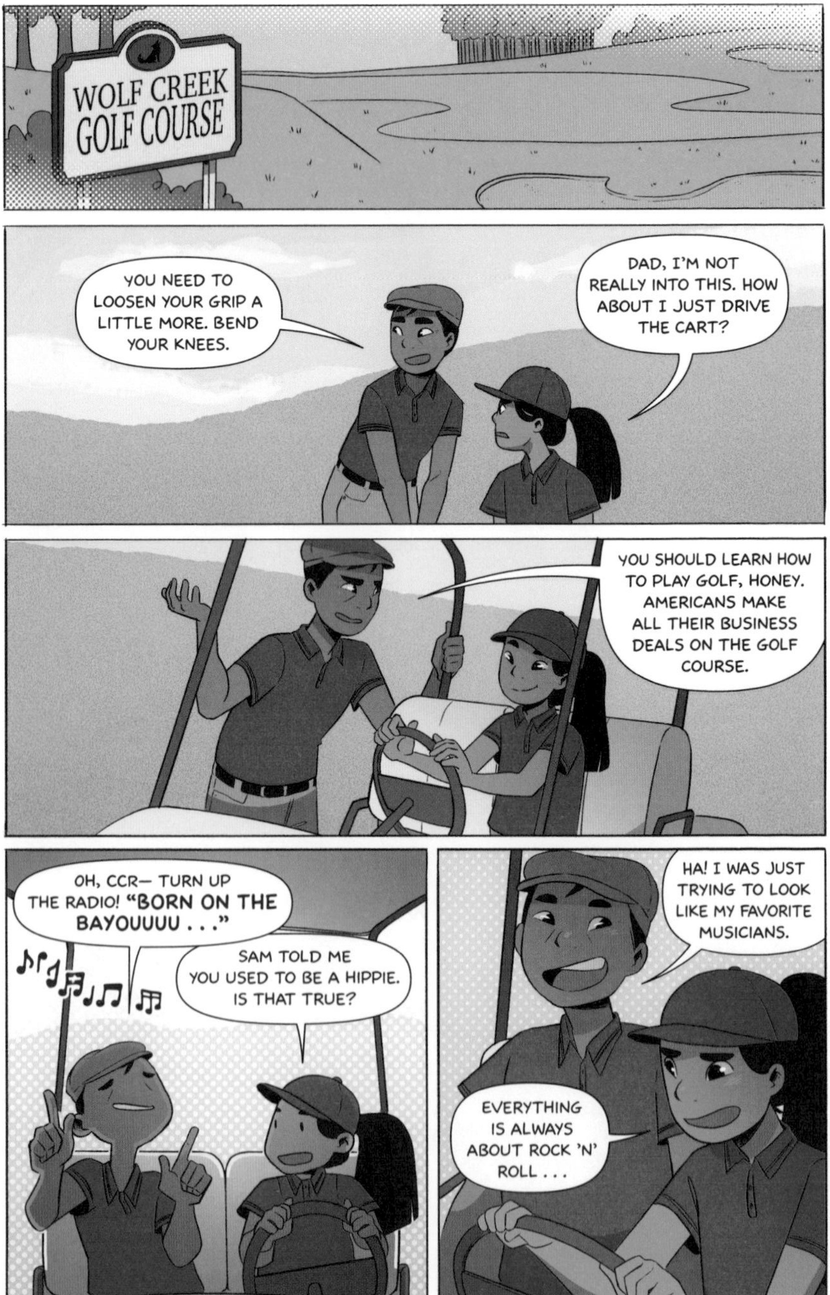
WOLF CREEK GOLF COURSE
YOU NEED TO LOOSEN YOUR GRIP A LITTLE MORE. BEND YOUR KNEES.
DAD, I'M NOT REALLY INTO THIS. HOW ABOUT I JUST DRIVE THE CART?
YOU SHOULD LEARN HOW TO PLAY GOLF, HONEY. AMERICANS MAKE ALL THEIR BUSINESS DEALS ON THE GOLF COURSE.
OH, CCR— TURN UP THE RADIO! "BORN ON THE BAYOUUUU . . ."
SAM TOLD ME YOU USED TO BE A HIPPIE. IS THAT TRUE?
HA! I WAS JUST TRYING TO LOOK LIKE MY FAVORITE MUSICIANS.
EVERYTHING IS ALWAYS ABOUT ROCK 'N' ROLL . . .

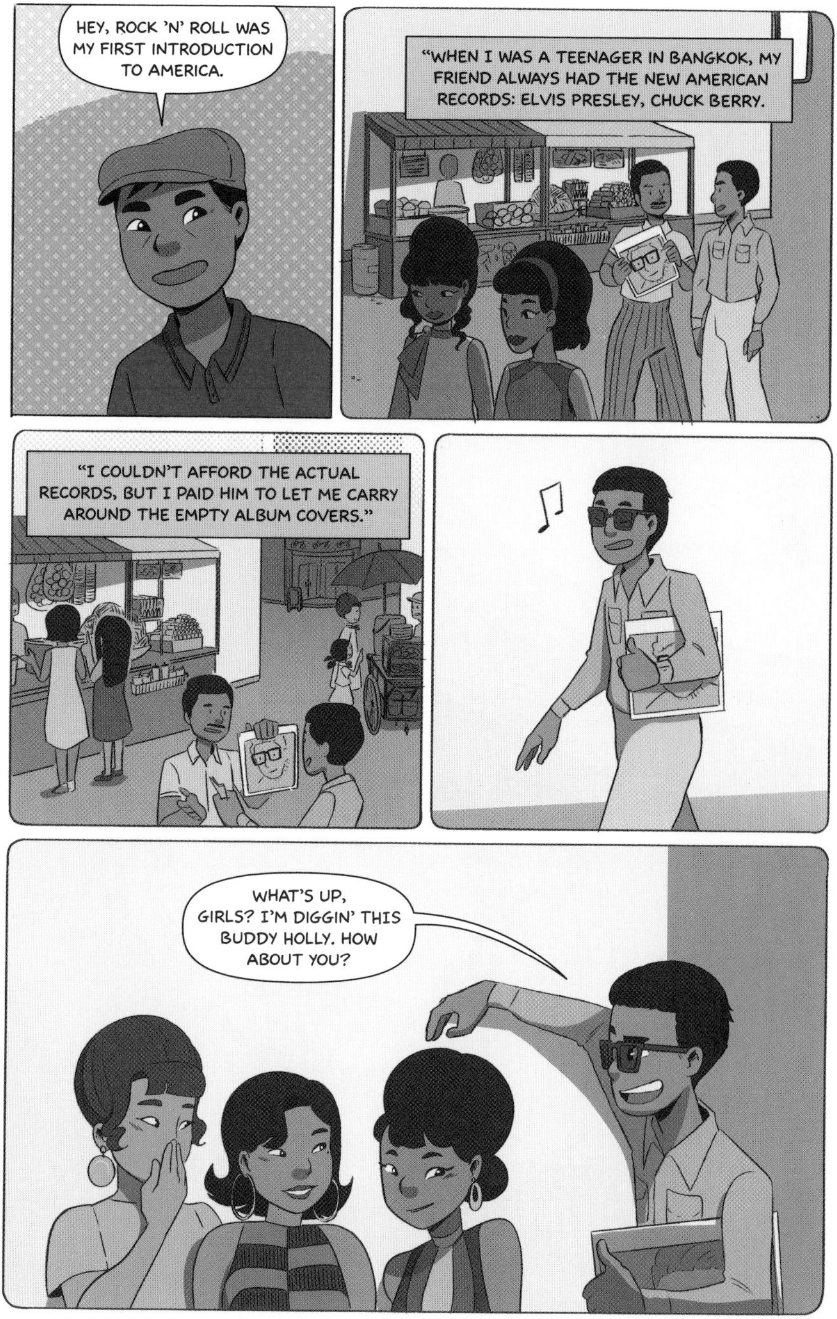
HEY, ROCK 'N' ROLL WAS MY FIRST INTRODUCTION TO AMERICA.
"WHEN I WAS A TEENAGER IN BANGKOK, MY FRIEND ALWAYS HAD THE NEW AMERICAN RECORDS: ELVIS PRESLEY, CHUCK BERRY.
"I COULDN'T AFFORD THE ACTUAL RECORDS, BUT I PAID HIM TO LET ME CARRY AROUND THE EMPTY ALBUM COVERS."
WHAT'S UP, GIRLS? I'M DIGGIN' THIS BUDDY HOLLY. HOW ABOUT YOU?

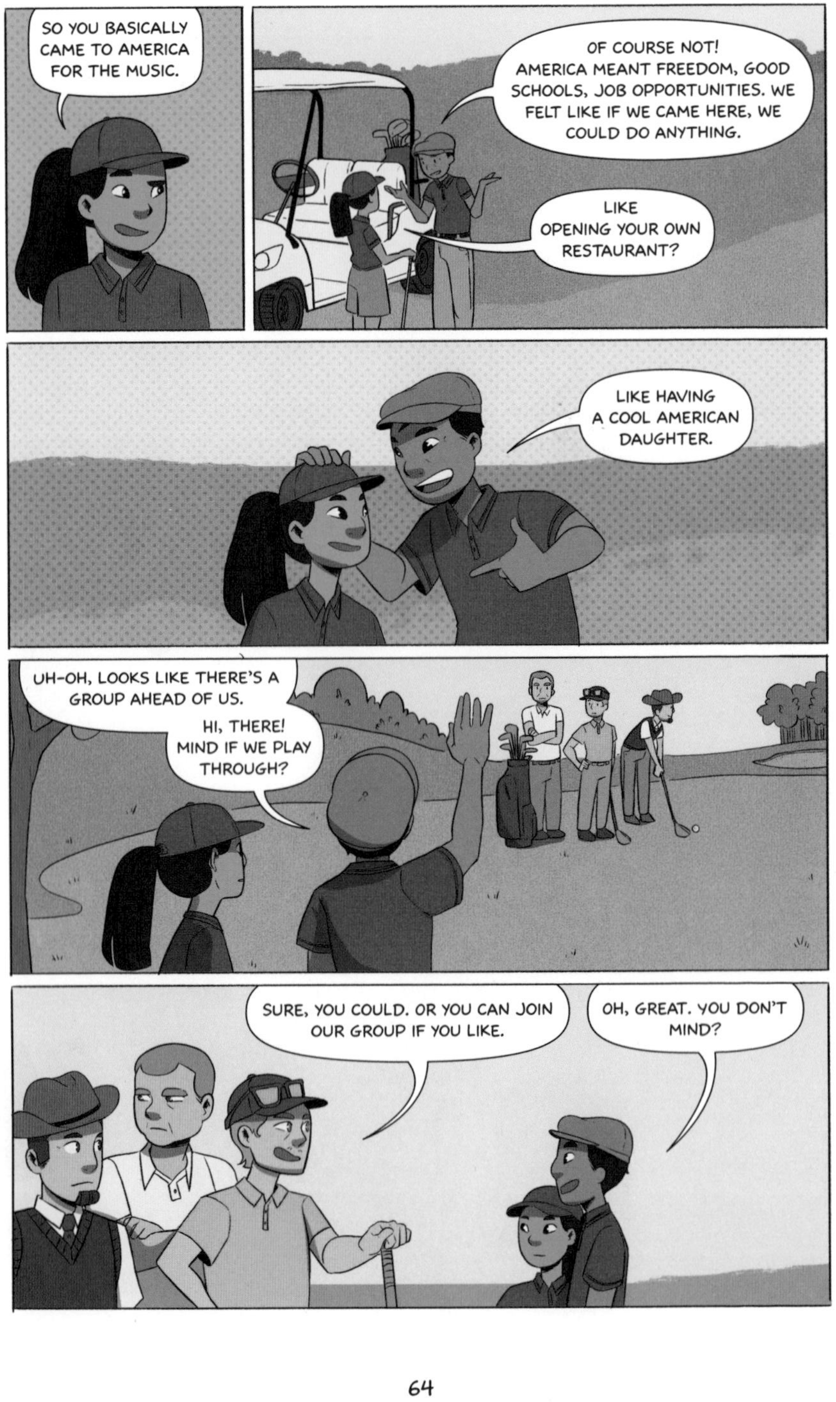
SO YOU BASICALLY CAME TO AMERICA FOR THE MUSIC.
OF COURSE NOT! AMERICA MEANT FREEDOM, GOOD SCHOOLS, JOB OPPORTUNITIES. WE FELT LIKE IF WE CAME HERE, WE COULD DO ANYTHING.
LIKE OPENING YOUR OWN RESTAURANT?
LIKE HAVING A COOL AMERICAN DAUGHTER.
UH-OH, LOOKS LIKE THERE'S A GROUP AHEAD OF US.
HI, THERE! MIND IF WE PLAY THROUGH?
SURE, YOU COULD. OR YOU CAN JOIN OUR GROUP IF YOU LIKE.
OH, GREAT. YOU DON'T MIND?

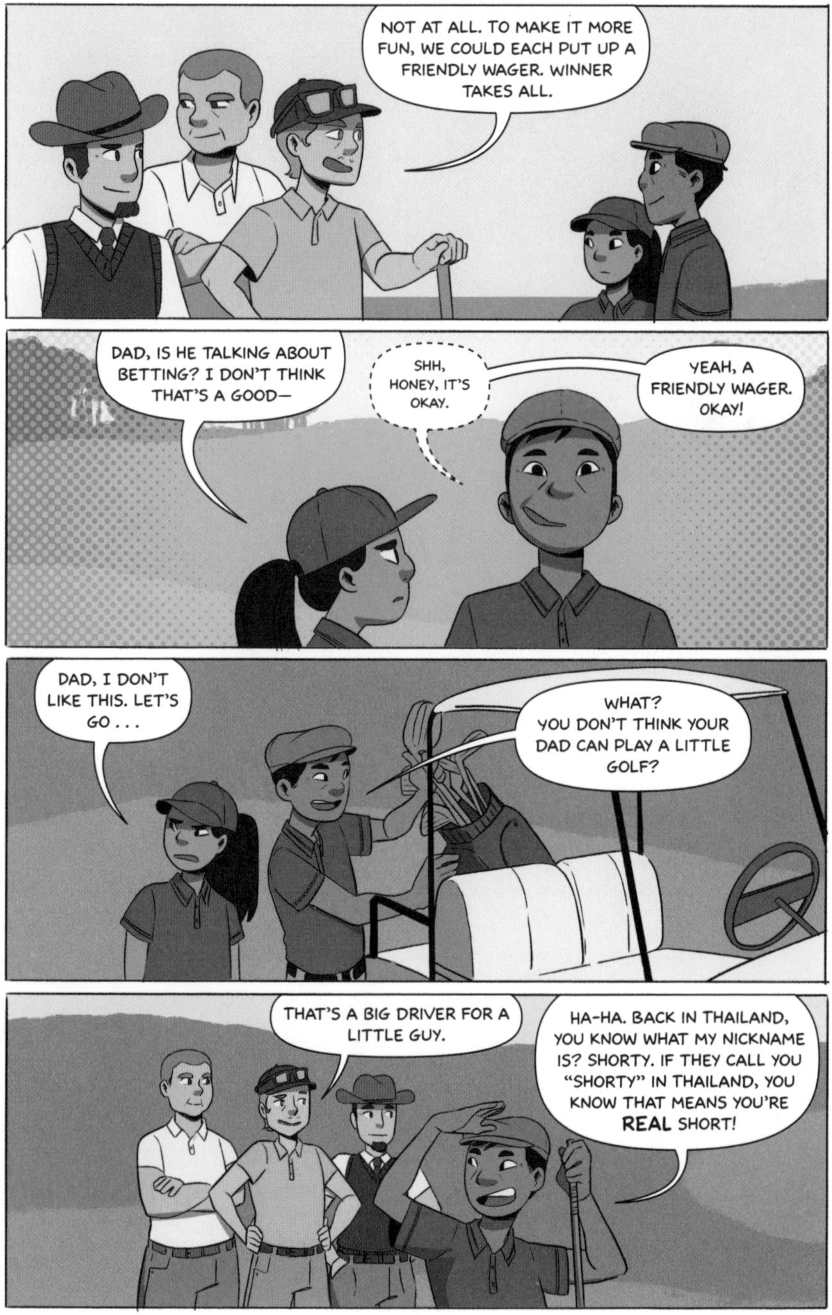
NOT AT ALL. TO MAKE IT MORE FUN, WE COULD EACH PUT UP A FRIENDLY WAGER. WINNER TAKES ALL.
DAD, IS HE TALKING ABOUT BETTING? I DON'T THINK THAT'S A GOOD—
SHH, HONEY, IT'S OKAY.
YEAH, A FRIENDLY WAGER. OKAY!
DAD, I DON'T LIKE THIS. LET'S GO . . .
WHAT? YOU DON'T THINK YOUR DAD CAN PLAY A LITTLE GOLF?
THAT'S A BIG DRIVER FOR A LITTLE GUY.
HA-HA. BACK IN THAILAND, YOU KNOW WHAT MY NICKNAME IS? SHORTY. IF THEY CALL YOU "SHORTY" IN THAILAND, YOU KNOW THAT MEANS YOU'RE **REAL** SHORT!

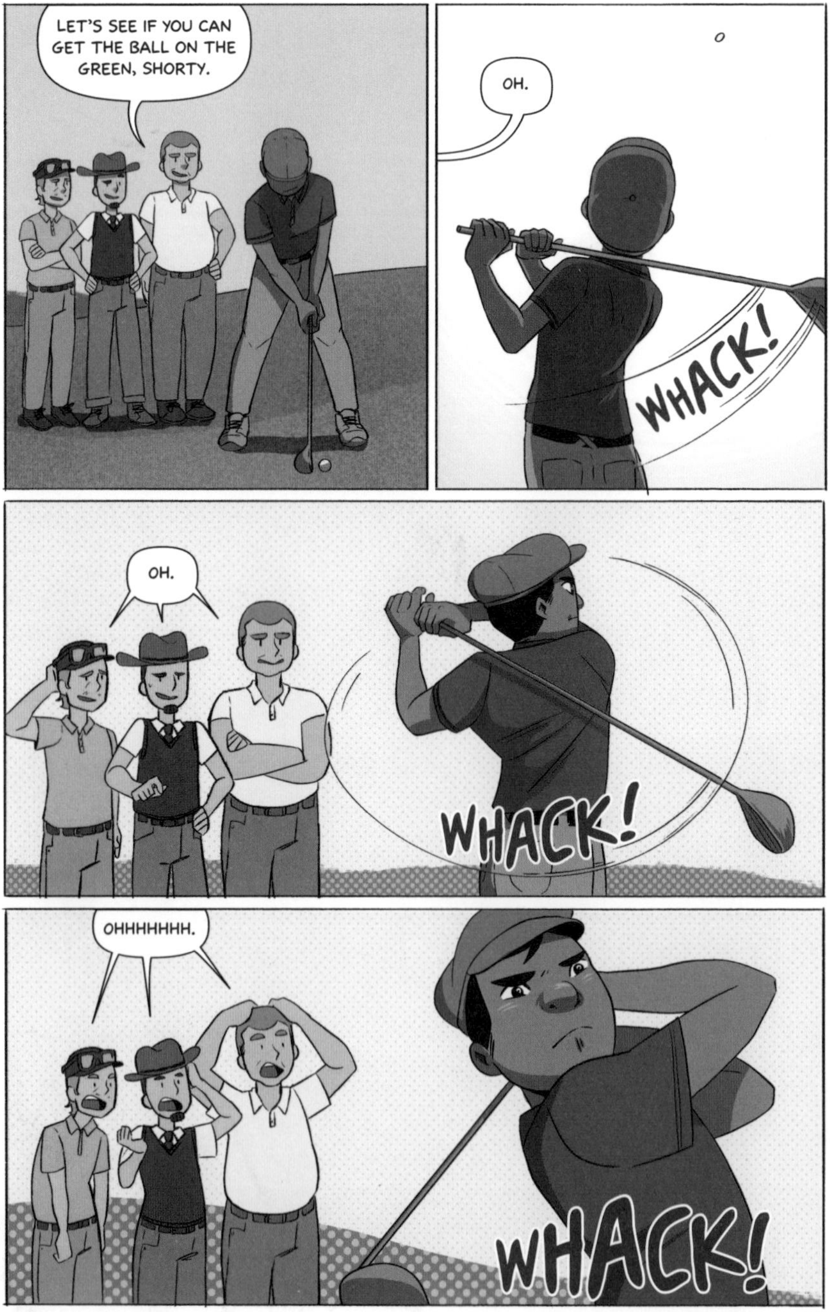
LET'S SEE IF YOU CAN GET THE BALL ON THE GREEN, SHORTY.
OH.
WHACK!
OH.
WHACK!
OHHHHHHH.
WHACK!

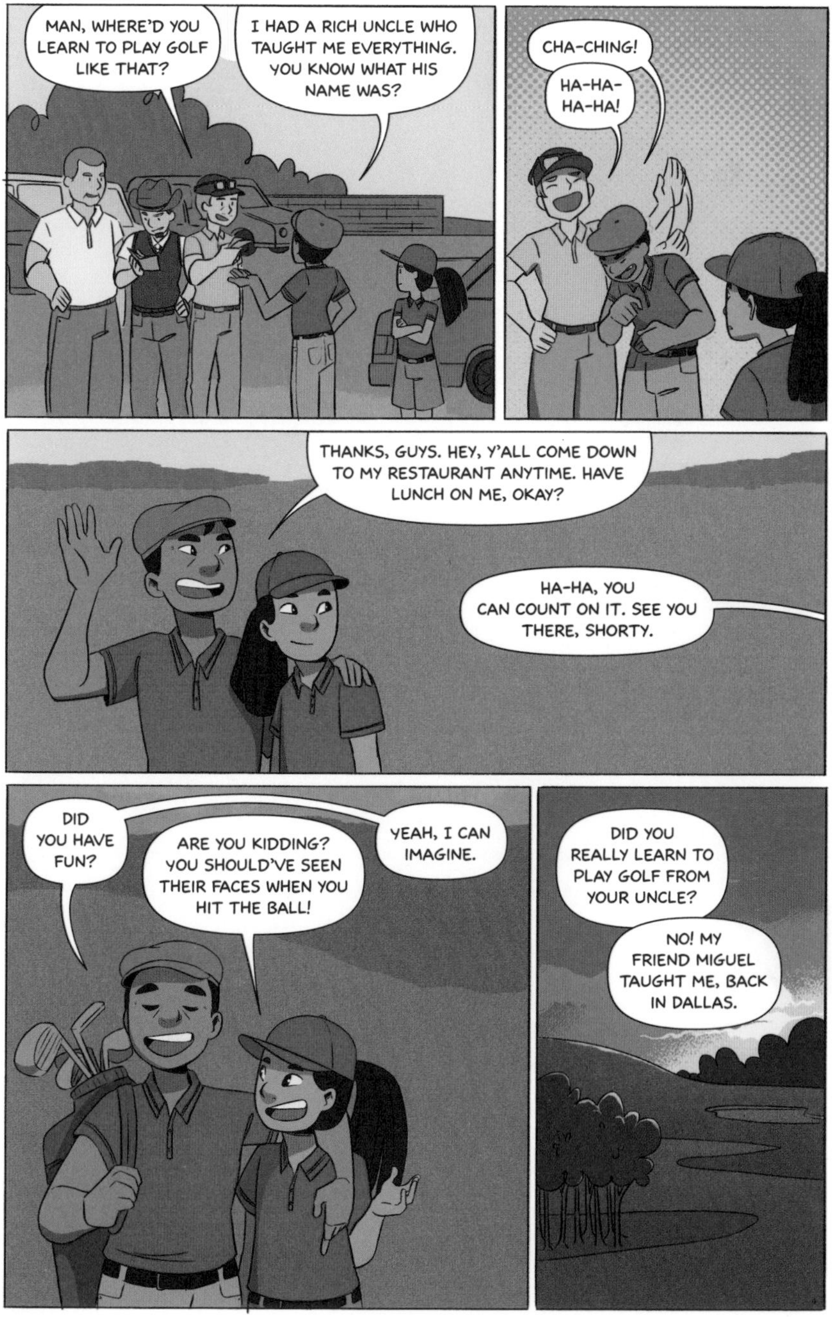
MAN, WHERE'D YOU LEARN TO PLAY GOLF LIKE THAT?
I HAD A RICH UNCLE WHO TAUGHT ME EVERYTHING. YOU KNOW WHAT HIS NAME WAS?
CHA-CHING!
HA-HA-HA-HA!
THANKS, GUYS. HEY, Y'ALL COME DOWN TO MY RESTAURANT ANYTIME. HAVE LUNCH ON ME, OKAY?
HA-HA, YOU CAN COUNT ON IT. SEE YOU THERE, SHORTY.
DID YOU HAVE FUN?
ARE YOU KIDDING? YOU SHOULD'VE SEEN THEIR FACES WHEN YOU HIT THE BALL!
YEAH, I CAN IMAGINE.
DID YOU REALLY LEARN TO PLAY GOLF FROM YOUR UNCLE?
NO! MY FRIEND MIGUEL TAUGHT ME, BACK IN DALLAS.

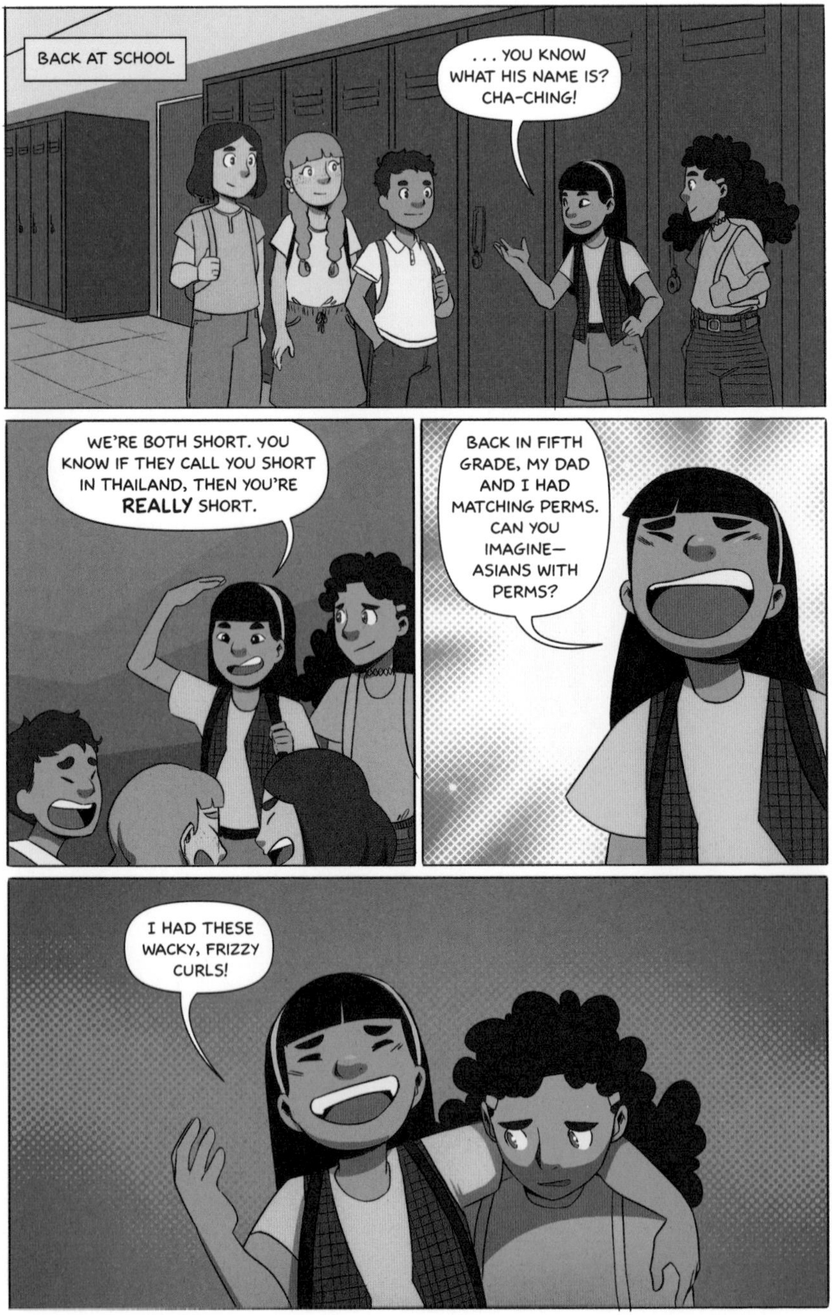
BACK AT SCHOOL
. . . YOU KNOW WHAT HIS NAME IS? CHA-CHING!
WE'RE BOTH SHORT. YOU KNOW IF THEY CALL YOU SHORT IN THAILAND, THEN YOU'RE **REALLY** SHORT.
BACK IN FIFTH GRADE, MY DAD AND I HAD MATCHING PERMS. CAN YOU IMAGINE— ASIANS WITH PERMS?
I HAD THESE WACKY, FRIZZY CURLS!

I LOOKED JUST LIKE MEGAN! WE WERE THE FRIZZ TWINS, RIGHT?

BRRRING

MEGAN, WAIT!

YOUNG LADY, WE **WALK** IN THE HALLS!

WHAT DID I JUST DO?

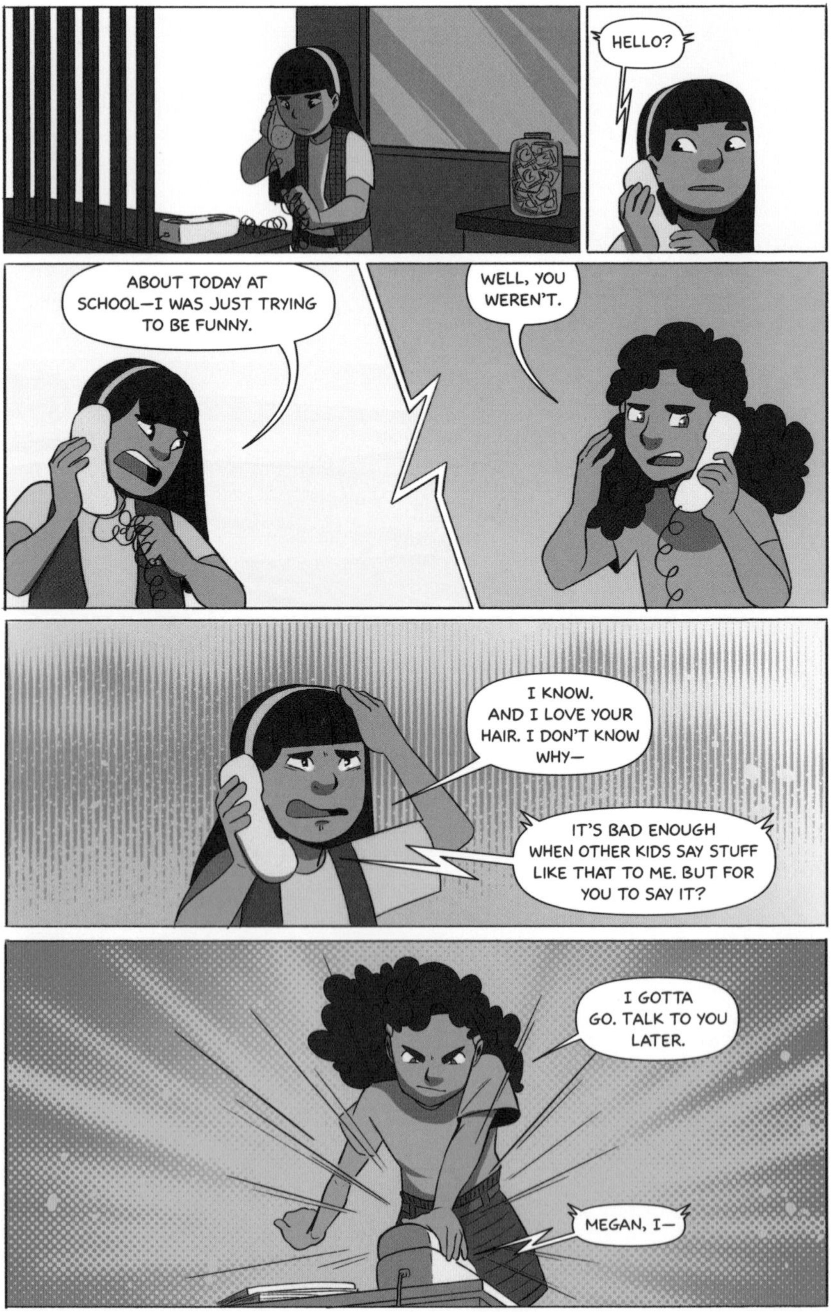
HELLO?
ABOUT TODAY AT SCHOOL—I WAS JUST TRYING TO BE FUNNY.
WELL, YOU WEREN'T.
I KNOW. AND I LOVE YOUR HAIR. I DON'T KNOW WHY—
IT'S BAD ENOUGH WHEN OTHER KIDS SAY STUFF LIKE THAT TO ME. BUT FOR YOU TO SAY IT?
I GOTTA GO. TALK TO YOU LATER.
MEGAN, I—

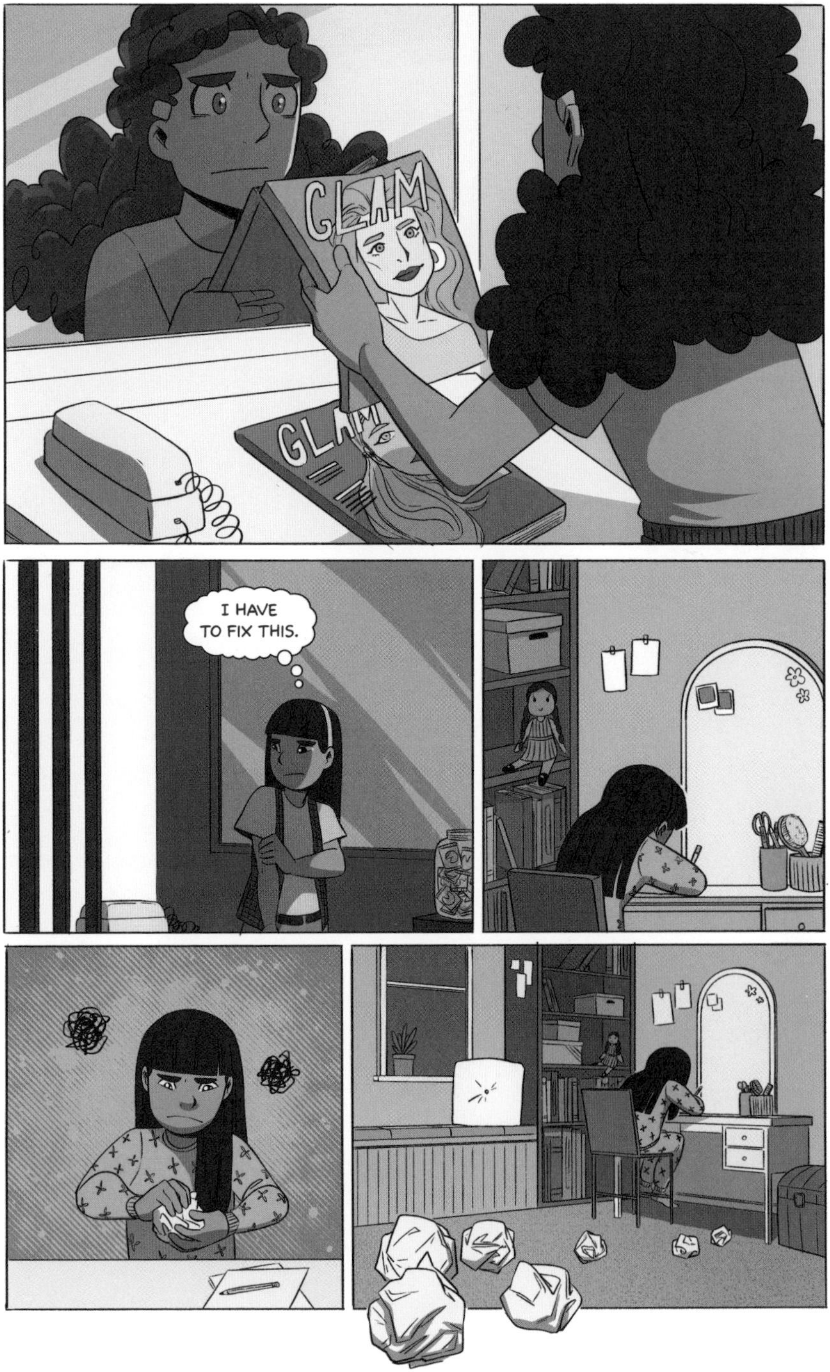
GLAM
GLAM
I HAVE
TO FIX THIS.

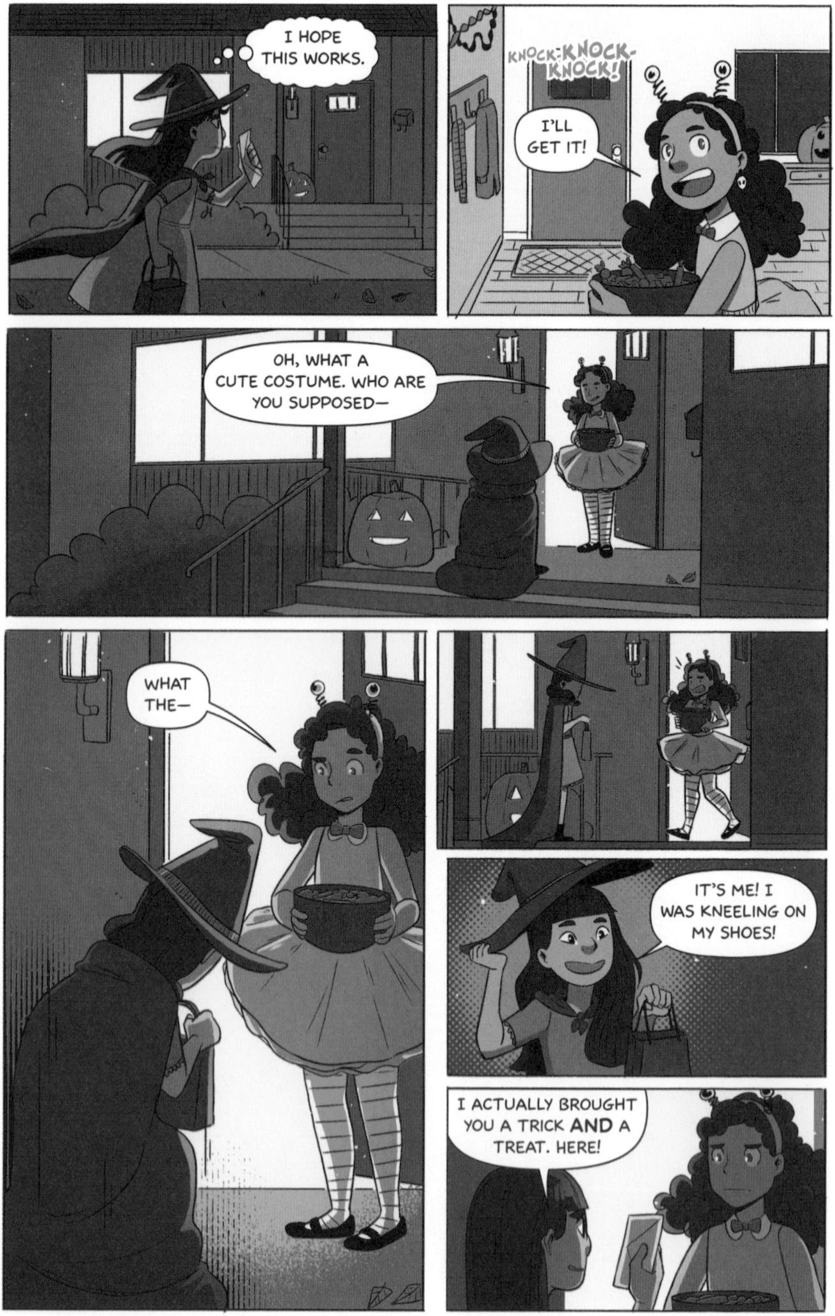
I HOPE THIS WORKS.
KNOCK-KNOCK-KNOCK!
I'LL GET IT!
OH, WHAT A CUTE COSTUME. WHO ARE YOU SUPPOSED—
WHAT THE—
IT'S ME! I WAS KNEELING ON MY SHOES!
I ACTUALLY BROUGHT YOU A TRICK AND A TREAT. HERE!

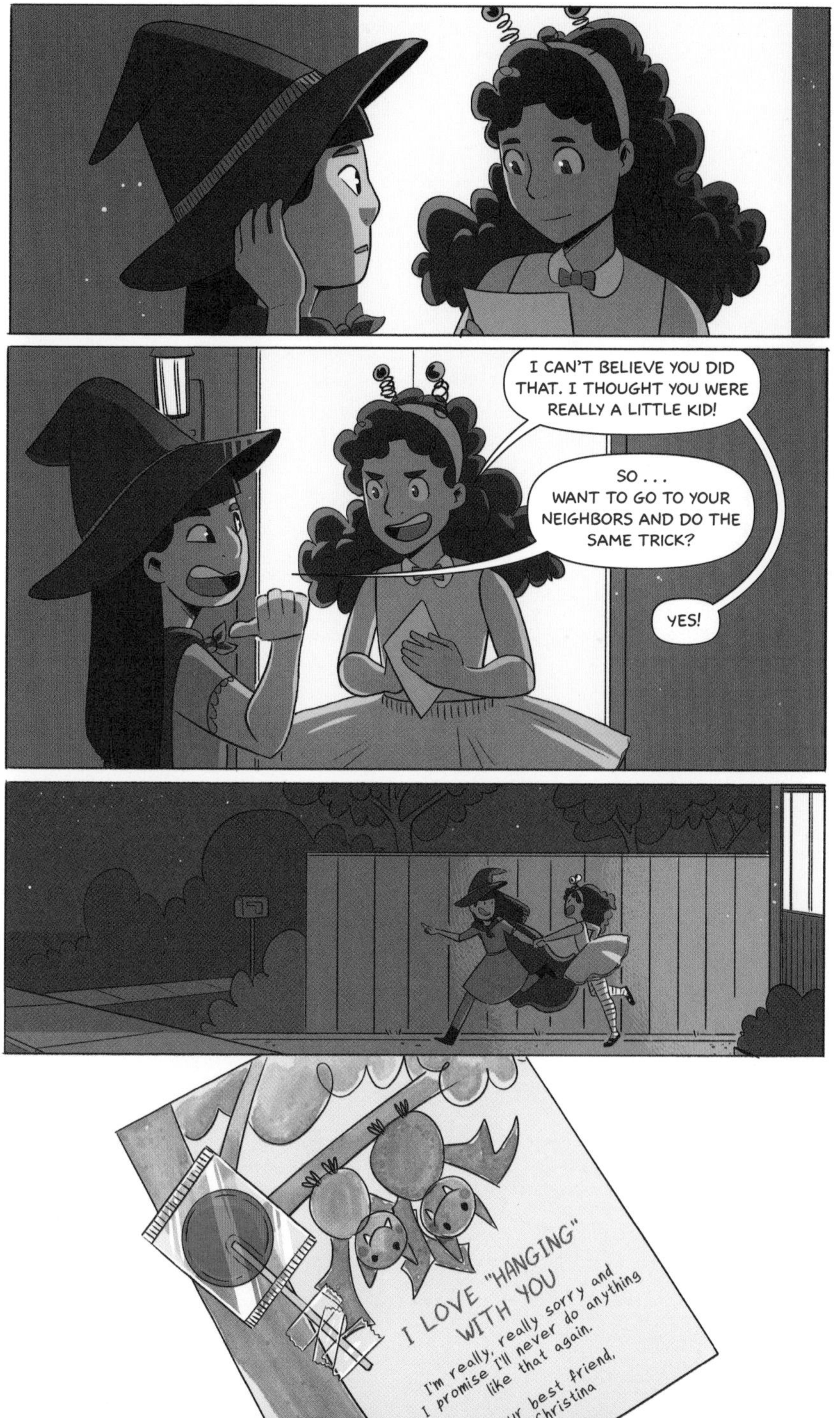
I CAN'T BELIEVE YOU DID THAT. I THOUGHT YOU WERE REALLY A LITTLE KID!
SO . . . WANT TO GO TO YOUR NEIGHBORS AND DO THE SAME TRICK?
YES!
I LOVE "HANGING" WITH YOU
I'm really, really sorry and I promise I'll never do anything like that again.
Your best friend, Christina

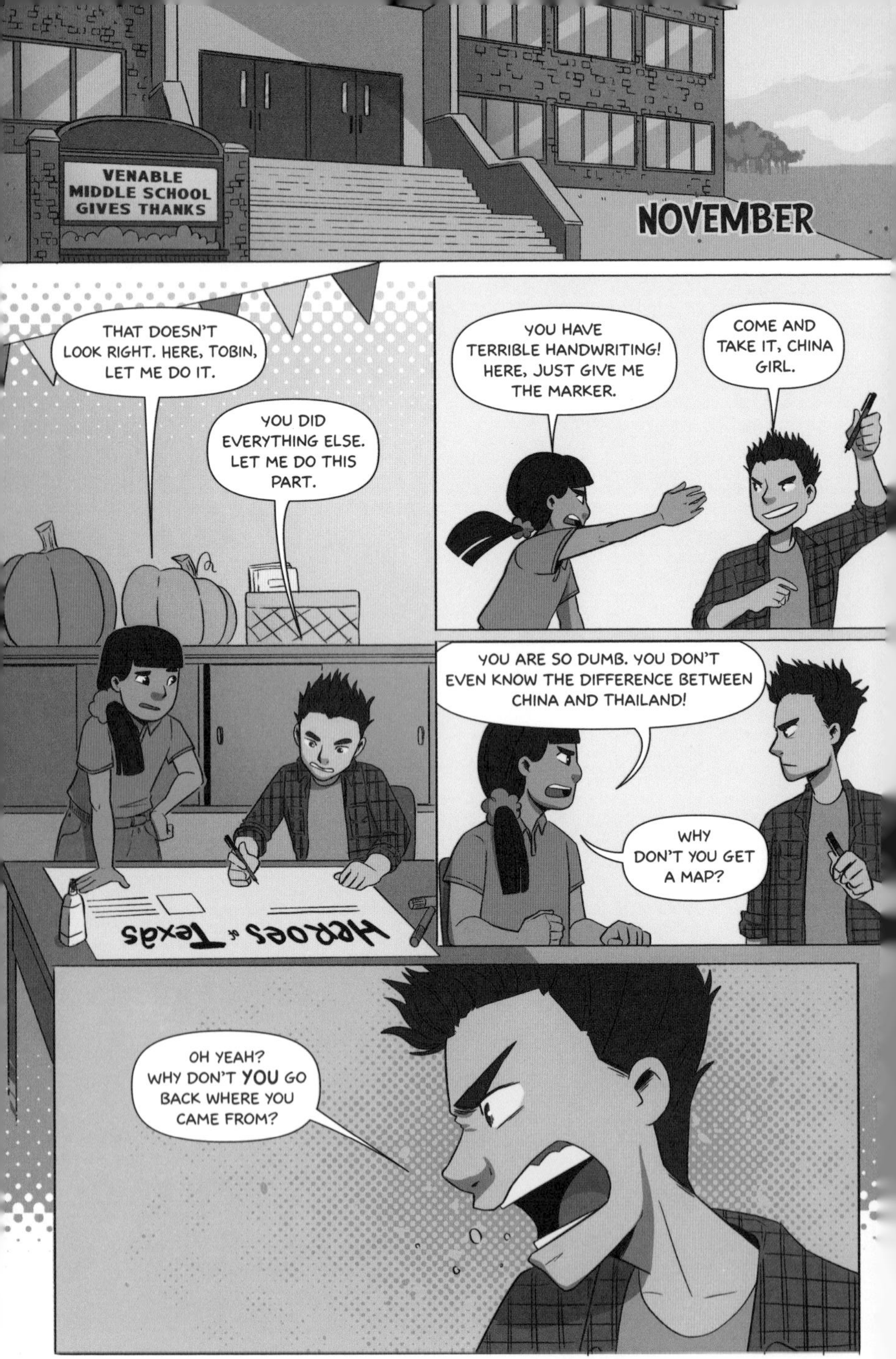
VENABLE MIDDLE SCHOOL GIVES THANKS
NOVEMBER
THAT DOESN'T LOOK RIGHT. HERE, TOBIN, LET ME DO IT.
YOU DID EVERYTHING ELSE. LET ME DO THIS PART.
Heroes of Texas
YOU HAVE TERRIBLE HANDWRITING! HERE, JUST GIVE ME THE MARKER.
COME AND TAKE IT, CHINA GIRL.
YOU ARE SO DUMB. YOU DON'T EVEN KNOW THE DIFFERENCE BETWEEN CHINA AND THAILAND!
WHY DON'T YOU GET A MAP?
OH YEAH? WHY DON'T YOU GO BACK WHERE YOU CAME FROM?

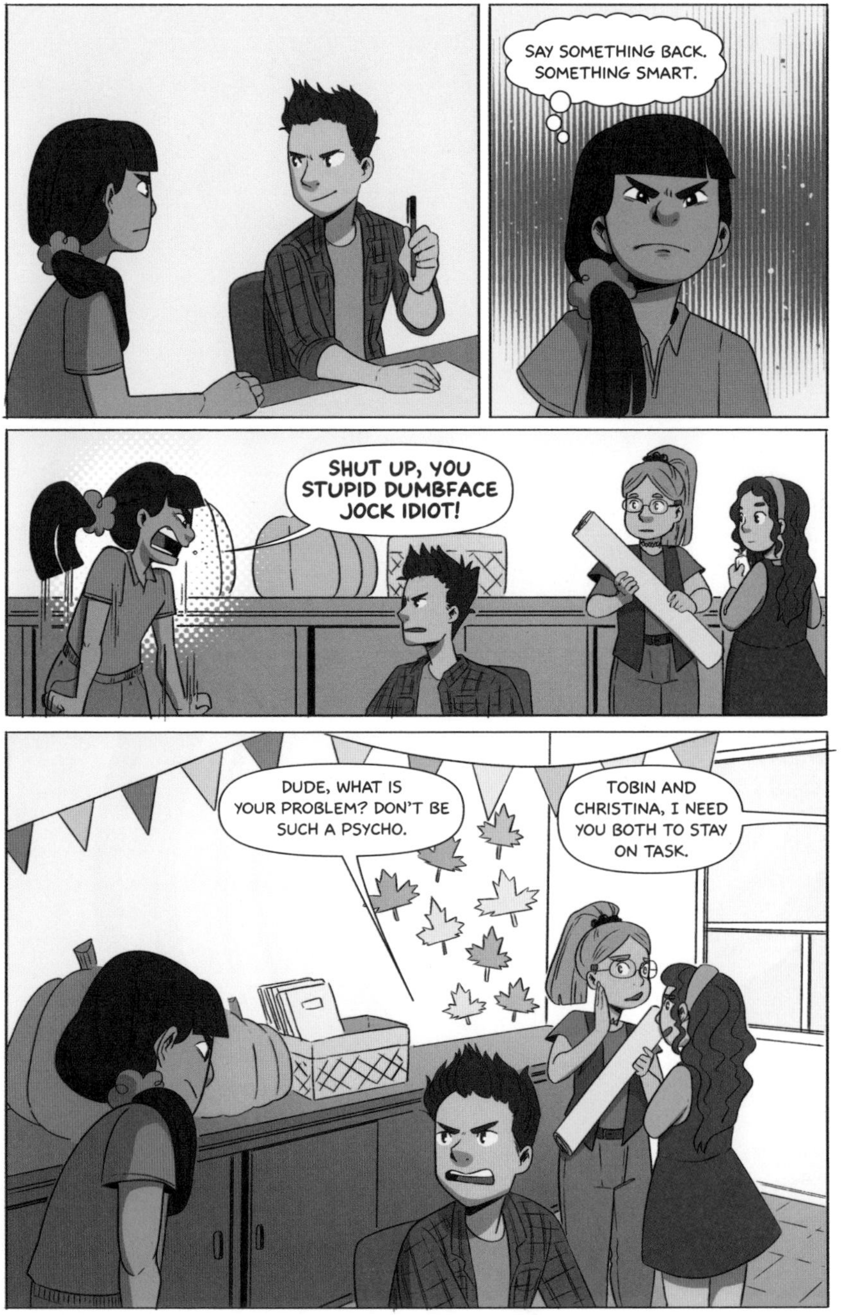
SAY SOMETHING BACK. SOMETHING SMART.
SHUT UP, YOU STUPID DUMBFACE JOCK IDIOT!
DUDE, WHAT IS YOUR PROBLEM? DON'T BE SUCH A PSYCHO.
TOBIN AND CHRISTINA, I NEED YOU BOTH TO STAY ON TASK.

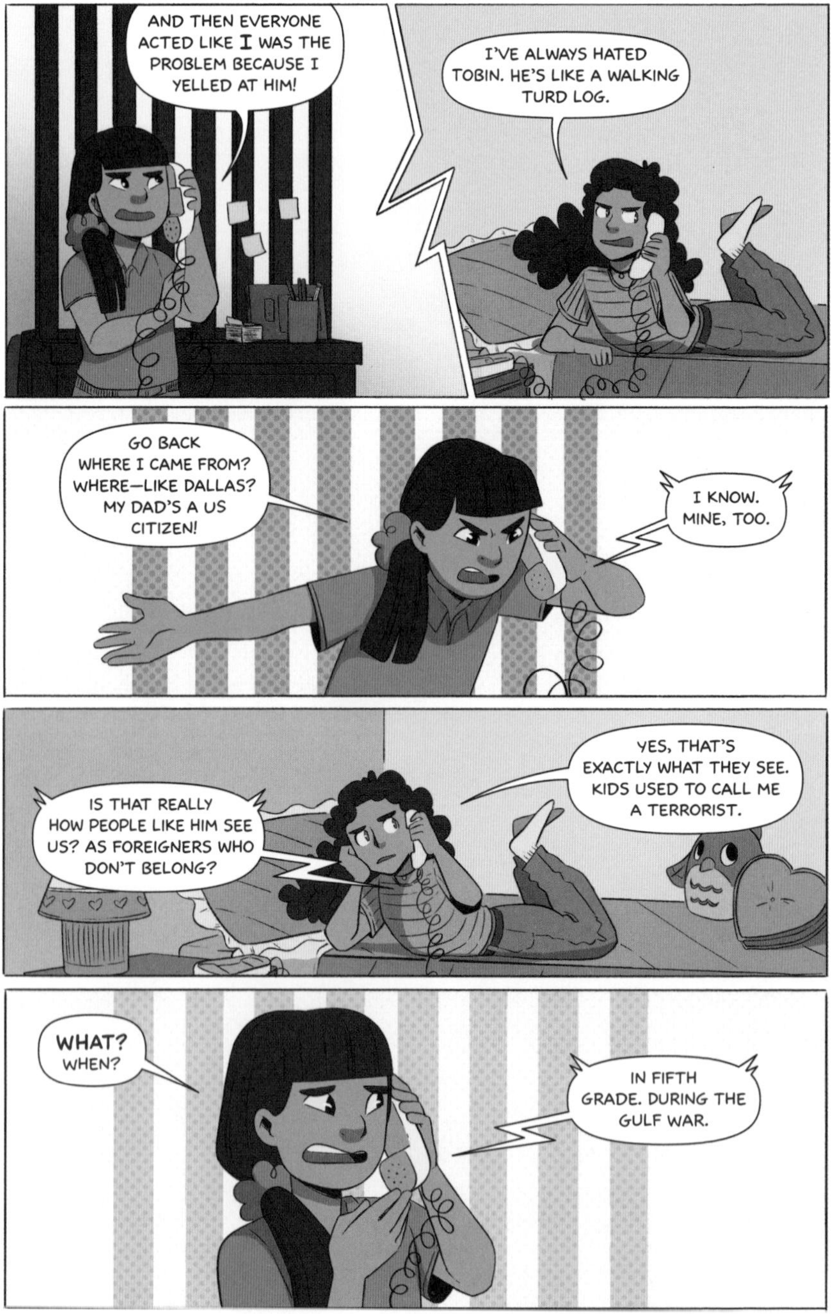
AND THEN EVERYONE ACTED LIKE I WAS THE PROBLEM BECAUSE I YELLED AT HIM!
I'VE ALWAYS HATED TOBIN. HE'S LIKE A WALKING TURD LOG.
GO BACK WHERE I CAME FROM? WHERE—LIKE DALLAS? MY DAD'S A US CITIZEN!
I KNOW. MINE, TOO.
IS THAT REALLY HOW PEOPLE LIKE HIM SEE US? AS FOREIGNERS WHO DON'T BELONG?
YES, THAT'S EXACTLY WHAT THEY SEE. KIDS USED TO CALL ME A TERRORIST.
WHAT? WHEN?
IN FIFTH GRADE. DURING THE GULF WAR.

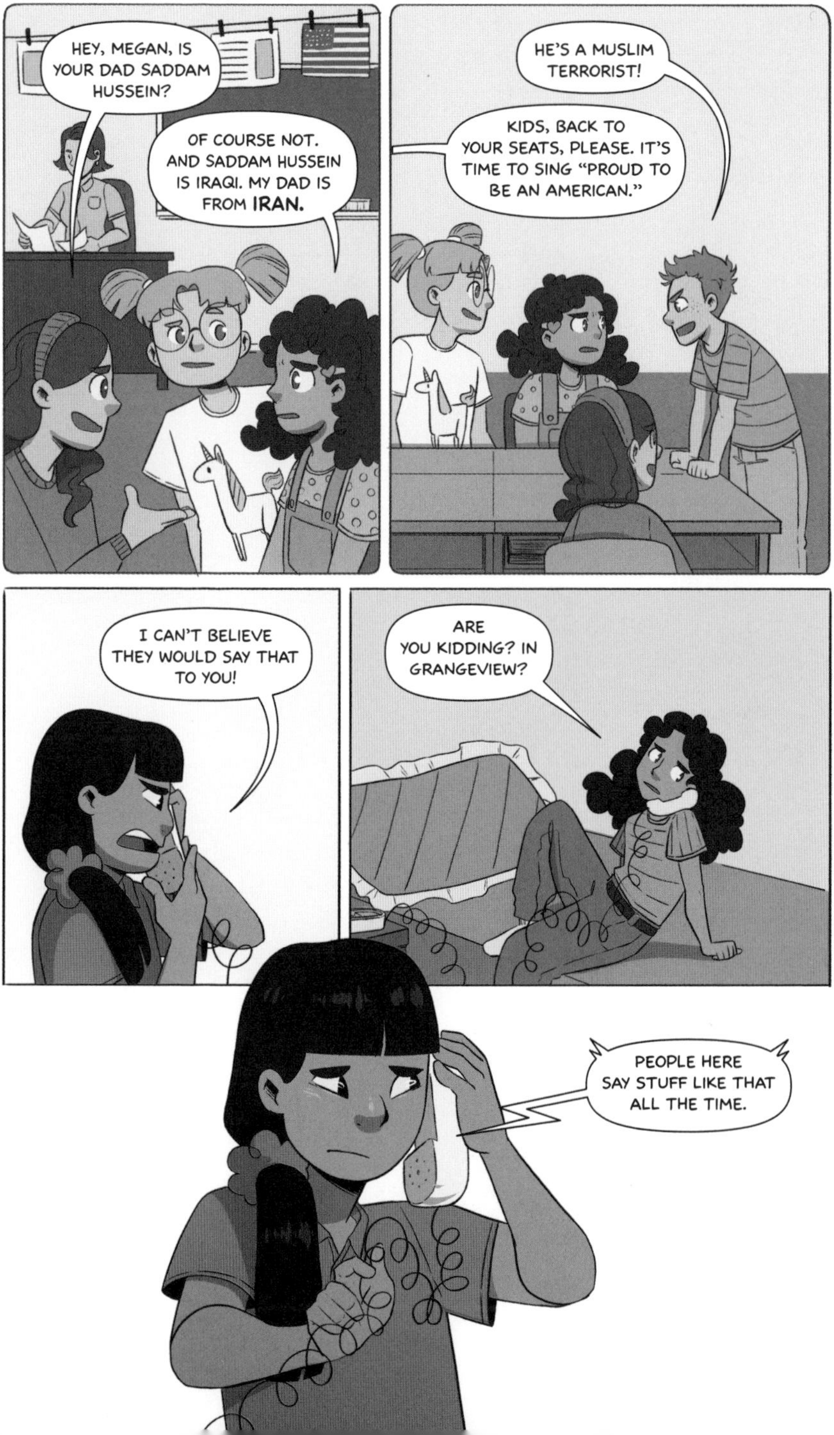
HEY, MEGAN, IS YOUR DAD SADDAM HUSSEIN?
OF COURSE NOT. AND SADDAM HUSSEIN IS IRAQI. MY DAD IS FROM **IRAN.**
HE'S A MUSLIM TERRORIST!
KIDS, BACK TO YOUR SEATS, PLEASE. IT'S TIME TO SING "PROUD TO BE AN AMERICAN."
I CAN'T BELIEVE THEY WOULD SAY THAT TO YOU!
ARE YOU KIDDING? IN GRANGEVIEW?
PEOPLE HERE SAY STUFF LIKE THAT ALL THE TIME.

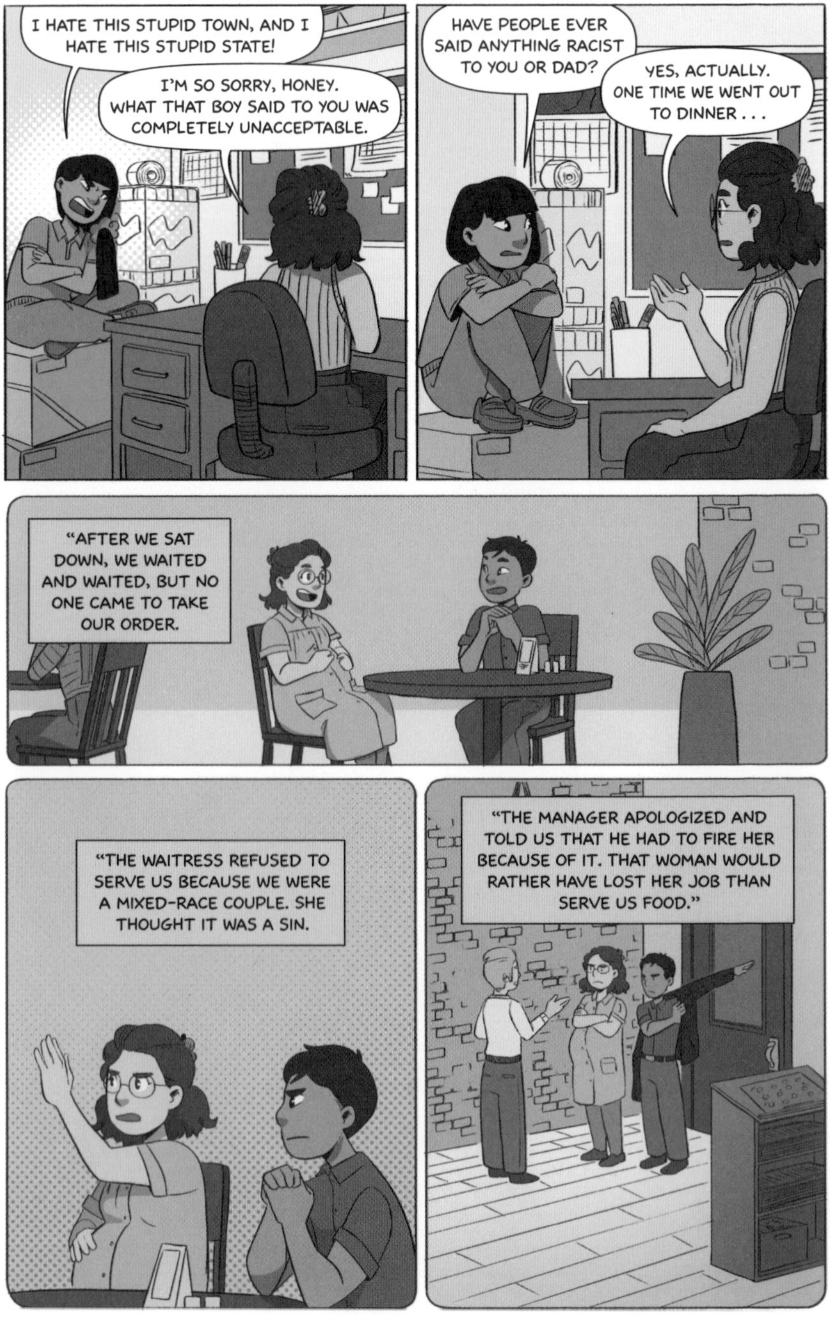
I HATE THIS STUPID TOWN, AND I HATE THIS STUPID STATE!
I'M SO SORRY, HONEY. WHAT THAT BOY SAID TO YOU WAS COMPLETELY UNACCEPTABLE.
HAVE PEOPLE EVER SAID ANYTHING RACIST TO YOU OR DAD?
YES, ACTUALLY. ONE TIME WE WENT OUT TO DINNER . . .
"AFTER WE SAT DOWN, WE WAITED AND WAITED, BUT NO ONE CAME TO TAKE OUR ORDER.
"THE WAITRESS REFUSED TO SERVE US BECAUSE WE WERE A MIXED-RACE COUPLE. SHE THOUGHT IT WAS A SIN.
"THE MANAGER APOLOGIZED AND TOLD US THAT HE HAD TO FIRE HER BECAUSE OF IT. THAT WOMAN WOULD RATHER HAVE LOST HER JOB THAN SERVE US FOOD."

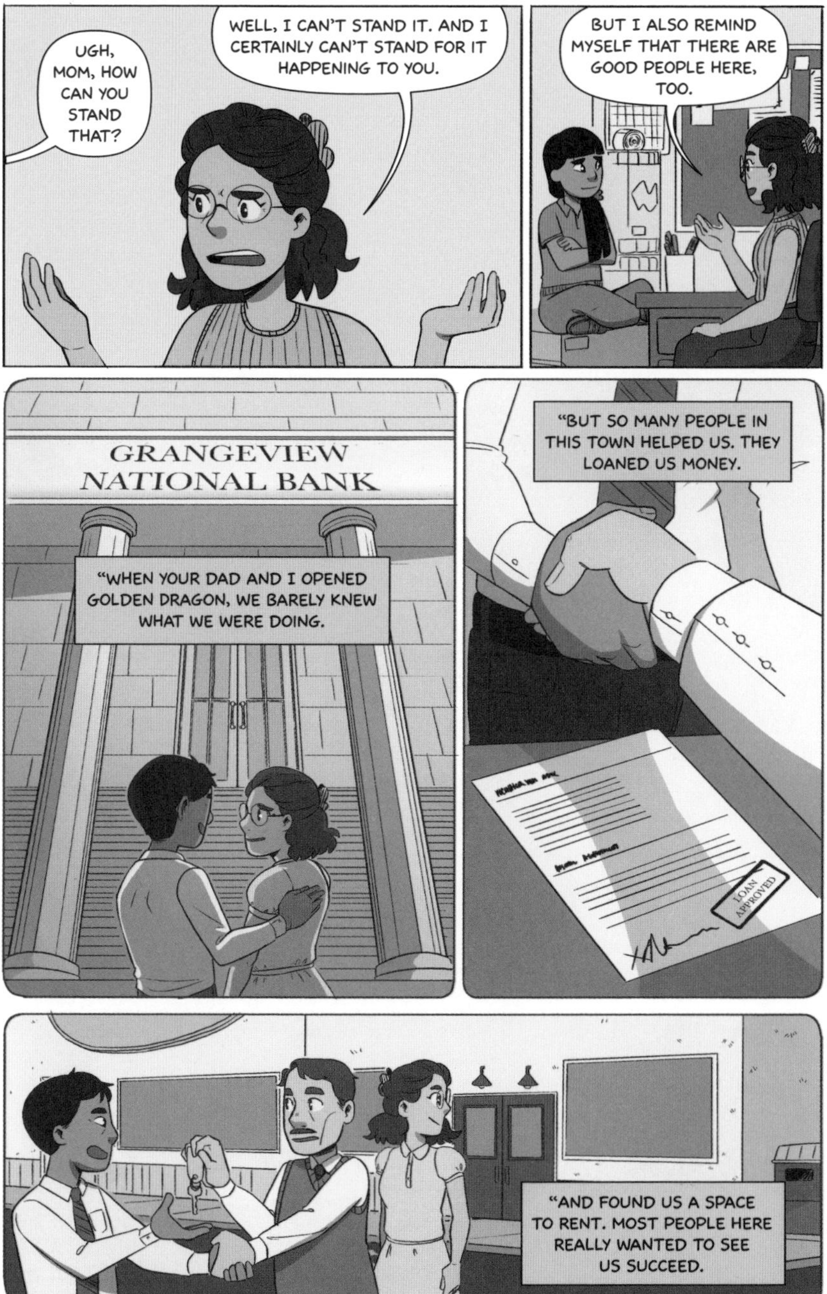
UGH, MOM, HOW CAN YOU STAND THAT?
WELL, I CAN'T STAND IT. AND I CERTAINLY CAN'T STAND FOR IT HAPPENING TO YOU.
BUT I ALSO REMIND MYSELF THAT THERE ARE GOOD PEOPLE HERE, TOO.
GRANGEVIEW NATIONAL BANK
"WHEN YOUR DAD AND I OPENED GOLDEN DRAGON, WE BARELY KNEW WHAT WE WERE DOING.
"BUT SO MANY PEOPLE IN THIS TOWN HELPED US. THEY LOANED US MONEY.
LOAN APPROVED
"AND FOUND US A SPACE TO RENT. MOST PEOPLE HERE REALLY WANTED TO SEE US SUCCEED.

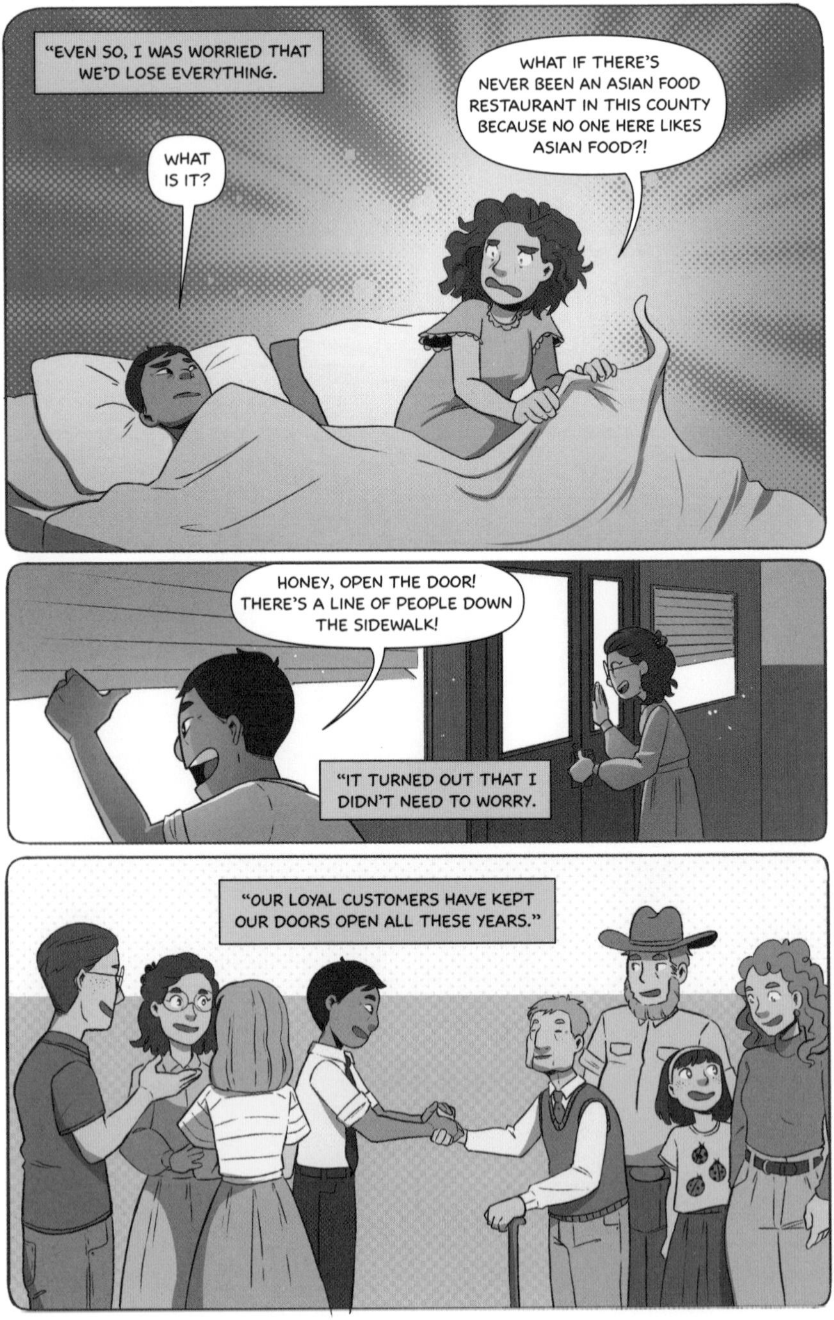
"EVEN SO, I WAS WORRIED THAT WE'D LOSE EVERYTHING.
WHAT IS IT?
WHAT IF THERE'S NEVER BEEN AN ASIAN FOOD RESTAURANT IN THIS COUNTY BECAUSE NO ONE HERE LIKES ASIAN FOOD?!
HONEY, OPEN THE DOOR! THERE'S A LINE OF PEOPLE DOWN THE SIDEWALK!
"IT TURNED OUT THAT I DIDN'T NEED TO WORRY.
"OUR LOYAL CUSTOMERS HAVE KEPT OUR DOORS OPEN ALL THESE YEARS."

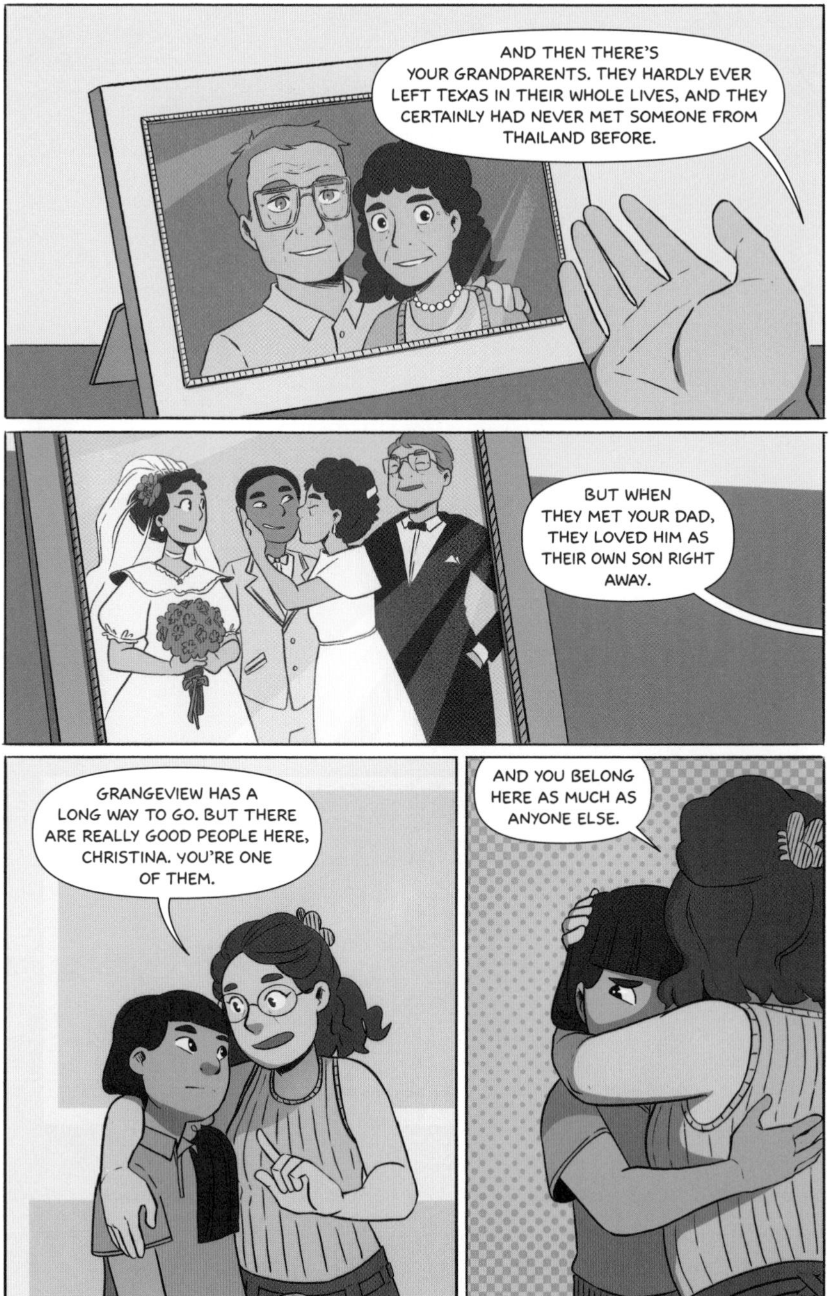
AND THEN THERE'S YOUR GRANDPARENTS. THEY HARDLY EVER LEFT TEXAS IN THEIR WHOLE LIVES, AND THEY CERTAINLY HAD NEVER MET SOMEONE FROM THAILAND BEFORE.
BUT WHEN THEY MET YOUR DAD, THEY LOVED HIM AS THEIR OWN SON RIGHT AWAY.
GRANGEVIEW HAS A LONG WAY TO GO. BUT THERE ARE REALLY GOOD PEOPLE HERE, CHRISTINA. YOU'RE ONE OF THEM.
AND YOU BELONG HERE AS MUCH AS ANYONE ELSE.

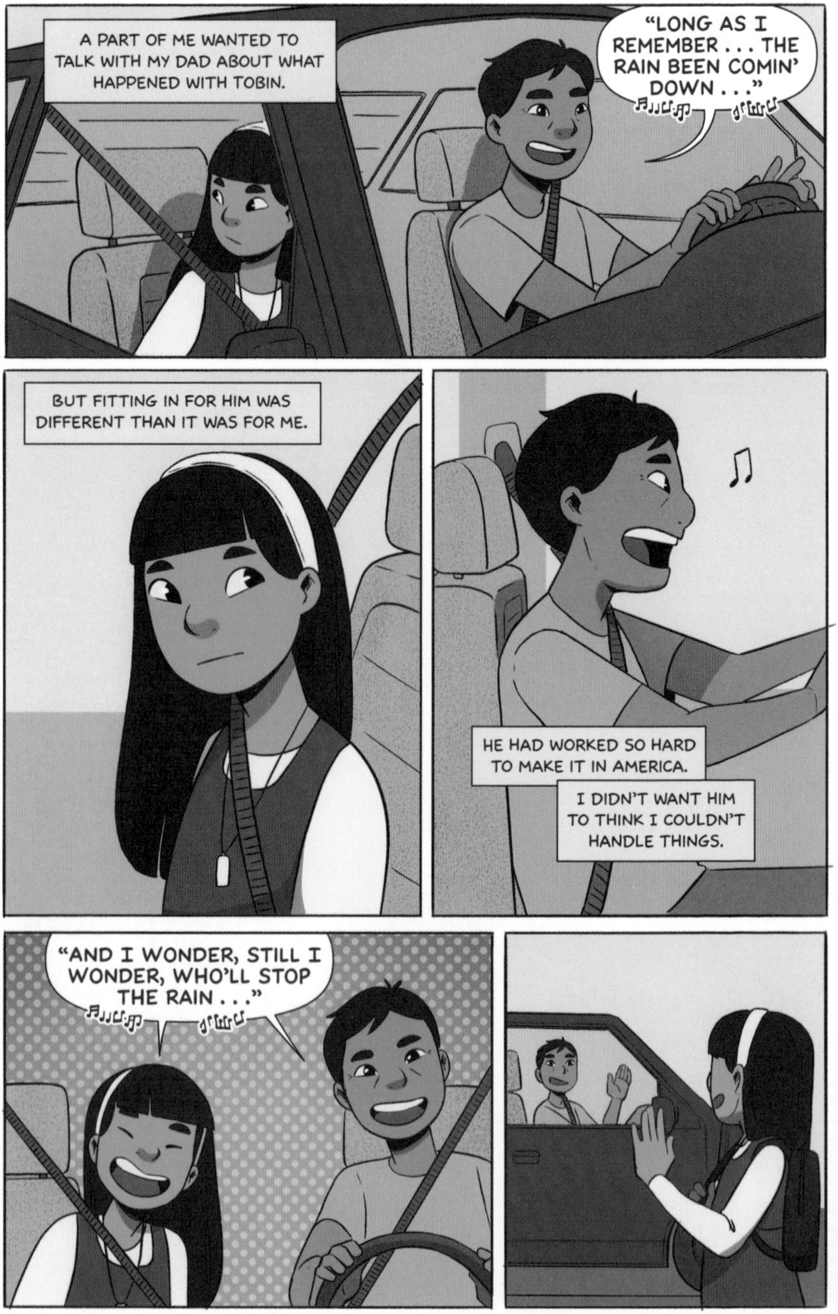

A PART OF ME WANTED TO TALK WITH MY DAD ABOUT WHAT HAPPENED WITH TOBIN.
"LONG AS I REMEMBER . . . THE RAIN BEEN COMIN' DOWN . . ."
BUT FITTING IN FOR HIM WAS DIFFERENT THAN IT WAS FOR ME.
HE HAD WORKED SO HARD TO MAKE IT IN AMERICA.
I DIDN'T WANT HIM TO THINK I COULDN'T HANDLE THINGS.
"AND I WONDER, STILL I WONDER, WHO'LL STOP THE RAIN . . ."

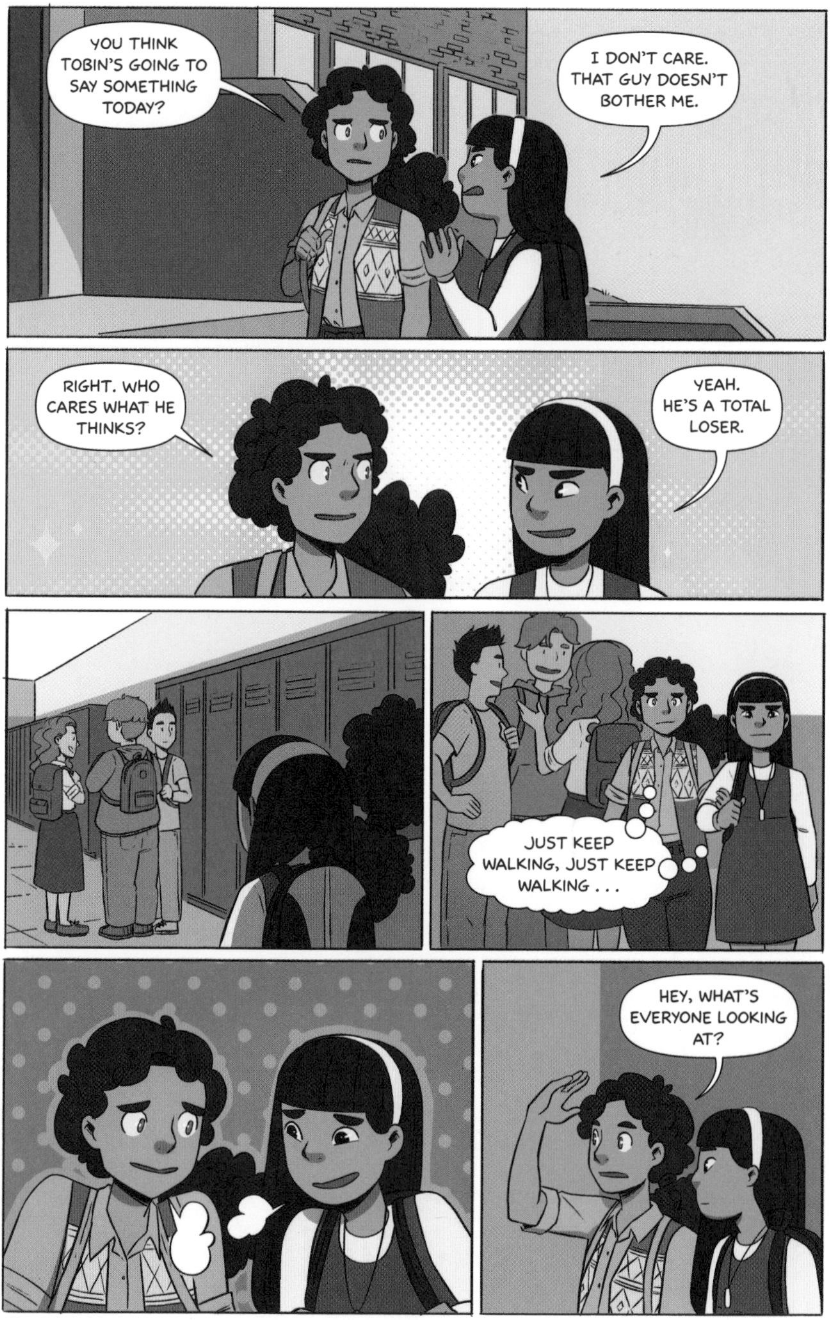
YOU THINK TOBIN'S GOING TO SAY SOMETHING TODAY?
I DON'T CARE. THAT GUY DOESN'T BOTHER ME.
RIGHT. WHO CARES WHAT HE THINKS?
YEAH. HE'S A TOTAL LOSER.
JUST KEEP WALKING, JUST KEEP WALKING . . .
HEY, WHAT'S EVERYONE LOOKING AT?

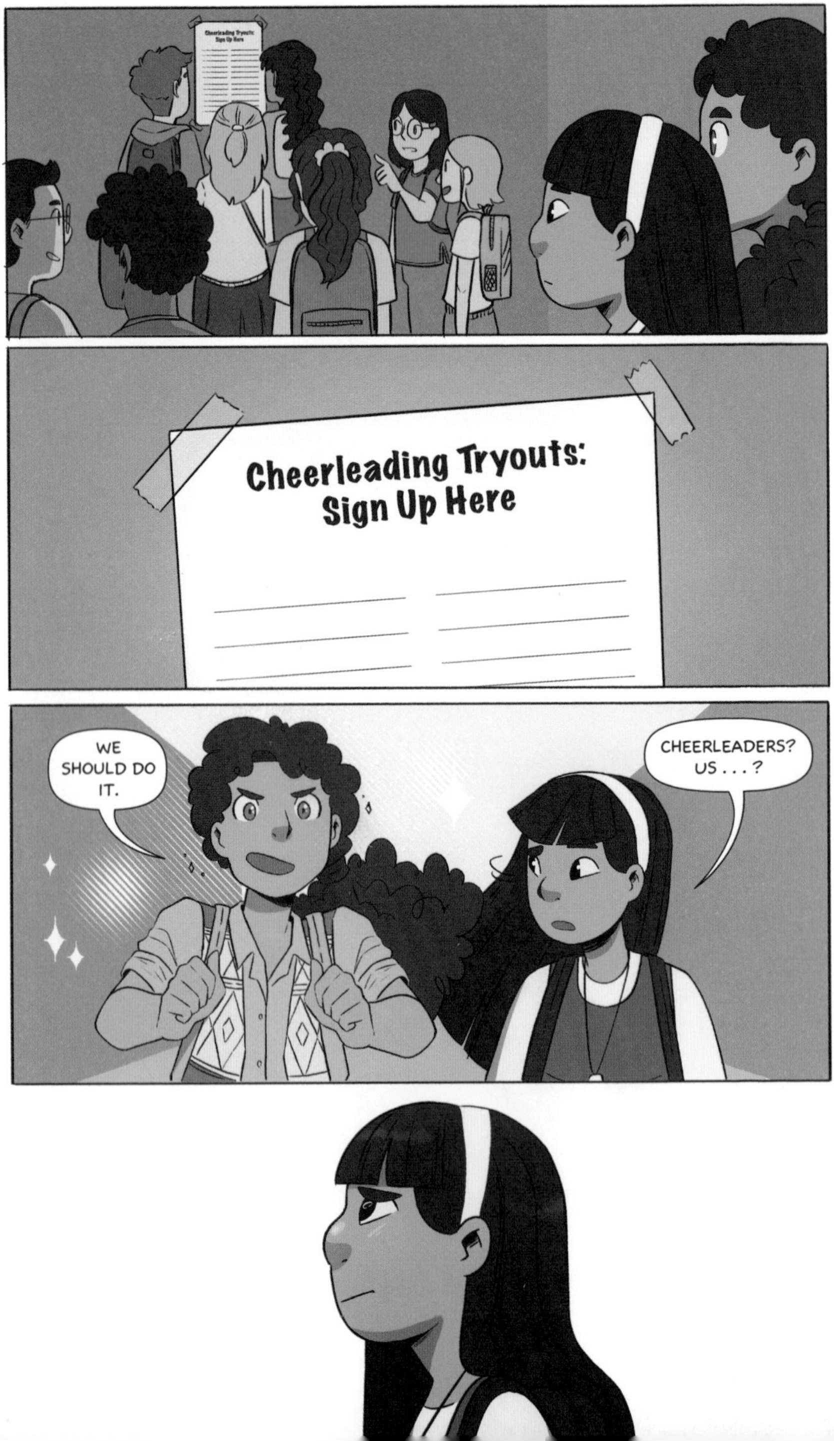
Cheerleading Tryouts: Sign Up Here
Cheerleading Tryouts: Sign Up Here
WE SHOULD DO IT.
CHEERLEADERS? US . . . ?

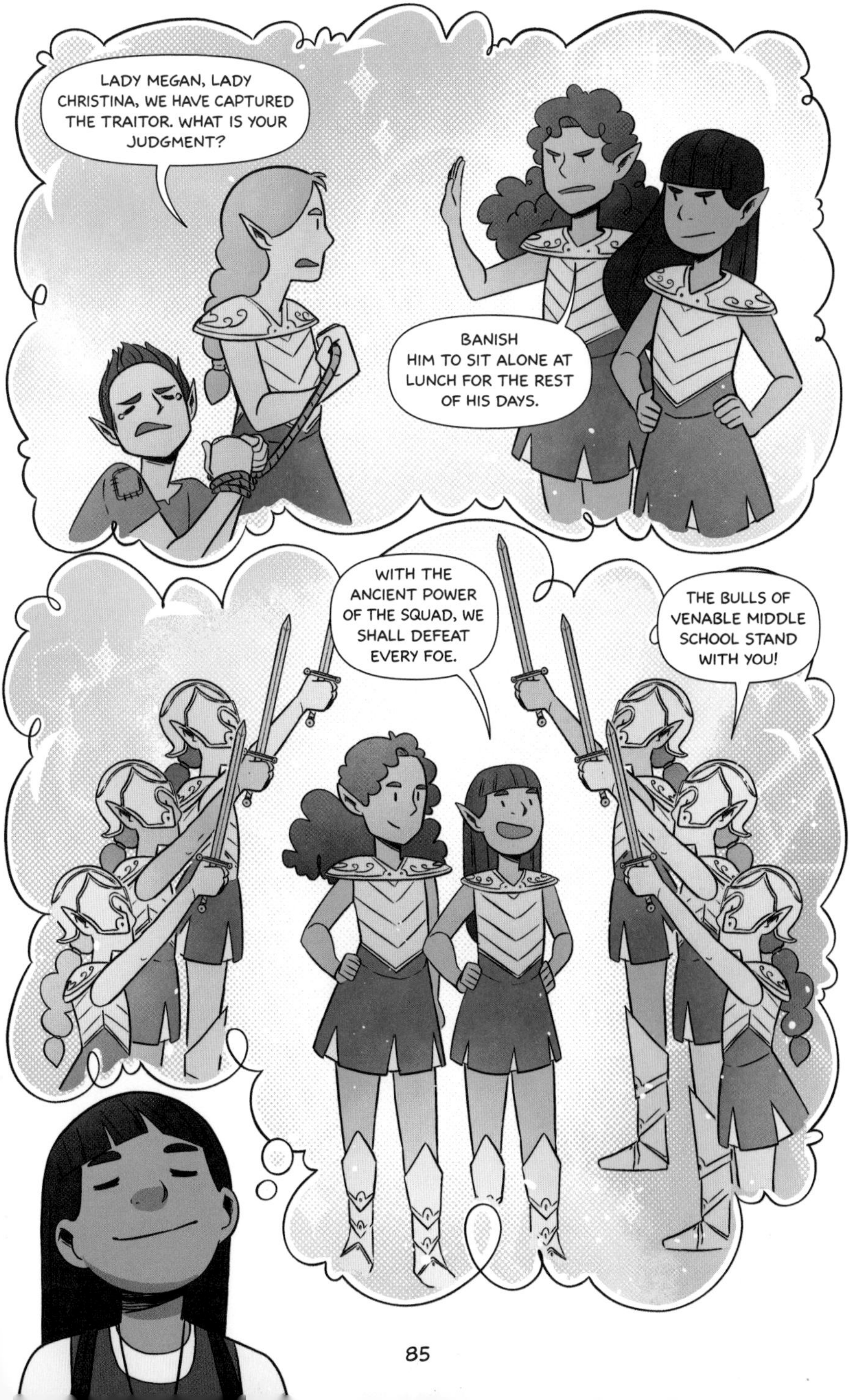
LADY MEGAN, LADY CHRISTINA, WE HAVE CAPTURED THE TRAITOR. WHAT IS YOUR JUDGMENT?
BANISH HIM TO SIT ALONE AT LUNCH FOR THE REST OF HIS DAYS.
WITH THE ANCIENT POWER OF THE SQUAD, WE SHALL DEFEAT EVERY FOE.
THE BULLS OF VENABLE MIDDLE SCHOOL STAND WITH YOU!

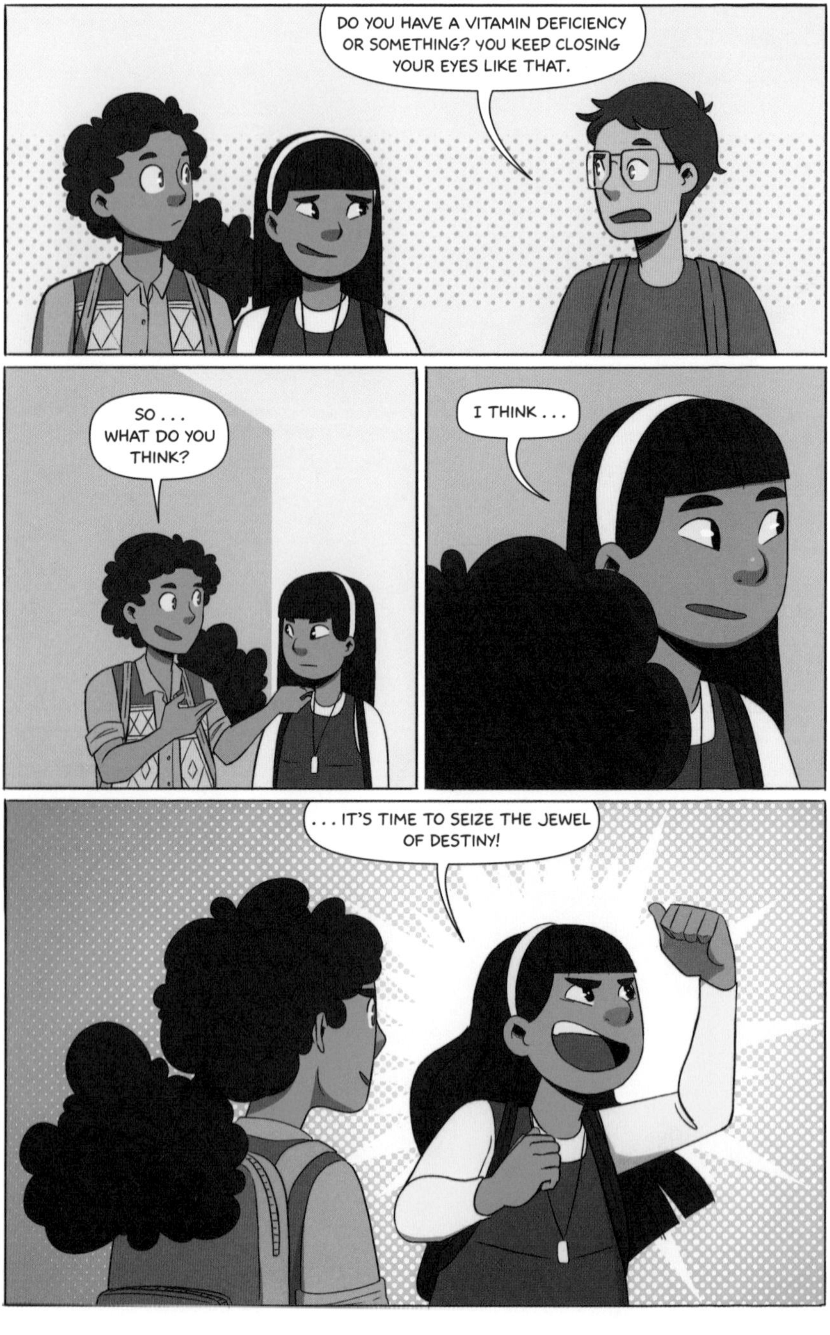
DO YOU HAVE A VITAMIN DEFICIENCY OR SOMETHING? YOU KEEP CLOSING YOUR EYES LIKE THAT.
SO . . . WHAT DO YOU THINK?
I THINK . . .
. . . IT'S TIME TO SEIZE THE JEWEL OF DESTINY!

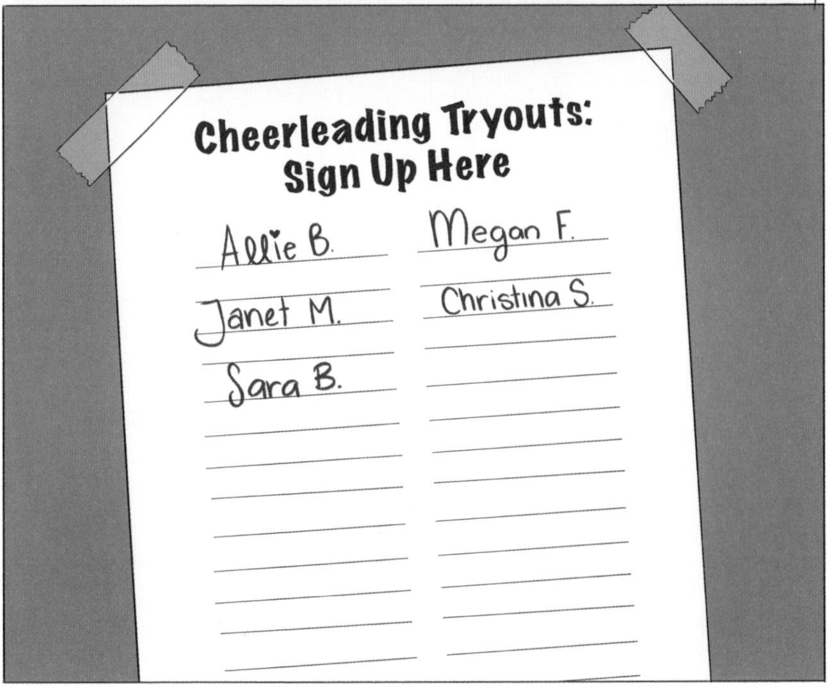

Cheerleading Tryouts:
Sign Up Here

Allie B.	Megan F.
Janet M.	Christina S.
Sara B.	

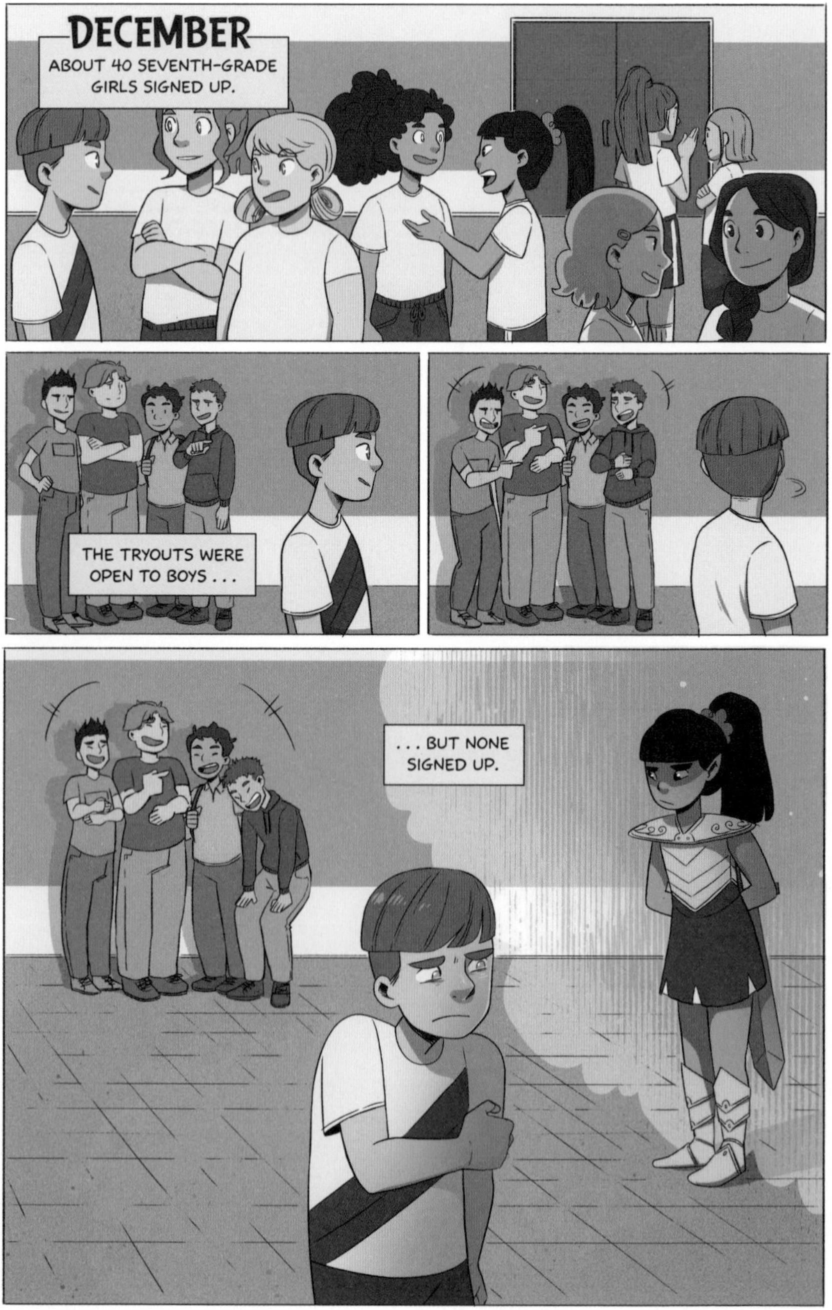
DECEMBER
ABOUT 40 SEVENTH-GRADE GIRLS SIGNED UP.
THE TRYOUTS WERE OPEN TO BOYS . . .
. . . BUT NONE SIGNED UP.

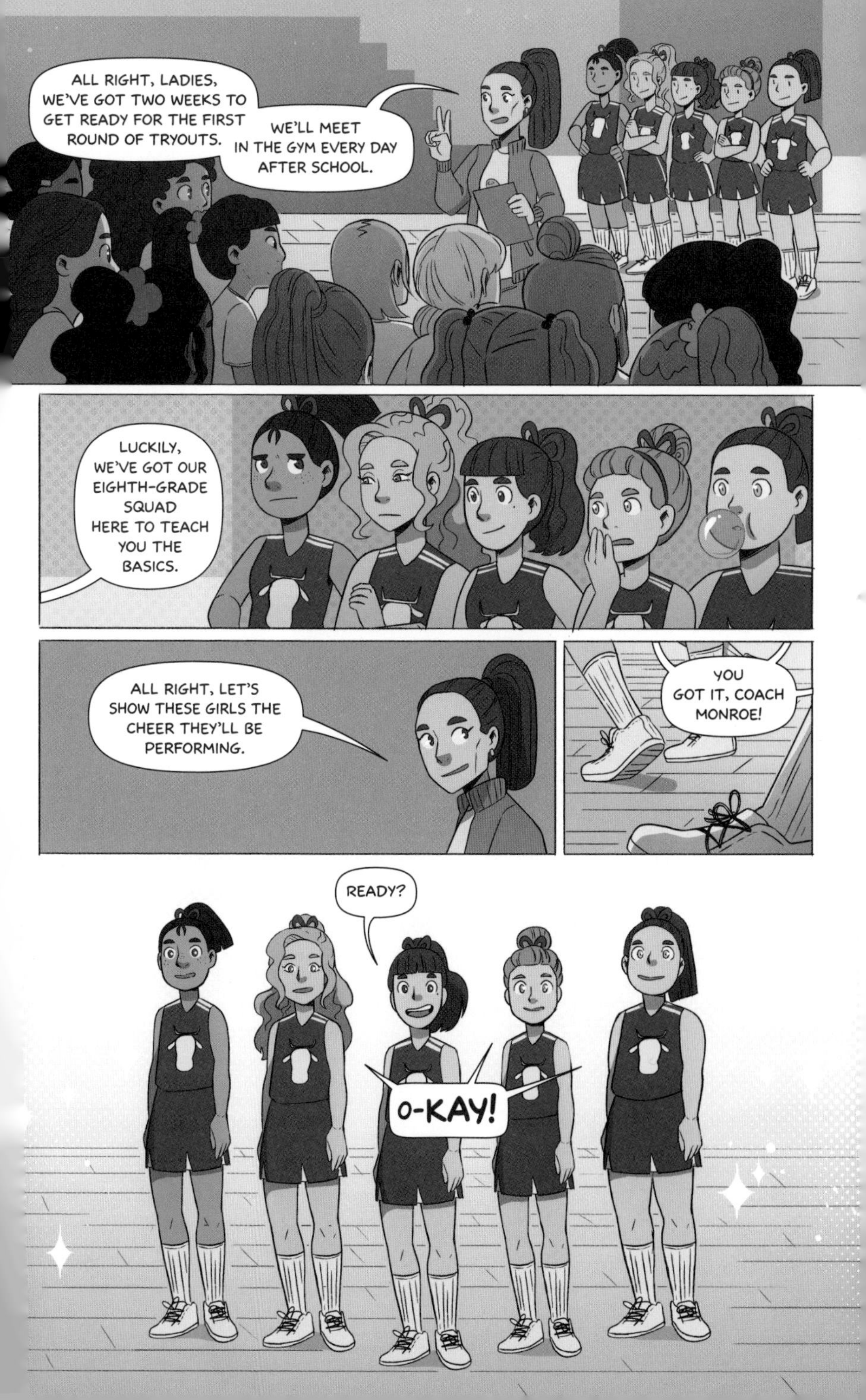
ALL RIGHT, LADIES, WE'VE GOT TWO WEEKS TO GET READY FOR THE FIRST ROUND OF TRYOUTS.
WE'LL MEET IN THE GYM EVERY DAY AFTER SCHOOL.
LUCKILY, WE'VE GOT OUR EIGHTH-GRADE SQUAD HERE TO TEACH YOU THE BASICS.
ALL RIGHT, LET'S SHOW THESE GIRLS THE CHEER THEY'LL BE PERFORMING.
YOU GOT IT, COACH MONROE!
READY?
O-KAY!

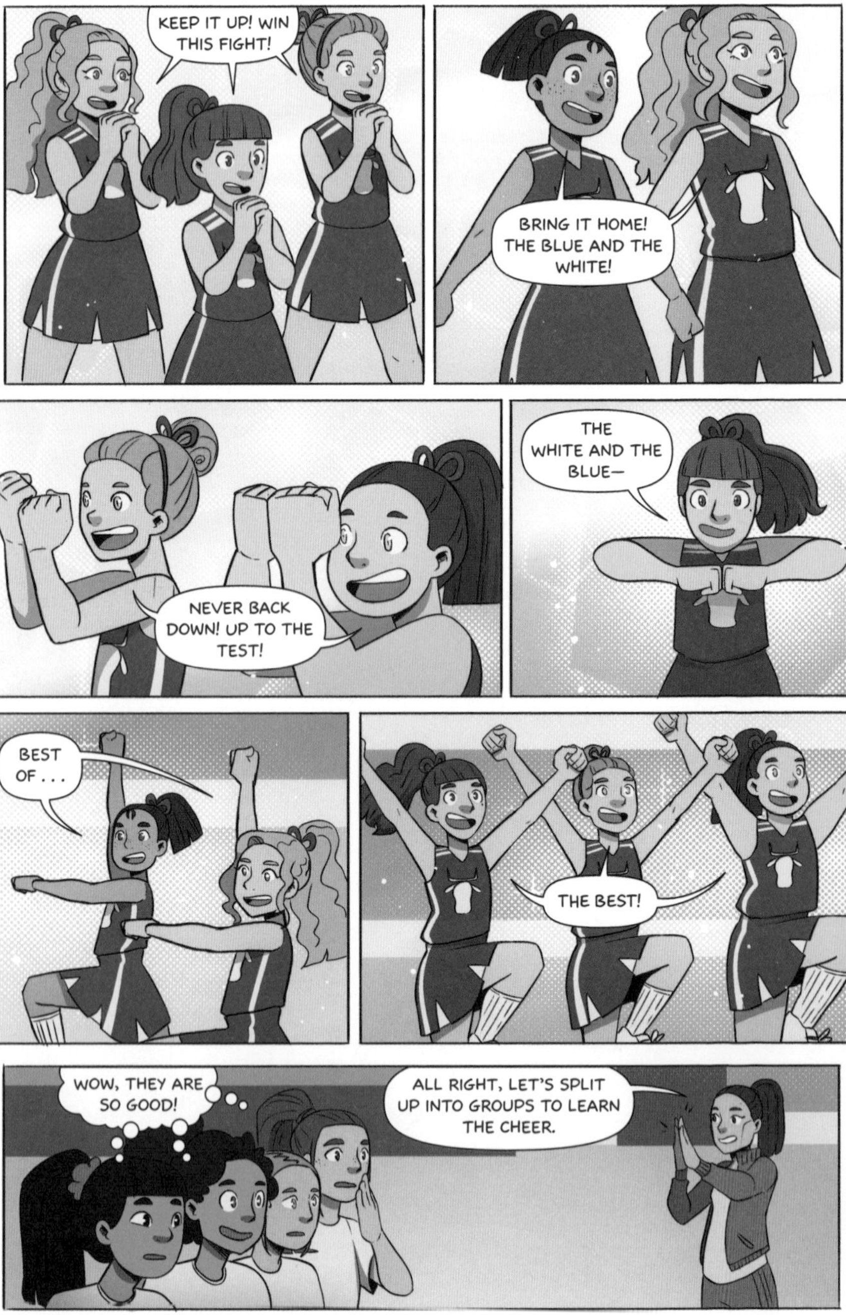
KEEP IT UP! WIN THIS FIGHT!
BRING IT HOME! THE BLUE AND THE WHITE!
NEVER BACK DOWN! UP TO THE TEST!
THE WHITE AND THE BLUE—
BEST OF . . .
THE BEST!
WOW, THEY ARE SO GOOD!
ALL RIGHT, LET'S SPLIT UP INTO GROUPS TO LEARN THE CHEER.

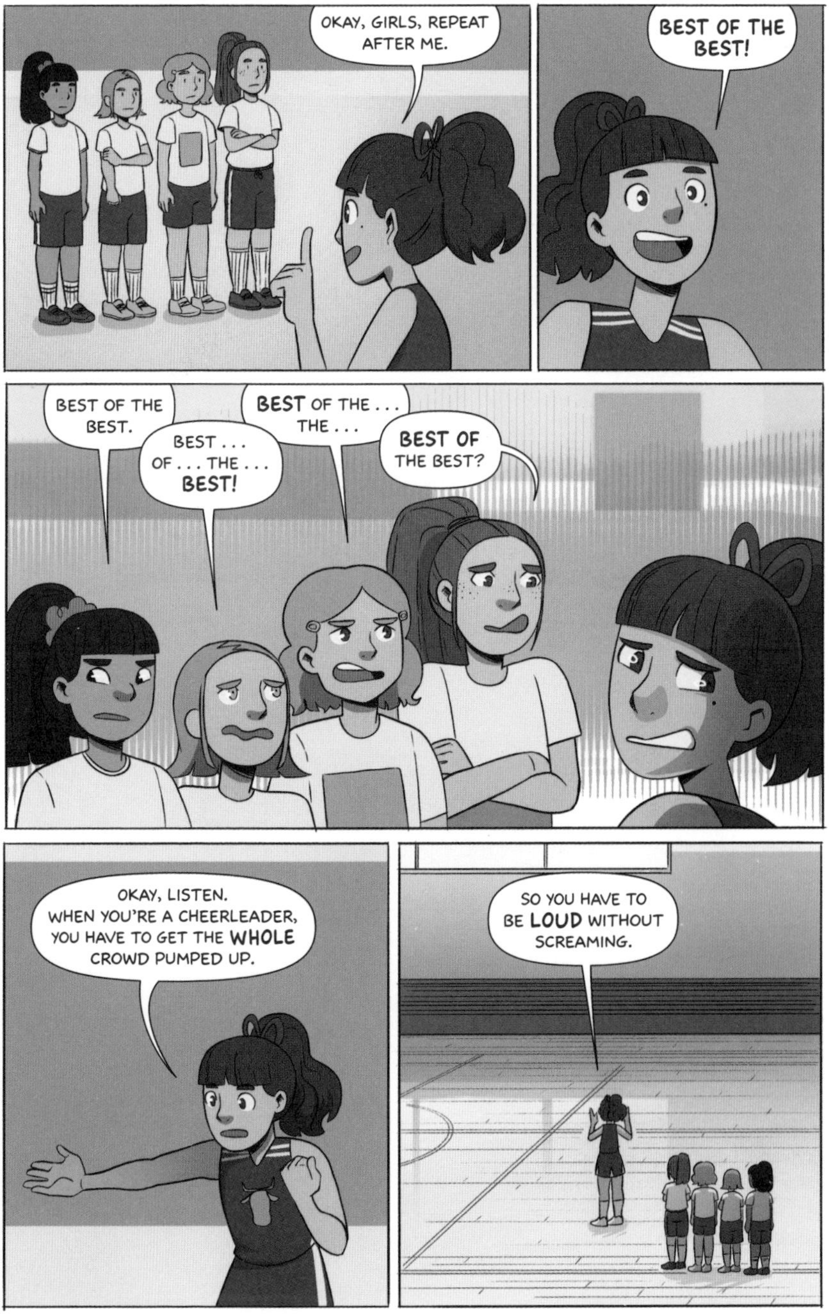
OKAY, GIRLS, REPEAT AFTER ME.
BEST OF THE BEST!
BEST OF THE BEST.
BEST . . . OF . . . THE . . . BEST!
BEST OF THE . . . THE . . .
BEST OF THE BEST?
OKAY, LISTEN. WHEN YOU'RE A CHEERLEADER, YOU HAVE TO GET THE WHOLE CROWD PUMPED UP.
SO YOU HAVE TO BE LOUD WITHOUT SCREAMING.

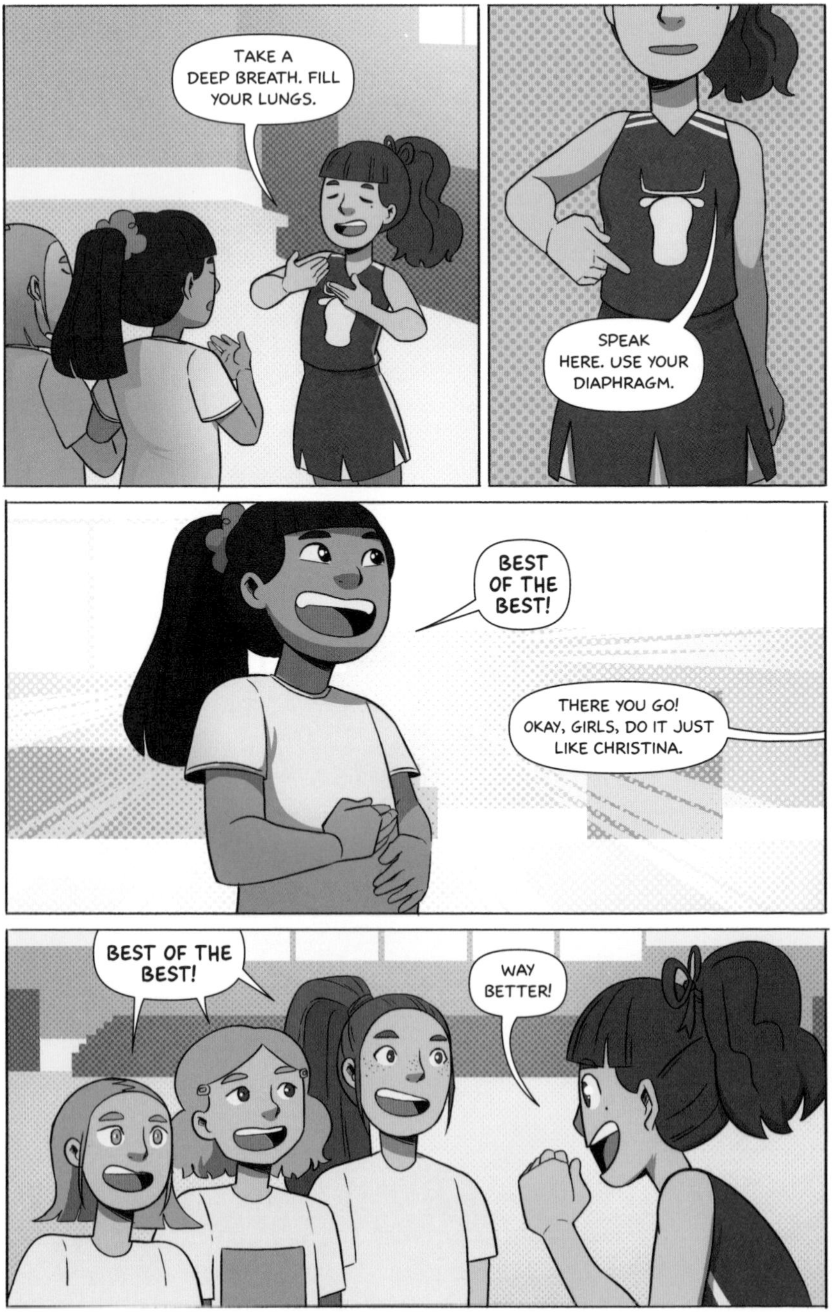
TAKE A DEEP BREATH. FILL YOUR LUNGS.
SPEAK HERE. USE YOUR DIAPHRAGM.
BEST OF THE BEST!
THERE YOU GO! OKAY, GIRLS, DO IT JUST LIKE CHRISTINA.
BEST OF THE BEST!
WAY BETTER!

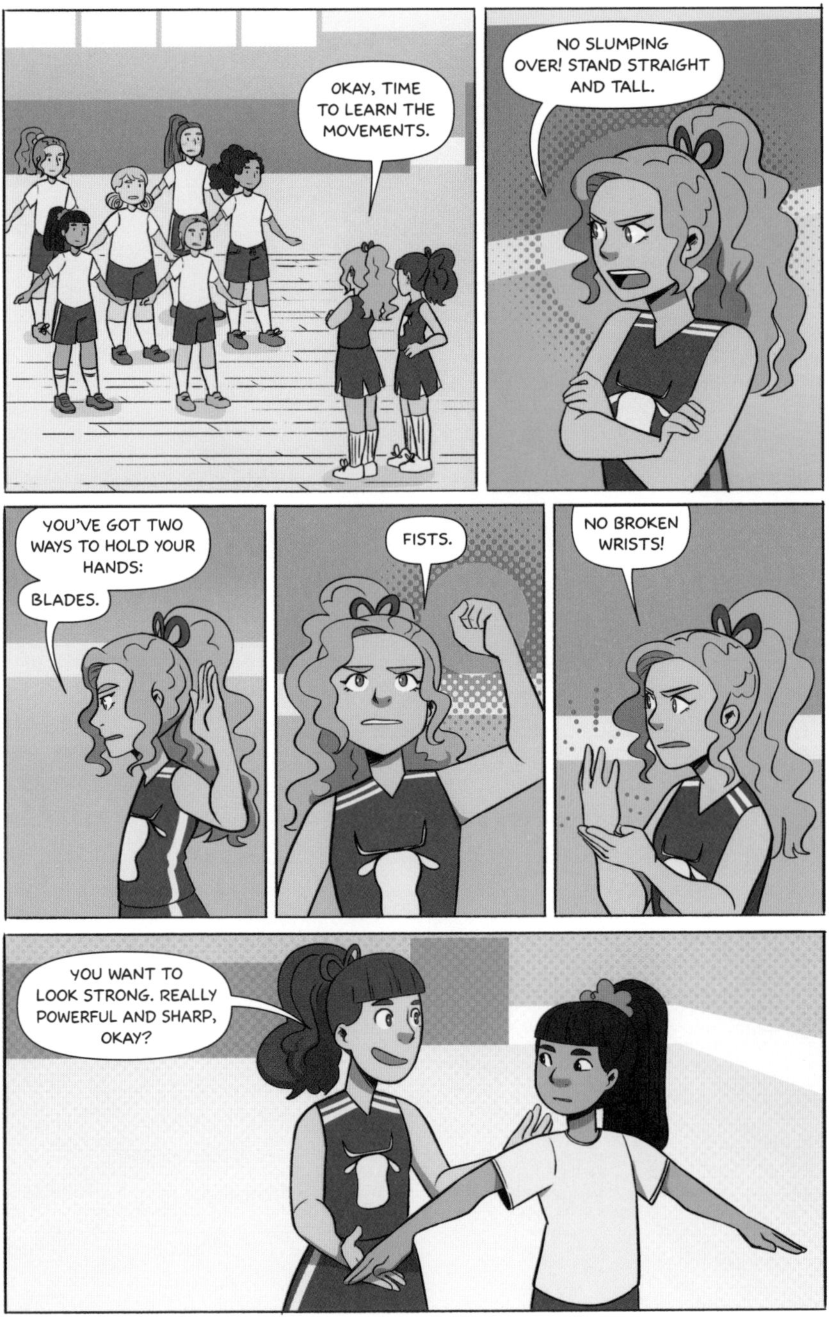
OKAY, TIME TO LEARN THE MOVEMENTS.
NO SLUMPING OVER! STAND STRAIGHT AND TALL.
YOU'VE GOT TWO WAYS TO HOLD YOUR HANDS:
BLADES.
FISTS.
NO BROKEN WRISTS!
YOU WANT TO LOOK STRONG. REALLY POWERFUL AND SHARP, OKAY?

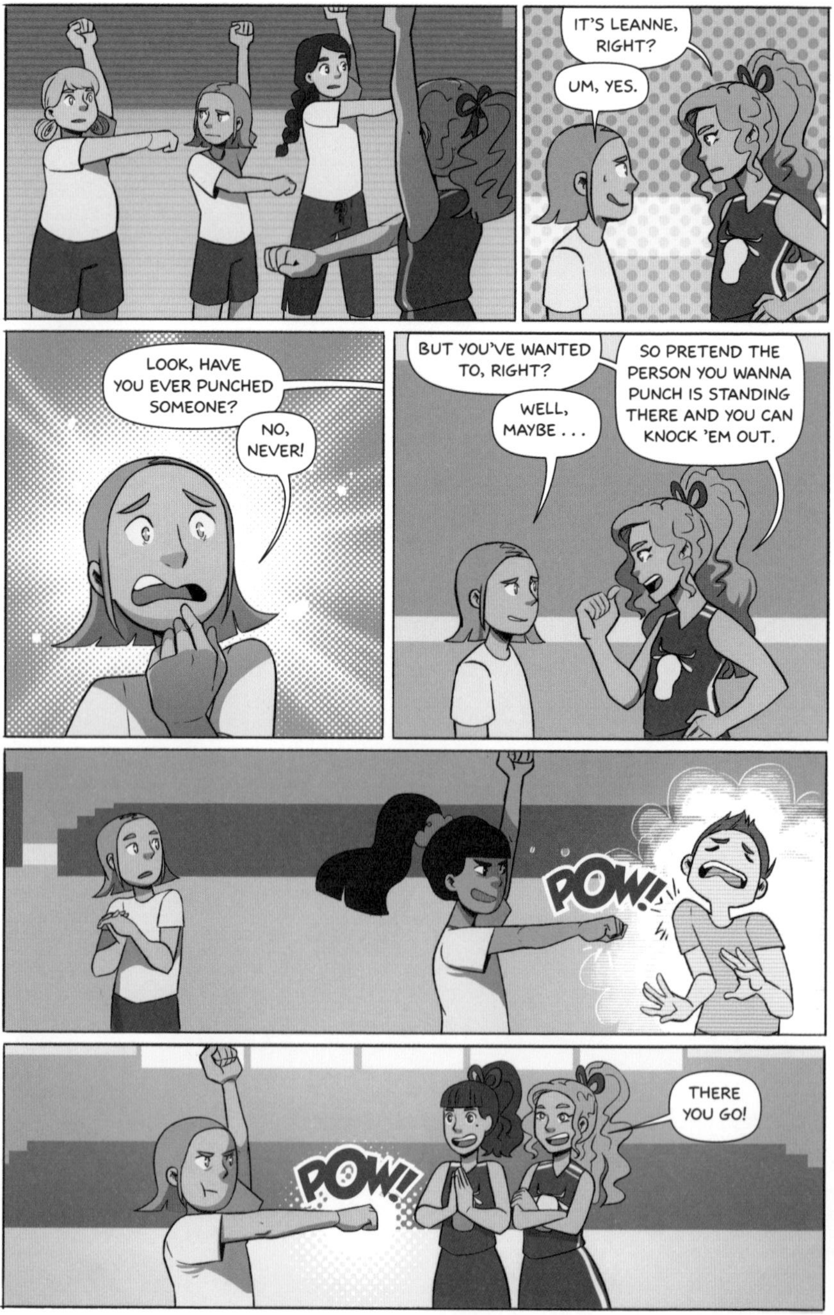
IT'S LEANNE, RIGHT?
UM, YES.
LOOK, HAVE YOU EVER PUNCHED SOMEONE?
NO, NEVER!
BUT YOU'VE WANTED TO, RIGHT?
WELL, MAYBE . . .
SO PRETEND THE PERSON YOU WANNA PUNCH IS STANDING THERE AND YOU CAN KNOCK 'EM OUT.
POW!
POW!
THERE YOU GO!

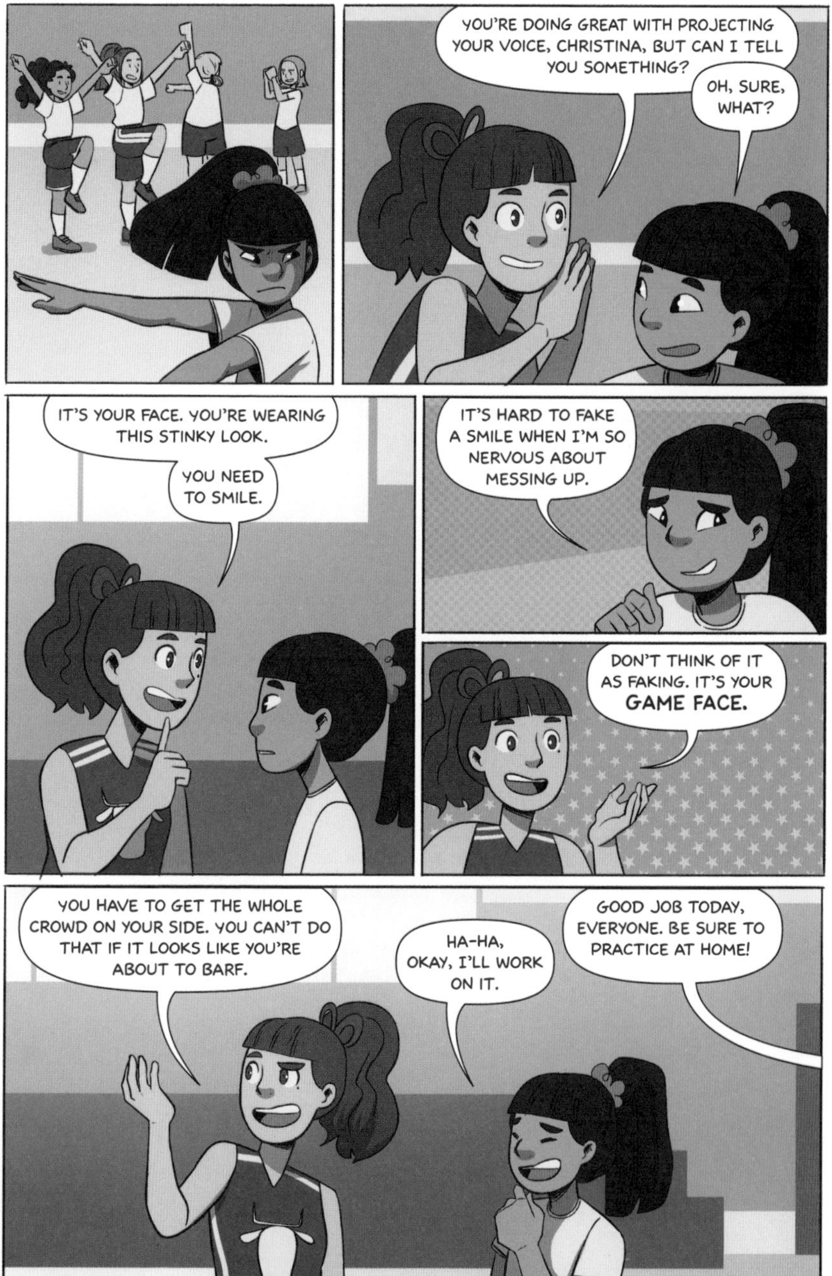

YOU'RE DOING GREAT WITH PROJECTING YOUR VOICE, CHRISTINA, BUT CAN I TELL YOU SOMETHING?
OH, SURE, WHAT?
IT'S YOUR FACE. YOU'RE WEARING THIS STINKY LOOK.
YOU NEED TO SMILE.
IT'S HARD TO FAKE A SMILE WHEN I'M SO NERVOUS ABOUT MESSING UP.
DON'T THINK OF IT AS FAKING. IT'S YOUR GAME FACE.
YOU HAVE TO GET THE WHOLE CROWD ON YOUR SIDE. YOU CAN'T DO THAT IF IT LOOKS LIKE YOU'RE ABOUT TO BARF.
HA-HA, OKAY, I'LL WORK ON IT.
GOOD JOB TODAY, EVERYONE. BE SURE TO PRACTICE AT HOME!

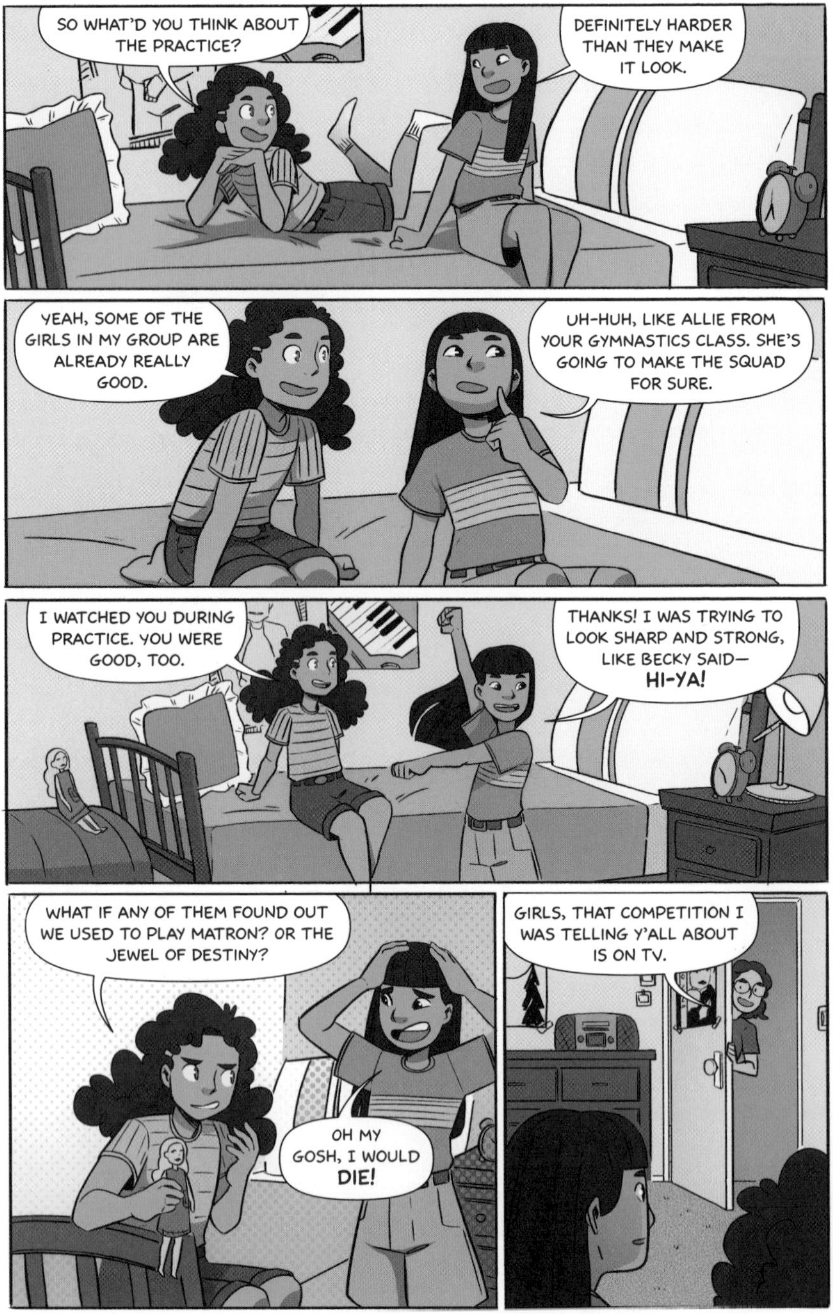
SO WHAT'D YOU THINK ABOUT THE PRACTICE?
DEFINITELY HARDER THAN THEY MAKE IT LOOK.
YEAH, SOME OF THE GIRLS IN MY GROUP ARE ALREADY REALLY GOOD.
UH-HUH, LIKE ALLIE FROM YOUR GYMNASTICS CLASS. SHE'S GOING TO MAKE THE SQUAD FOR SURE.
I WATCHED YOU DURING PRACTICE. YOU WERE GOOD, TOO.
THANKS! I WAS TRYING TO LOOK SHARP AND STRONG, LIKE BECKY SAID— **HI-YA!**
WHAT IF ANY OF THEM FOUND OUT WE USED TO PLAY MATRON? OR THE JEWEL OF DESTINY?
OH MY GOSH, I WOULD **DIE!**
GIRLS, THAT COMPETITION I WAS TELLING Y'ALL ABOUT IS ON TV.

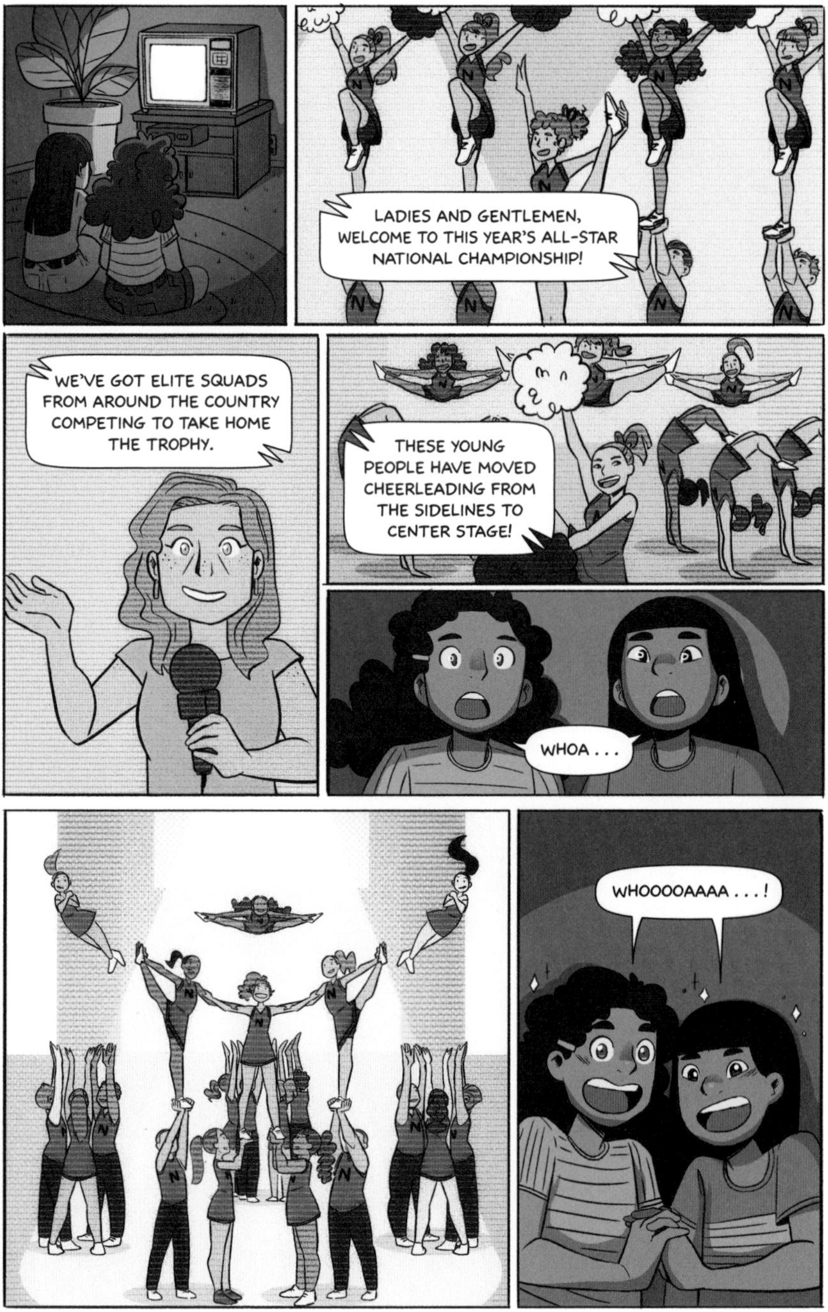
LADIES AND GENTLEMEN, WELCOME TO THIS YEAR'S ALL-STAR NATIONAL CHAMPIONSHIP!
WE'VE GOT ELITE SQUADS FROM AROUND THE COUNTRY COMPETING TO TAKE HOME THE TROPHY.
THESE YOUNG PEOPLE HAVE MOVED CHEERLEADING FROM THE SIDELINES TO CENTER STAGE!
WHOA . . .
WHOOOOAAAA . . .!

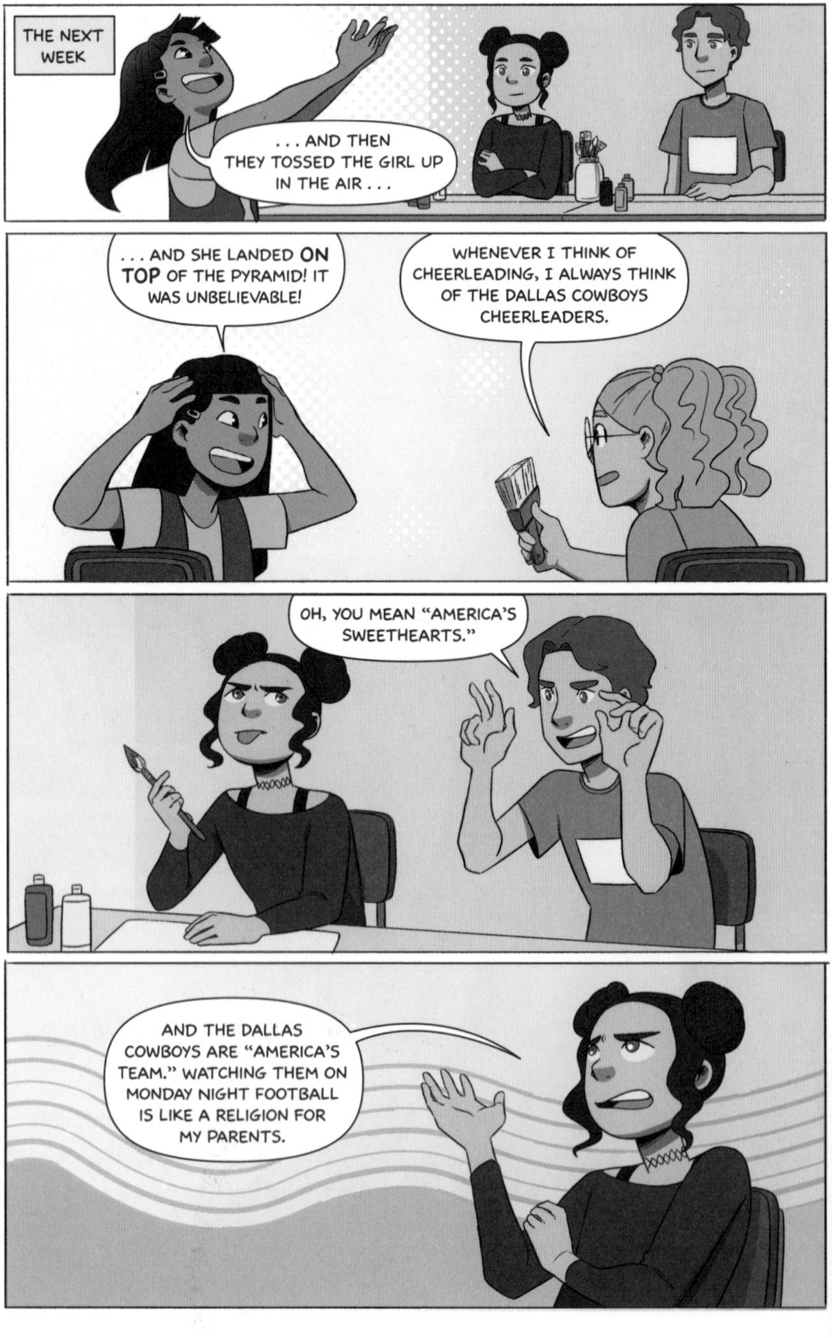
THE NEXT WEEK
. . . AND THEN THEY TOSSED THE GIRL UP IN THE AIR . . .
. . . AND SHE LANDED ON TOP OF THE PYRAMID! IT WAS UNBELIEVABLE!
WHENEVER I THINK OF CHEERLEADING, I ALWAYS THINK OF THE DALLAS COWBOYS CHEERLEADERS.
OH, YOU MEAN "AMERICA'S SWEETHEARTS."
AND THE DALLAS COWBOYS ARE "AMERICA'S TEAM." WATCHING THEM ON MONDAY NIGHT FOOTBALL IS LIKE A RELIGION FOR MY PARENTS.

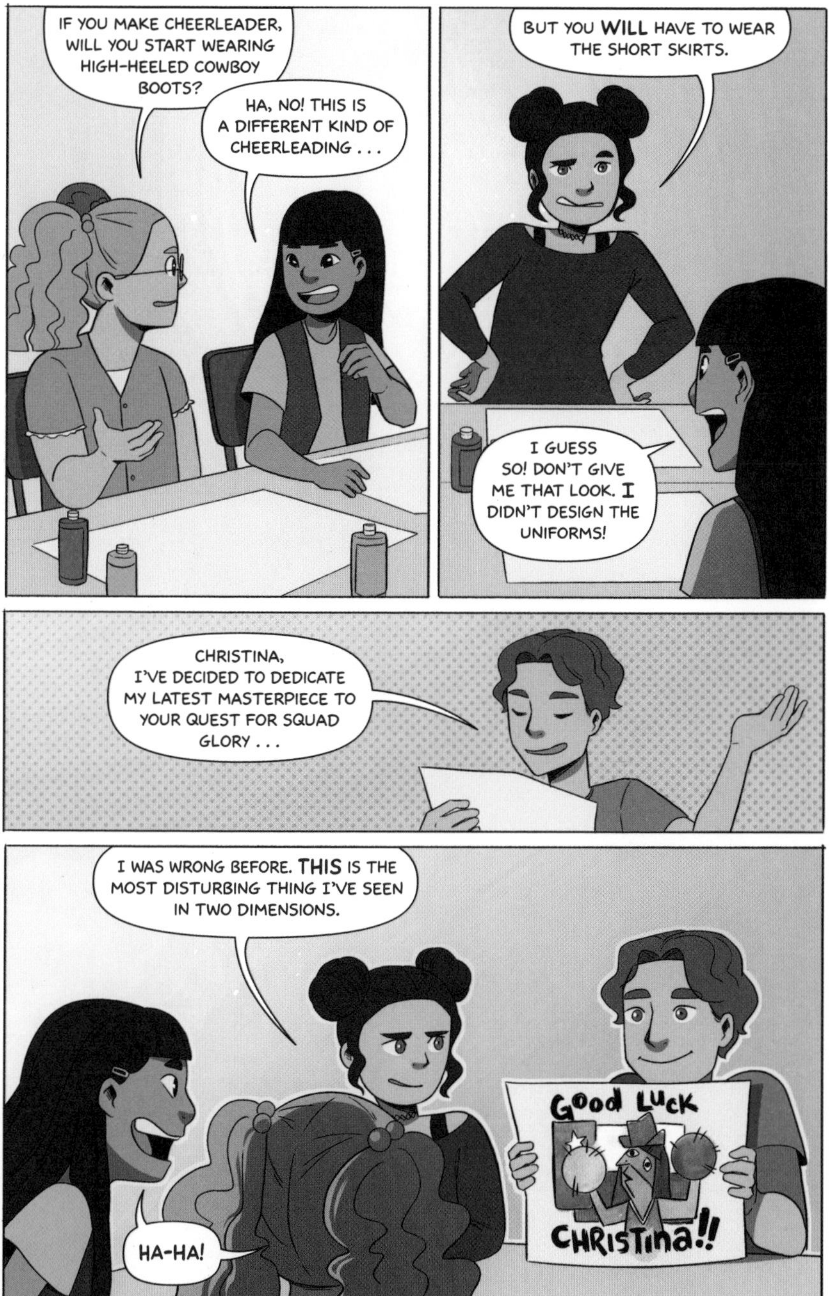
IF YOU MAKE CHEERLEADER, WILL YOU START WEARING HIGH-HEELED COWBOY BOOTS?
HA, NO! THIS IS A DIFFERENT KIND OF CHEERLEADING . . .
BUT YOU **WILL** HAVE TO WEAR THE SHORT SKIRTS.
I GUESS SO! DON'T GIVE ME THAT LOOK. **I** DIDN'T DESIGN THE UNIFORMS!
CHRISTINA, I'VE DECIDED TO DEDICATE MY LATEST MASTERPIECE TO YOUR QUEST FOR SQUAD GLORY . . .
I WAS WRONG BEFORE. **THIS** IS THE MOST DISTURBING THING I'VE SEEN IN TWO DIMENSIONS.
Good Luck CHRISTina!!
HA-HA!

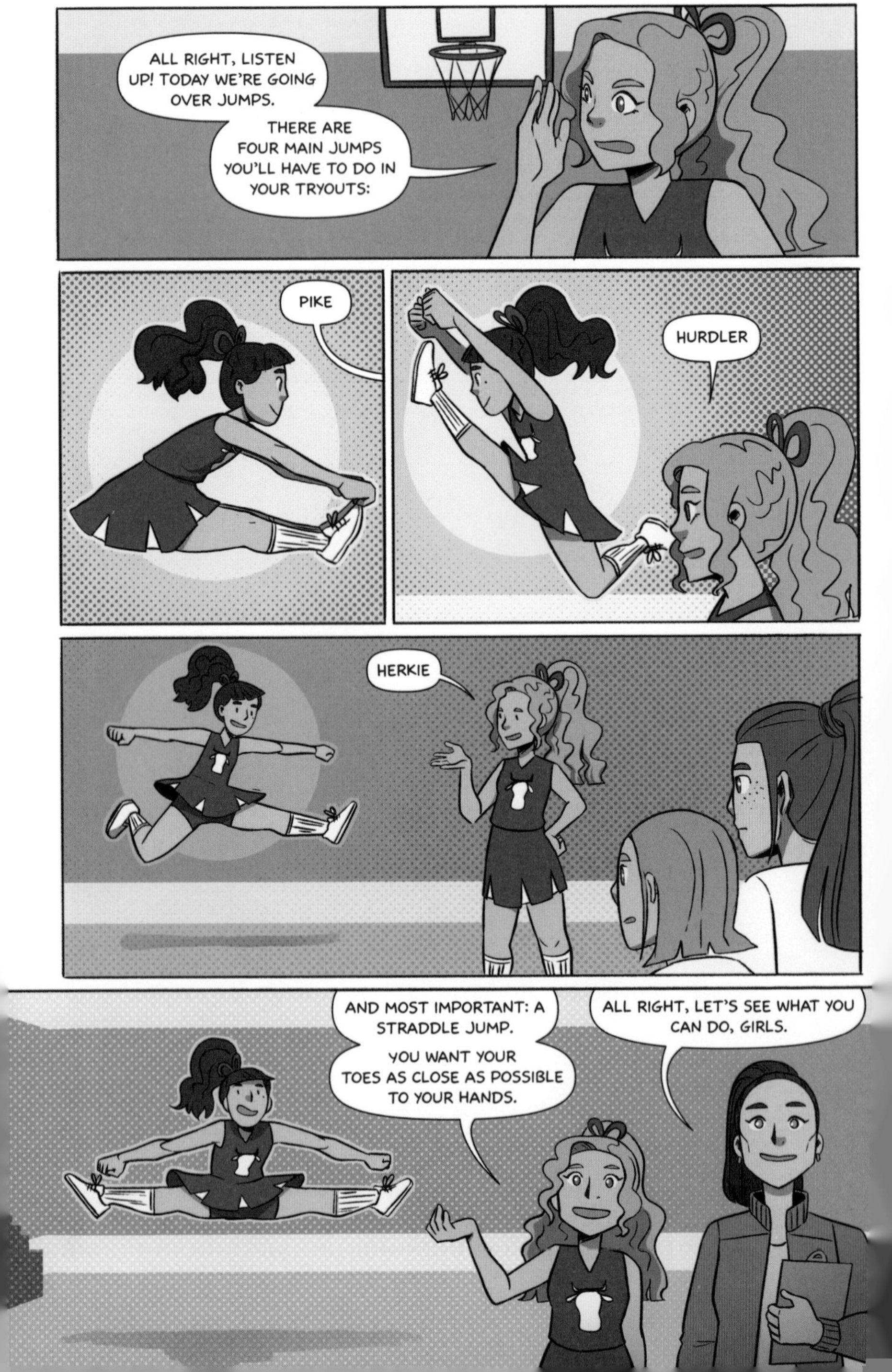
ALL RIGHT, LISTEN UP! TODAY WE'RE GOING OVER JUMPS.
THERE ARE FOUR MAIN JUMPS YOU'LL HAVE TO DO IN YOUR TRYOUTS:
PIKE
HURDLER
HERKIE
AND MOST IMPORTANT: A STRADDLE JUMP.
YOU WANT YOUR TOES AS CLOSE AS POSSIBLE TO YOUR HANDS.
ALL RIGHT, LET'S SEE WHAT YOU CAN DO, GIRLS.

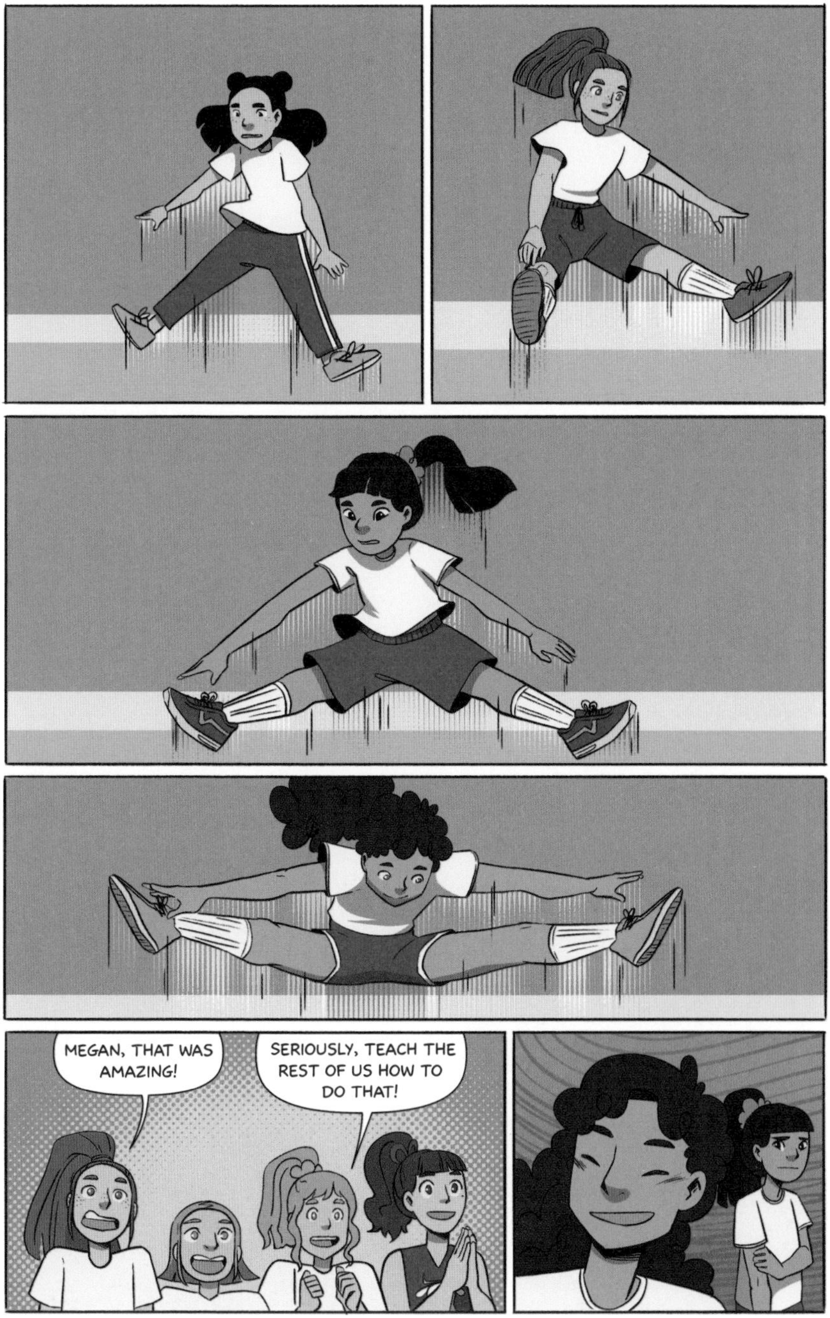
MEGAN, THAT WAS AMAZING!
SERIOUSLY, TEACH THE REST OF US HOW TO DO THAT!

ALL RIGHT, Y'ALL, LET'S GO OVER HOW YOU'LL RUN IN DURING YOUR TRYOUT.

TUMBLERS OVER HERE.

NON-TUMBLERS OVER THERE.

IF YOU CAN'T TUMBLE, YOU'LL SASHAY IN AND DO SPIRIT FINGERS.

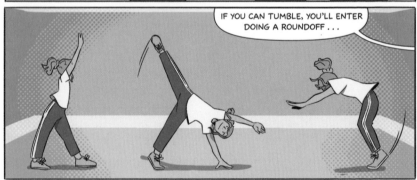

IF YOU CAN TUMBLE, YOU'LL ENTER DOING A ROUNDOFF . . .

. . . OR A ROUNDOFF BACK HANDSPRING . . .

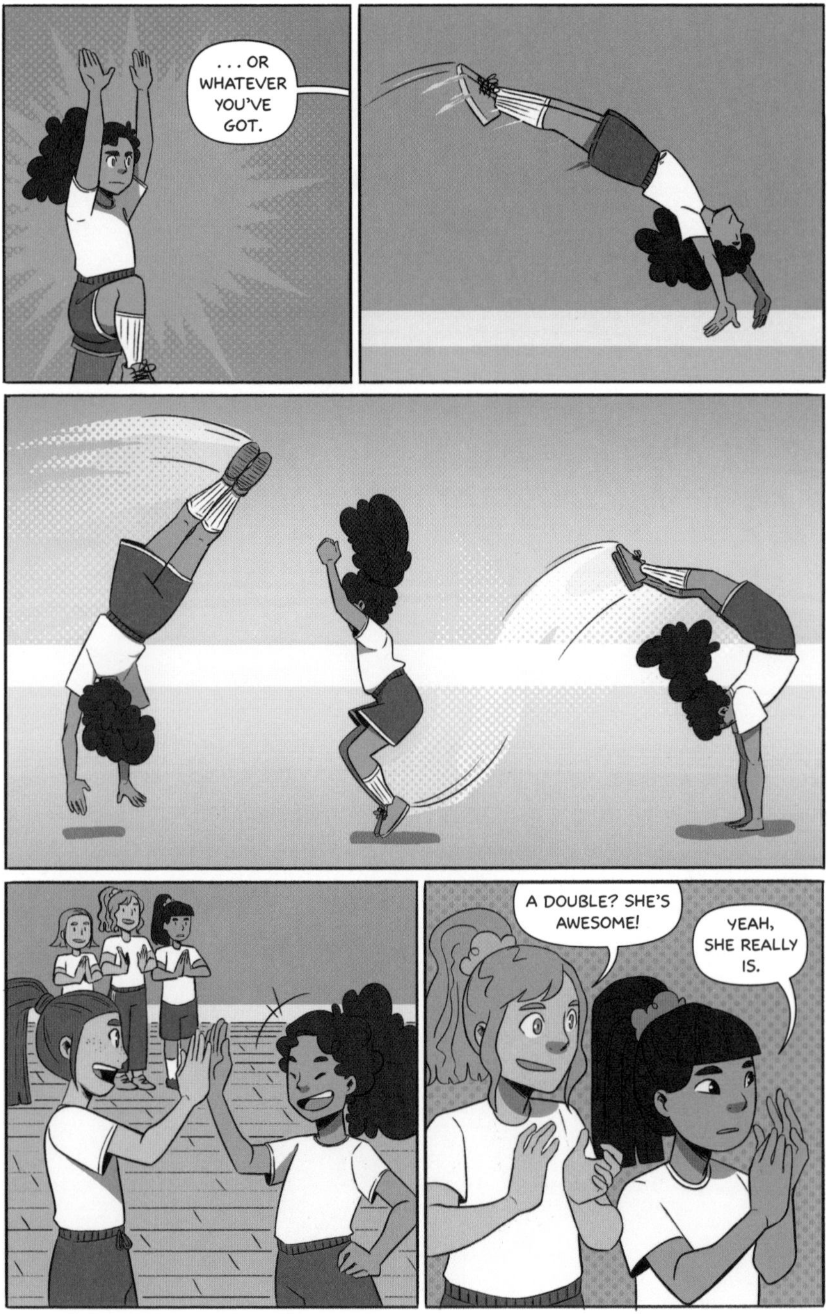
. . . OR WHATEVER YOU'VE GOT.
A DOUBLE? SHE'S AWESOME!
YEAH, SHE REALLY IS.

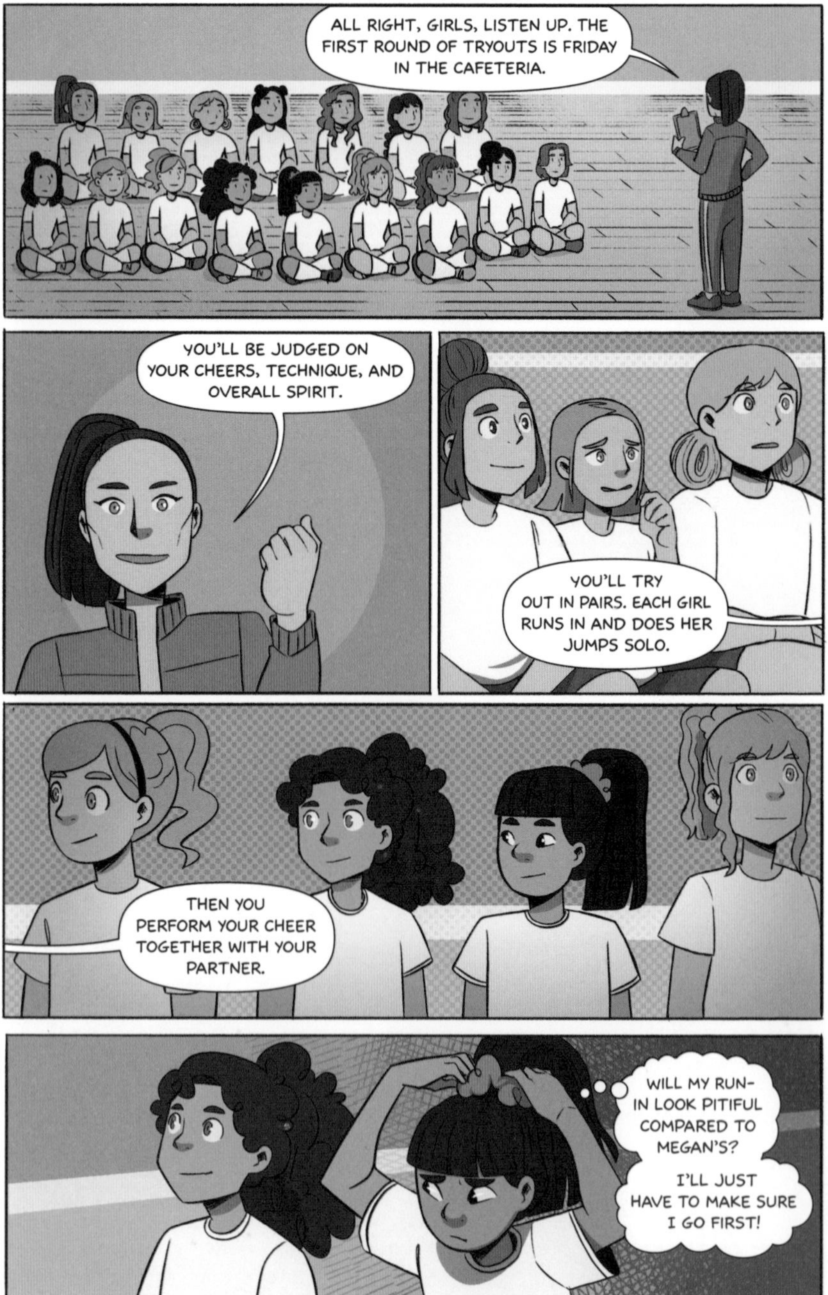
ALL RIGHT, GIRLS, LISTEN UP. THE FIRST ROUND OF TRYOUTS IS FRIDAY IN THE CAFETERIA.
YOU'LL BE JUDGED ON YOUR CHEERS, TECHNIQUE, AND OVERALL SPIRIT.
YOU'LL TRY OUT IN PAIRS. EACH GIRL RUNS IN AND DOES HER JUMPS SOLO.
THEN YOU PERFORM YOUR CHEER TOGETHER WITH YOUR PARTNER.
WILL MY RUN-IN LOOK PITIFUL COMPARED TO MEGAN'S?
I'LL JUST HAVE TO MAKE SURE I GO FIRST!

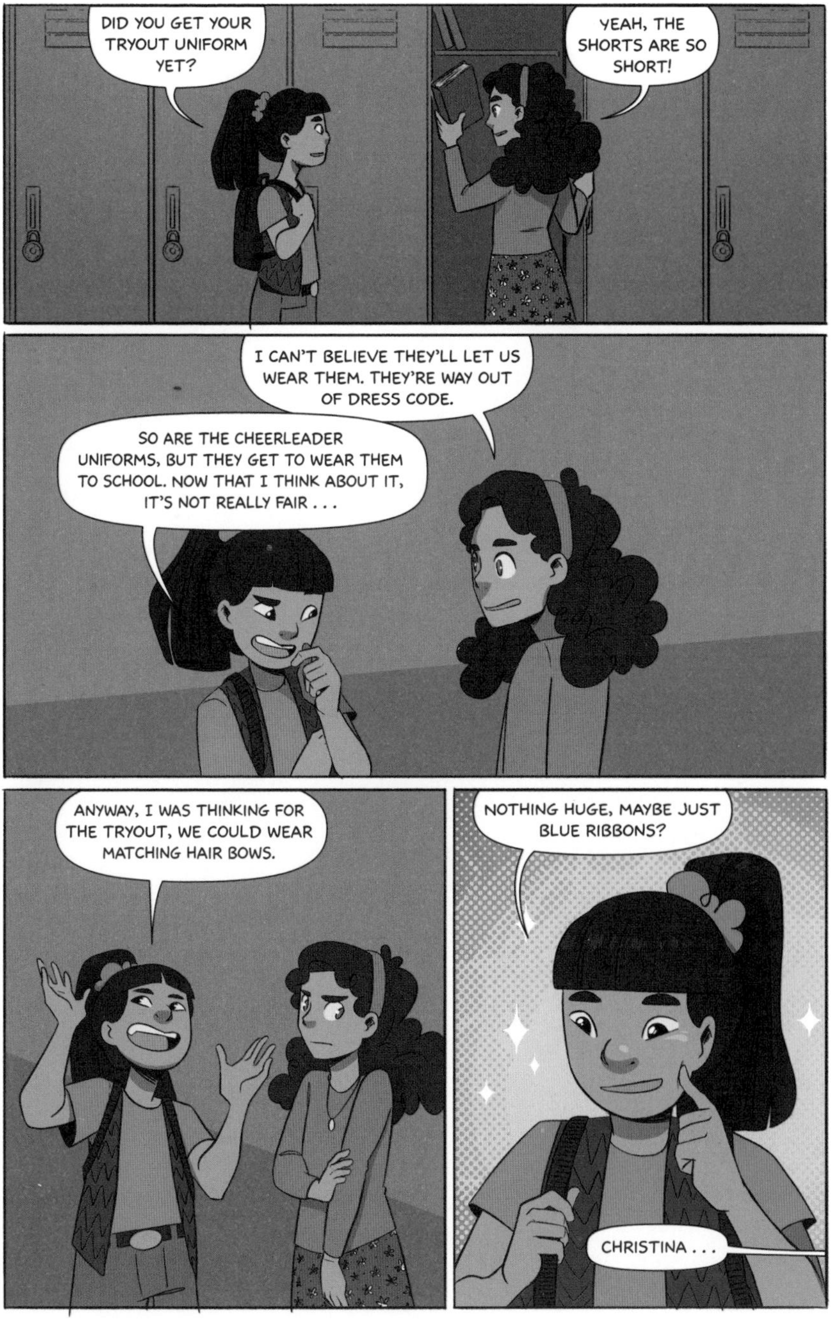
DID YOU GET YOUR TRYOUT UNIFORM YET?
YEAH, THE SHORTS ARE SO SHORT!
I CAN'T BELIEVE THEY'LL LET US WEAR THEM. THEY'RE WAY OUT OF DRESS CODE.
SO ARE THE CHEERLEADER UNIFORMS, BUT THEY GET TO WEAR THEM TO SCHOOL. NOW THAT I THINK ABOUT IT, IT'S NOT REALLY FAIR . . .
ANYWAY, I WAS THINKING FOR THE TRYOUT, WE COULD WEAR MATCHING HAIR BOWS.
NOTHING HUGE, MAYBE JUST BLUE RIBBONS?
CHRISTINA . . .

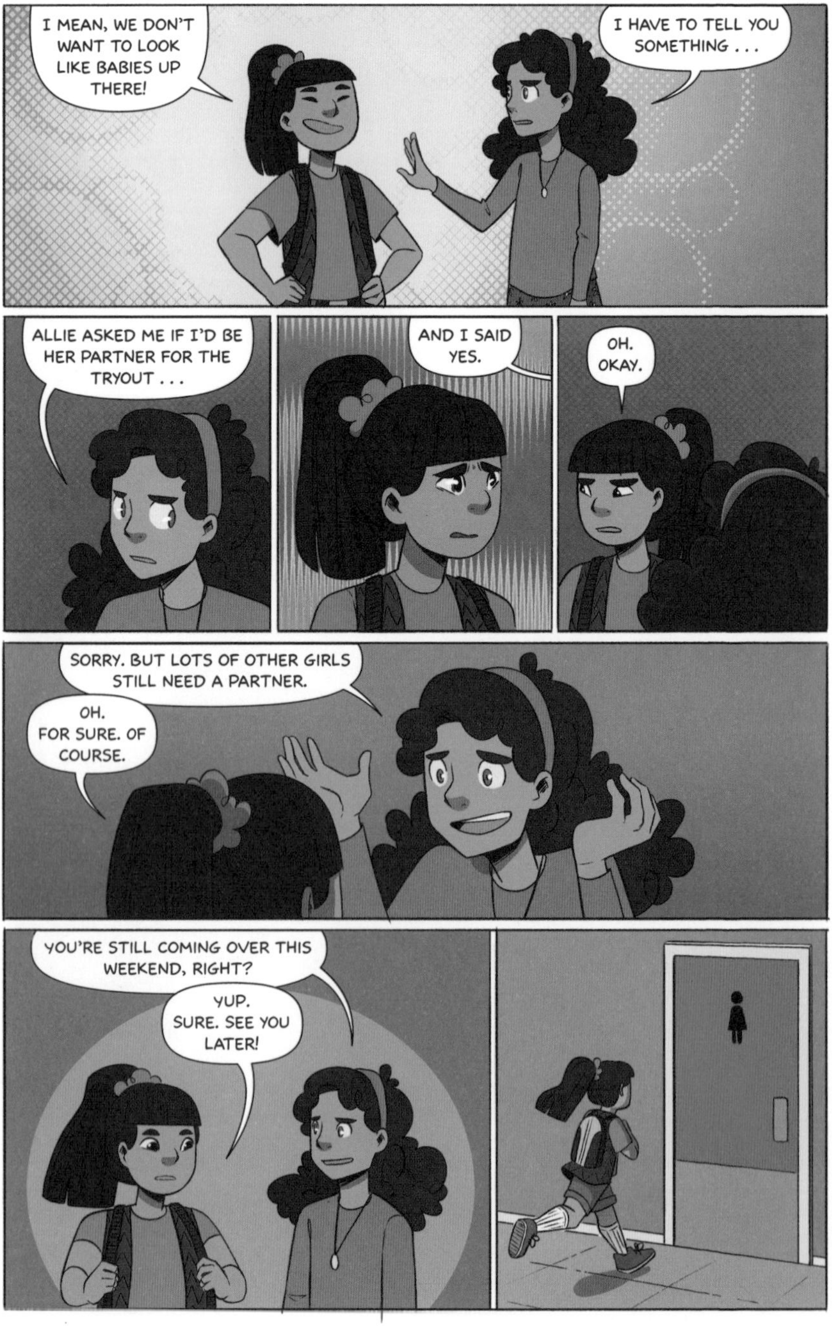
I MEAN, WE DON'T WANT TO LOOK LIKE BABIES UP THERE!
I HAVE TO TELL YOU SOMETHING . . .
ALLIE ASKED ME IF I'D BE HER PARTNER FOR THE TRYOUT . . .
AND I SAID YES.
OH. OKAY.
SORRY. BUT LOTS OF OTHER GIRLS STILL NEED A PARTNER.
OH. FOR SURE. OF COURSE.
YOU'RE STILL COMING OVER THIS WEEKEND, RIGHT?
YUP. SURE. SEE YOU LATER!

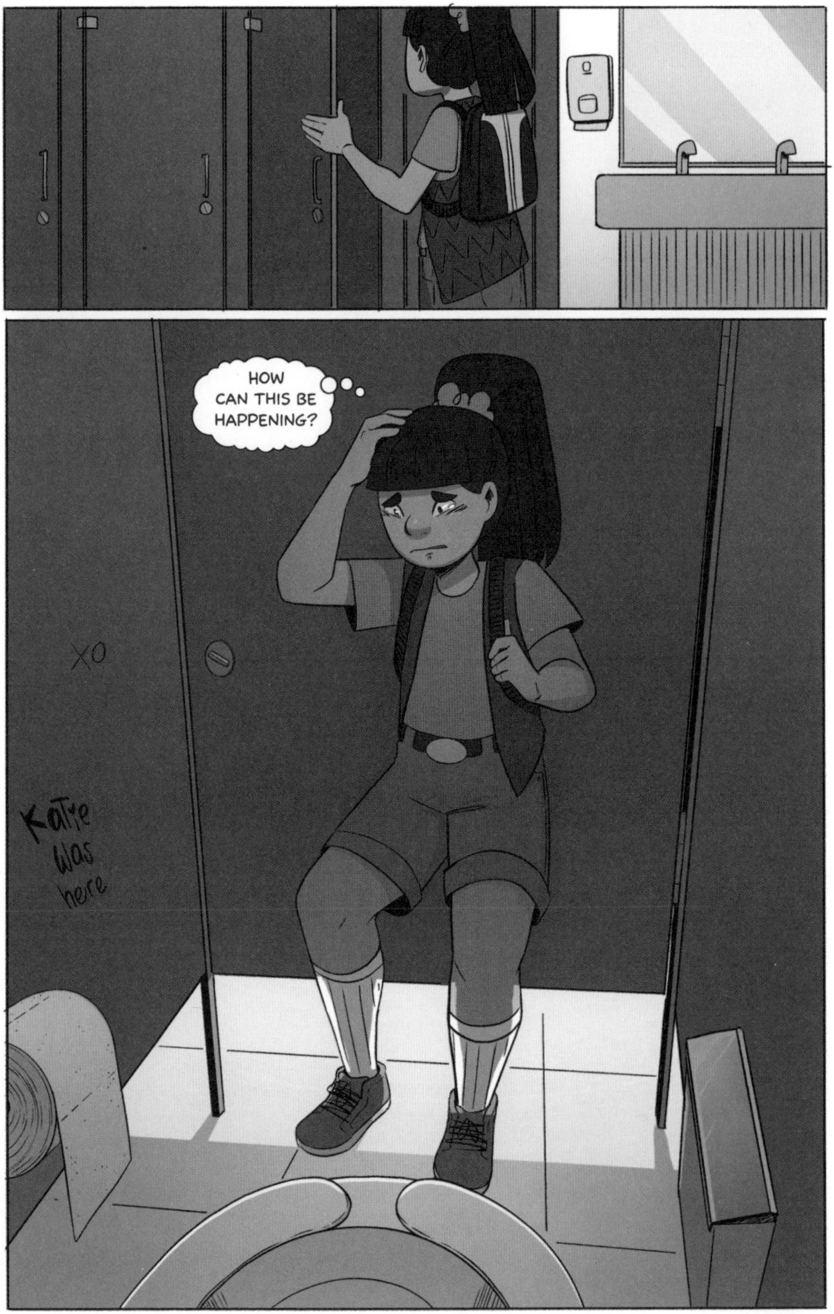
HOW CAN THIS BE HAPPENING?
XO
Katie Was here

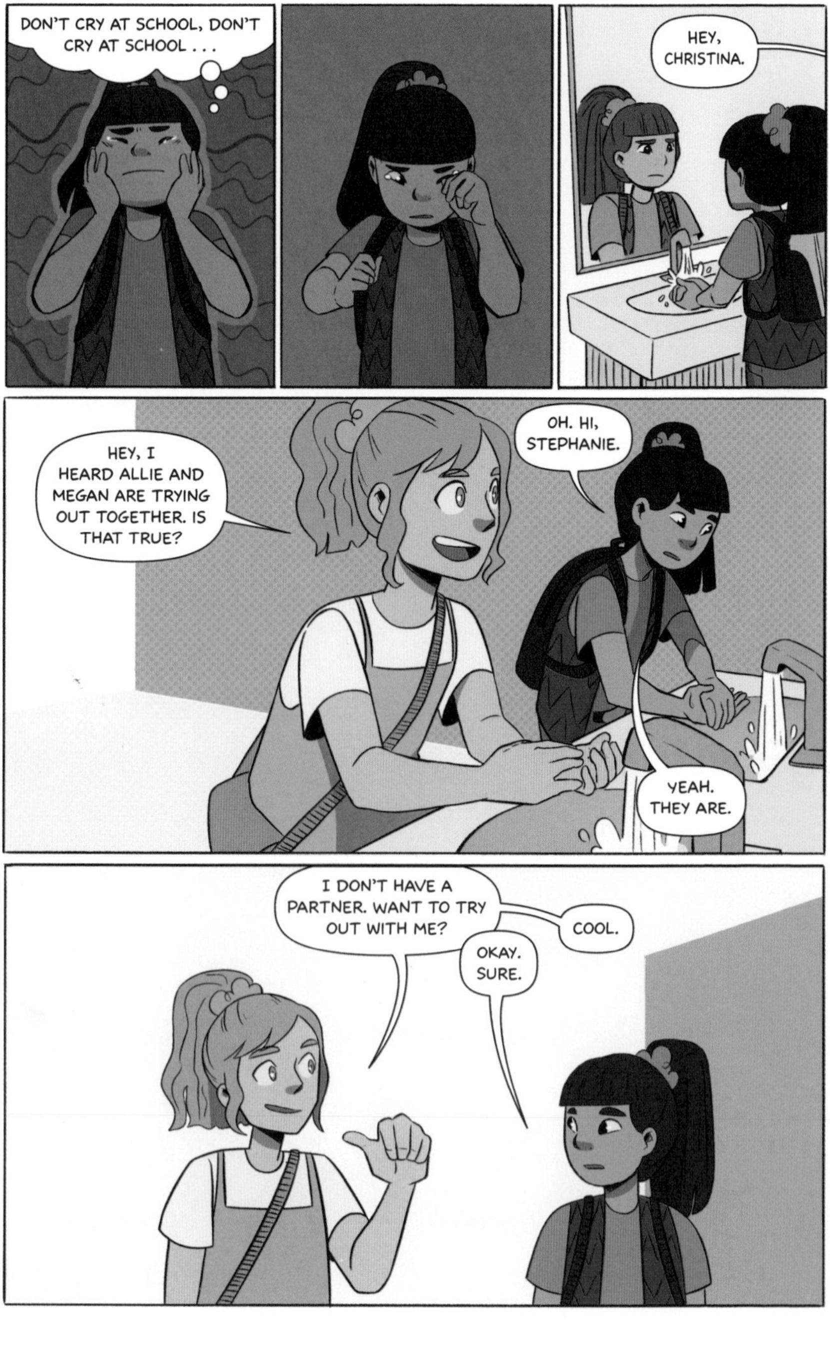
DON'T CRY AT SCHOOL, DON'T CRY AT SCHOOL . . .
HEY, CHRISTINA.
OH. HI, STEPHANIE.
HEY, I HEARD ALLIE AND MEGAN ARE TRYING OUT TOGETHER. IS THAT TRUE?
YEAH. THEY ARE.
I DON'T HAVE A PARTNER. WANT TO TRY OUT WITH ME?
OKAY. SURE.
COOL.

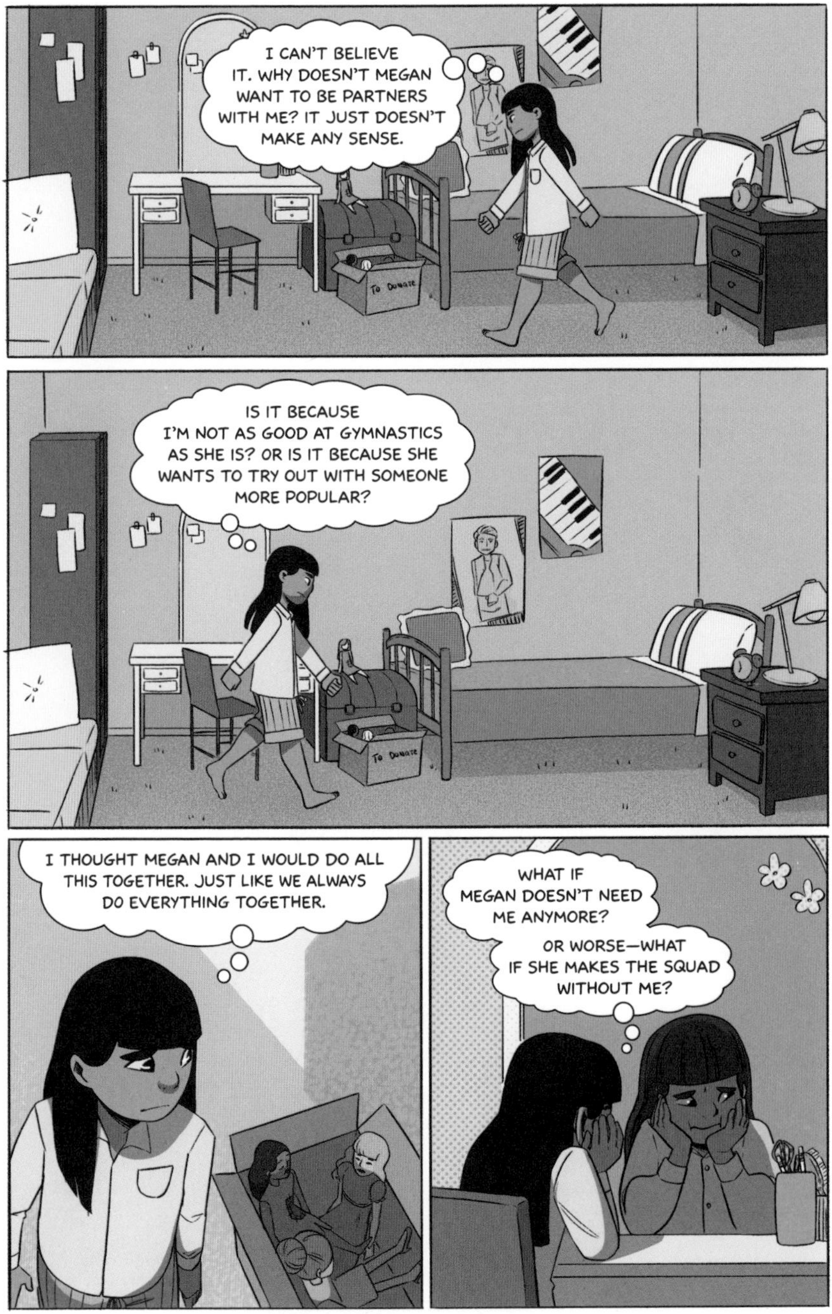
I CAN'T BELIEVE IT. WHY DOESN'T MEGAN WANT TO BE PARTNERS WITH ME? IT JUST DOESN'T MAKE ANY SENSE.
TO DONATE
IS IT BECAUSE I'M NOT AS GOOD AT GYMNASTICS AS SHE IS? OR IS IT BECAUSE SHE WANTS TO TRY OUT WITH SOMEONE MORE POPULAR?
TO DONATE
I THOUGHT MEGAN AND I WOULD DO ALL THIS TOGETHER. JUST LIKE WE ALWAYS DO EVERYTHING TOGETHER.
WHAT IF MEGAN DOESN'T NEED ME ANYMORE?
OR WORSE—WHAT IF SHE MAKES THE SQUAD WITHOUT ME?

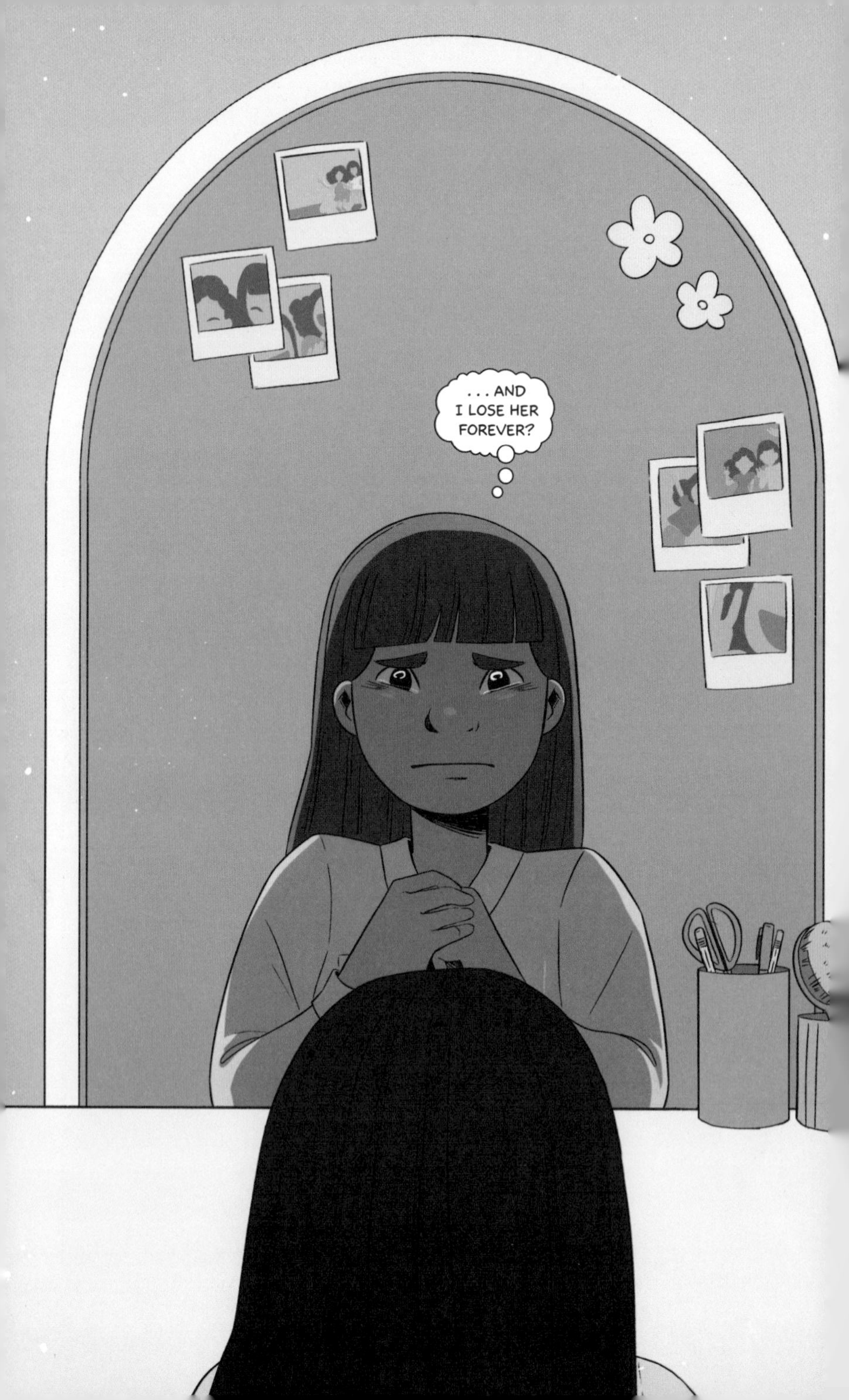
. . . AND I LOSE HER FOREVER?

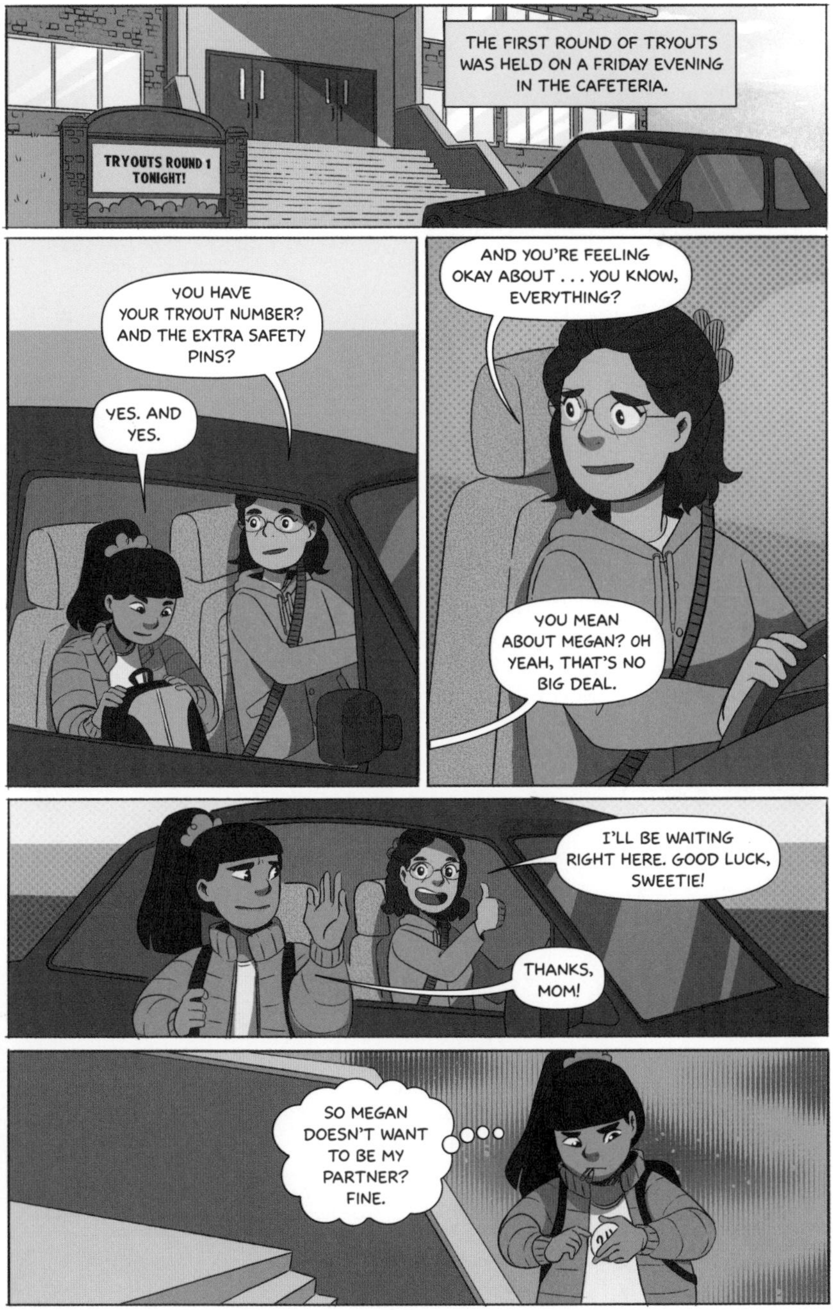
THE FIRST ROUND OF TRYOUTS WAS HELD ON A FRIDAY EVENING IN THE CAFETERIA.
TRYOUTS ROUND 1 TONIGHT!
YOU HAVE YOUR TRYOUT NUMBER? AND THE EXTRA SAFETY PINS?
YES. AND YES.
AND YOU'RE FEELING OKAY ABOUT . . . YOU KNOW, EVERYTHING?
YOU MEAN ABOUT MEGAN? OH YEAH, THAT'S NO BIG DEAL.
I'LL BE WAITING RIGHT HERE. GOOD LUCK, SWEETIE!
THANKS, MOM!
SO MEGAN DOESN'T WANT TO BE MY PARTNER? FINE.

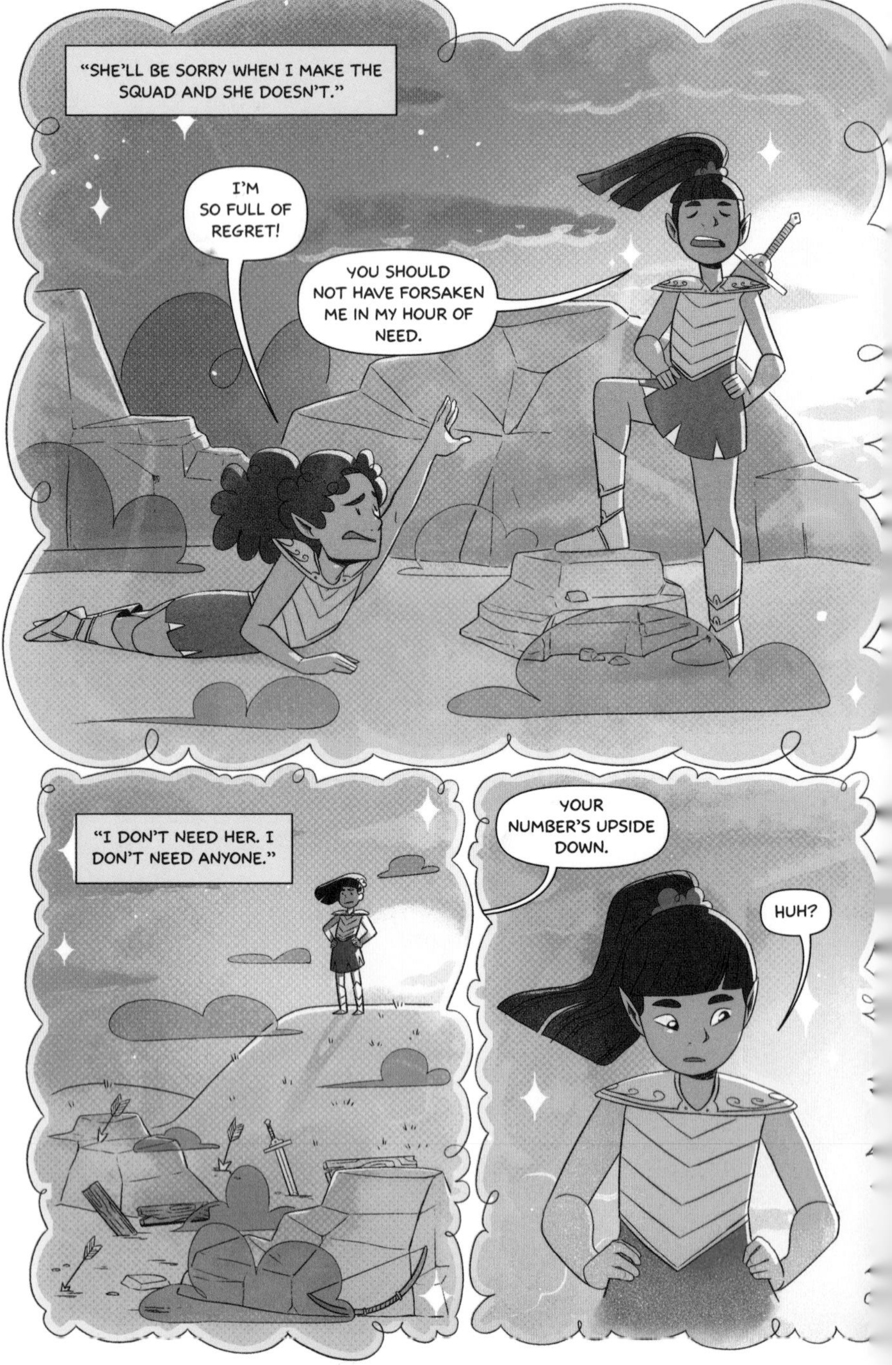
"SHE'LL BE SORRY WHEN I MAKE THE SQUAD AND SHE DOESN'T."
I'M SO FULL OF REGRET!
YOU SHOULD NOT HAVE FORSAKEN ME IN MY HOUR OF NEED.
"I DON'T NEED HER. I DON'T NEED ANYONE."
YOUR NUMBER'S UPSIDE DOWN.
HUH?

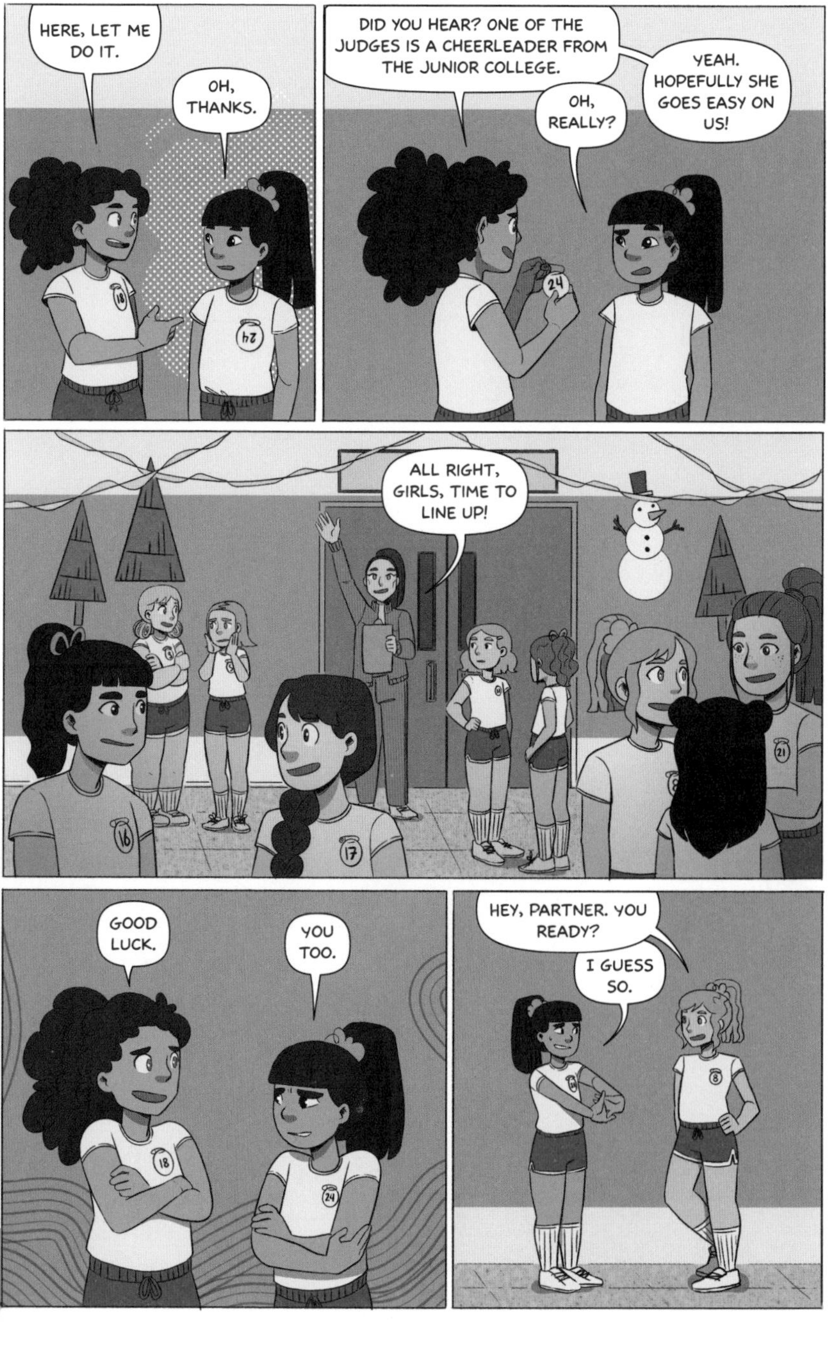
HERE, LET ME DO IT.
OH, THANKS.
DID YOU HEAR? ONE OF THE JUDGES IS A CHEERLEADER FROM THE JUNIOR COLLEGE.
OH, REALLY?
YEAH. HOPEFULLY SHE GOES EASY ON US!
ALL RIGHT, GIRLS, TIME TO LINE UP!
GOOD LUCK.
YOU TOO.
HEY, PARTNER. YOU READY?
I GUESS SO.

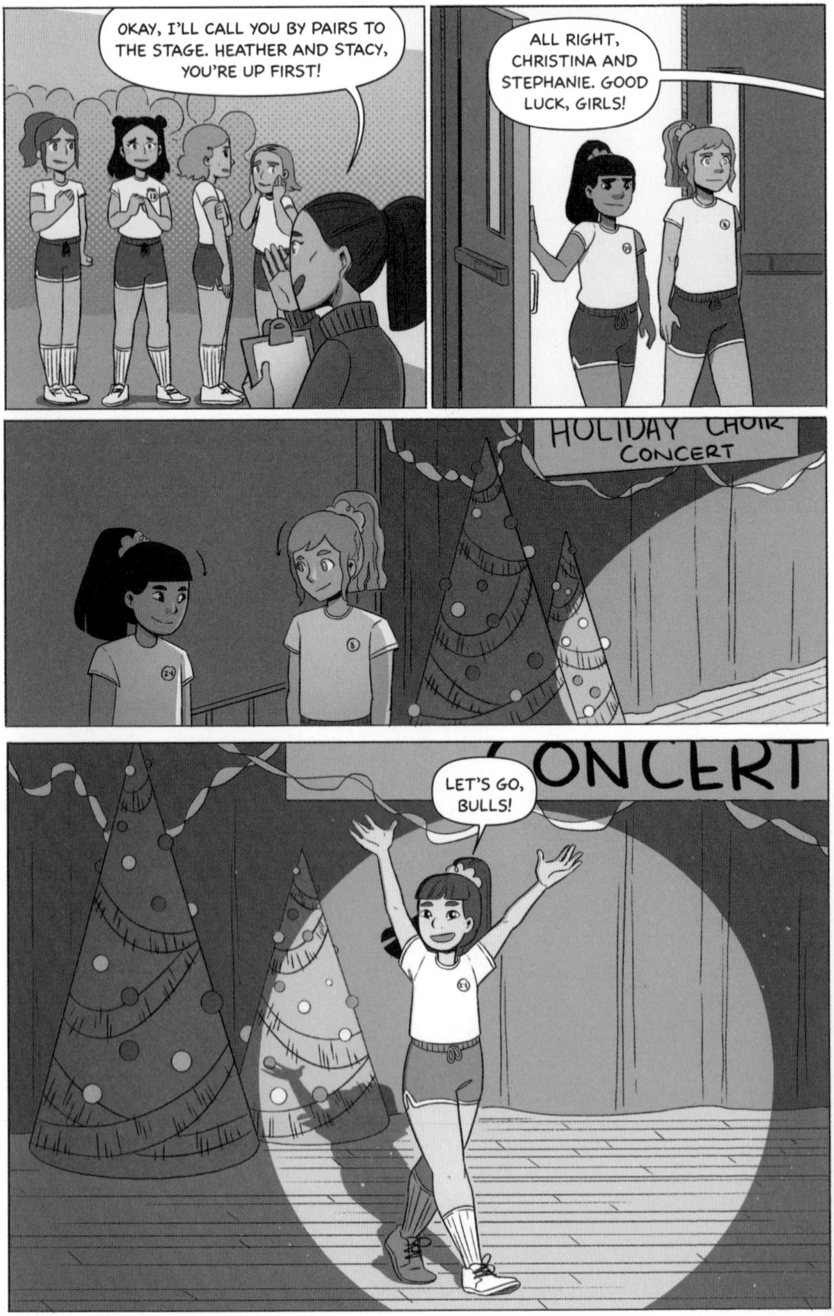
OKAY, I'LL CALL YOU BY PAIRS TO THE STAGE. HEATHER AND STACY, YOU'RE UP FIRST!
ALL RIGHT, CHRISTINA AND STEPHANIE. GOOD LUCK, GIRLS!
HOLIDAY CHOIR CONCERT
CONCERT
LET'S GO, BULLS!

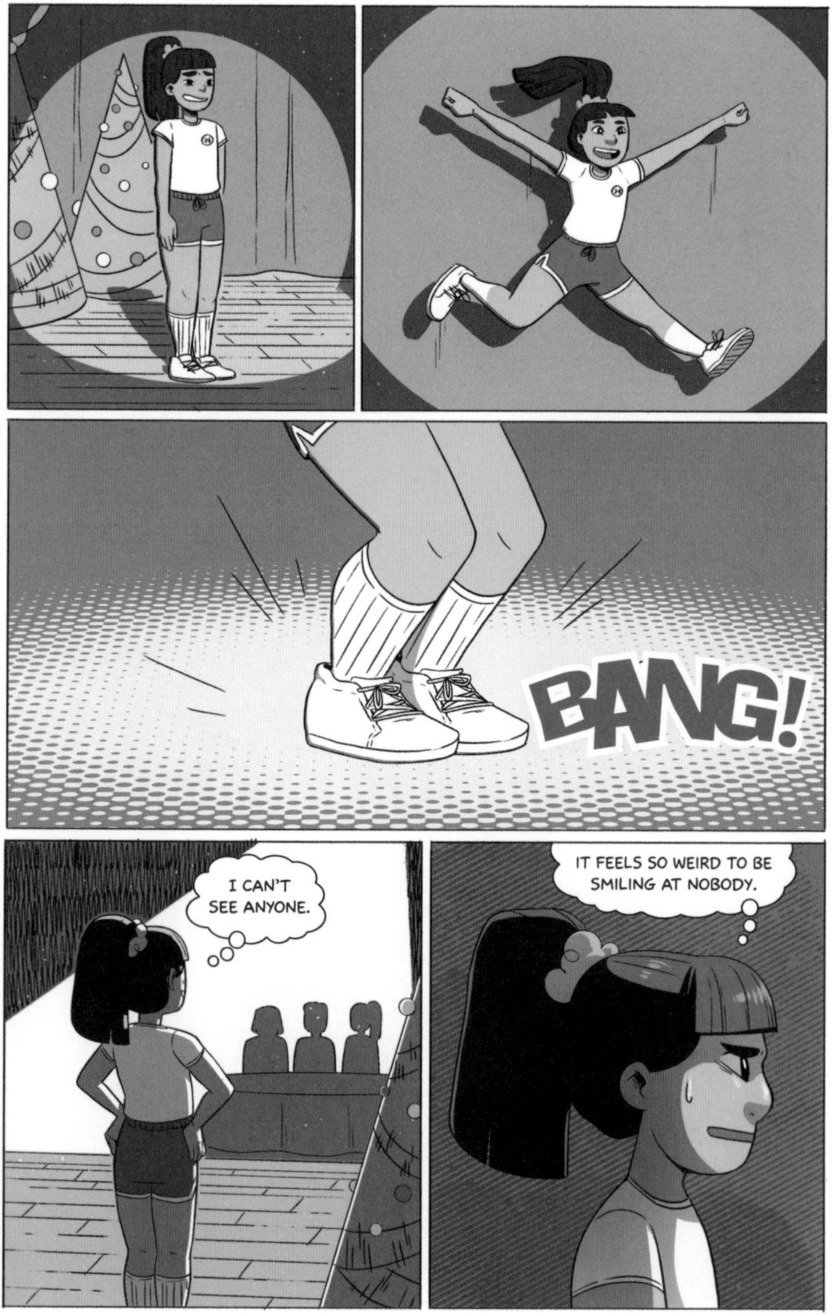
BANG!
I CAN'T SEE ANYONE.
IT FEELS SO WEIRD TO BE SMILING AT NOBODY.

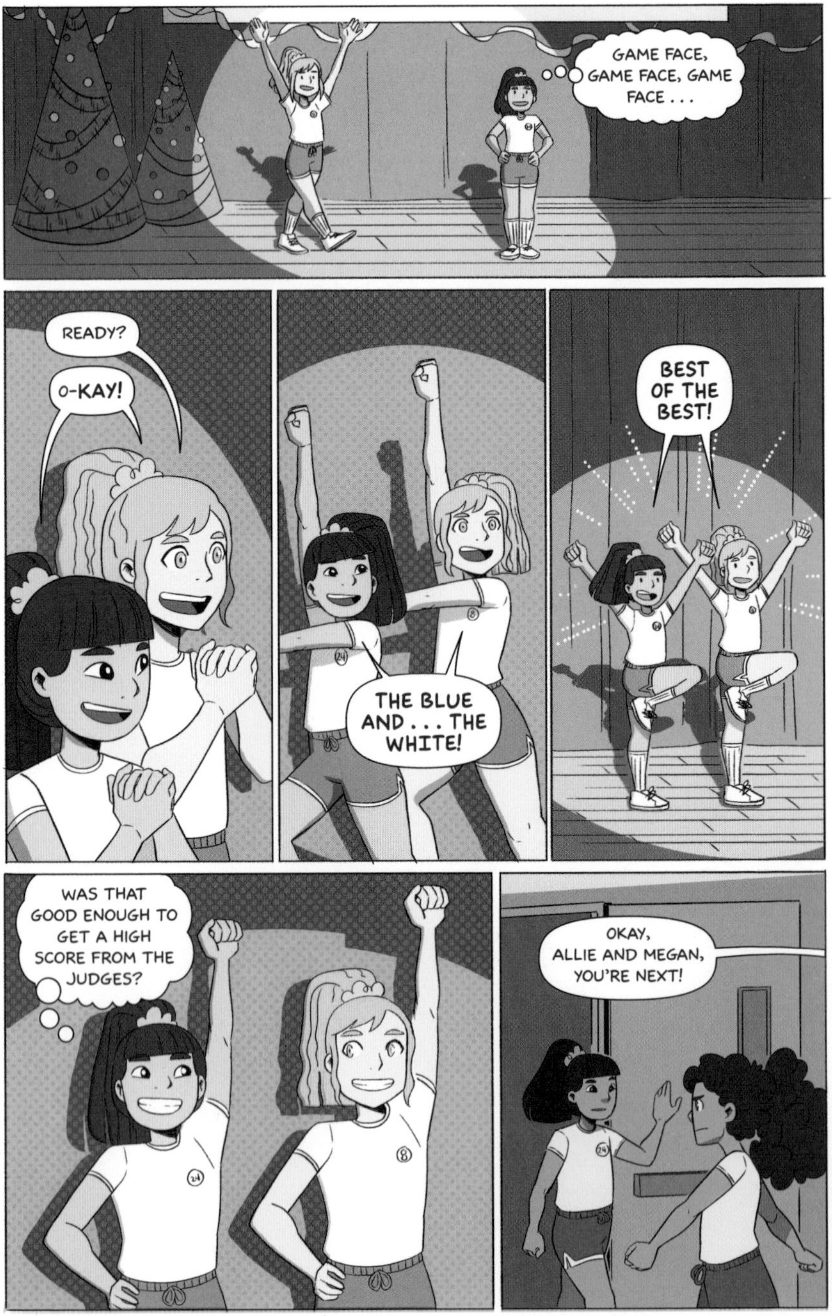
GAME FACE, GAME FACE, GAME FACE . . .
READY?
O-KAY!
THE BLUE AND . . . THE WHITE!
BEST OF THE BEST!
WAS THAT GOOD ENOUGH TO GET A HIGH SCORE FROM THE JUDGES?
OKAY, ALLIE AND MEGAN, YOU'RE NEXT!

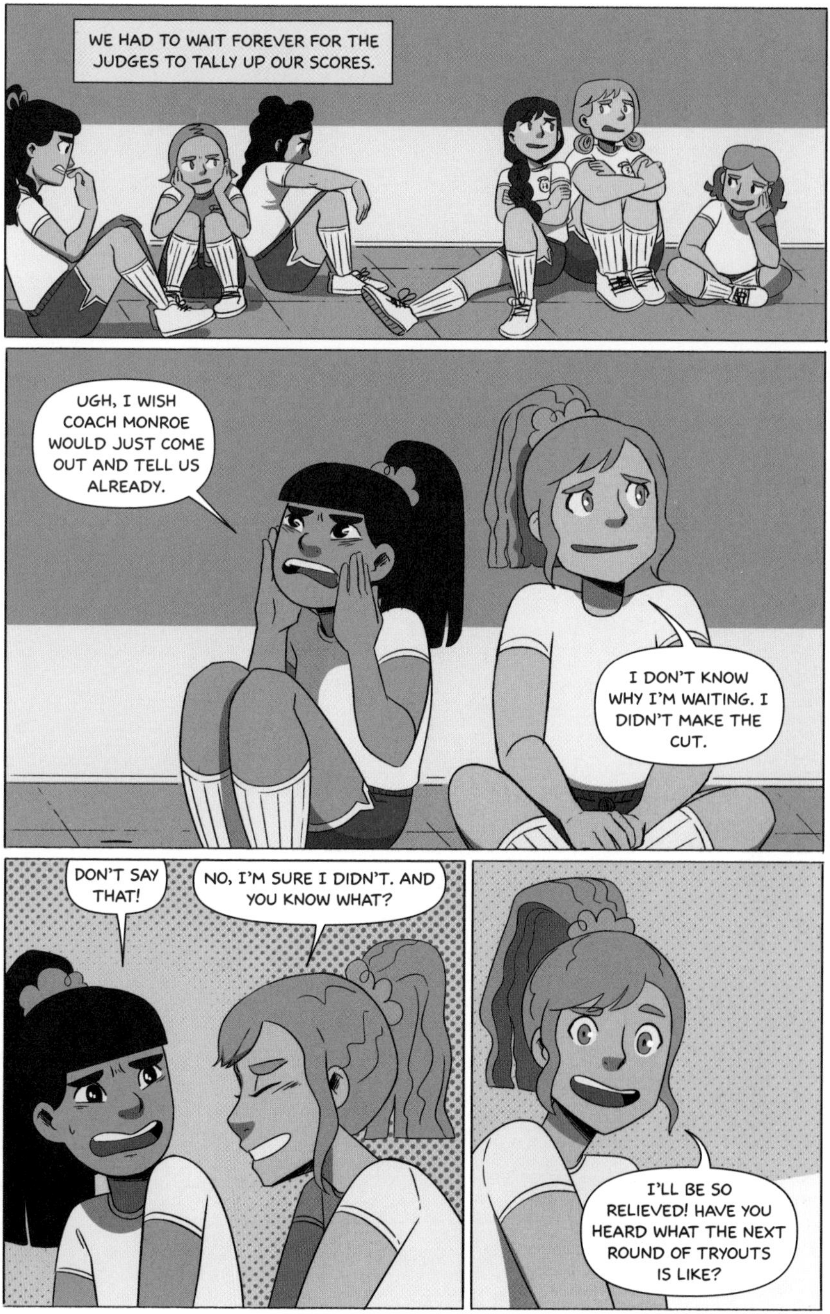
WE HAD TO WAIT FOREVER FOR THE JUDGES TO TALLY UP OUR SCORES.
UGH, I WISH COACH MONROE WOULD JUST COME OUT AND TELL US ALREADY.
I DON'T KNOW WHY I'M WAITING. I DIDN'T MAKE THE CUT.
DON'T SAY THAT!
NO, I'M SURE I DIDN'T. AND YOU KNOW WHAT?
I'LL BE SO RELIEVED! HAVE YOU HEARD WHAT THE NEXT ROUND OF TRYOUTS IS LIKE?

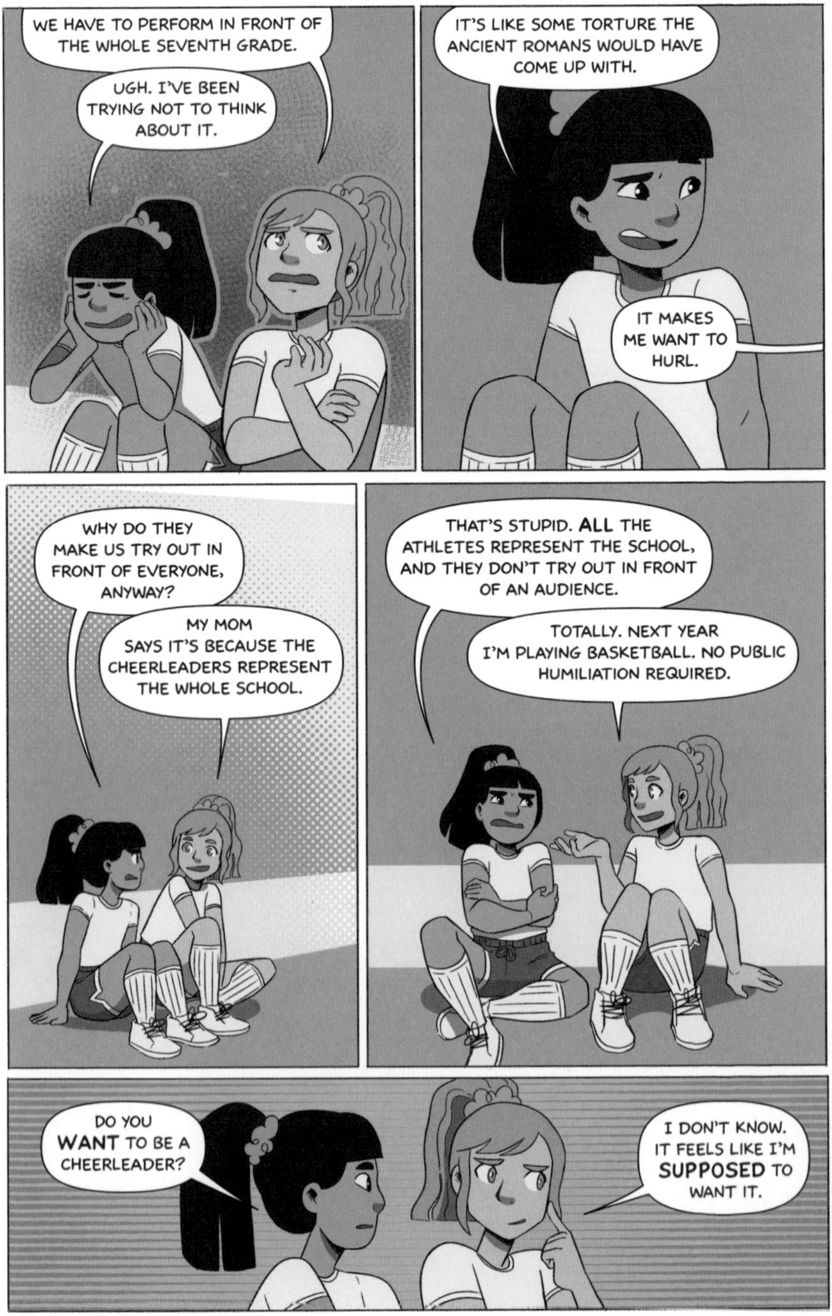
WE HAVE TO PERFORM IN FRONT OF THE WHOLE SEVENTH GRADE.
UGH. I'VE BEEN TRYING NOT TO THINK ABOUT IT.
IT'S LIKE SOME TORTURE THE ANCIENT ROMANS WOULD HAVE COME UP WITH.
IT MAKES ME WANT TO HURL.
WHY DO THEY MAKE US TRY OUT IN FRONT OF EVERYONE, ANYWAY?
MY MOM SAYS IT'S BECAUSE THE CHEERLEADERS REPRESENT THE WHOLE SCHOOL.
THAT'S STUPID. **ALL** THE ATHLETES REPRESENT THE SCHOOL, AND THEY DON'T TRY OUT IN FRONT OF AN AUDIENCE.
TOTALLY. NEXT YEAR I'M PLAYING BASKETBALL. NO PUBLIC HUMILIATION REQUIRED.
DO YOU **WANT** TO BE A CHEERLEADER?
I DON'T KNOW. IT FEELS LIKE I'M **SUPPOSED** TO WANT IT.

I WAS SURPRISED **YOU** WERE TRYING OUT. YOU DON'T REALLY SEEM LIKE THE CHEERLEADER TYPE.

OH? WHAT TYPE DO I SEEM LIKE?

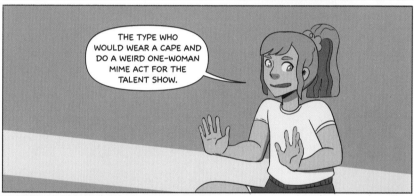

THE TYPE WHO WOULD WEAR A CAPE AND DO A WEIRD ONE-WOMAN MIME ACT FOR THE TALENT SHOW.

HA-HA, THAT ACTUALLY SOUNDS KIND OF AWESOME!

SEE? I PEGGED YOU RIGHT.

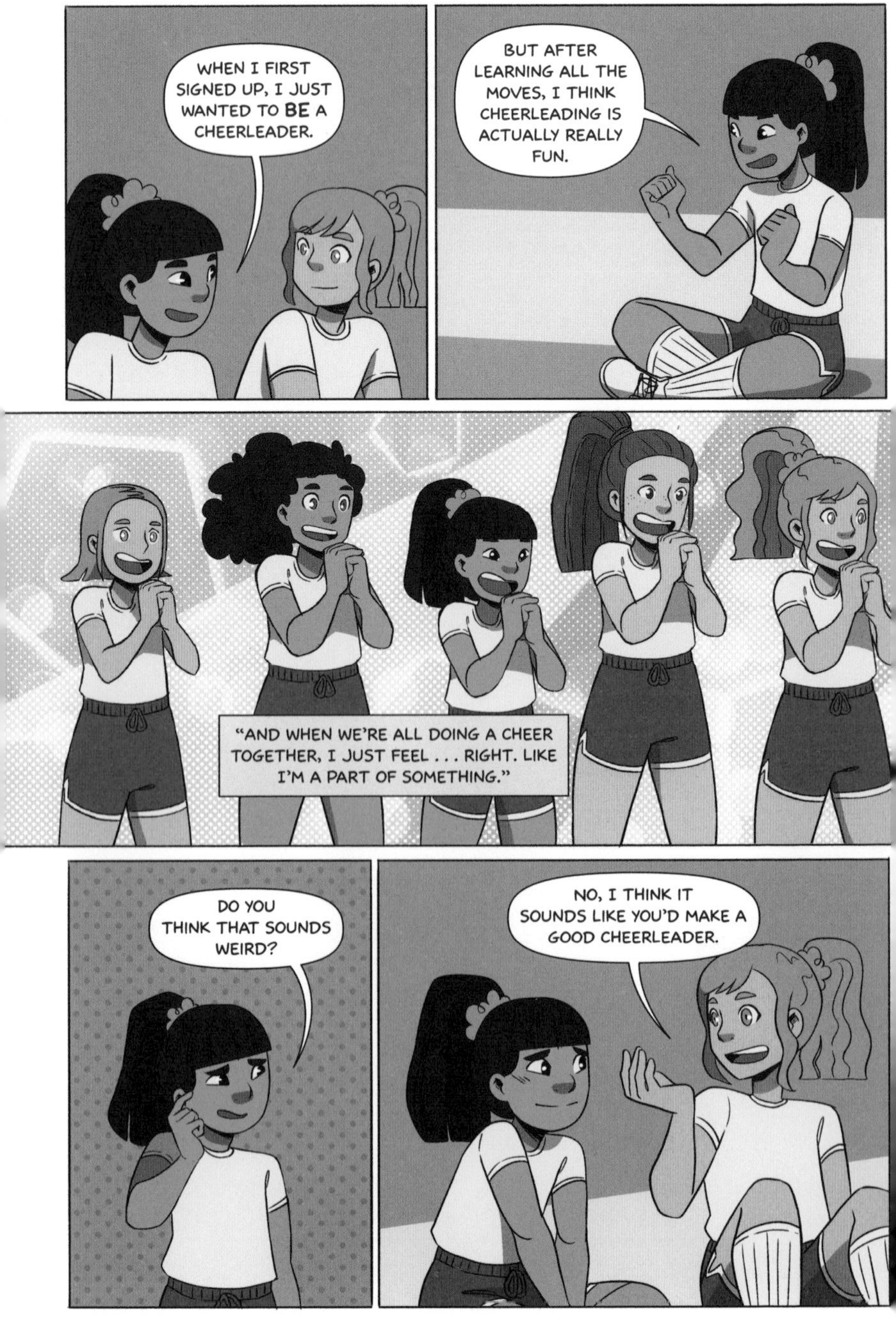
WHEN I FIRST SIGNED UP, I JUST WANTED TO **BE** A CHEERLEADER.
BUT AFTER LEARNING ALL THE MOVES, I THINK CHEERLEADING IS ACTUALLY REALLY FUN.
"AND WHEN WE'RE ALL DOING A CHEER TOGETHER, I JUST FEEL . . . RIGHT. LIKE I'M A PART OF SOMETHING."
DO YOU THINK THAT SOUNDS WEIRD?
NO, I THINK IT SOUNDS LIKE YOU'D MAKE A GOOD CHEERLEADER.

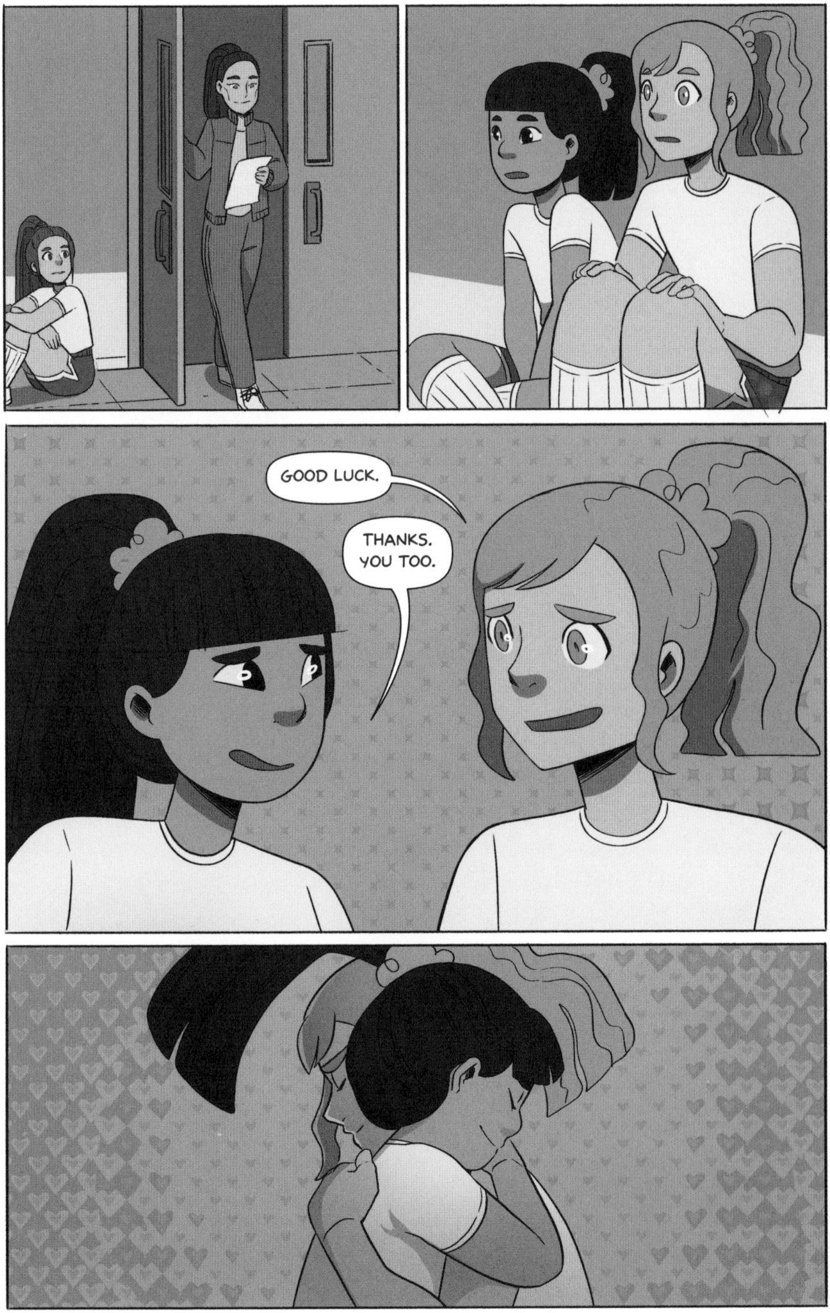
GOOD LUCK.
THANKS. YOU TOO.

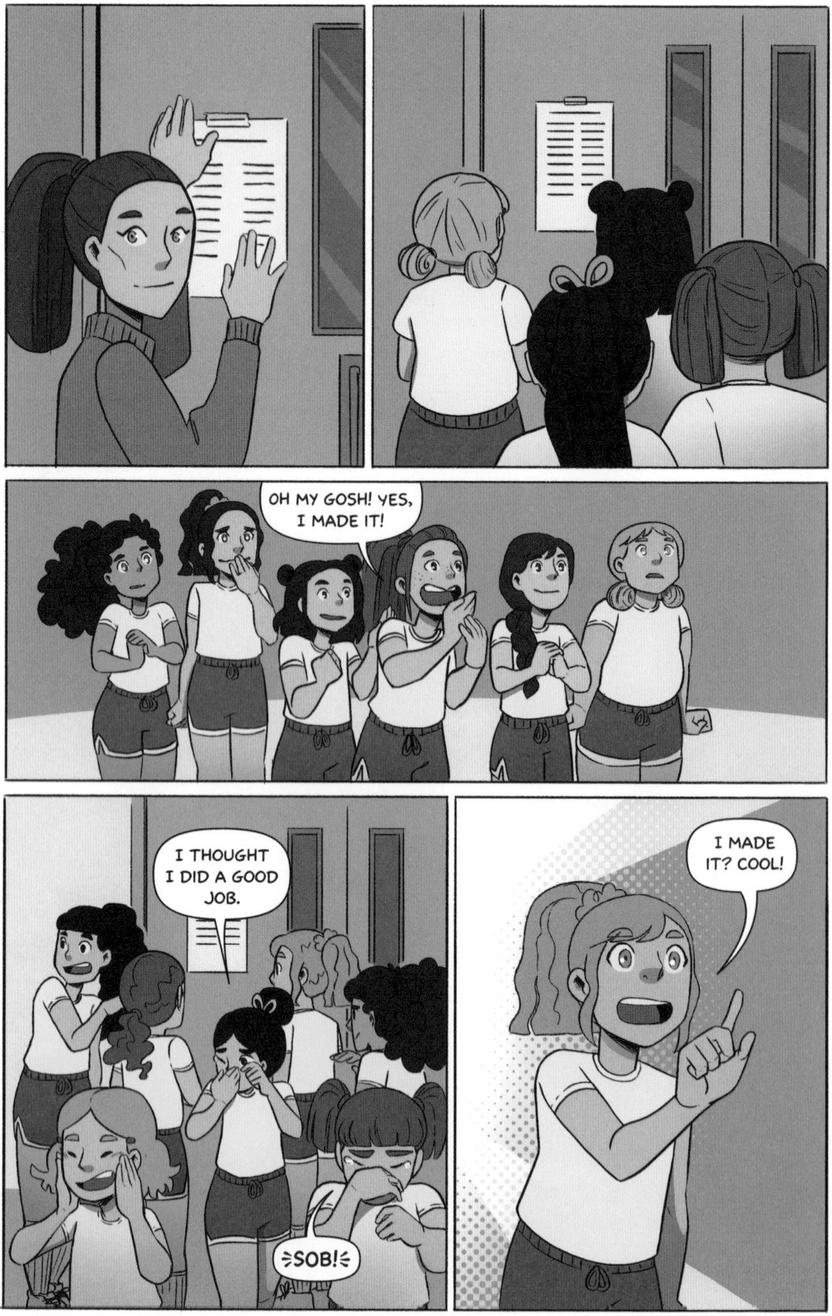
OH MY GOSH! YES, I MADE IT!
I THOUGHT I DID A GOOD JOB.
SOB!
I MADE IT? COOL!

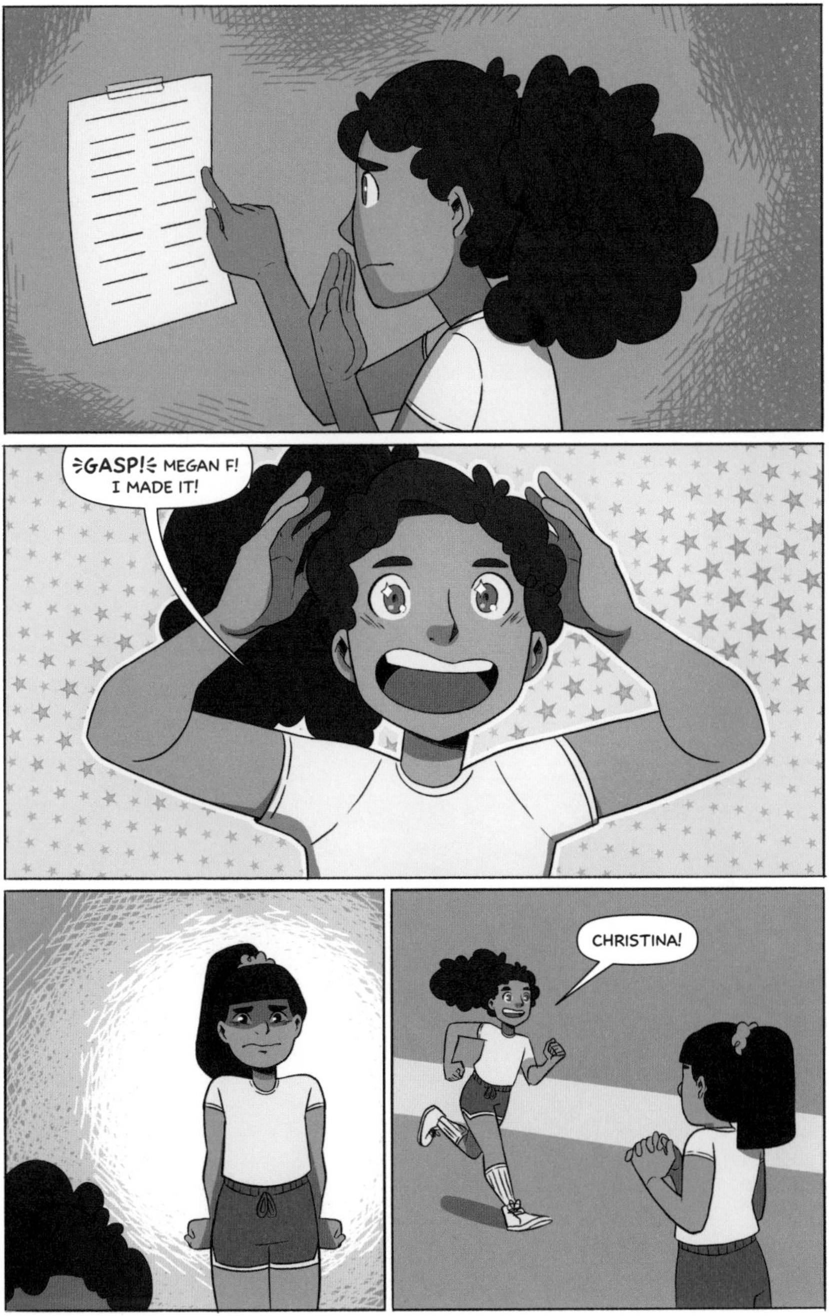

GASP! MEGAN F! I MADE IT!
CHRISTINA!

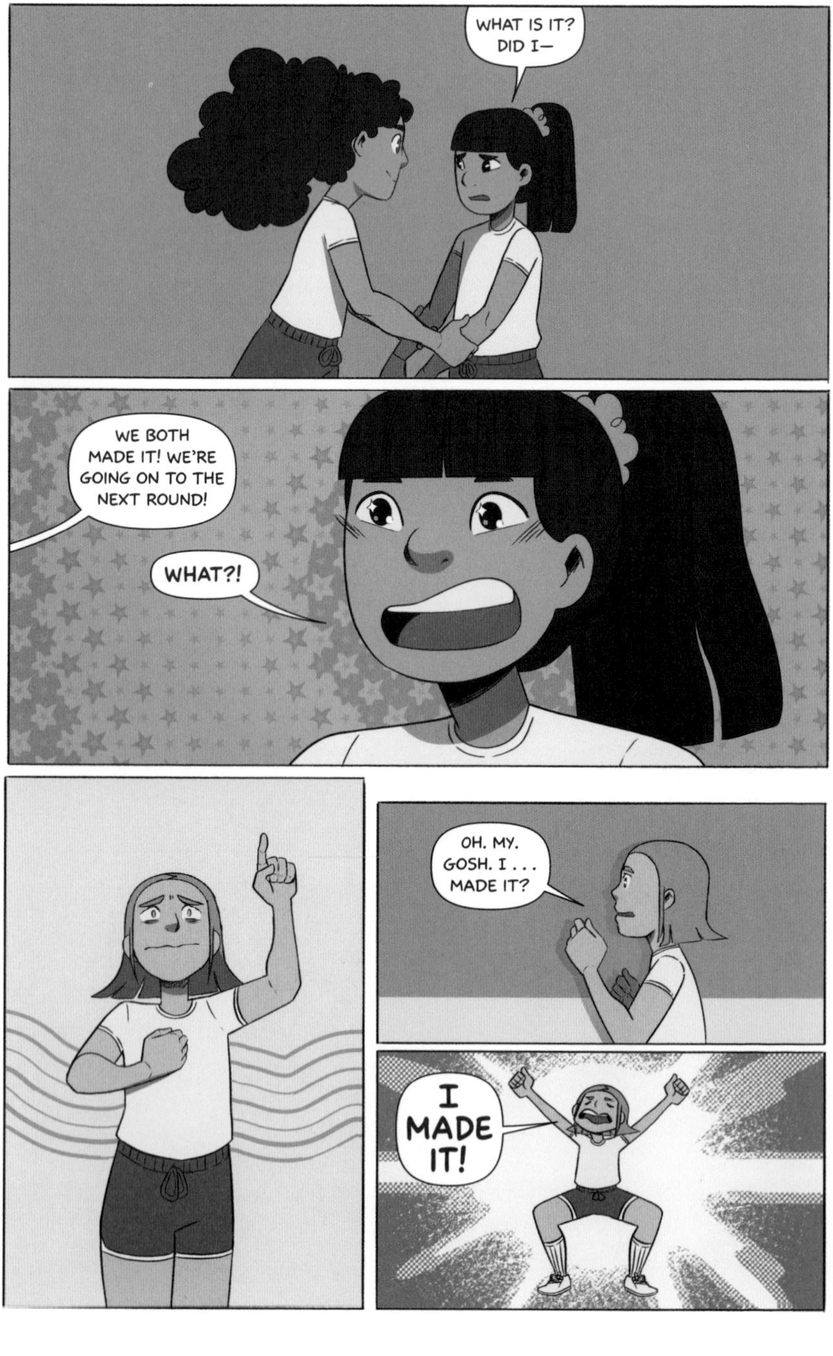
WHAT IS IT? DID I—
WE BOTH MADE IT! WE'RE GOING ON TO THE NEXT ROUND!
WHAT?!
OH. MY. GOSH. I . . . MADE IT?
I MADE IT!

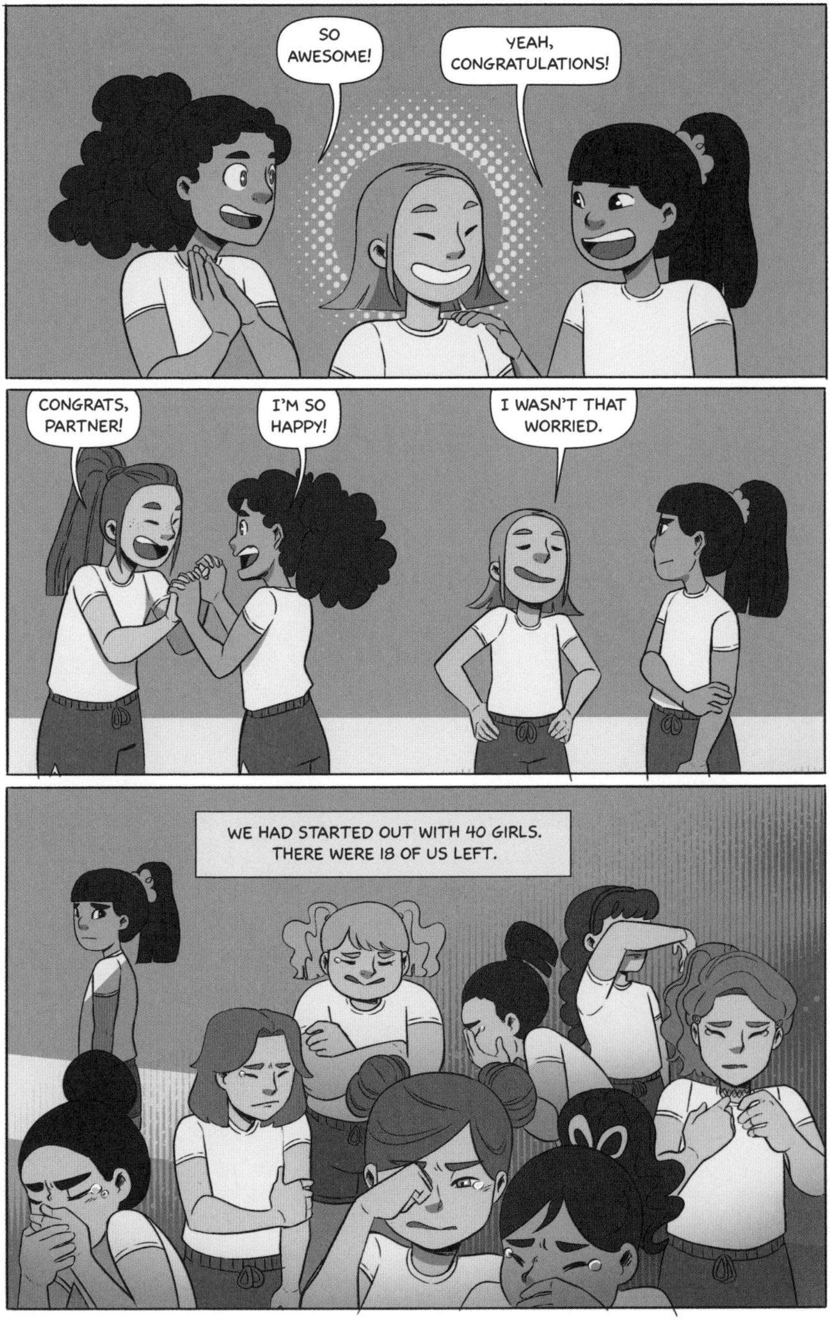
SO AWESOME!
YEAH, CONGRATULATIONS!
CONGRATS, PARTNER!
I'M SO HAPPY!
I WASN'T THAT WORRIED.
WE HAD STARTED OUT WITH 40 GIRLS. THERE WERE 18 OF US LEFT.

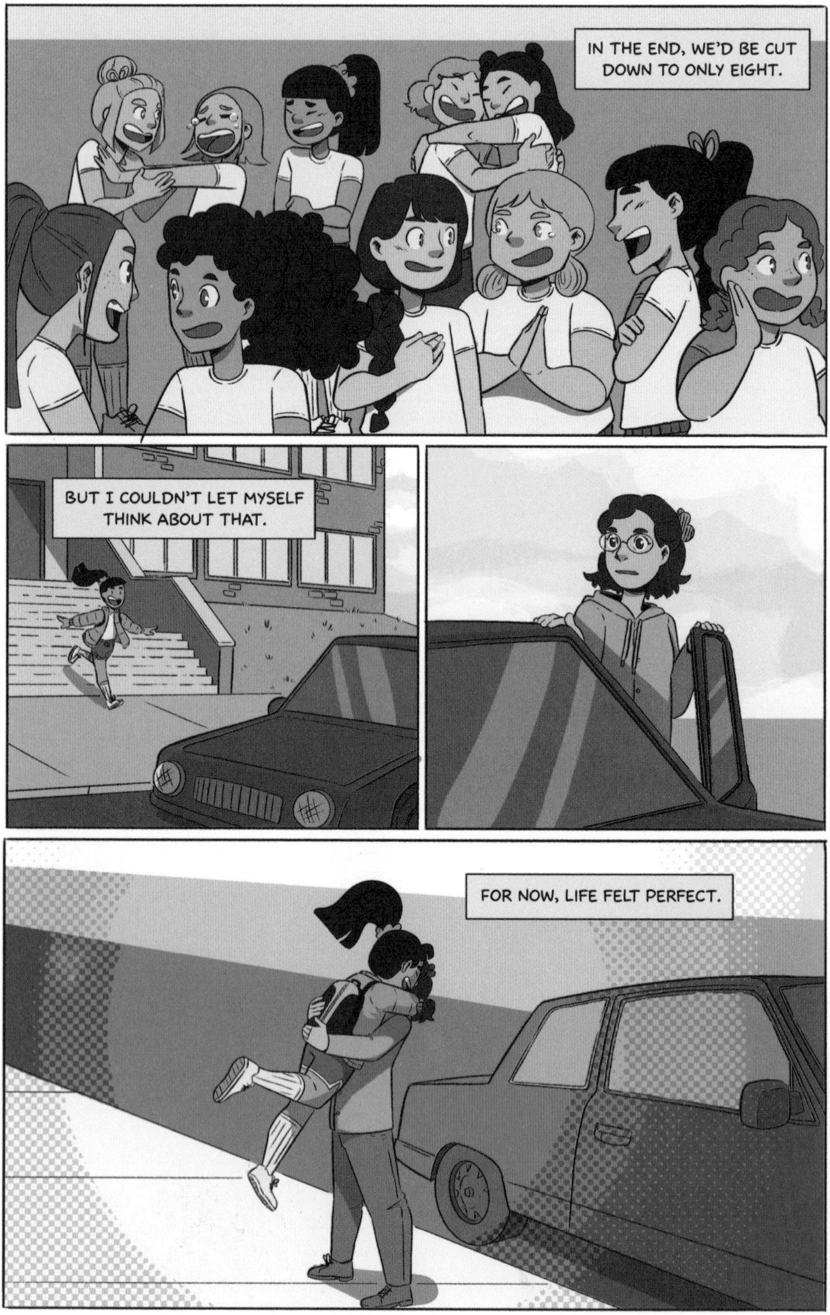
IN THE END, WE'D BE CUT DOWN TO ONLY EIGHT.
BUT I COULDN'T LET MYSELF THINK ABOUT THAT.
FOR NOW, LIFE FELT PERFECT.

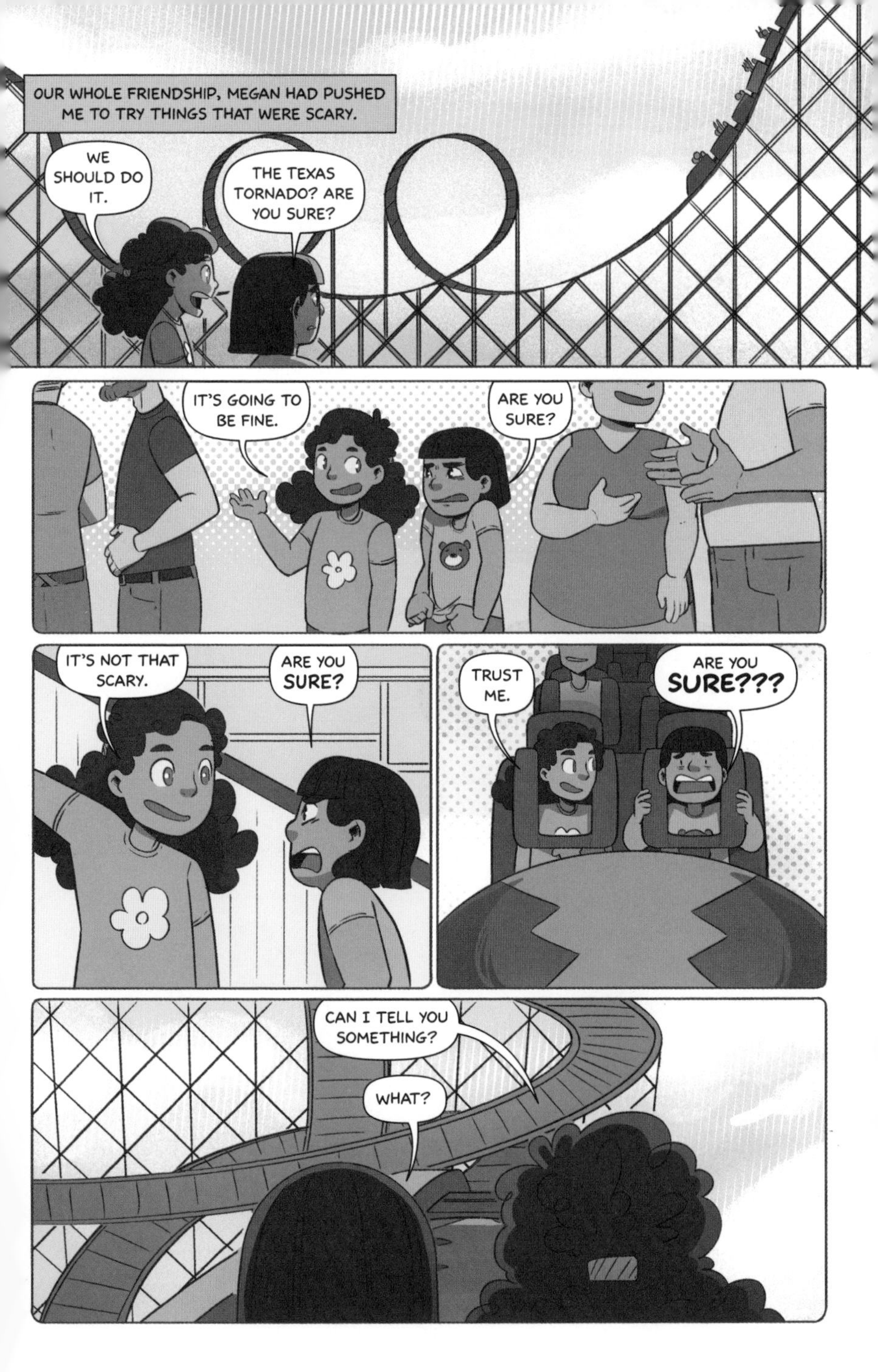
OUR WHOLE FRIENDSHIP, MEGAN HAD PUSHED ME TO TRY THINGS THAT WERE SCARY.
WE SHOULD DO IT.
THE TEXAS TORNADO? ARE YOU SURE?
IT'S GOING TO BE FINE.
ARE YOU SURE?
IT'S NOT THAT SCARY.
ARE YOU **SURE?**
TRUST ME.
ARE YOU **SURE???**
CAN I TELL YOU SOMETHING?
WHAT?

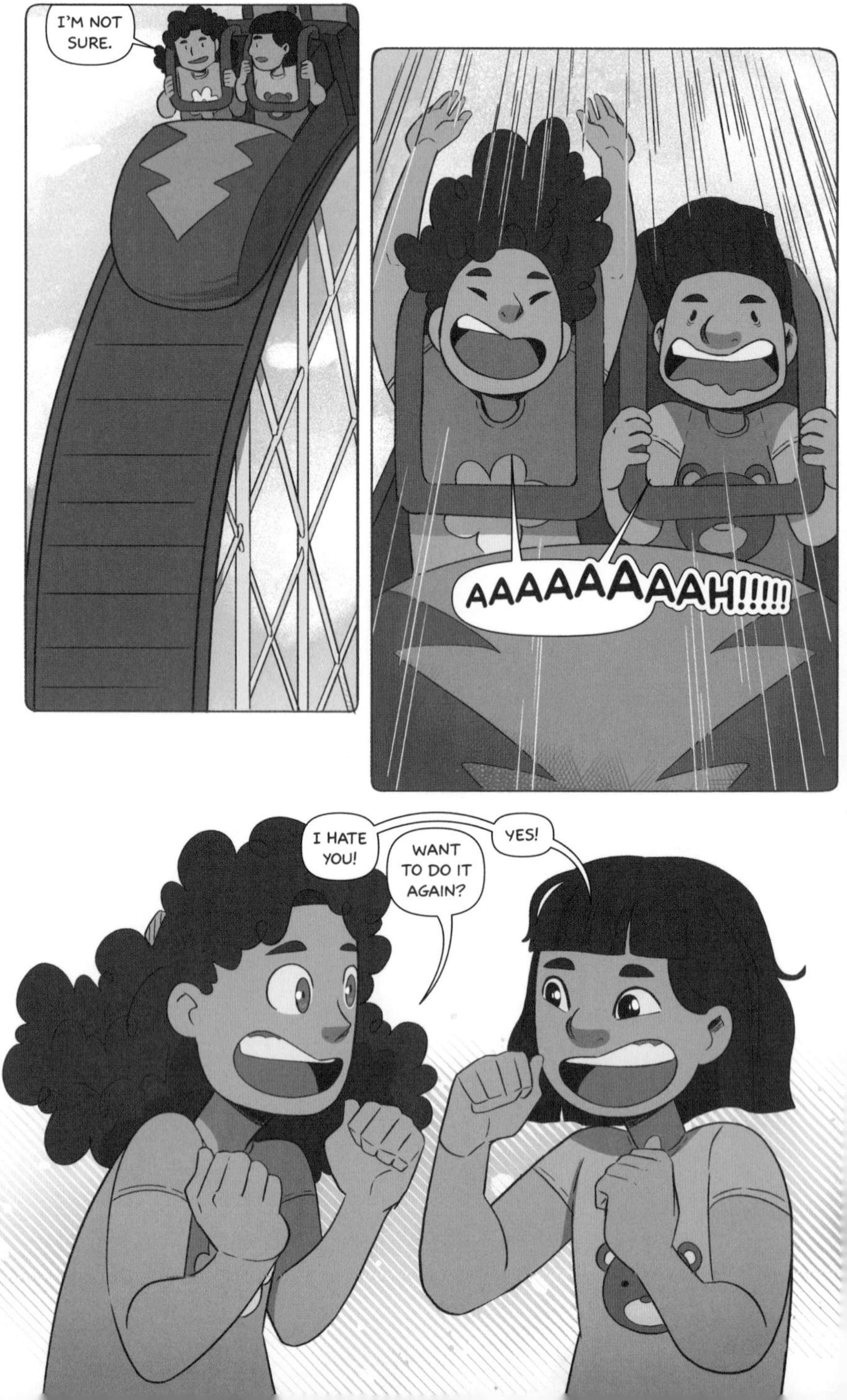
I'M NOT SURE.
AAAAAAAAH!!!!!!
I HATE YOU!
WANT TO DO IT AGAIN?
YES!

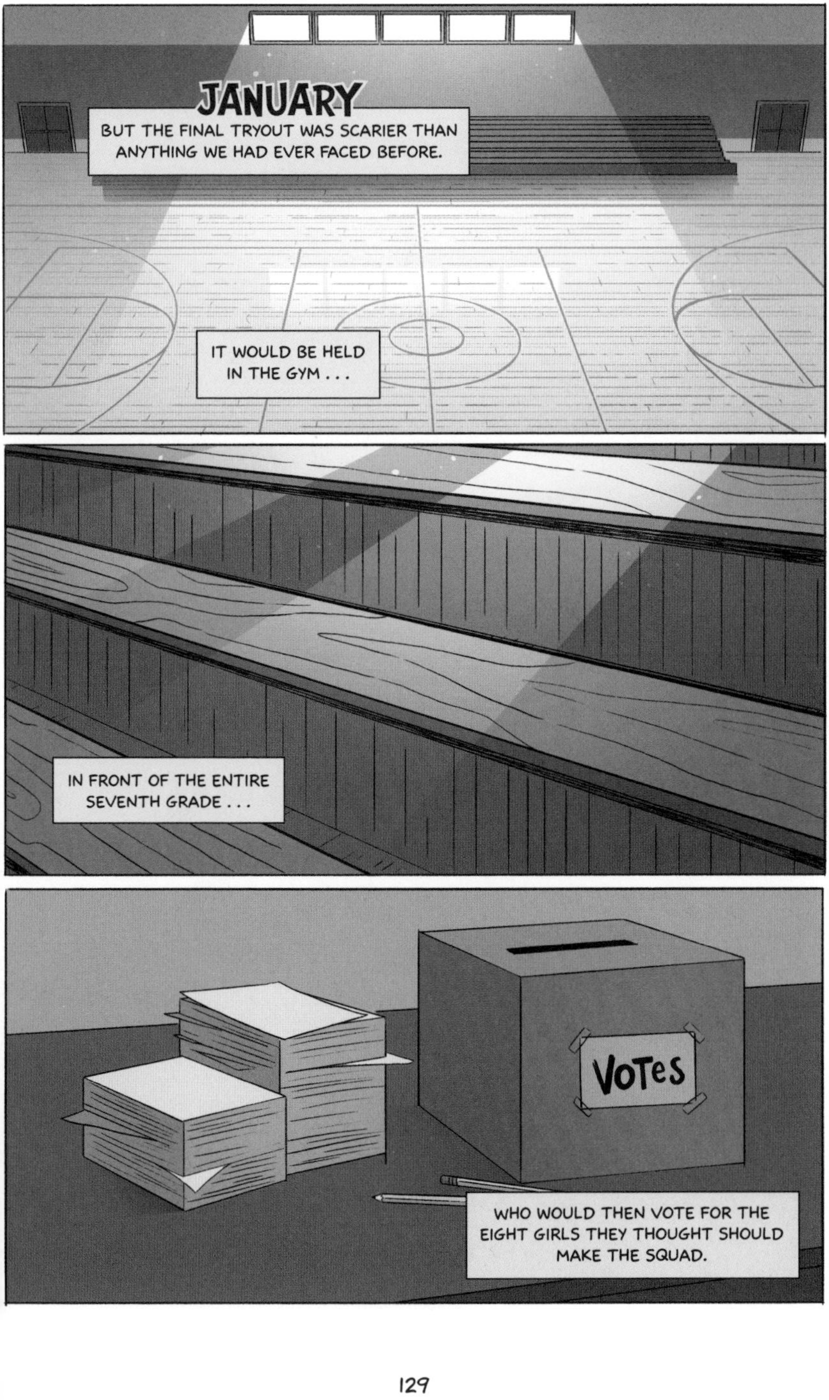
JANUARY
BUT THE FINAL TRYOUT WAS SCARIER THAN ANYTHING WE HAD EVER FACED BEFORE.
IT WOULD BE HELD IN THE GYM . . .
IN FRONT OF THE ENTIRE SEVENTH GRADE . . .
VOTES
WHO WOULD THEN VOTE FOR THE EIGHT GIRLS THEY THOUGHT SHOULD MAKE THE SQUAD.

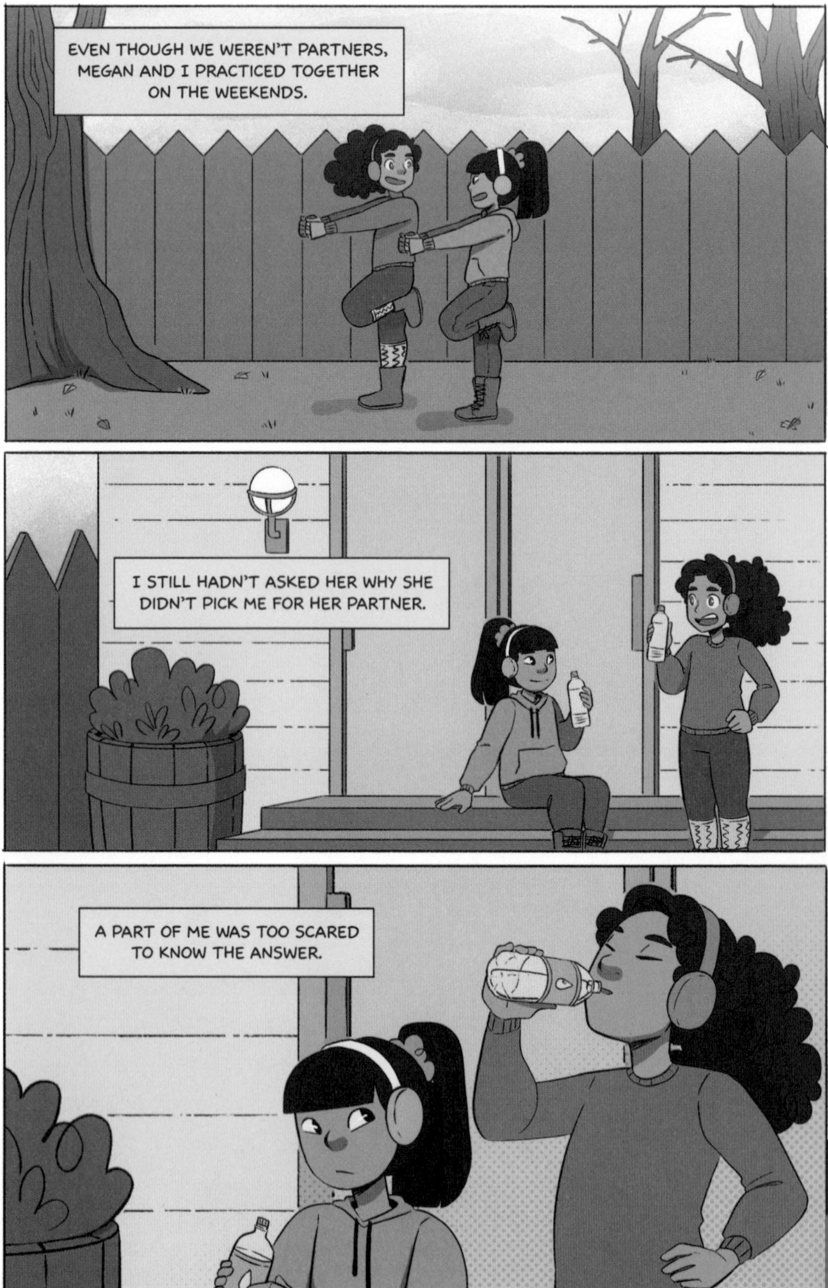
EVEN THOUGH WE WEREN'T PARTNERS, MEGAN AND I PRACTICED TOGETHER ON THE WEEKENDS.
I STILL HADN'T ASKED HER WHY SHE DIDN'T PICK ME FOR HER PARTNER.
A PART OF ME WAS TOO SCARED TO KNOW THE ANSWER.

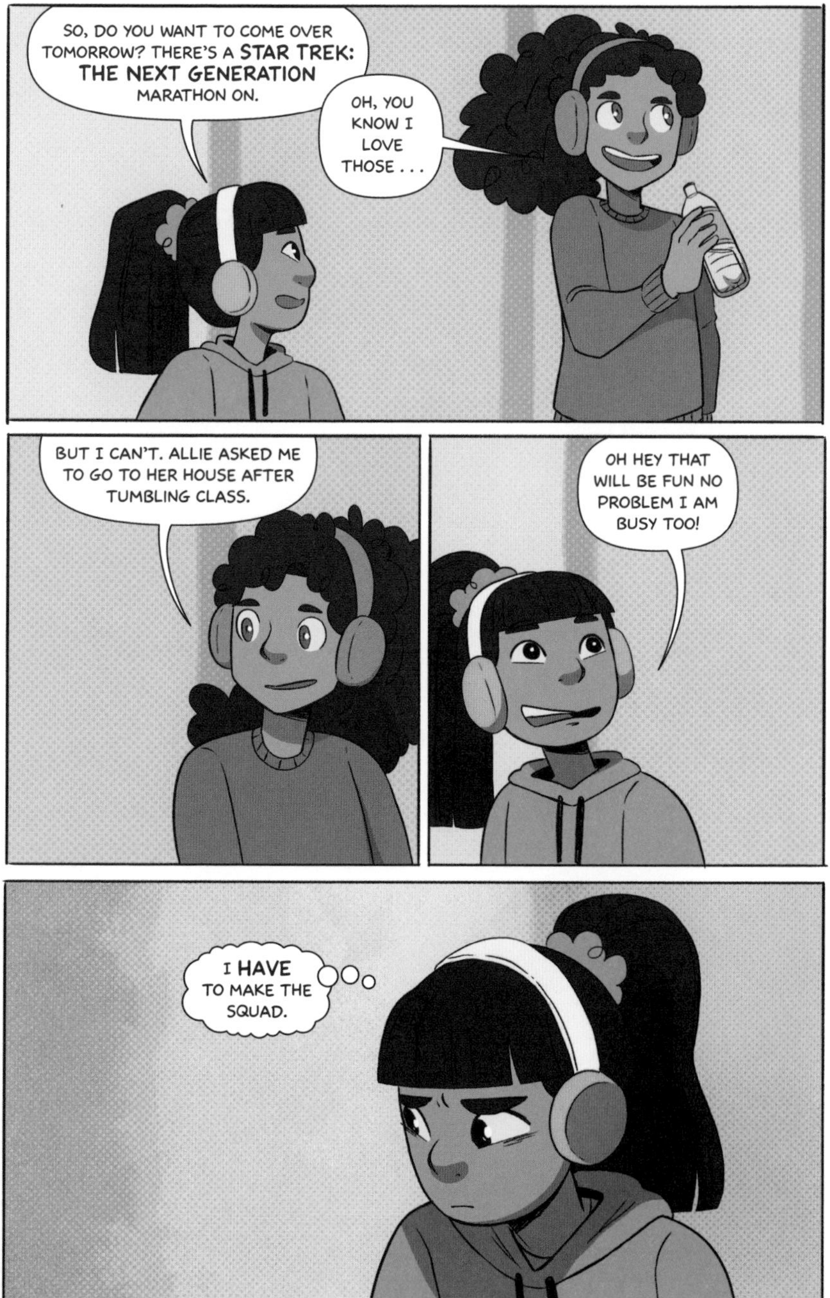
SO, DO YOU WANT TO COME OVER TOMORROW? THERE'S A **STAR TREK: THE NEXT GENERATION** MARATHON ON.
OH, YOU KNOW I LOVE THOSE . . .
BUT I CAN'T. ALLIE ASKED ME TO GO TO HER HOUSE AFTER TUMBLING CLASS.
OH HEY THAT WILL BE FUN NO PROBLEM I AM BUSY TOO!
I **HAVE** TO MAKE THE SQUAD.

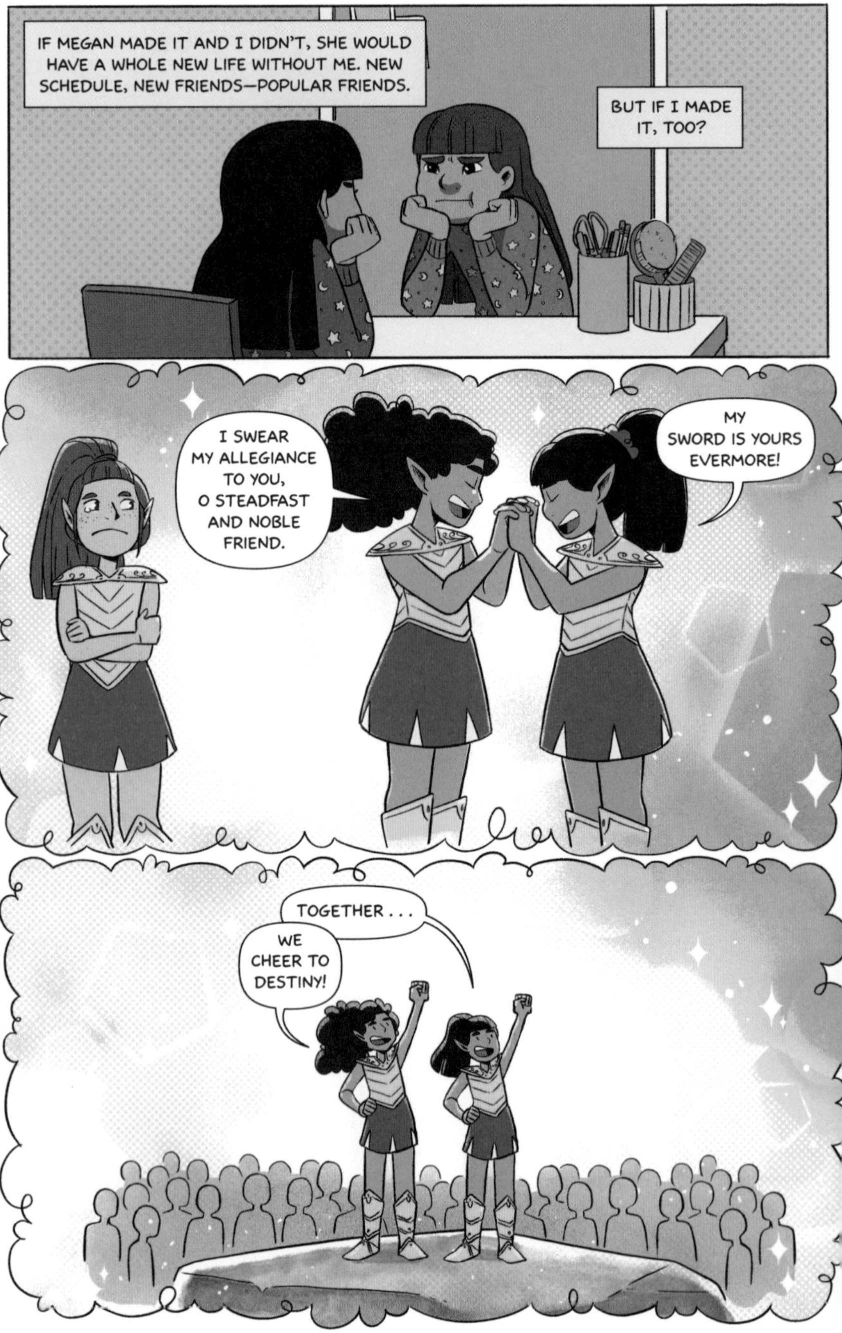
IF MEGAN MADE IT AND I DIDN'T, SHE WOULD HAVE A WHOLE NEW LIFE WITHOUT ME. NEW SCHEDULE, NEW FRIENDS—POPULAR FRIENDS.
BUT IF I MADE IT, TOO?
I SWEAR MY ALLEGIANCE TO YOU, O STEADFAST AND NOBLE FRIEND.
MY SWORD IS YOURS EVERMORE!
TOGETHER . . .
WE CHEER TO DESTINY!

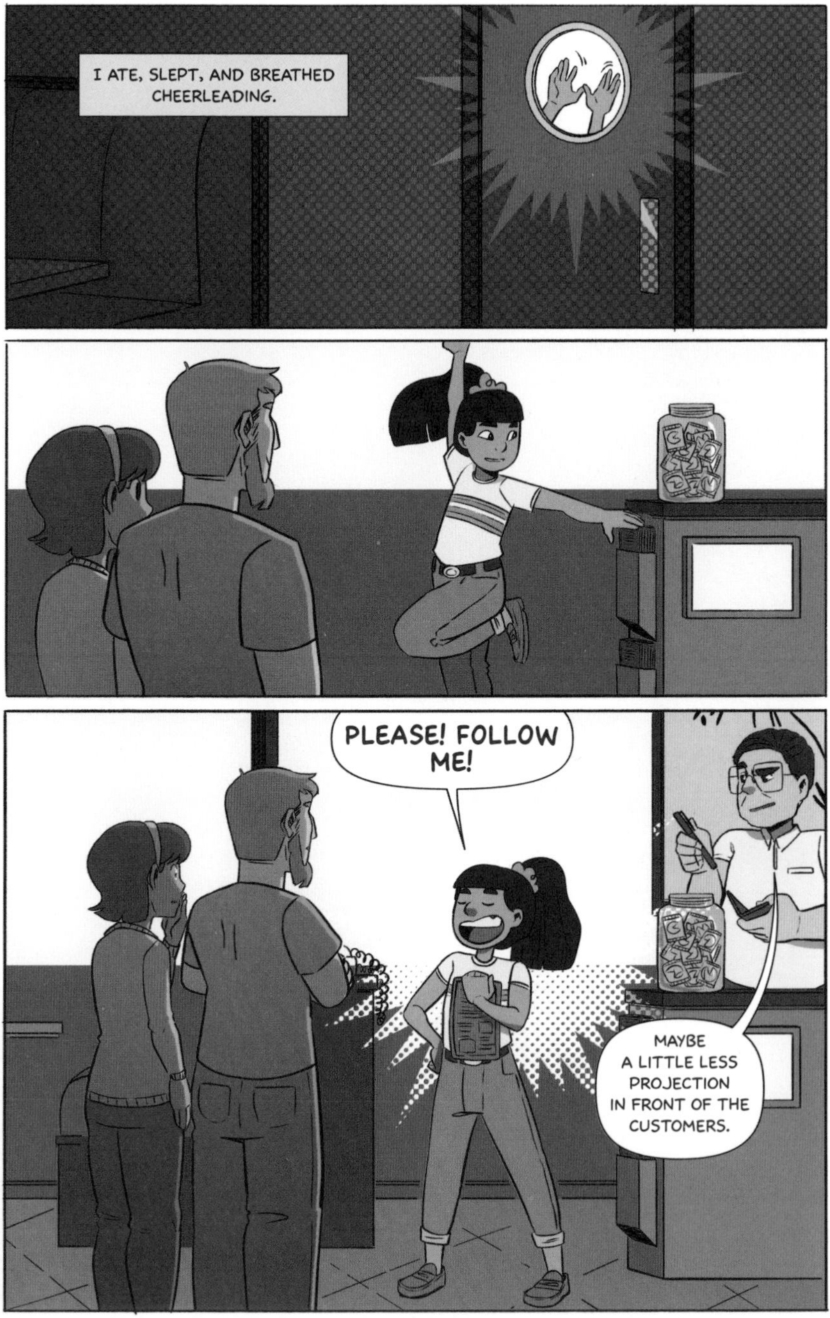
I ATE, SLEPT, AND BREATHED CHEERLEADING.
PLEASE! FOLLOW ME!
MAYBE A LITTLE LESS PROJECTION IN FRONT OF THE CUSTOMERS.

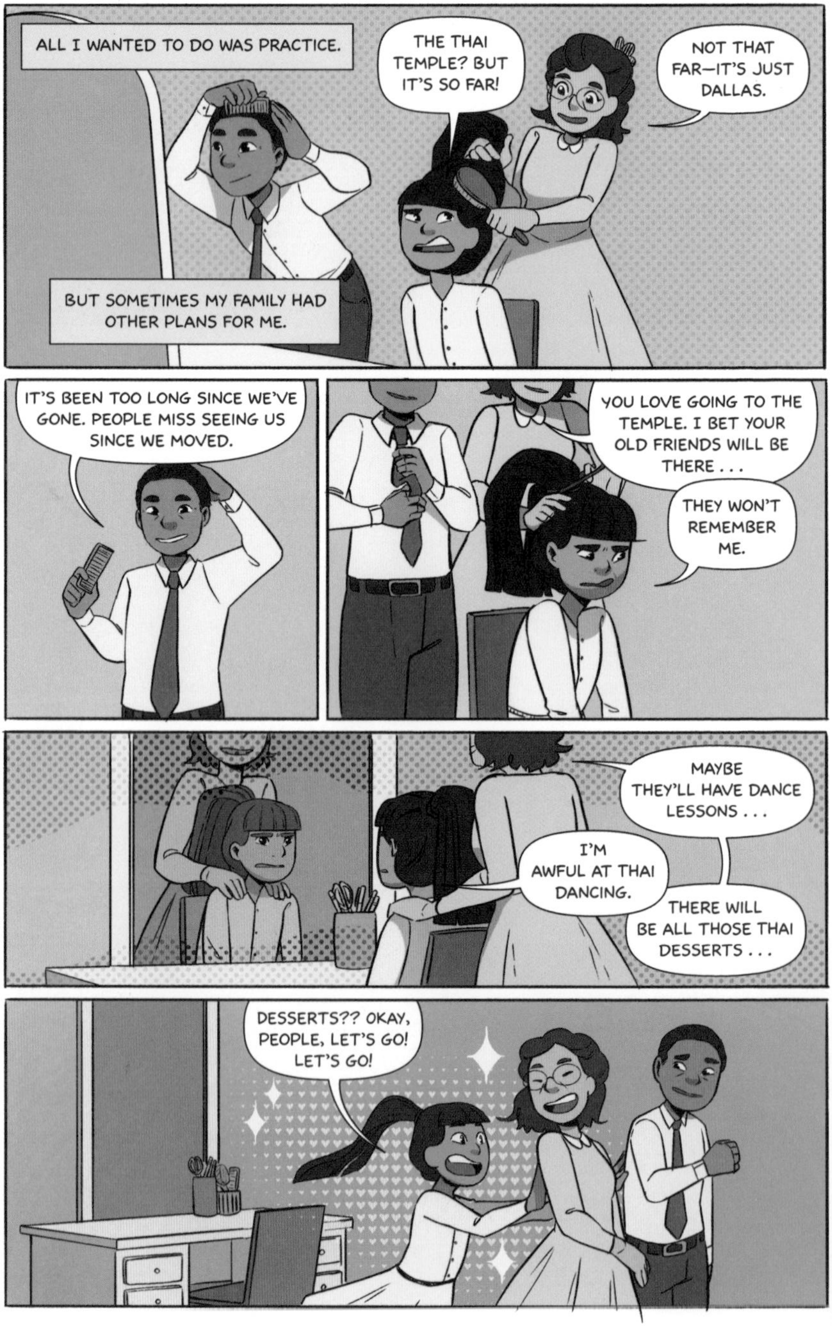
ALL I WANTED TO DO WAS PRACTICE.
THE THAI TEMPLE? BUT IT'S SO FAR!
NOT THAT FAR—IT'S JUST DALLAS.
BUT SOMETIMES MY FAMILY HAD OTHER PLANS FOR ME.
IT'S BEEN TOO LONG SINCE WE'VE GONE. PEOPLE MISS SEEING US SINCE WE MOVED.
YOU LOVE GOING TO THE TEMPLE. I BET YOUR OLD FRIENDS WILL BE THERE . . .
THEY WON'T REMEMBER ME.
MAYBE THEY'LL HAVE DANCE LESSONS . . .
I'M AWFUL AT THAI DANCING.
THERE WILL BE ALL THOSE THAI DESSERTS . . .
DESSERTS?? OKAY, PEOPLE, LET'S GO! LET'S GO!

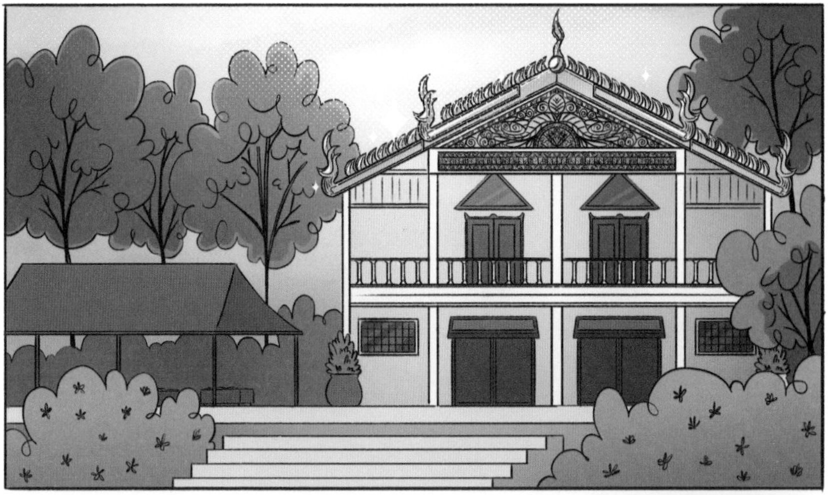

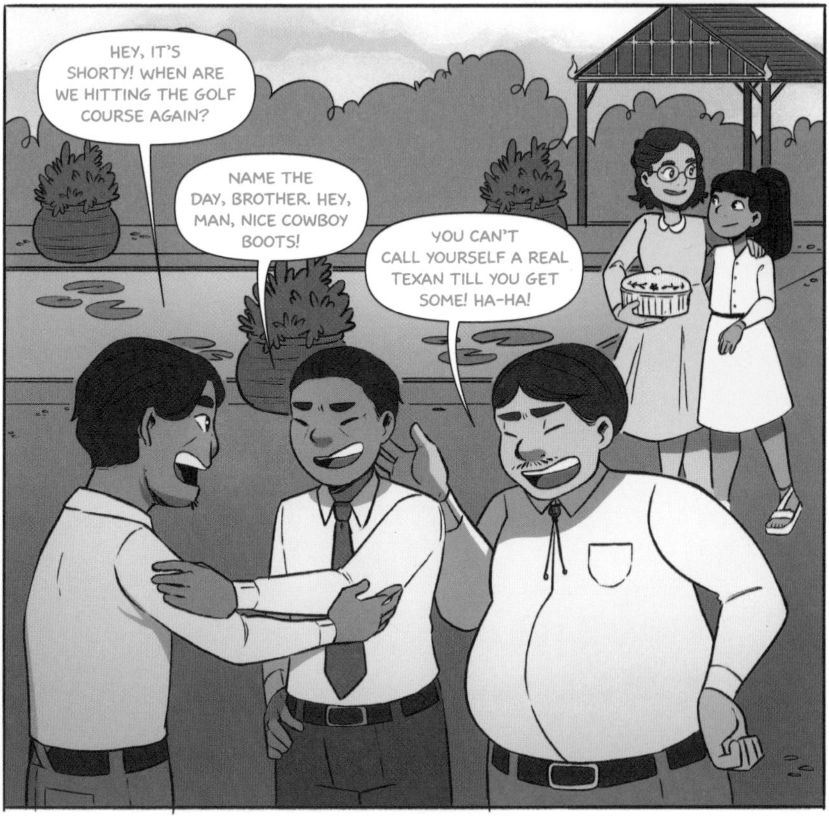
HEY, IT'S SHORTY! WHEN ARE WE HITTING THE GOLF COURSE AGAIN?
NAME THE DAY, BROTHER. HEY, MAN, NICE COWBOY BOOTS!
YOU CAN'T CALL YOURSELF A REAL TEXAN TILL YOU GET SOME! HA-HA!

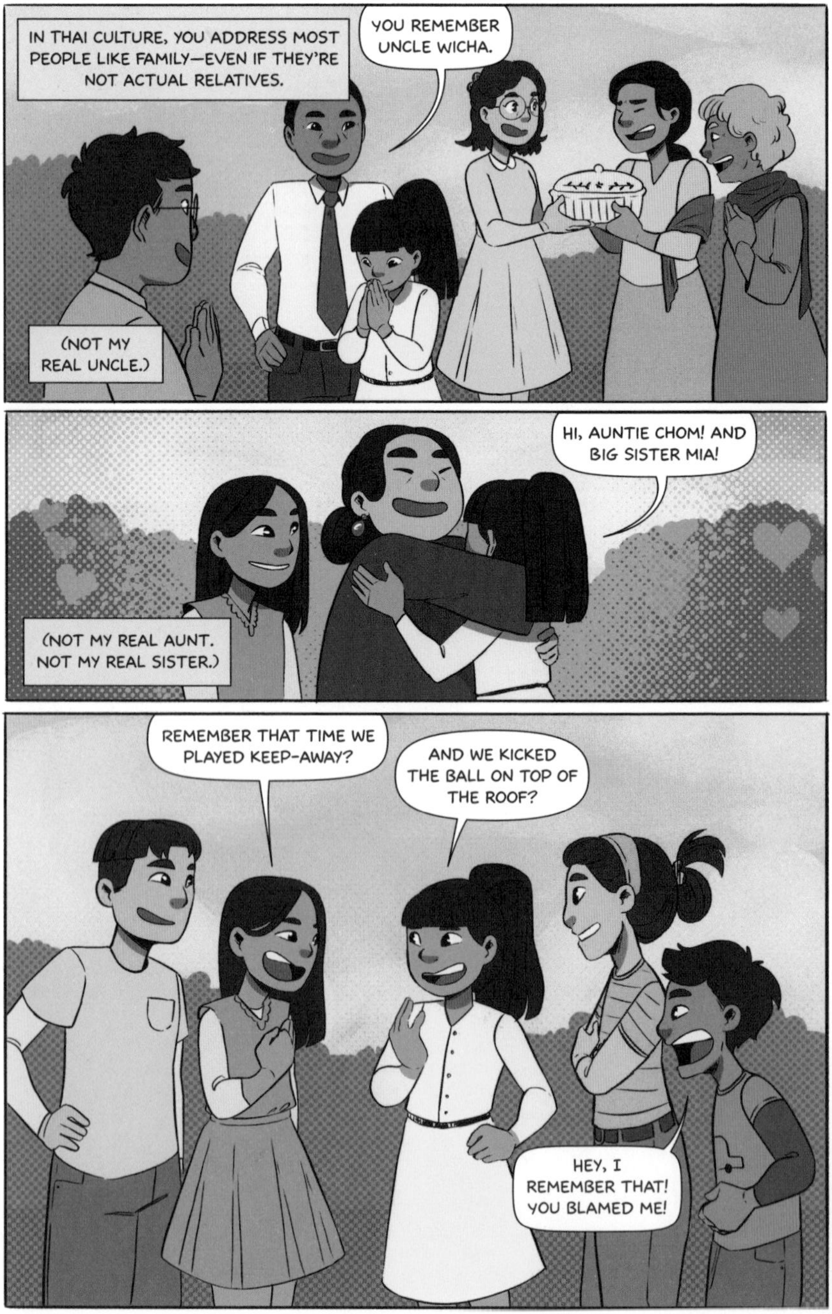
IN THAI CULTURE, YOU ADDRESS MOST PEOPLE LIKE FAMILY—EVEN IF THEY'RE NOT ACTUAL RELATIVES.
YOU REMEMBER UNCLE WICHA.
(NOT MY REAL UNCLE.)
HI, AUNTIE CHOM! AND BIG SISTER MIA!
(NOT MY REAL AUNT. NOT MY REAL SISTER.)
REMEMBER THAT TIME WE PLAYED KEEP-AWAY?
AND WE KICKED THE BALL ON TOP OF THE ROOF?
HEY, I REMEMBER THAT! YOU BLAMED ME!

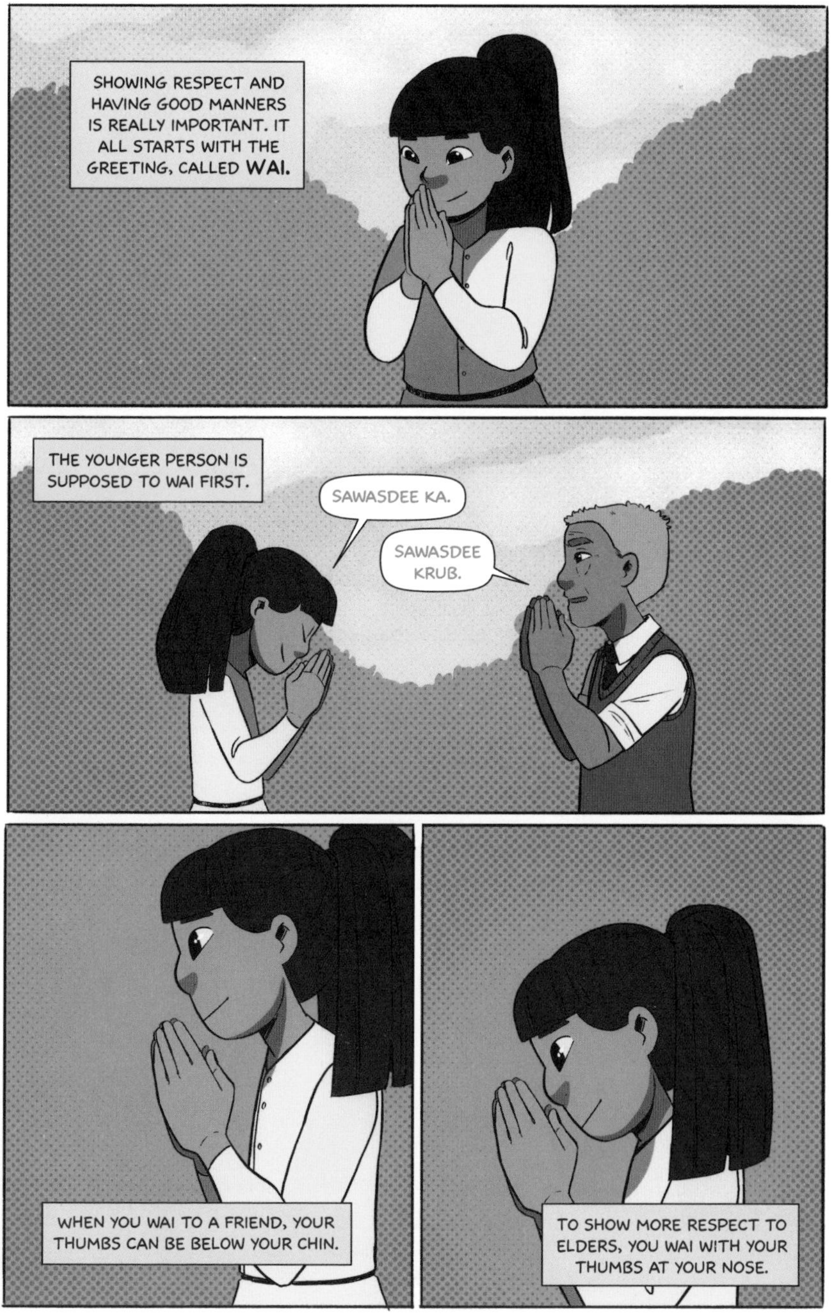
SHOWING RESPECT AND HAVING GOOD MANNERS IS REALLY IMPORTANT. IT ALL STARTS WITH THE GREETING, CALLED **WAI.**
THE YOUNGER PERSON IS SUPPOSED TO WAI FIRST.
SAWASDEE KA.
SAWASDEE KRUB.
WHEN YOU WAI TO A FRIEND, YOUR THUMBS CAN BE BELOW YOUR CHIN.
TO SHOW MORE RESPECT TO ELDERS, YOU WAI WITH YOUR THUMBS AT YOUR NOSE.

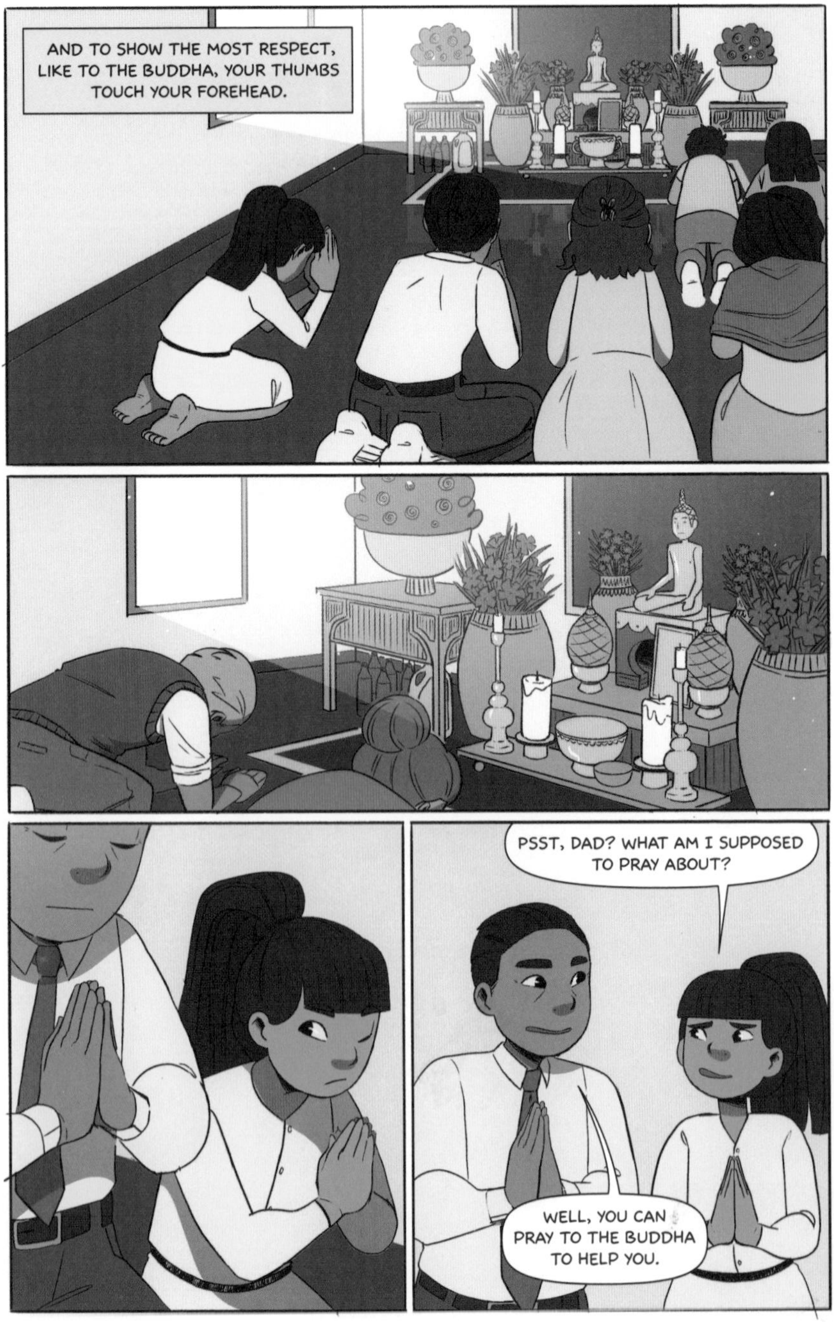
AND TO SHOW THE MOST RESPECT, LIKE TO THE BUDDHA, YOUR THUMBS TOUCH YOUR FOREHEAD.
PSST, DAD? WHAT AM I SUPPOSED TO PRAY ABOUT?
WELL, YOU CAN PRAY TO THE BUDDHA TO HELP YOU.

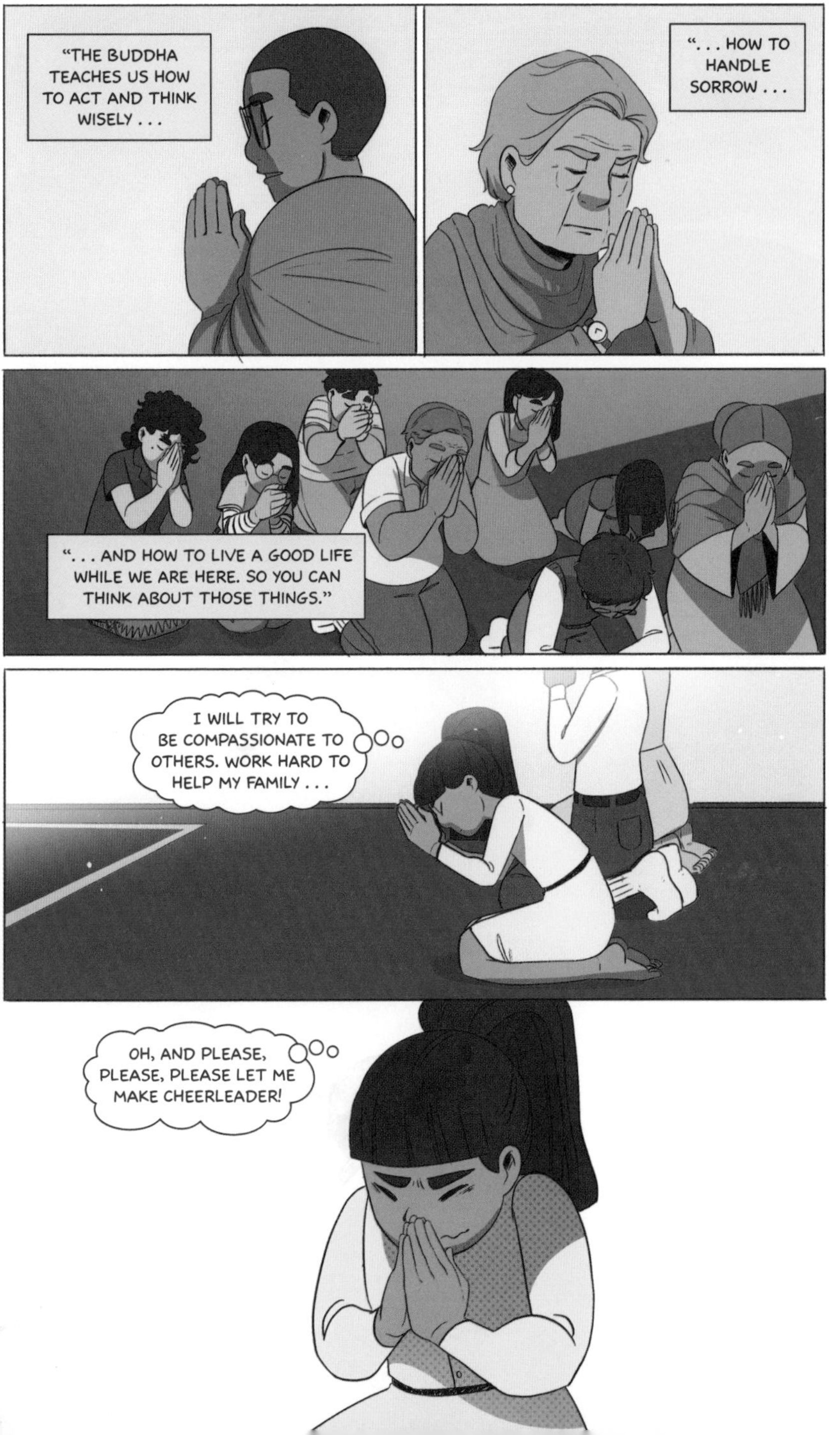
"THE BUDDHA TEACHES US HOW TO ACT AND THINK WISELY . . .
". . . HOW TO HANDLE SORROW . . .
". . . AND HOW TO LIVE A GOOD LIFE WHILE WE ARE HERE. SO YOU CAN THINK ABOUT THOSE THINGS."
I WILL TRY TO BE COMPASSIONATE TO OTHERS. WORK HARD TO HELP MY FAMILY . . .
OH, AND PLEASE, PLEASE, PLEASE LET ME MAKE CHEERLEADER!

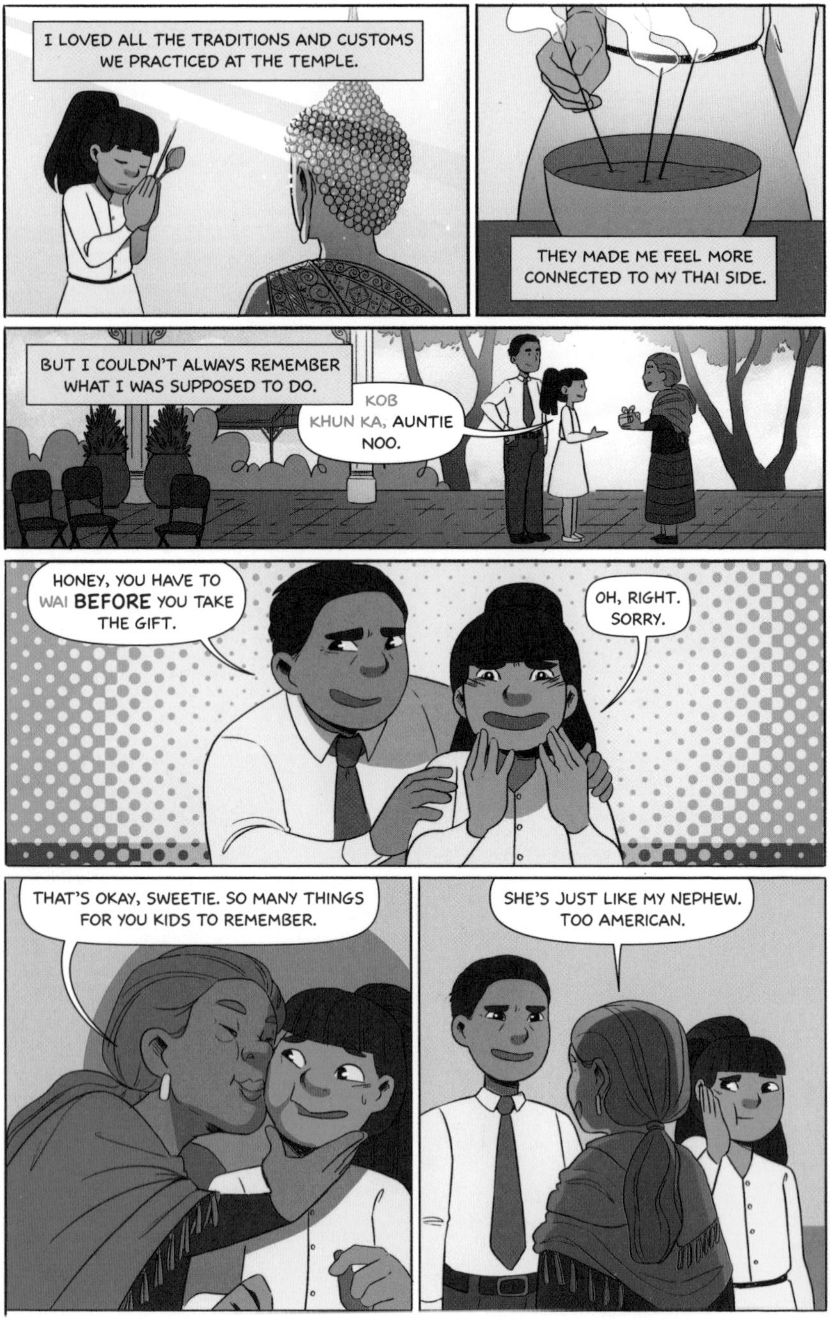
I LOVED ALL THE TRADITIONS AND CUSTOMS WE PRACTICED AT THE TEMPLE.
THEY MADE ME FEEL MORE CONNECTED TO MY THAI SIDE.
BUT I COULDN'T ALWAYS REMEMBER WHAT I WAS SUPPOSED TO DO.
KOB KHUN KA, AUNTIE NOO.
HONEY, YOU HAVE TO WAI **BEFORE** YOU TAKE THE GIFT.
OH, RIGHT. SORRY.
THAT'S OKAY, SWEETIE. SO MANY THINGS FOR YOU KIDS TO REMEMBER.
SHE'S JUST LIKE MY NEPHEW. TOO AMERICAN.

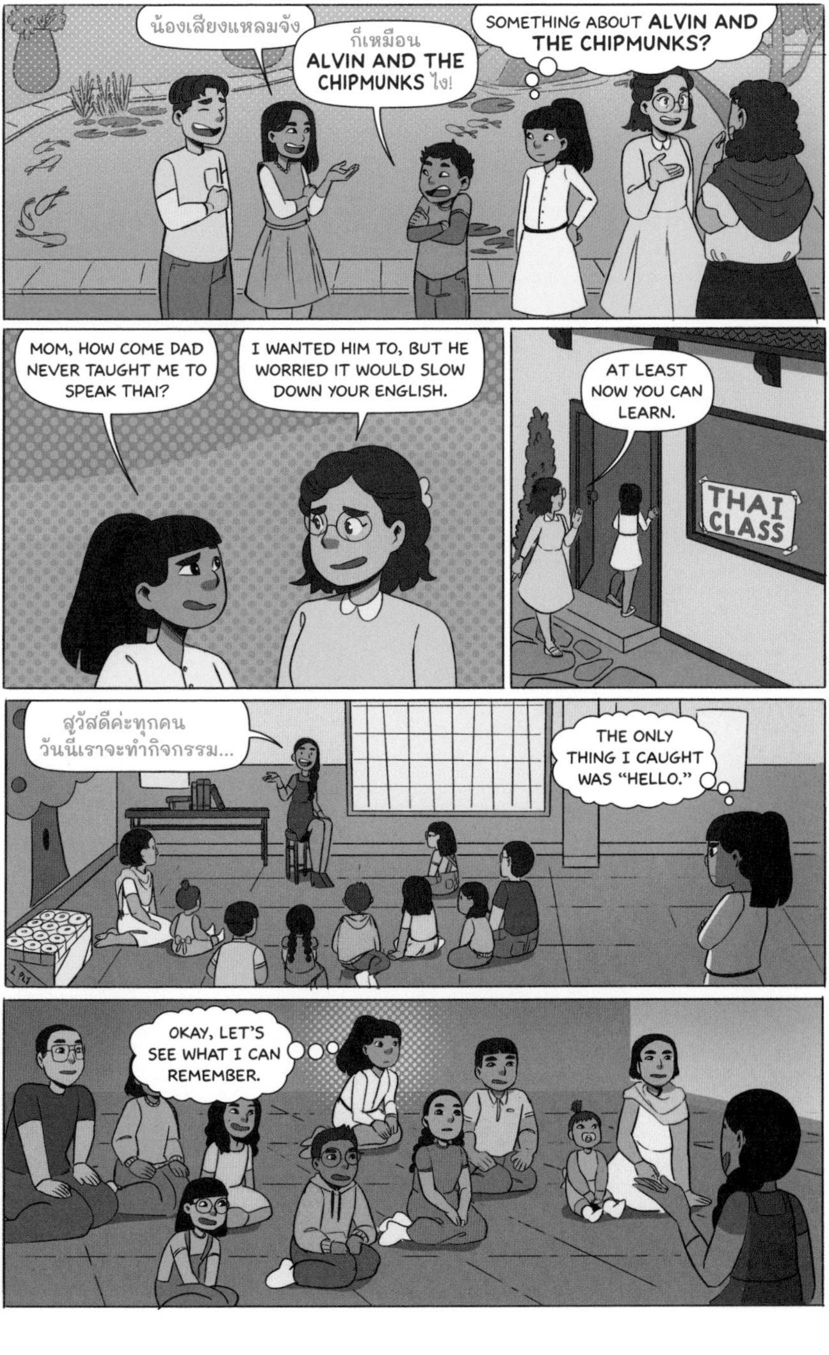
น้องเสียงแหลมจัง
ก็เหมือน ALVIN AND THE CHIPMUNKS ไง!
SOMETHING ABOUT ALVIN AND THE CHIPMUNKS?
MOM, HOW COME DAD NEVER TAUGHT ME TO SPEAK THAI?
I WANTED HIM TO, BUT HE WORRIED IT WOULD SLOW DOWN YOUR ENGLISH.
AT LEAST NOW YOU CAN LEARN.
THAI CLASS
สูวัสดีค่ะทุกคน วันนี้เราจะทำกิจกรรม...
THE ONLY THING I CAUGHT WAS "HELLO."
OKAY, LET'S SEE WHAT I CAN REMEMBER.

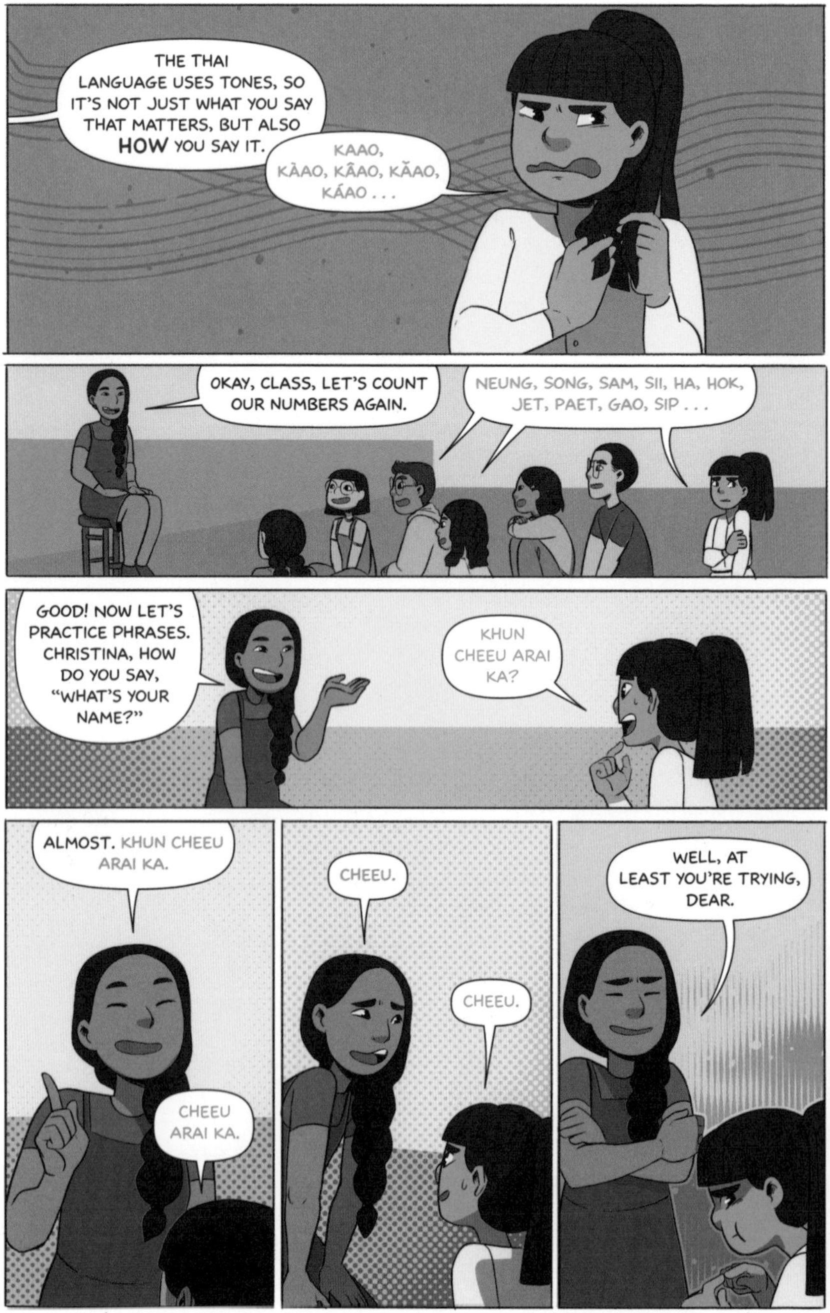
THE THAI LANGUAGE USES TONES, SO IT'S NOT JUST WHAT YOU SAY THAT MATTERS, BUT ALSO **HOW** YOU SAY IT.
KAAO, KÀAO, KÂAO, KǍAO, KÁAO . . .
OKAY, CLASS, LET'S COUNT OUR NUMBERS AGAIN.
NEUNG, SONG, SAM, SII, HA, HOK, JET, PAET, GAO, SIP . . .
GOOD! NOW LET'S PRACTICE PHRASES. CHRISTINA, HOW DO YOU SAY, "WHAT'S YOUR NAME?"
KHUN CHEEU ARAI KA?
ALMOST. KHUN CHEEU ARAI KA.
CHEEU ARAI KA.
CHEEU.
CHEEU.
WELL, AT LEAST YOU'RE TRYING, DEAR.

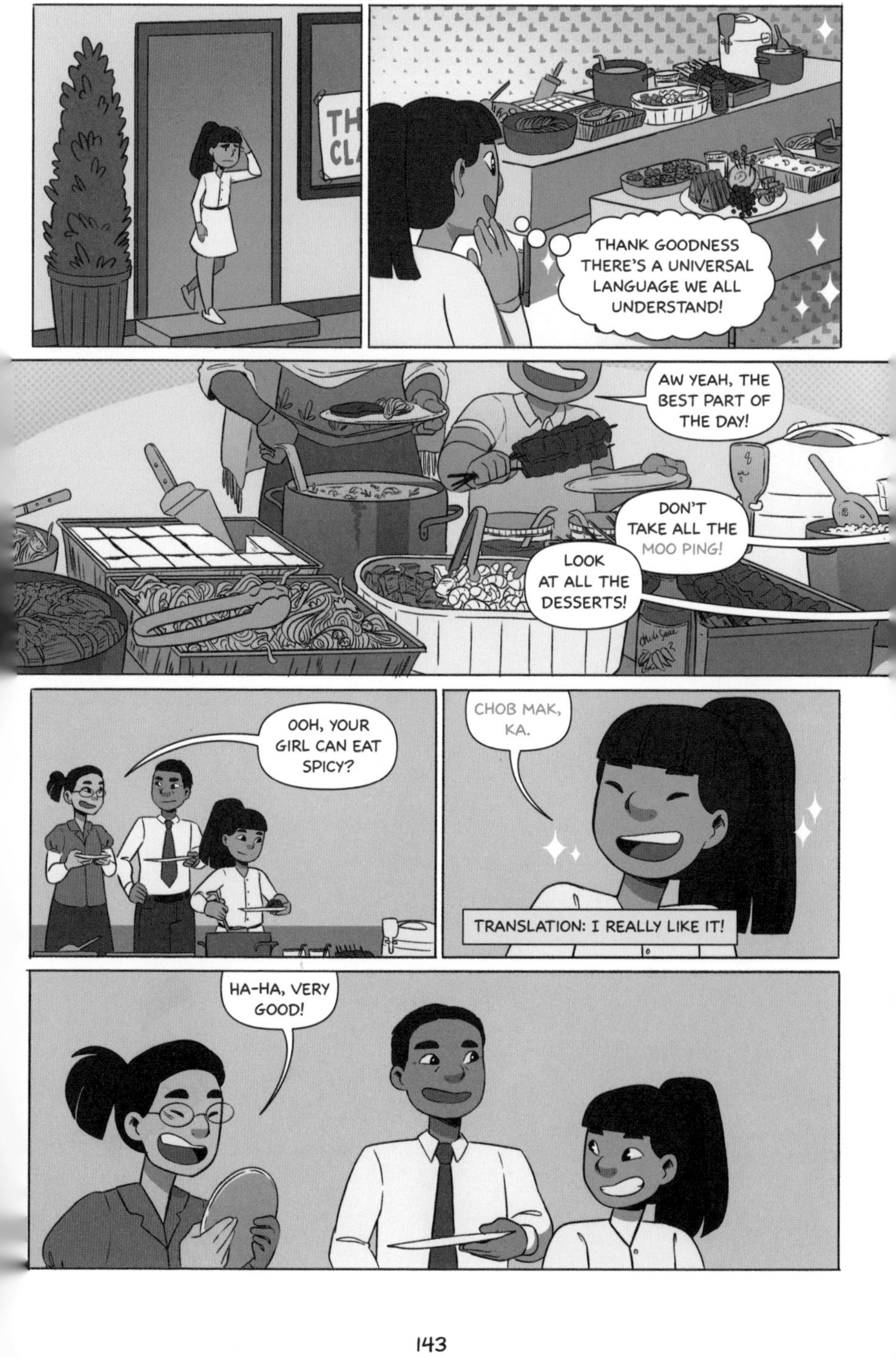
THANK GOODNESS THERE'S A UNIVERSAL LANGUAGE WE ALL UNDERSTAND!
AW YEAH, THE BEST PART OF THE DAY!
DON'T TAKE ALL THE MOO PING!
LOOK AT ALL THE DESSERTS!
OOH, YOUR GIRL CAN EAT SPICY?
CHOB MAK, KA.
TRANSLATION: I REALLY LIKE IT!
HA-HA, VERY GOOD!

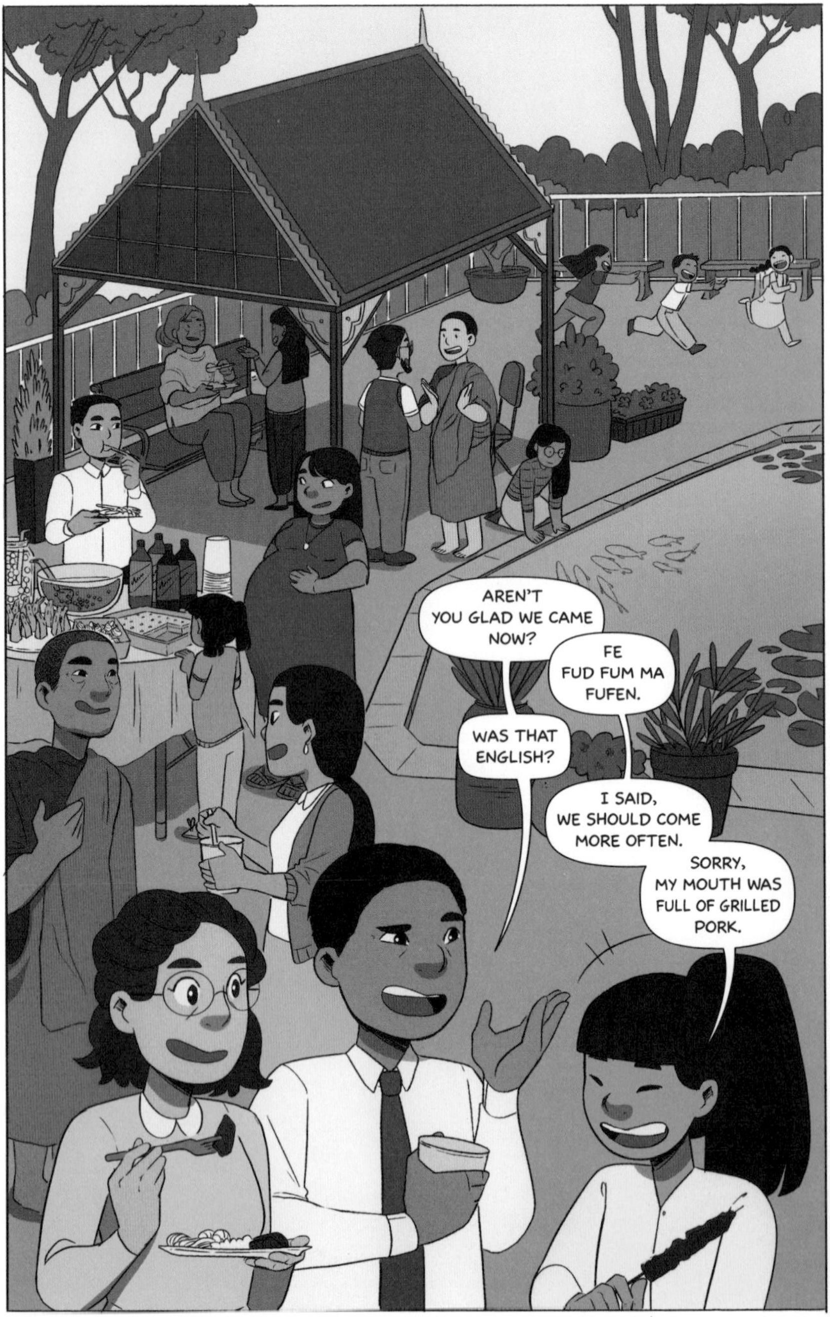
AREN'T YOU GLAD WE CAME NOW?
FE FUD FUM MA FUFEN.
WAS THAT ENGLISH?
I SAID, WE SHOULD COME MORE OFTEN.
SORRY, MY MOUTH WAS FULL OF GRILLED PORK.

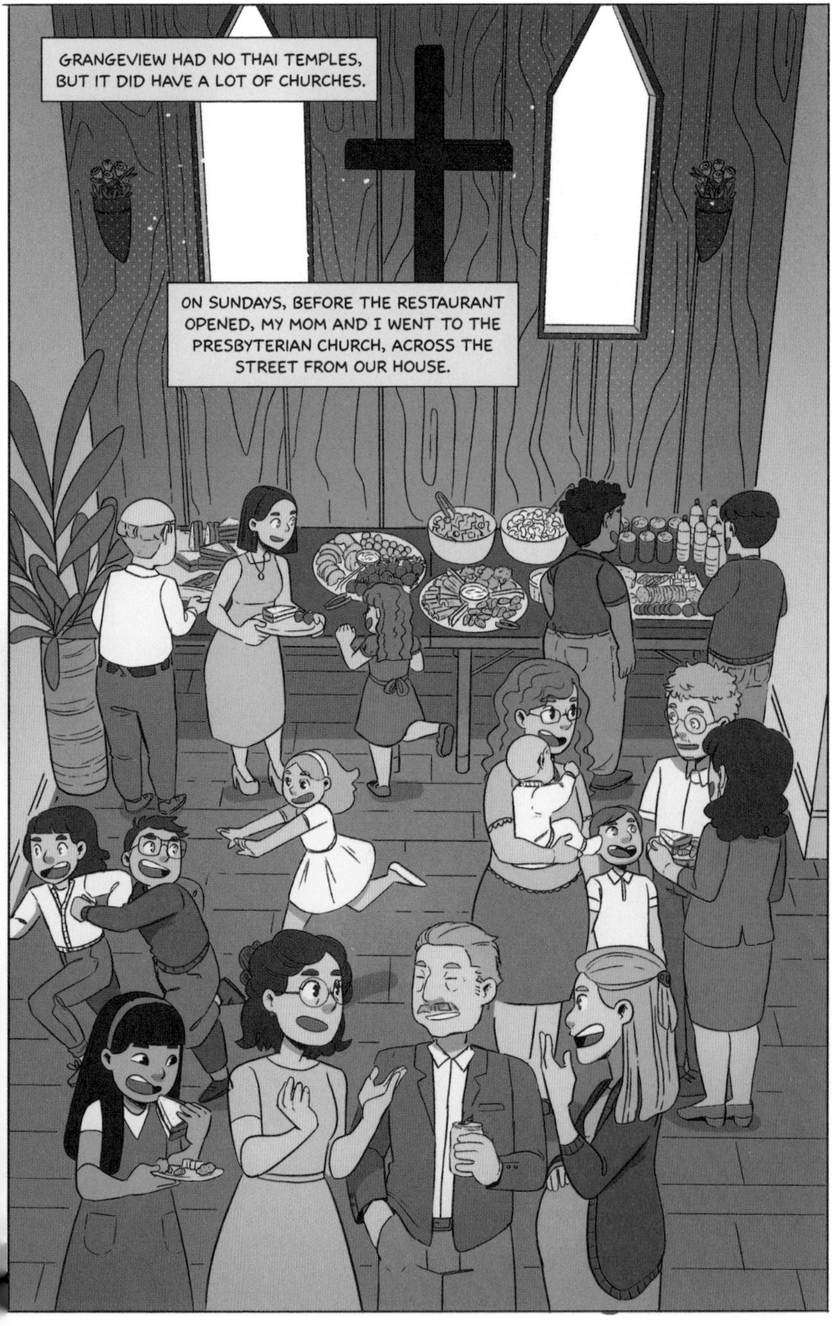
GRANGEVIEW HAD NO THAI TEMPLES, BUT IT DID HAVE A LOT OF CHURCHES.
ON SUNDAYS, BEFORE THE RESTAURANT OPENED, MY MOM AND I WENT TO THE PRESBYTERIAN CHURCH, ACROSS THE STREET FROM OUR HOUSE.

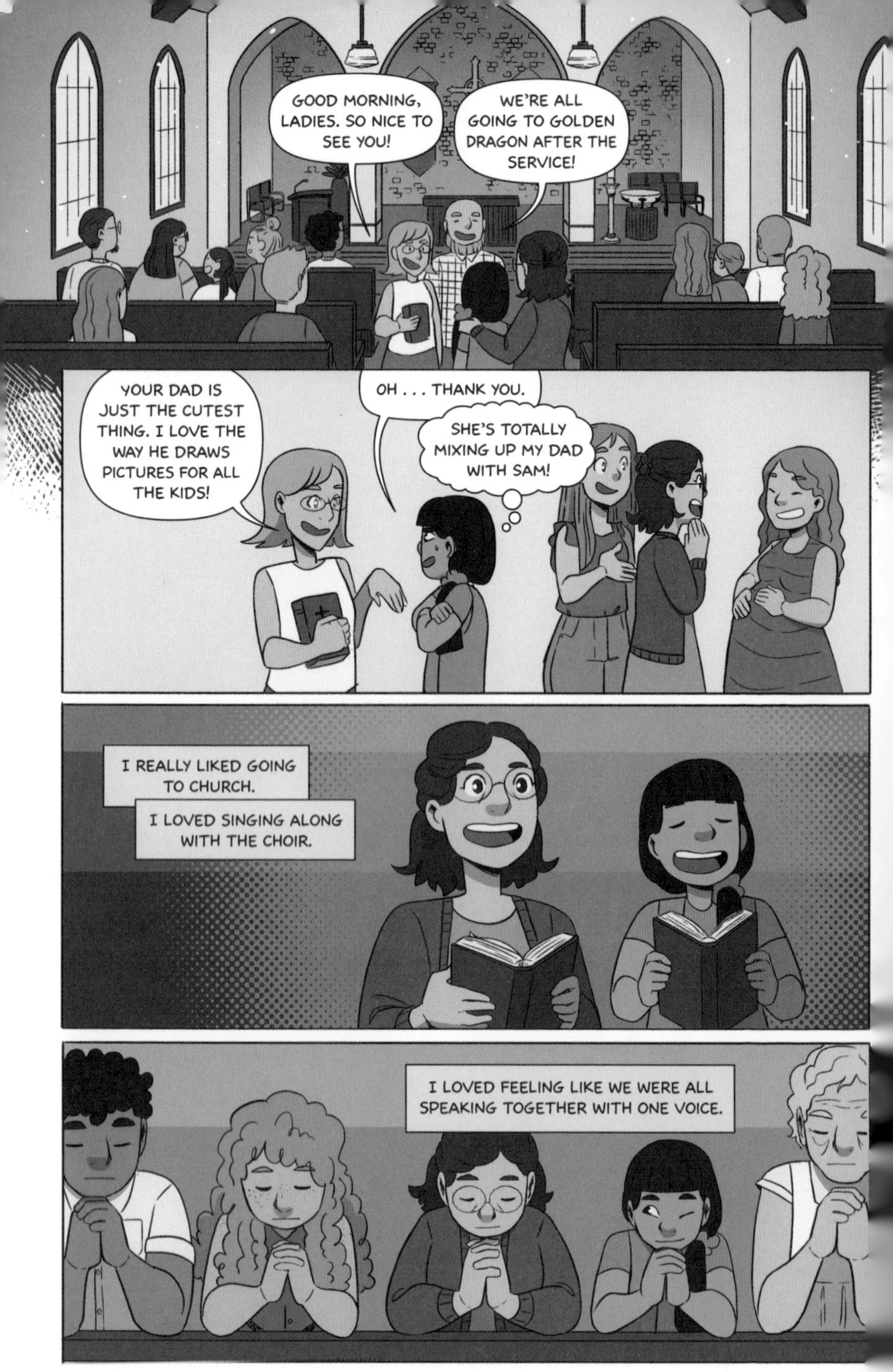
GOOD MORNING, LADIES. SO NICE TO SEE YOU!
WE'RE ALL GOING TO GOLDEN DRAGON AFTER THE SERVICE!
YOUR DAD IS JUST THE CUTEST THING. I LOVE THE WAY HE DRAWS PICTURES FOR ALL THE KIDS!
OH . . . THANK YOU.
SHE'S TOTALLY MIXING UP MY DAD WITH SAM!
I REALLY LIKED GOING TO CHURCH.
I LOVED SINGING ALONG WITH THE CHOIR.
I LOVED FEELING LIKE WE WERE ALL SPEAKING TOGETHER WITH ONE VOICE.

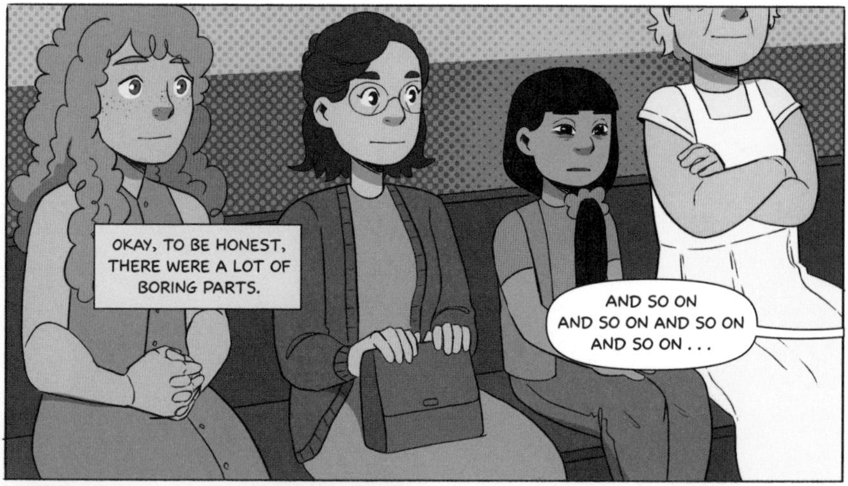
OKAY, TO BE HONEST, THERE WERE A LOT OF BORING PARTS.
AND SO ON AND SO ON AND SO ON AND SO ON . . .

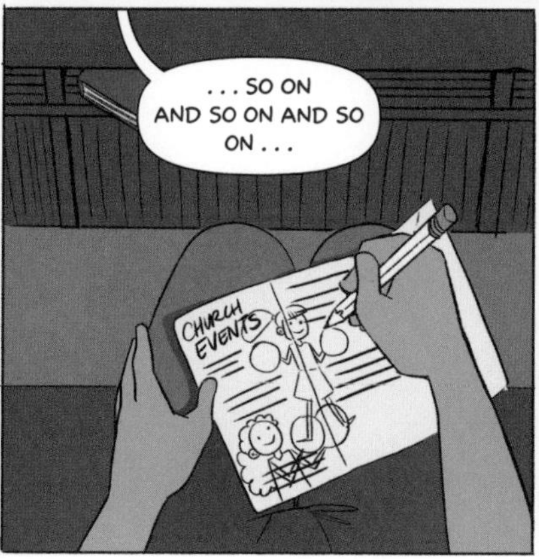
. . . SO ON AND SO ON AND SO ON . . .
CHURCH EVENTS

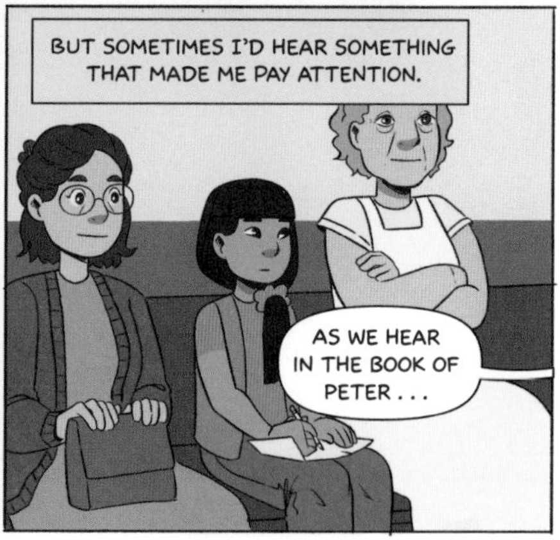
BUT SOMETIMES I'D HEAR SOMETHING THAT MADE ME PAY ATTENTION.
AS WE HEAR IN THE BOOK OF PETER . . .

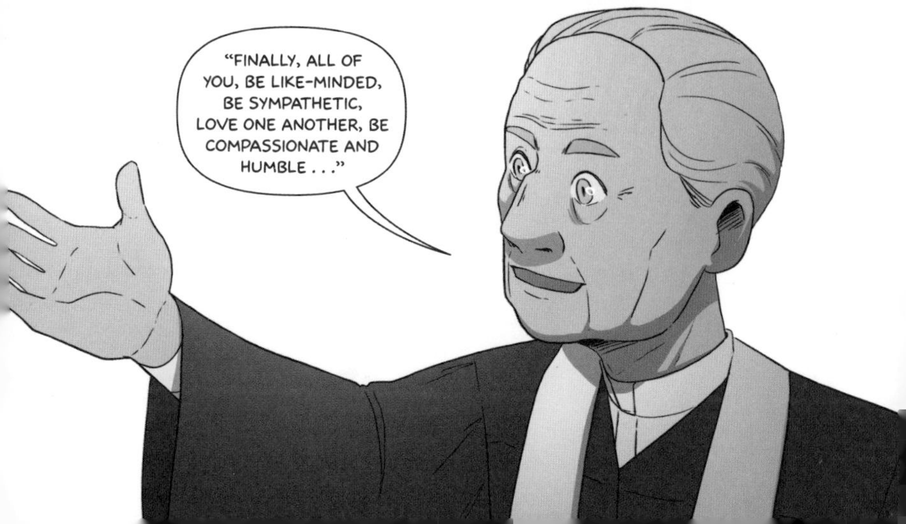
"FINALLY, ALL OF YOU, BE LIKE-MINDED, BE SYMPATHETIC, LOVE ONE ANOTHER, BE COMPASSIONATE AND HUMBLE . . ."

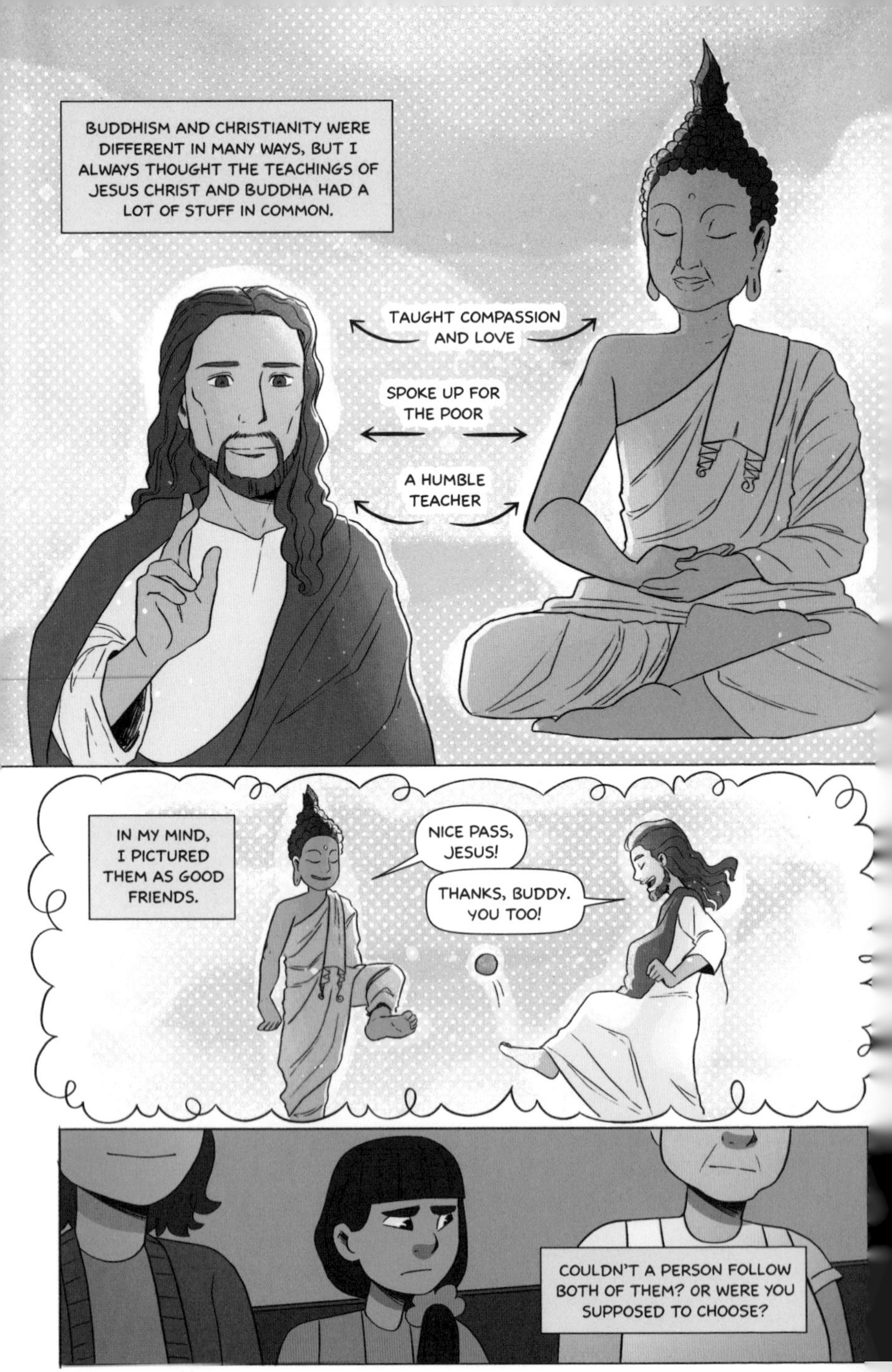
BUDDHISM AND CHRISTIANITY WERE DIFFERENT IN MANY WAYS, BUT I ALWAYS THOUGHT THE TEACHINGS OF JESUS CHRIST AND BUDDHA HAD A LOT OF STUFF IN COMMON.
TAUGHT COMPASSION AND LOVE
SPOKE UP FOR THE POOR
A HUMBLE TEACHER
IN MY MIND, I PICTURED THEM AS GOOD FRIENDS.
NICE PASS, JESUS!
THANKS, BUDDY. YOU TOO!
COULDN'T A PERSON FOLLOW BOTH OF THEM? OR WERE YOU SUPPOSED TO CHOOSE?

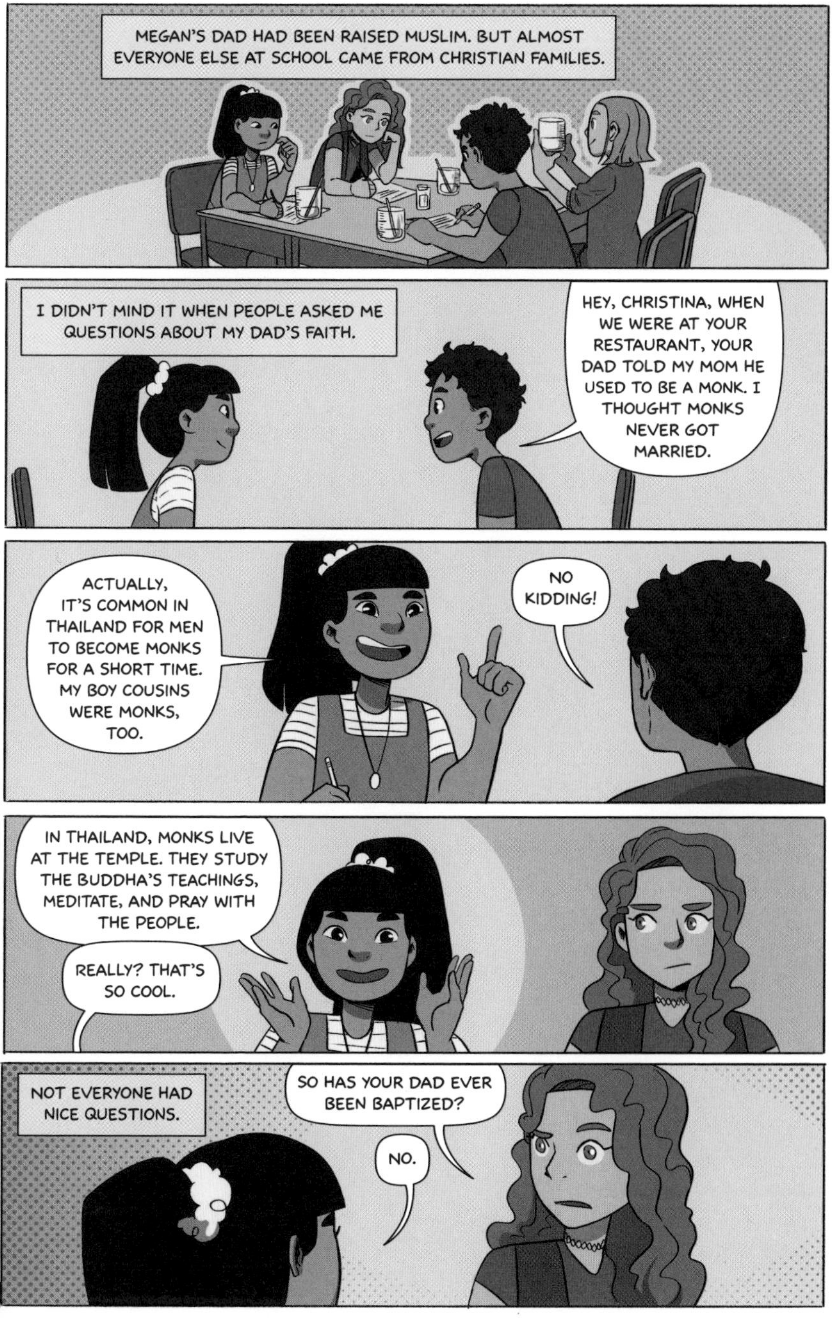
MEGAN'S DAD HAD BEEN RAISED MUSLIM. BUT ALMOST EVERYONE ELSE AT SCHOOL CAME FROM CHRISTIAN FAMILIES.
I DIDN'T MIND IT WHEN PEOPLE ASKED ME QUESTIONS ABOUT MY DAD'S FAITH.
HEY, CHRISTINA, WHEN WE WERE AT YOUR RESTAURANT, YOUR DAD TOLD MY MOM HE USED TO BE A MONK. I THOUGHT MONKS NEVER GOT MARRIED.
ACTUALLY, IT'S COMMON IN THAILAND FOR MEN TO BECOME MONKS FOR A SHORT TIME. MY BOY COUSINS WERE MONKS, TOO.
NO KIDDING!
IN THAILAND, MONKS LIVE AT THE TEMPLE. THEY STUDY THE BUDDHA'S TEACHINGS, MEDITATE, AND PRAY WITH THE PEOPLE.
REALLY? THAT'S SO COOL.
NOT EVERYONE HAD NICE QUESTIONS.
SO HAS YOUR DAD EVER BEEN BAPTIZED?
NO.

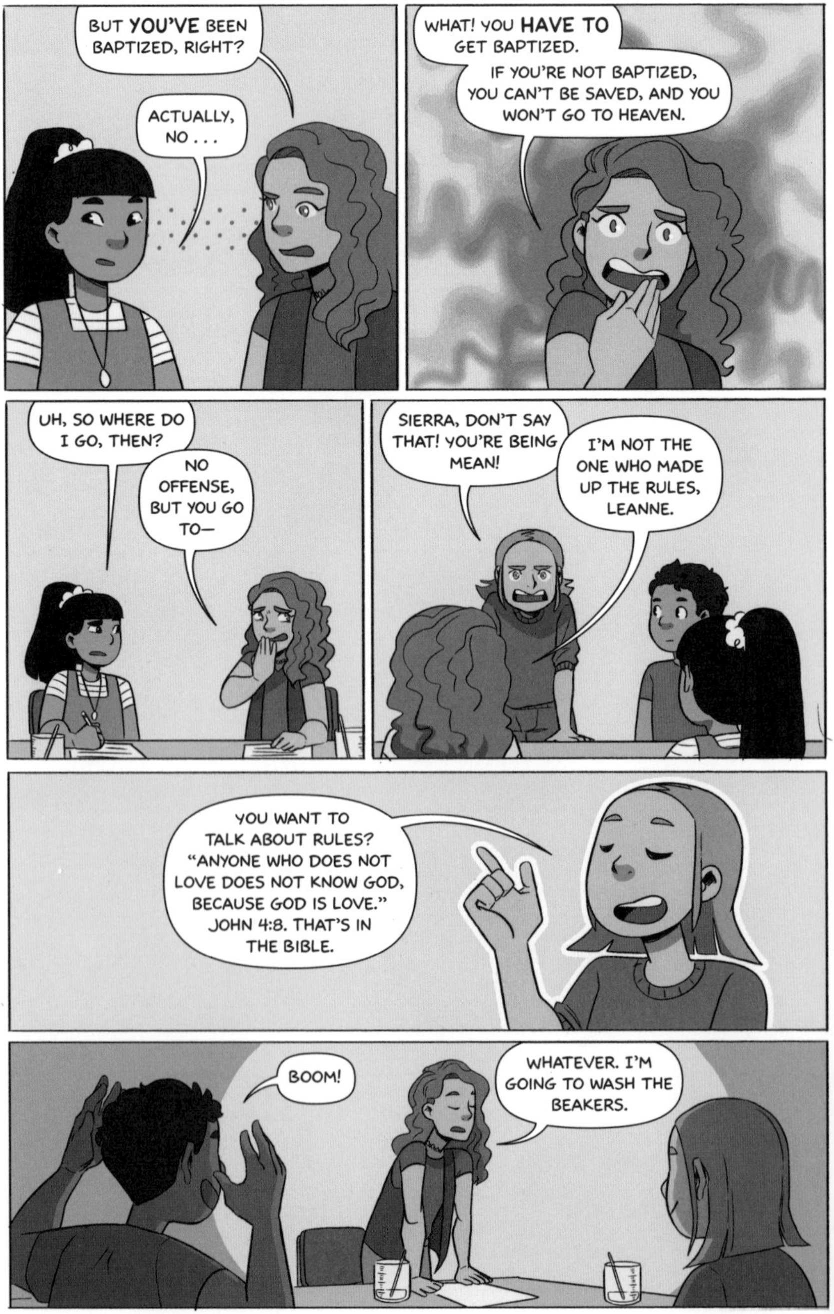
BUT **YOU'VE** BEEN BAPTIZED, RIGHT?
ACTUALLY, NO . . .
WHAT! YOU **HAVE TO** GET BAPTIZED.
IF YOU'RE NOT BAPTIZED, YOU CAN'T BE SAVED, AND YOU WON'T GO TO HEAVEN.
UH, SO WHERE DO I GO, THEN?
NO OFFENSE, BUT YOU GO TO—
SIERRA, DON'T SAY THAT! YOU'RE BEING MEAN!
I'M NOT THE ONE WHO MADE UP THE RULES, LEANNE.
YOU WANT TO TALK ABOUT RULES? "ANYONE WHO DOES NOT LOVE DOES NOT KNOW GOD, BECAUSE GOD IS LOVE." JOHN 4:8. THAT'S IN THE BIBLE.
BOOM!
WHATEVER. I'M GOING TO WASH THE BEAKERS.

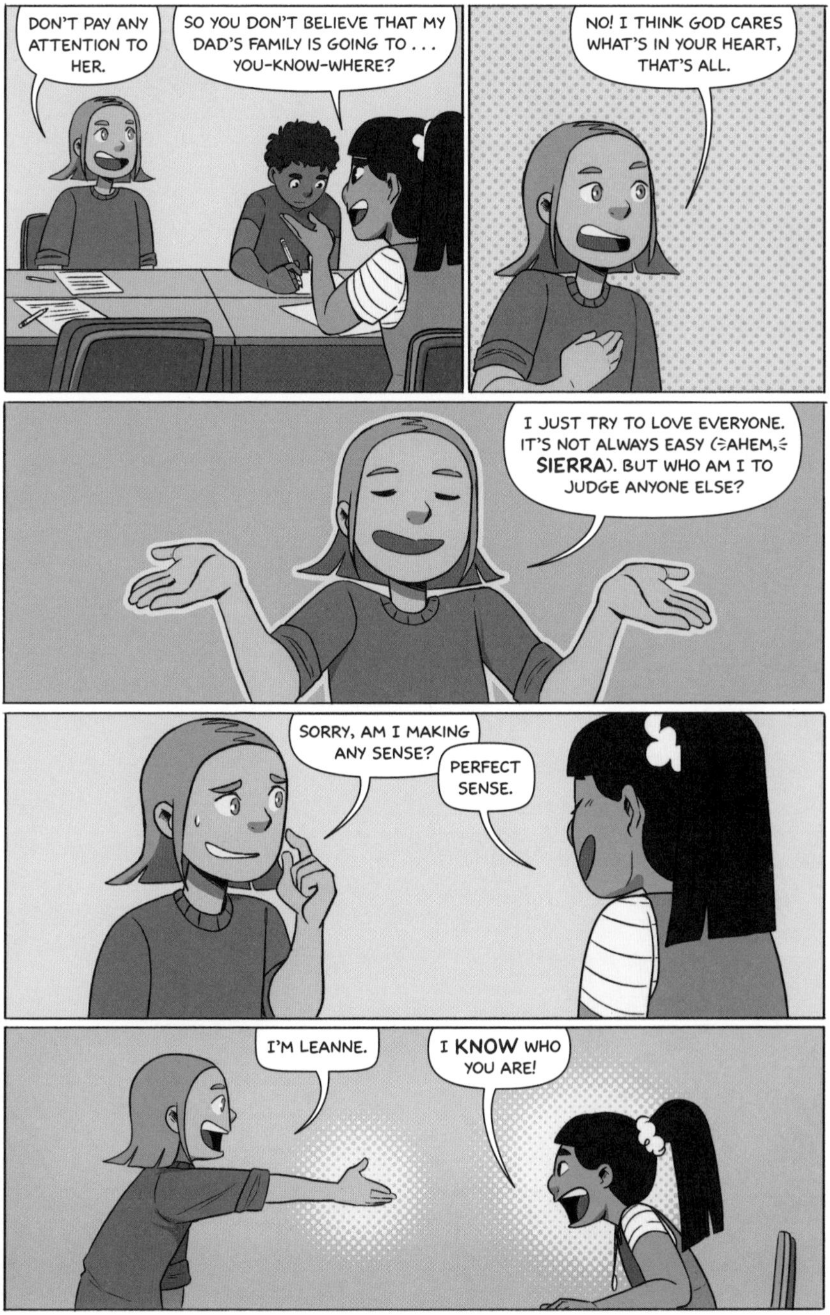
DON'T PAY ANY ATTENTION TO HER.
SO YOU DON'T BELIEVE THAT MY DAD'S FAMILY IS GOING TO . . . YOU-KNOW-WHERE?
NO! I THINK GOD CARES WHAT'S IN YOUR HEART, THAT'S ALL.
I JUST TRY TO LOVE EVERYONE. IT'S NOT ALWAYS EASY (AHEM, SIERRA). BUT WHO AM I TO JUDGE ANYONE ELSE?
SORRY, AM I MAKING ANY SENSE?
PERFECT SENSE.
I'M LEANNE.
I KNOW WHO YOU ARE!

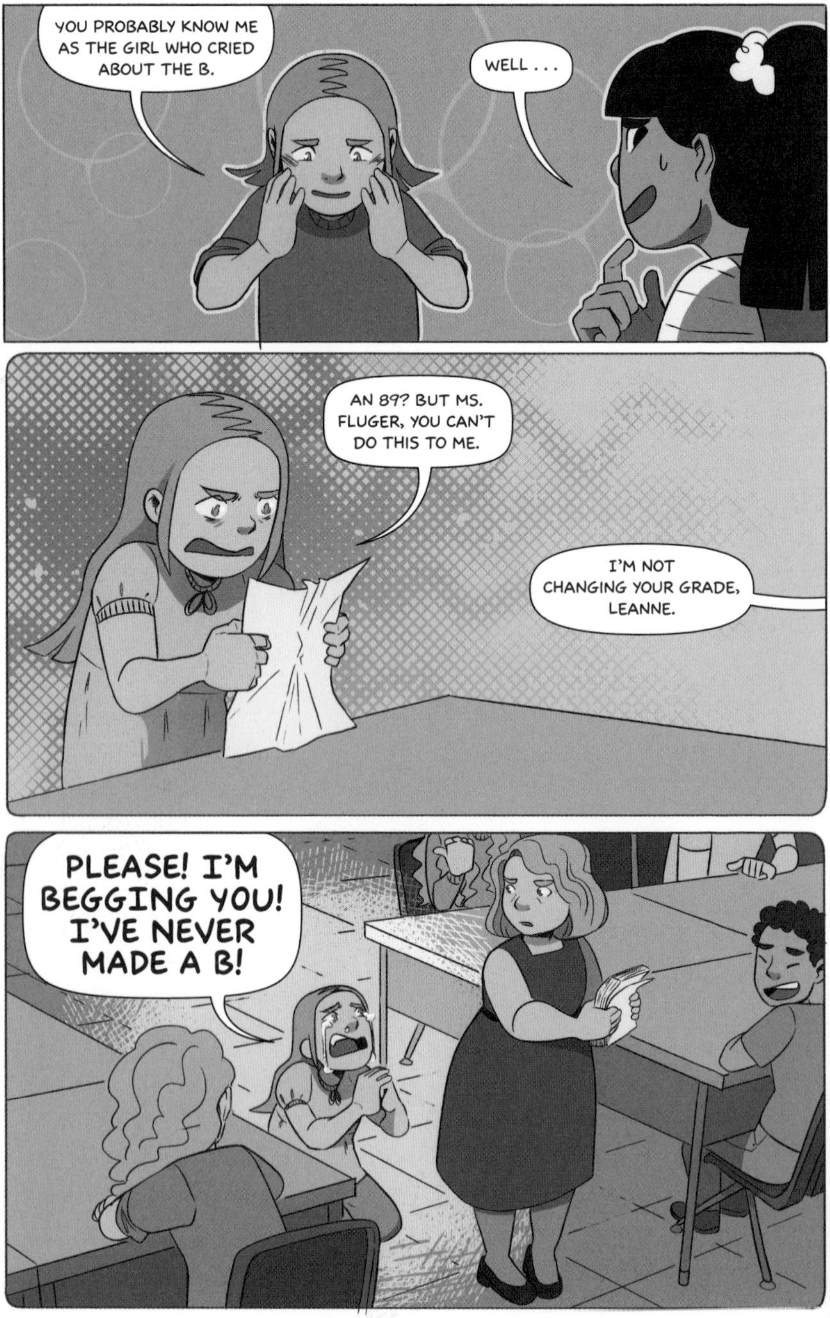

YOU PROBABLY KNOW ME AS THE GIRL WHO CRIED ABOUT THE B.
WELL . . .
AN 89? BUT MS. FLUGER, YOU CAN'T DO THIS TO ME.
I'M NOT CHANGING YOUR GRADE, LEANNE.
PLEASE! I'M BEGGING YOU! I'VE NEVER MADE A B!

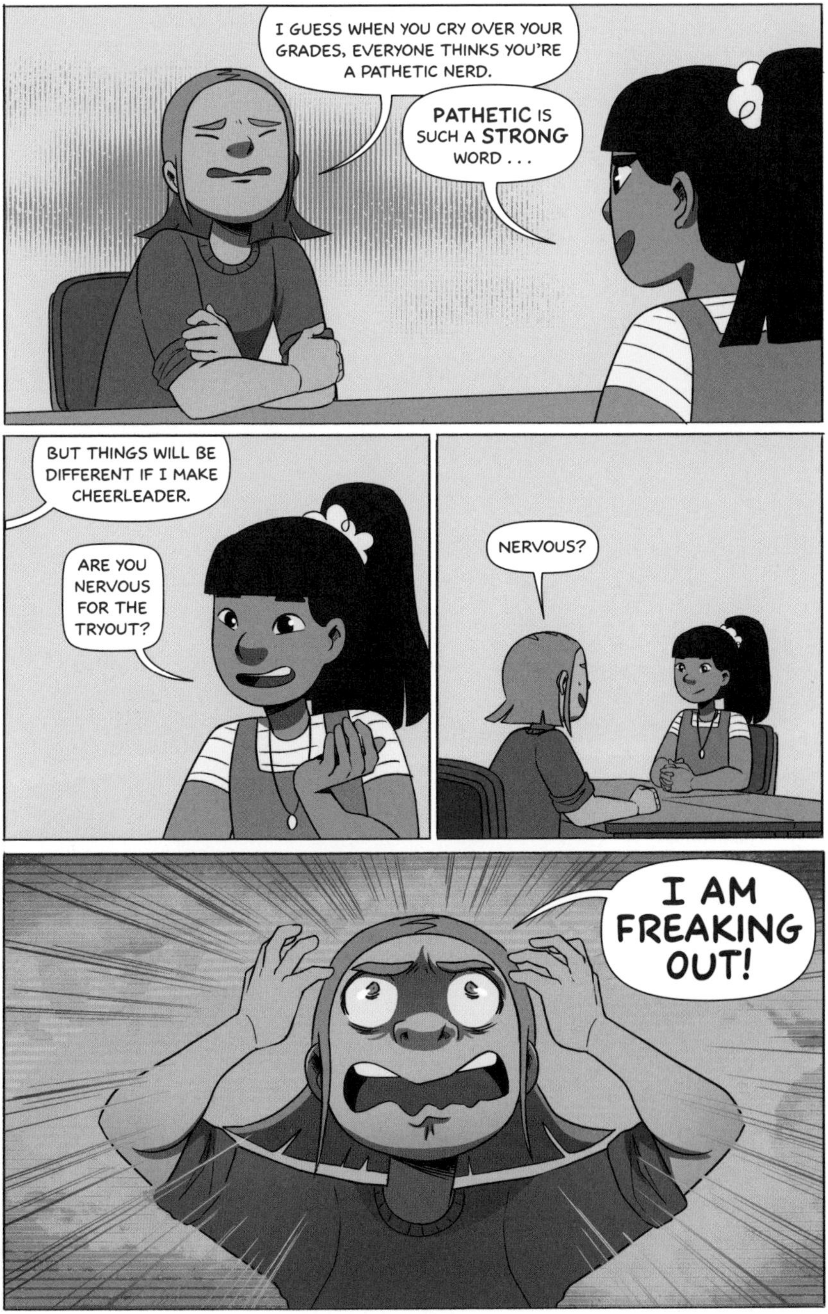
I GUESS WHEN YOU CRY OVER YOUR GRADES, EVERYONE THINKS YOU'RE A PATHETIC NERD.
PATHETIC IS SUCH A STRONG WORD . . .
BUT THINGS WILL BE DIFFERENT IF I MAKE CHEERLEADER.
ARE YOU NERVOUS FOR THE TRYOUT?
NERVOUS?
I AM FREAKING OUT!

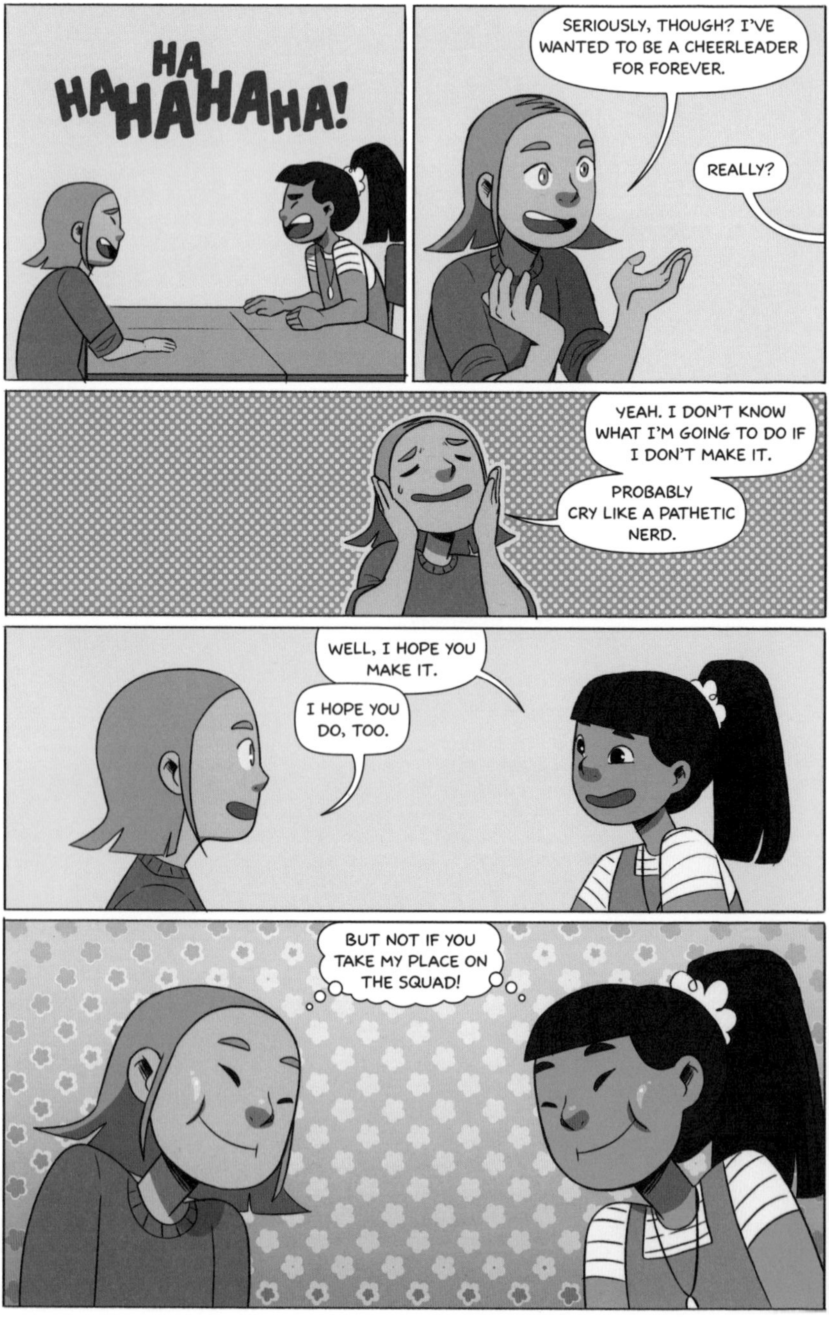
HA HA HA HA HA HA!
SERIOUSLY, THOUGH? I'VE WANTED TO BE A CHEERLEADER FOR FOREVER.
REALLY?
YEAH. I DON'T KNOW WHAT I'M GOING TO DO IF I DON'T MAKE IT.
PROBABLY CRY LIKE A PATHETIC NERD.
WELL, I HOPE YOU MAKE IT.
I HOPE YOU DO, TOO.
BUT NOT IF YOU TAKE MY PLACE ON THE SQUAD!

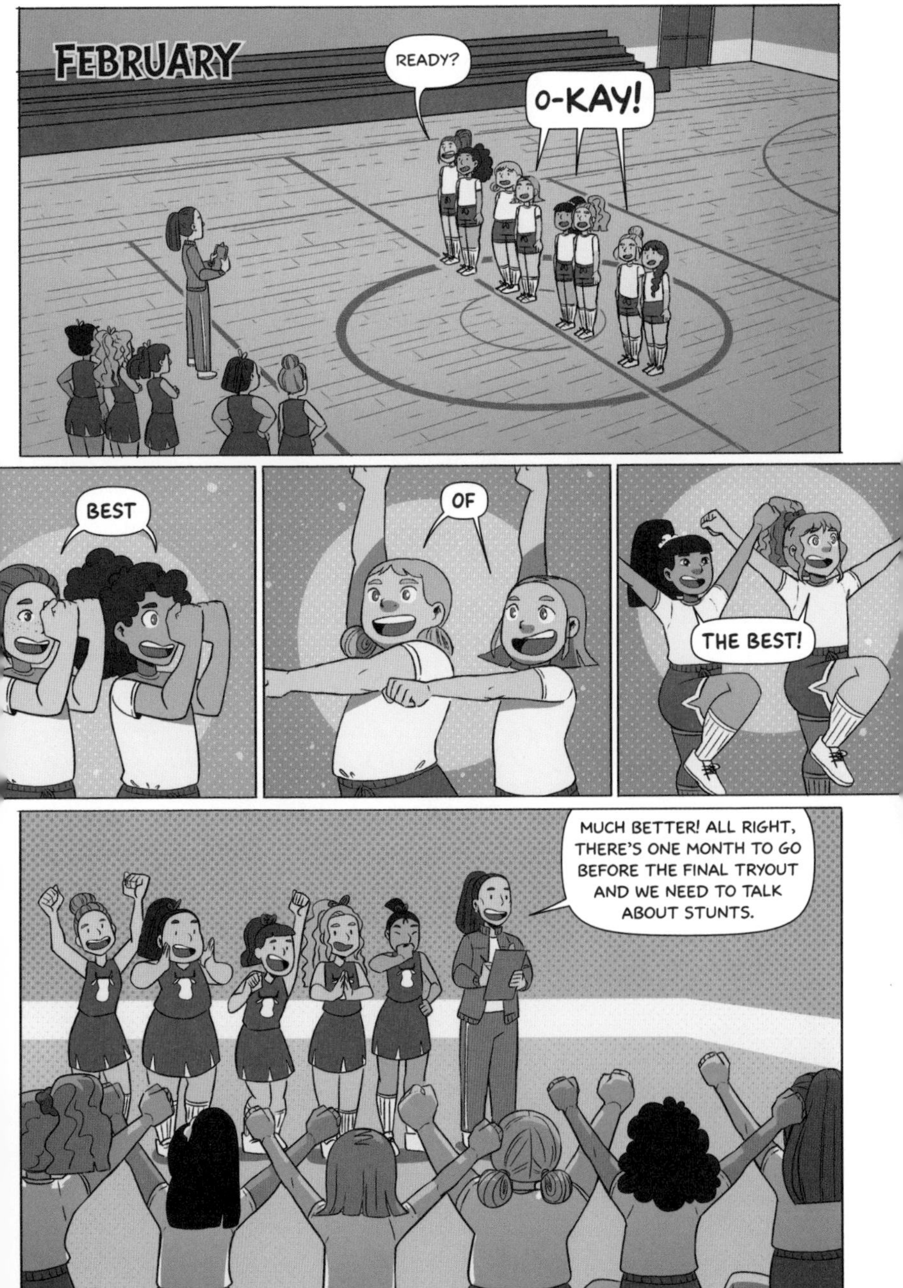
FEBRUARY
READY?
O-KAY!
BEST
OF
THE BEST!
MUCH BETTER! ALL RIGHT, THERE'S ONE MONTH TO GO BEFORE THE FINAL TRYOUT AND WE NEED TO TALK ABOUT STUNTS.

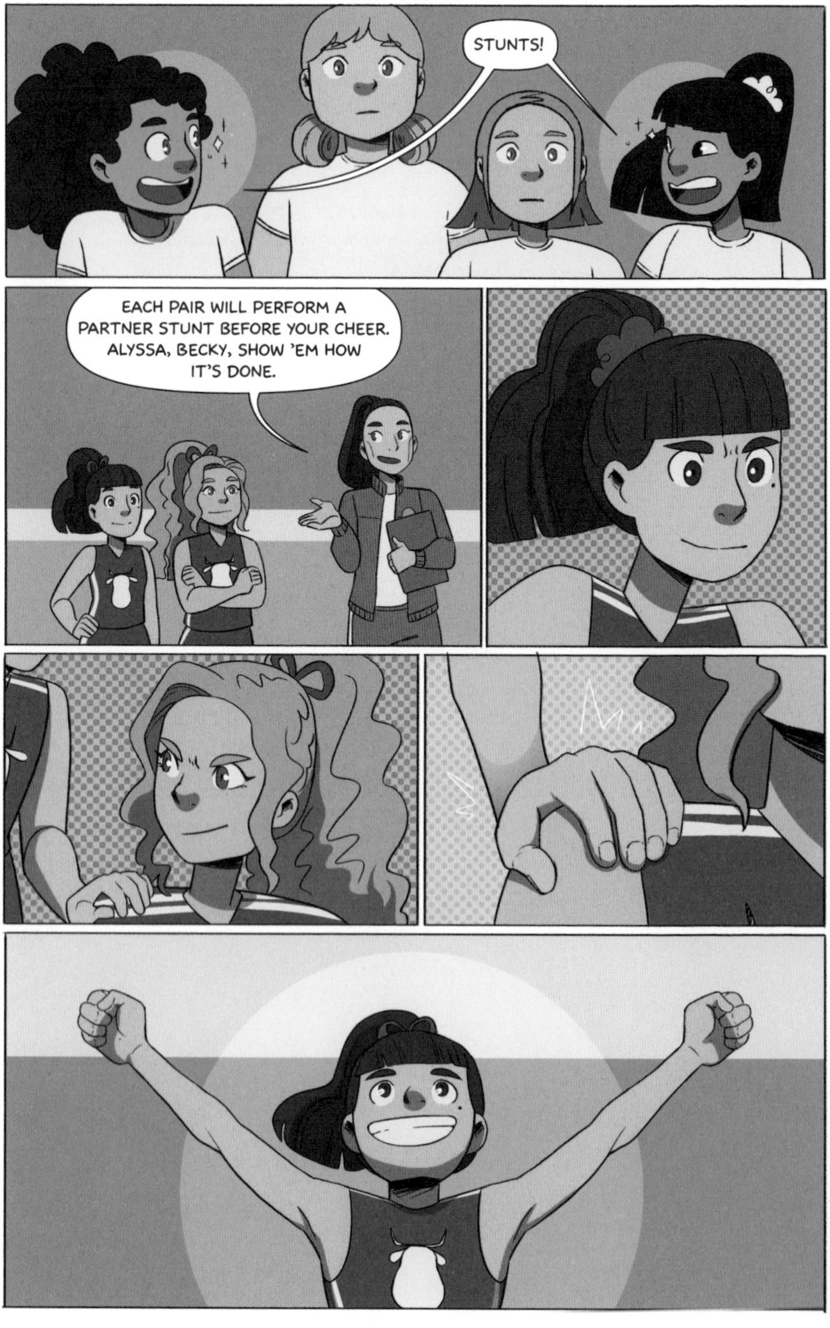
STUNTS!
EACH PAIR WILL PERFORM A PARTNER STUNT BEFORE YOUR CHEER. ALYSSA, BECKY, SHOW 'EM HOW IT'S DONE.

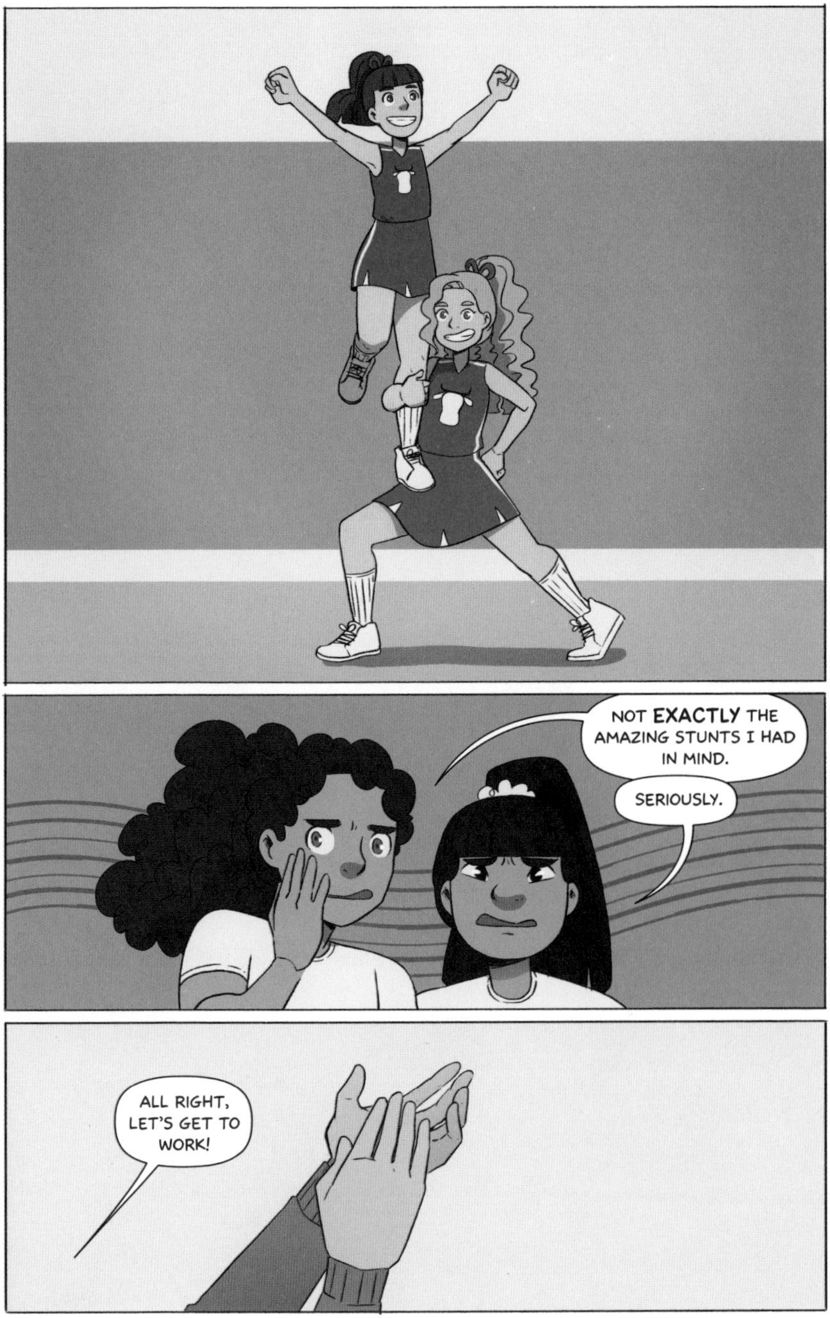
NOT EXACTLY THE AMAZING STUNTS I HAD IN MIND.
SERIOUSLY.
ALL RIGHT, LET'S GET TO WORK!

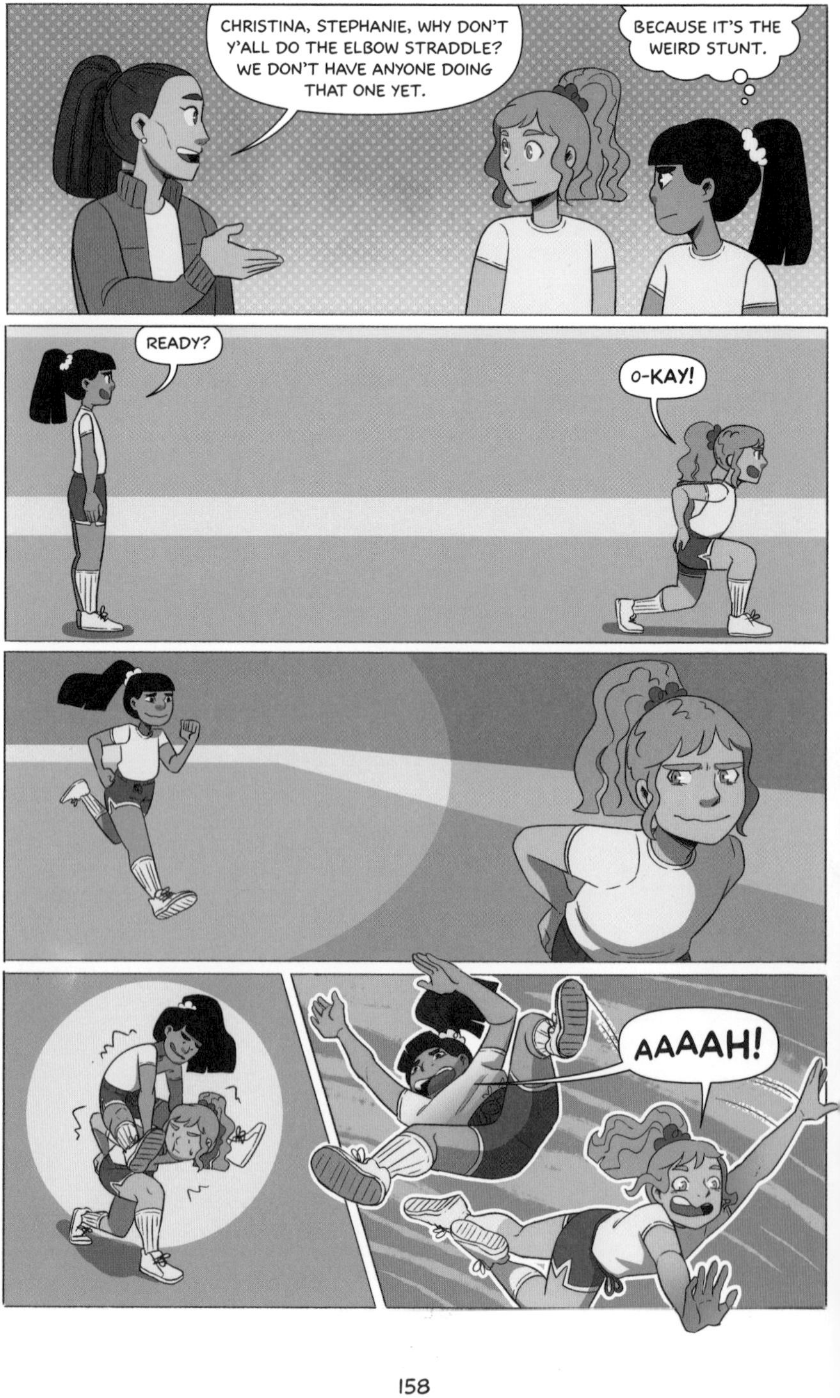
CHRISTINA, STEPHANIE, WHY DON'T Y'ALL DO THE ELBOW STRADDLE? WE DON'T HAVE ANYONE DOING THAT ONE YET.
BECAUSE IT'S THE WEIRD STUNT.
READY?
O-KAY!
AAAAH!

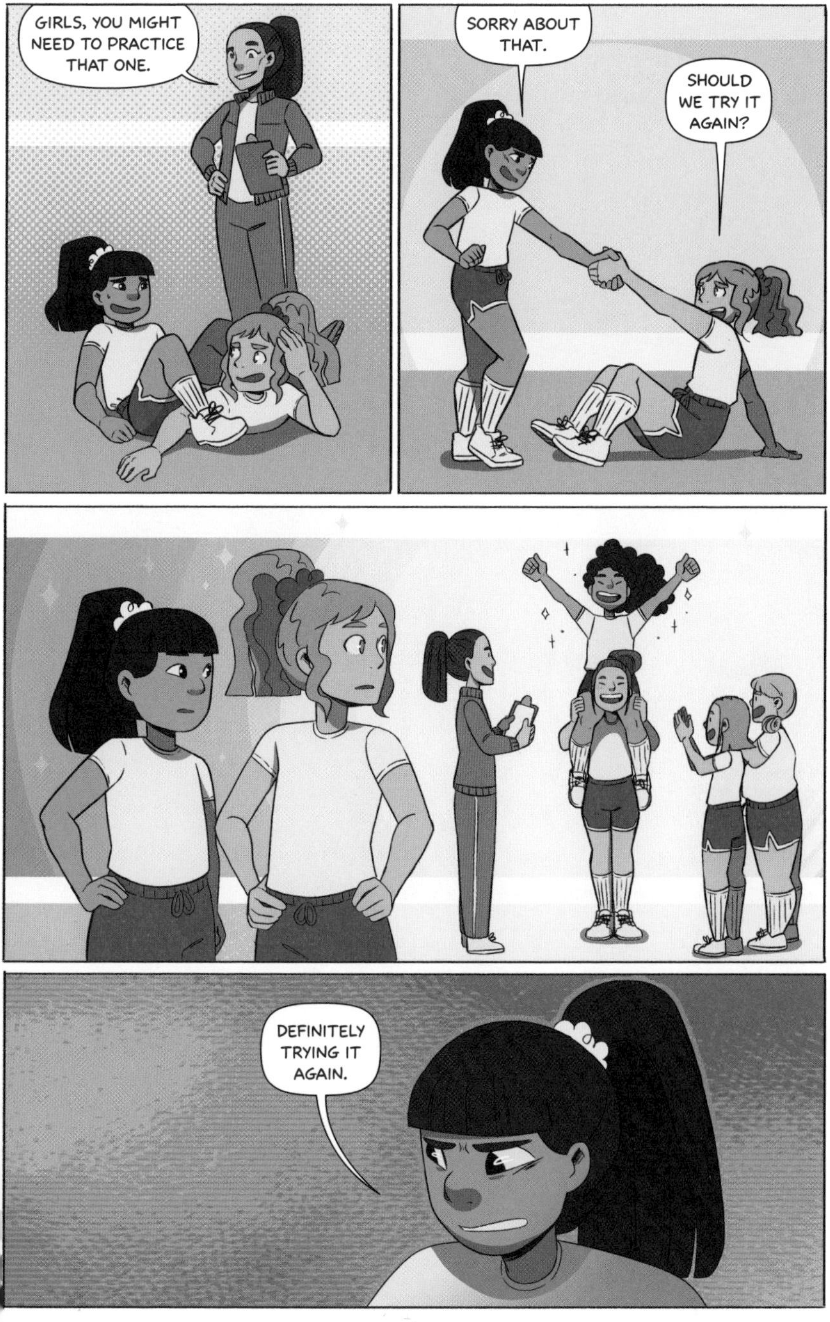
GIRLS, YOU MIGHT NEED TO PRACTICE THAT ONE.
SORRY ABOUT THAT.
SHOULD WE TRY IT AGAIN?
DEFINITELY TRYING IT AGAIN.

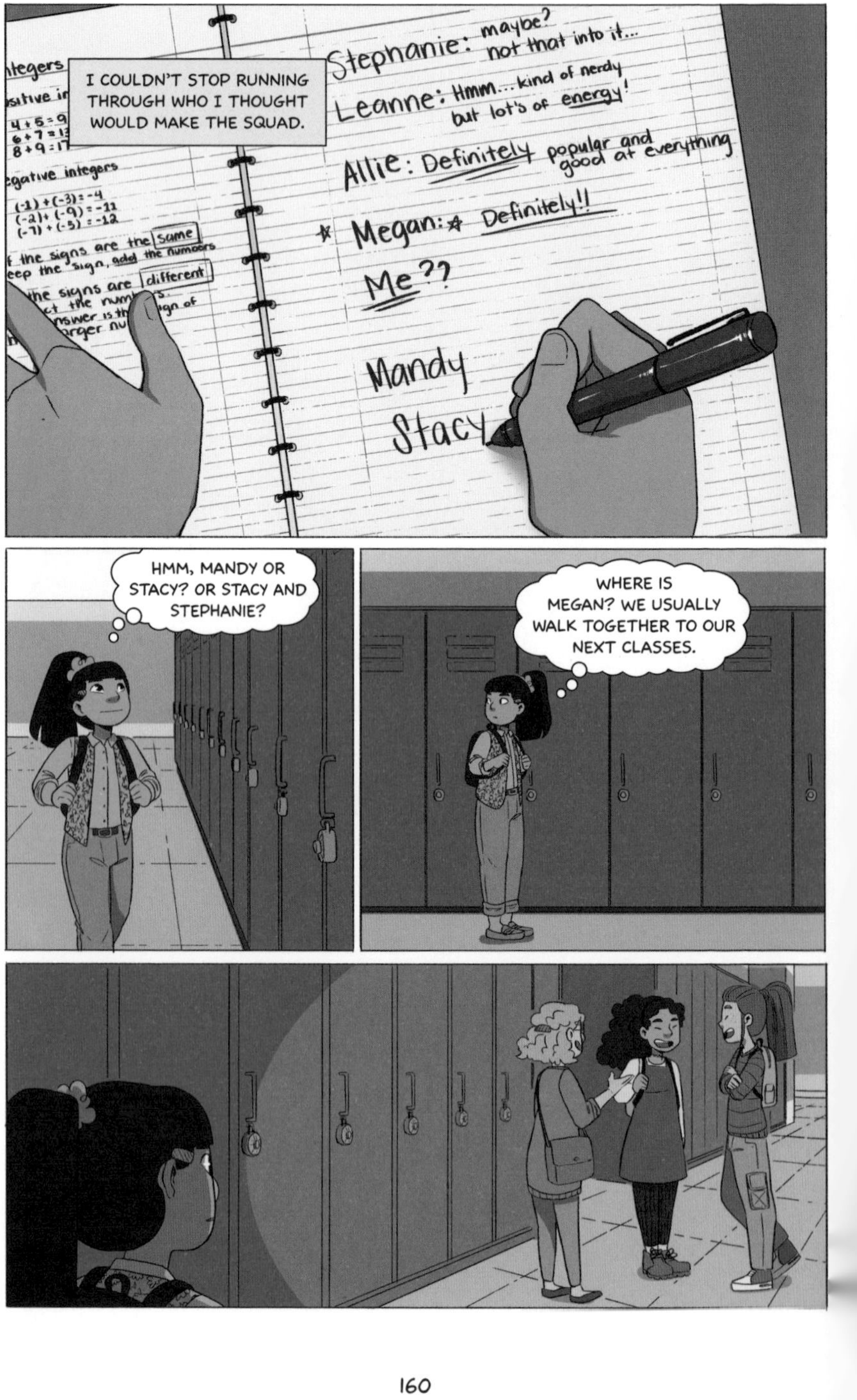
I COULDN'T STOP RUNNING THROUGH WHO I THOUGHT WOULD MAKE THE SQUAD.
Stephanie: maybe? not that into it...
Leanne: Hmm... kind of nerdy but lot's of energy!
Allie: Definitely popular and good at everything
Megan: Definitely!!
Me??
Mandy
Stacy
HMM, MANDY OR STACY? OR STACY AND STEPHANIE?
WHERE IS MEGAN? WE USUALLY WALK TOGETHER TO OUR NEXT CLASSES.

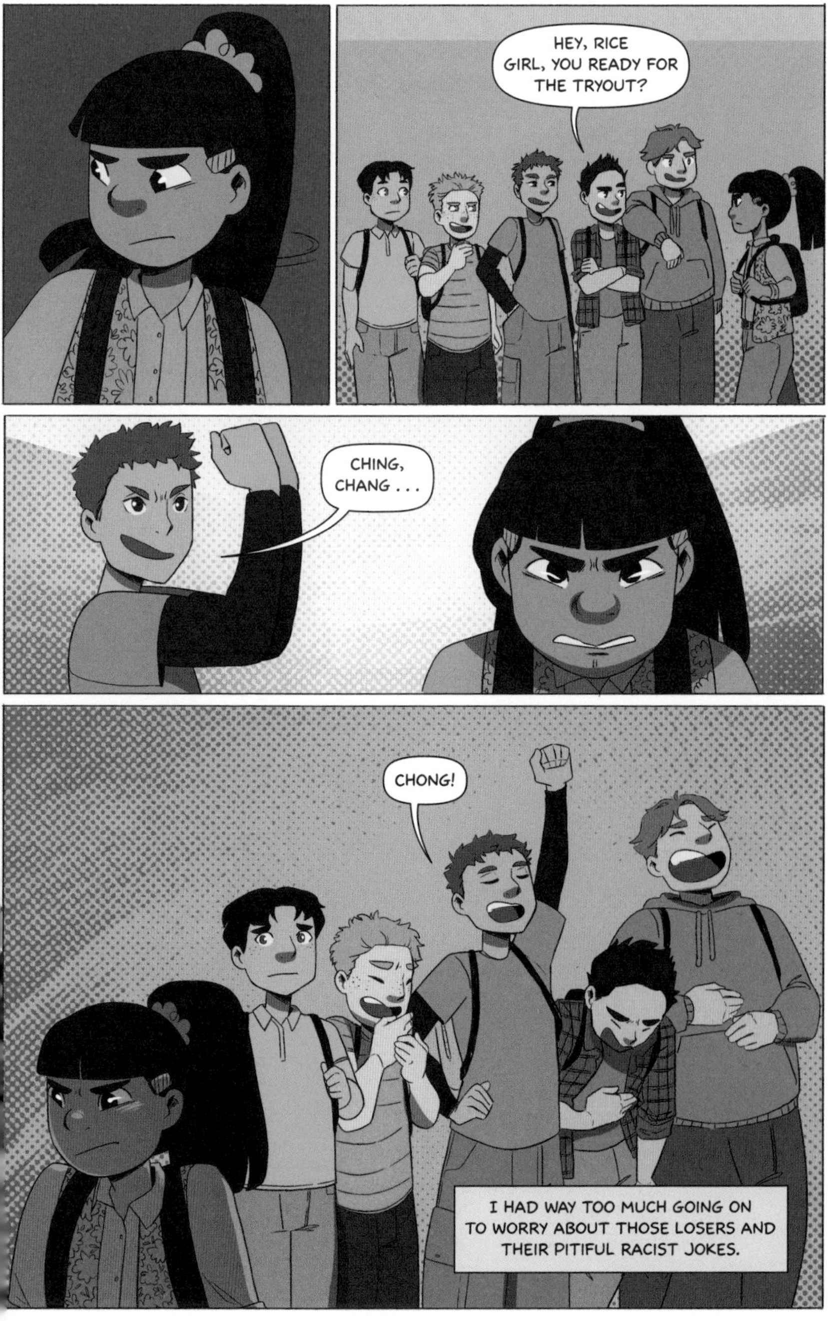
HEY, RICE GIRL, YOU READY FOR THE TRYOUT?
CHING, CHANG . . .
CHONG!
I HAD WAY TOO MUCH GOING ON TO WORRY ABOUT THOSE LOSERS AND THEIR PITIFUL RACIST JOKES.

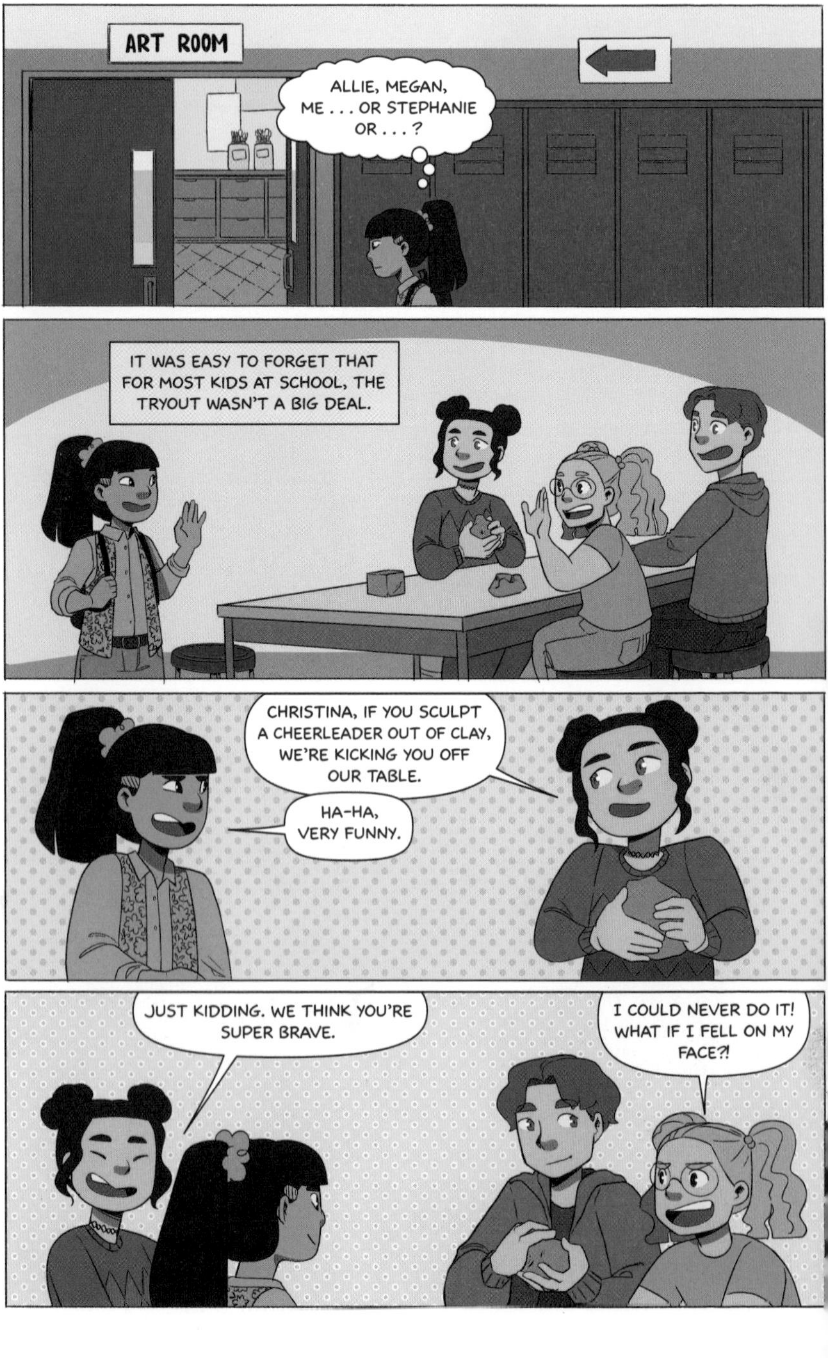
ART ROOM
ALLIE, MEGAN, ME . . . OR STEPHANIE OR . . . ?
IT WAS EASY TO FORGET THAT FOR MOST KIDS AT SCHOOL, THE TRYOUT WASN'T A BIG DEAL.
CHRISTINA, IF YOU SCULPT A CHEERLEADER OUT OF CLAY, WE'RE KICKING YOU OFF OUR TABLE.
HA-HA, VERY FUNNY.
JUST KIDDING. WE THINK YOU'RE SUPER BRAVE.
I COULD NEVER DO IT! WHAT IF I FELL ON MY FACE?!

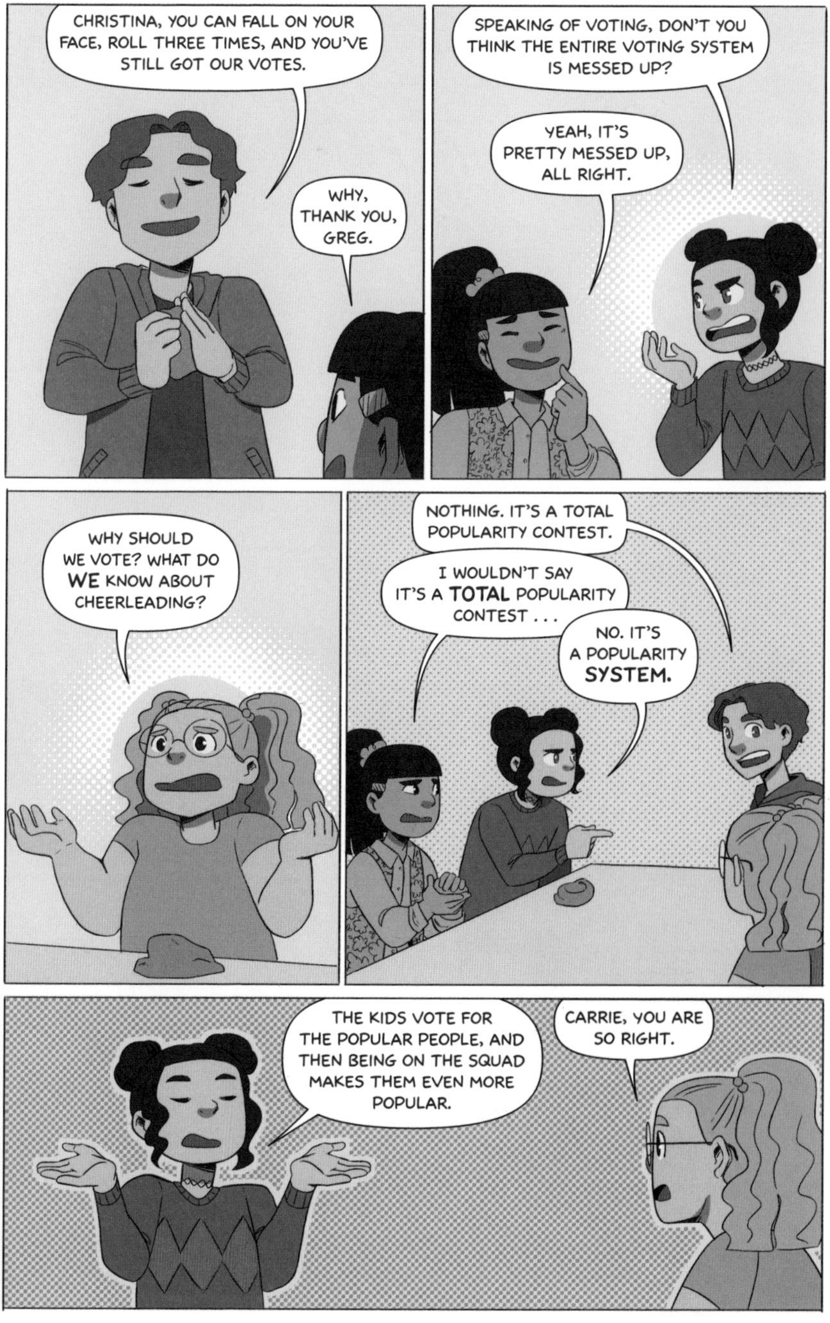
CHRISTINA, YOU CAN FALL ON YOUR FACE, ROLL THREE TIMES, AND YOU'VE STILL GOT OUR VOTES.
WHY, THANK YOU, GREG.
SPEAKING OF VOTING, DON'T YOU THINK THE ENTIRE VOTING SYSTEM IS MESSED UP?
YEAH, IT'S PRETTY MESSED UP, ALL RIGHT.
WHY SHOULD WE VOTE? WHAT DO WE KNOW ABOUT CHEERLEADING?
NOTHING. IT'S A TOTAL POPULARITY CONTEST.
I WOULDN'T SAY IT'S A TOTAL POPULARITY CONTEST . . .
NO. IT'S A POPULARITY SYSTEM.
THE KIDS VOTE FOR THE POPULAR PEOPLE, AND THEN BEING ON THE SQUAD MAKES THEM EVEN MORE POPULAR.
CARRIE, YOU ARE SO RIGHT.

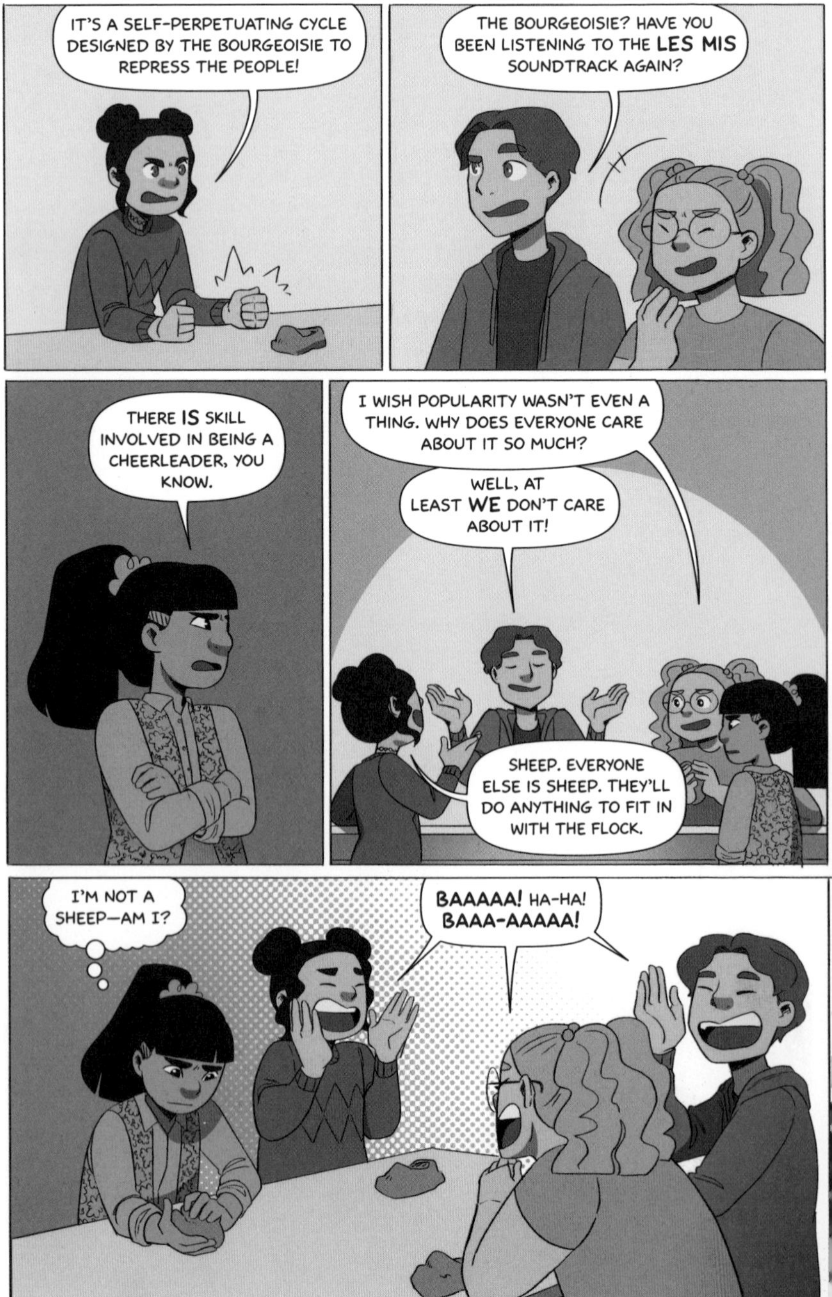
IT'S A SELF-PERPETUATING CYCLE DESIGNED BY THE BOURGEOISIE TO REPRESS THE PEOPLE!
THE BOURGEOISIE? HAVE YOU BEEN LISTENING TO THE LES MIS SOUNDTRACK AGAIN?
THERE IS SKILL INVOLVED IN BEING A CHEERLEADER, YOU KNOW.
I WISH POPULARITY WASN'T EVEN A THING. WHY DOES EVERYONE CARE ABOUT IT SO MUCH?
WELL, AT LEAST WE DON'T CARE ABOUT IT!
SHEEP. EVERYONE ELSE IS SHEEP. THEY'LL DO ANYTHING TO FIT IN WITH THE FLOCK.
I'M NOT A SHEEP—AM I?
BAAAAA! HA-HA! BAAA-AAAAA!

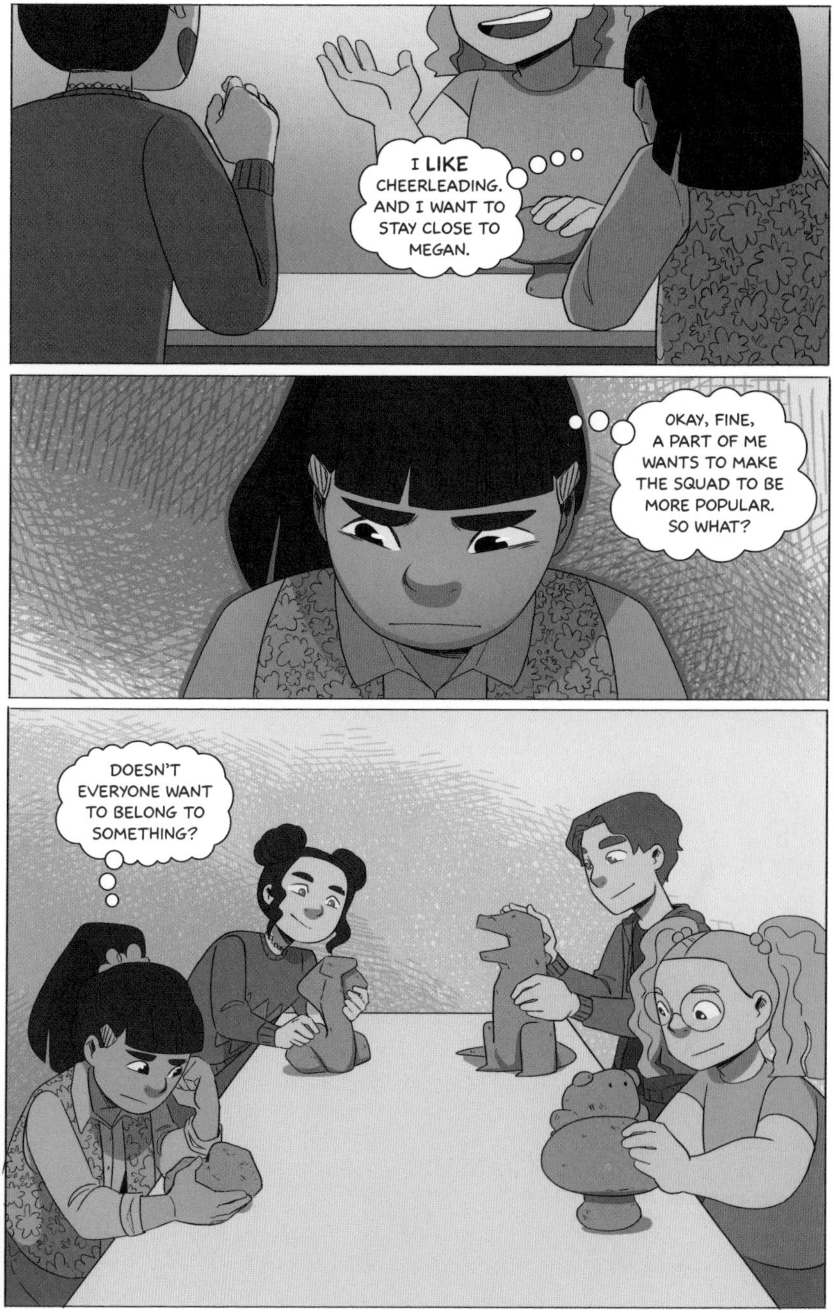
I **LIKE** CHEERLEADING. AND I WANT TO STAY CLOSE TO MEGAN.
OKAY, FINE, A PART OF ME WANTS TO MAKE THE SQUAD TO BE MORE POPULAR. SO WHAT?
DOESN'T EVERYONE WANT TO BELONG TO SOMETHING?

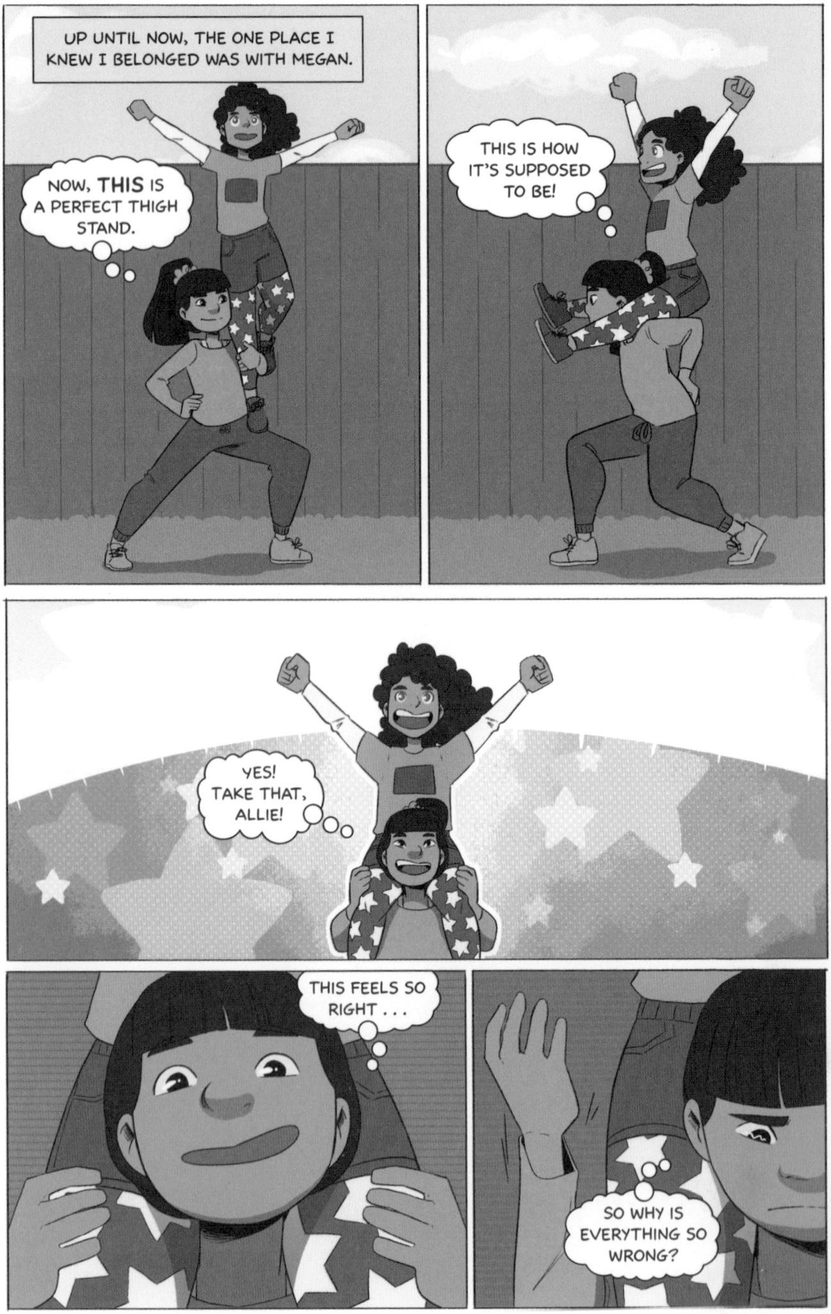
UP UNTIL NOW, THE ONE PLACE I KNEW I BELONGED WAS WITH MEGAN.
NOW, **THIS** IS A PERFECT THIGH STAND.
THIS IS HOW IT'S SUPPOSED TO BE!
YES! TAKE THAT, ALLIE!
THIS FEELS SO RIGHT . . .
SO WHY IS EVERYTHING SO WRONG?

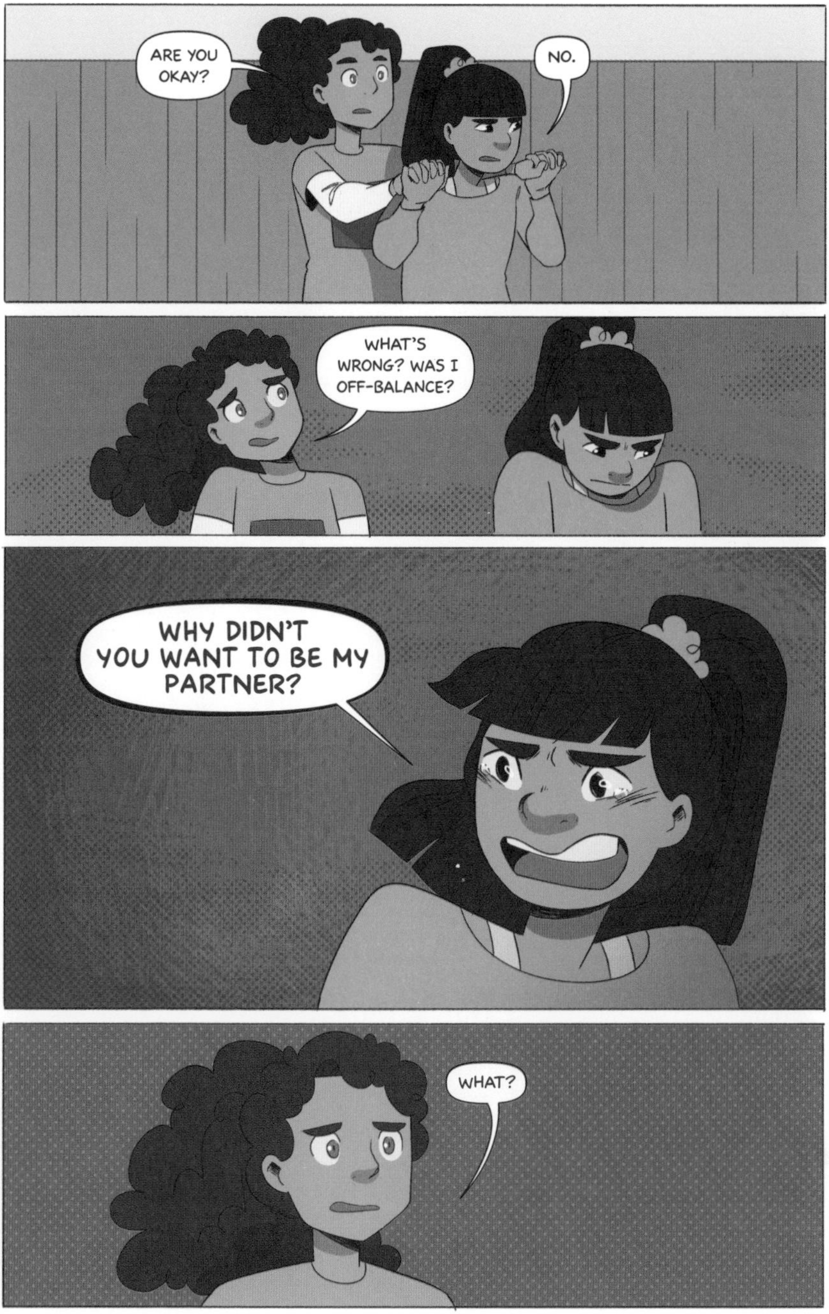

ARE YOU OKAY?
NO.
WHAT'S WRONG? WAS I OFF-BALANCE?
WHY DIDN'T YOU WANT TO BE MY PARTNER?
WHAT?

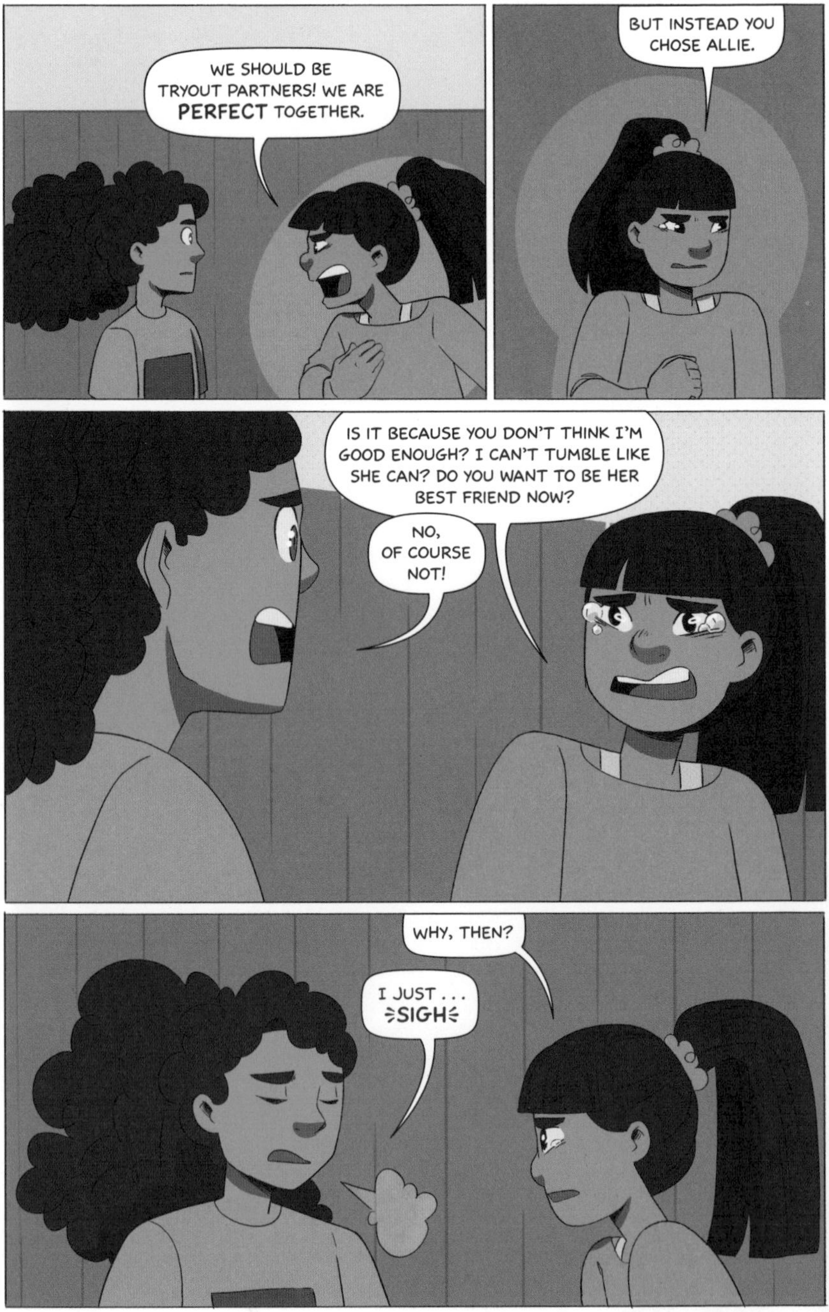
WE SHOULD BE TRYOUT PARTNERS! WE ARE **PERFECT** TOGETHER.
BUT INSTEAD YOU CHOSE ALLIE.
IS IT BECAUSE YOU DON'T THINK I'M GOOD ENOUGH? I CAN'T TUMBLE LIKE SHE CAN? DO YOU WANT TO BE HER BEST FRIEND NOW?
NO, OF COURSE NOT!
WHY, THEN?
I JUST . . .
SIGH

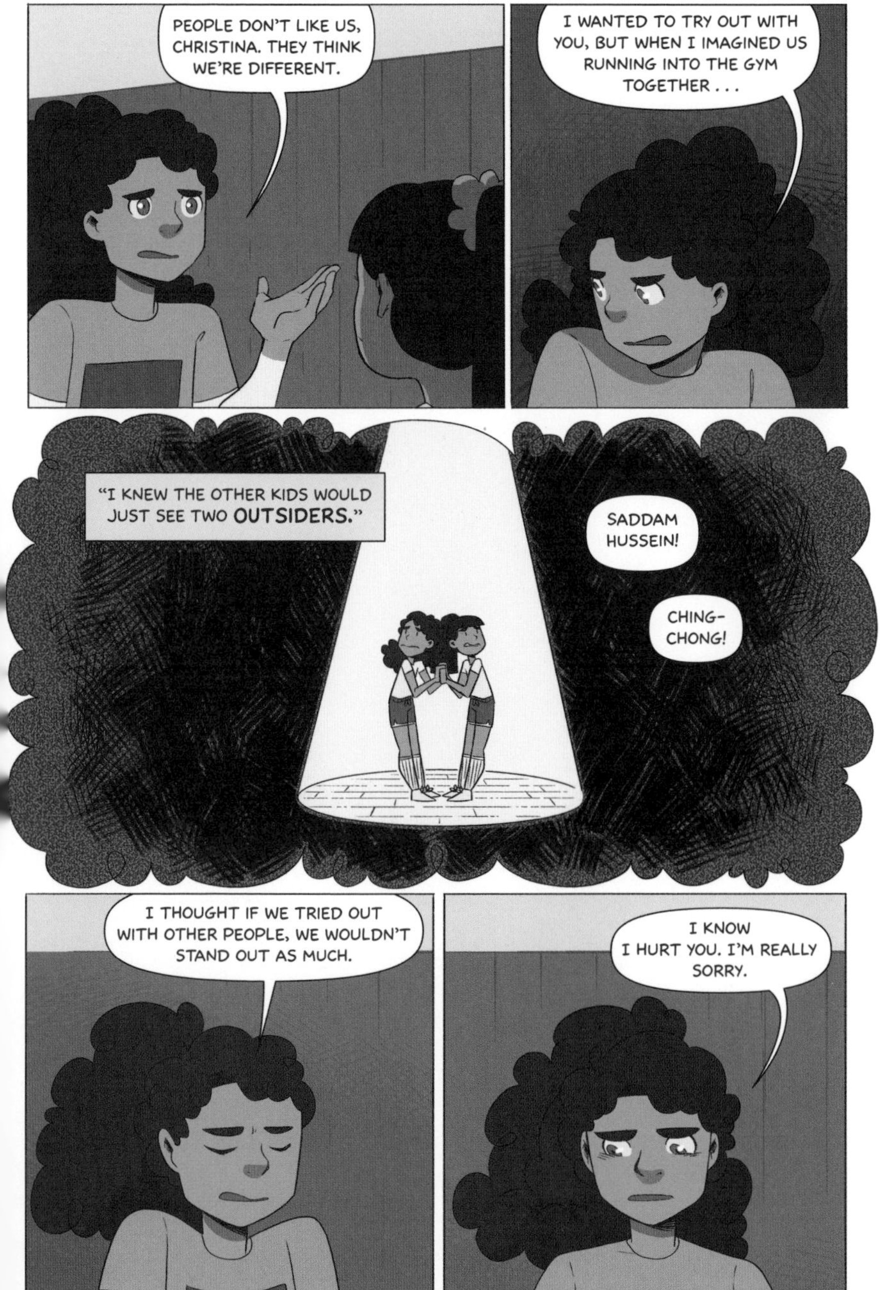
PEOPLE DON'T LIKE US, CHRISTINA. THEY THINK WE'RE DIFFERENT.
I WANTED TO TRY OUT WITH YOU, BUT WHEN I IMAGINED US RUNNING INTO THE GYM TOGETHER . . .
"I KNEW THE OTHER KIDS WOULD JUST SEE TWO OUTSIDERS."
SADDAM HUSSEIN!
CHING-CHONG!
I THOUGHT IF WE TRIED OUT WITH OTHER PEOPLE, WE WOULDN'T STAND OUT AS MUCH.
I KNOW I HURT YOU. I'M REALLY SORRY.

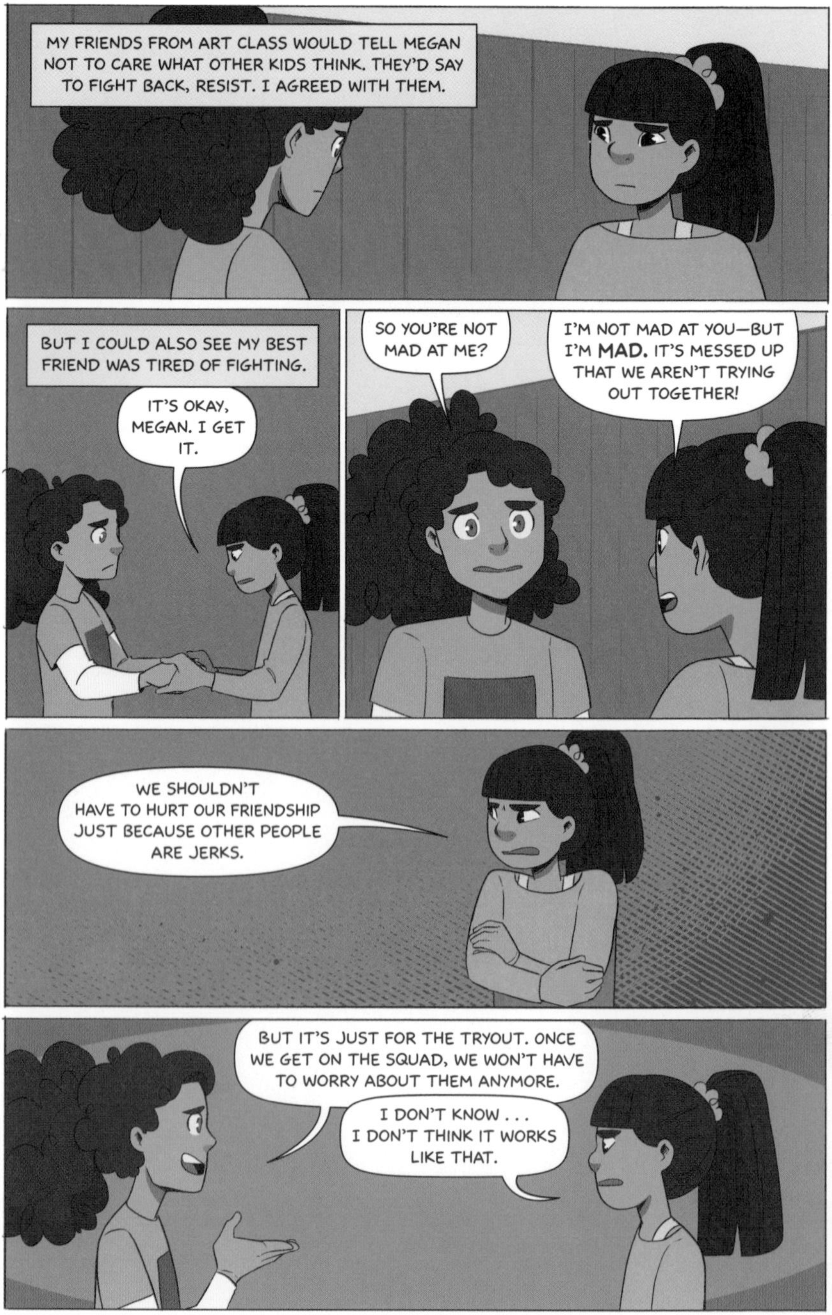
MY FRIENDS FROM ART CLASS WOULD TELL MEGAN NOT TO CARE WHAT OTHER KIDS THINK. THEY'D SAY TO FIGHT BACK, RESIST. I AGREED WITH THEM.
BUT I COULD ALSO SEE MY BEST FRIEND WAS TIRED OF FIGHTING.
IT'S OKAY, MEGAN. I GET IT.
SO YOU'RE NOT MAD AT ME?
I'M NOT MAD AT YOU—BUT I'M **MAD.** IT'S MESSED UP THAT WE AREN'T TRYING OUT TOGETHER!
WE SHOULDN'T HAVE TO HURT OUR FRIENDSHIP JUST BECAUSE OTHER PEOPLE ARE JERKS.
BUT IT'S JUST FOR THE TRYOUT. ONCE WE GET ON THE SQUAD, WE WON'T HAVE TO WORRY ABOUT THEM ANYMORE.
I DON'T KNOW . . . I DON'T THINK IT WORKS LIKE THAT.

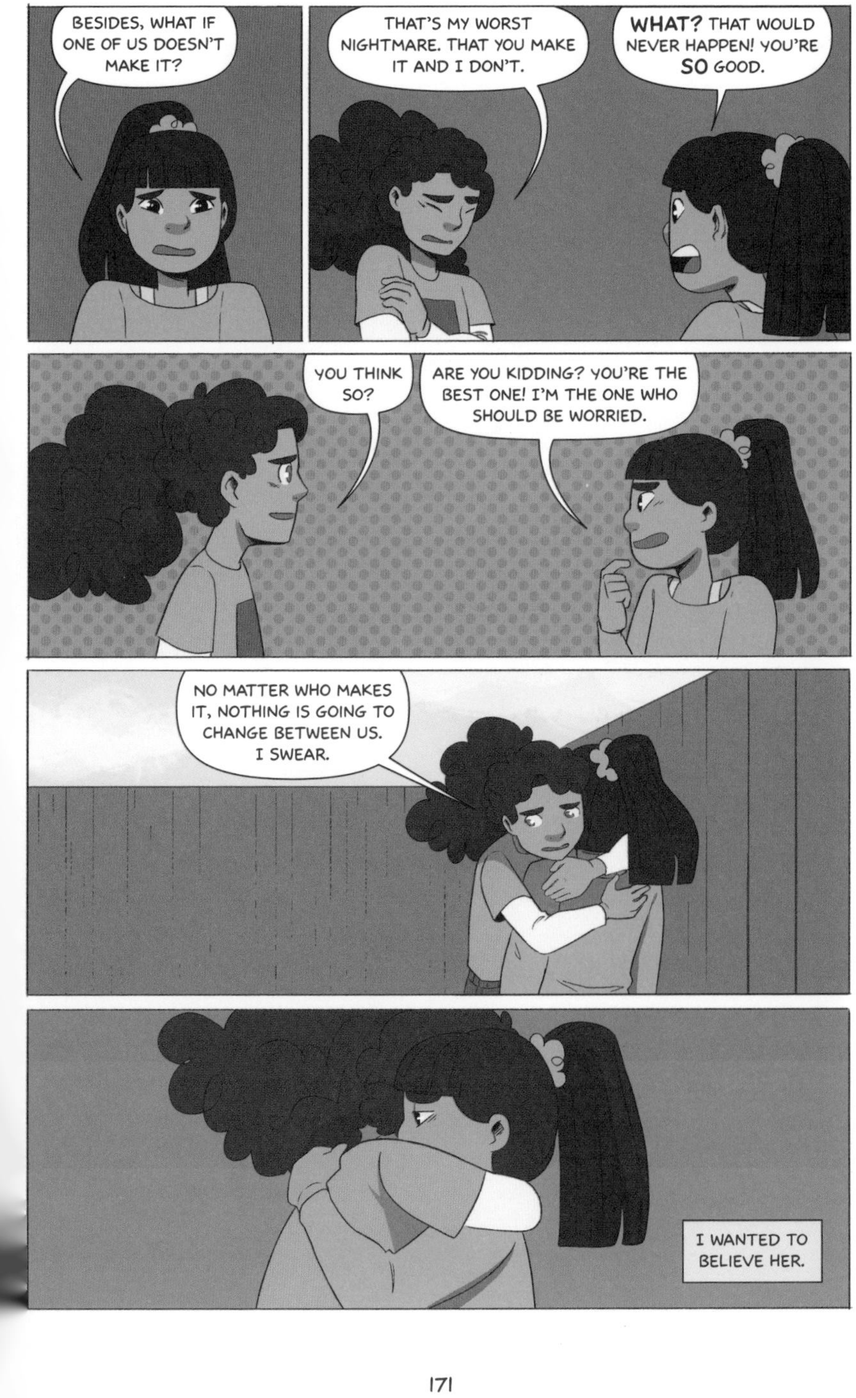
BESIDES, WHAT IF ONE OF US DOESN'T MAKE IT?
THAT'S MY WORST NIGHTMARE. THAT YOU MAKE IT AND I DON'T.
WHAT? THAT WOULD NEVER HAPPEN! YOU'RE SO GOOD.
YOU THINK SO?
ARE YOU KIDDING? YOU'RE THE BEST ONE! I'M THE ONE WHO SHOULD BE WORRIED.
NO MATTER WHO MAKES IT, NOTHING IS GOING TO CHANGE BETWEEN US. I SWEAR.
I WANTED TO BELIEVE HER.

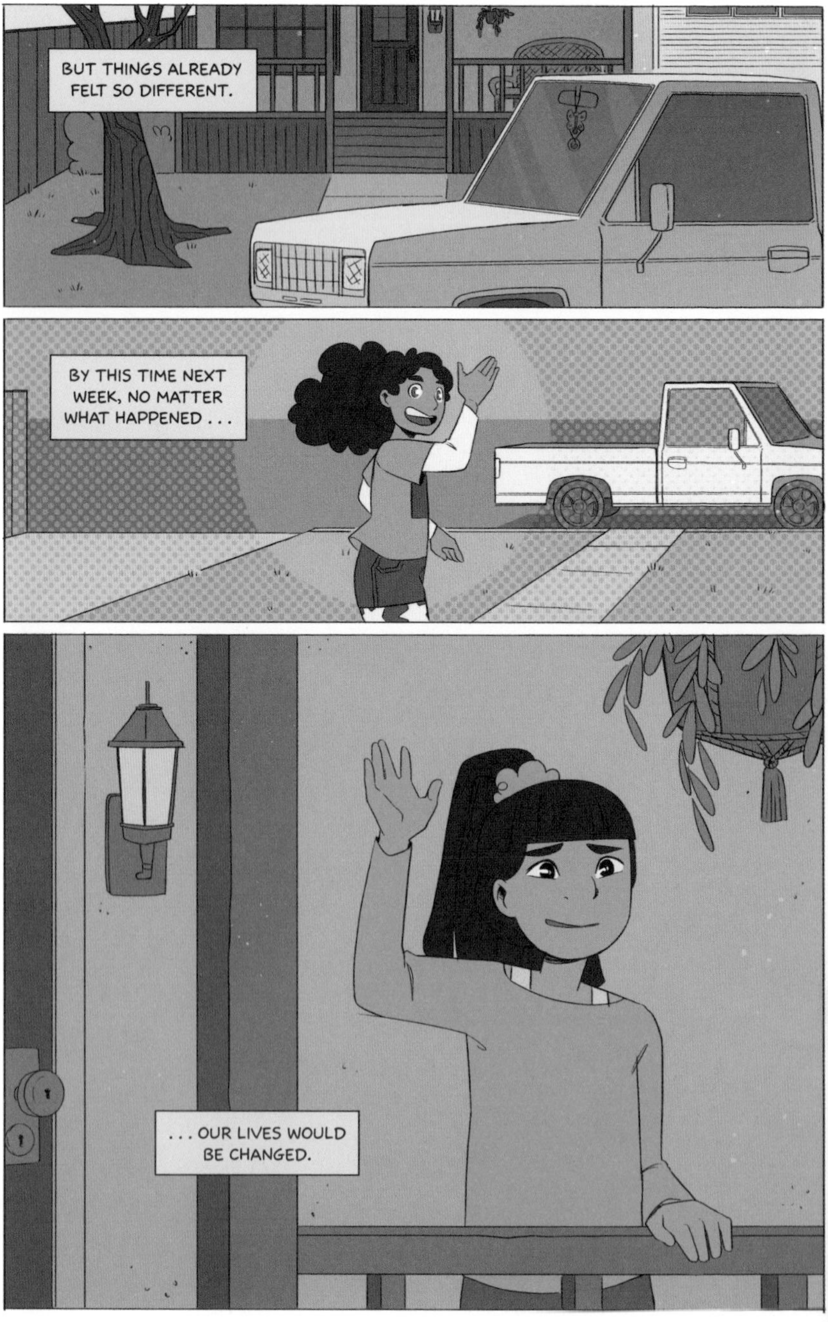
BUT THINGS ALREADY FELT SO DIFFERENT.
BY THIS TIME NEXT WEEK, NO MATTER WHAT HAPPENED . . .
. . . OUR LIVES WOULD BE CHANGED.

MARCH
TRYOUT DAY

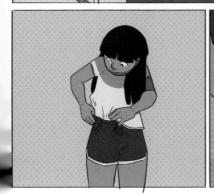

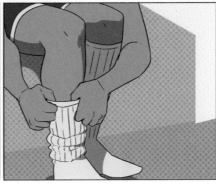

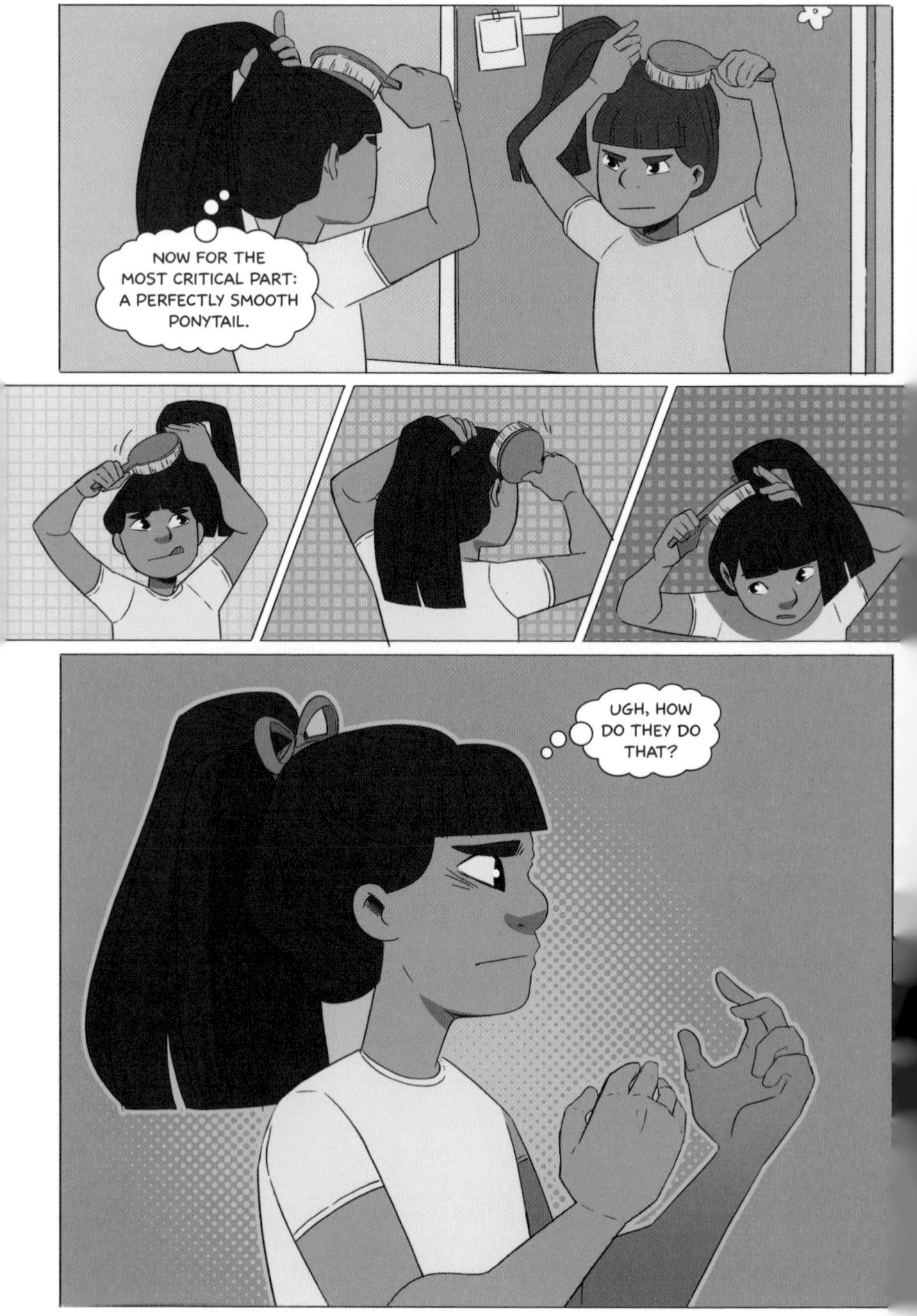
NOW FOR THE MOST CRITICAL PART: A PERFECTLY SMOOTH PONYTAIL.
UGH, HOW DO THEY DO THAT?

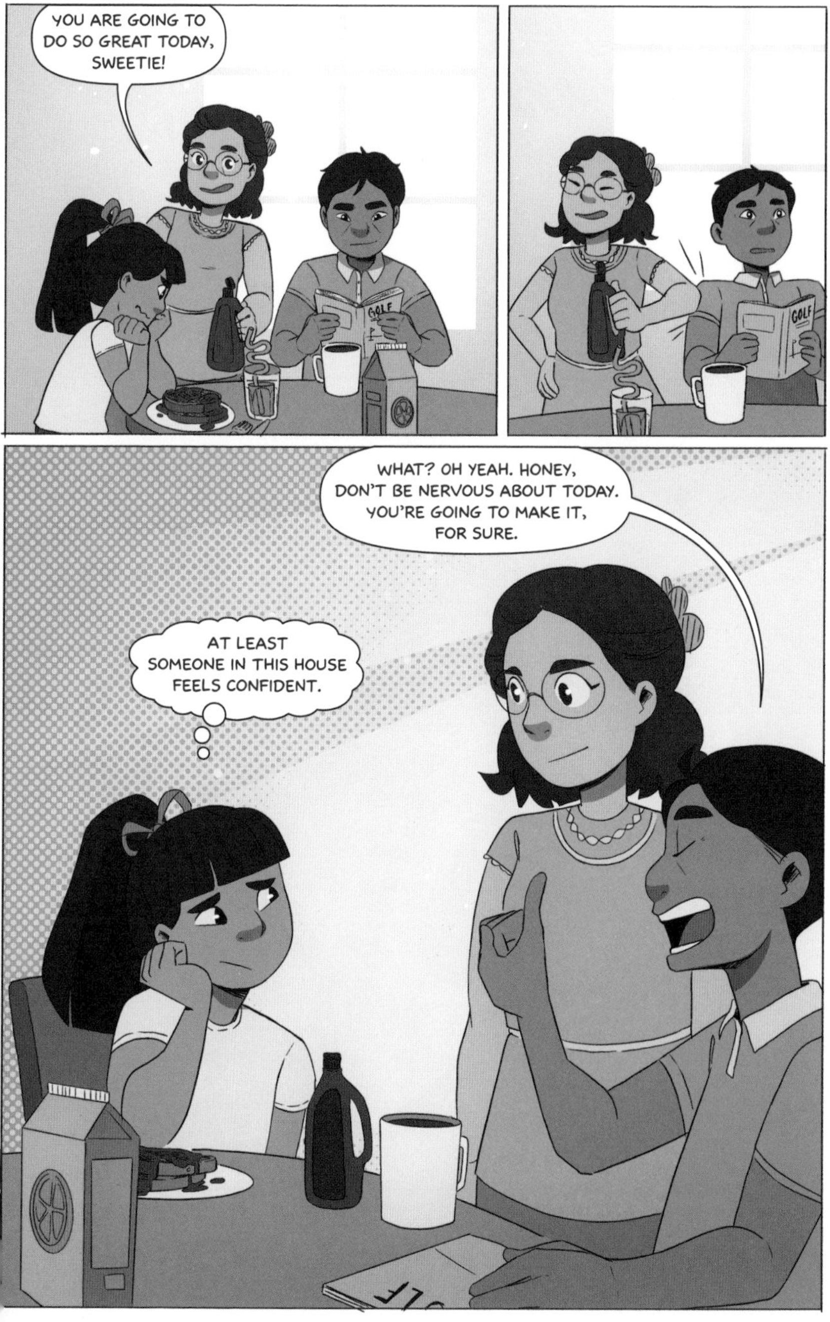
YOU ARE GOING TO DO SO GREAT TODAY, SWEETIE!
GOLF
WHAT? OH YEAH. HONEY, DON'T BE NERVOUS ABOUT TODAY. YOU'RE GOING TO MAKE IT, FOR SURE.
AT LEAST SOMEONE IN THIS HOUSE FEELS CONFIDENT.

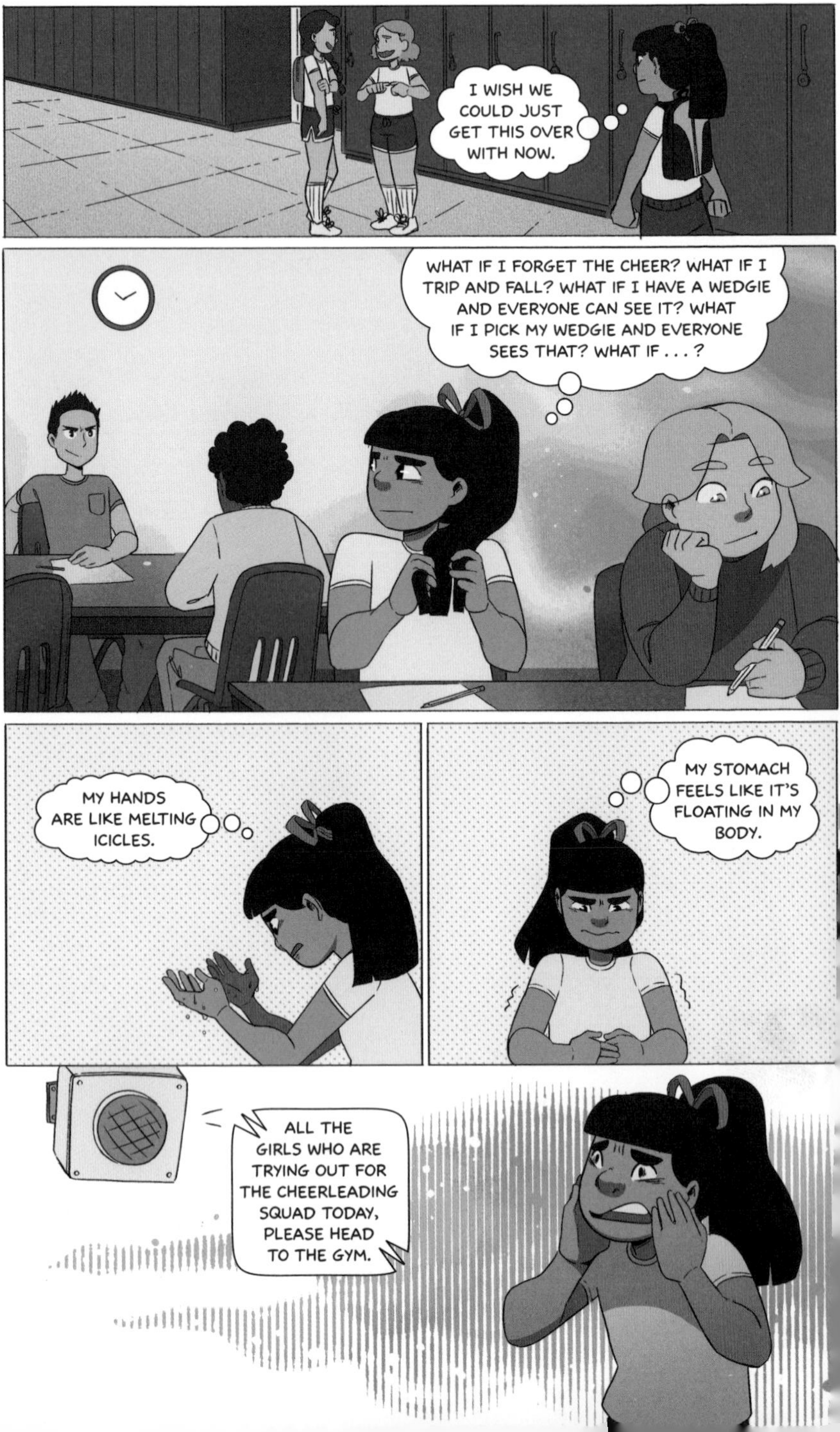
I WISH WE COULD JUST GET THIS OVER WITH NOW.
WHAT IF I FORGET THE CHEER? WHAT IF I TRIP AND FALL? WHAT IF I HAVE A WEDGIE AND EVERYONE CAN SEE IT? WHAT IF I PICK MY WEDGIE AND EVERYONE SEES THAT? WHAT IF . . . ?
MY HANDS ARE LIKE MELTING ICICLES.
MY STOMACH FEELS LIKE IT'S FLOATING IN MY BODY.
ALL THE GIRLS WHO ARE TRYING OUT FOR THE CHEERLEADING SQUAD TODAY, PLEASE HEAD TO THE GYM.

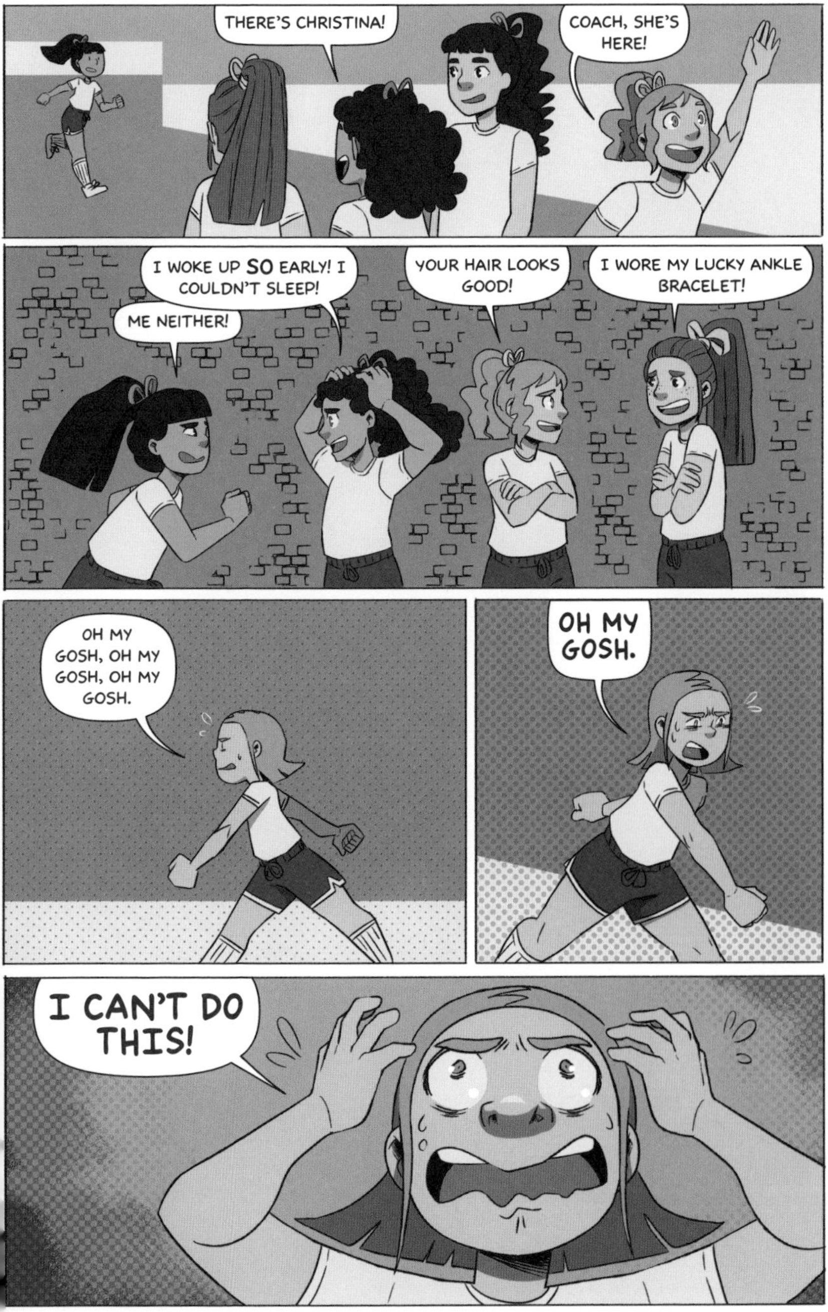
THERE'S CHRISTINA!
COACH, SHE'S HERE!
I WOKE UP SO EARLY! I COULDN'T SLEEP!
ME NEITHER!
YOUR HAIR LOOKS GOOD!
I WORE MY LUCKY ANKLE BRACELET!
OH MY GOSH, OH MY GOSH, OH MY GOSH.
OH MY GOSH.
I CAN'T DO THIS!

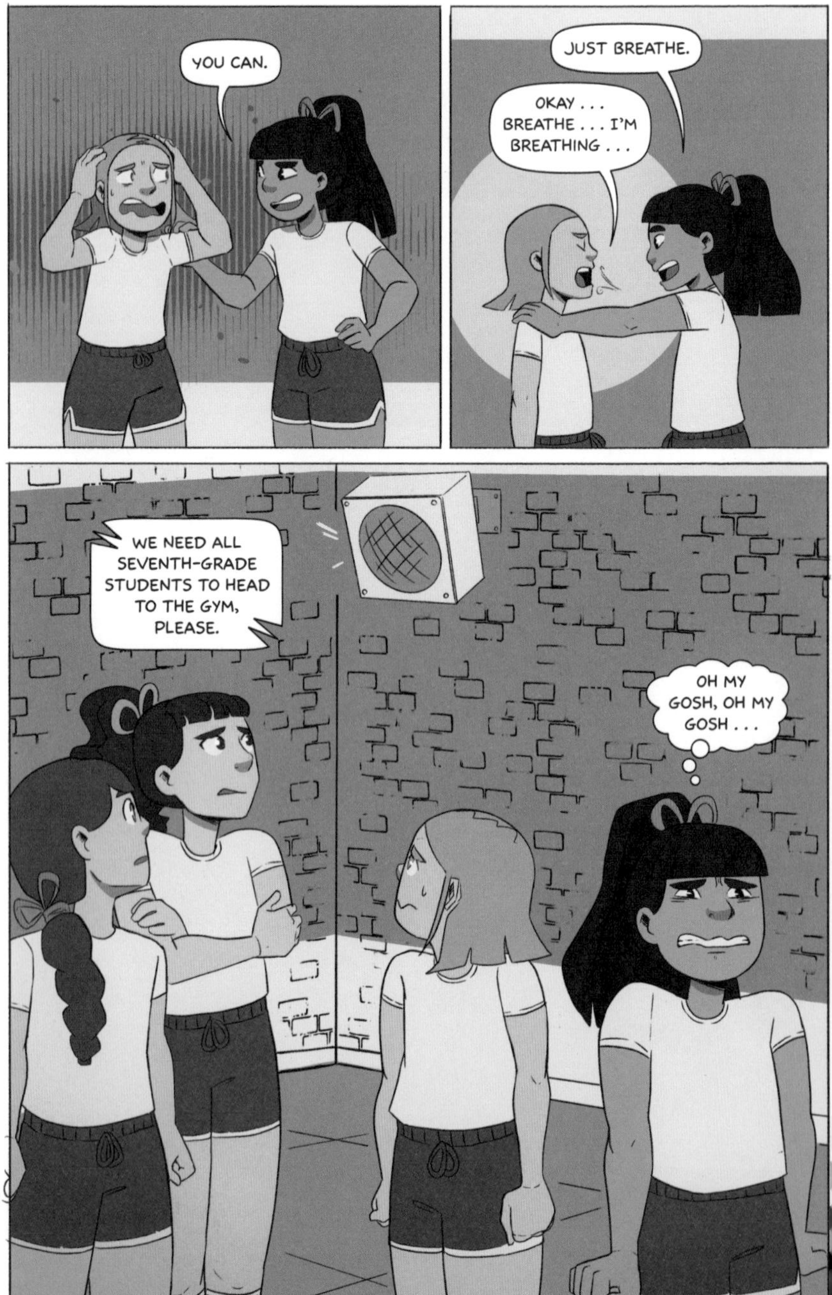
YOU CAN.
JUST BREATHE.
OKAY . . . BREATHE . . . I'M BREATHING . . .
WE NEED ALL SEVENTH-GRADE STUDENTS TO HEAD TO THE GYM, PLEASE.
OH MY GOSH, OH MY GOSH . . .

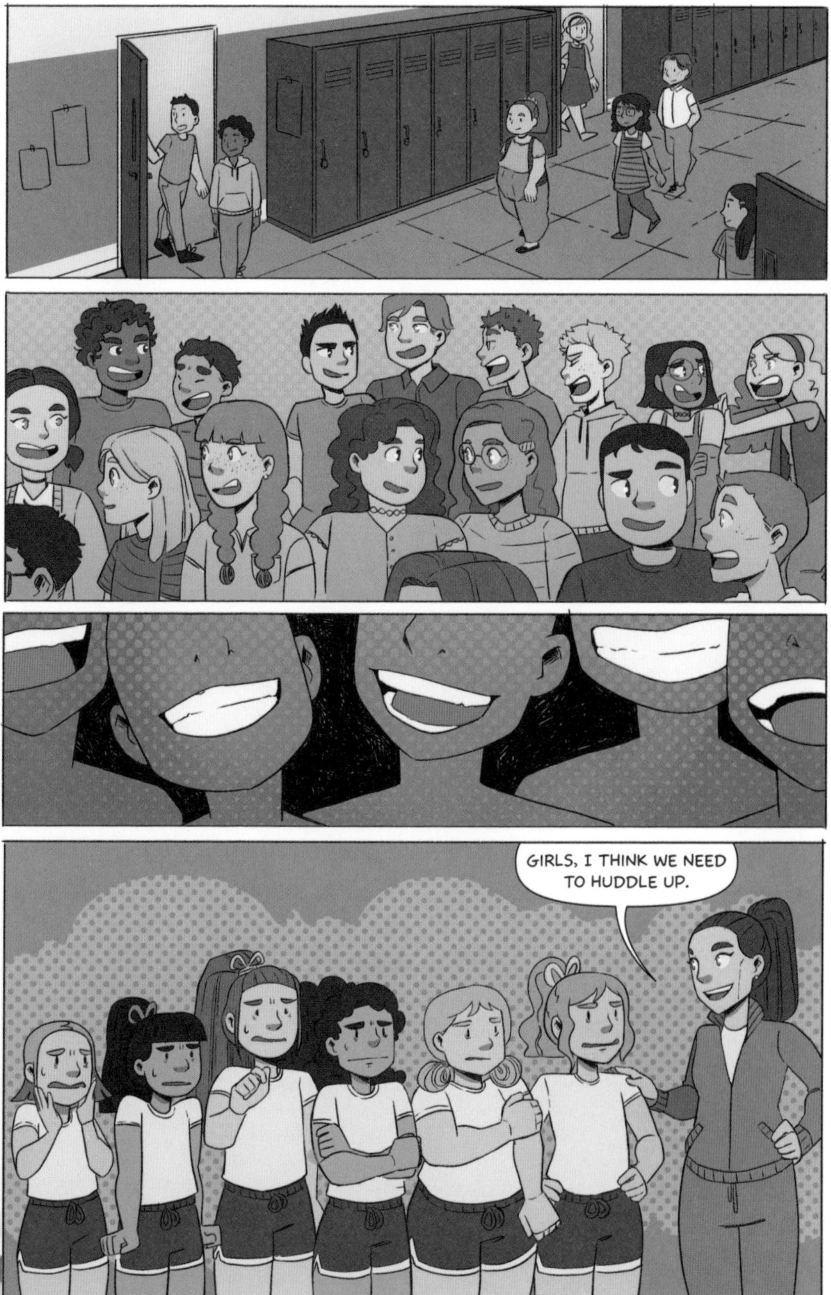
GIRLS, I THINK WE NEED TO HUDDLE UP.

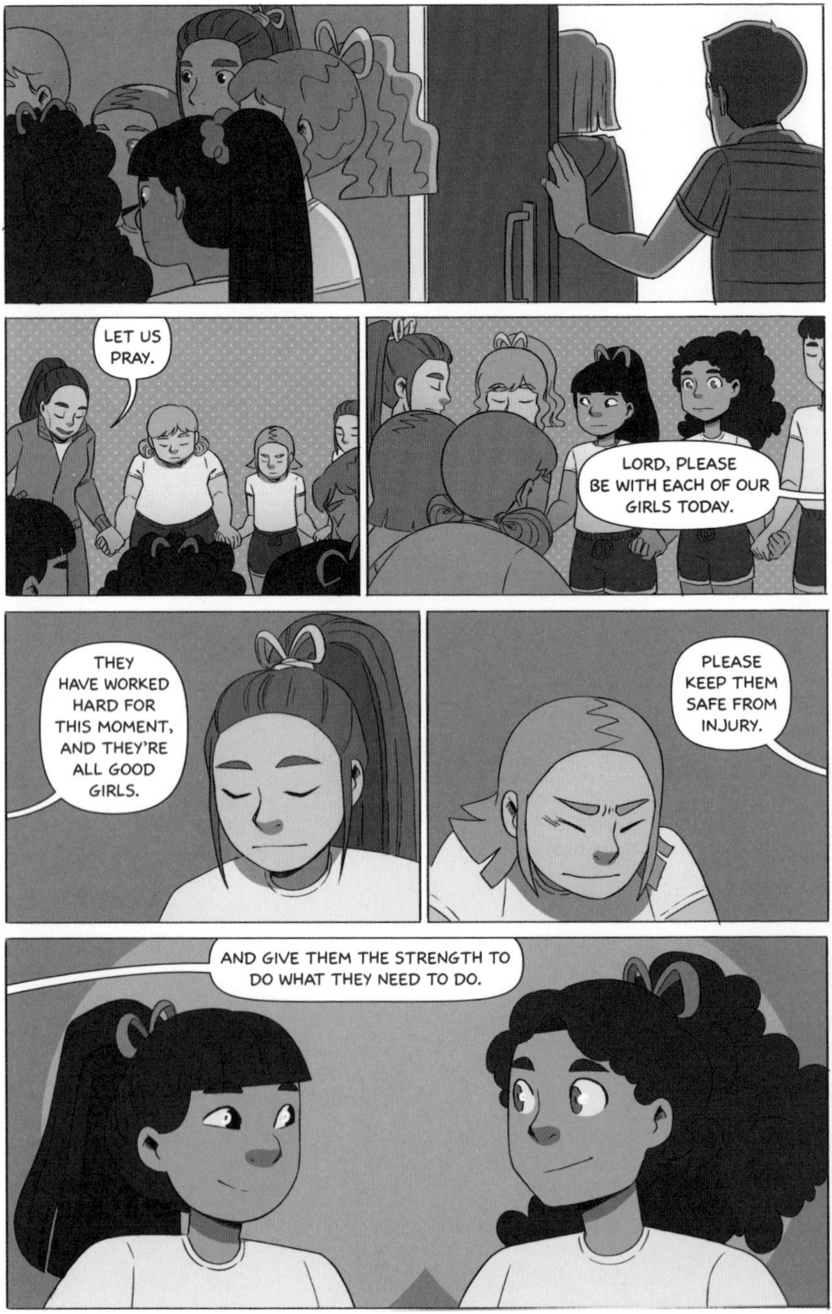
LET US PRAY.
LORD, PLEASE BE WITH EACH OF OUR GIRLS TODAY.
THEY HAVE WORKED HARD FOR THIS MOMENT, AND THEY'RE ALL GOOD GIRLS.
PLEASE KEEP THEM SAFE FROM INJURY.
AND GIVE THEM THE STRENGTH TO DO WHAT THEY NEED TO DO.

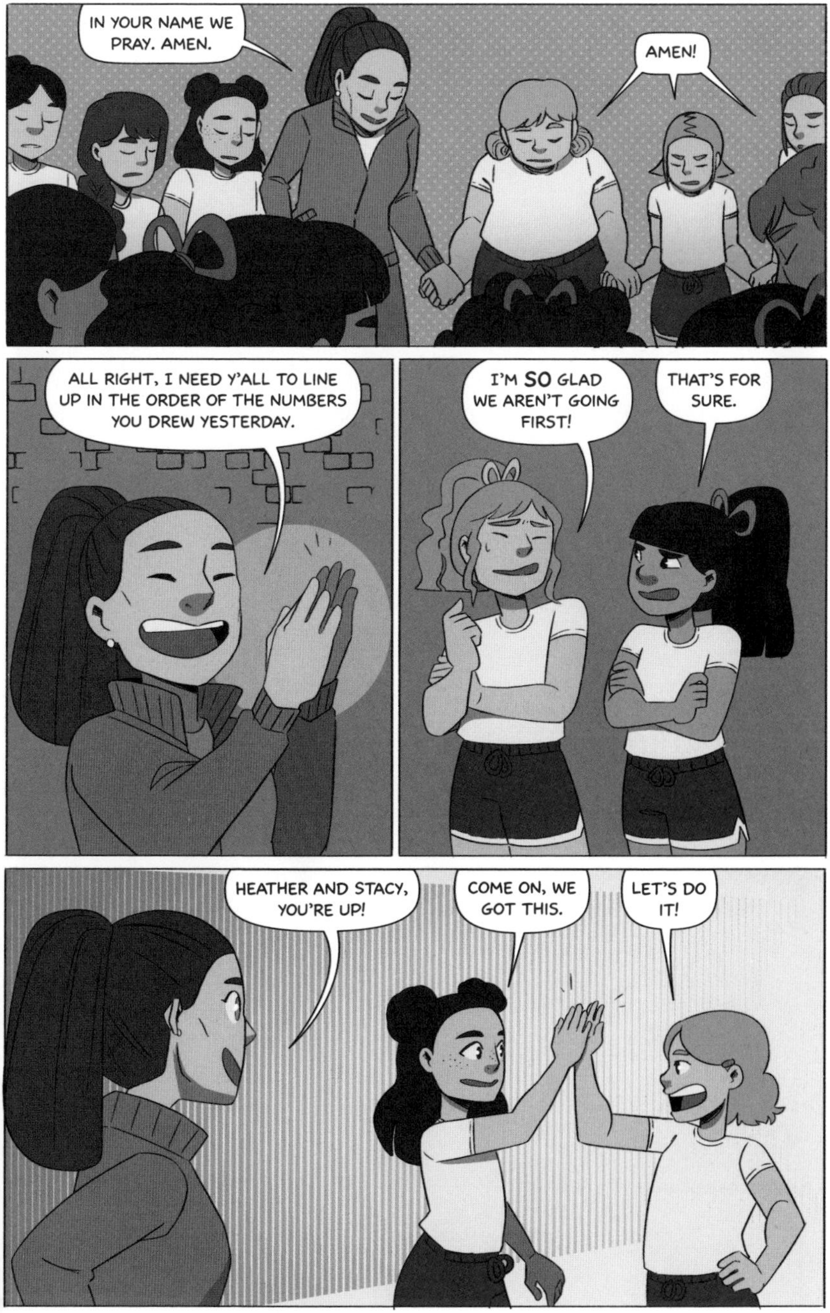
IN YOUR NAME WE PRAY. AMEN.
AMEN!
ALL RIGHT, I NEED Y'ALL TO LINE UP IN THE ORDER OF THE NUMBERS YOU DREW YESTERDAY.
I'M SO GLAD WE AREN'T GOING FIRST!
THAT'S FOR SURE.
HEATHER AND STACY, YOU'RE UP!
COME ON, WE GOT THIS.
LET'S DO IT!

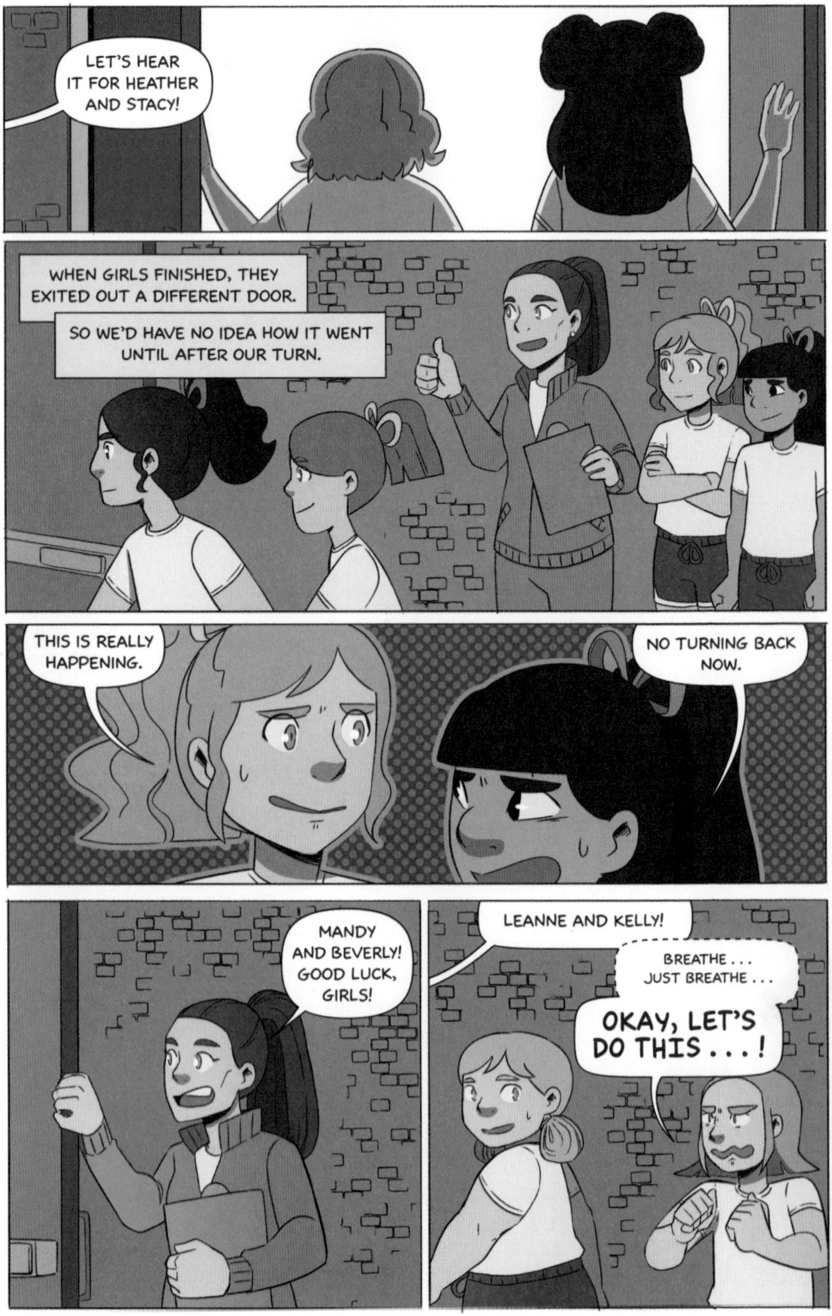
LET'S HEAR IT FOR HEATHER AND STACY!
WHEN GIRLS FINISHED, THEY EXITED OUT A DIFFERENT DOOR.
SO WE'D HAVE NO IDEA HOW IT WENT UNTIL AFTER OUR TURN.
THIS IS REALLY HAPPENING.
NO TURNING BACK NOW.
MANDY AND BEVERLY! GOOD LUCK, GIRLS!
LEANNE AND KELLY!
BREATHE . . . JUST BREATHE . . .
OKAY, LET'S DO THIS . . . !

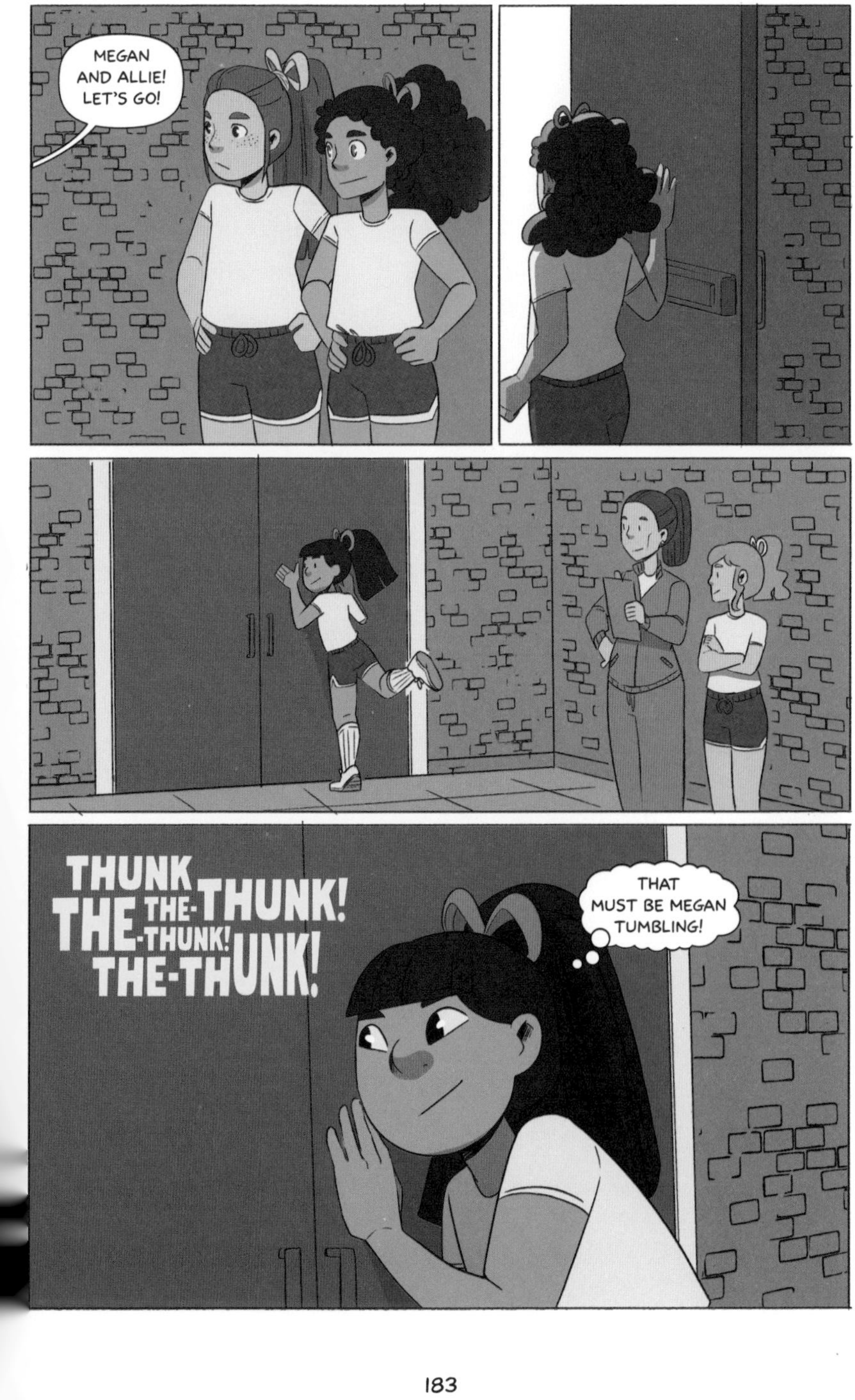
MEGAN AND ALLIE! LET'S GO!
THUNK THE THE-THUNK! THE-THUNK! THE-THUNK!
THAT MUST BE MEGAN TUMBLING!

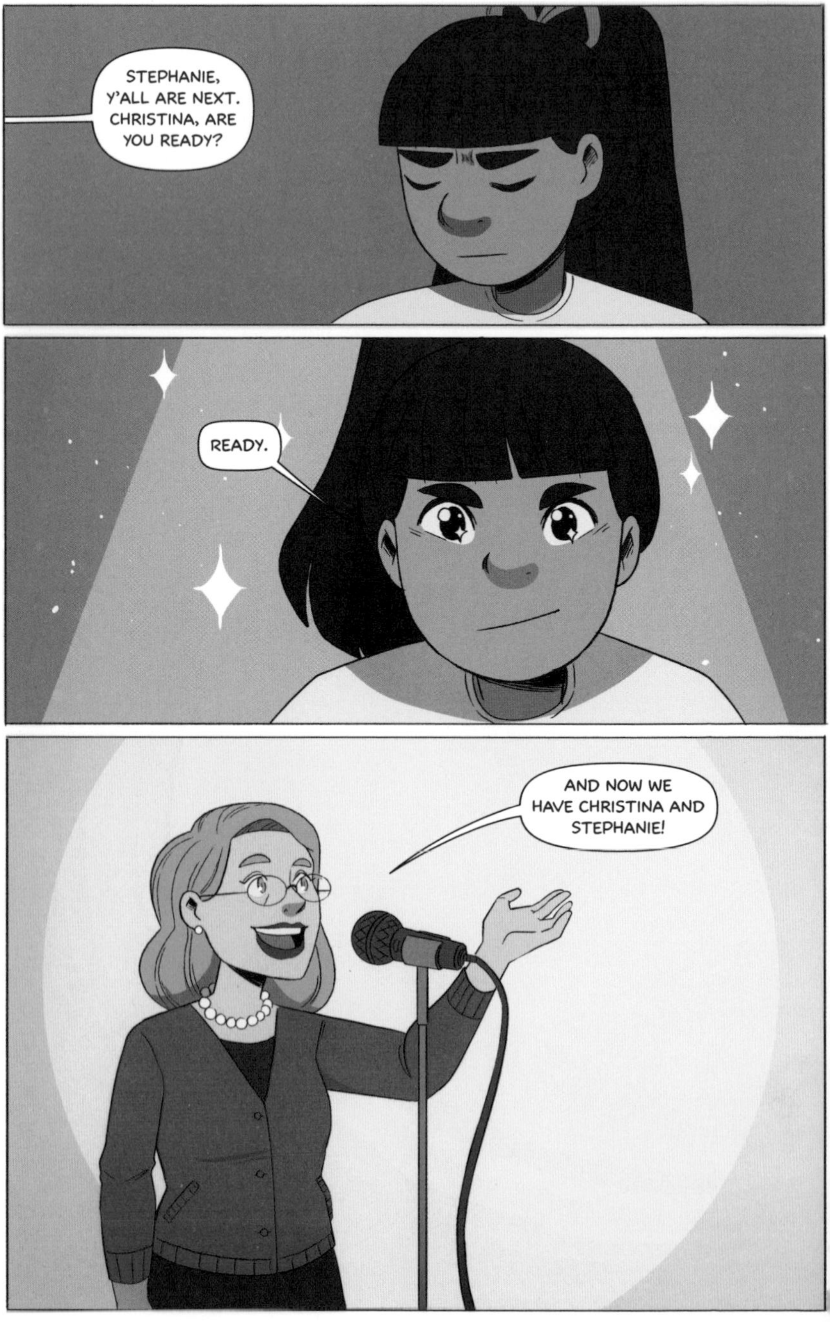
STEPHANIE, Y'ALL ARE NEXT. CHRISTINA, ARE YOU READY?
READY.
AND NOW WE HAVE CHRISTINA AND STEPHANIE!

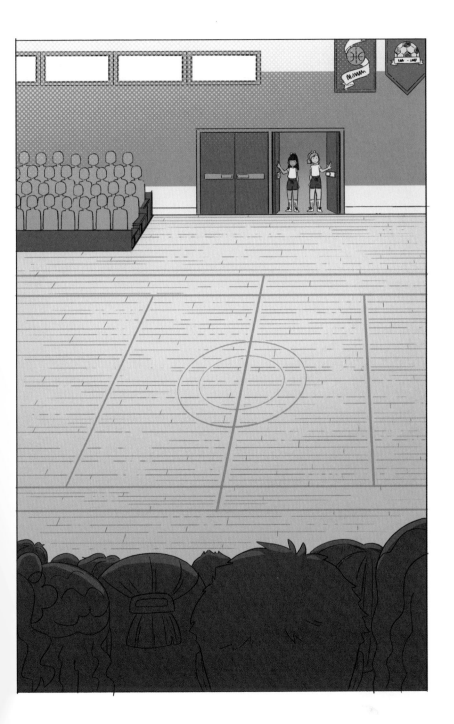

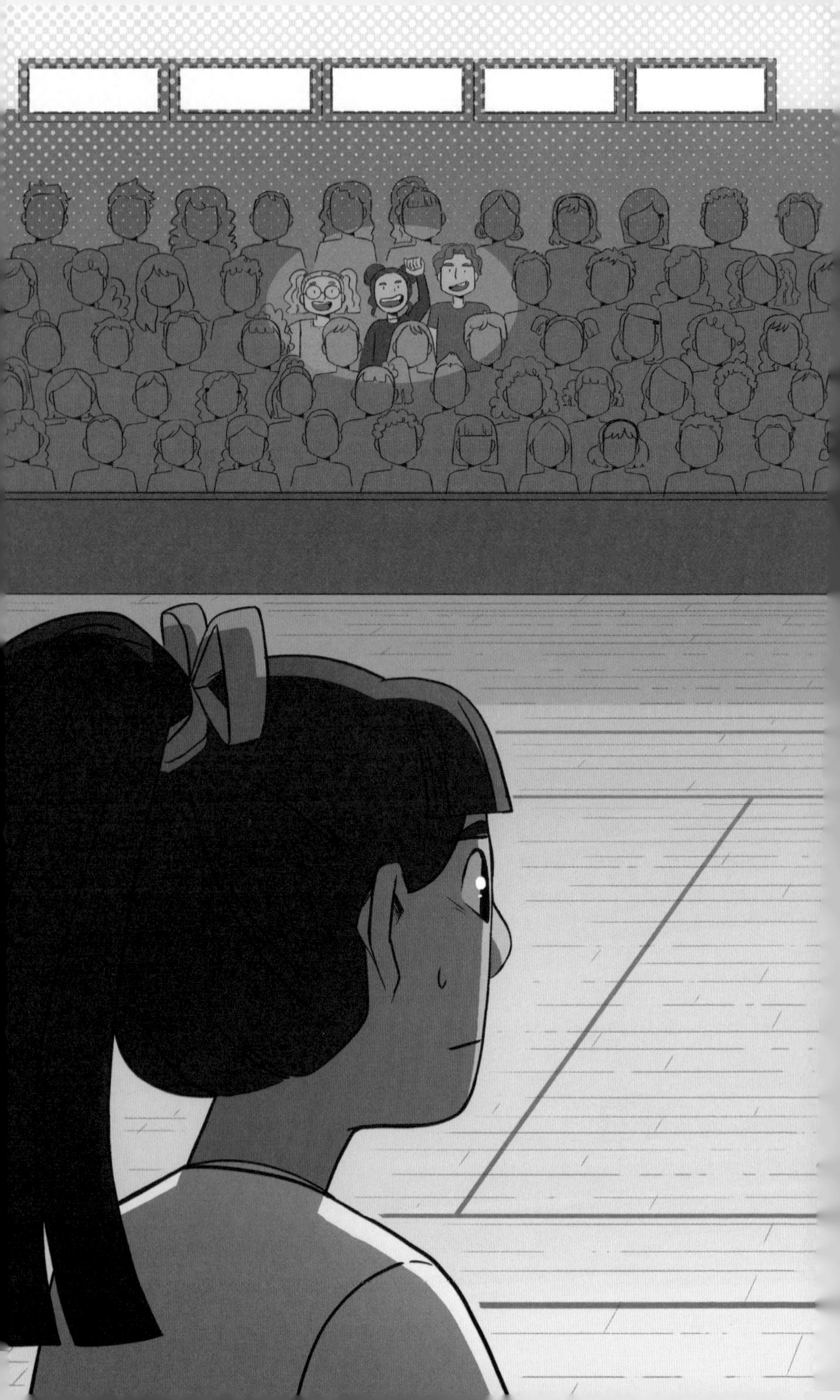

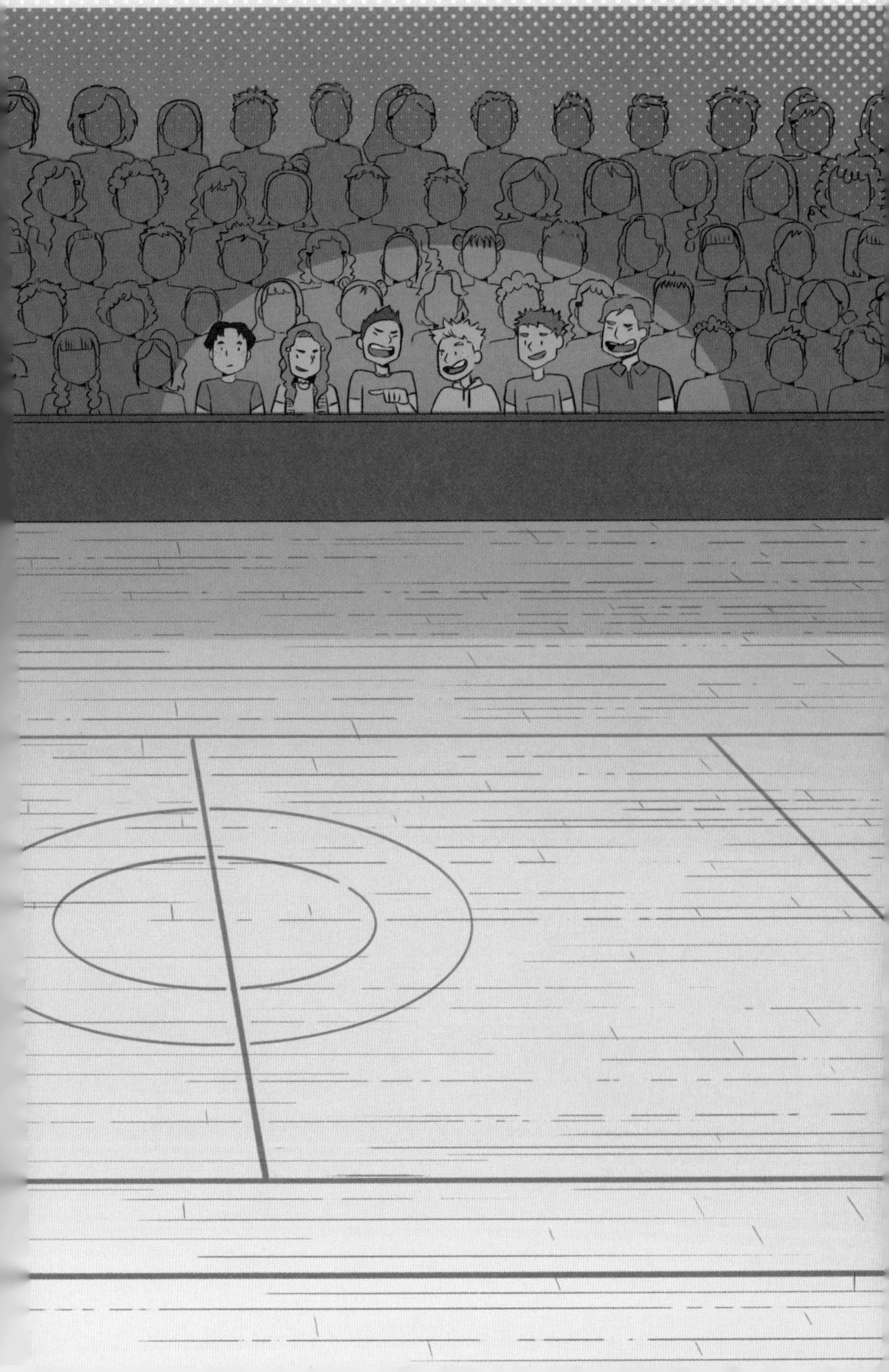

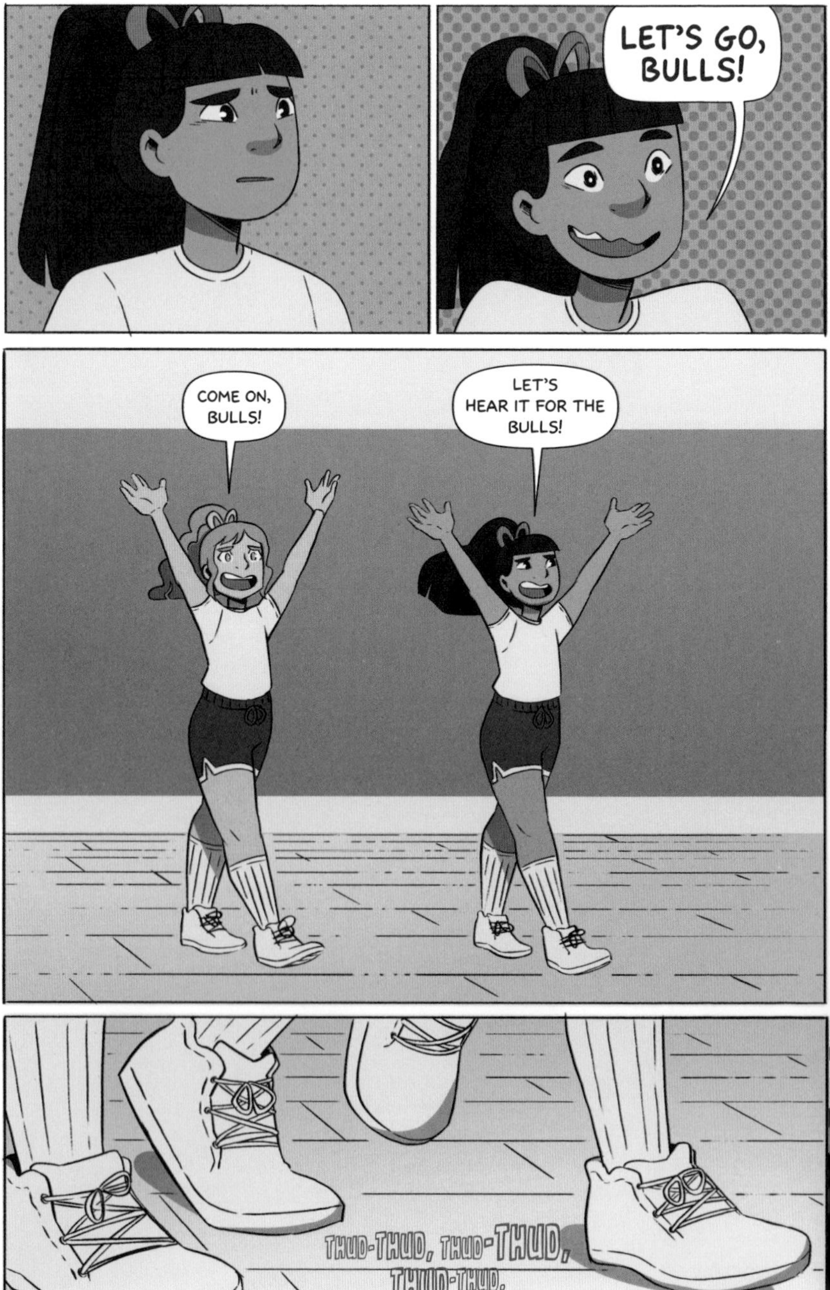
LET'S GO, BULLS!
COME ON, BULLS!
LET'S HEAR IT FOR THE BULLS!
THUD-THUD, THUD-THUD, THUD-THUD.

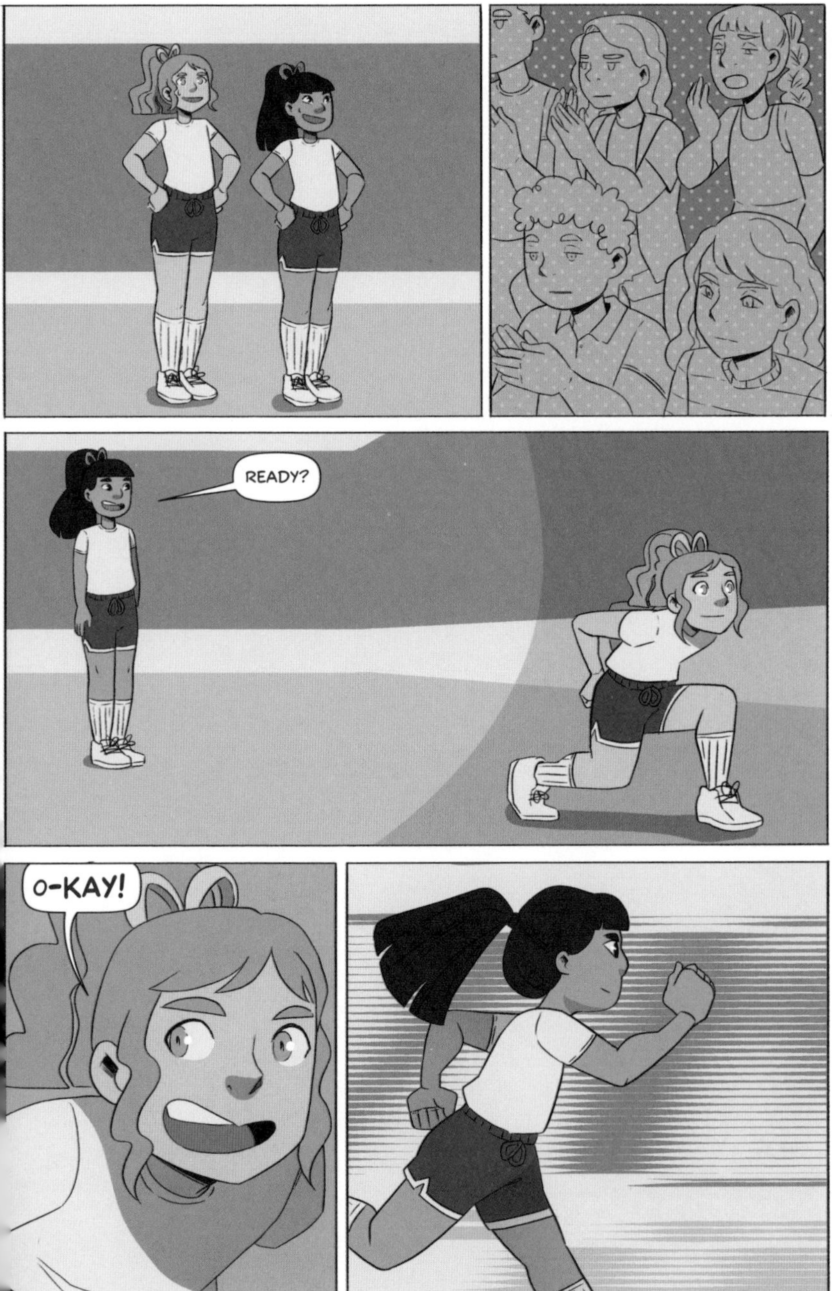
READY?
O-KAY!

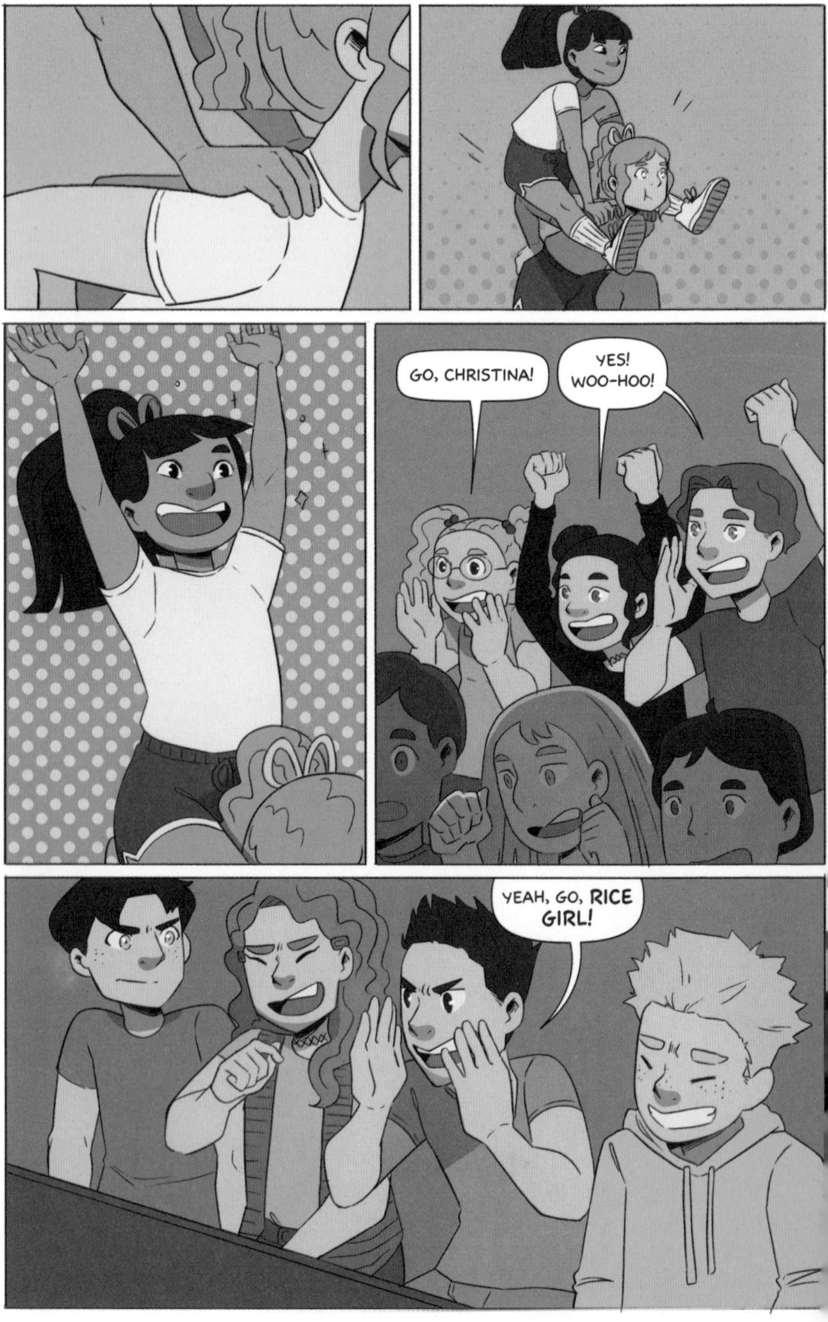
GO, CHRISTINA!
YES! WOO-HOO!
YEAH, GO, RICE GIRL!

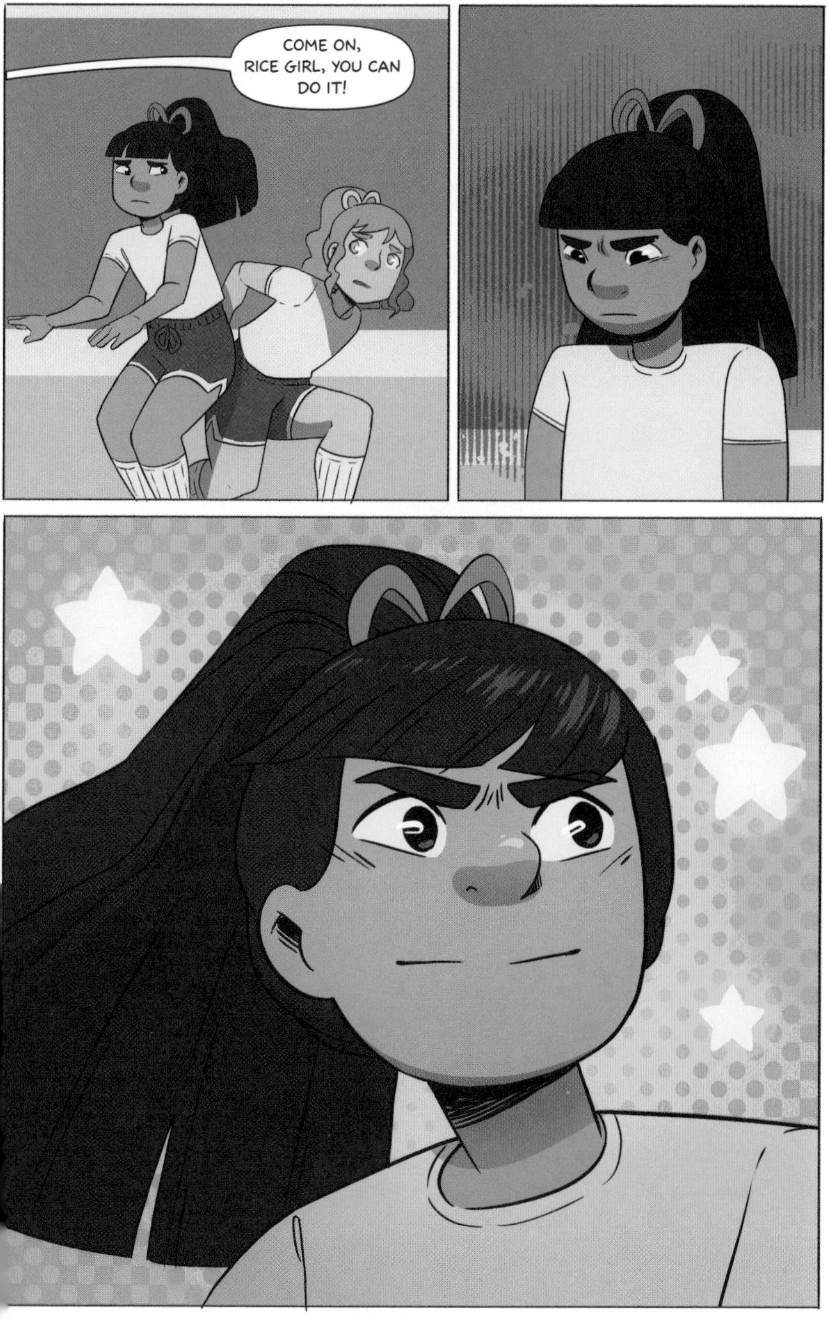
COME ON, RICE GIRL, YOU CAN DO IT!

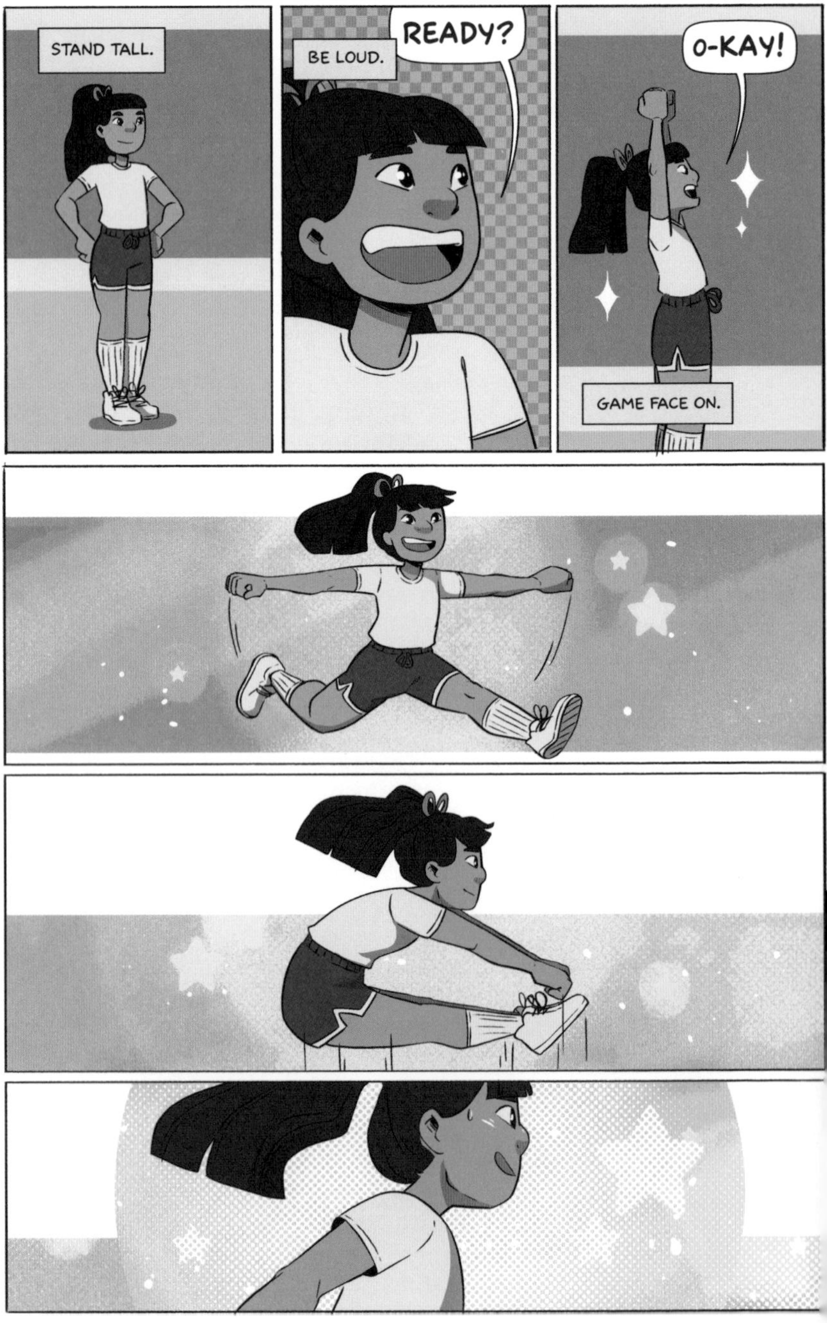
STAND TALL.
BE LOUD.
READY?
O-KAY!
GAME FACE ON.

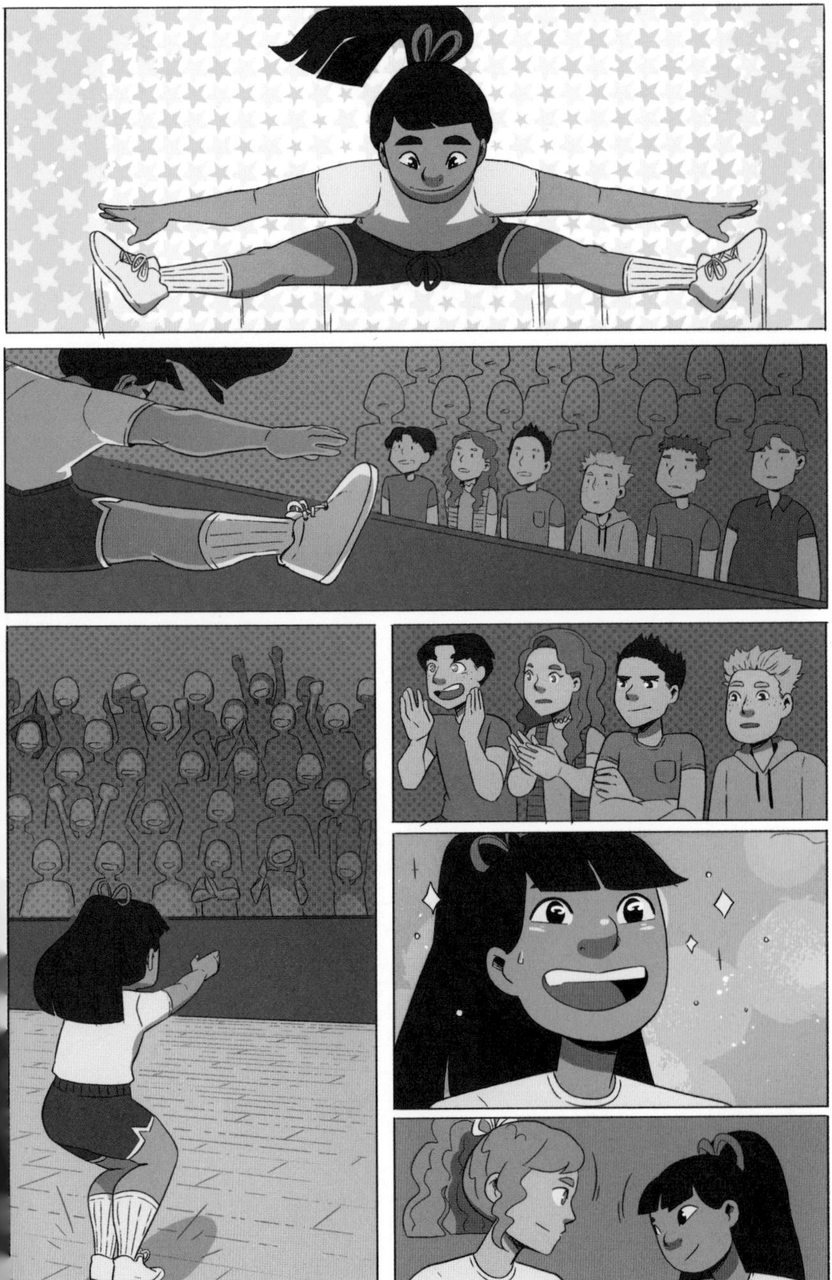

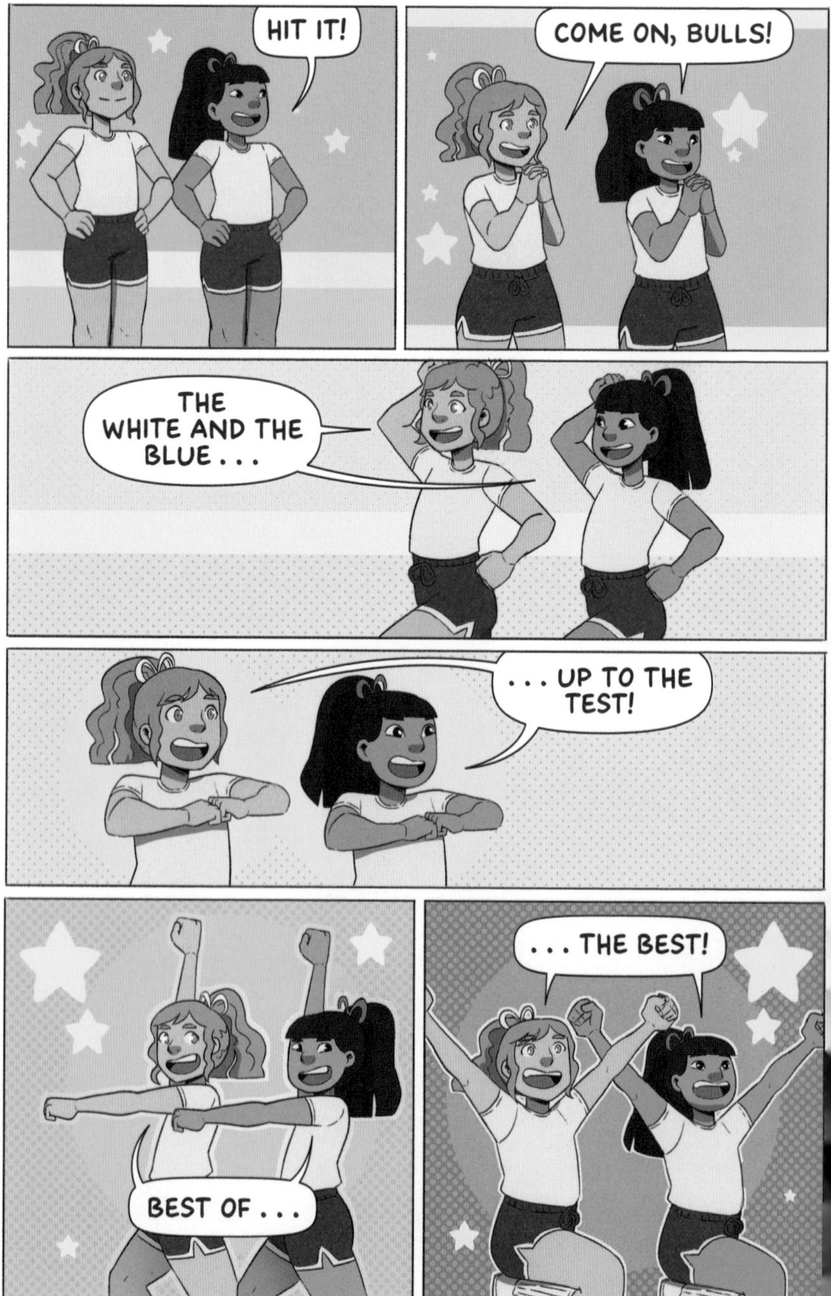
HIT IT!
COME ON, BULLS!
THE WHITE AND THE BLUE . . .
. . . UP TO THE TEST!
BEST OF . . .
. . . THE BEST!

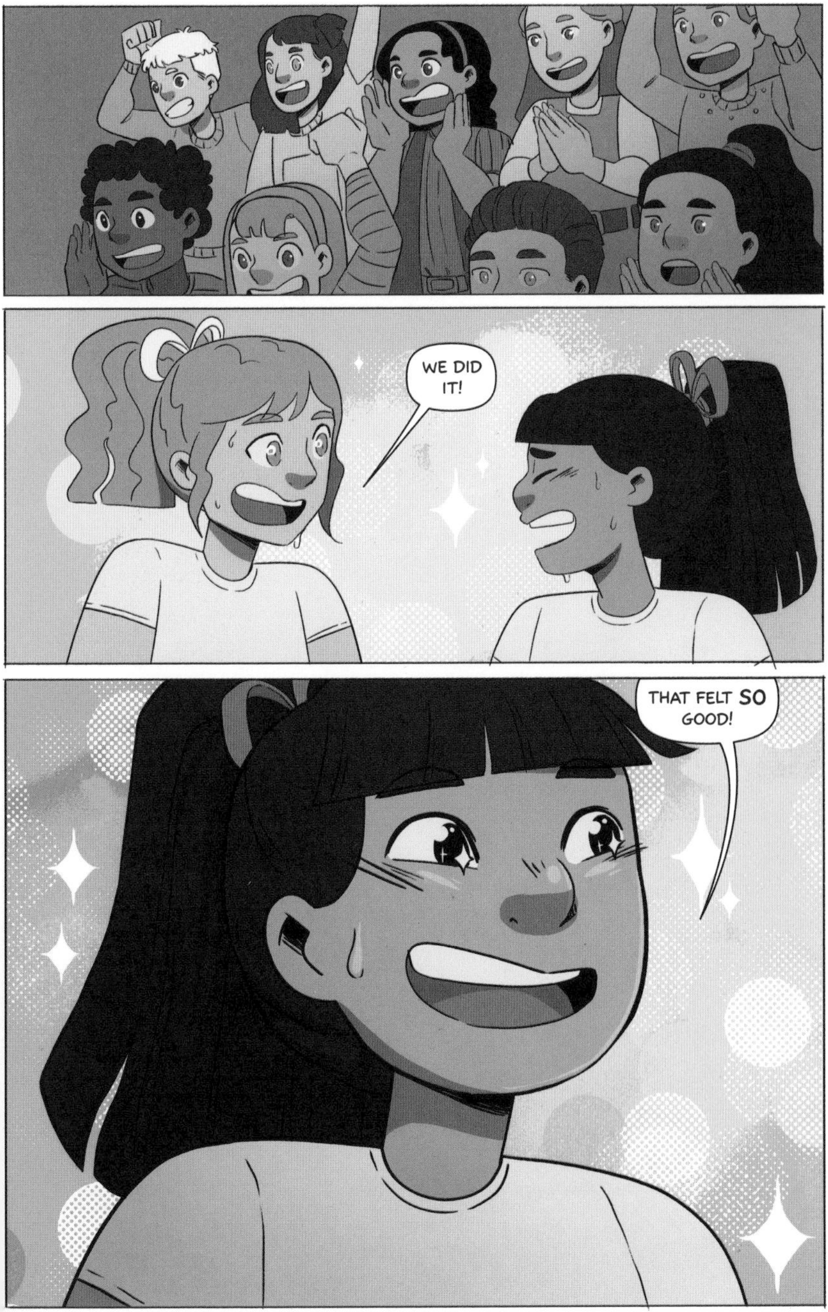
WE DID IT!
THAT FELT SO GOOD!

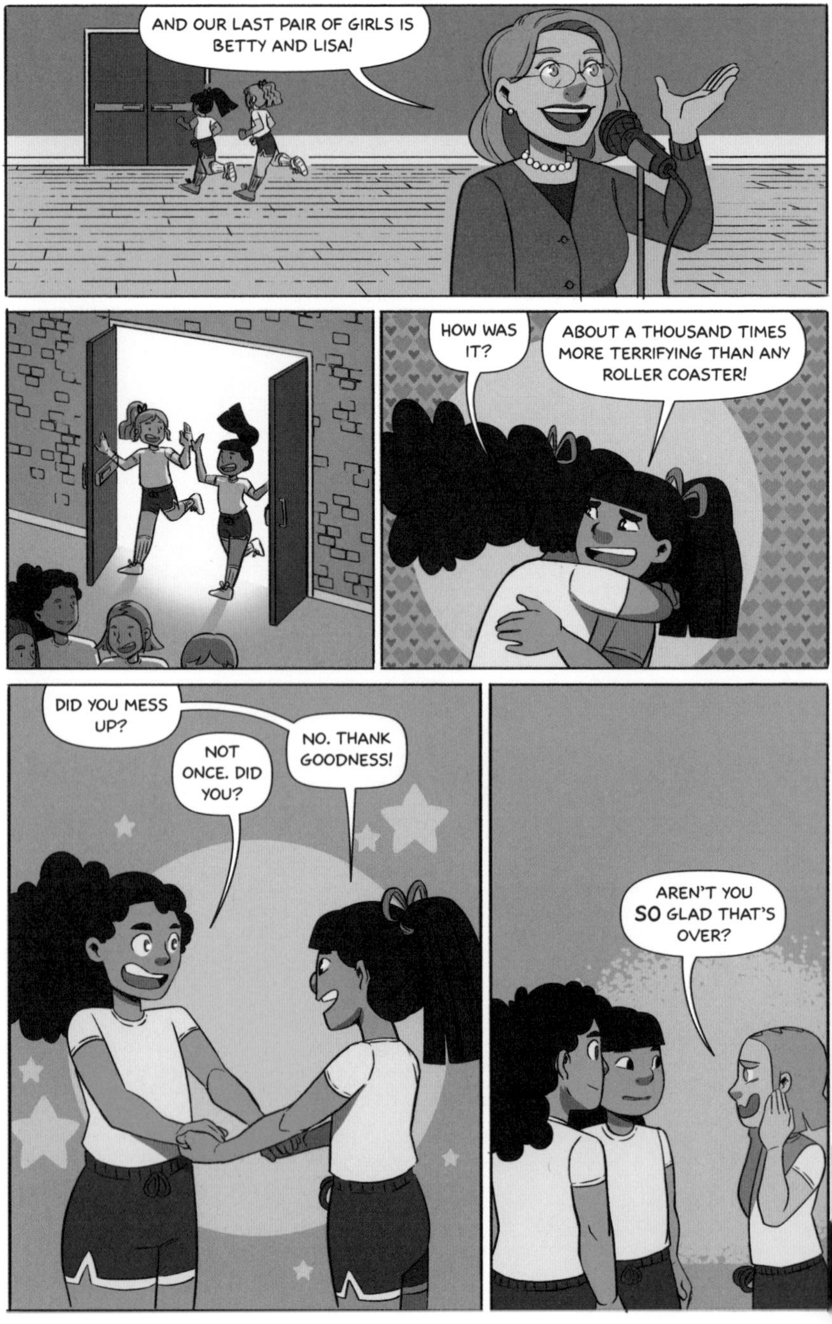
AND OUR LAST PAIR OF GIRLS IS BETTY AND LISA!
HOW WAS IT?
ABOUT A THOUSAND TIMES MORE TERRIFYING THAN ANY ROLLER COASTER!
DID YOU MESS UP?
NOT ONCE. DID YOU?
NO. THANK GOODNESS!
AREN'T YOU SO GLAD THAT'S OVER?

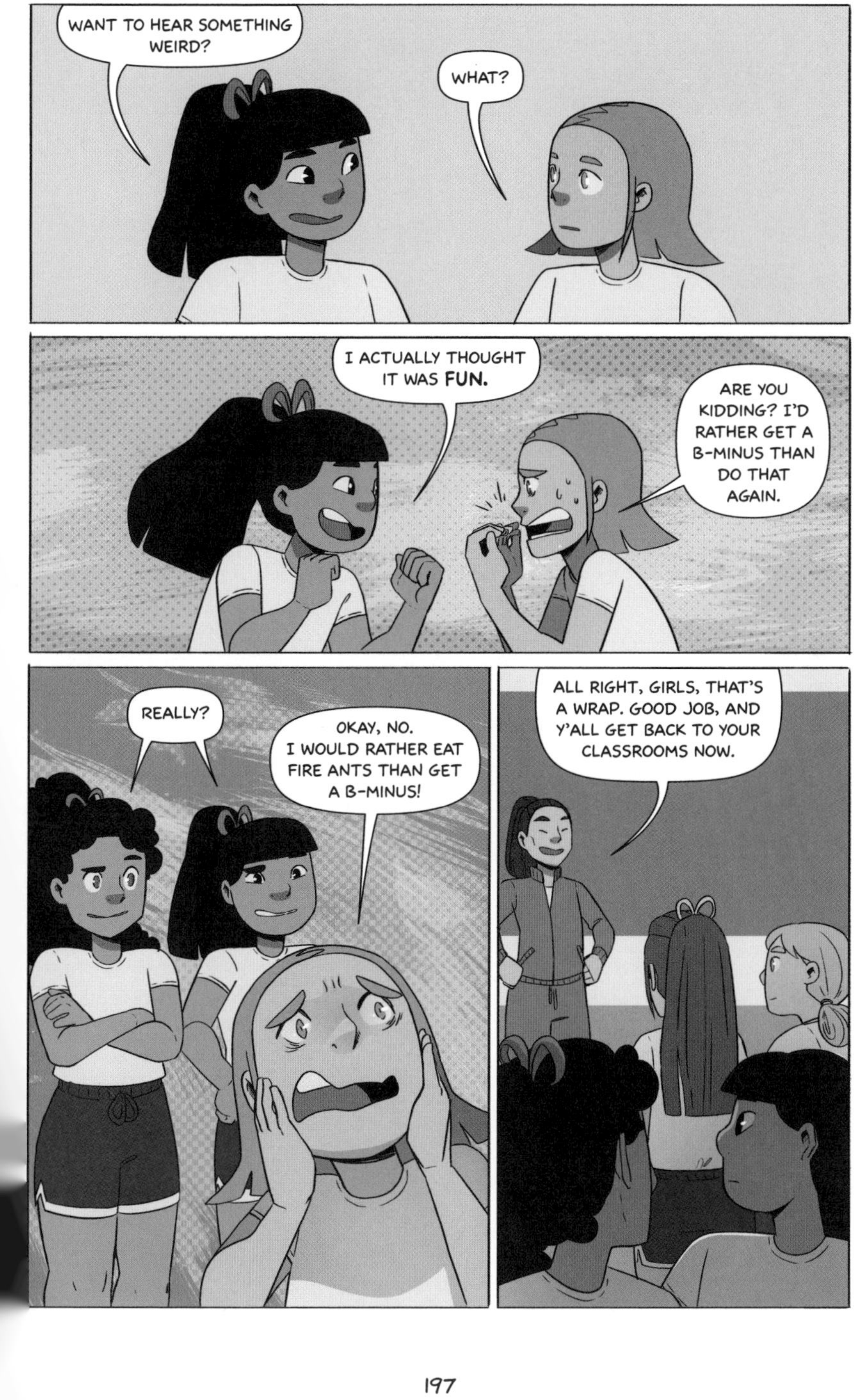

WANT TO HEAR SOMETHING WEIRD?
WHAT?
I ACTUALLY THOUGHT IT WAS FUN.
ARE YOU KIDDING? I'D RATHER GET A B-MINUS THAN DO THAT AGAIN.
REALLY?
OKAY, NO. I WOULD RATHER EAT FIRE ANTS THAN GET A B-MINUS!
ALL RIGHT, GIRLS, THAT'S A WRAP. GOOD JOB, AND Y'ALL GET BACK TO YOUR CLASSROOMS NOW.

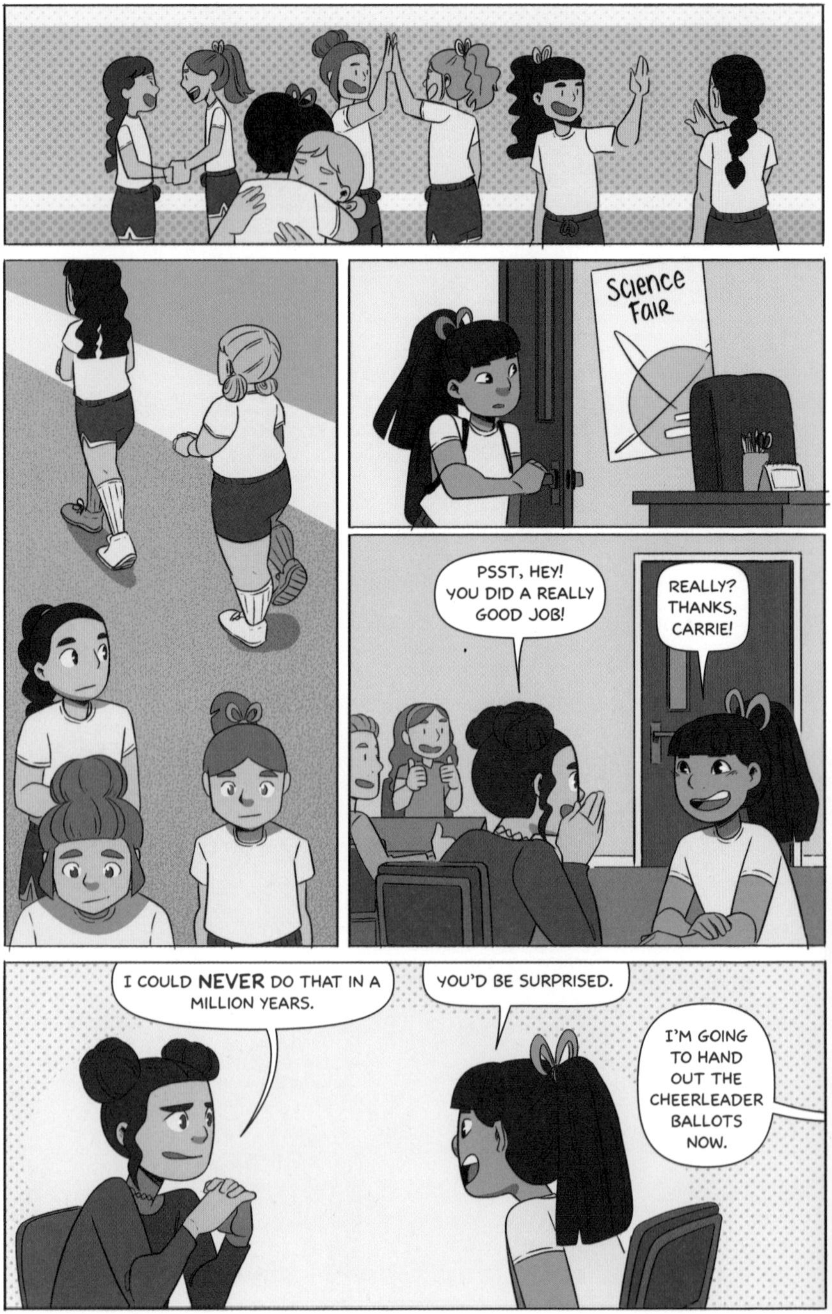
Science Fair
PSST, HEY! YOU DID A REALLY GOOD JOB!
REALLY? THANKS, CARRIE!
I COULD **NEVER** DO THAT IN A MILLION YEARS.
YOU'D BE SURPRISED.
I'M GOING TO HAND OUT THE CHEERLEADER BALLOTS NOW.

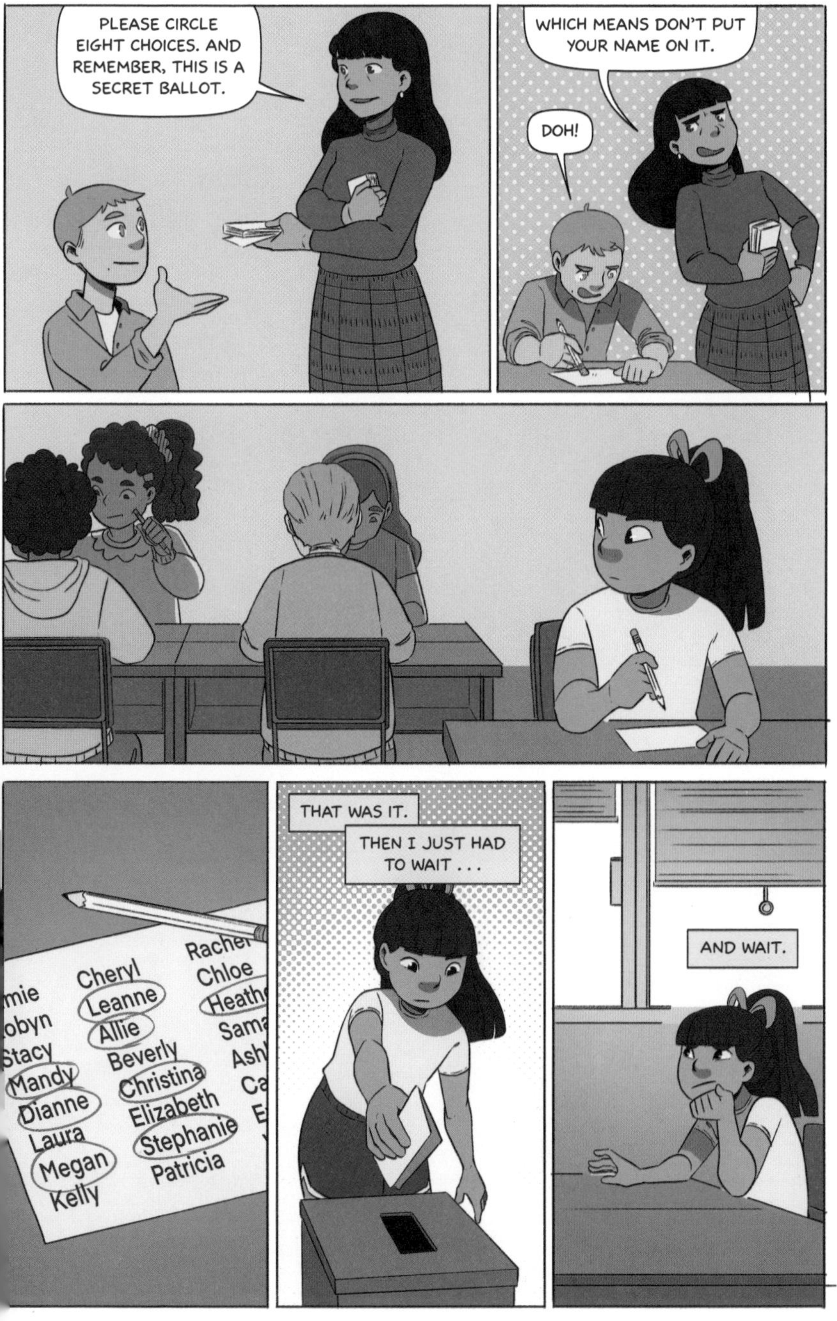
PLEASE CIRCLE EIGHT CHOICES. AND REMEMBER, THIS IS A SECRET BALLOT.
WHICH MEANS DON'T PUT YOUR NAME ON IT.
DOH!
Cheryl
Leanne
Allie
Beverly
Christina
Elizabeth
Stephanie
Patricia
Chloe
Stacy
Mandy
Dianne
Laura
Megan
Kelly
THAT WAS IT.
THEN I JUST HAD TO WAIT . . .
AND WAIT.

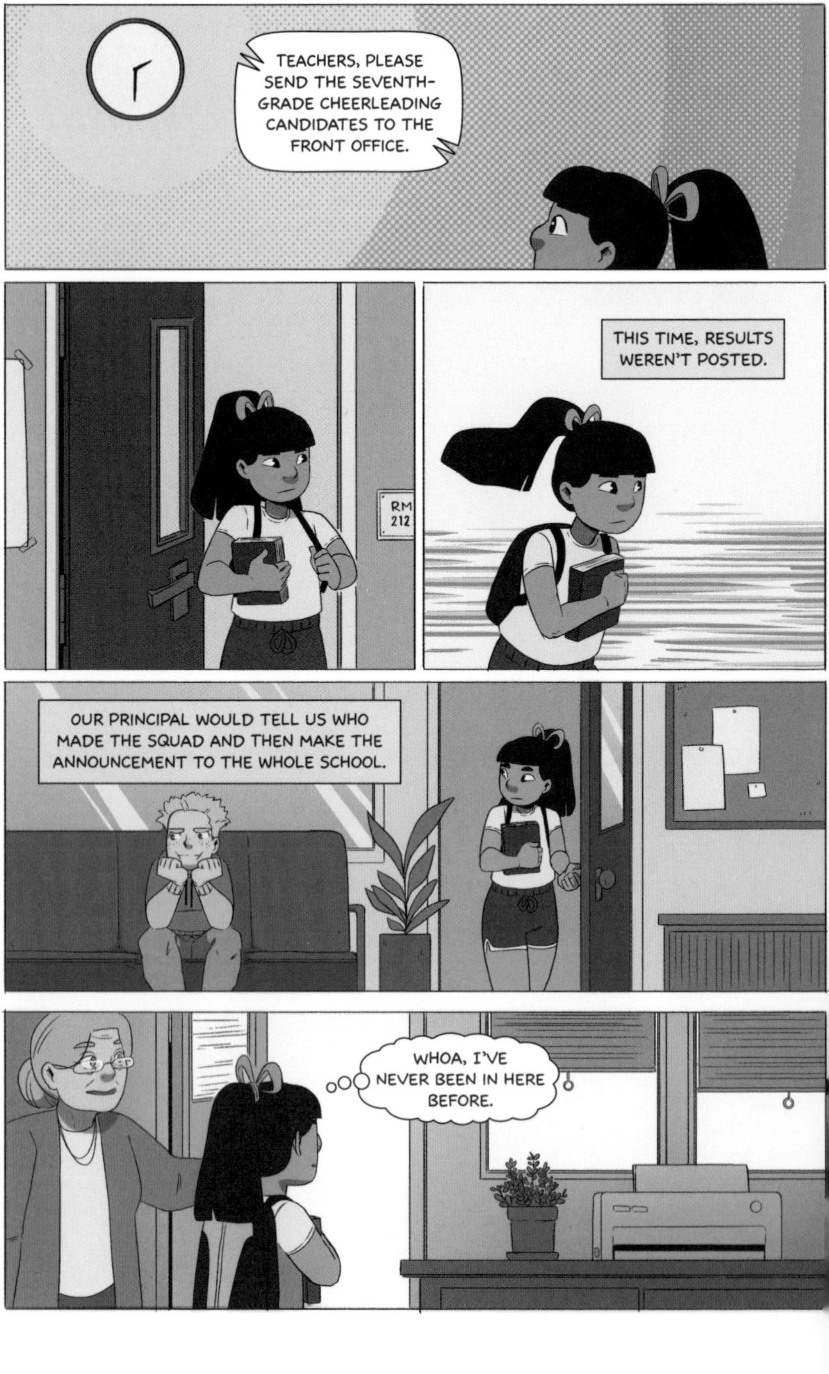
TEACHERS, PLEASE SEND THE SEVENTH-GRADE CHEERLEADING CANDIDATES TO THE FRONT OFFICE.
RM 212
THIS TIME, RESULTS WEREN'T POSTED.
OUR PRINCIPAL WOULD TELL US WHO MADE THE SQUAD AND THEN MAKE THE ANNOUNCEMENT TO THE WHOLE SCHOOL.
WHOA, I'VE NEVER BEEN IN HERE BEFORE.

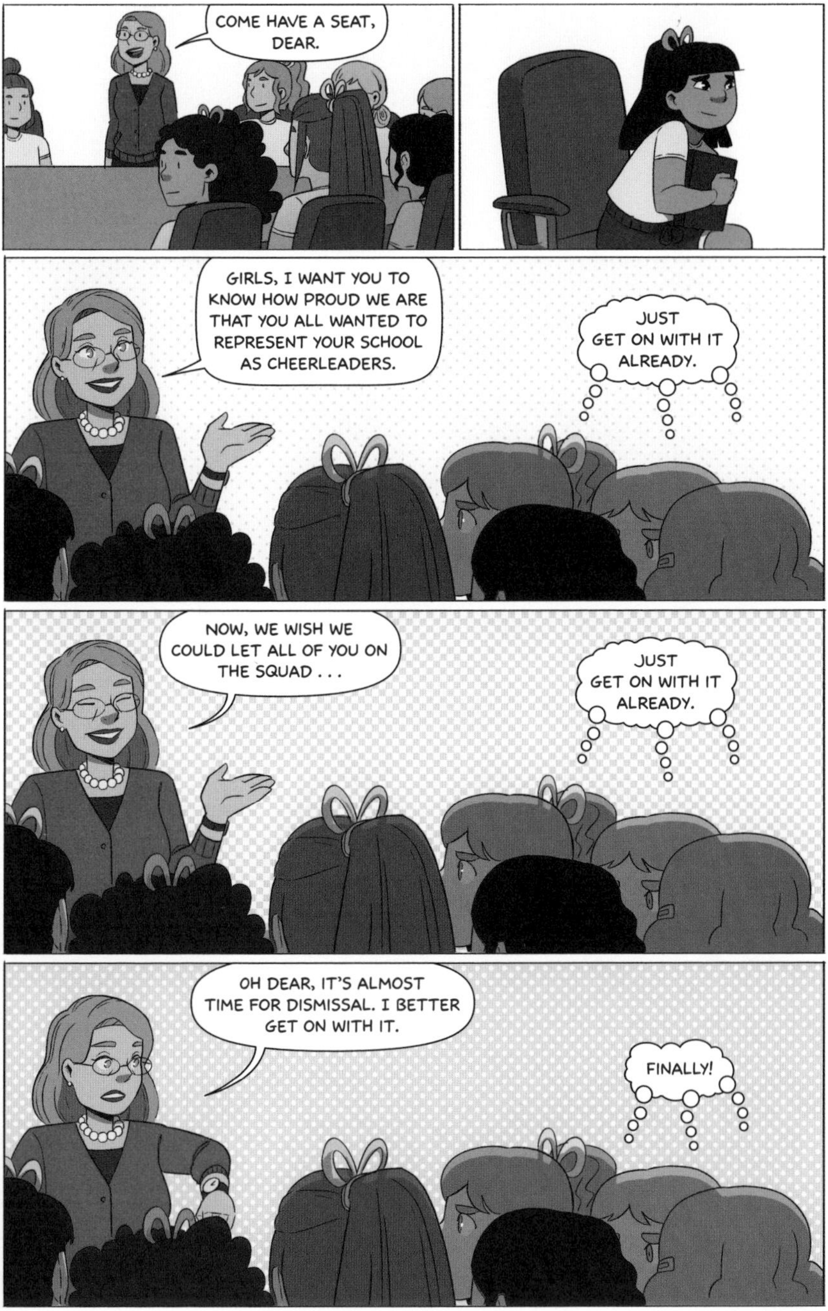
COME HAVE A SEAT, DEAR.
GIRLS, I WANT YOU TO KNOW HOW PROUD WE ARE THAT YOU ALL WANTED TO REPRESENT YOUR SCHOOL AS CHEERLEADERS.
JUST GET ON WITH IT ALREADY.
NOW, WE WISH WE COULD LET ALL OF YOU ON THE SQUAD . . .
JUST GET ON WITH IT ALREADY.
OH DEAR, IT'S ALMOST TIME FOR DISMISSAL. I BETTER GET ON WITH IT.
FINALLY!

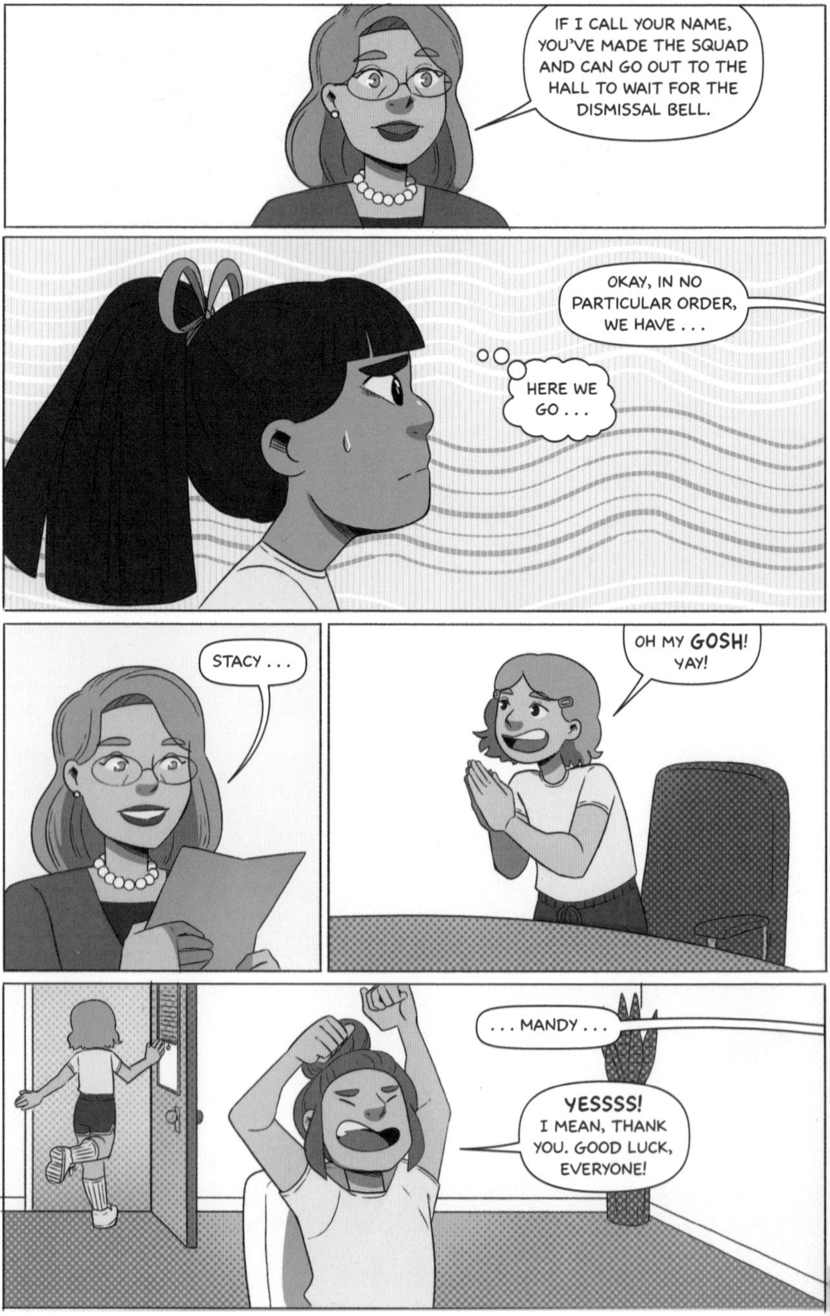
IF I CALL YOUR NAME, YOU'VE MADE THE SQUAD AND CAN GO OUT TO THE HALL TO WAIT FOR THE DISMISSAL BELL.
OKAY, IN NO PARTICULAR ORDER, WE HAVE . . .
HERE WE GO . . .
STACY . . .
OH MY GOSH! YAY!
. . . MANDY . . .
YESSSS! I MEAN, THANK YOU. GOOD LUCK, EVERYONE!

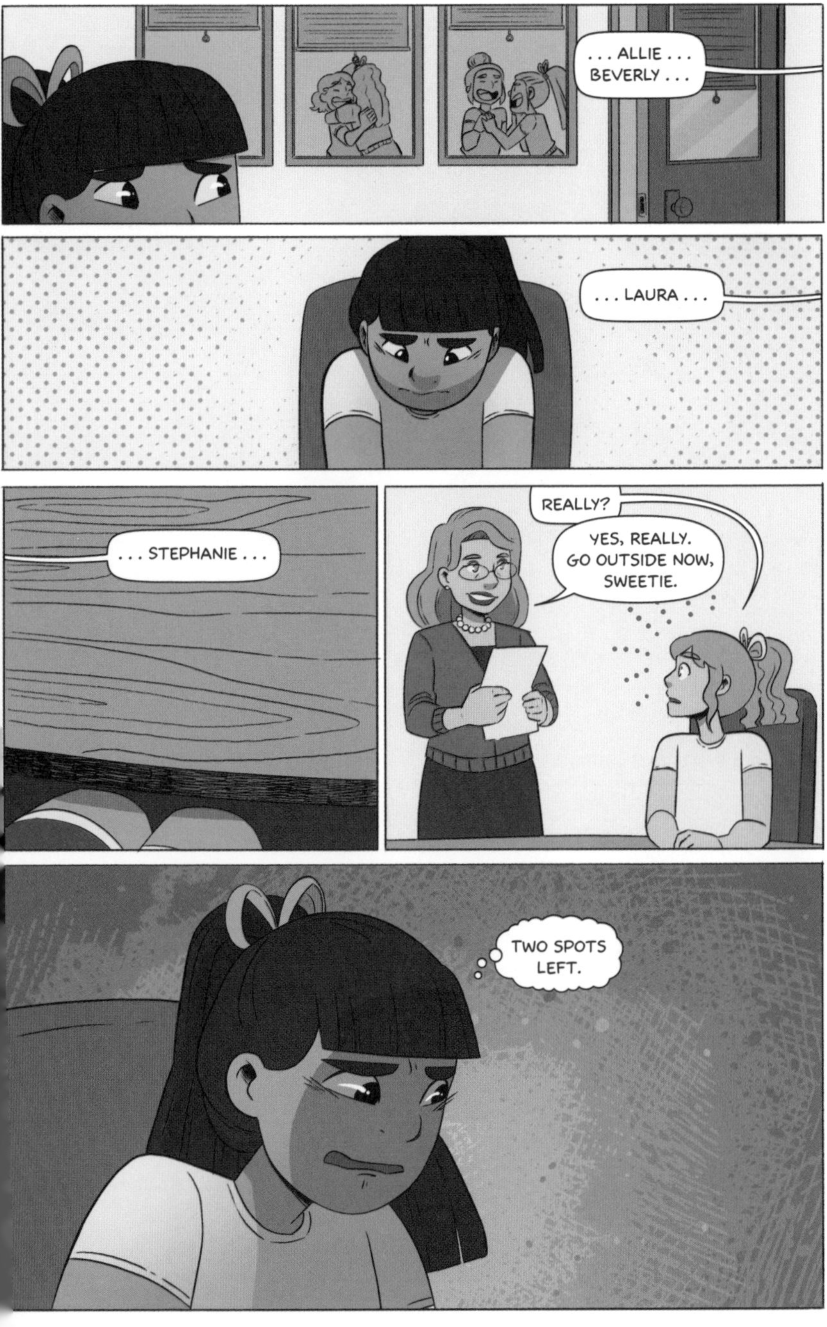
. . . ALLIE . . . BEVERLY . . .
. . . LAURA . . .
. . . STEPHANIE . . .
REALLY?
YES, REALLY. GO OUTSIDE NOW, SWEETIE.
TWO SPOTS LEFT.

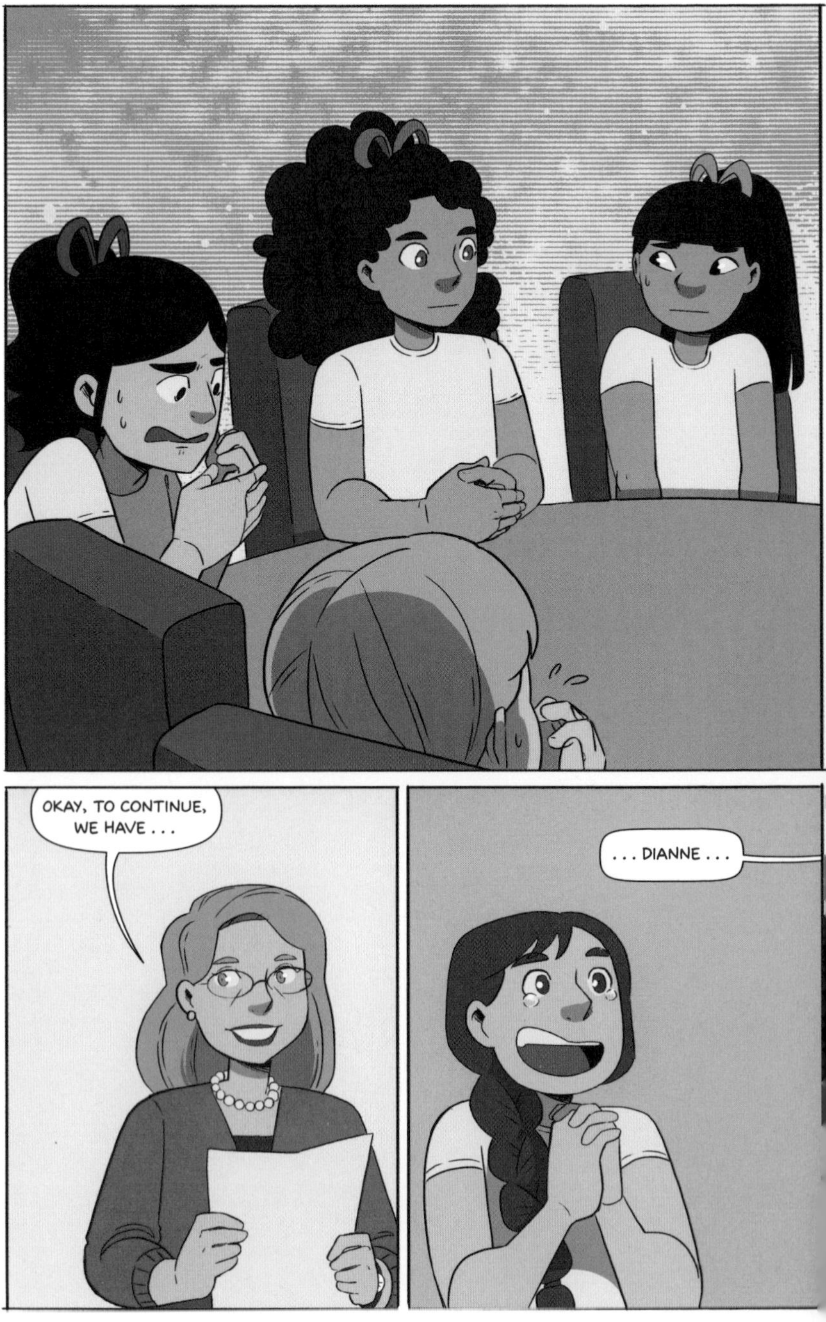
OKAY, TO CONTINUE, WE HAVE . . .
. . . DIANNE . . .

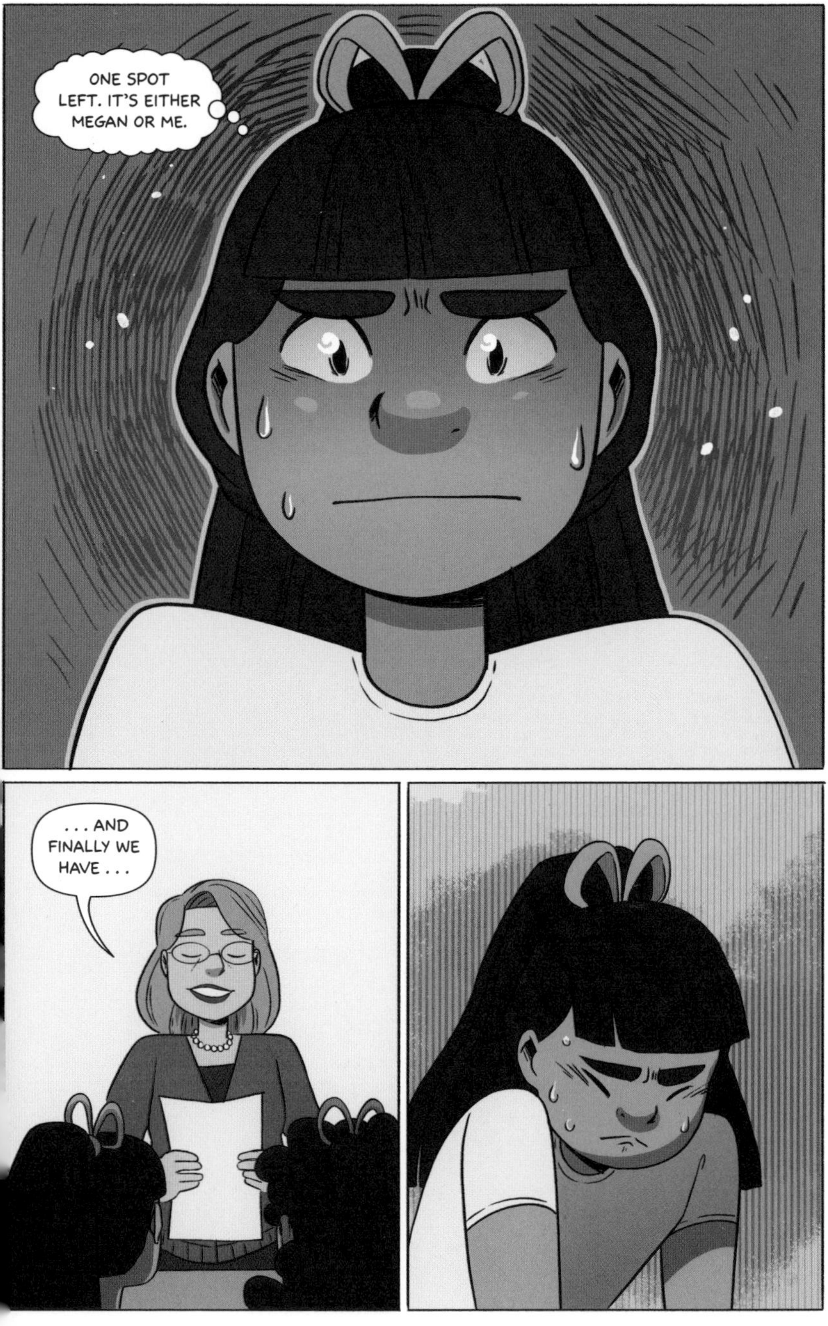
ONE SPOT LEFT. IT'S EITHER MEGAN OR ME.
. . . AND FINALLY WE HAVE . . .

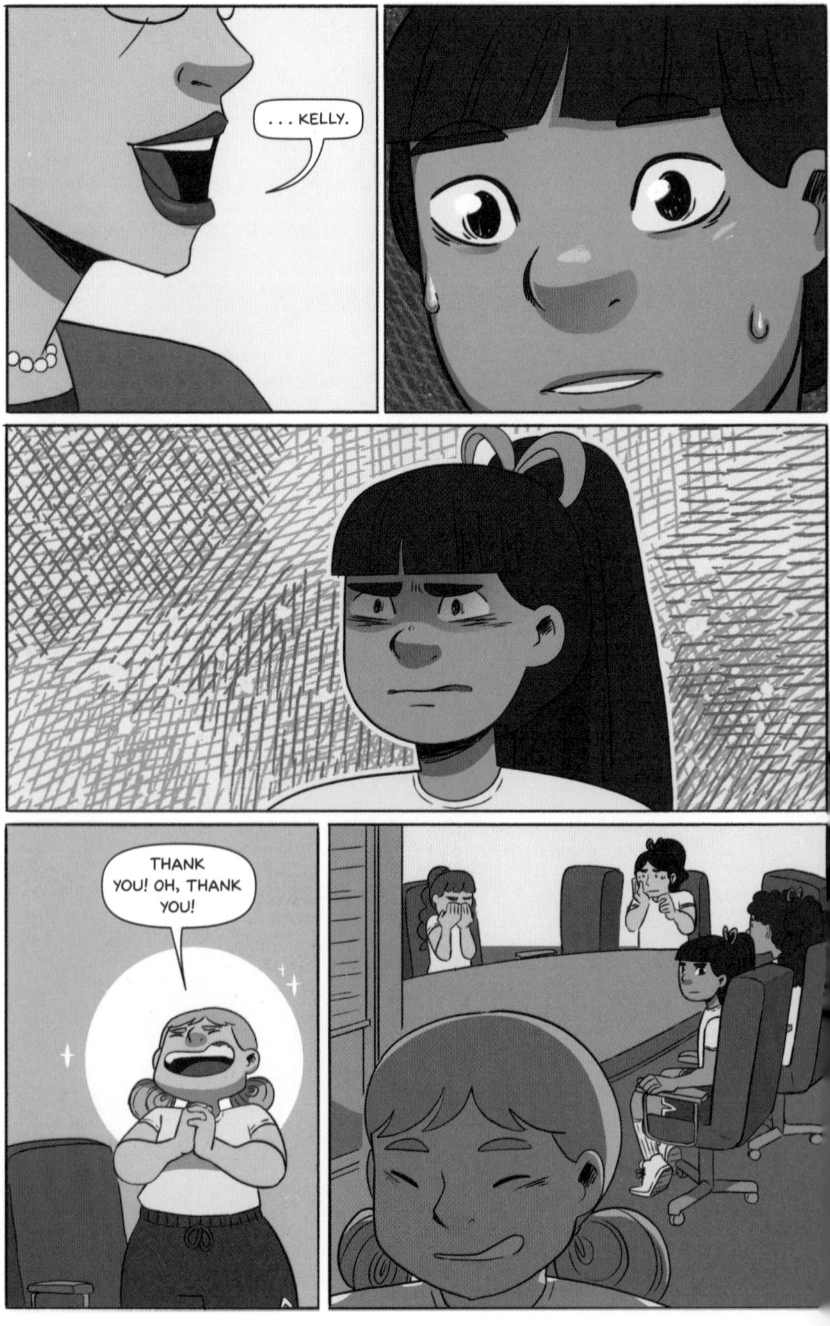
. . . KELLY.
THANK YOU! OH, THANK YOU!

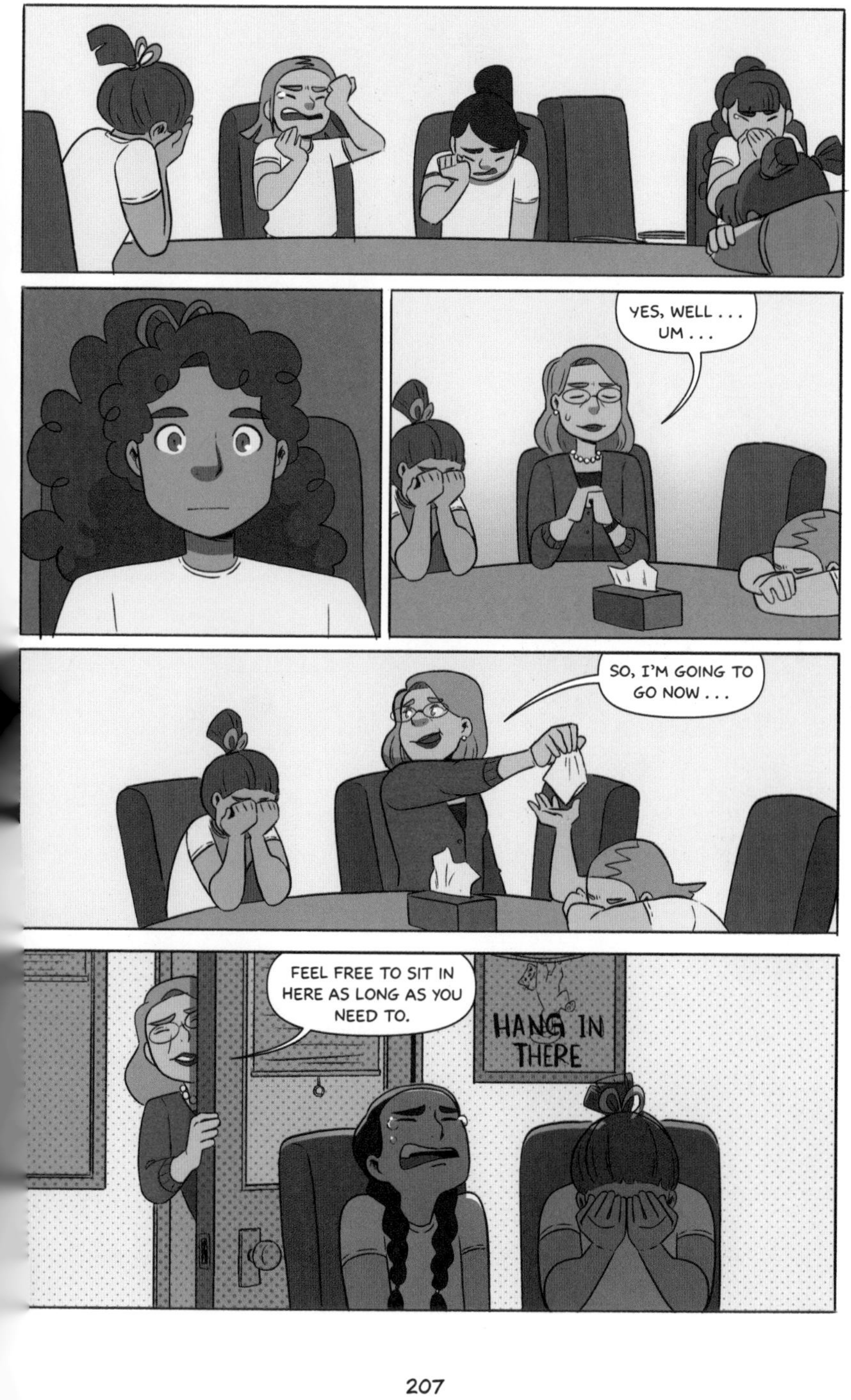
YES, WELL . . .
UM . . .
SO, I'M GOING TO GO NOW . . .
FEEL FREE TO SIT IN HERE AS LONG AS YOU NEED TO.
HANG IN THERE

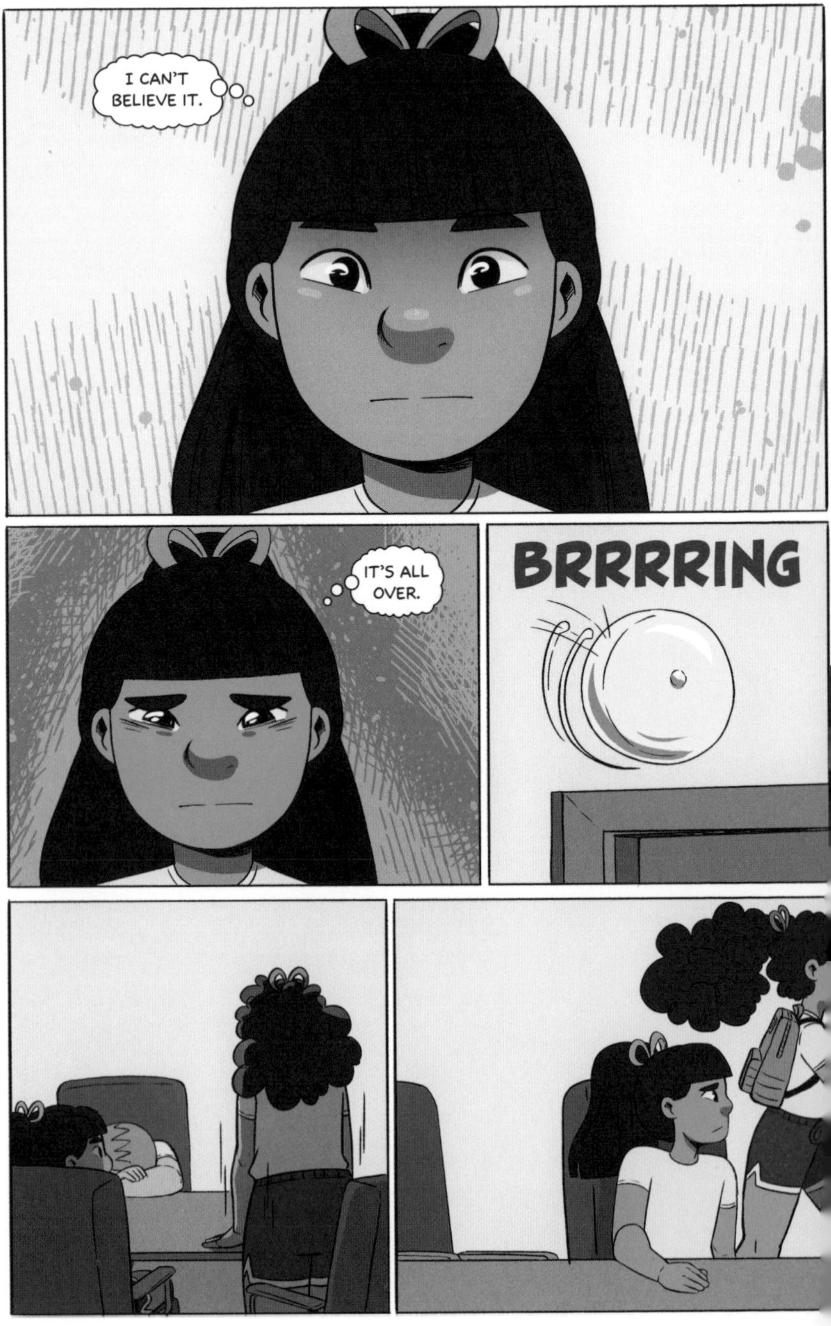
I CAN'T BELIEVE IT.
IT'S ALL OVER.
BRRRRING

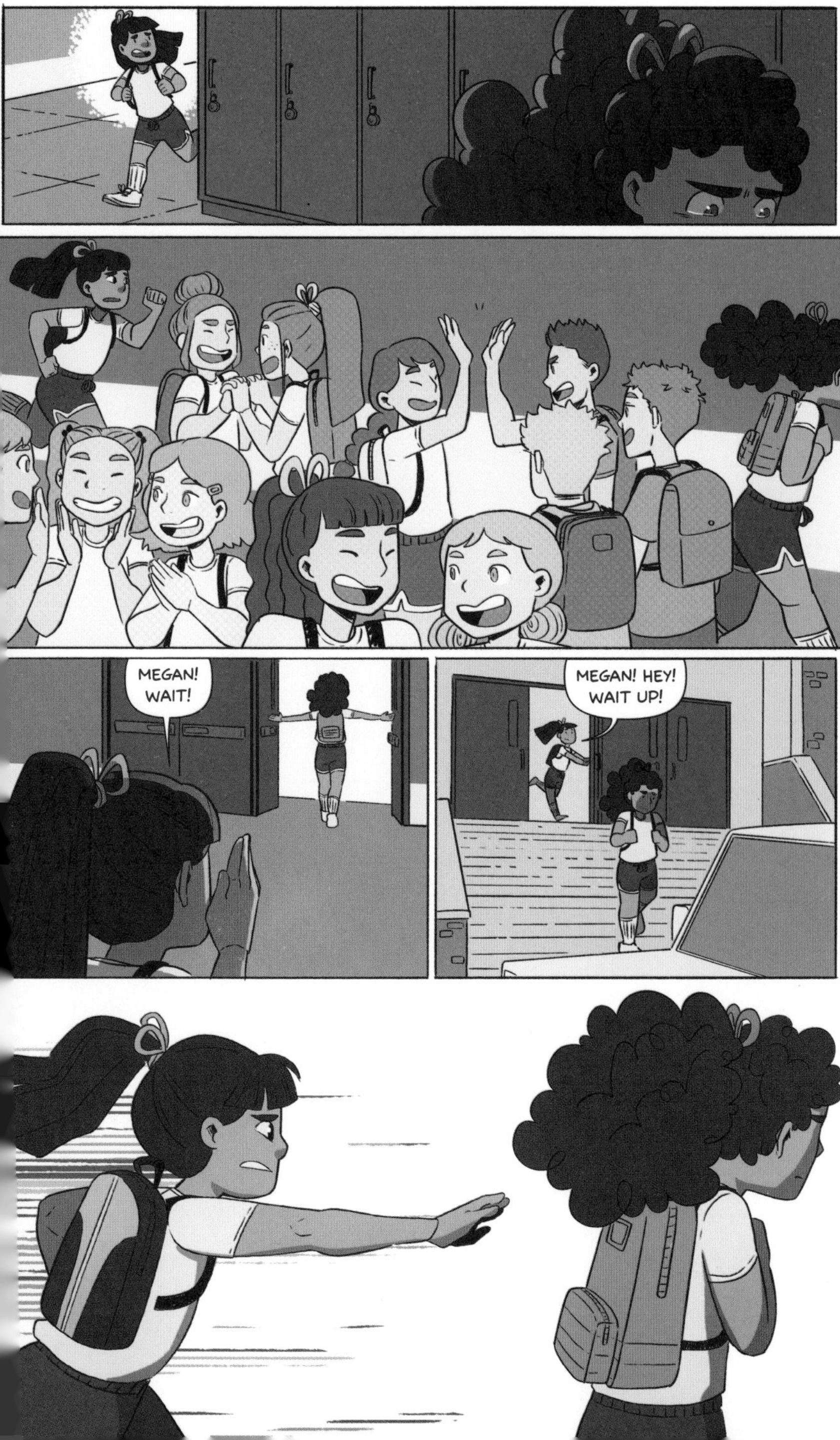
MEGAN! WAIT!
MEGAN! HEY! WAIT UP!

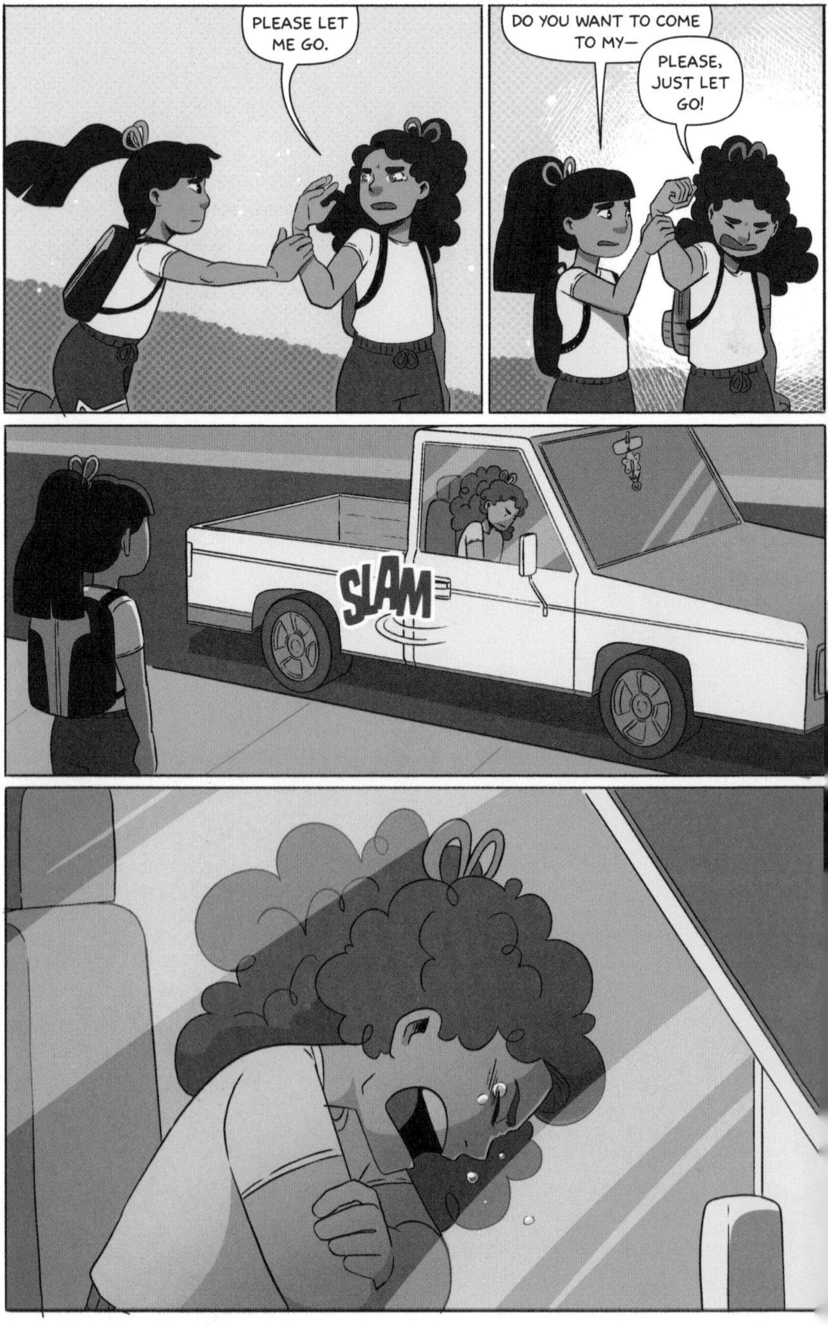

PLEASE LET ME GO.
DO YOU WANT TO COME TO MY—
PLEASE, JUST LET GO!
SLAM

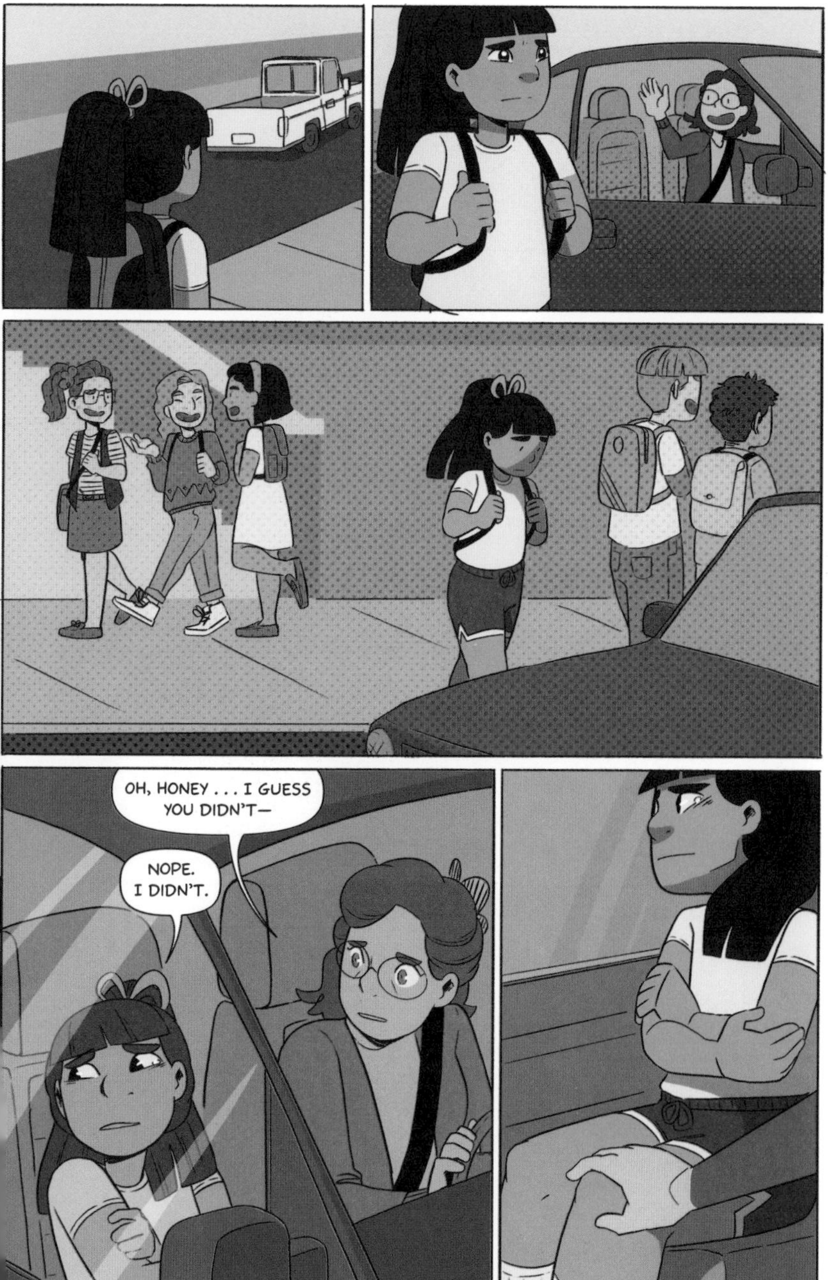
OH, HONEY . . . I GUESS YOU DIDN'T—
NOPE. I DIDN'T.

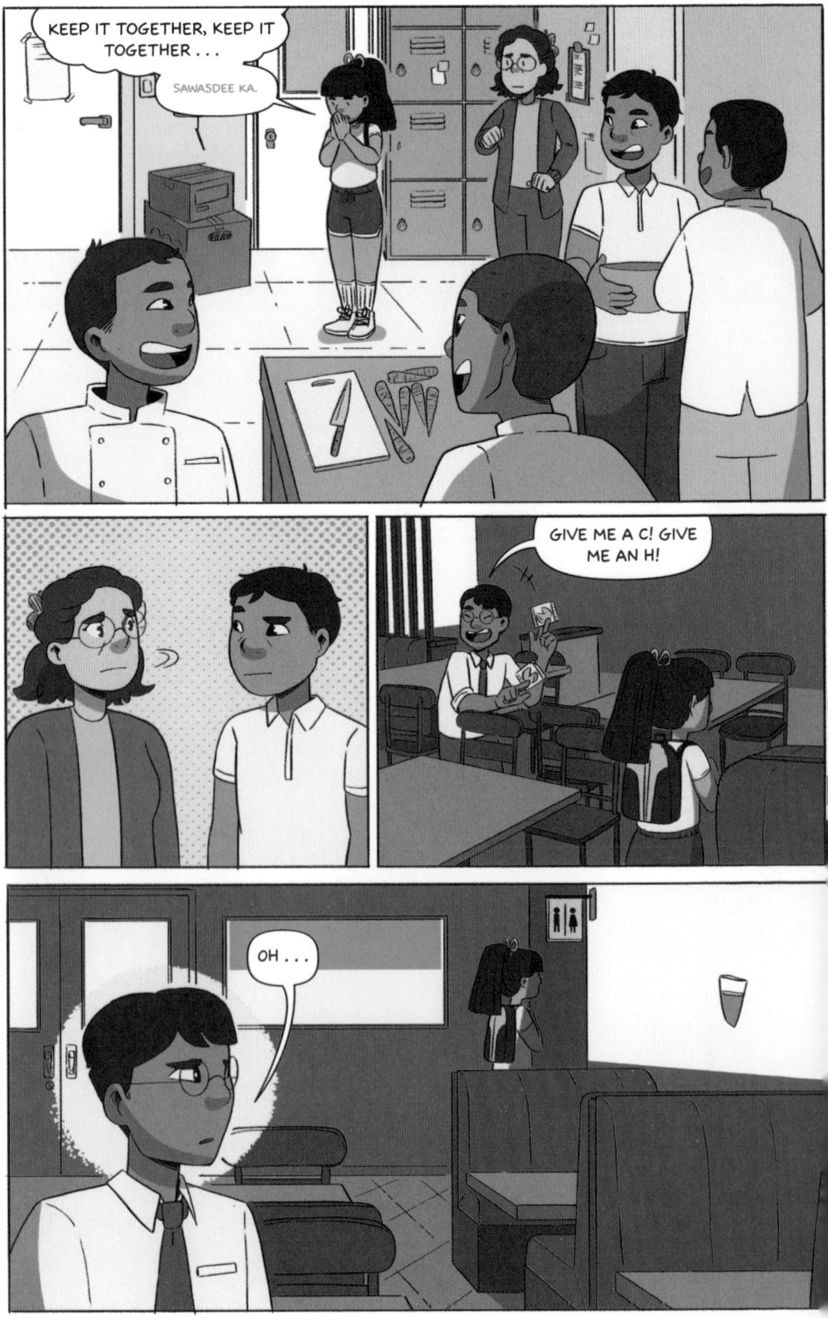
KEEP IT TOGETHER, KEEP IT TOGETHER . . .
SAWASDEE KA.
GIVE ME A C! GIVE ME AN H!
OH . . .

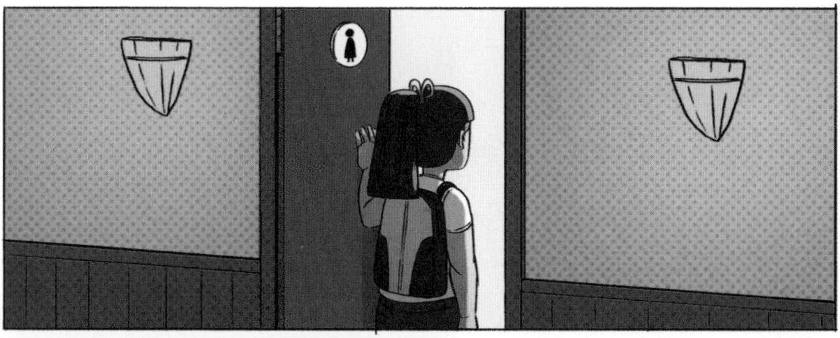

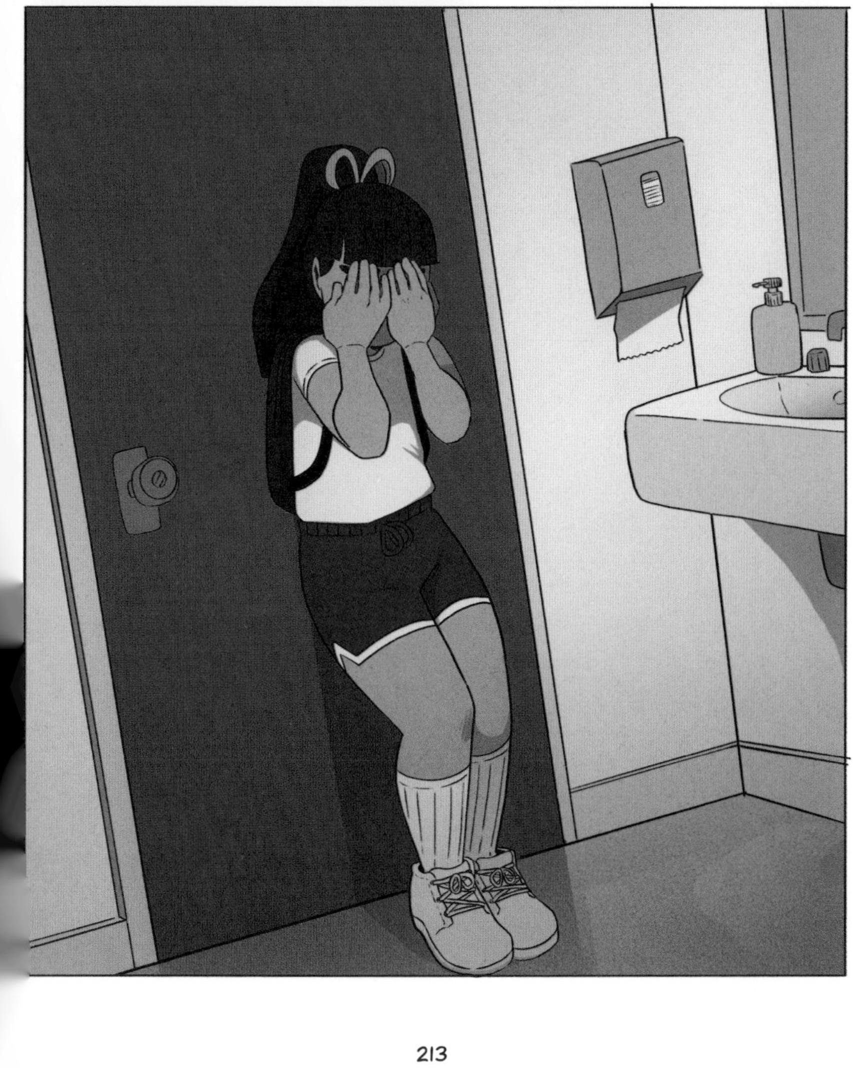

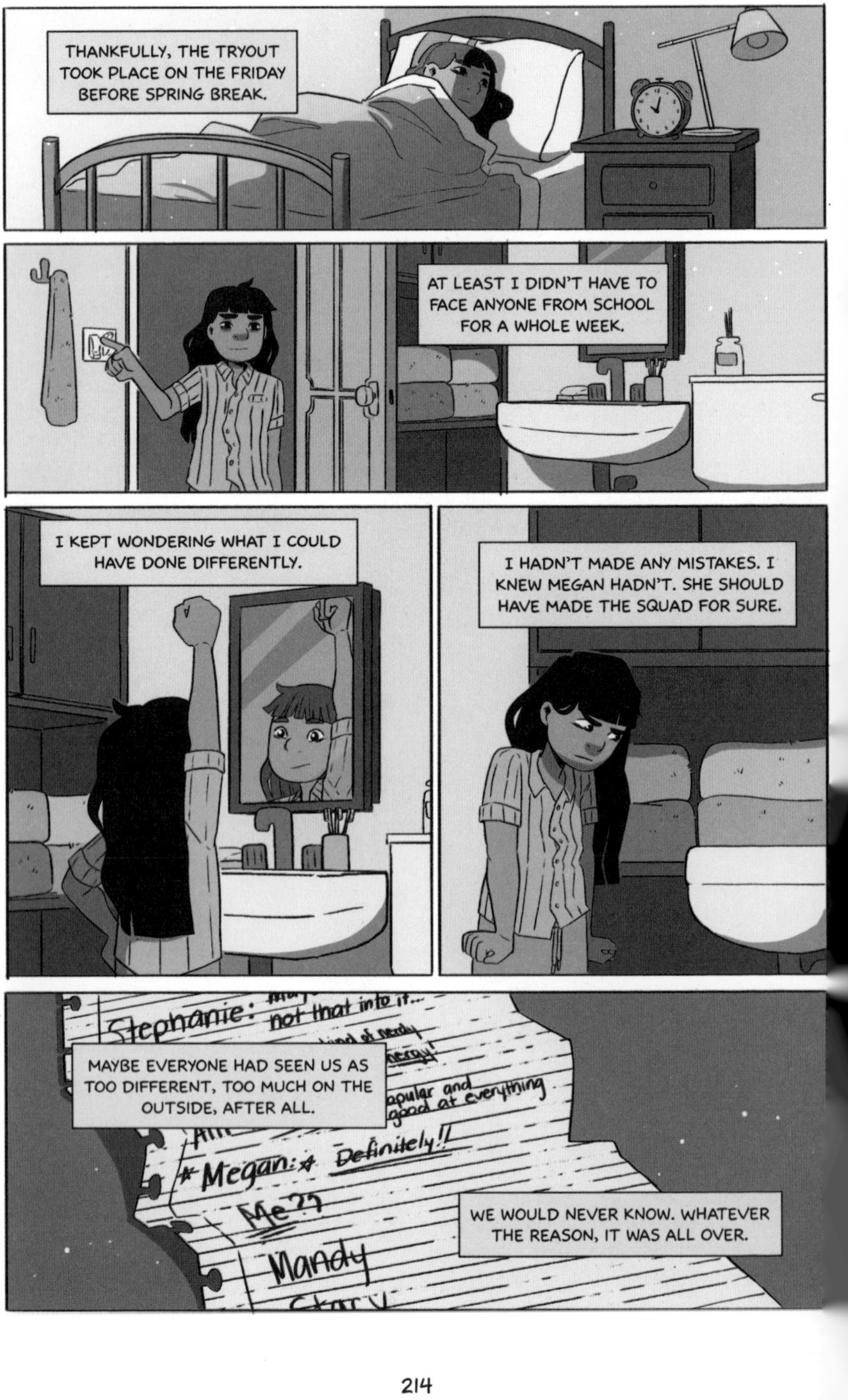
THANKFULLY, THE TRYOUT TOOK PLACE ON THE FRIDAY BEFORE SPRING BREAK.
AT LEAST I DIDN'T HAVE TO FACE ANYONE FROM SCHOOL FOR A WHOLE WEEK.
I KEPT WONDERING WHAT I COULD HAVE DONE DIFFERENTLY.
I HADN'T MADE ANY MISTAKES. I KNEW MEGAN HADN'T. SHE SHOULD HAVE MADE THE SQUAD FOR SURE.
Stephanie:
not that into it...
MAYBE EVERYONE HAD SEEN US AS TOO DIFFERENT, TOO MUCH ON THE OUTSIDE, AFTER ALL.
good at everything
Megan: Definitely!!
Me??
WE WOULD NEVER KNOW. WHATEVER THE REASON, IT WAS ALL OVER.
Mandy

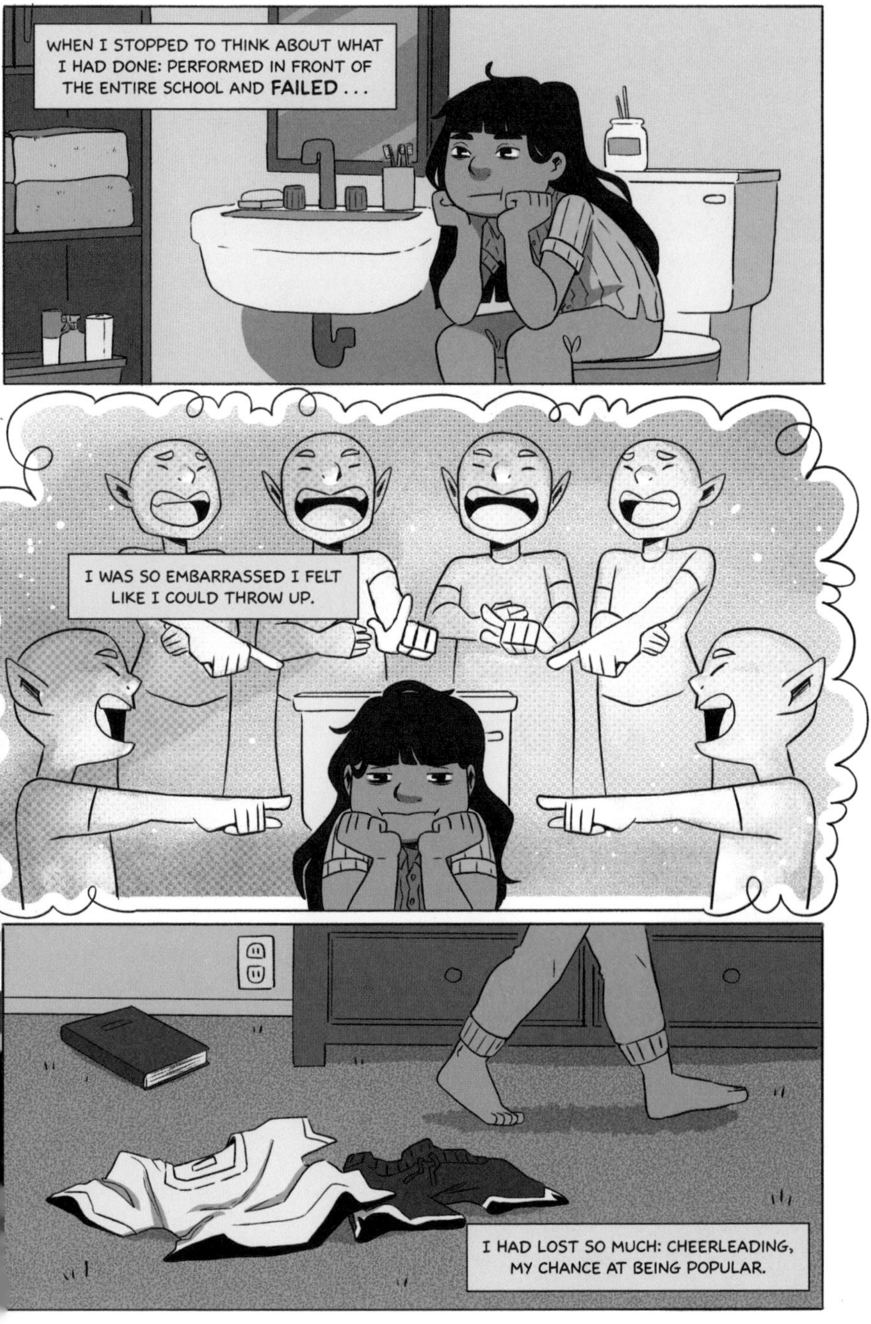
WHEN I STOPPED TO THINK ABOUT WHAT I HAD DONE: PERFORMED IN FRONT OF THE ENTIRE SCHOOL AND **FAILED** . . .
I WAS SO EMBARRASSED I FELT LIKE I COULD THROW UP.
I HAD LOST SO MUCH: CHEERLEADING, MY CHANCE AT BEING POPULAR.

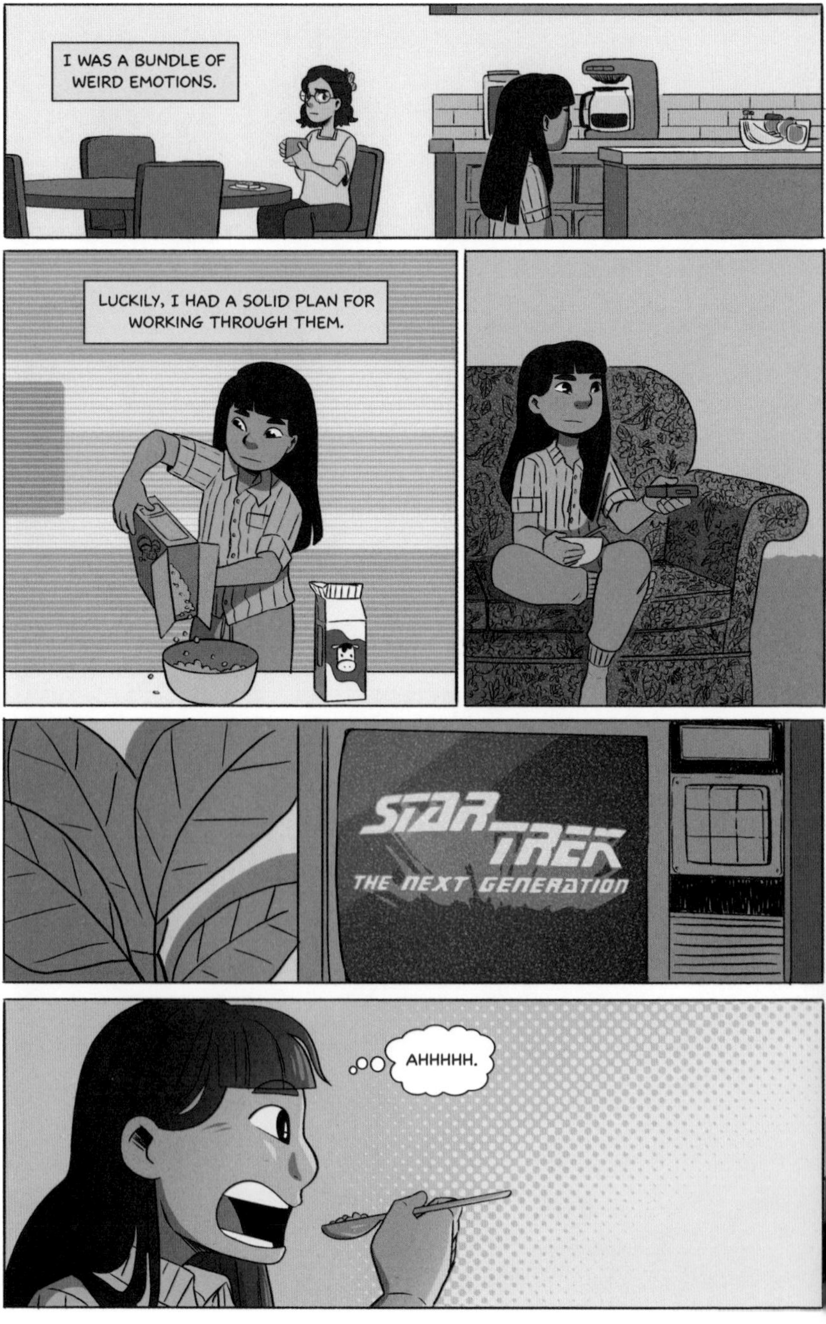
I WAS A BUNDLE OF WEIRD EMOTIONS.
LUCKILY, I HAD A SOLID PLAN FOR WORKING THROUGH THEM.
STAR TREK
THE NEXT GENERATION
AHHHHH.

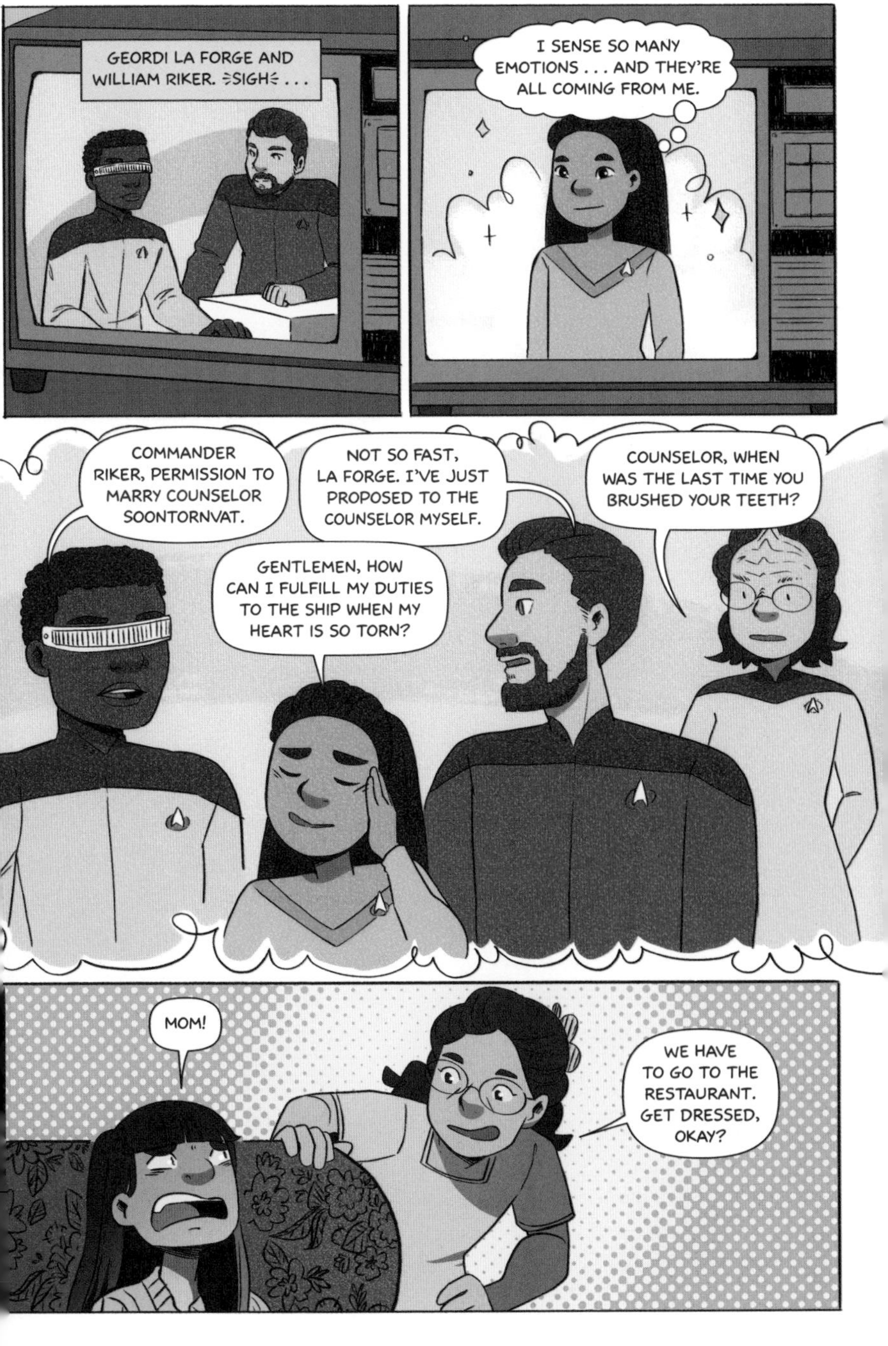
GEORDI LA FORGE AND WILLIAM RIKER. ⋟SIGH⋞ . . .
I SENSE SO MANY EMOTIONS . . . AND THEY'RE ALL COMING FROM ME.
COMMANDER RIKER, PERMISSION TO MARRY COUNSELOR SOONTORNVAT.
NOT SO FAST, LA FORGE. I'VE JUST PROPOSED TO THE COUNSELOR MYSELF.
GENTLEMEN, HOW CAN I FULFILL MY DUTIES TO THE SHIP WHEN MY HEART IS SO TORN?
COUNSELOR, WHEN WAS THE LAST TIME YOU BRUSHED YOUR TEETH?
MOM!
WE HAVE TO GO TO THE RESTAURANT. GET DRESSED, OKAY?

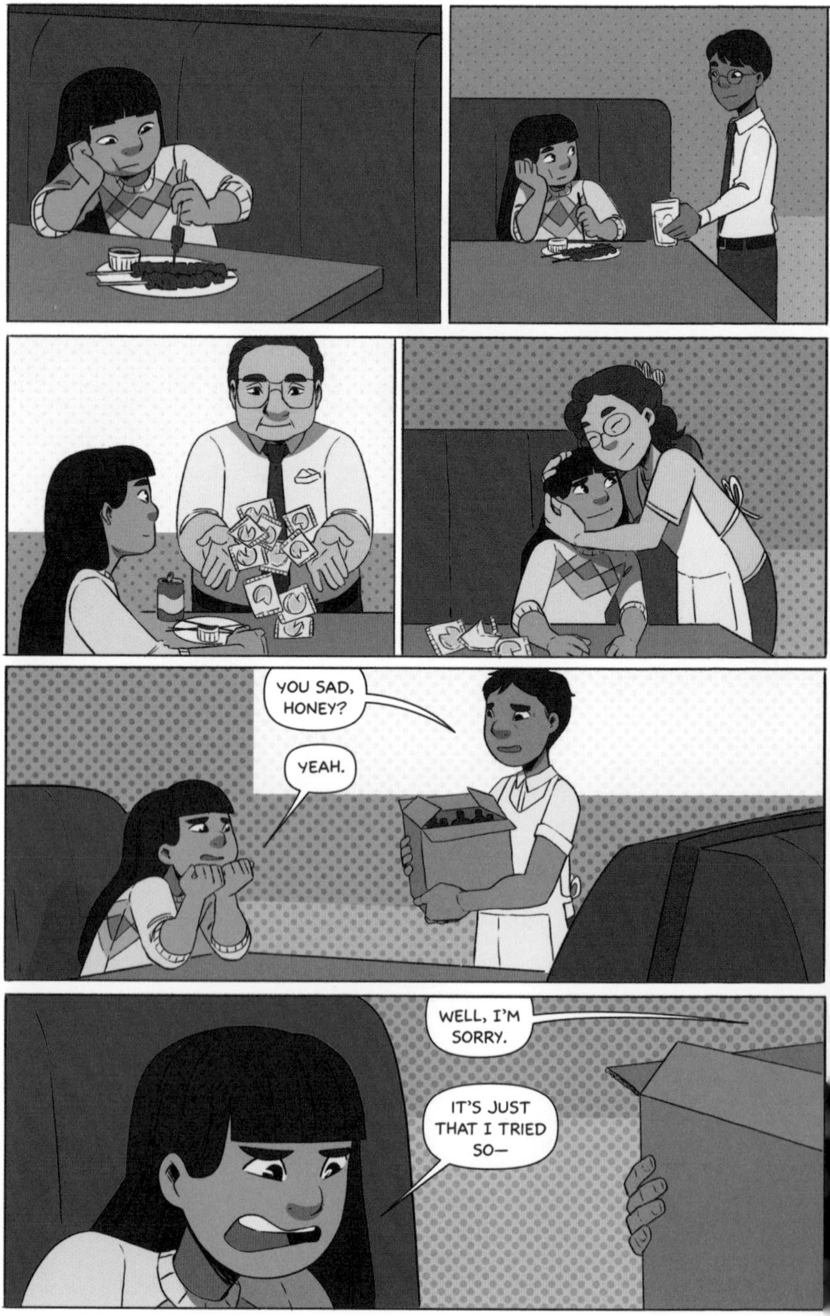
YOU SAD, HONEY?
YEAH.
WELL, I'M SORRY.
IT'S JUST THAT I TRIED SO—

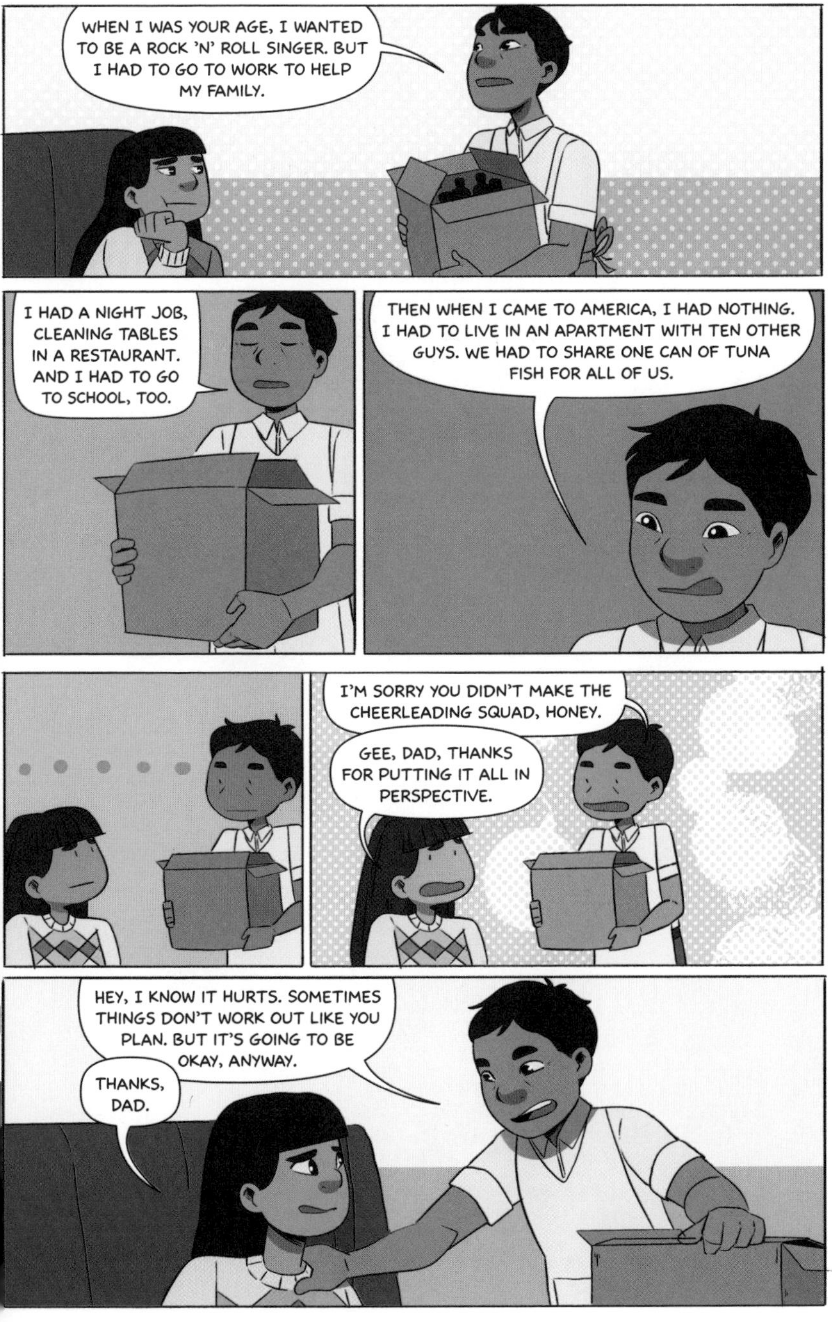
WHEN I WAS YOUR AGE, I WANTED TO BE A ROCK 'N' ROLL SINGER. BUT I HAD TO GO TO WORK TO HELP MY FAMILY.
I HAD A NIGHT JOB, CLEANING TABLES IN A RESTAURANT. AND I HAD TO GO TO SCHOOL, TOO.
THEN WHEN I CAME TO AMERICA, I HAD NOTHING. I HAD TO LIVE IN AN APARTMENT WITH TEN OTHER GUYS. WE HAD TO SHARE ONE CAN OF TUNA FISH FOR ALL OF US.
I'M SORRY YOU DIDN'T MAKE THE CHEERLEADING SQUAD, HONEY.
GEE, DAD, THANKS FOR PUTTING IT ALL IN PERSPECTIVE.
HEY, I KNOW IT HURTS. SOMETIMES THINGS DON'T WORK OUT LIKE YOU PLAN. BUT IT'S GOING TO BE OKAY, ANYWAY.
THANKS, DAD.

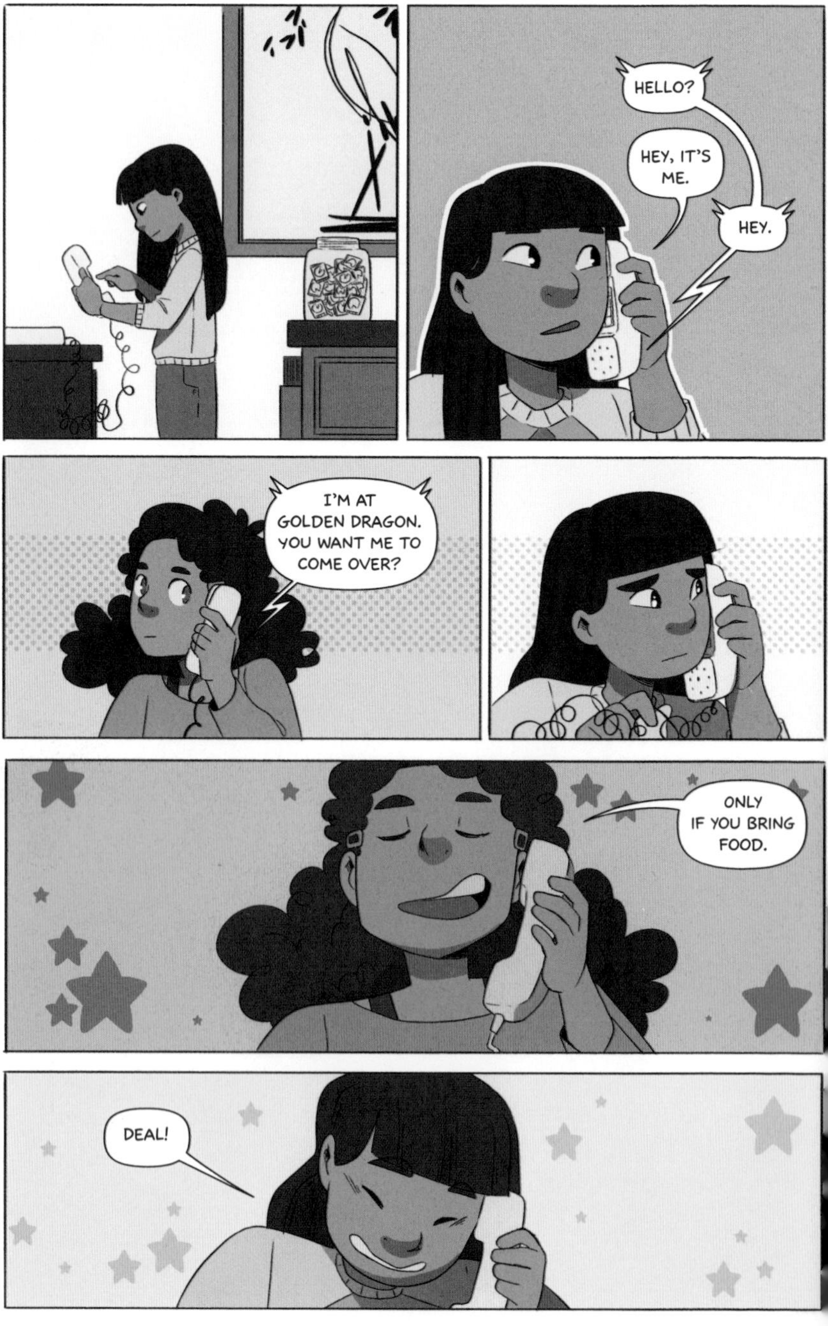
HELLO?
HEY, IT'S ME.
HEY.
I'M AT GOLDEN DRAGON. YOU WANT ME TO COME OVER?
ONLY IF YOU BRING FOOD.
DEAL!

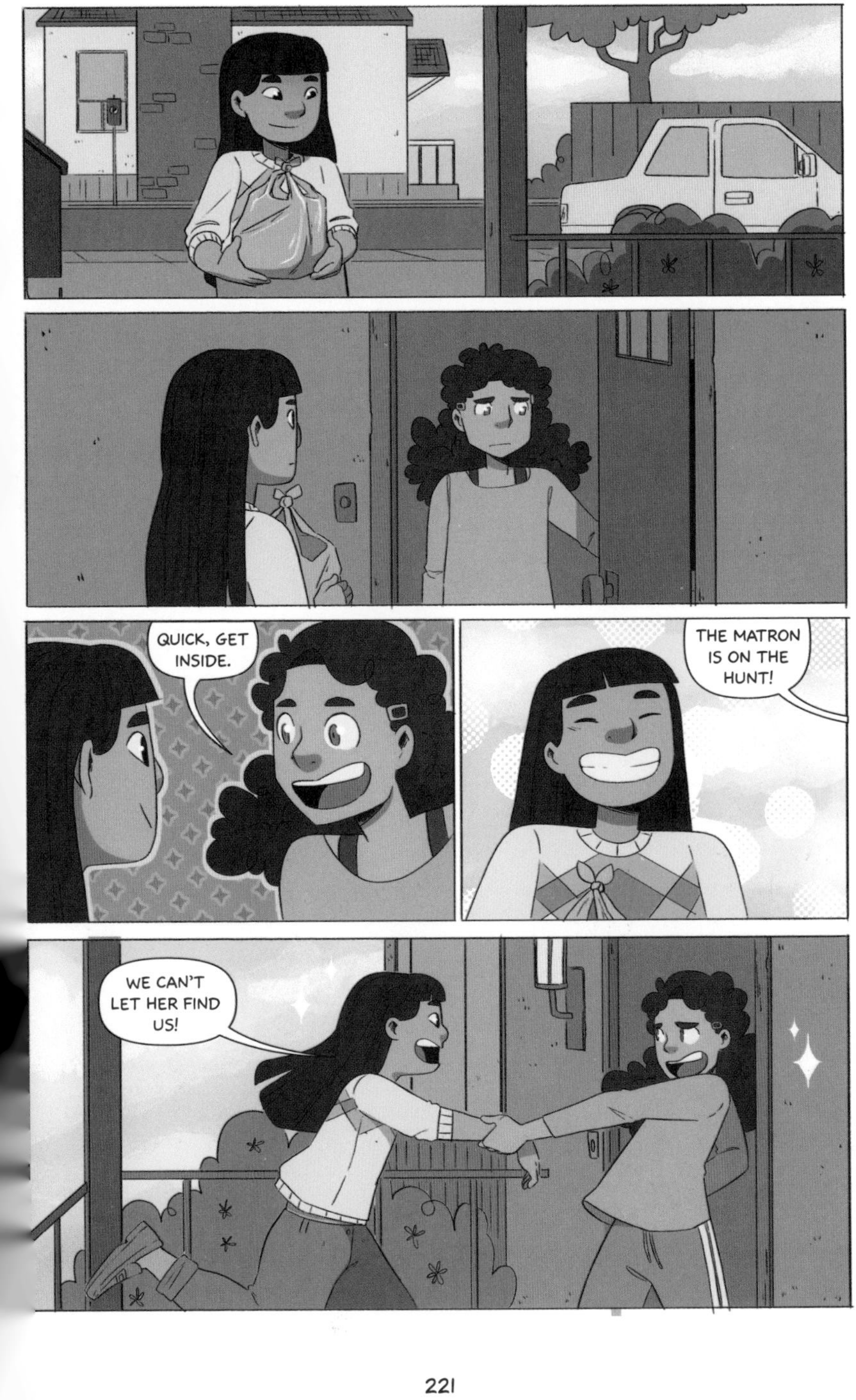
QUICK, GET INSIDE.
THE MATRON IS ON THE HUNT!
WE CAN'T LET HER FIND US!

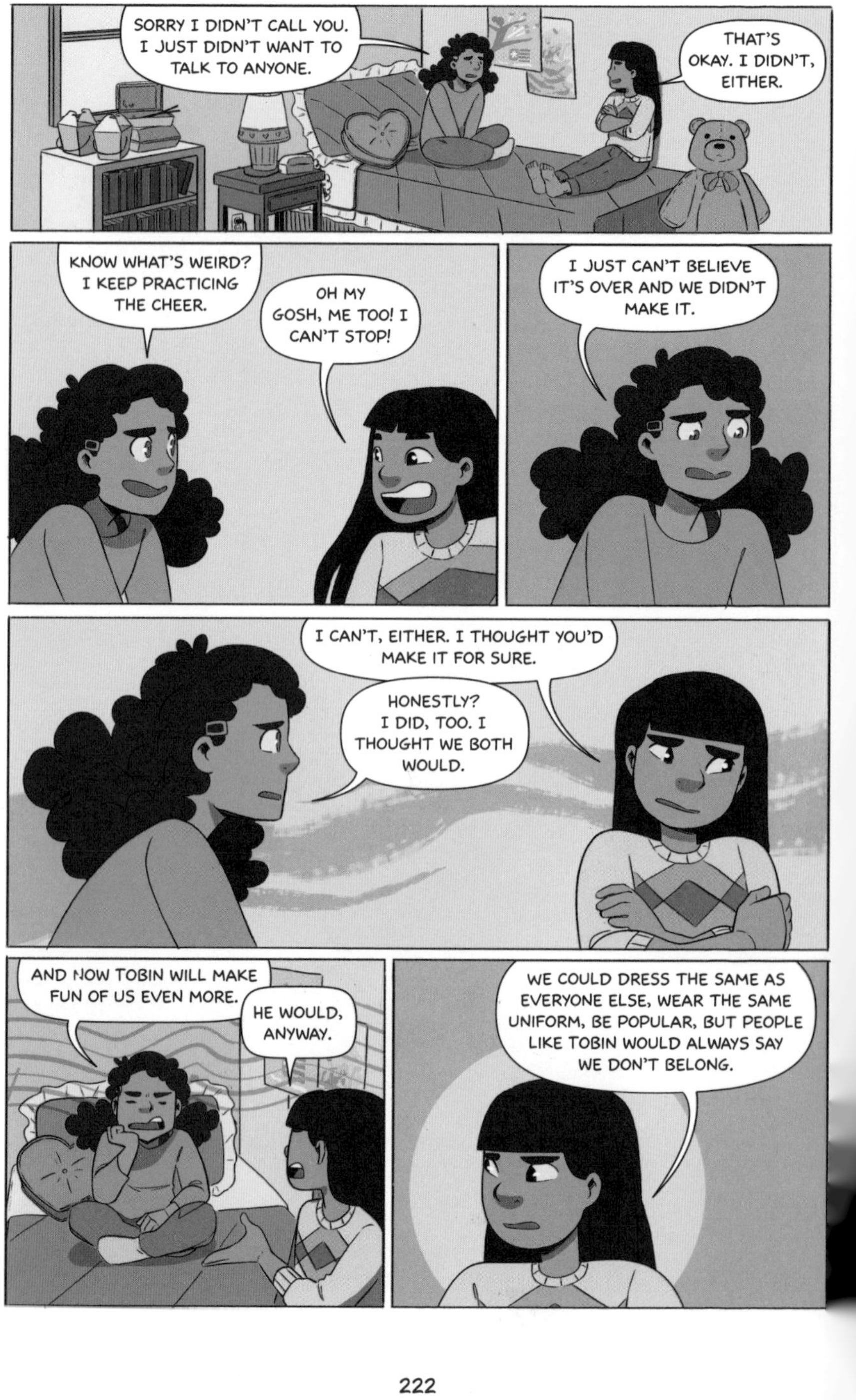
SORRY I DIDN'T CALL YOU. I JUST DIDN'T WANT TO TALK TO ANYONE.
THAT'S OKAY. I DIDN'T, EITHER.
KNOW WHAT'S WEIRD? I KEEP PRACTICING THE CHEER.
OH MY GOSH, ME TOO! I CAN'T STOP!
I JUST CAN'T BELIEVE IT'S OVER AND WE DIDN'T MAKE IT.
I CAN'T, EITHER. I THOUGHT YOU'D MAKE IT FOR SURE.
HONESTLY? I DID, TOO. I THOUGHT WE BOTH WOULD.
AND NOW TOBIN WILL MAKE FUN OF US EVEN MORE.
HE WOULD, ANYWAY.
WE COULD DRESS THE SAME AS EVERYONE ELSE, WEAR THE SAME UNIFORM, BE POPULAR, BUT PEOPLE LIKE TOBIN WOULD ALWAYS SAY WE DON'T BELONG.

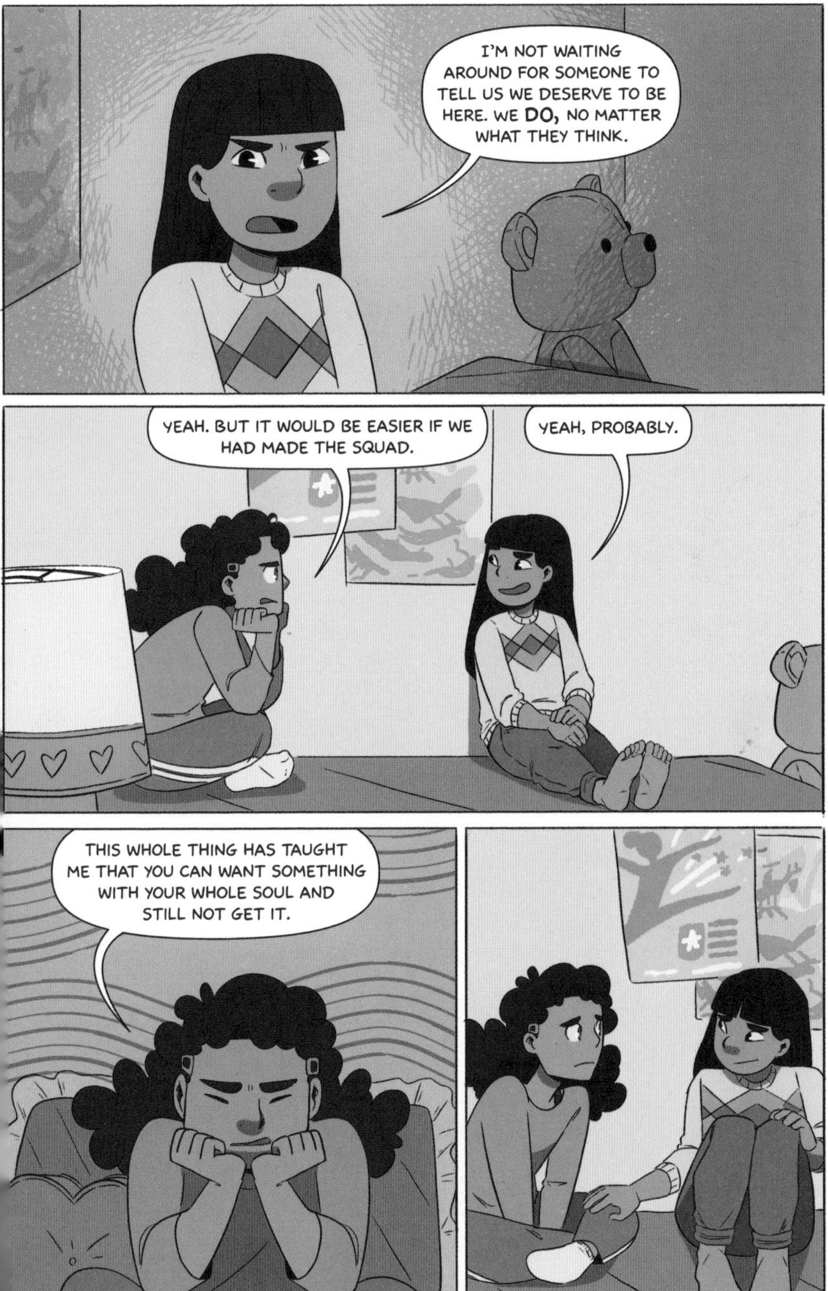
I'M NOT WAITING AROUND FOR SOMEONE TO TELL US WE DESERVE TO BE HERE. WE DO, NO MATTER WHAT THEY THINK.
YEAH. BUT IT WOULD BE EASIER IF WE HAD MADE THE SQUAD.
YEAH, PROBABLY.
THIS WHOLE THING HAS TAUGHT ME THAT YOU CAN WANT SOMETHING WITH YOUR WHOLE SOUL AND STILL NOT GET IT.

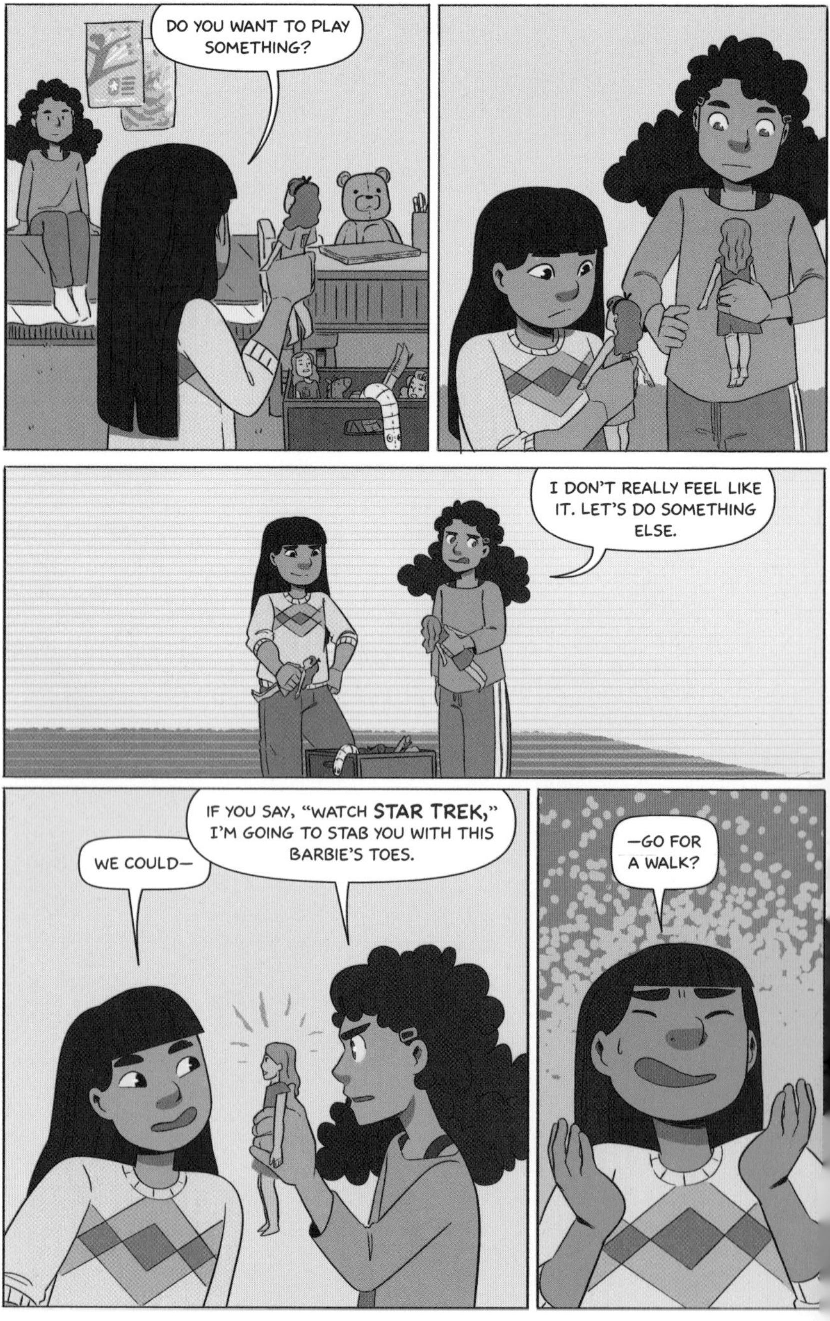
DO YOU WANT TO PLAY SOMETHING?
I DON'T REALLY FEEL LIKE IT. LET'S DO SOMETHING ELSE.
WE COULD—
IF YOU SAY, "WATCH STAR TREK," I'M GOING TO STAB YOU WITH THIS BARBIE'S TOES.
—GO FOR A WALK?

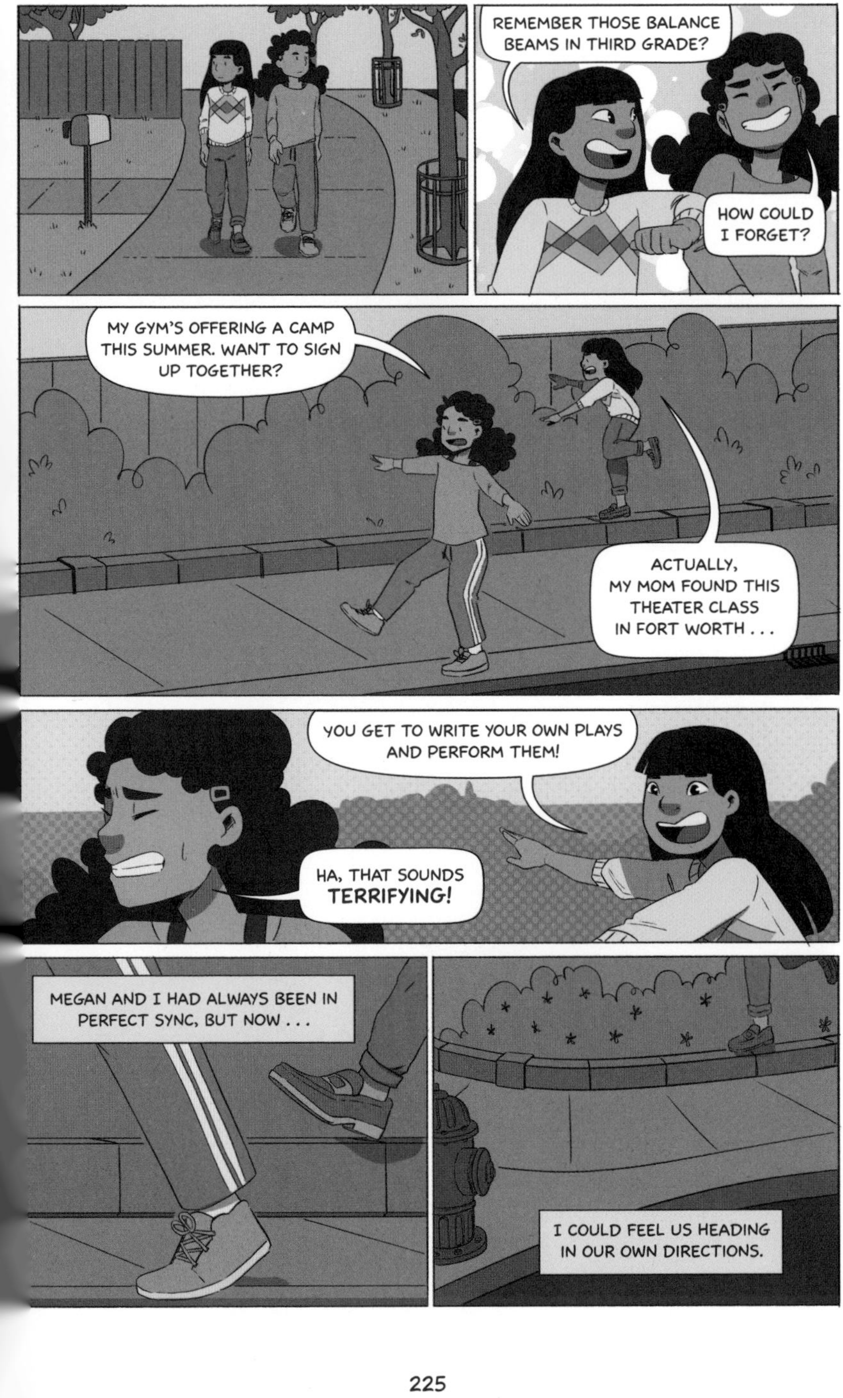

REMEMBER THOSE BALANCE BEAMS IN THIRD GRADE?
HOW COULD I FORGET?
MY GYM'S OFFERING A CAMP THIS SUMMER. WANT TO SIGN UP TOGETHER?
ACTUALLY, MY MOM FOUND THIS THEATER CLASS IN FORT WORTH . . .
YOU GET TO WRITE YOUR OWN PLAYS AND PERFORM THEM!
HA, THAT SOUNDS **TERRIFYING!**
MEGAN AND I HAD ALWAYS BEEN IN PERFECT SYNC, BUT NOW . . .
I COULD FEEL US HEADING IN OUR OWN DIRECTIONS.

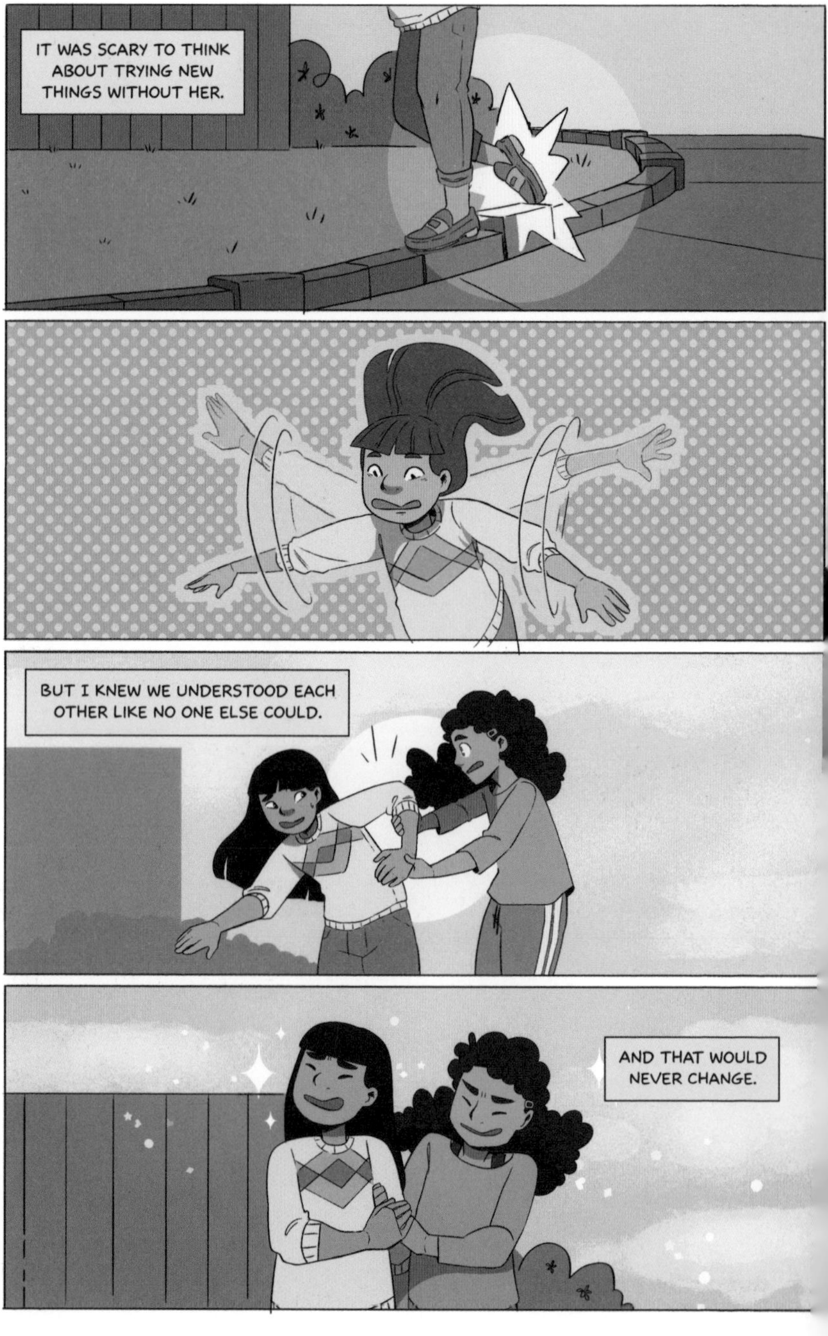
IT WAS SCARY TO THINK ABOUT TRYING NEW THINGS WITHOUT HER.
BUT I KNEW WE UNDERSTOOD EACH OTHER LIKE NO ONE ELSE COULD.
AND THAT WOULD NEVER CHANGE.

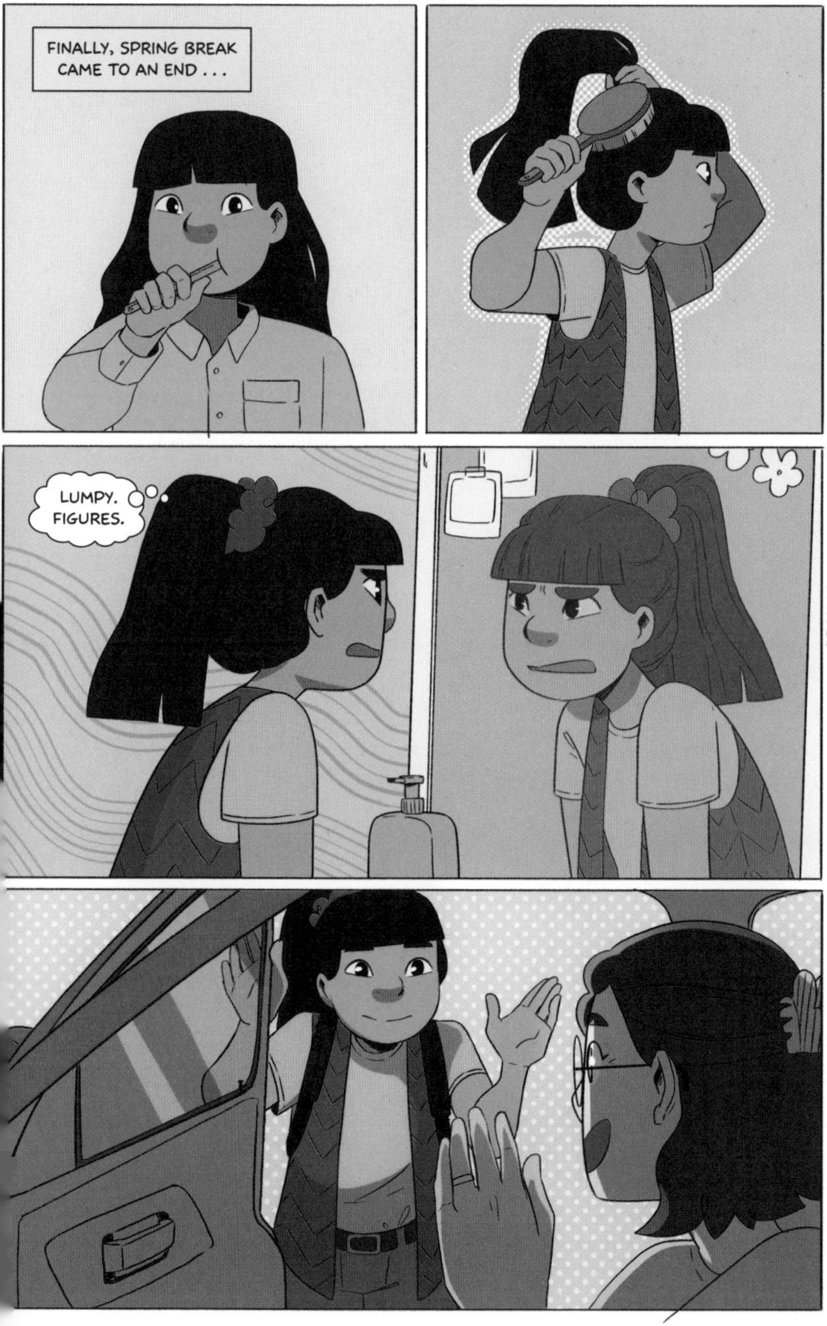
FINALLY, SPRING BREAK CAME TO AN END . . .
LUMPY. FIGURES.

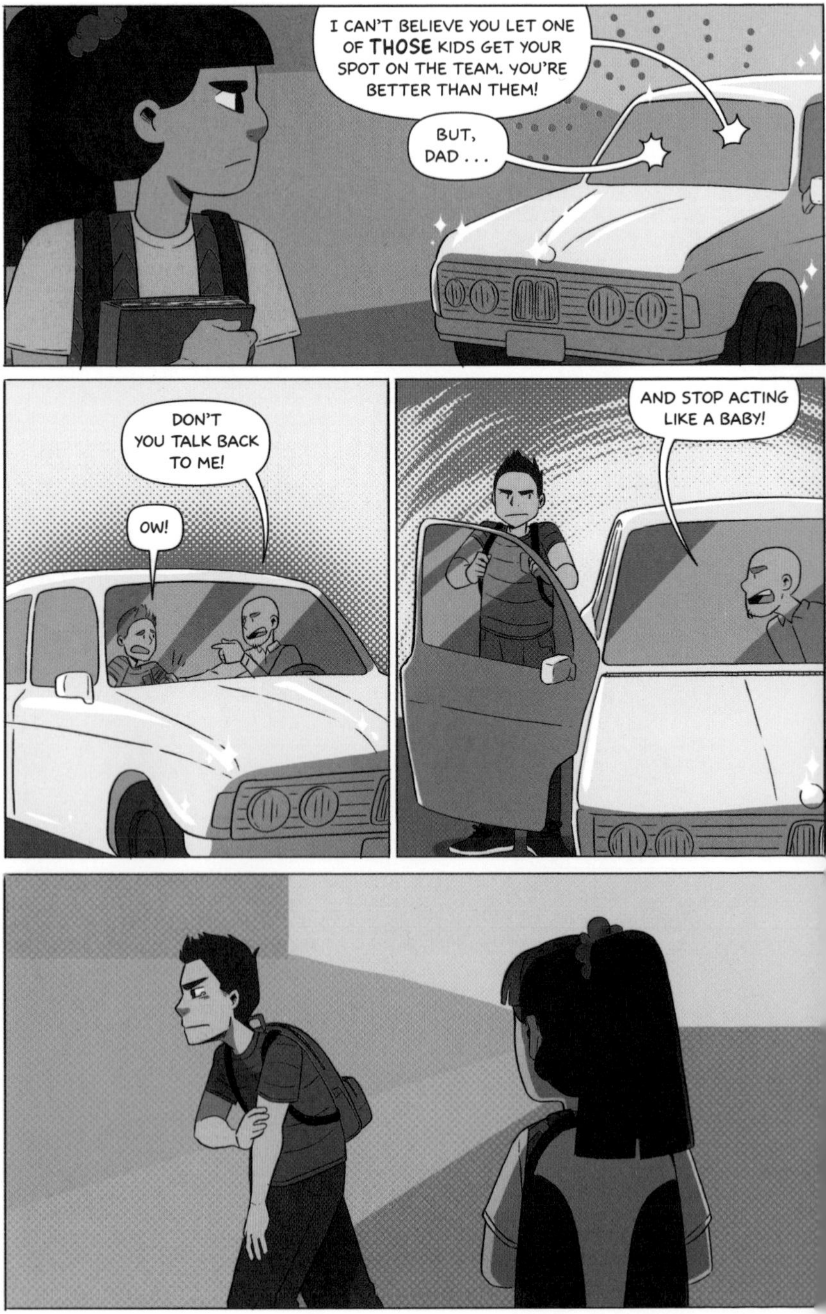
I CAN'T BELIEVE YOU LET ONE OF **THOSE** KIDS GET YOUR SPOT ON THE TEAM. YOU'RE BETTER THAN THEM!
BUT, DAD . . .
DON'T YOU TALK BACK TO ME!
OW!
AND STOP ACTING LIKE A BABY!

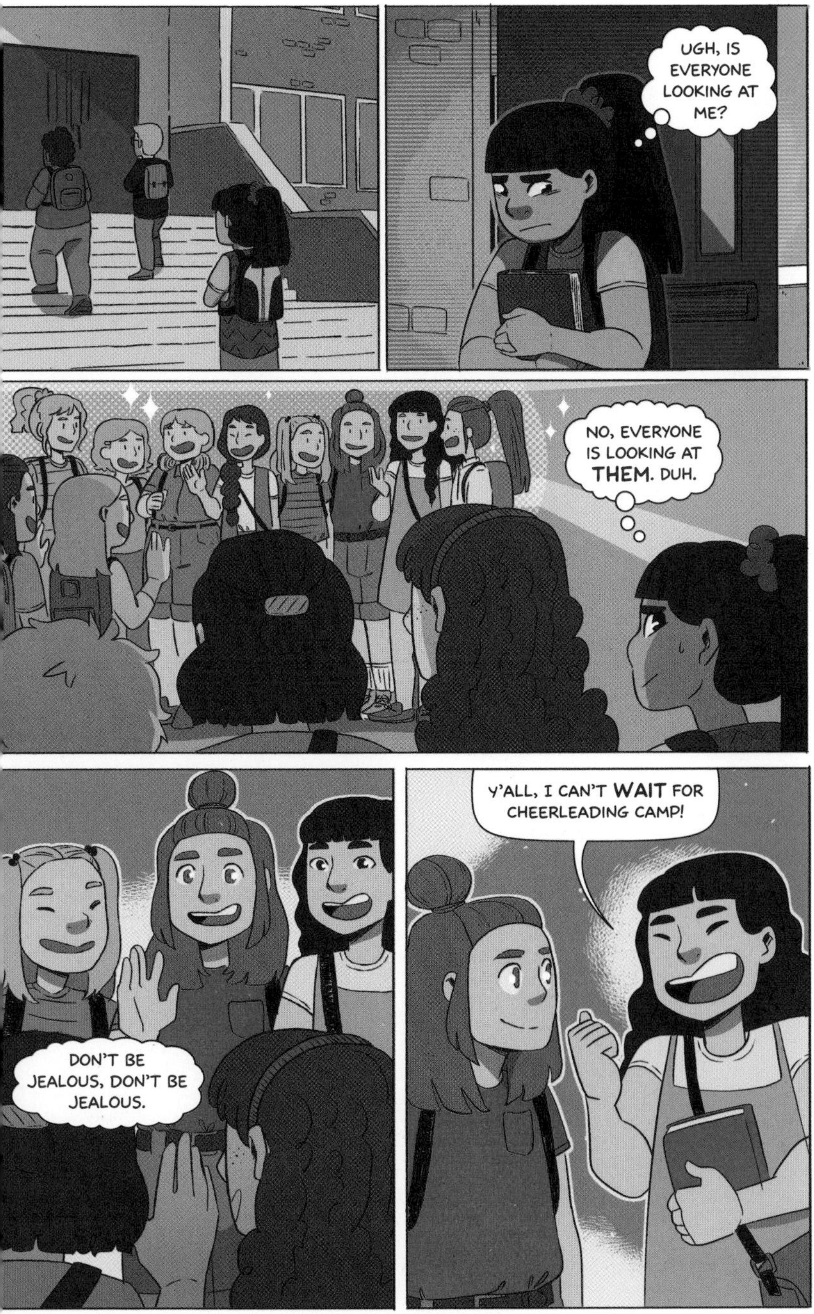
UGH, IS EVERYONE LOOKING AT ME?
NO, EVERYONE IS LOOKING AT THEM. DUH.
DON'T BE JEALOUS, DON'T BE JEALOUS.
Y'ALL, I CAN'T WAIT FOR CHEERLEADING CAMP!

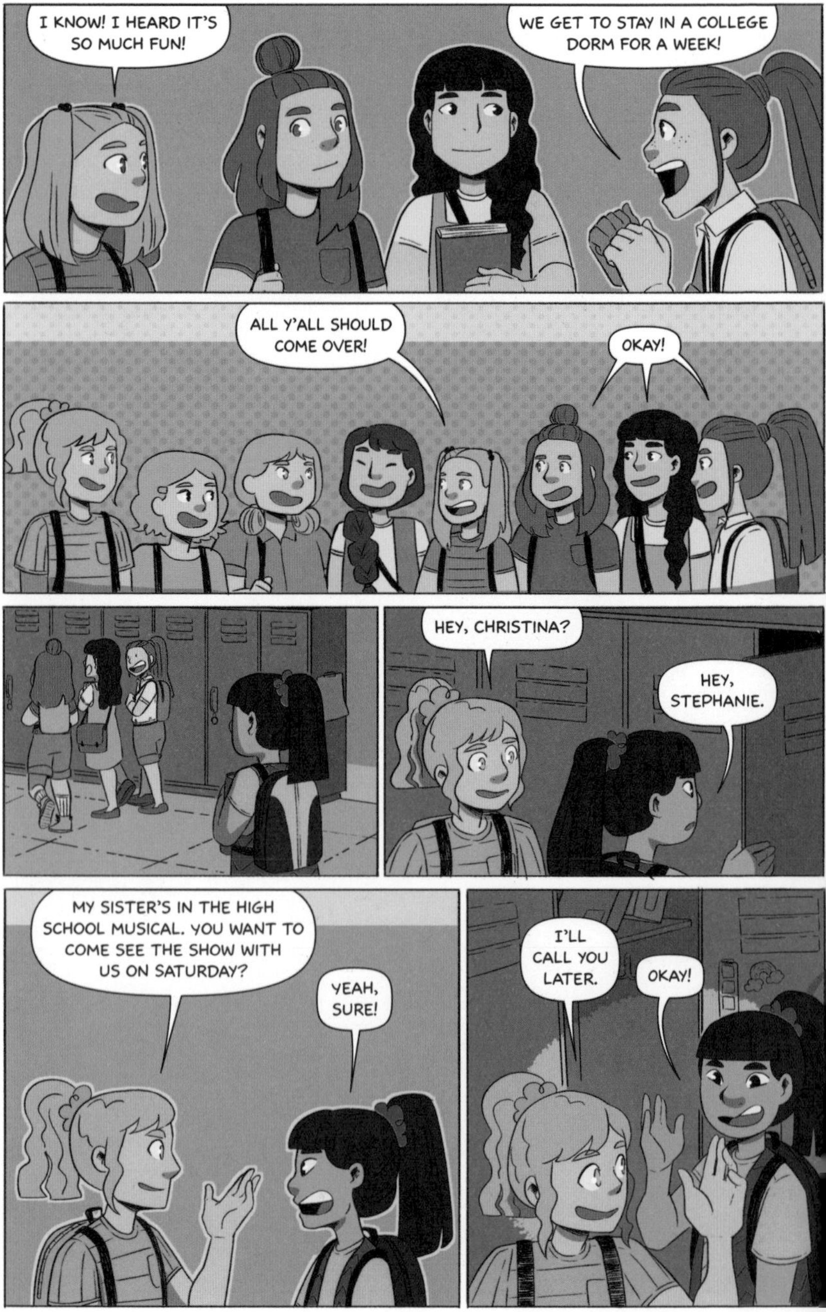
I KNOW! I HEARD IT'S SO MUCH FUN!
WE GET TO STAY IN A COLLEGE DORM FOR A WEEK!
ALL Y'ALL SHOULD COME OVER!
OKAY!
HEY, CHRISTINA?
HEY, STEPHANIE.
MY SISTER'S IN THE HIGH SCHOOL MUSICAL. YOU WANT TO COME SEE THE SHOW WITH US ON SATURDAY?
YEAH, SURE!
I'LL CALL YOU LATER.
OKAY!

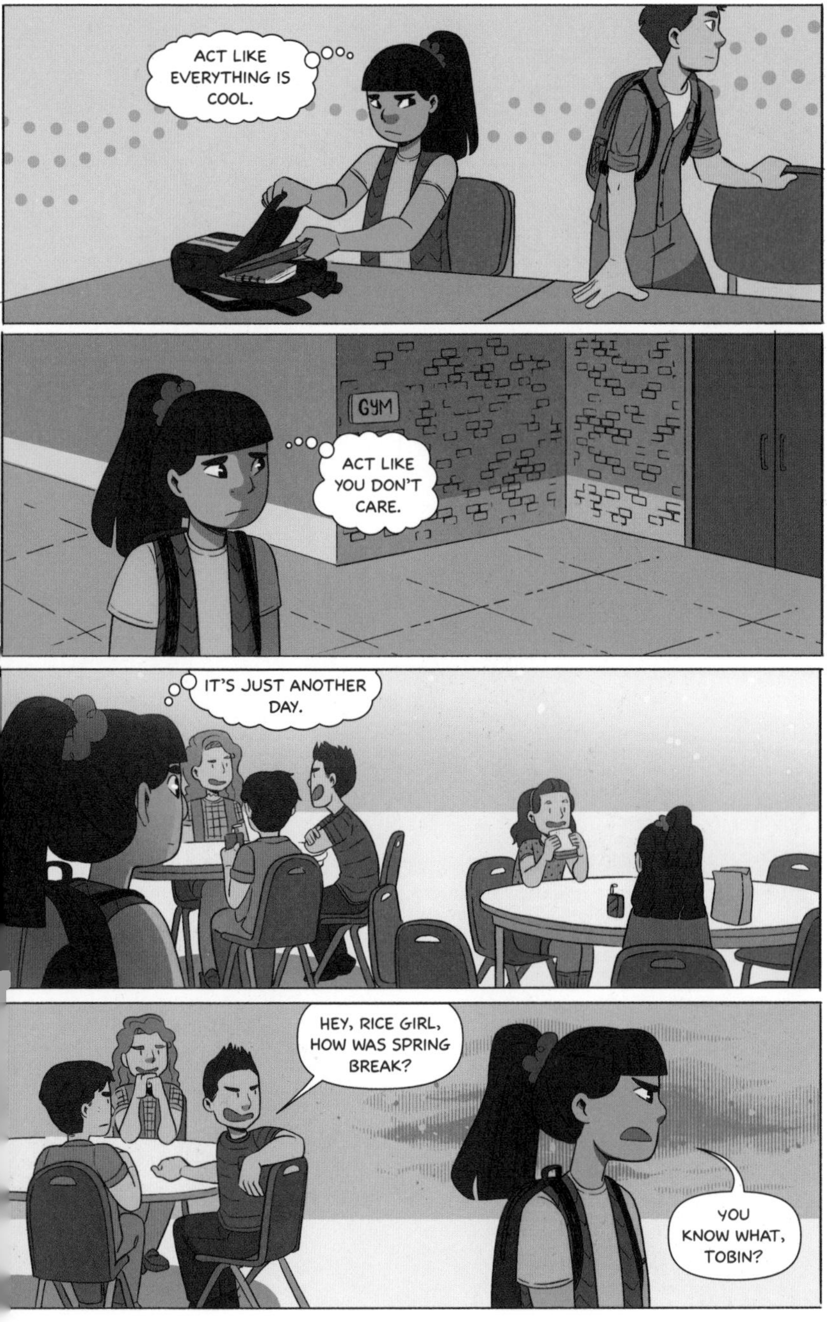
ACT LIKE EVERYTHING IS COOL.
ACT LIKE YOU DON'T CARE.
GYM
IT'S JUST ANOTHER DAY.
HEY, RICE GIRL, HOW WAS SPRING BREAK?
YOU KNOW WHAT, TOBIN?

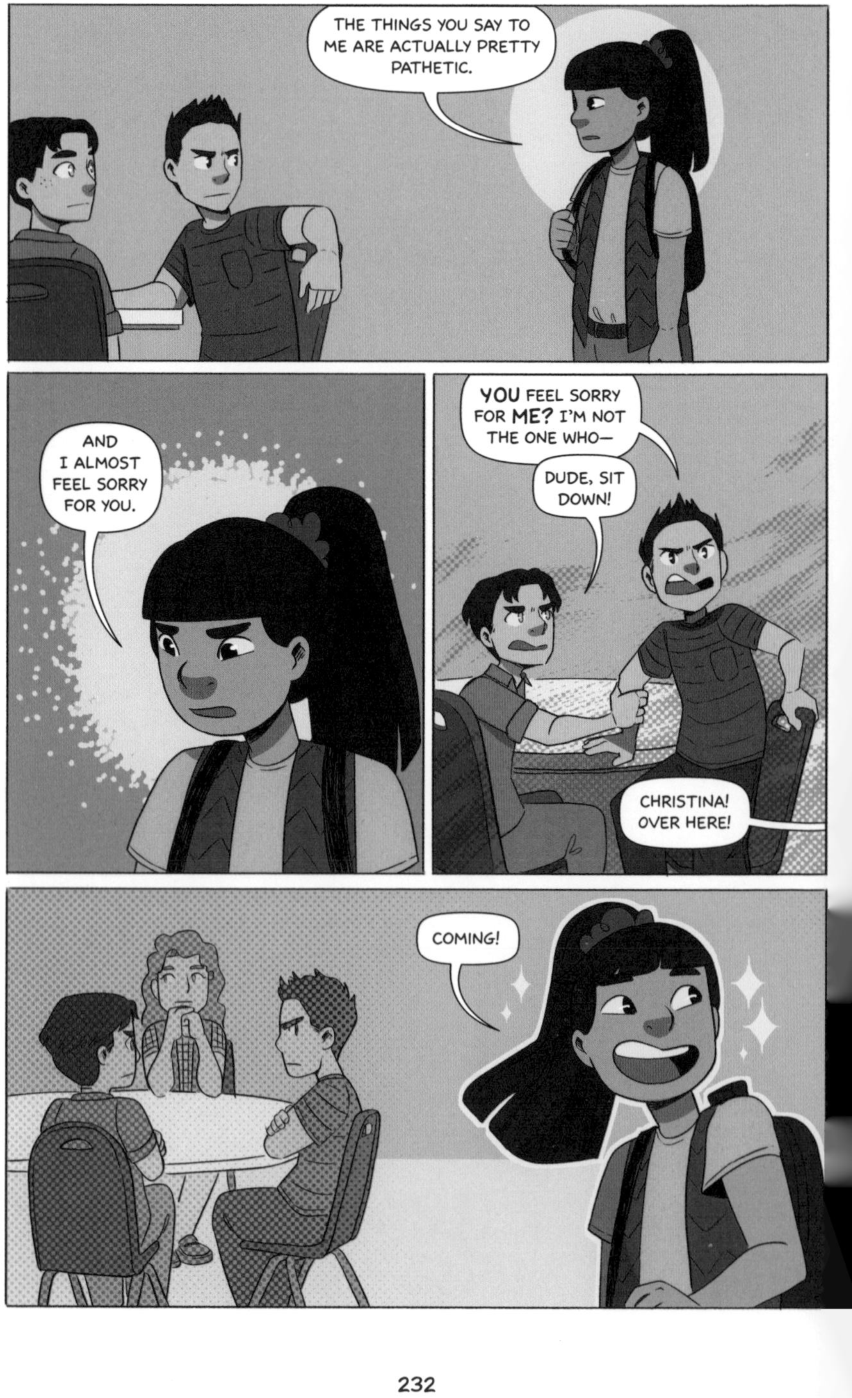
THE THINGS YOU SAY TO ME ARE ACTUALLY PRETTY PATHETIC.
AND I ALMOST FEEL SORRY FOR YOU.
YOU FEEL SORRY FOR ME? I'M NOT THE ONE WHO—
DUDE, SIT DOWN!
CHRISTINA! OVER HERE!
COMING!

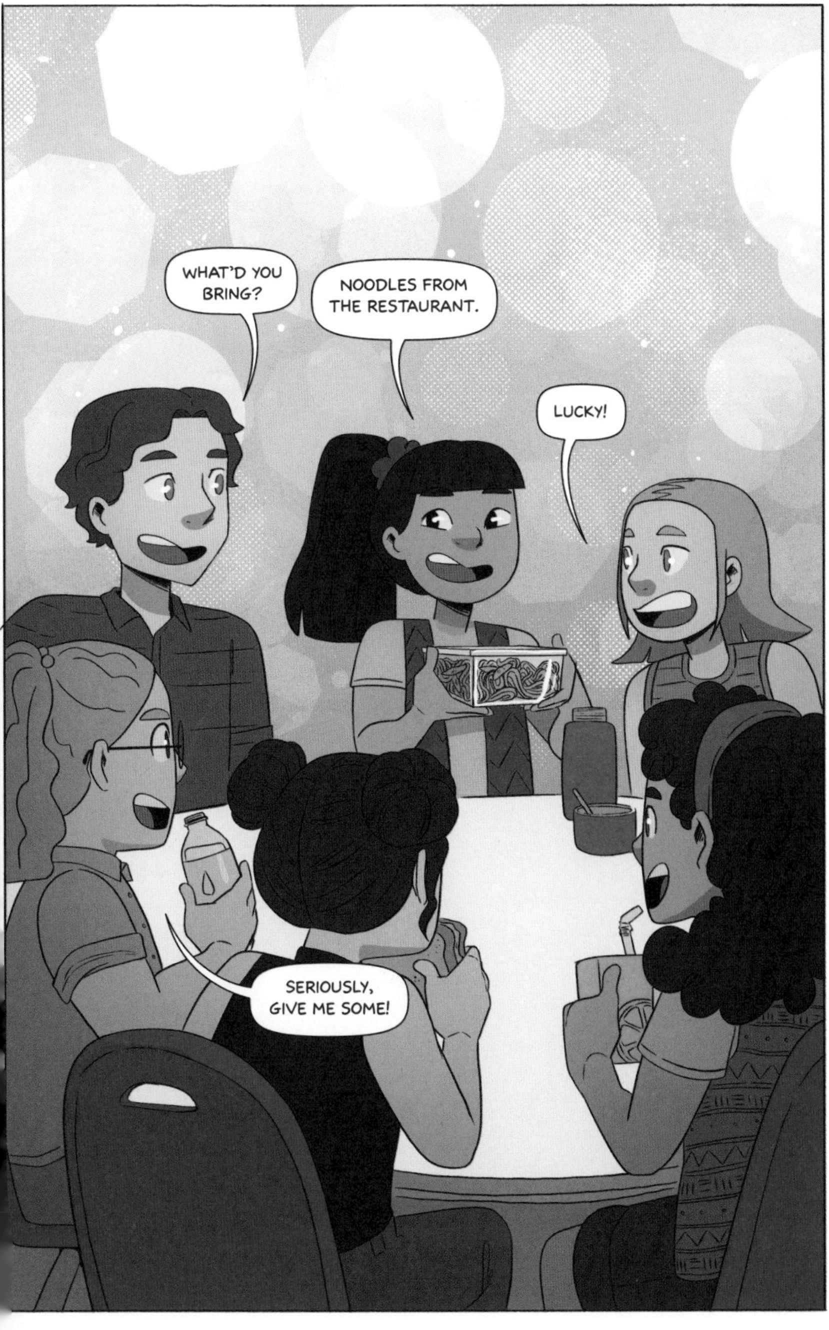
WHAT'D YOU BRING?
NOODLES FROM THE RESTAURANT.
LUCKY!
SERIOUSLY, GIVE ME SOME!

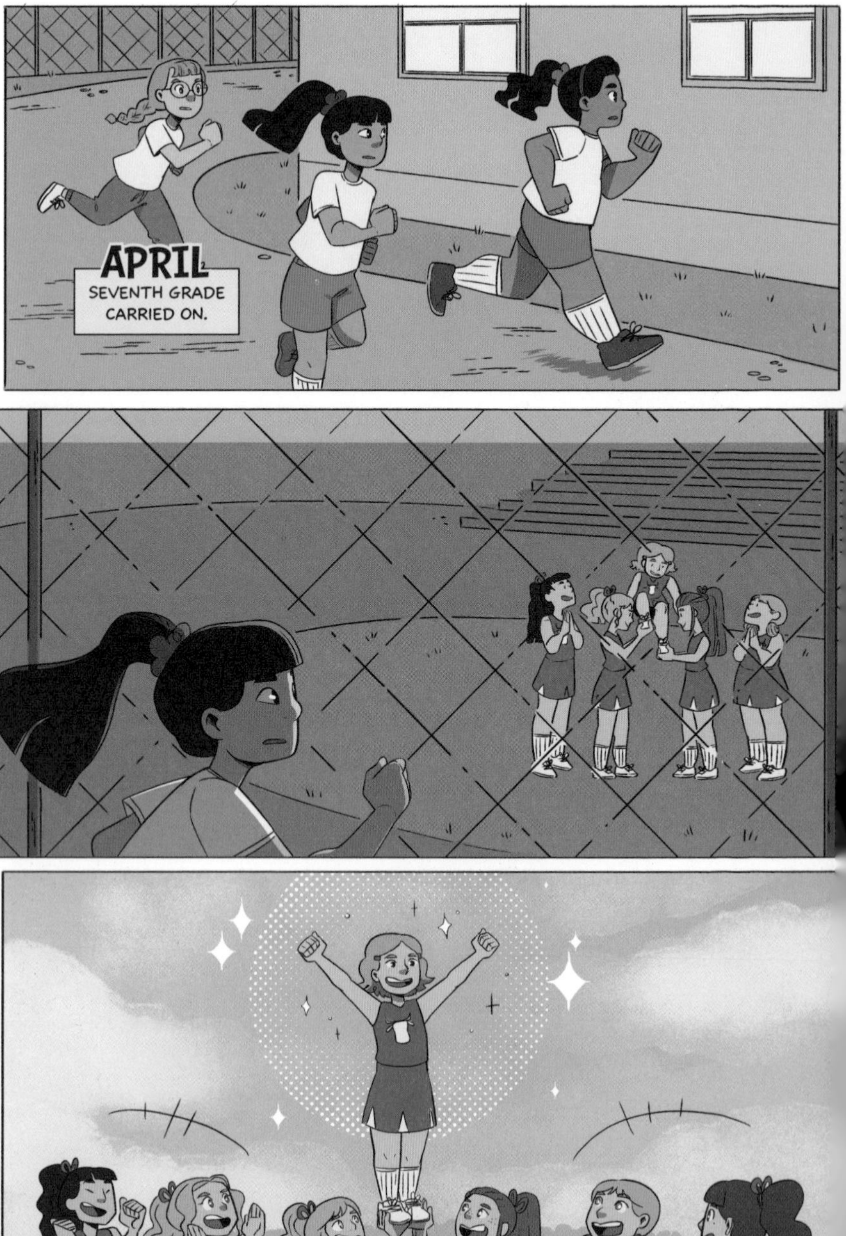
APRIL
SEVENTH GRADE CARRIED ON.

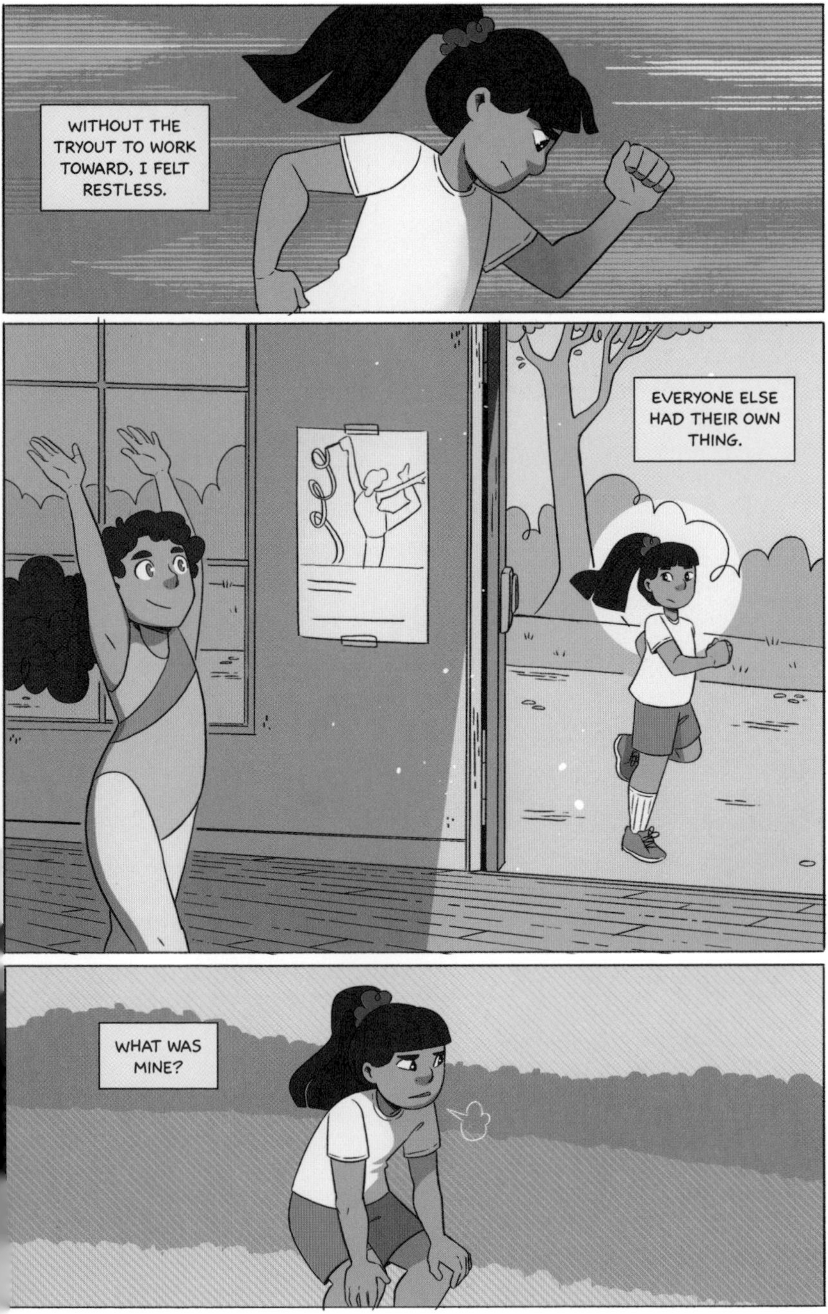
WITHOUT THE TRYOUT TO WORK TOWARD, I FELT RESTLESS.
EVERYONE ELSE HAD THEIR OWN THING.
WHAT WAS MINE?

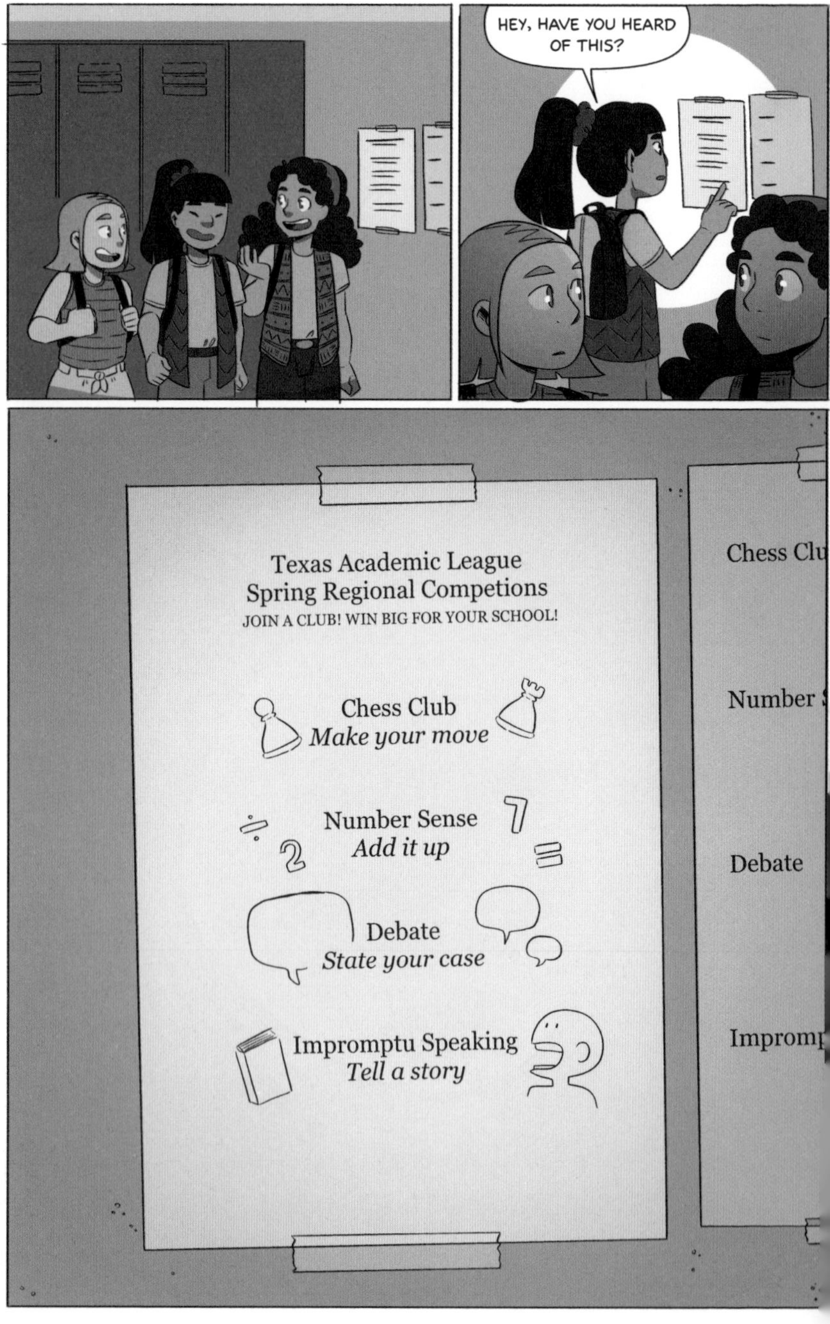
HEY, HAVE YOU HEARD OF THIS?
Texas Academic League
Spring Regional Competions
JOIN A CLUB! WIN BIG FOR YOUR SCHOOL!
Chess Club
Make your move
Number Sense
Add it up
Debate
State your case
Impromptu Speaking
Tell a story
Chess Clu
Number
Debate
Impromp

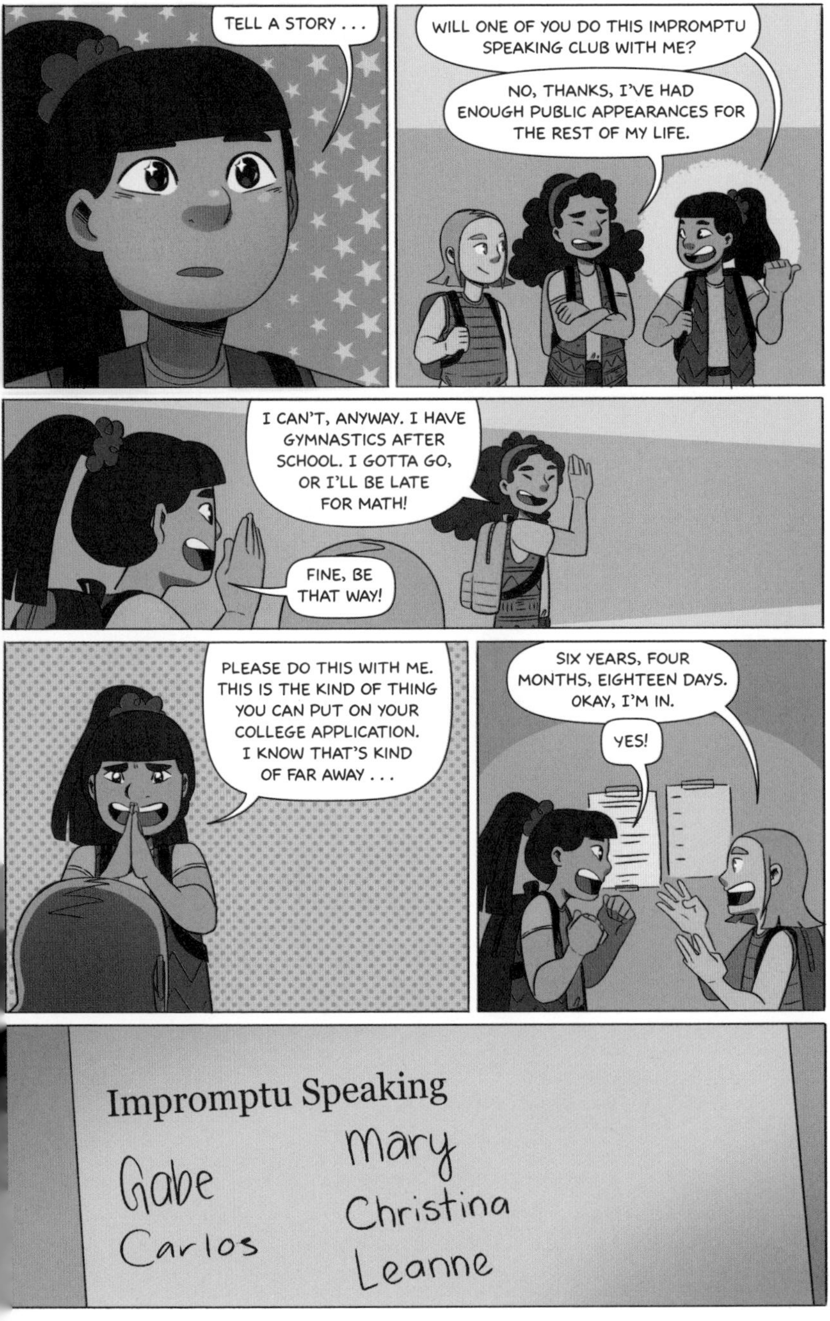
TELL A STORY . . .
WILL ONE OF YOU DO THIS IMPROMPTU SPEAKING CLUB WITH ME?
NO, THANKS, I'VE HAD ENOUGH PUBLIC APPEARANCES FOR THE REST OF MY LIFE.
I CAN'T, ANYWAY. I HAVE GYMNASTICS AFTER SCHOOL. I GOTTA GO, OR I'LL BE LATE FOR MATH!
FINE, BE THAT WAY!
PLEASE DO THIS WITH ME. THIS IS THE KIND OF THING YOU CAN PUT ON YOUR COLLEGE APPLICATION. I KNOW THAT'S KIND OF FAR AWAY . . .
SIX YEARS, FOUR MONTHS, EIGHTEEN DAYS. OKAY, I'M IN.
YES!
Impromptu Speaking
Gabe
Carlos
Mary
Christina
Leanne

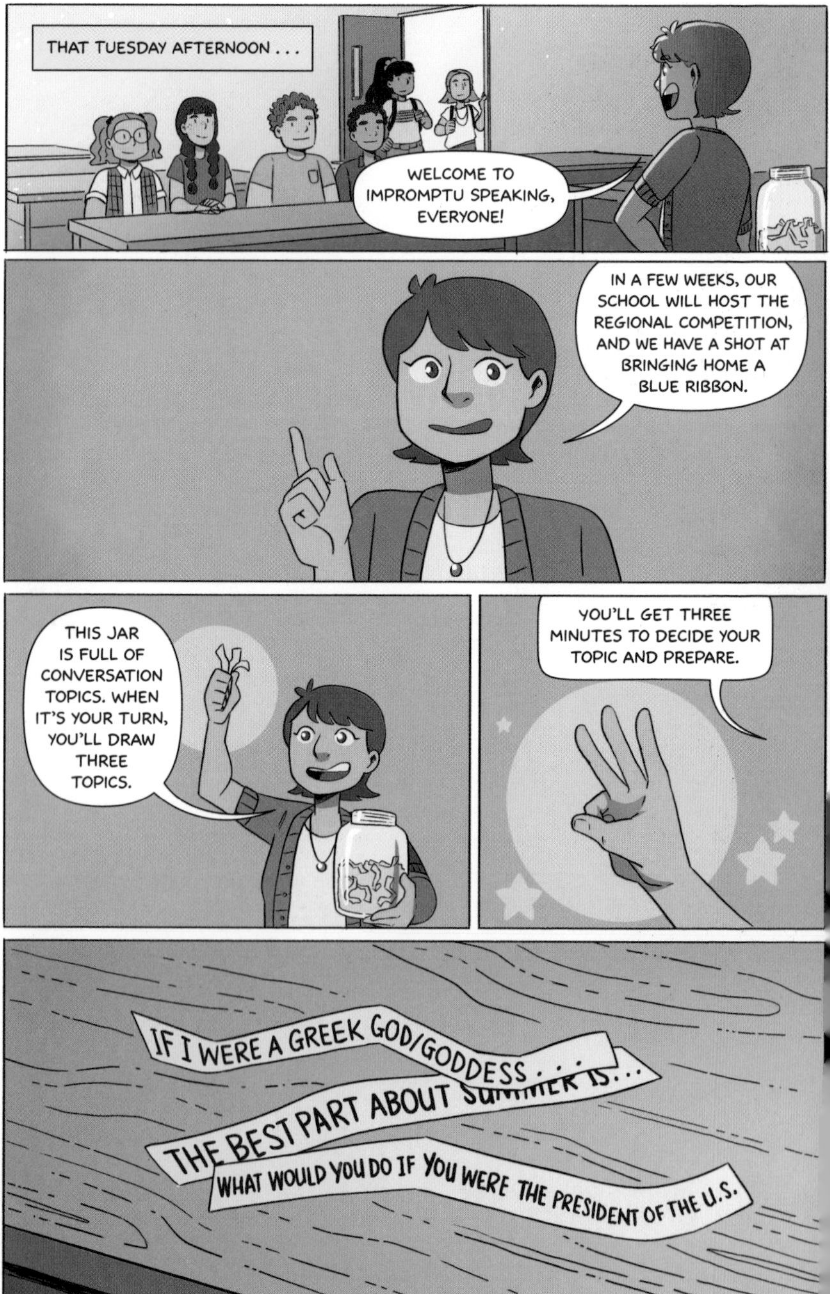
THAT TUESDAY AFTERNOON . . .
WELCOME TO IMPROMPTU SPEAKING, EVERYONE!
IN A FEW WEEKS, OUR SCHOOL WILL HOST THE REGIONAL COMPETITION, AND WE HAVE A SHOT AT BRINGING HOME A BLUE RIBBON.
THIS JAR IS FULL OF CONVERSATION TOPICS. WHEN IT'S YOUR TURN, YOU'LL DRAW THREE TOPICS.
YOU'LL GET THREE MINUTES TO DECIDE YOUR TOPIC AND PREPARE.
IF I WERE A GREEK GOD/GODDESS . . .
THE BEST PART ABOUT SUMMER IS . . .
WHAT WOULD YOU DO IF YOU WERE THE PRESIDENT OF THE U.S.

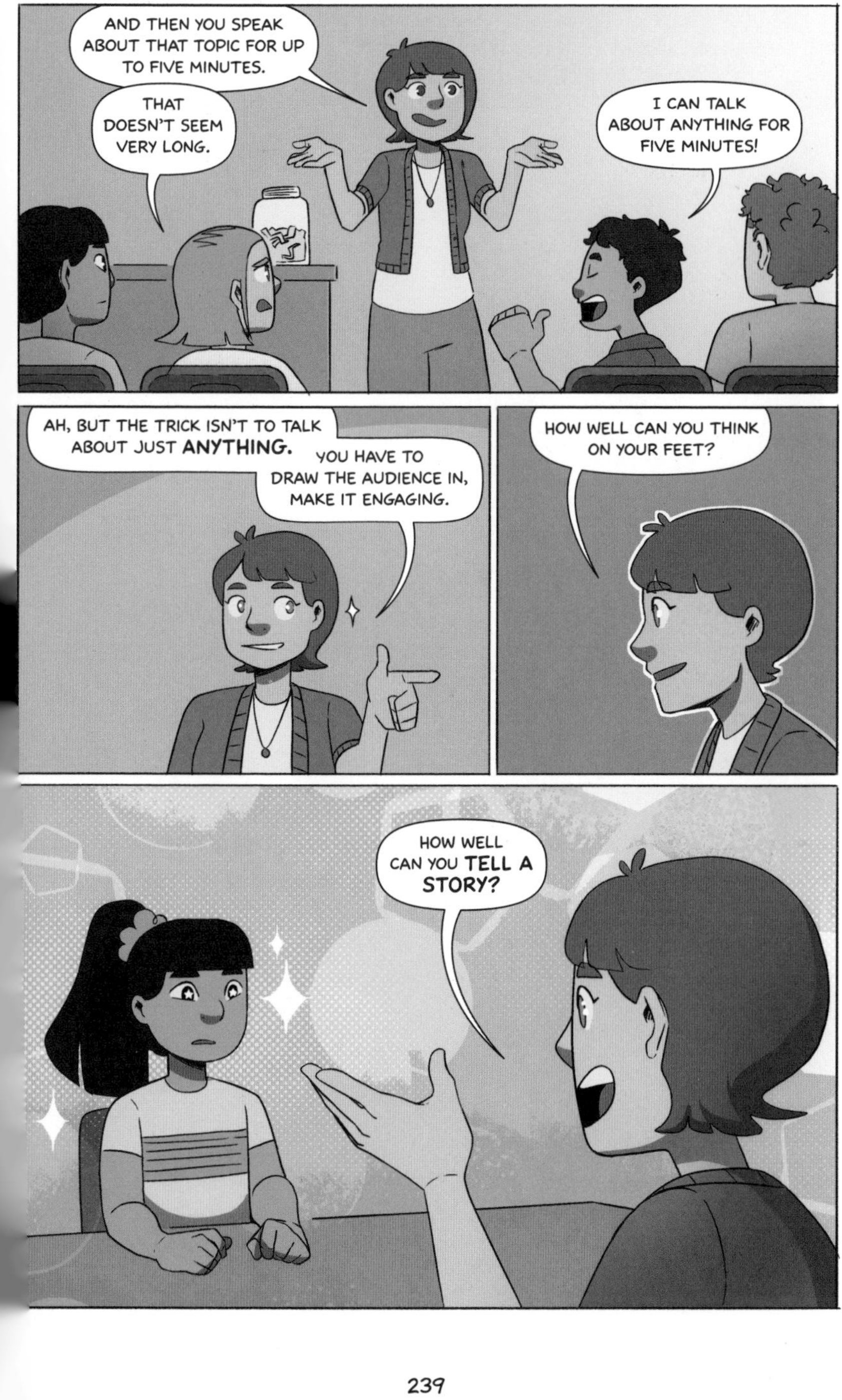
AND THEN YOU SPEAK ABOUT THAT TOPIC FOR UP TO FIVE MINUTES.
THAT DOESN'T SEEM VERY LONG.
I CAN TALK ABOUT ANYTHING FOR FIVE MINUTES!
AH, BUT THE TRICK ISN'T TO TALK ABOUT JUST ANYTHING.
YOU HAVE TO DRAW THE AUDIENCE IN, MAKE IT ENGAGING.
HOW WELL CAN YOU THINK ON YOUR FEET?
HOW WELL CAN YOU TELL A STORY?

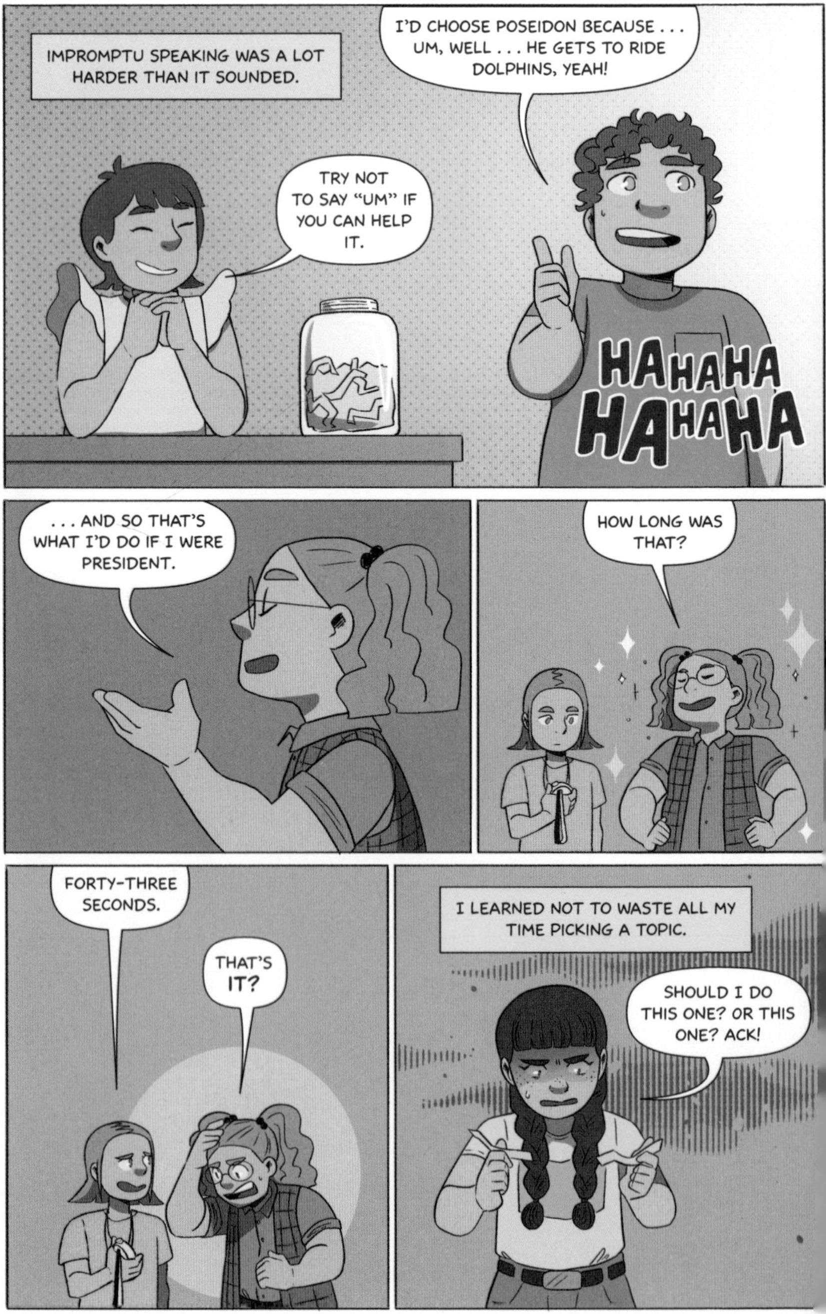
IMPROMPTU SPEAKING WAS A LOT HARDER THAN IT SOUNDED.
I'D CHOOSE POSEIDON BECAUSE . . . UM, WELL . . . HE GETS TO RIDE DOLPHINS, YEAH!
TRY NOT TO SAY "UM" IF YOU CAN HELP IT.
HAHAHA HAHAHA
. . . AND SO THAT'S WHAT I'D DO IF I WERE PRESIDENT.
HOW LONG WAS THAT?
FORTY-THREE SECONDS.
THAT'S IT?
I LEARNED NOT TO WASTE ALL MY TIME PICKING A TOPIC.
SHOULD I DO THIS ONE? OR THIS ONE? ACK!

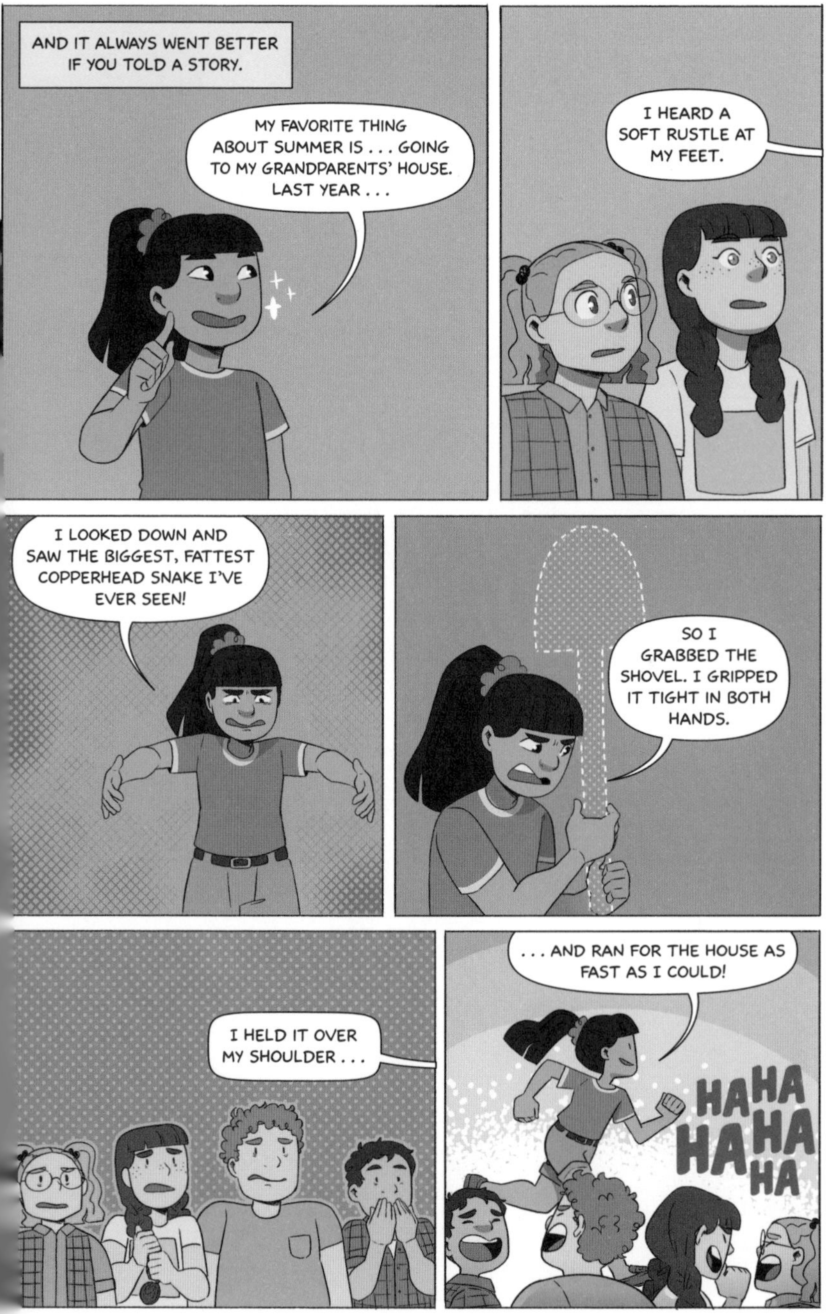
AND IT ALWAYS WENT BETTER IF YOU TOLD A STORY.
MY FAVORITE THING ABOUT SUMMER IS . . . GOING TO MY GRANDPARENTS' HOUSE. LAST YEAR . . .
I HEARD A SOFT RUSTLE AT MY FEET.
I LOOKED DOWN AND SAW THE BIGGEST, FATTEST COPPERHEAD SNAKE I'VE EVER SEEN!
SO I GRABBED THE SHOVEL. I GRIPPED IT TIGHT IN BOTH HANDS.
I HELD IT OVER MY SHOULDER . . .
. . . AND RAN FOR THE HOUSE AS FAST AS I COULD!
HAHA HAHA HAHA

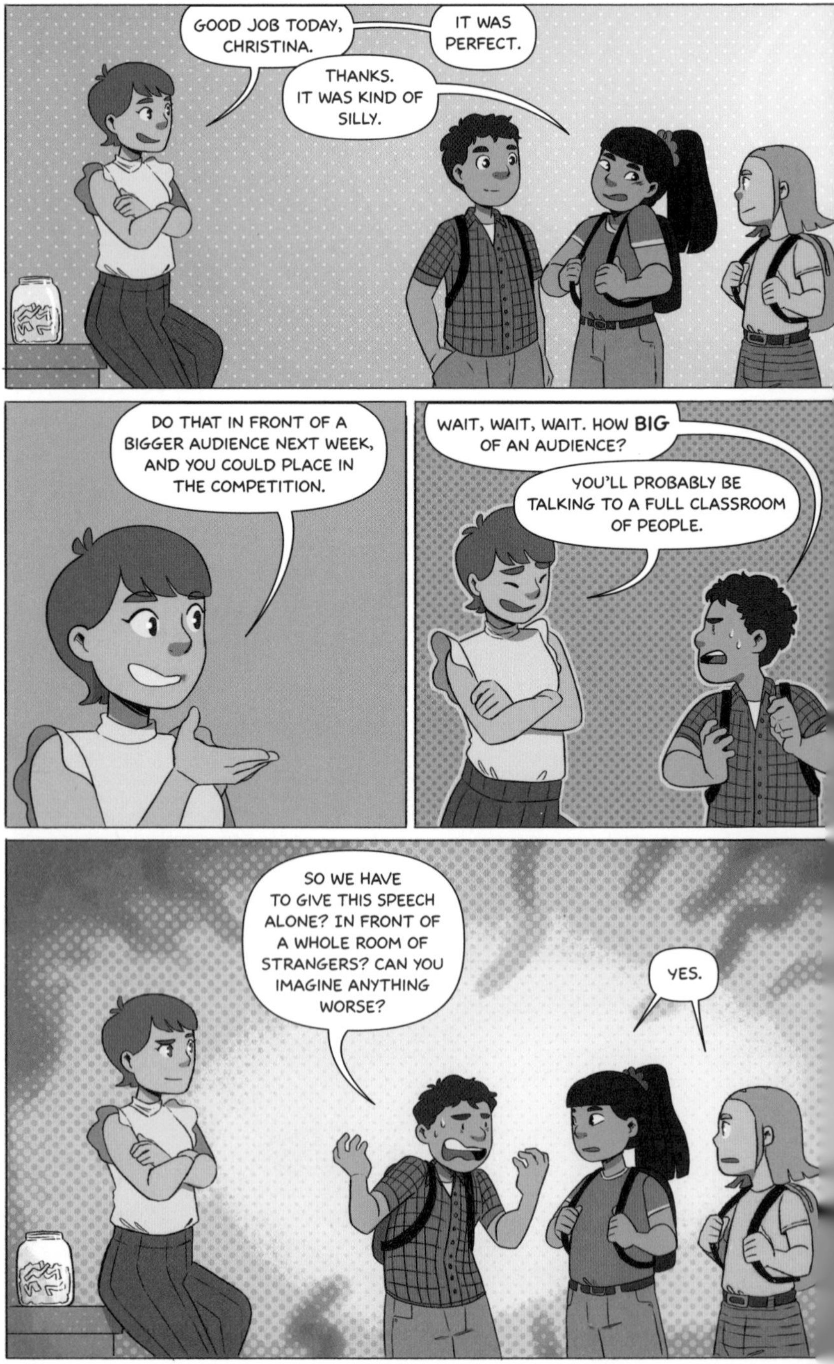
GOOD JOB TODAY, CHRISTINA.
IT WAS PERFECT.
THANKS. IT WAS KIND OF SILLY.
DO THAT IN FRONT OF A BIGGER AUDIENCE NEXT WEEK, AND YOU COULD PLACE IN THE COMPETITION.
WAIT, WAIT, WAIT. HOW **BIG** OF AN AUDIENCE?
YOU'LL PROBABLY BE TALKING TO A FULL CLASSROOM OF PEOPLE.
SO WE HAVE TO GIVE THIS SPEECH ALONE? IN FRONT OF A WHOLE ROOM OF STRANGERS? CAN YOU IMAGINE ANYTHING WORSE?
YES.

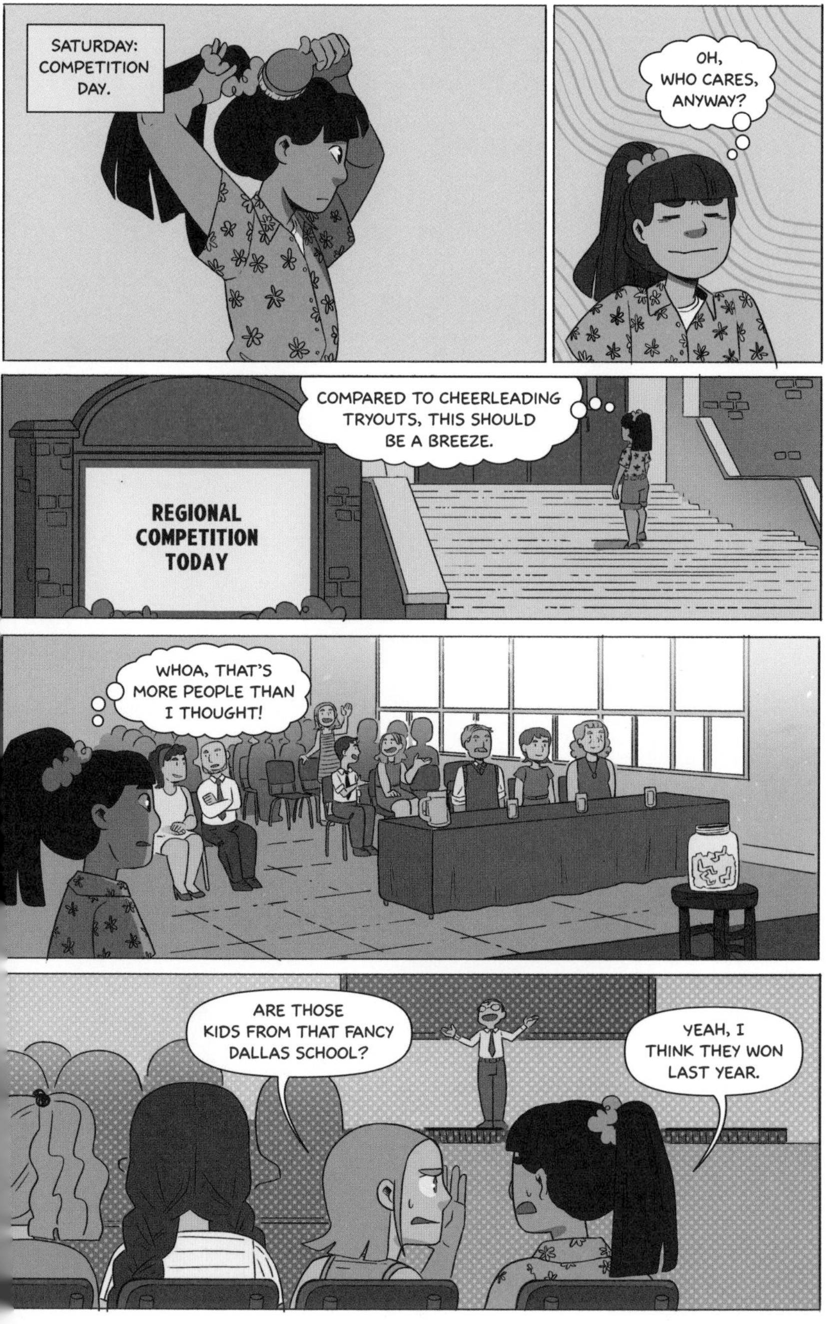
SATURDAY: COMPETITION DAY.
OH, WHO CARES, ANYWAY?
COMPARED TO CHEERLEADING TRYOUTS, THIS SHOULD BE A BREEZE.
REGIONAL COMPETITION TODAY
WHOA, THAT'S MORE PEOPLE THAN I THOUGHT!
ARE THOSE KIDS FROM THAT FANCY DALLAS SCHOOL?
YEAH, I THINK THEY WON LAST YEAR.

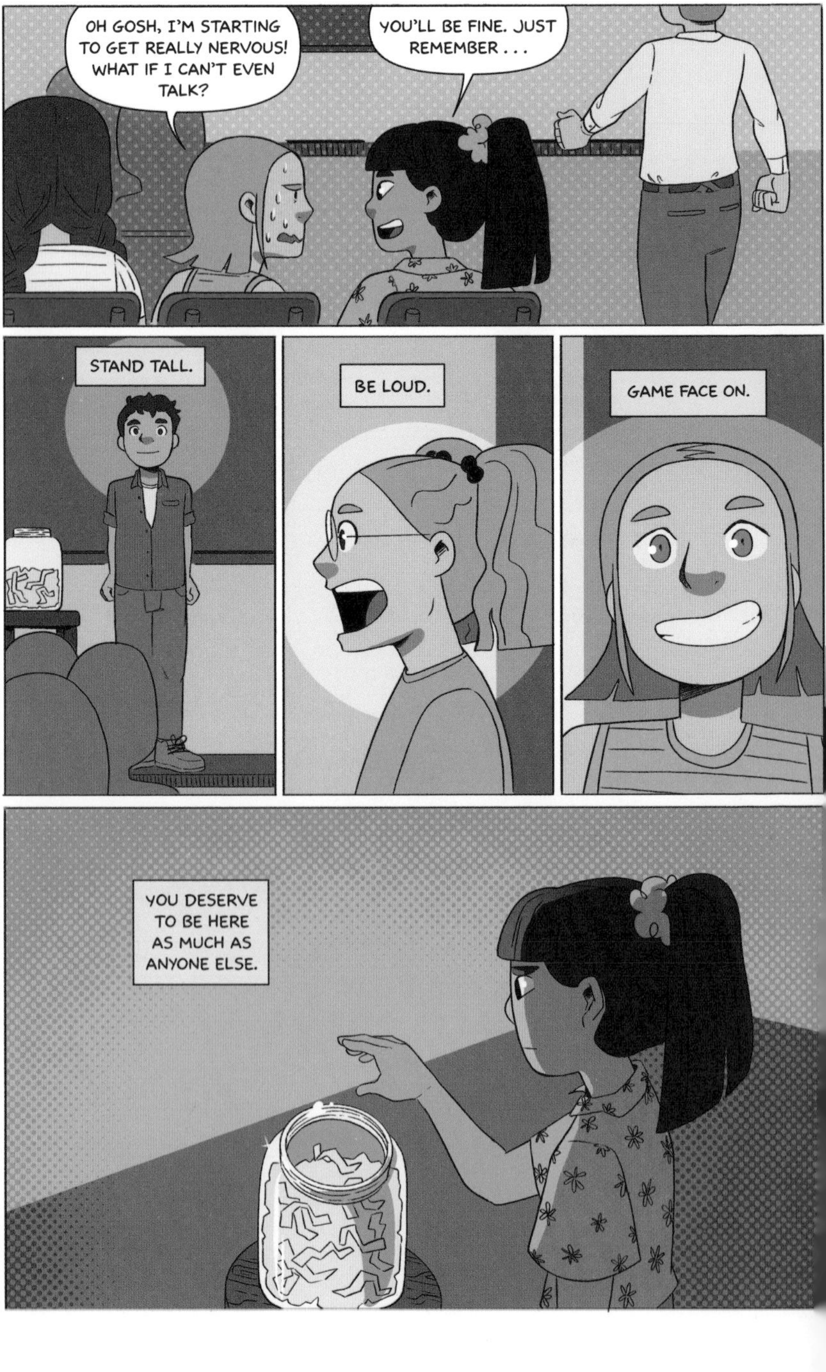
OH GOSH, I'M STARTING TO GET REALLY NERVOUS! WHAT IF I CAN'T EVEN TALK?
YOU'LL BE FINE. JUST REMEMBER . . .
STAND TALL.
BE LOUD.
GAME FACE ON.
YOU DESERVE TO BE HERE AS MUCH AS ANYONE ELSE.

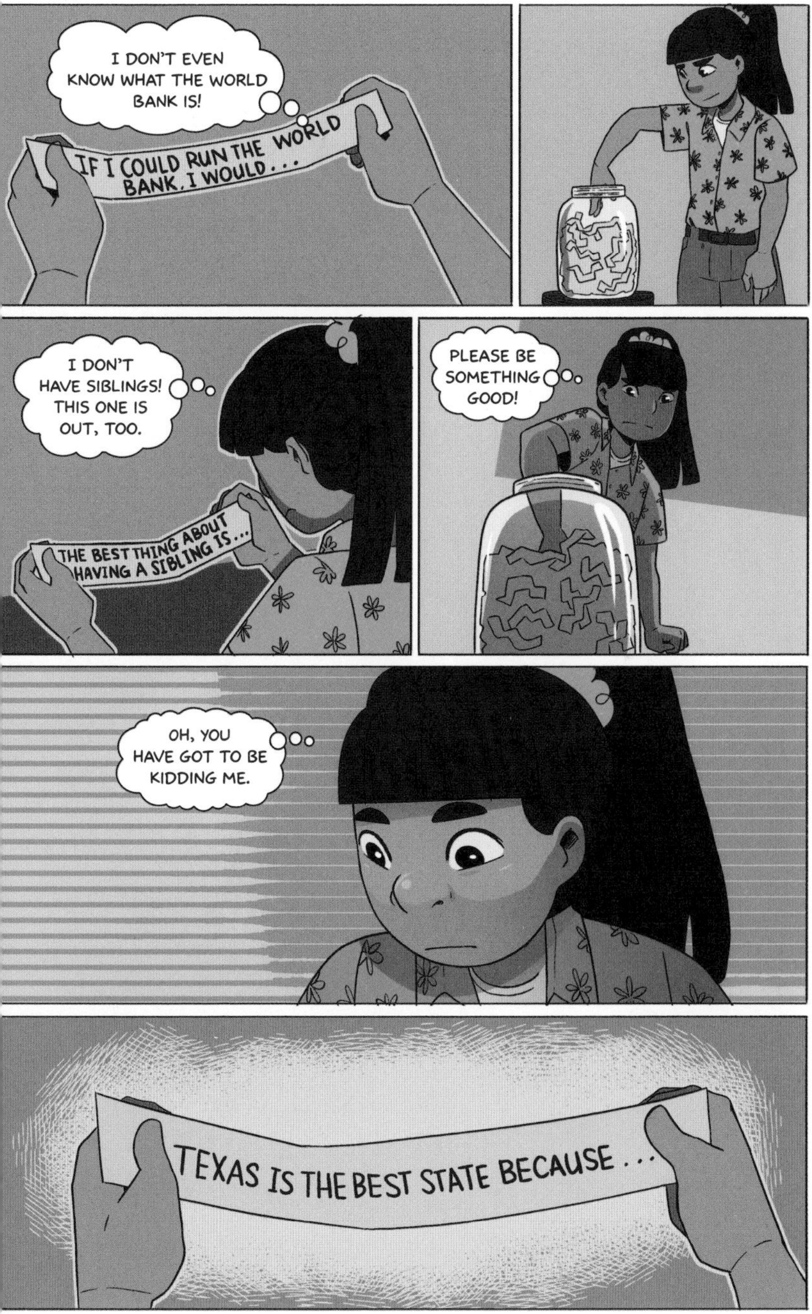
I DON'T EVEN KNOW WHAT THE WORLD BANK IS!
IF I COULD RUN THE WORLD BANK, I WOULD . . .
I DON'T HAVE SIBLINGS! THIS ONE IS OUT, TOO.
THE BEST THING ABOUT HAVING A SIBLING IS . . .
PLEASE BE SOMETHING GOOD!
OH, YOU HAVE GOT TO BE KIDDING ME.
TEXAS IS THE BEST STATE BECAUSE . . .

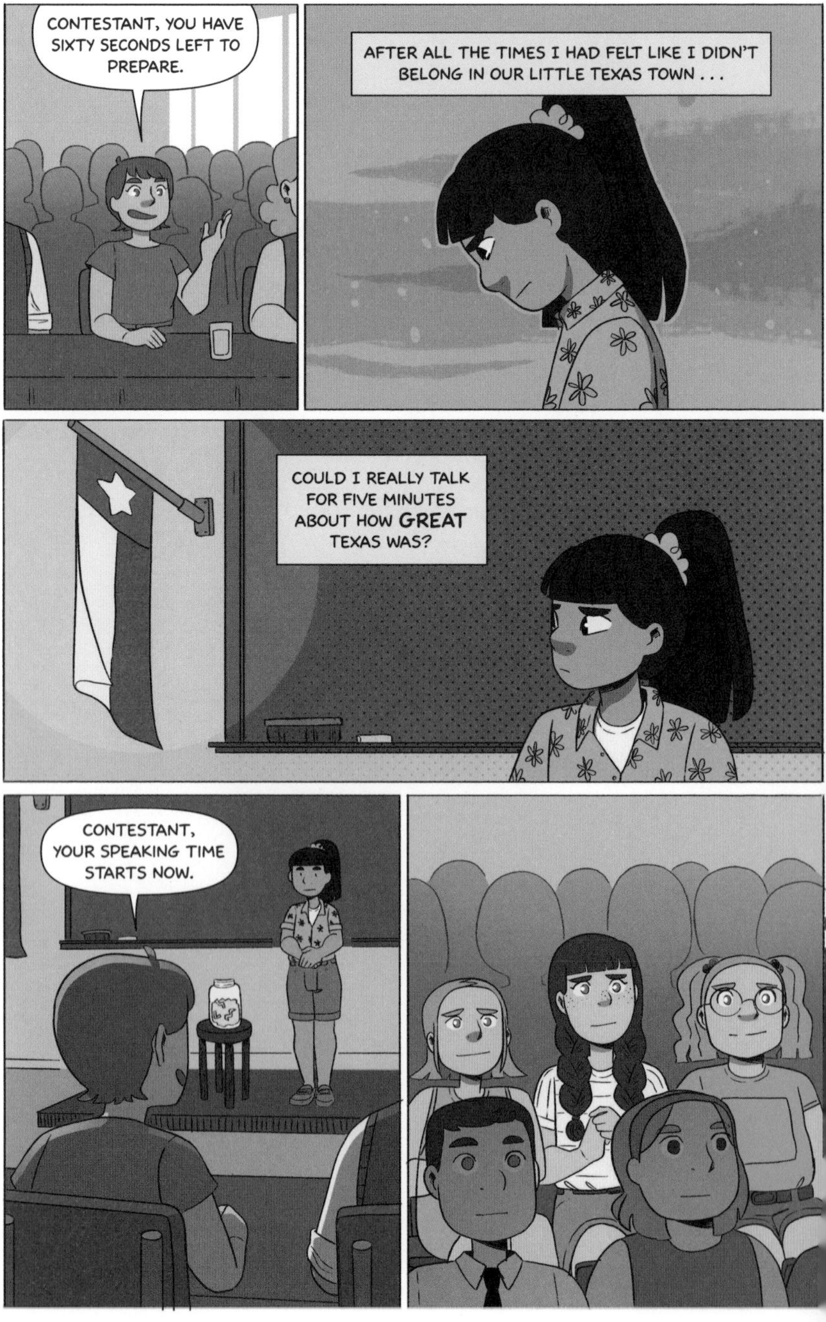

CONTESTANT, YOU HAVE SIXTY SECONDS LEFT TO PREPARE.
AFTER ALL THE TIMES I HAD FELT LIKE I DIDN'T BELONG IN OUR LITTLE TEXAS TOWN . . .
COULD I REALLY TALK FOR FIVE MINUTES ABOUT HOW **GREAT** TEXAS WAS?
CONTESTANT, YOUR SPEAKING TIME STARTS NOW.

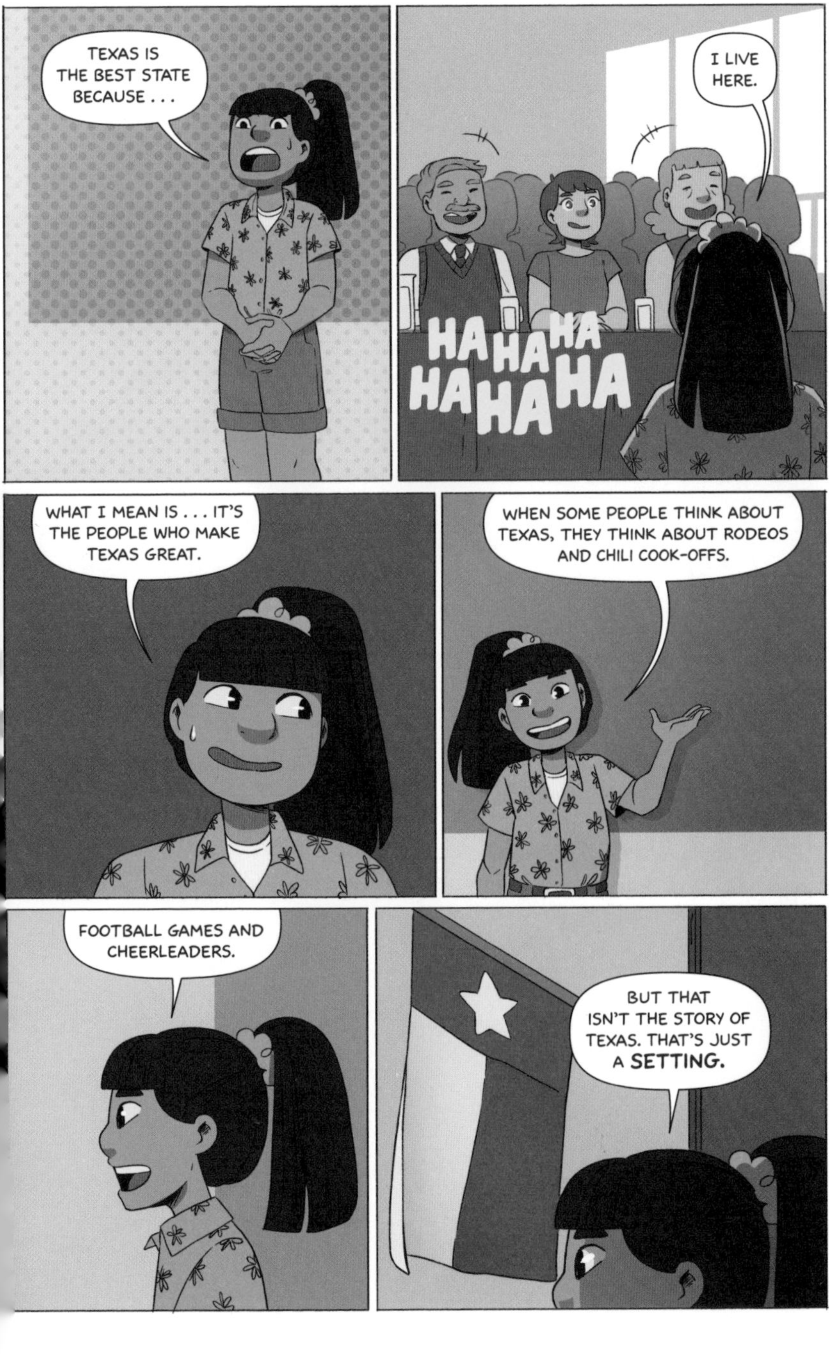
TEXAS IS THE BEST STATE BECAUSE . . .
I LIVE HERE.
HAHAHAHA HAHAHAHA
WHAT I MEAN IS . . . IT'S THE PEOPLE WHO MAKE TEXAS GREAT.
WHEN SOME PEOPLE THINK ABOUT TEXAS, THEY THINK ABOUT RODEOS AND CHILI COOK-OFFS.
FOOTBALL GAMES AND CHEERLEADERS.
BUT THAT ISN'T THE STORY OF TEXAS. THAT'S JUST A **SETTING.**

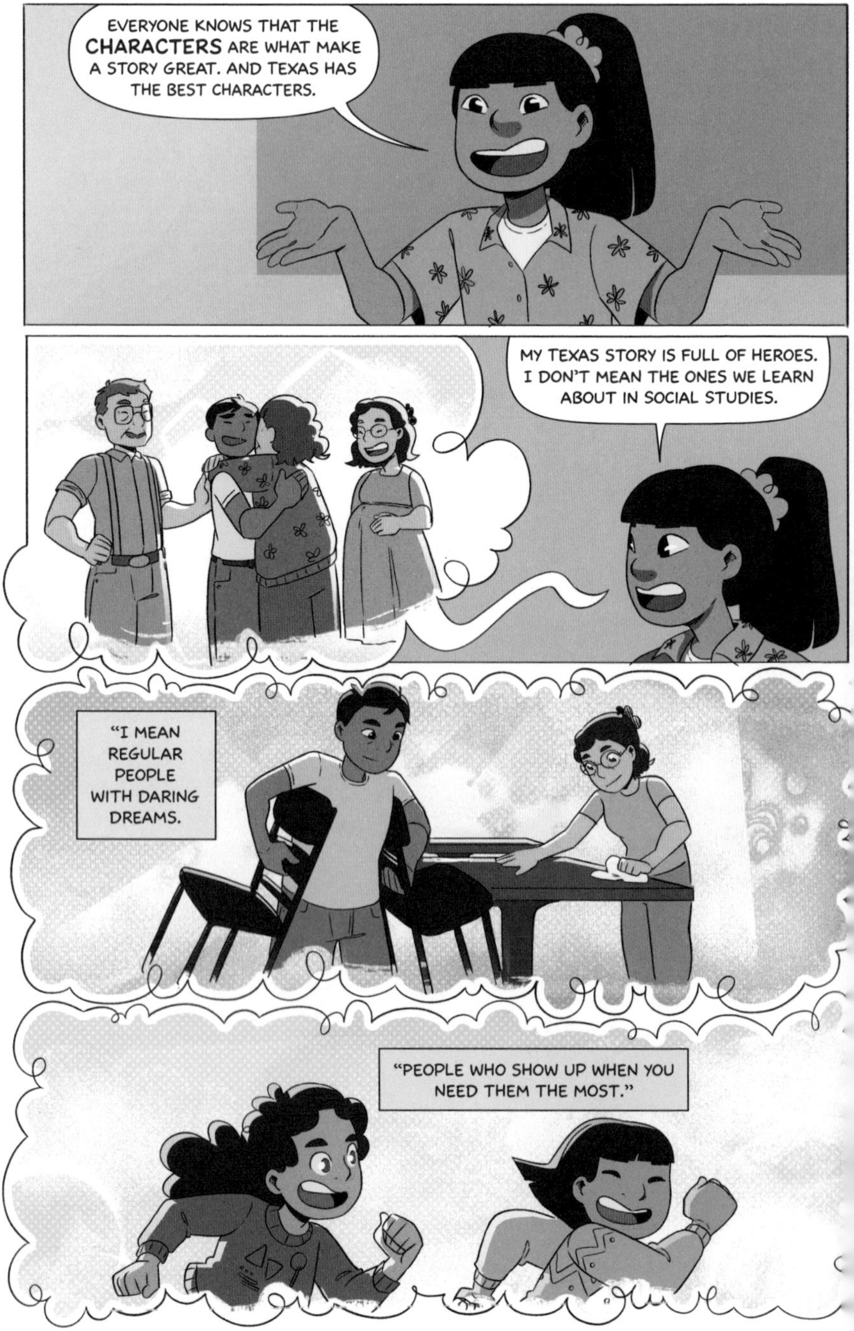
EVERYONE KNOWS THAT THE CHARACTERS ARE WHAT MAKE A STORY GREAT. AND TEXAS HAS THE BEST CHARACTERS.
MY TEXAS STORY IS FULL OF HEROES. I DON'T MEAN THE ONES WE LEARN ABOUT IN SOCIAL STUDIES.
"I MEAN REGULAR PEOPLE WITH DARING DREAMS.
"PEOPLE WHO SHOW UP WHEN YOU NEED THEM THE MOST."

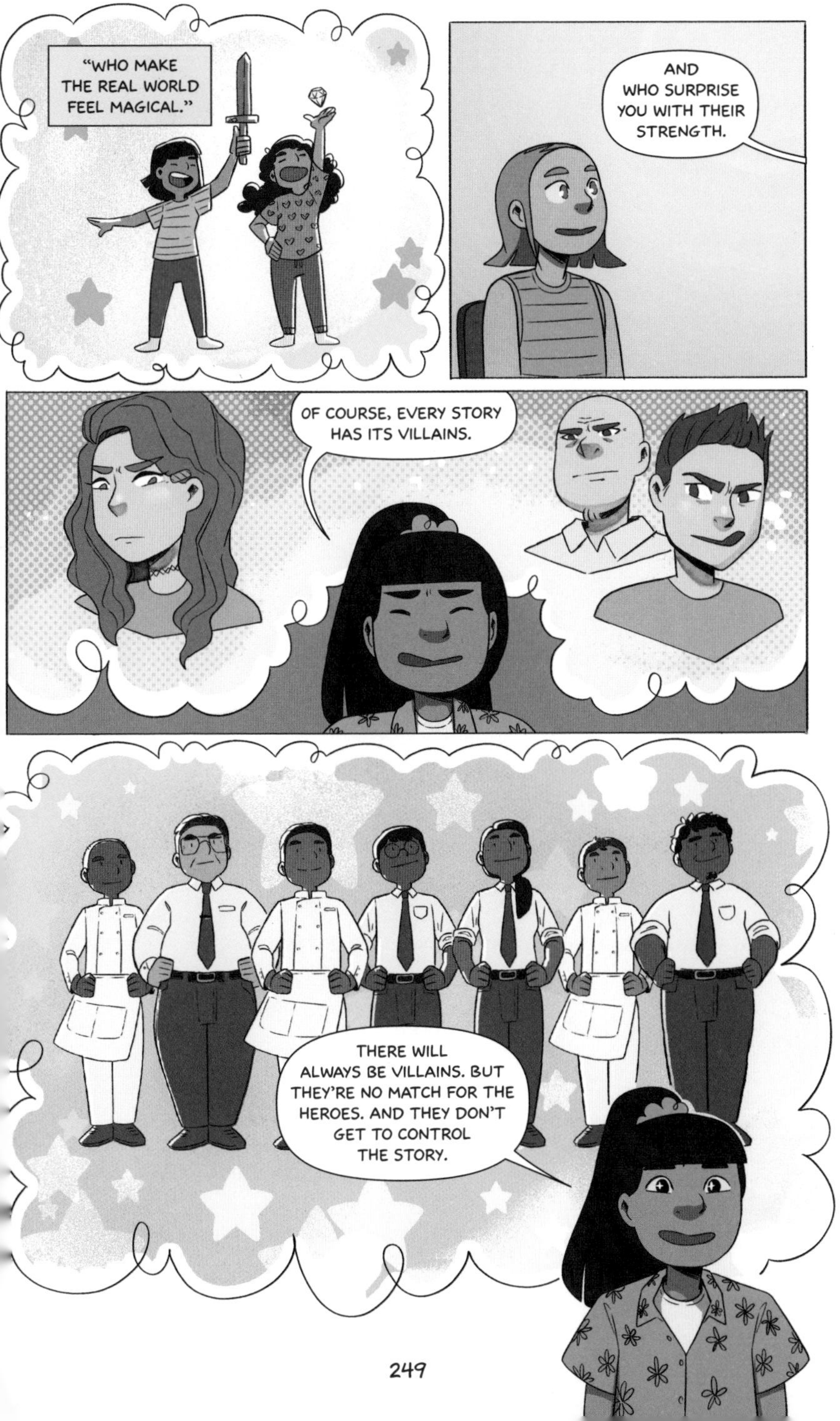
"WHO MAKE THE REAL WORLD FEEL MAGICAL."
AND WHO SURPRISE YOU WITH THEIR STRENGTH.
OF COURSE, EVERY STORY HAS ITS VILLAINS.
THERE WILL ALWAYS BE VILLAINS. BUT THEY'RE NO MATCH FOR THE HEROES. AND THEY DON'T GET TO CONTROL THE STORY.

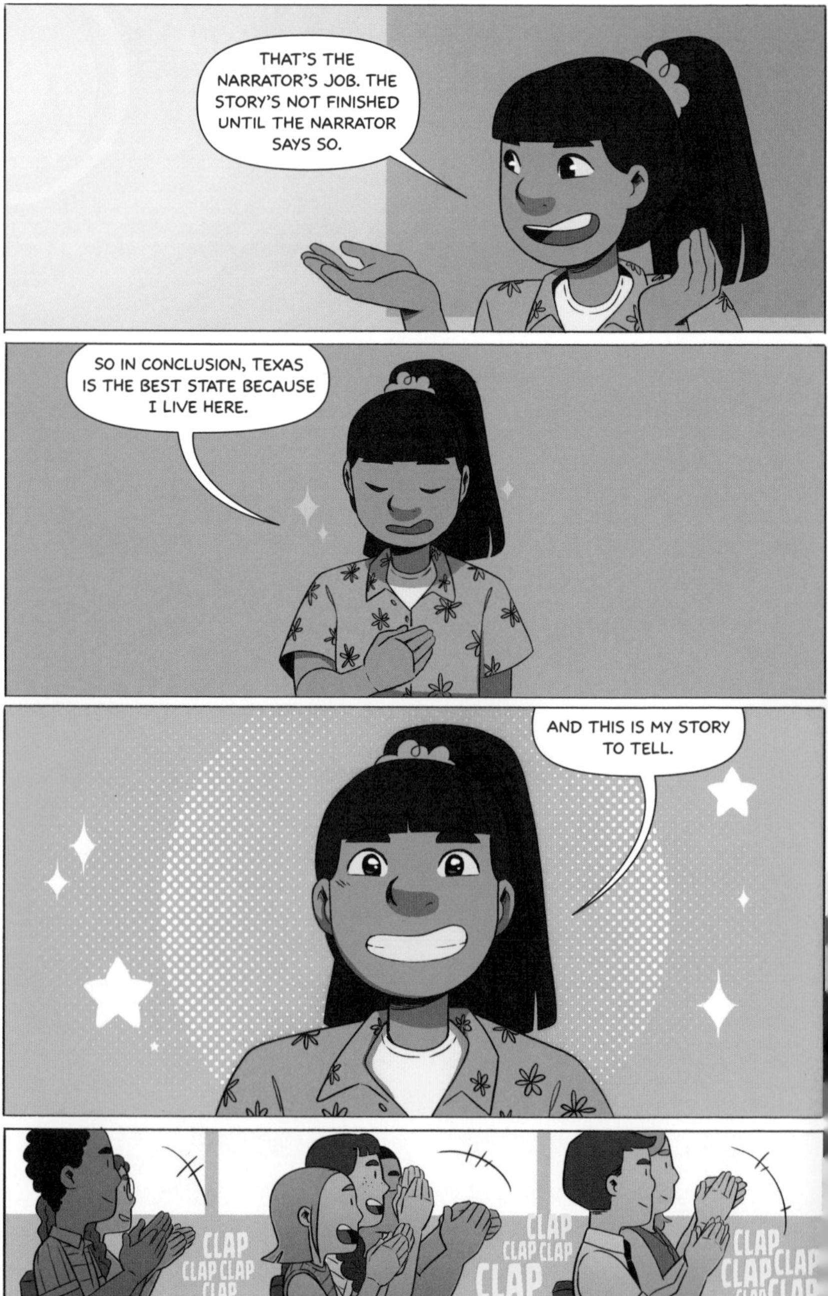
THAT'S THE NARRATOR'S JOB. THE STORY'S NOT FINISHED UNTIL THE NARRATOR SAYS SO.
SO IN CONCLUSION, TEXAS IS THE BEST STATE BECAUSE I LIVE HERE.
AND THIS IS MY STORY TO TELL.
CLAP CLAP CLAP CLAP
CLAP CLAP CLAP CLAP
CLAP CLAP CLAP CLAP CLAP

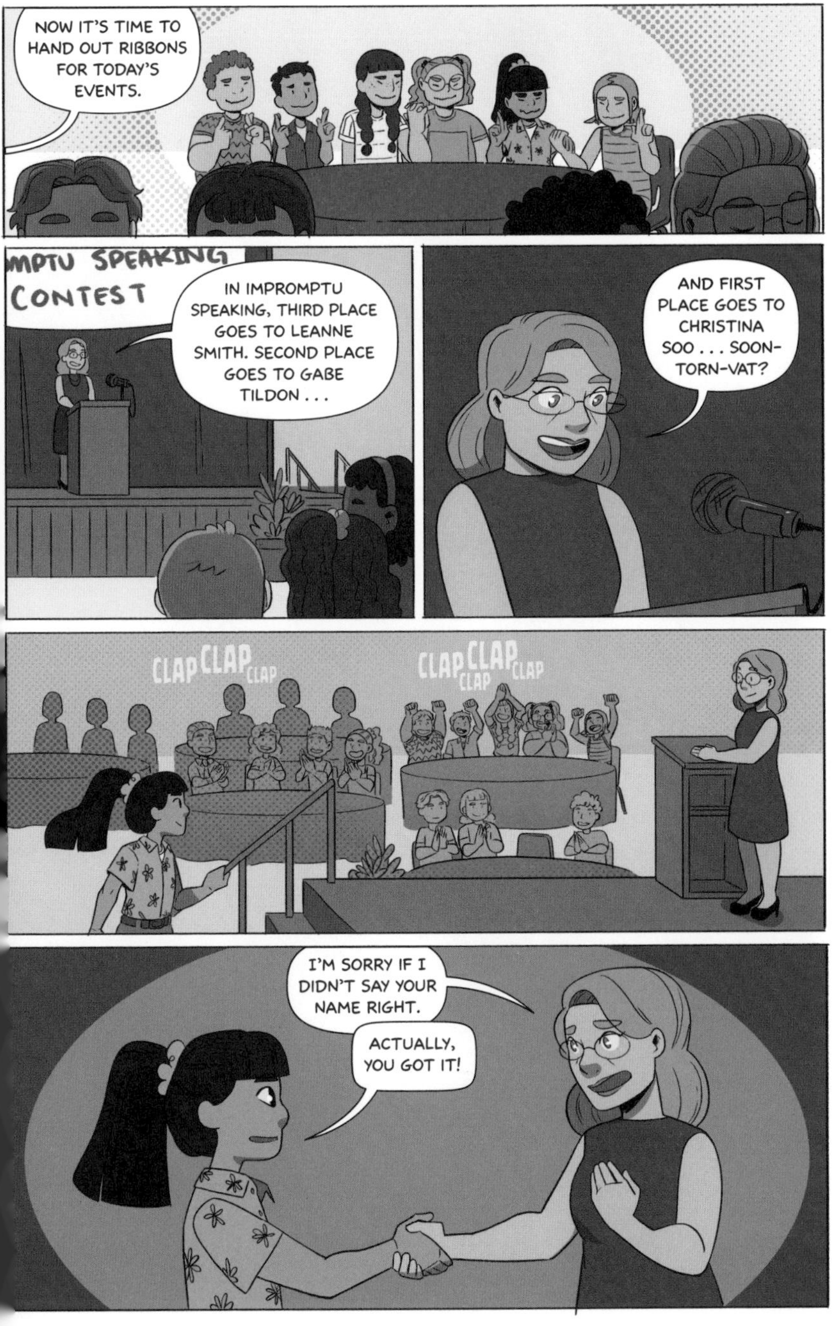
NOW IT'S TIME TO HAND OUT RIBBONS FOR TODAY'S EVENTS.
MPTU SPEAKING CONTEST
IN IMPROMPTU SPEAKING, THIRD PLACE GOES TO LEANNE SMITH. SECOND PLACE GOES TO GABE TILDON . . .
AND FIRST PLACE GOES TO CHRISTINA SOO . . . SOON-TORN-VAT?
CLAP CLAP CLAP
CLAP CLAP CLAP CLAP
I'M SORRY IF I DIDN'T SAY YOUR NAME RIGHT.
ACTUALLY, YOU GOT IT!

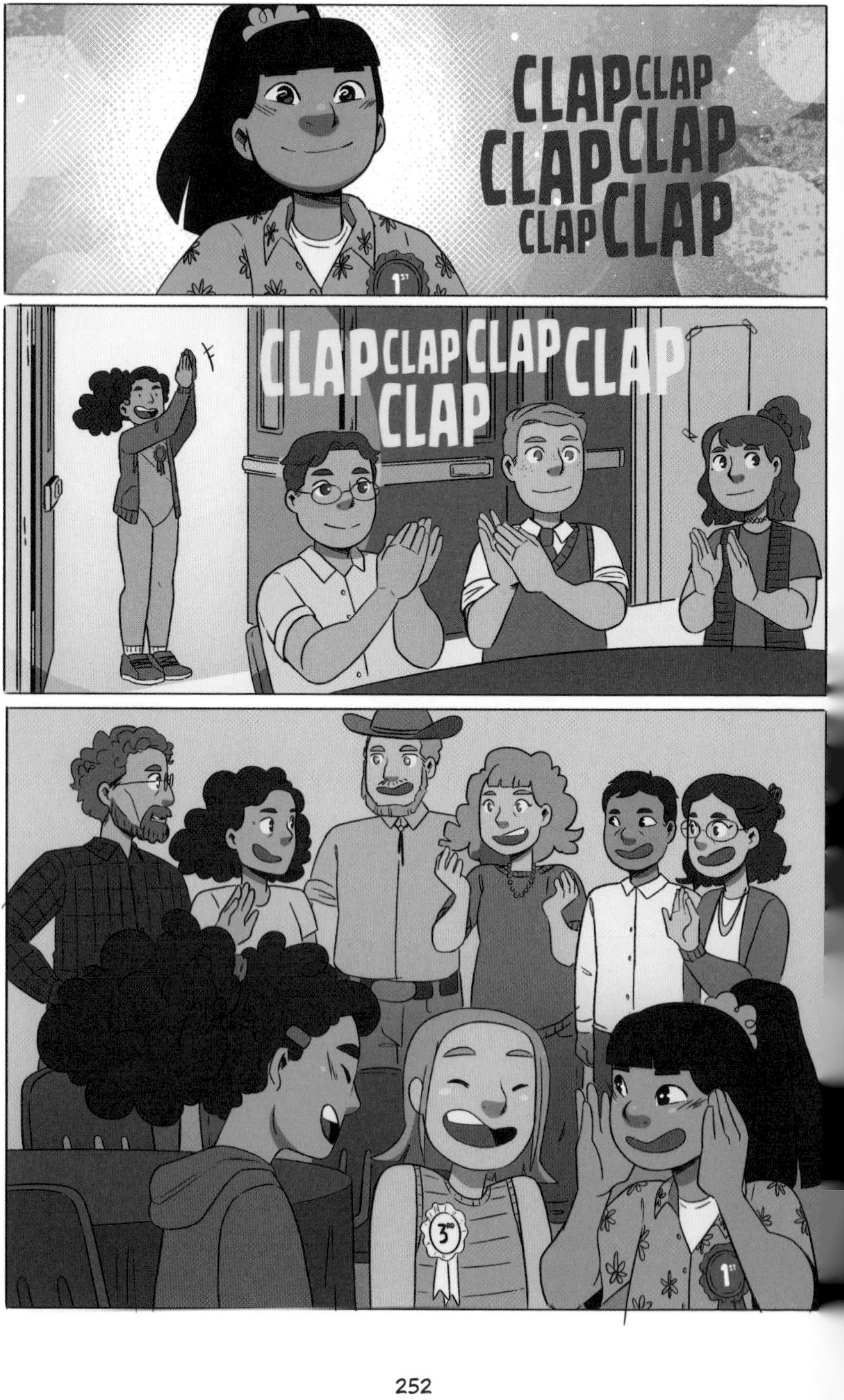
CLAP CLAP
CLAP CLAP
CLAP CLAP
CLAP CLAP CLAP CLAP
CLAP

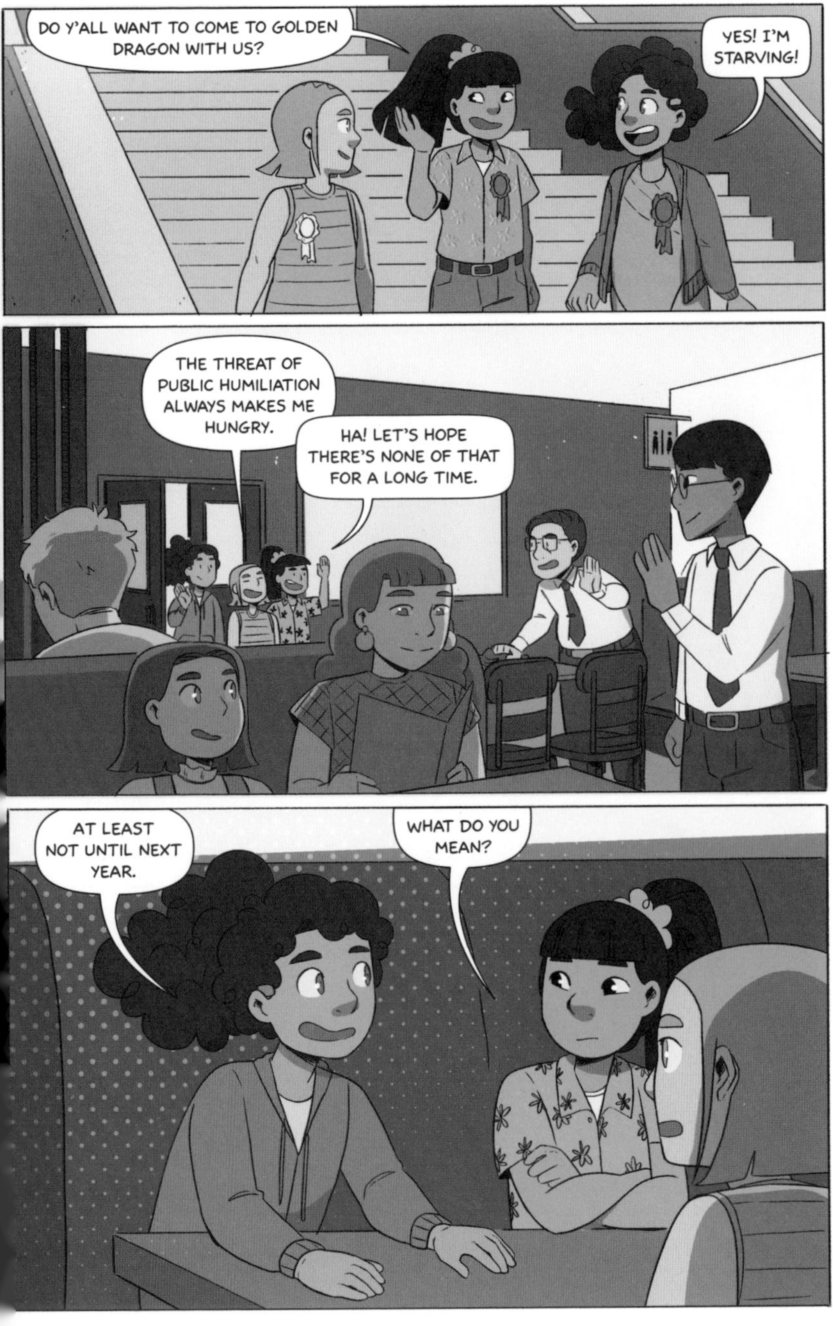
DO Y'ALL WANT TO COME TO GOLDEN DRAGON WITH US?
YES! I'M STARVING!
THE THREAT OF PUBLIC HUMILIATION ALWAYS MAKES ME HUNGRY.
HA! LET'S HOPE THERE'S NONE OF THAT FOR A LONG TIME.
AT LEAST NOT UNTIL NEXT YEAR.
WHAT DO YOU MEAN?

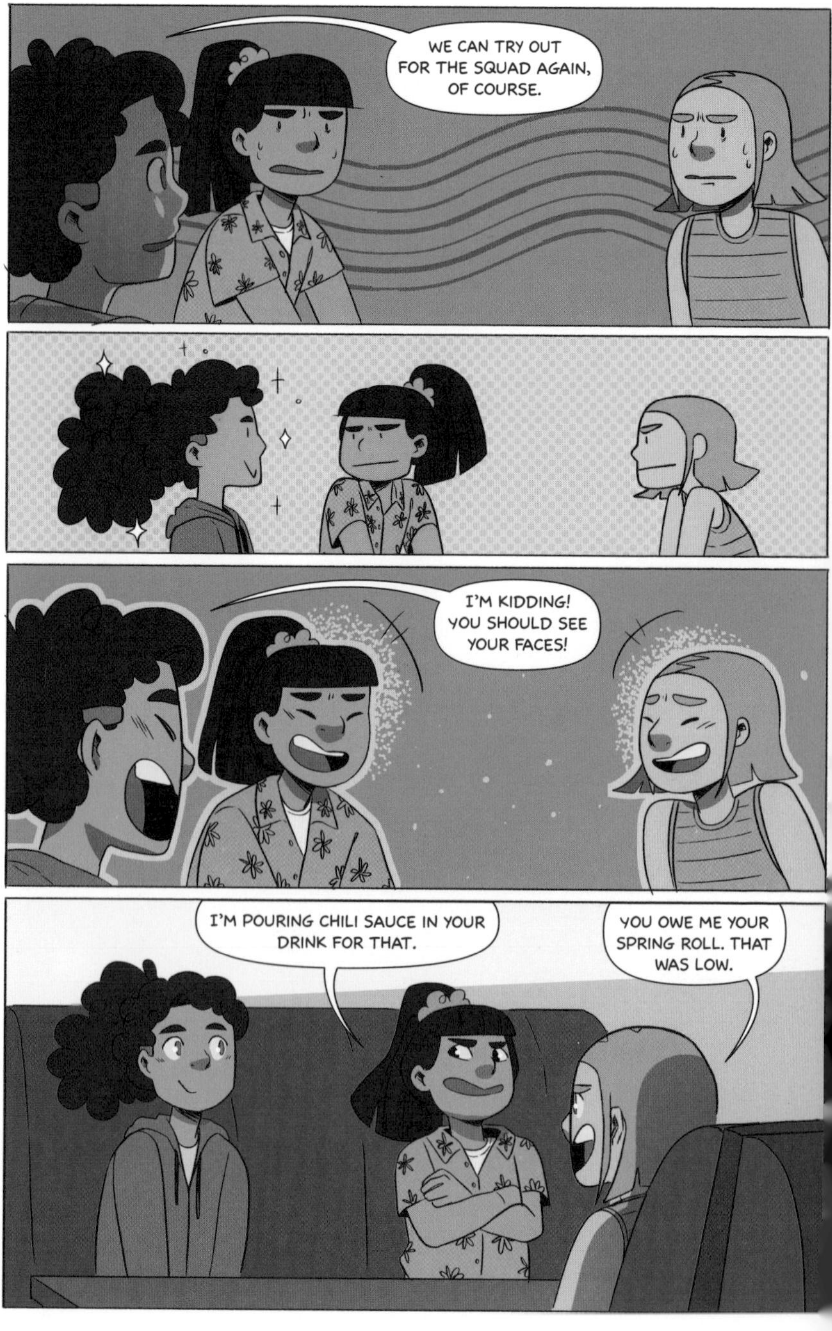
WE CAN TRY OUT FOR THE SQUAD AGAIN, OF COURSE.
I'M KIDDING! YOU SHOULD SEE YOUR FACES!
I'M POURING CHILI SAUCE IN YOUR DRINK FOR THAT.
YOU OWE ME YOUR SPRING ROLL. THAT WAS LOW.

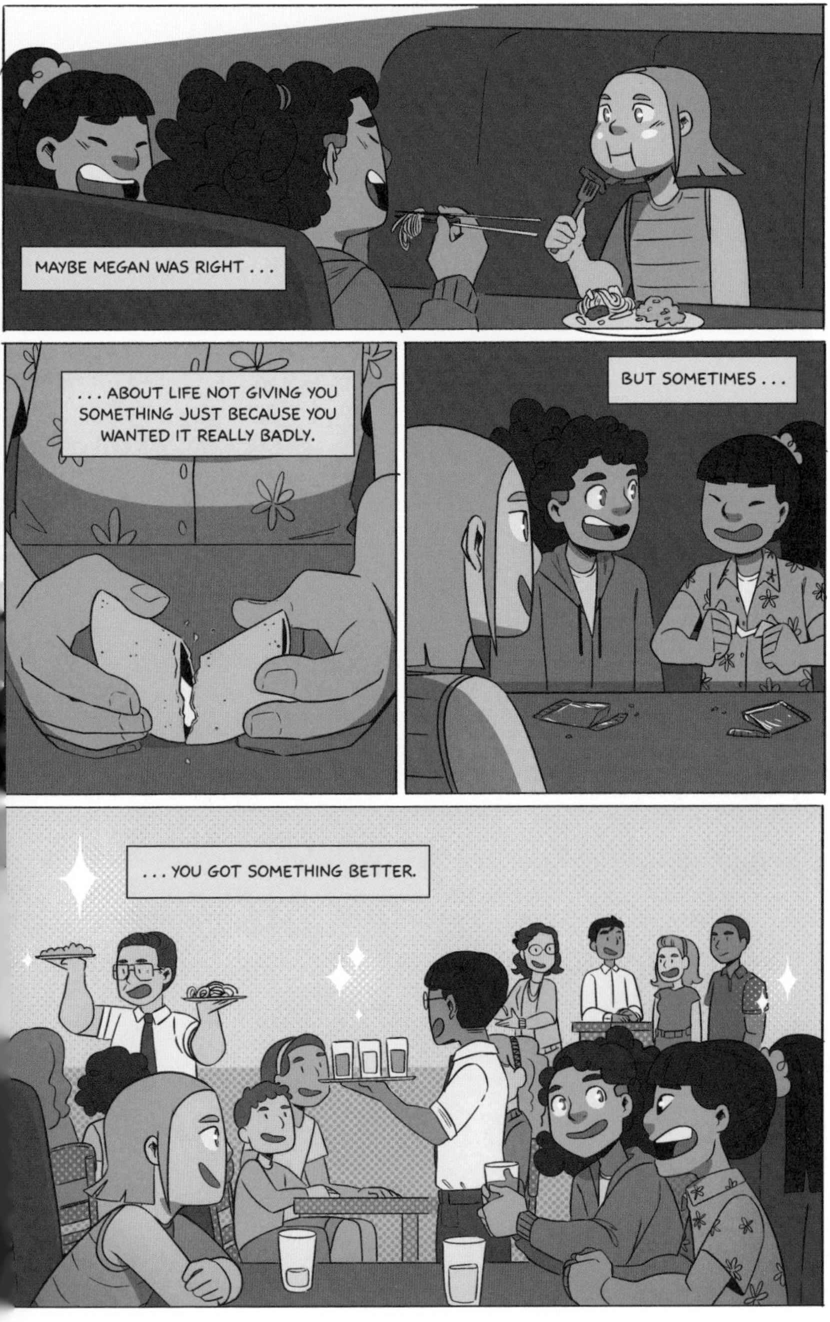
MAYBE MEGAN WAS RIGHT . . .
. . . ABOUT LIFE NOT GIVING YOU SOMETHING JUST BECAUSE YOU WANTED IT REALLY BADLY.
BUT SOMETIMES . . .
. . . YOU GOT SOMETHING BETTER.

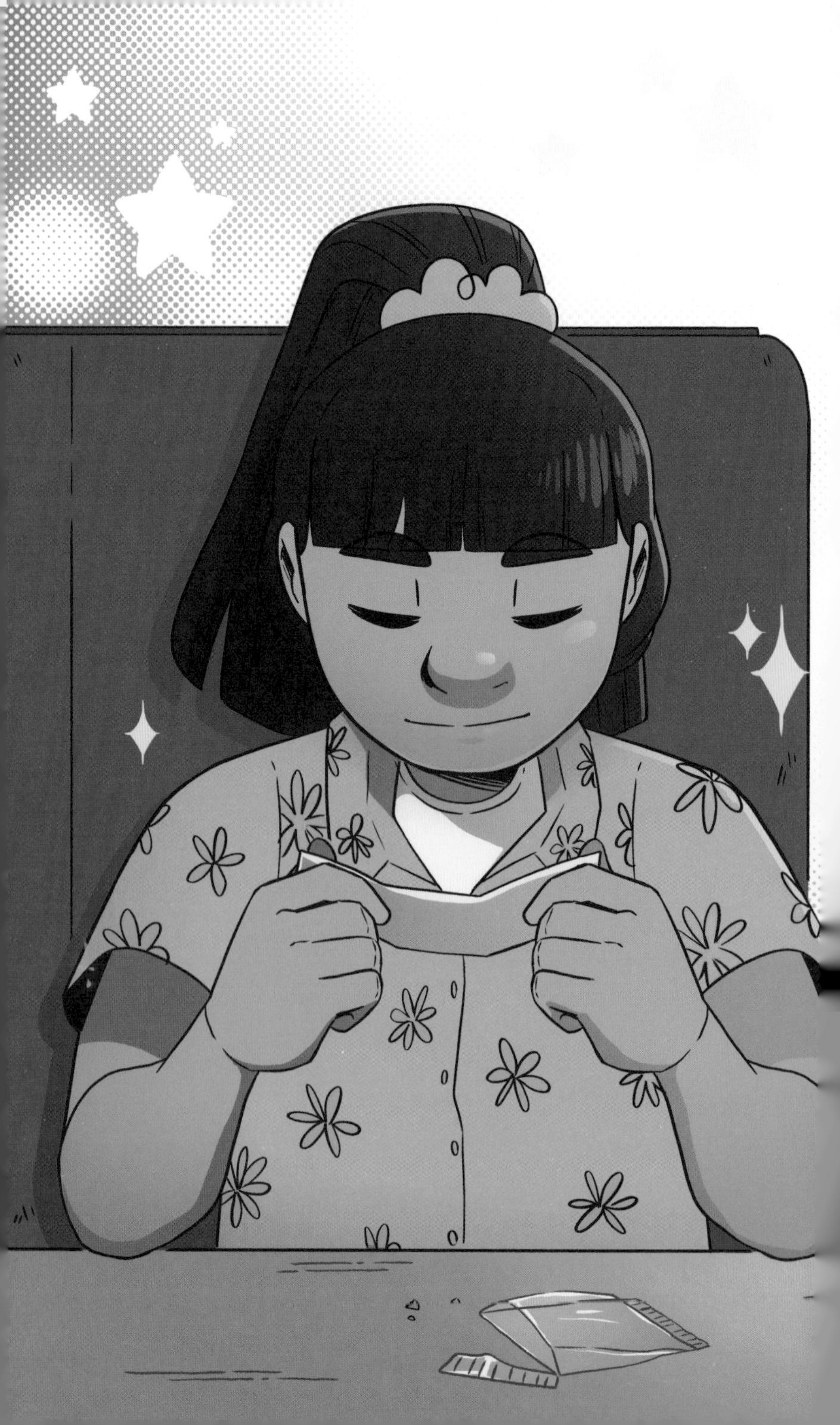

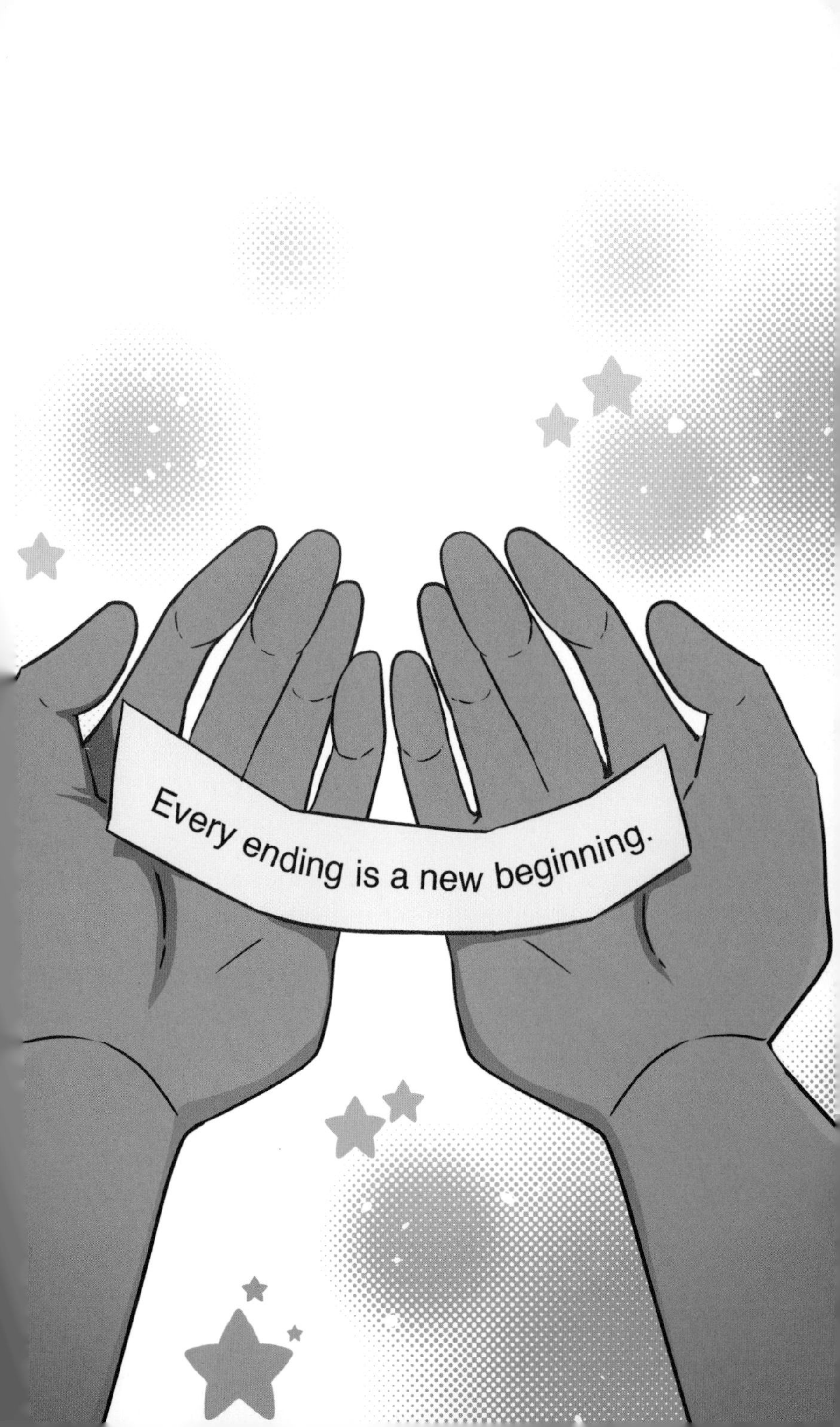
Every ending is a new beginning.

AUTHOR'S NOTE

I never planned to write a book like this. For the most part, I'm a fantasy writer and feel way more comfortable making up stories about magic or dragons than writing about myself. But for years, whenever I recounted my tale of trying out for cheerleader in middle school, the people listening would recoil or cringe, as if I were telling the plot of a horror movie. And when I would talk about what it was like to grow up in a small Texas town, they would lean in and want to know more. It took me a long time to realize that maybe these reactions were a sign I had a story that needed to be told. And maybe somewhere out there was a young person who needed to read it.

My feelings about my hometown are complicated and include things that I wish had been different. Most of all, I wish the community had done more to make everyone feel welcome, no matter their race, religion, sexual orientation, or gender identity. But I also feel proud to have grown up there. Our restaurant is still open and serving up yummy food (my family recently sold the business to our dear friends). My grandparents are buried there. I made some of the very best friends of my life there. Overall, it was a place where I saw the power of good hearts at work.

The hardest part of writing this book was being honest about how it felt to deal with racism and my identity as an Asian American. I worried: That was so long ago. Will it even resonate with today's readers? And there were other kids at my school, particularly Black, Latine, and LGBTQIA2+ kids, who dealt with much worse discrimination than I did. And what does it even mean for someone of white and immigrant heritage to feel "belonging" when they live on land that was taken from Native Americans? Sometimes I wondered, "Does my little story matter?" And then current events and conversations with other writers and friends changed my mind. Maybe my own personal story was small, but the conversation about race and belonging in America is a very big one.

In my middle school, hardly anyone talked about race unless they were making a joke, or it was one of the few days we were covering it in history class. It was as though everyone hoped that if they didn't talk about it, it wouldn't exist. And whenever other people (kids or adults) said something racist to me, I didn't tell my teachers because I'd accepted and internalized that that's just the way things were. But I was wrong. Talking to one another and sharing our stories is how we make change.

(And on that note, if anyone is saying hurtful things to you or someone you know, definitely tell an adult who can support you in addressing it. You deserve to be treated with respect.)

I didn't keep a journal in middle school, so I have had to construct the events of this book as best as I can from my own memory and from the memories of friends. I am sure I have made mistakes. I am sure that my memories differ from those of other people who were there. And I am definitely sure that my prize-winning Impromptu Speaking speech about Texas wasn't nearly that eloquent!

To respect the privacy of the people in this story, everyone's name has been changed except for mine. Some of the characters are written exactly as I remember them in real life (like Megan and Leanne, still some of my best friends today), while other characters (like Tobin) represent several people mashed into one. And there are some real-life friends who were very important to me, who couldn't make it into this book at all because I didn't have room. Here and there, I moved up a few scenes to fit them into the timeline of the story. And I stretched out the timeline of the cheerleading tryout to give it the hefty weight that it felt like it held in real life. But every word is true to my emotional experience.

If I could go back in time, there are so many things I would change about my own behavior in middle school. I would not have been so cruel to other kids, like Deanna. I would have stuck up for other people more often, like the boys who were bullied for wanting to be cheerleaders (or for just wanting to be themselves). These regrets still gnaw at me. But the tryout itself (aka the most devastating moment of my young life)—would I go back and sit it out if I could? Hmm, I don't know . . .

A few years after we graduated from middle school, the administration changed the rules so that the cheerleaders are now treated more like the athletes they are, and the selection process is based solely on judges' votes. Thank goodness. It should have always been that way. But if there is a silver lining to that harrowing event, it's that I really did walk away feeling like I could tackle anything.

So many adults forget how much courage it takes to just be a kid. If you are reading this and you are facing something that seems impossible, I'm here to tell you that you can get through it.

So take a deep breath. Get your game face on. I believe in you.

Christina

PHOTOS FROM CHRISTINA'S CHILDHOOD

Me, the year we moved from Dallas

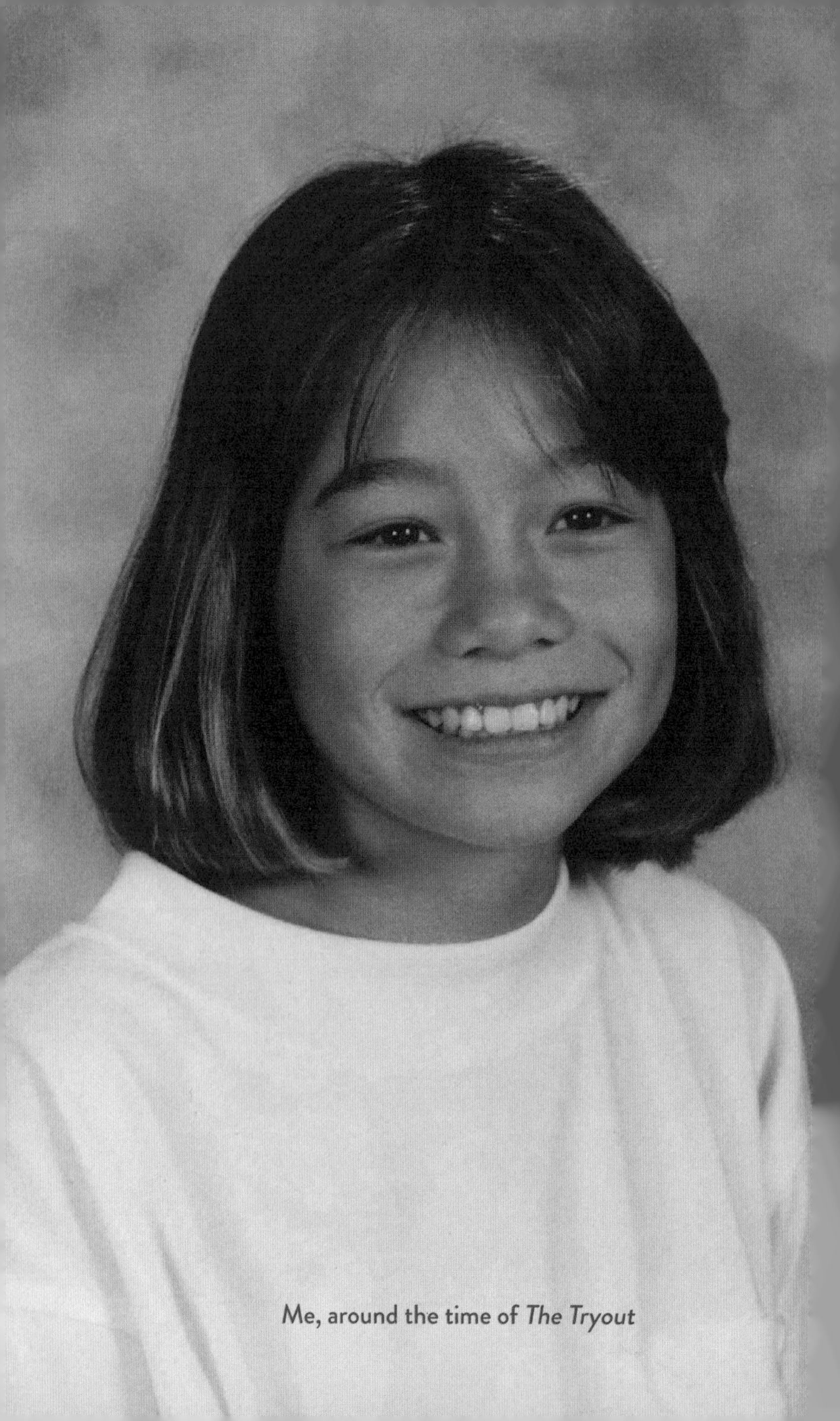

Me, around the time of *The Tryout*

My dad and his brother on the day they immigrated to the United States

My dad, when we first opened the restaurant

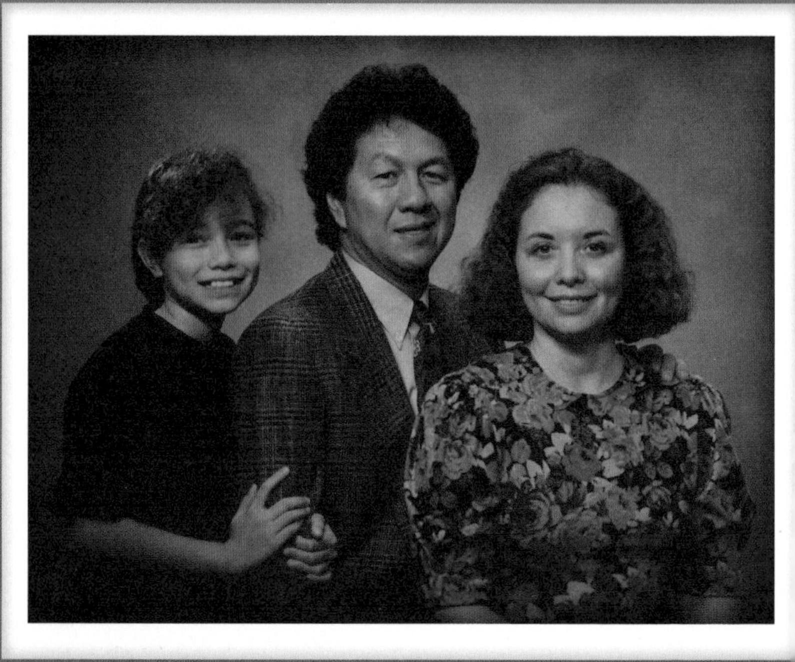

Mom, Dad, and me with our matching perms

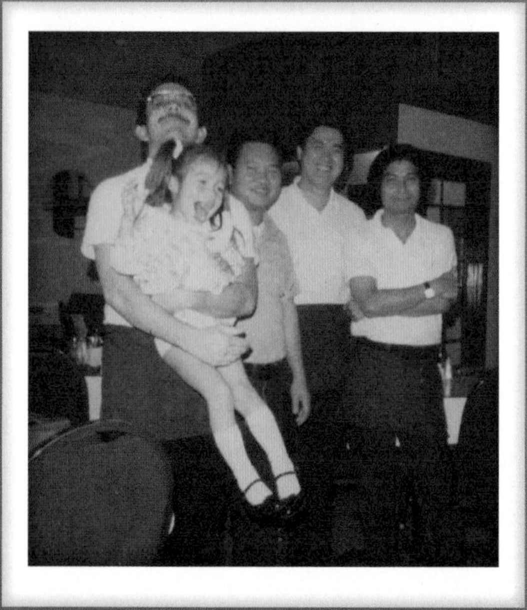

Me, with my restaurant uncles

Megan and me, dancing at a party at the restaurant

AUTHOR'S ACKNOWLEDGMENTS

Tremendous thanks to Joanna Cacao, for bringing this story to life through your incredible illustrations. I am so grateful for your humor, empathy, and your overwhelming talent. I count myself as the luckiest author to get to work with you on this!

Thank you also to letterer Jesse Post and colorist Amanda Lafrenais for your beautiful work. Many thanks to expert readers Quincy Surasmith and Solmaz Sharif for helping us make this book as strong as possible.

Thank you to Tracy Mack, my amazing editor. You saw the heart of this story right away, and your passion for it kept me going when the writing was hard. I'm so happy we get to work on books together!

Thank you to the wonderful team at Scholastic and Graphix: Leslie Owusu, Ben Gartenberg, Phil Falco, Shivana Sookdeo, David Saylor, Cassandra Pelham Fulton, Elizabeth Krych, Jordana Kulak, Emily Heddleson, Lizette Serrano, Erin Berger, Matt Poulter, and Meaghan Finnerty. You are the best squad I could have hoped for!

So many thanks to my extraordinary agent, Stephanie Fretwell-Hill. One day you and I will perform a partner stunt together!

Thank you to Neal Porter, who told me this story was not a picture book. I was mad at you then, but hey, you were right. Thank you Varian Johnson, for helping me when I had zero clue about how to write a graphic novel. You are kind and generous, always.

To all my old friends from back home: I treasure our memories together so very much. I would travel back in time and relive those days in a heartbeat. Shauna, I'm beyond grateful for our friendship. Erica, thank you for every single moment. We had so many great ones. I love you.

Thank you to all my wonderful teachers, with a special shout-out to Ms. Starnes, Ms. Bailey, Ms. Smith, Ms. Sullivan, and Ms. Bruno. And thank you to all the teachers and librarians out there who work so hard to get books into the hands of kids. I'm forever grateful for you.

Thank you to my restaurant family, especially my beloved "uncles," Chris and Adrian. Uncle Donis, we miss you every day. Mom and Dad, you gave me everything, and I can never thank you enough. Bob and Liz, thank you for your love and support. Thank you to my wonderful husband, Tom. You are far and away my biggest and best cheerleader. Thank you to my daughters, Elowyn and Aven, for sharing your love of graphic novels with me and for inspiring me to make one for you.

ILLUSTRATOR'S ACKNOWLEDGMENTS

The Tryout is my very first collaboration on a project of this size, and am so grateful for the opportunity and being able to draw these characters and story. I've learned so much and am so excited for what's to come.

Thank you so much to Christina Soontornvat for trusting me and my skills with her amazing story, as well as Tracy Mack, Leslie Owusu, Phil Falco, Shivana Sookdeo, and everyone at Scholastic for believing in this book and helping to make this happen. Thank you to Tara Gilbert, for being one of my biggest cheerleaders and always being in my corner. Thank you to Amanda Lafrenais for doing the colors and Jesse Post for the great lettering work. I'd also like to thank my family and friends, who love and root for me.

And last but certainly not least, I'd like to thank my love and partner, Warren, for always being there and supporting me.

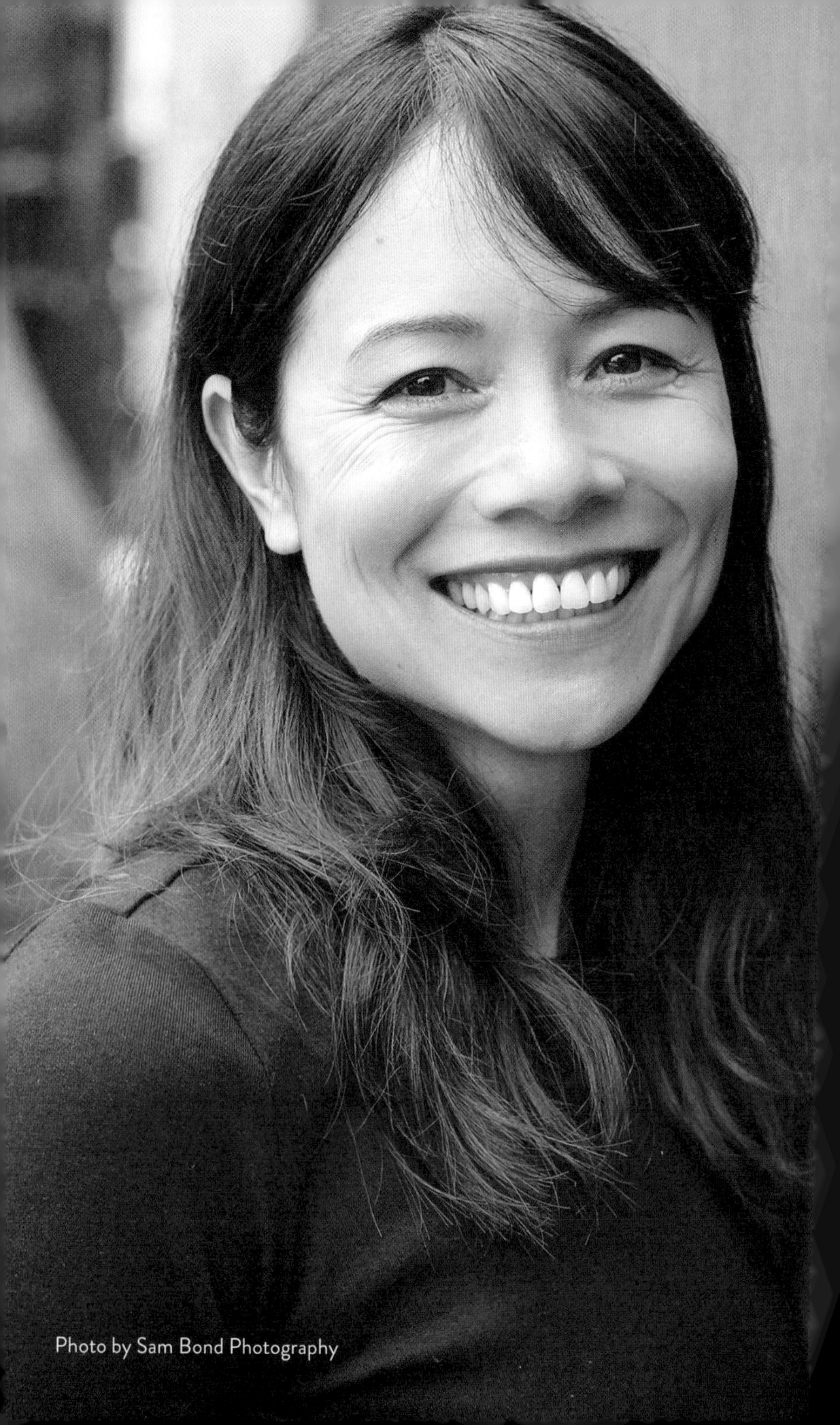

Photo by Sam Bond Photography

CHRISTINA SOONTORNVAT is the two-time Newbery Honor–winning author of *A Wish in the Dark* and *All Thirteen: The Incredible Cave Rescue of the Thai Boys' Soccer Team*, for which she also won a Sibert Honor and the Kirkus Prize. Christina grew up reading books behind the counter of her parents' Thai/Chinese restaurant in a small Texas town. Of the climactic event at the center of this book, she says, "Trying out for cheerleader in the seventh grade was exhilarating, horrifying, empowering, and nauseating all at once. In other words, it makes for an epic story." Christina currently resides in Austin, Texas, with her husband, two young daughters, and one old cat.

JOANNA CACAO is a Canadian Filipino artist and illustrator who loves working on magical and fantastical stories. She gets her visual inspiration from the TV shows and cartoons she watched growing up, especially *Full House*. Her biggest influences come from various manga, as well as Ghibli and Disney films. Though Joanna was never a cheerleader, her eldest sister was, so the world is familiar. She attended predominantly white schools, where she experienced very similar situations to Christina. Joanna lives in Winnipeg, Canada, with her Pomeranian, Danny.

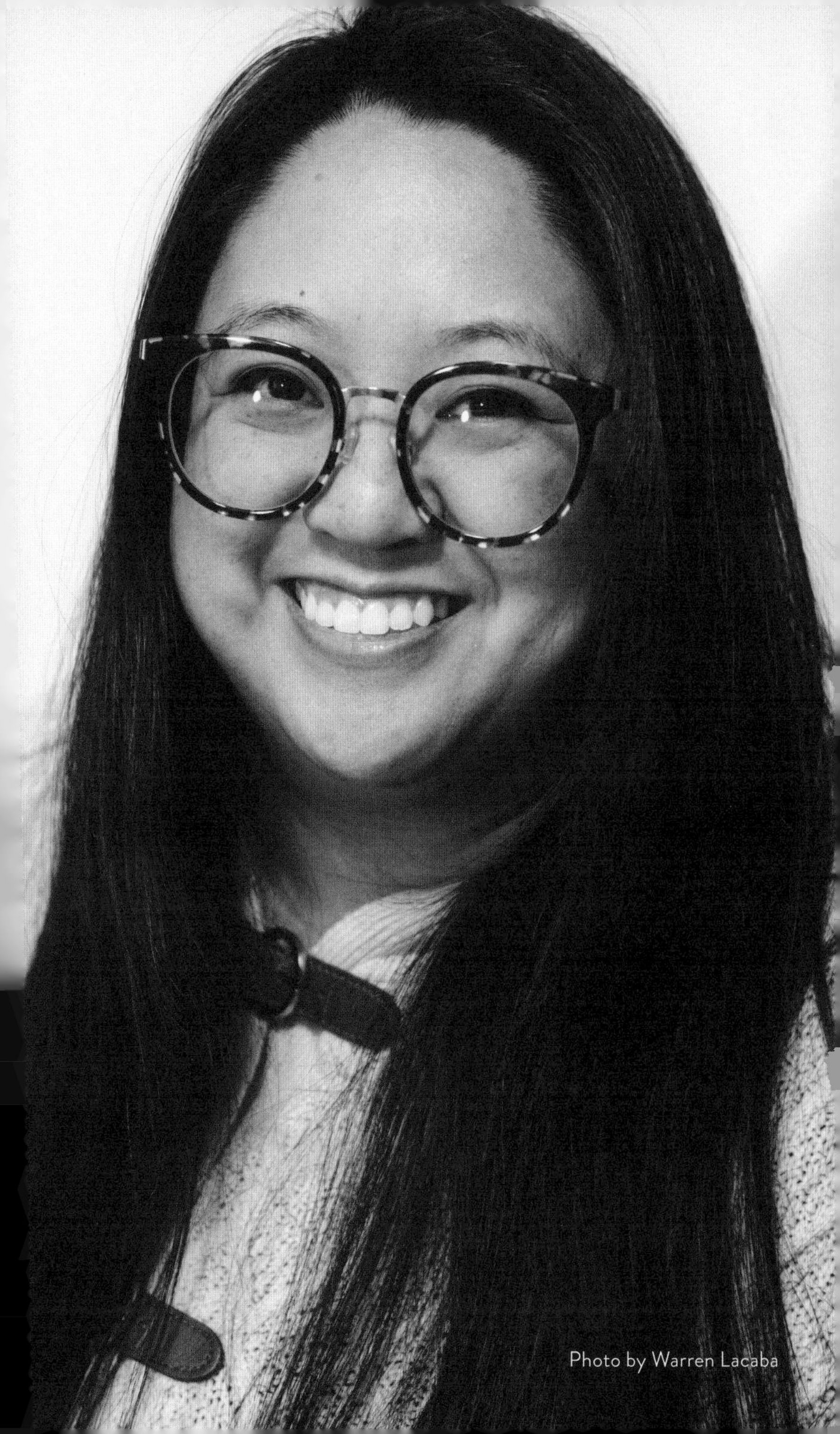

Photo by Warren Lacaba

For my friends from back home.
CS

For my love, Warren, who was there for
me every step of the way.
JC

Text copyright © 2022 by Christina Soontornvat
Art copyright © 2022 by Joanna Cacao

All rights reserved. Published by Graphix, an imprint of Scholastic Inc.,
Publishers since 1920. SCHOLASTIC, GRAPHIX, and associated logos are trademarks
and/or registered trademarks of Scholastic Inc. The publisher does not have any
control over and does not assume any responsibility for author or
third-party websites or their content.

Library of Congress Control Number: 2021044117

ISBN 978-1-338-74130-8 (hardcover)
ISBN 978-1-338-74126-1 (paperback)

10 9 8 7 6 5 4 3 2 1   22 23 24 25 26

Printed in China 62
First edition, September 2022

Edited by Tracy Mack
Lettering by Jesse Post
Coloring by Amanda Lafrenais
Book Design by Phil Falco & Shivana Sookdeo
Creative Director: Phil Falco
Publisher: David Saylor